Eleanor's Daughter

Other Books by
JUNE HALL MCCASH

Marguerite's Landing

The Boys of Shiloh

The Thread Box: A Collection of Poems

A Titanic Love Story: Ida and Isidor Straus

Plum Orchard
winner of the 2013 Georgia Author of the Year Award for Best Novel

Almost to Eden
winner of the 2011 Georgia Author of the Year Award for First Novel

The Jekyll Island Club:
Southern Haven for America's Millionaires
(co-author William Barton McCash)

Jekyll Island's Early Years:
From Prehistory through Reconstruction

The Jekyll Island Cottage Colony

The Jekyll Island CLub Hotel
(co-author Brenden Martin)

The Cultural Patronage of Medieval Women
(edited by June Hall McCash)

The Life of Saint Audrey: A Text of Marie de France
(co-edited and co-trans., with Judith Clark Barban)

Love's Fools: Troilus, Aucassin, Calisto and the Parody of the Courtly Love

Eleanor's Daughter

A novel of Marie de Champagne

June Hall McCash

TWIN
OAKS
PRESS

ISBN-13: 978-1-937937-20-1

Corrected Paperback Edition 2019
Originally published November 2018

Twin Oaks Press
twinoakspress@gmail.com
www.twinoakspress.com

Design
Art Growden

To Michael and Bren,
with love,
in remembrance of your school days in Troyes.
Thanks for being such great troopers.

Genealogical Chart of France

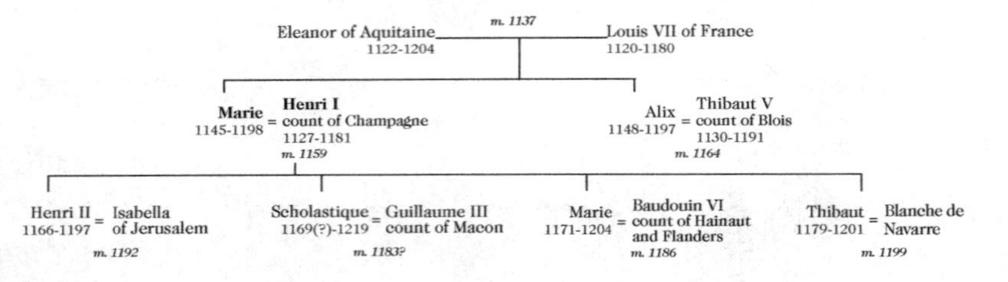

Genealogical Chart of Champagne

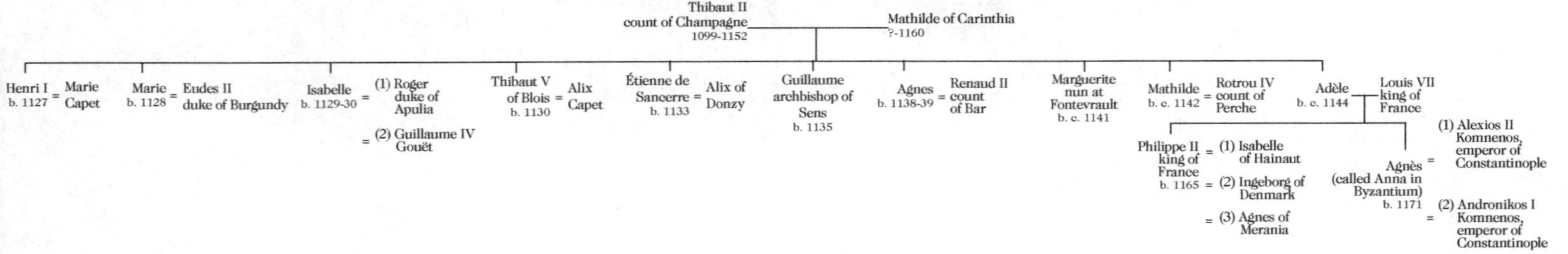

Genealogical Chart of England

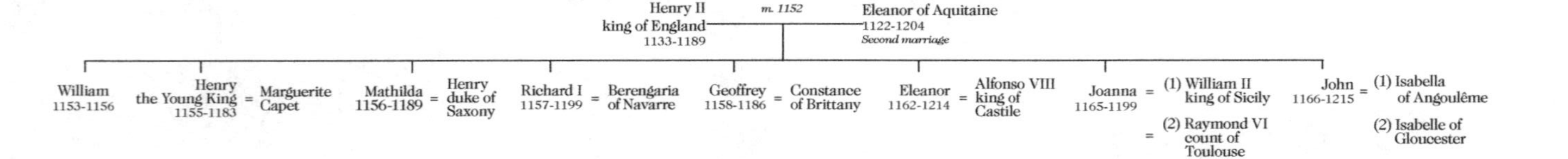

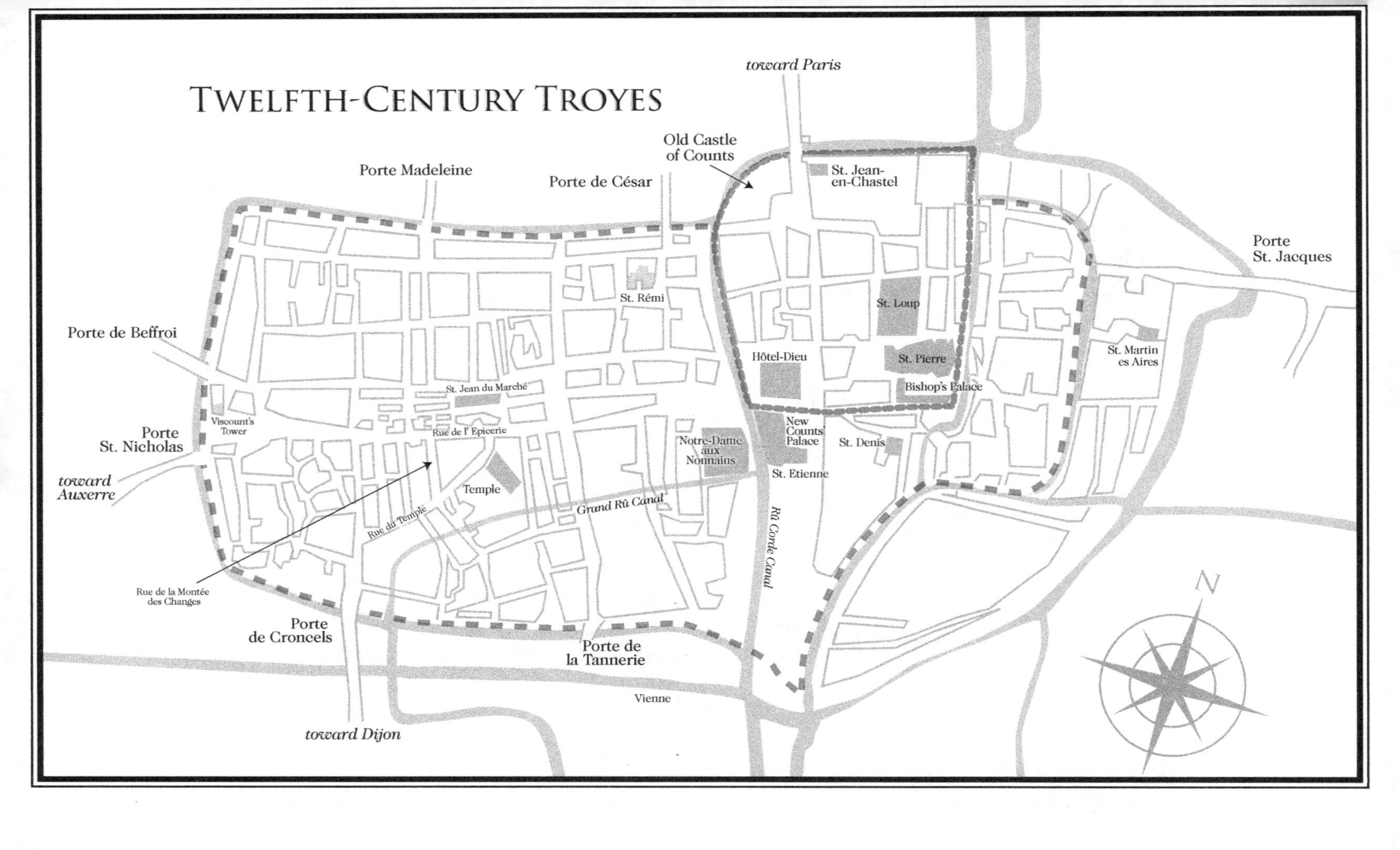
Twelfth-Century Troyes
toward Paris
Old Castle of Counts
St. Jean-en-Chastel
Porte Madeleine
Porte de César
Porte St. Jacques
St. Rémi
St. Loup
St. Martin es Aires
Porte de Beffroi
Hôtel-Dieu
St. Pierre
Bishop's Palace
St. Jean du Marché
Viscount's Tower
Porte St. Nicholas
Rue de l' Epicerie
New Counts' Palace
Notre-Dame aux Nonnains
St. Denis
toward Auxerre
Temple
St. Etienne
Grand Rû Canal
Rue du Temple
Rû Corde Canal
N
Rue de la Montée des Changes
Porte de Croncels
Porte de la Tannerie
Vienne
toward Dijon

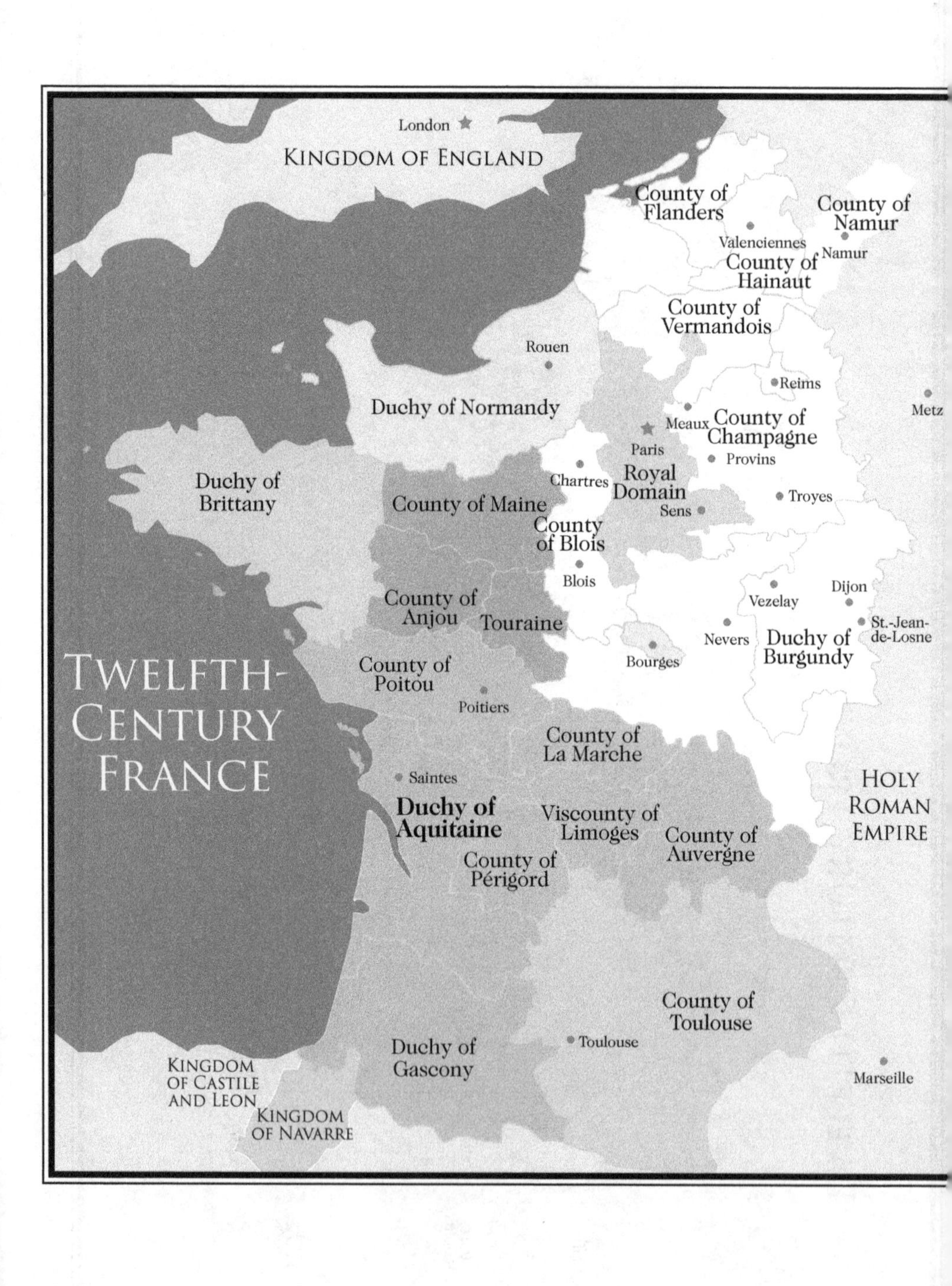

London
Kingdom of England
County of Flanders
County of Namur
Valenciennes
Namur
County of Hainaut
County of Vermandois
Rouen
Reims
Metz
Duchy of Normandy
Meaux
County of Champagne
Paris
Provins
Duchy of Brittany
Chartres
Royal Domain
Troyes
County of Maine
Sens
County of Blois
Blois
County of Anjou
Touraine
Vezelay
Dijon
Nevers
Duchy of Burgundy
St.-Jean-de-Losne
Bourges
Twelfth-Century France
County of Poitou
Poitiers
County of La Marche
Saintes
Holy Roman Empire
Duchy of Aquitaine
Viscounty of Limoges
County of Auvergne
County of Périgord
County of Toulouse
Toulouse
Duchy of Gascony
Marseille
Kingdom of Castile and Leon
Kingdom of Navarre

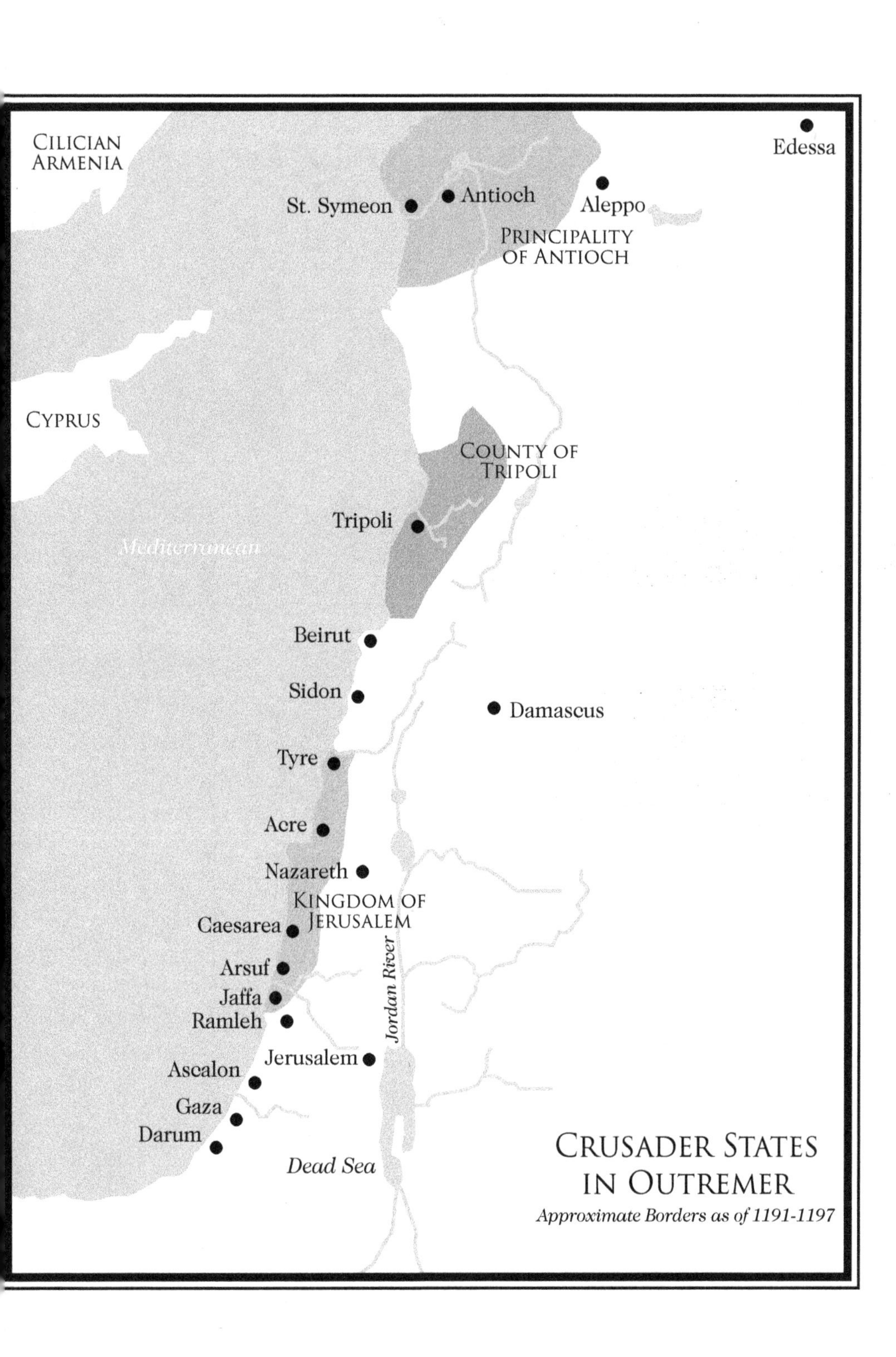
CILICIAN
ARMENIA
Edessa
St. Symeon
Antioch
Aleppo
PRINCIPALITY
OF ANTIOCH
CYPRUS
COUNTY OF
TRIPOLI
Tripoli
Mediterranean
Beirut
Sidon
Damascus
Tyre
Acre
Nazareth
KINGDOM OF
JERUSALEM
Caesarea
Arsuf
Jaffa
Ramleh
Jordan River
Jerusalem
Ascalon
Gaza
Darum
Dead Sea
CRUSADER STATES
IN OUTREMER
Approximate Borders as of 1191-1197

PROLOGUE

Vitry, Champagne, January 1143

Early morning mists were beginning to clear by the time the church bells rang the hour of terce. People in the town of Vitry, nestled peacefully on the banks of the Marne River, already scurried about their tasks—merchants arranging their stalls, women setting up their looms or kneading dough to make bread for their families, yawning children beginning their daily chores. The pale winter sun illumined the hilltop castle, a favorite home of the rich and powerful Count Thibaut de Champagne. The count was away, and it stood empty except for the caretakers, but it was the place where he had chosen to raise his children. The bustling town and fertile fields that stretched beyond bore witness to his prosperity.

At first the townspeople heard only a distant rumble. They knew it was not thunder, for the skies were clear and the east side of the church steeple reflected the rays of the morning sun. As the ground began to vibrate, Hervé, the burly blacksmith, looked up from his anvil where he was hammering a glowing horseshoe.

"What the devil?" He could see dust from approaching hoof beats rising from the west and the glint of chain mail on the riders.

"Soldiers.... Boy, hand me my sledgehammer," he said gruffly to the thin, young orphan boy, who was pumping the bellows to keep the coals hot. The boy fetched the tool. It was all the smith had to use as a weapon.

The two stood peering apprehensively out the wide door of the forge, as dozens of mounted knights swept along the roads. Their swords gleamed in the early brightness, ready to slash at anything that blocked their path. Foot soldiers, shouting now, raced toward the village and flowed into the narrow streets like a floodtide drowning everything in its path.

Townspeople ran for safety as the attackers swarmed through the village. People screamed and scurried here and there to avoid being trampled. Simon, the woodsman, dropped the load of firewood he was carrying and bolted toward the open door of a nearby house. The baker's son, Baudri, on his way to deliver the four warm loaves of bread under his arm, stood wide-eyed and frozen in the middle of the street. Amice, the cobbler's wife, snatched up her small daughter just in time to keep her from being crushed beneath the galloping hooves. Hervé thought furiously. *Was there any place they would be safe?*

He felt a rising surge of panic. There seemed nowhere to run. The roads were blocked. Even the fields surrounding the little town were full of foot soldiers wielding flails and pikes. Bodies already lay here and there in the streets and paths, hacked down by passing swordsmen—the woodcutter, the baker's son, and an unrecognizable woman who had been struck in the face.

"Who are they?" asked the boy, his teeth beginning to chatter in fear as he stood behind the burly blacksmith.

"Don't know for sure. Probably the king's men. He's the count's only enemy I know of." *Who else would have such a well-equipped army?*

"Come on, boy. We can't stay here," Hervé said when the first wave of troops had passed by. "Let's make for the church before they're back." It was their only hope. He felt sure the pious King Louis VII, once destined for the life of the clergy, would not defile the house of God. It was their only possible sanctuary.

The blacksmith and his helper joined a wave of terrified townspeople hurrying toward the church, its bell tolling as both warning and summons. The priest held the door open, motioning for them to come inside. Mothers hastily herded their children through the welcoming portals. Old people, some leaning on canes or crutches, hobbled into the cool emptiness of the nave. Men, armed with pruning hooks and carving knives, helped the wounded inside and, once they were sure there was no one else, they barred the heavy wooden doors behind them. All that was left of the town's population, more than a thousand people, crowded together in the church.

They prayed and waited, trembling at the yells and threats of the soldiers outside and their pounding on the heavy wooden doors of the church. Suddenly it grew quiet. The people inside the church waited and listened, hoping it was all over.

Then, to their horror, they began to hear the crackling of flames, to smell smoke, to feel the heat. The king's men were torching their town—everything the villagers owned. They knew their wooden houses and thatched roofs would burn like dry tinder and that a wall of fire would soon surround their sanctuary. The priest began to intone a prayer, asking God for the miracle of rain to save the town. The people joined in with a solemn "Amen."

But rain did not come, and they could already see through the small high windows of the church an orange glow rising outside. As they waited, aware there was nothing else they could do, they suddenly realized that even the church was on fire. They had to get out. But try as they might, they could not open the doors. Too late they realized that the pounding they had heard was the soldiers nailing them shut. They were trapped. There would be no escape. Their only hope was in God. The smoke grew worse and the heat more intense. They could see flames leaping along the wooden supports of the church roof.

People began to kneel and moan their anguished prayers. Children screamed in fear, as their parents sought to shield them from the inevitable agony. Hervé could feel the trembling boy huddled next to him—a child really, not more than ten or eleven years old. He put his strong arm around the boy as they knelt side-by-side.

"*Courage, Jacquot,*" he whispered gently, drawing the boy closer. He realized suddenly that it was the first time he had ever called the child by name.

Astride his horse in an open field at a safe distance from the tumult, King Louis watched with satisfaction as his soldiers ravaged the town. Vitry was now his. His revenge against his insolent and meddlesome vassal, Thibaut de Champagne, though not yet complete, had begun. Caught up in the excitement of the battle, he had given the order: *Burn the town*. He watched the flames hungrily devour the rooftops of wood and thatch. Only when he began to hear the screams coming from inside the church did he realize what was happening.

"Why don't they come out and beg for mercy?" he asked his sergeant-at-arms, seated on a spirited stallion at his side. He hadn't meant for them to die. All he wanted was for them to see that real power lay with the king and not with their count. He wanted them on their knees and at his mercy.

"The soldiers have nailed shut the church doors, my lord," the man answered.

"God have mercy," the king cried, his eyes widening in disbelief. But there was nothing he could do. The church was already in flames. It was too late. He was too far away. He could only sit and watch in horror as the fire blazed ever higher and licked its way up to the roof. He was mesmerized until he heard the crash of the hot lead roof cave in on those trapped inside. Then he closed his eyes and let his head fall forward on his chest. He could no longer hear their screams. There was only deadly silence from the burning village.

King Louis covered his face with his hands and rocked back and forth in the saddle, moaning "God have mercy" again and again, until he was almost unable to breathe. How many had there been? Unfriendly chroniclers would write the tale, he knew, and they would probably exaggerate the number of Christian souls locked in the church in Vitry. He would be blamed.

"The king refused to hear their cries," they would write. They would never know that it was not really his fault, that he had not meant the church to burn. It was his soldiers who did the evil deed. All he had wanted was to punish Thibaut, to let him feel the force of the king's wrath. But he knew their blood was on his hands, that with this horrible act, the death of so many guiltless people, he had made himself an enemy of God.

Overwhelmed and in terror for his soul, the king dismounted heavily. The stench of burned flesh in his nostrils, he looked once more over the still-flaming embers of Vitry. Suddenly he could no longer stand.

"God help me," he cried out, as he fell to his knees and wept.

CHAPTER 1

June 11, 1144, Abbey Church of St. Denis, France

The queen waited alone in the dark nave. Her fingers played nervously on the leather binding of her psalter, and she could almost hear the pounding of her heart. She carried the psalter in hopes that the abbot would view it as a sign of her devotion to God. *More likely,* she thought, *he will interpret it as a gesture of false piety.* He always seemed to judge her in the worst possible light. She couldn't decide now whether she felt more nervous or foolish at having requested this meeting. What could she say to the abbot that he didn't already know? What would she be willing to tell him? Could he help her? *Would he?*

During the consecration ceremony earlier in the day, a rainbow of light had poured through the stained-glass windows of the apse in the newly built east end of the abbey church of St. Denis. Even the light of the west façade's rose window was fading now, along with her confidence, as she heard one of the heavy doors of the church swing open followed by the thud of its closing. There was no sign of the colors that had washed over the stone floors earlier in the day, only a dull gray as the light continued to dim. She could hear footsteps approaching now, and she took a deep breath.

Suddenly he stood before her—Bernard, Abbot of Clairvaux.

"Father Abbot," the queen said softly, curtseying deeply before him.

"*Ma dame,*" he nodded. "You asked to speak with me?"

"Yes, Father." She hoped her voice did not convey her uncertainty.

Nothing about the abbot looked imposing. Although he was fairly tall, he was a frail man physically, his head bent forward in a familiar gesture of humility. The gray fringe of his tonsured head matched his thin beard. He wore the plain white robe of the Cistercians, which glowed faintly in the darkening church. On the surface he appeared to be a simple and unassuming man, yet even the queen, whenever she heard his voice as he delivered his extraordinary sermons, could not help but be impressed. He was transformed at such moments. Everyone within reach of his words was compelled to listen, mesmerized by his intellect and his persuasiveness. He could sway the mind and the emotions of anyone who listened. Above all, he could work miracles.

Queen Eleanor had heard the many stories that circulated throughout Christendom of the miracles of Bernard de Clairvaux, how he cured the sick, made the lame to walk, and the mute to speak. And in spite of his attitude toward her, she stood in awe of the man, whom many took for a saint. He gazed at her thoughtfully before he broke the silence.

"And what concerns you on this auspicious occasion? You seem a young woman who already has all that God can grant." She could feel his eyes appraising her silken gown and her jeweled gold coronet studded with rubies, but she refused to wince under his scrutiny.

"All but one thing, Father," she replied in a soft voice.

"And what is that?"

Her voice grew strong in its conviction. "A son."

"Ah…" He touched his hand to his heart and smiled faintly. "Ah, yes. A child. A queen does need to produce an heir, doesn't she? It is her duty." Eleanor knew of many noble ladies who had been put aside for their barrenness. Even her husband's father, Louis the Fat, had ended his marriage to his first and childless wife after only three years. She did not intend to share that fate if she could avoid it. So far, her husband, Louis the Young, as some called him, had been patient, but how much longer would he be willing to wait? Abbot Bernard was her last hope, and she was willing to overcome her pride to beg for his help if that was what it took.

The darkening of the church seemed ominous as Abbot Bernard continued to gaze at her in silence, as though waiting for her to say more. His piercing eyes seemed to contain an unspoken accusation.

Finally, it was he who spoke first, "And what do you need from me, my lady?" His voice echoed in the empty nave, as she sought the words to make her request.

She wished it were Suger, the abbot of St. Denis, to whom she could turn. With him she felt more secure. While she could not say they were friends, at least he understood her ways and her love of worldly things. It did not mean she was not concerned with the salvation of her soul, but he and she were in agreement that visible splendor could lift one's spirit to higher levels, even toward God. His magnificent renovation of the abbey church was a testimony to his beliefs. He himself had donated the gilded bronze doors of the façade to provide a welcoming portal to pilgrims who flocked to the church every feast day. He saw them as a reflection of God's glory, inviting the worshipper to enter through the light of those magnificent doors to the True Light and the True Door, which was Christ.

Abbot Suger was also a practical man, grateful for her generous donations of funds, workmen, and jewels to support the rebuilding of his church. He had seen from the very beginning the advantages to France of her marriage to the young Capetian prince, now the king—Louis VII. As heiress of Aquitaine and the richest woman in Christendom, she could also claim a bloodline that dated back to Charlemagne. For years, he had sought to spread the idea that the French king, not the German emperor, was the true successor to Charlemagne, and just as he had worked for the *renovatio* of the abbey church, so he worked tirelessly for the *renovatio imperii Karoli Magni*, the renewal of the Carolingian empire with the French king as its rightful heir. Her son would restore that bloodline. But unfortunately, Suger was not known for his miracles.

Abbot Bernard no doubt viewed her contributions to the abbey's "superfluity" as yet another of her misguided ways, helping to lure the thoughts of Christians away from their devotion to God. His own Cistercian order had long since revolted against such material splendor and the increasing laxity of the Benedictine Order in an effort to restore the fundamental rule of St. Benedict and return to a simpler, more agrarian way of life.

He did not admire the magnificence of the renovated ambulatory, the pointed arches and fine open chapels, but rather condemned it all as a material distraction from spiritual concerns. So far during the consecration festivities, he had kept his judgments mostly to himself. But his expressions were not difficult to read. Whenever he left behind the simple life of his Cistercian brothers at Clairvaux to come to Paris, he brought his frowning displeasure with him. He made no effort to hide it. And he seemed to disapprove of everything about her—what he considered her worldliness, her love of the troubadour songs from her native Poitou, the pleasure she took in the laughter of her ladies, in dances like the *carole*, and in sweetmeats and fine wines, of which she found all too little at the cold Capetian court. His was a temperament alien to the young Queen Eleanor, who wanted to drink in every pleasure of this world before she turned her thoughts to the next.

Yet now she and Abbot Bernard, despite their differences, stood face-to-face beneath the soaring vaults of St. Denis. And regardless of his disapproval, she needed his help—a miracle that only he could perform. *But would he?*

"Father, I beseech you," she began. "King Louis and I have been wed more than seven years, and I have not given birth. And now, I fear… I fear that God may have sealed my womb..." In spite of her efforts, she could feel herself on the verge of tears, remembering, when she was only fifteen and not long after the marriage, her one pregnancy, which had ended in a flow of blood after only a few months. But now she was determined. She would not show weakness. "I am here to ask for your help. Why does God not give me a child?"

The abbot's face was impassive as he gave his answer. "The ways of God are not our ways. Perhaps there is something… some impediment you must overcome," he said thoughtfully.

She was uncertain how much she should tell him, but now that she was here she wanted him to understand that the fault was not solely hers.

"The problem..." She spoke almost in a whisper. *Would he understand? Was it appropriate to bring up the issue that concerned her most?* "The problem, I think... is that the king does not often lie with me." She had hoped that at the very least Abbot Bernard would be willing to speak to her husband and remind him of his conjugal duties.

The abbot said nothing for a moment, his face bearing an expression of distaste. Then he nodded. "Yes, that is essential if married couples hope to conceive." He frowned and pressed his lips together as he considered her words.

"But perhaps you do not encourage him sufficiently. Perhaps you have made it difficult for him to approach you. There is a rumor about that you have accused him to others," he said dryly. "Your exact words, as they were reported to me, my lady, were, 'I thought I had wed a king; but I find I have married a monk.'" He peered at her sternly as though the fault were hers alone. "Is that true, my lady?"

Eleanor could feel her face and throat redden with embarrassment and anger at his words. She only hoped the diaphanous wimple that floated around her neck would conceal her resentment. So it was *she* he would hold responsible. But she could not deny it. Those had been her exact words, and she had said them to only one of her ladies, who had obviously repeated them to others, a lady who, beginning with the morrow, would no longer be in her retinue at court.

"I fear it *is* true." She sought to control her pride and, at least outwardly, accepted his blame. But she went on to add, "I don't expect him to join me in the dances or sit in the great hall listening to tales or songs he finds not to his liking... but," she added, "he must join me occasionally in bed if I am to bear his child."

The abbot nodded. "That is indeed an impediment," he said, "but I think you need to be more... persuasive, more encouraging. I will grant that is certainly one of your problems. But..." he paused, leaving the space between them heavy with anticipation. "Perhaps it is not the only one. I think there is another, even more serious, impediment." The nave was growing ever darker as they spoke.

"What do you mean? What other impediment?"

The old abbot stood silent for a moment, his eyes fixed on the queen. Then he pointed to a pair of wooden stools that sat against the wall near the doors of the north transept.

"Shall we sit down for a while?" It was not a question, but a command. Usually there were no seats for the congregation, but today the consecration service had been long and the crowded church hot. The monks had brought in a few benches and stools for the most elderly among the throng so that they might rest for a few moments rather than faint from the heat and the thick air.

Queen Eleanor nodded, and together they walked farther into the cool depths of the church and sat, facing one another. The abbot had chosen a stool with his back to the ambulatory. The queen leaned away from the thick stone wall of the side aisle and asked once more, "What other impediment do you mean?" She was anxious to know his answer.

The abbot was silent for a long time and closed his eyes, as though in prayer. He bowed his head, put the fingertips of his two hands together, and brought them thoughtfully to his lips. Finally, he opened his eyes once more to look intently at the queen.

"Vitry," he said, his voice firm and resonant. "Vitry-le-Brûlé is an example." Vitry the Burned. It was what everyone called it now. He let the name resonate for a moment before he added in his most commanding voice, "The king must stop making war on the count of Champagne before he can find approval with God… and before you can bear a child. You must be what a woman is supposed to be—a peacemaker. You must stop supporting this war and bring about peace between the count and the king."

Eleanor was astonished. He was speaking to her—a woman—about the king's policies, about the king's fury with the count of Champagne? And he dared ask *her* to make peace with a man she and her husband both despised? No doubt the abbot was well aware that she had encouraged the king in his war against the obstreperous count. And she had every reason for doing so. Thibaut de Champagne—the very thought of him left a bitter taste in her mouth—was a sworn vassal of the crown, and yet he had refused to do his military duty and help in

Louis's efforts to secure her well-founded hereditary claims to the rich city of Toulouse.

Even more infuriating were Count Thibaut's attempts to interfere in her sister's marriage. Eleanor herself had encouraged the union between her younger sister, who throughout her childhood had been called by her saint's name, Petronilla, and the king's seneschal, Raoul de Vermandois. King Louis was equally enthusiastic about the marriage, for it would strengthen his alliance with the rich house of Vermandois. And the couple were fond of one another, despite the vast difference in their ages.

There was one problem, however. Raoul was already married. And unfortunately, his wife was the niece of Thibaut de Champagne.

Repudiating a wife was not usually an insurmountable obstacle if a nobleman wished to marry elsewhere. It was merely a matter of finding a few bishops prepared to show grounds for annulment. Thus, at the king's request, the bishops of Laon, Senlis, and Noyon were called together and quickly concluded, as they were supposed to do and as Eleanor knew they would, that the marriage of Thibaut's niece and Raoul was consanguineous, of too close a kinship—a common excuse for annulment among the noble families of France. Thus, the annulment was granted, and Raoul and Petronilla, or Aelith as she now preferred to call herself, were soon married. That should have ended the matter.

But Count Thibaut refused to bow to either the king's will or the judgment of the bishops, contending that they violated his family's honor and that the marriage between Petronilla and Raoul was invalid. He had the audacity to take his complaints directly to the pope. Innocent II had listened sympathetically—with the result that a papal council had not only ruled the first marriage still binding, but also excommunicated all those involved—Raoul, Petronilla, and the three bishops.

Queen Eleanor was furious. The count's efforts had damned her sister and made her officially an adulteress. Only after the death of Pope Innocent on September 23, 1143, did the new Pope Celestine II recognize Petronilla's marriage as lawful. Only then were they relieved of the family scandal caused by Thibaut. Now Abbot Bernard wanted her to forgive the count and make peace between him and her husband. Every fiber of her being resisted. She hated the man.

Bernard always sides with the count. Little wonder, Eleanor thought with disdain. *Thibaut is always fawning over the abbot. He might as well kiss the hem of his chasuble.* The count had even gone so far as to declare his intention to take Cistercian vows in his later life and to be buried in Cistercian vestments. *Such an obvious ploy.* It may have been obvious to everyone else, but Abbot Bernard seemed to preen at the count's attentions and professed piety.

All these thoughts and memories swirled in Eleanor's head. How could the abbot ask this of her? She had not expected it. She was silent for a long time as he awaited her answer. She could understand why Bernard wanted peace between the king, whom he served as counselor, and the count, whom he obviously loved as a brother. Perhaps he saw this bargain with the queen as a final opportunity, however faint, to end the hostility between the two men. Perhaps, just as he was her last desperate hope, she may also have been his.

It was Abbot Bernard who broke the long silence. "My lady," he began urgently. "Consider my request carefully. You must stop stirring up the king against the Church and the count. Find in your heart the strength to overcome your own will and urge him to do the right thing. Become an agent for God's kingdom and help lead your husband's soul to salvation. It is a wife's duty."

Duty. Once more a wife's duty, Eleanor thought with disgust. "But, Father, I…" she began to protest, for she knew such a task would be onerous and against her nature. She was anything but a peacemaker, and she knew that her husband despised Thibaut as much as she did. Perhaps more. He had his own reasons.

The abbot raised a finger to silence her.

"If you do what I ask, my lady, I will implore our merciful God to answer your prayer." He spoke slowly, emphasizing every word. "Seek peace, and I promise, in confidence of His great mercy, that you will bear a child. I will pray to God to unseal your womb and make fertile your barrenness."

She drew in a sudden breath. Her miracle. He was offering her a miracle. This was what she wanted, what she had come for, and she felt her body flood with joy. It was like the dew of divine grace. But could she do it? Could she bring peace between Louis and Thibaut? Louis's reasons for hating Thibaut were as valid as her own. Even if she wanted to, could she end this quarrel, for which she had served as bellows to the flame for so many years? In her heart she knew that this might be her only chance for the miracle she so desperately needed. Even her hatred of Thibaut faded by comparison to her fervent desire for a child.

Thus, with all the humility she could muster, she uttered her sincere reply. "I will try, Father Abbot. I will try."

CHAPTER 2

Eleanor waited impatiently for the right moment to approach her husband. The evening after their return to the royal castle on the Île de la Cité in Paris, once supper had been served in the great hall and the trestle tables cleared away, the queen suggested, as she frequently did, that one of the troubadours from her homeland of Aquitaine grace the court with a song or two. Although the king appeared to listen to the first *canso*, a love lament composed in the queen's native language of the south, the *langue d'oc*, he fidgeted with impatience. Eleanor had heard him say many times that these lyrics, which he did not understand, all sounded alike to him. He had no interest in such frivolous entertainment.

As soon as the song ended, the king rose abruptly and left the great hall to go up to the solar, the royal couple's private living space, to enjoy the rest of the evening alone. The queen watched him leave and excused herself at the earliest opportunity to follow him up the narrow stone steps.

When she entered the solar, he was already seated, propped on plush pillows, a goblet of spiced wine within his reach.

"How fare you tonight, husband?" she asked.

"Well enough. I'm just weary of all the noise and merriment."

"It is always good to have a quiet moment to oneself after a long day." She tried to make her voice sympathetic. "These last days at St.

Denis were trying, weren't they?"

"I rather enjoyed them myself, and I had an opportunity to talk with some old friends among the monks." He had been educated at St. Denis in preparation for a life in the Church. But all that had changed when his older brother, Philippe, was killed in a bizarre accident and his horse was tripped by a black pig in the marketplace. At his brother's death, eleven-year-old Louis found himself whisked from the safety and quiet of the abbey cloister and thrust abruptly into his new role as heir apparent to the throne—a role he did not relish.

"I found being back at the abbey rather peaceful, though the consecration festivities did seem rather long in such heat."

"Yes, I agree." She let silence gather in the room as she refilled his goblet from the flagon that sat on the table beside him. Then, in a quiet voice, she announced, "I met privately with Abbot Bernard while we were there." He lifted his eyebrows in amazement.

"You met with the abbot?" He seemed incredulous. "I didn't think the two of you ever found much to talk about. What, pray tell, was the occasion?"

"I asked for his help," she replied, her voice still quiet. "I asked for a miracle."

"A miracle?"

"Yes."

"And what did this miracle entail?"

"That he would ask God to grant me fertility."

"A good cause, if ever there was one. And what did he say?"

She hesitated a moment. "He promised to ask God for the miracle only if I could persuade you to make peace with Count Thibaut."

He laughed, but the laugh was grim. "Make peace with Thibaut? I've tried. Never again," he said. "He's betrayed me more than once. His sheltering Pierre de la Châtre in Champagne was the last straw."

Eleanor remembered the incident all too well. It was what had finally propelled the king to take such aggressive action against his vassal. And for once, it was the king alone whom Thibaut's actions offended. She cared little for such matters. But when the archbishop of Bourges had died in 1141, Louis had seen it as an opportunity to promote his new chancellor, Cadurc, to the position. Pope Innocent II had favored the nephew of his own chancellor—a man named Pierre de La Châtre. But the king was adamant; it was to be Cadurc and no other. When the canons of the cathedral chapter elected Pierre despite Louis's explicit demands, he was furious and swore on holy relics that as long as he lived, Pierre de La Châtre would never enter the city of Bourges.

At the time Eleanor thought her husband foolish to give the incident such importance, but he felt it called his royal prerogatives into question. The pope, equally adamant and wroth with King Louis over the matter, excommunicated him and placed his lands under interdict. That was when Count Thibaut, who had no business in the matter at all, interjected himself into the situation and agreed to shelter the new archbishop in Champagne, where he could preside over his episcopal see from afar.

Louis was enraged. It was the final insult that had set him on his savage attacks on Thibaut's lands and brought about the burning of Vitry.

"Why should I make peace? I've tried before and been betrayed."

"I know your feelings about him, and I share them. We both have good reason to despise him. But if the abbot can help—"

"Thibaut is nothing but an *upstart usurper*," the king raged. "He shouldn't even *be* count. He has no right to any of his lands. He has an older brother."

It was true. Guillaume de Sully, his older brother, had the misfortune of stuttering. It disgusted his mother, who concluded that anyone who couldn't talk properly was feeble-minded and worthless and excluded him from his inheritance in favor of his younger brother Thibaut.

"Besides, Brie and Champagne didn't even belong to his father," Louis added.

That too was true. Thibaut had inherited his easternmost lands from his uncle Hugh, who still had a living son, born in his father's old age from his second nuptials to a much younger woman. Although he'd been told by his doctors he could not father a child, he assumed the son his wife bore was his—until one night when he called the child to come sit on his knee. The two-year-old turned away and ran instead to his mother. She folded him in her arms and said, "You are right to come to me, my son. What do you have to do with that old man?"

Hugh took his wife's words as a public denial of his paternity. He rose, snatched the boy from his mother's arms, and tried to throw him into the fire. Courtiers saved the child's life, but the count's bitterness remained. He repudiated his wife and disinherited the boy as a bastard.

"I remember. Count Hugh was an impulsive fool," Eleanor said.

Louis nodded in agreement. Instead of calming down, the angry count left his land to his nephew Thibaut and went to live out his life in the Holy Land in an environment more suited to his temperament—among warrior-knights called the Templars.

"*Thibaut le Grand*," Louis scoffed at his nickname—Thibaut the Great. "He's nothing but a great pain in the royal backside."

Eleanor gave a sardonic laugh at the king's pun. "At least he doesn't sit on the English throne," she offered. "It was a real possibility, you know."

"Thank God for that." Louis grimaced and crossed himself. As the grandson of William the Conqueror—or William the Bastard, as Louis preferred to call him—Thibaut might have inherited the English throne at the death of his uncle, Henry I. The drowning of Henry's only son in the sinking of the White Ship in 1135 had left Thibaut the next male in line. But for once it was he who felt the sting of rejection.

Although his uncle had left his crown to his daughter Matilda, his barons rebelled at the idea of a woman ruler and turned to the sons of King Henry's sister Adela. Norman barons urged Thibaut to rush to England to assume the throne. But the English barons had already crowned his younger brother Stephen, who was among the retinue of their uncle and well known to his courtiers.

"It's amazing, nevertheless, how he managed to profit from the situation," Louis observed.

"He's a master at doing that," Eleanor said wryly.

In exchange for renouncing his claim to the English throne, Thibaut had enriched his coffers by demanding a portion of the English royal treasure and an annual compensation from Stephen of 2,000 silver marks. He also forced his brother to give up any claims to family territories in France.

"Avoid war and acquire the wealth," Louis said. "It could have been the motto on his coat of arms."

"But your harassment in Champagne upset his plans, I think."

"I thank God that the world was spared the existence of 'King' Thibaut," Louis said in an acid tone, "but he's still making trouble everywhere I turn."

"I know, and perhaps he brought Vitry upon himself."

At the mention of Vitry, Louis's face crumpled. He stared into the embers and took another gulp of wine. Tears welled in his eyes.

Eleanor moved closer to the king, sat down beside him, and touched his hand as it encircled the stem of the goblet. She spoke in a soft but steady voice.

"What's past is past, Louis. We can't undo what's already done. But it has to end. I know it torments you. You still wake up, crying out, with nightmares of Vitry." She would comfort him like a small child, as he whimpered in her arms. "Perhaps making peace would—"

Louis interrupted. "What you're asking is impossible. We tried making peace once before, remember?"

It was true. Eleanor had previously urged Louis to stop his harassment against Champagne and return Vitry to the count on one condition—that Thibaut agree to seek a levy of the sentence of excommunication against Raoul and Petronilla. They expected him to refuse. But after the count talked it over with Abbot Bernard, surprisingly he agreed.

"We should have been wary," the king said. "It was much too easy."

"Yes," she murmured, standing now, gazing out the open window into the darkness, and remembering their naïve trust.

At Thibaut's request, the pope had indeed lifted the interdict and the excommunication, and, in exchange, the king returned Vitry to Count Thibaut. The only problem was that, as soon as it was over, Pope Innocent once again ordered Raoul to take back his "legitimate" wife.

"We realized our mistake too late," Eleanor murmured.

Louis nodded. "Too late," he echoed.

They had failed to state in their negotiations that the marriage between Raoul and Petronilla must be recognized as valid, assuming it was implicit in their demands. When Raoul refused once again to take back his first wife, the pope excommunicated the ill-starred couple for a second time. By then, however, Thibaut was once more in possession of Vitry.

"I'm still certain it was Abbot Bernard who suggested the trickery," Eleanor said. "He was Thibaut's advisor in the matter,"

"You're probably right," Louis said. He still felt stung by the betrayal.

Pope Innocent's death in September 1143 finally brought a conclusion to the matter. Louis was able to persuade the new pope, Celestine II, to lift the excommunication and recognize the new marriage. But Celestine's death, after a papacy of only five months and twelve days, was a blow to the king, who thought he finally had an ally in the Holy See.

"You know I can't trust Thibaut. Even now, he's trying to strengthen his military position against me by forming alliances with the counts of Flanders and Soissons and planning to marry his sons to their daughters. It's another act of aggression."

"But there are other ways to interpret these things, Louis," Eleanor said. "The counts of Flanders and Soissons are, after all, your vassals. It isn't necessarily an effort to undermine the kingdom. His sons have to marry someone sooner or later. Better that they marry the daughters of your own vassals than those of the emperor or the English king." She could hardly believe she was spouting words he had already heard from Abbot Bernard.

Louis sat silently, still staring into the embers, not yet swept clean from last evening's fire. She took his silence as a softening of his position. She hoped it was.

"Besides, Louis, these alliances are still not settled. Perhaps they can be stopped. It's time to listen to Abbot Bernard and try to make a permanent peace with Thibaut," Eleanor urged.

It was hard for her to say such things, for she agreed with her husband that the count was nothing but a troublemaker. But she was now desperate to make herself the ally of the abbot of Clairvaux in order to bring about the miracle he had promised. "Please think about it," she pleaded.

"Whatever I do, he will always want something else. How do you know you can trust him?"

"The abbot always keeps his word, Louis—at least to the *letter* of the law—and he has promised me this miracle," Eleanor reminded him.

He sat quietly, thinking about her words.

"Louis, you need an heir. A son to follow in the Capetian line. We must do everything possible. Please. Just some small gesture of peace toward Thibaut."

Louis continued to stare at the dead fireplace.

She persisted. "Do you remember the old prediction—that in the seventh generation, the throne of France would return to the line of Charlemagne?"

The King pressed his lips together.

"You are well aware that you are the sixth generation. We need a son from the line of Charlemagne, and I am of that line. This may be our only chance. If you won't listen to Abbot Bernard, listen to Abbot Suger. You know he hopes we can blend the Capetian bloodline with that of Charlemagne. For once, be practical. You have enough experience in the Church to know how things work. And you have the power to bring Abbot Bernard to your side. Please," she implored, "please use it."

He looked up at her. She was standing beside the great fireplace, her eyes fixed on his.

He was silent for a long moment. Then he said, "I will think about it."

Almost four months later, on the feast day of St. Denis, King Louis and Count Thibaut finally met in the presence of Abbots Suger and Bernard to negotiate the peace. Thibaut agreed to withdraw his offers of betrothal between his sons and the daughters of Louis's vassals to the north and vowed to complain no more about the marriage of Raoul and Petronilla. Louis agreed, albeit a bit grudgingly, to accept without further complaint the new archbishop of Bourges and to cease harassing the people of Champagne.

The two men exchanged the kiss of peace on the lips, as the abbots smiled with benevolence upon the two of them. Queen Eleanor had kept her part of the bargain. Now she could only hope that Abbot Bernard would keep his.

CHAPTER 3

Early April 1145, near Saintes, Aquitaine

The spring air was deliciously warm behind the linen curtains, and the rocking of the litter was almost putting her to sleep. Eleanor lay back on the plush embroidered pillows that cushioned the movements of the wooden litter in which she and her sister were riding. The slow but regular pace of the horses was rhythmic. Her eyes closed in relaxation until she felt a firm kick in her belly, which startled her and made her laugh.

"He's a hearty little fellow, don't you think, Petronilla," she said aloud.

"Aelith, remember?" her sister corrected her. Eleanor had still not grown accustomed to the new name her sister preferred to call herself. Although it was her birth name, her parents had always used her saint's name instead.

"Aelith," Eleanor repeated. She planned to make every effort to accede to her sister's wishes.

Aelith pulled the curtain aside and peered out. "We're almost there. I can see the tower of the abbey church in the distance."

"Thank God," Eleanor said. Louis had not wanted her to accompany him on this trip into the Saintonge, where he had been called to settle a dispute that involved the Benedictine nuns at Notre-Dame de Saintes, the wealthy convent where her paternal great-aunt, Agnès de Barbezieux, was abbess.

"It's far too dangerous in your condition," he argued. But she was adamant. If she had persuaded him to make peace with Count Thibaut, surely she could persuade him to see this matter her way.

"I want to have this child in my own lands, and since you are going there anyhow, I'll come along."

"It's foolhardy."

"I'll bring my sister with me, and my aunt will look after me for the lying-in." Eleanor knew she would feel safer and more comfortable under the watchful eyes of the nuns and her great-aunt Agnès than she would in the royal household in Paris, where Louis's mother would no doubt be in charge. The abbess, or Madame de Saintes as she was called, was delighted with the idea. Louis, on the other hand, fumed over the matter until Eleanor thought of a wonderful ploy she felt sure would convince him that she was right.

"Remember the story of the barren lances that Abbot Suger read to us—the one from the book by Archbishop Turpin that tells of the conquests of my ancestor, Charlemagne?" She rarely missed an opportunity to remind him of her connection to the emperor. "Remember the story of the soldiers who planted their lances in the soil of Saintes the night before the battle, and the next morning the lances had grown branches and taken root in the soil."

The king nodded. Of course he remembered. Abbot Suger was proud to own at least a partial copy of a manuscript owned by the Cathedral of Santiago and known as the *Codex Calixtinus.* He was especially interested in the parts about St. Denis and Charlemagne. The abbot often read from them and encouraged discussion whenever he was at the royal court.

"But why is that important?"

"Think of it. At Saintes, from the barren lances came life. People will be reminded when I give birth there. From the queen whom everyone had taken for barren, there will also come new life—our son. It's a sign and a new connection with the Carolingian line. I think it would please Abbot Bernard, who gave us this miracle. Not to mention Abbot Suger."

The king looked at her and smiled with unfeigned admiration. She loved to amaze him with her intellect, and she could tell that he was struck by the analogy. It would be one, she was sure, with which he himself would try to impress Abbot Bernard, probably even taking credit for having thought of it himself. She didn't mind, especially if it was enough to win the argument.

Now here she was, with the king's entourage, on her way to Saintes. They had been traveling for more than two weeks now, following the well-worn pilgrim road that led from Paris by way of Tours—known as the Via Turonensis. At last they were finally drawing near to the Abbaye-aux-Dames, as people called the convent of Notre-Dame de Saintes, just outside the town on the opposite bank of the Charente River.

Once they had arrived, Louis and his retinue, which included his brother-in-law, Raoul de Vermandois, remained only one day and night before they left the ladies in care of the nuns in order to conduct business elsewhere. Eleanor was relieved to see them go. Now she and Aelith were free to do whatever they liked. Though the nuns kept a watchful eye on the pregnant queen, the two sisters went out occasionally to explore the sites on the other side of the river.

The afternoon was pleasant, and there was much to see. They rode with the curtains of their litter open as they crossed the stone bridge that spanned the Charente and connected the abbey with the town. The double arch of Germanicus, built so many years ago by the Romans, loomed over them as they passed beneath one of its bays.

The most prominent sight inside the city walls was the Cathedral of Saint-Pierre, which was still in the process of being rebuilt after a disastrous fire the previous century. The streets of the town teemed with people on this sunny spring day—mostly pilgrims, Eleanor judged. Saintes was a lively stop on the popular route that their father had followed on his pilgrimage to Santiago de Compostella in Spain, where he had died eight years earlier.

They visited the tomb of Saint Eutropius on the hill outside the town walls where the saint had lived for many years as a hermit and where he was martyred. Leaving the site, they gazed down on the ruins of a Roman amphitheater, now overgrown with weeds, where children played among the rubble.

The sisters reveled in their little jaunt outside the convent in this glorious weather. The town, they observed, was just as the pilgrim's guide at the end of the *Codex Calixtinus* described it, "surrounded with ancient walls and high towers, situated in the best place, equally broad and long, with all good things and a profusion of foods, the best meadows, clear springs, protected by a huge river, with gardens and orchards and vineyards all around the city, with healthy air, open spaces and streets, charming in many ways."

On most days, however, rather than venture far outside the convent, Eleanor and Aelith preferred to walk in the meadows and orchards surrounding the abbey or sit in the sunshine of the cloister garden, where the flowering plants were largely for medicinal use—calendula, lavender, chamomile, rosemary, and even roses—while the herbs found their way into the nuns' kitchen. The sisters spent much of their time reading together the saints' lives in books borrowed from the abbey library, doing needlework, talking, gossiping, and just passing the hours.

The friendly nuns at the Abbaye-aux-Dames followed the order of Saint Benedict, devoting their lives to work and prayer, but they also took pleasure in the fruits of their labors. They dined well in the refectory and enjoyed the regional wines, not unlike their Benedictine brothers.

One mid-July evening after vespers, Eleanor, now bloated and uncomfortable, walked in the garden with Aelith as they waited for the stars to come out. Although the light was failing and the warmth of the day was beginning to diminish, they were reluctant to go inside. The queen took a deep breath and turned to her sister.

"I have enjoyed this time together—just the two of us," she said. "And the nuns, of course." She reached out to touch her sister's hand. "I hope you are happy in your marriage."

"I'm very happy. I too have found pleasure in our time together, but I miss Raoul. I wish you could say the same for Louis."

"Marriage is what it is, my sister. There were happy moments at the beginning, but things change."

"I'm sure they'll never change between Raoul and me," Aelith said in a satisfied voice, as she leaned over to breathe in the fragrance of a mid-summer rose.

Eleanor looked at her almost sadly. "I hope you are right, my dear." But she had her doubts. She'd never understood what made her sister fall in love so impulsively with Raoul. He was more than twice her age and had lost an eye in one of his youthful battles. But she had seen Aelith's growing desire for the man and, knowing her sister's impetuous nature, did all she could to make certain that any babies from the liaison would be born in wedlock. So far, they had already produced two children—Elisabeth, born soon after the marriage and, more recently, a son named for his father.

Eleanor gestured toward a stone bench, and the two women sat to listen to the breathing of the night and the sound of crickets starting their raucous songs in the garden.

"Aelith," Eleanor spoke softly, "I've wondered. Why did you decide you no longer wanted to be called Petronilla?"

"It was my saint's name, given at baptism, my childhood name—and I much prefer my ordinary given name, Aelith."

"Quite frankly, so do I. But why did you change it now? Petronilla was what *Papa* always called you."

"I know, and that's why I used it as long as I did. But I thought it sounded childish. I've never liked Petronilla." Her tone made the name sound distasteful. "Such an ugly name. Raoul didn't like it either. He thought Aelith had a softer sound." She paused for a moment of reflection. "What finally decided me, though, was that it was Petronilla who was excommunicated by the pope. Since that is the name in all the official records, I decided to stop using it. Aelith was never excommunicated."

Eleanor gave a grim laugh and nodded. "A good reason if ever there was one."

At that moment, she was startled by a sudden gush of water that flowed down her legs and soaked her gown. She drew in a deep breath as she anticipated the tight unease of her first labor pain.

The night was long, but thank God it was finally over. Now it was morning, and the sun streaked the room with light. The birth had been an ordeal that lasted too many hours as far as Eleanor was concerned, but Aelith and Aunt Agnès had stayed by her side throughout the night. It had finally ended with unspeakable anguish. Aelith had dried her sister's tears and was now sitting beside her bed, holding her hand for consolation.

"Don't feel bad, sister. You can have others. At least it's proof that you're not barren."

Aelith's words were little solace. Eleanor's hopes had been so high. She was so confident in Bernard's promise that she had never doubted for an instant that she would bear the king a son and heir. But now she recalled the abbot's exact words. "Seek peace, and I promise, in confidence of His great mercy, that you will bear a child." Once again he had tricked her with the precision of his words. He had only promised a child—not a son. She had not really noticed his careful phrasing at the time, for he was well aware that she needed a son, not a useless daughter.

"What will you name her?" Aelith asked.

"I haven't thought about any names for a girl."

"Why not let the nuns decide?"

Agnès de Barbezieux was delighted with the idea, and she already knew the name they would choose—the name of Our Lady, the queen of Heaven, the patron saint of their convent—Marie. The abbess proclaimed it the most beautiful name in all the world and suggested that, perhaps one day, this child would become a nun here at the abbey.

"You mustn't mourn the birth of a daughter, Eleanor," the abbess said. "She will bring you much comfort in your old age."

Eleanor groaned. That was the last thing she needed at the moment—a daughter to comfort her in her old age. She needed a strong, healthy son to be his father's heir to the throne of France. Nevertheless, she was grateful to her aunt and to the nuns for taking her in and caring for her during these final months of her pregnancy. She was glad she was here, where the nuns were rejoicing at a safe delivery and the birth of a daughter, and not in Paris, where the queen mother, Adelaide de Maurienne, would be blaming her for yet another failure. Eleanor would reward the convent well with her benevolence, for the sisters had seen her through one of the most difficult moments of her life.

She dreaded returning to Paris—humiliated—for expectations had been so high among the courtiers and throughout the kingdom. She wondered if the chroniclers would even bother to mention that she had at last given birth—to a disappointing daughter. It was just as well the king was not present. He would learn soon enough, even before he returned to the convent, she hoped. She didn't want to see his initial displeasure and frustration.

"Bring her to me, Aelith. I might as well see what she looks like."

Aelith fetched the baby from her cradle across the room and laid her in the crook of her mother's arm.

"Daughters are not so bad. She will be a playmate for Elisabeth and Raoul," Aelith said.

In spite of herself, Eleanor smiled. "She is rather sweet, isn't she?"

She unwrapped the small bundle and counted her fingers and toes, looking her over thoroughly, to make sure all the necessary parts were in place. Then she gazed at the baby's face intently and frowned thoughtfully, "I don't think she looks like me. Do you?"

"I agree. More's the pity… to have the most beautiful mother in Christendom and to look like one's father instead," Aelith said, sorrow in her voice.

Abbess Agnès, seated nearby, frowned, then leaned forward and added, "But she will change as she grows older. I'm sure she will become a lovely woman."

"Oh, well," said Eleanor, turning to her sister. "She is what she is. At least, as you said, she's proof that I'm not barren."

Louis was even more disappointed than Eleanor had expected. He was morose and barely spoke to her for a week after his return, having learned of the birth of a daughter before he arrived back at the abbey. Eleanor hoped that some of the initial displeasure might have worn off before his return, but if it had, she could hardly tell it. He even refused to see the child at first, despite the nuns' encouragement, until the queen forced the issue and had the baby brought to his bedchamber.

"This is your daughter, Marie," she said. "*Our* daughter."

Louis scarcely glanced at her.

"She resembles you, husband."

He looked a bit more closely. "She has no hair," he said.

"It will grow."

"So this is the abbot's miracle, the one for which I groveled to make peace with Thibaut de Champagne," he said bitterly. "A rather paltry miracle. What good is a daughter?"

"Louis, there will be others. And a daughter is by no means worthless. She will make a good marriage and be a blessing to us." She hoped it was true.

"Perhaps," he said, then fell once more into silence.

Eleanor was in no hurry to return to the Île de France. The royal household lingered for a time at the abbey, where the good cheer of the nuns sustained them. Then, by early September, when Eleanor was fully recovered from childbirth and could think of no more excuses to stay, they returned to the ducal castle in Poitiers. She basked in the familiar comfort and relative warmth of early fall in the region, where the grape harvest, known as the *vendange*, was about to begin. The grapes were abundant that year and promised a rich yield. How well she remembered those heady days from her childhood, when the vintners sent samples of their grapes to the duke and stood back with pride, waiting for his judgment. She remembered their smiles of pleasure when he would nod and give the new harvest his approval, indicating it would be a good year for wine.

How she dreaded going back to Paris.

The birth of a daughter had not made Louis any more attentive to his conjugal duties. In fact, he seemed increasingly disgusted by the act, but he was bound by his word to Abbot Bernard to fulfill his duties.

He was eager to get back to Paris before the worst of the winter set in, but the queen had set her heart on spending the fall and winter in Aquitaine, away from the Paris chill. She needed the comfort and familiar surroundings of her native land now more than ever. She tried to persuade Louis that he could conduct business there as well as he could from Paris and that he needed to make his presence felt in this part of the royal domain. But she was unable to convince him.

"You may stay if you like, but I am needed in the Île de France," he insisted. It was a compromise that pleased Eleanor. She and her daughter, along with her sister, would remain behind in Poitiers.

Without Louis's dour presence, she began to take a somewhat greater interest in her baby. Although the child clung more to her wet nurse than to her mother, Eleanor began to look forward to the brief time she spent each day with her daughter, exclaiming over her first tooth, her first smile, and clapping her hands along with little Marie when she was finally able to sit up on her own. Motherhood was not something that came naturally to the queen, but she was still amazed that she had managed to produce this perfect little creature—well, almost perfect—from her own body.

"You're not beautiful, my sweet," Eleanor said to her daughter, who was listening wide-eyed to the voice she was far too young to understand, "so you must learn the art of being charming." The child's hair did not shine with the golden hue of her mother's. In fact, Eleanor judged it, what little there was, to be a mousy brown, but Marie's wide-spaced eyes were blue-gray and sparkled with a liveliness her mother took for intelligence.

"I think you will not be a dullard," she reassured her daughter with a smile. "You must use what talents you have, and I will teach you." The child clapped her hands and returned her mother's smile. But she reached for her nursemaid, Claudine, the moment she returned to the nursery, and Eleanor went back to her reading in the garden.

The troubadours of the region flocked to Poitiers during her sojourn there. The evenings were filled with the new *cansos* they were composing, along with an occasional parodic song called a *sirventes* or a *pastorela*, which told of the meeting between a knight and a shepherdess. Such songs could lead to all sorts of amusing or titillating outcomes for the pleasure of the court. Eleanor thrived on the rich culture of the region, and she generously welcomed and rewarded the troubadours and jongleurs who constantly showed up on her doorstep.

Their songs echoed throughout the castle, drifting even to the nursery, where Marie's nursemaid would rock the cradle in time to the music. The baby would listen attentively and look about in wide-eyed wonder until the rocking lulled her to sleep.

CHAPTER 4

Poitiers, November 1145

A messenger from the king arrived, the hooves of his horse echoing sharply off the stones of the courtyard of the Maubergeonne Tower in Poitiers, where Eleanor was residing with her sister. The young man presented a letter to the queen with a low bow. She broke the seal and read it hastily, frowned, then shrugged, and turned to Aelith.

"Louis is summoning me to Bourges for a Christmas court," Eleanor said. "He has apparently decided…," she hesitated for a moment, "to lead an army to the Holy Land to rescue Edessa from the Saracens!" Her voice was incredulous at the announcement. "*Mordieu*!" She almost laughed.

Louis had never been a good military commander, and this was a monumental undertaking. Everyone had heard by now about the fall of Edessa on Christmas Eve, 1144, and the terrible slaughter of many Christians there by the Saracen governor of Aleppo and Masul, a man named Imad ad-Din Zengi. *But a holy war… led by Louis?*

"Why would he do such a thing?" Aelith asked.

Eleanor glanced once more at the letter, which she still held in her hand. "Abbot Bernard has told him it would expiate his sin at Vitry. Evidently, making peace with Thibaut was not enough. And Louis has decided to do it. He thinks announcing his intent to undertake a Holy

War on the anniversary of Edessa's capture would inspire his vassals to participate. And he expects me… and you as well, I'm sure, to be present."

"It's a bit of a surprise, isn't it?" Aelith asked.

"To say the least. He's not exactly the model of a warrior king. Remember what happened when I persuaded him to take up arms and finally make an effort to recapture the city of Toulouse, which belonged to our grandmother."

Aelith listened only half-heartedly. She had heard the story many times.

Eleanor went on. "It was a fiasco. A miserable failure. And another impertinent act by Thibaut de Champagne, who refused to participate. As the king's vassal, he owes—"

"I know… forty days of military service each year, but he didn't show up to help the king. And you didn't get back the city of Toulouse." Aelith's voice was weary.

"The only thing that made his later skirmishes against Thibaut fairly successful was the soldiers' desire for plunder. It certainly wasn't because of any great leadership on Louis's part. Now he wants me to be at his side in Bourges when he announces this absurd attempt at a holy war."

"Will you go?" Aelith asked.

"Of course. I am the queen. I need to be there."

At first Eleanor was puzzled as to why Louis chose to celebrate his Christmas court in Bourges, but he knew how she hated to travel in mid-winter and supposed he was making an effort to minimize the distance for each of them. That way they could be together in a show of solidarity for the royal marriage. Christmas Day would also be the anniversary of his coronation there in 1137 after his father's death. As the southernmost city in the royal domain, it stood almost squarely in the center of the lands controlled by his vassals in northern France and those in Aquitaine, whom he also wanted to attract to his cause. *Perhaps it's even part of his effort to get back in the good graces of Bernard,* she thought, since she felt certain that Pierre de La Châtre, now solidly ensconced as archbishop of Bourges, would be present. That would no doubt be an interesting confrontation.

The horses plodded over the cold ground toward the city of Bourges, and Eleanor rode beside her friend and most loyal vassal, Geoffrey de Rancon, whom she trusted with her life. Aelith preferred to travel, at least for this stage of the trip, in the litter with her three-year-old daughter, Elisabeth, and her baby, Raoul, whom she had brought along because she intended to return home with her husband.

"We've been separated far too long," she told her sister, who tried to persuade her to return with her to Poitiers. But Aelith was determined.

Eleanor, on the other hand, had no intention of going back to Paris in the middle of winter and had taken the precaution of leaving little Marie in Poitiers in the care of Claudine. Surely Louis wouldn't expect her to go with him and leave her child behind.

One of the first guests to arrive was the new archbishop of Bourges whom Louis greeted hospitably, though Eleanor could see from the false smile he wore that it cost him quite an effort. Louis had invited more people than usual, and the hall was growing crowded. The Christmas court promised to be festive, even though almost as many clerics as noblemen had come. From her seat on the dais, Eleanor watched the colorful array of guests, some seated at the trestle tables, drinking spiced wine and talking loudly, others standing, chatting before the blazing fire in the center of the room. The hall was abuzz with voices, movement, and musicians playing from the balcony.

Noble ladies were dressed in their finest winter clothing and mantles lined with miniver or fox fur, while Eleanor's lining was ermine, which only the queen was allowed to wear. Beneath it, she wore a *bliaut* of vermilion silk brocade, laced on both sides and cinched at the waist with a belt of *orfrois* to echo the bands of gold embroidery ornamenting the neckline and wide sleeves. Her hair, braided with golden ribbons in the fashionable style called *trecheure*, hung to her waist and was covered by a white silk wimple, anchored by her queen's crown of gold encrusted with rubies. Crown-wearing ceremonies were relatively rare, special occasions emphasizing the king's authority and dignity. Eleanor always enjoyed the pomp of such events.

As she gazed around the room, she spotted her sister Aelith near the fireplace, hanging onto the arm of Raoul and looking up at him with adoring eyes. *She will soon be pregnant again*, Eleanor thought.

When Louis mounted the dais to stand beside her, he signaled to the herald to call the meeting to order. He wanted to speak now before the courtiers were too drunk to respond with what he hoped would be enthusiasm. The musicians hushed, as the clerics and nobles settled down, took their seats at the various long tables, and turned their attention to the king. Among them was a monk from St. Denis, a confidant of Abbot Suger by the name of Odo de Deuil, now the king's chaplain, whose job it was to observe and record the events.

Louis began in a low tone, making an earnest effort to reveal what Odo would later describe as "the secret of his heart"—his desire to lead the crusade and make a personal pilgrimage to Jerusalem. Eleanor strained to hear his words, for he was not an articulate speaker and tended to ramble without making his points clearly and forcefully. She noticed that those in the assembly began to shift uncomfortably in their seats as they tried to listen politely. *Thank God*, she thought, when he finally sat down and nodded to Godfrey, the bishop of Langres, who stood and looked sternly out over the gathering until everyone was still and attentive once more. He began to speak, and his words rang out with clarity and authority over the great hall as he described the suffering and slaughter of the Christians in Edessa by the arrogant Saracens. His words were effective. Soon the ladies in the room were crying, and even some of the men began to dab at their eyes.

When he finally blessed the gathering and sat down, Louis stood up again to ask his vassals to join him in his glorious crusade. Moved as they might have been by the bishop's rhetoric, the king's inarticulate zeal did not have the same effect. Instead of leaning forward with eagerness, his vassals leaned back to whisper to their wives or speak with others at their table. A murmur went around the room, but not a single man rose to join the king. Eleanor could see Louis's shoulders beginning to droop in disappointment. Finally, Raoul de Vermandois, sensing that the matter was about to end badly, rose to his feet and requested permission to speak.

"My lord, clearly there are many matters to consider and arrangements to be made before committing to such a journey. Most of us here have lands to tend and families to look after," he said, touching Aelith's shoulder. "Let me propose that we delay the decision until Easter in order to give all your vassals time to consider what must be done." Eleanor could see that he was trying to save the king embarrassment.

Bishop Godfrey leaned toward the king and whispered something in his ear. The king nodded and stood once more. The hall quieted again.

"What my seneschal has proposed seems to make a great deal of sense," he said. His voice was clearer now. "We all need time to make arrangements. Let us delay the taking of the cross until Easter. Then we shall gather again at Vézelay and see what each of us has decided." *He hides his disappointment well,* Eleanor thought. *And Vézelay is a good choice.* As an important spiritual center and one of four starting points for the popular pilgrimage to Santiago, it was also the site of a Benedictine abbey that boasted the relics of Mary Magdalene.

A murmur of approval went through the crowd, relieved that no one was forced to make a commitment here and now. The king, equally relieved to avoid their refusals, signaled for the musicians once again to strike up their *vielles*, *gitterns*, and lutes and for the feast to begin.

The feasting lasted throughout the afternoon and into the evening, as guests dined upon the delicacies the squires carried ceremoniously into the hall one after another and served on their trenchers—roasted swan, wild boar, pheasants, eels in saffron sauce, salmon pie, St. John's rice, cheeses of all types, dates in comfit, figs, and *doucettes*, sweetmeats that came near the end of the meal, and much, much more—all served with wines that complemented each course. It was one of the more splendid feasts given by King Louis that she could recall. He often shied away from such festivity, but he had wanted to make this Christmas court very special.

Well past the hour of compline, long after the feast ended, the trestle tables were removed, and the sopping trenchers were thrown to the dogs, Louis and Eleanor were finally alone in their private rooms. Only then did the king inquire about his daughter.

"I see you have not brought the child. Does that mean you don't plan to return with me to Paris?" he asked, clearly disgruntled.

"It's much too cold and hard a trip for a baby at this time of year," she replied, with a barely stifled yawn. It was too late for a serious discussion, and she was exhausted.

"Nevertheless, your sister brought her own children."

"They are a bit older than Marie."

"The boy, Raoul, is older only by a few months," he reminded her.

"Six months, to be exact. That's quite a difference."

"I have missed you," he said, a trace of tenderness in his voice. She was surprised, even touched, by his words.

"And I have missed you," she replied, more out of duty than sentiment. "I promise I will join you at Easter at Vézelay, and Marie and I will return to Paris with you then." He nodded, seeming, for the moment at least, satisfied by her words. Eleanor thought it a propitious time to change the subject.

"What will you do to make the gathering at Vézelay more successful in getting your vassals to agree to this venture?"

"Bishop Godfrey suggested that a meeting at Easter would better remind people of the sacrifice of our Lord and incline them more to make one of their own. I also plan to invite Bernard de Clairvaux to join us there to help to persuade everyone."

"An excellent choice. He can, as you well know, persuade anyone to do almost anything."

The king smiled a rueful smile, "As we both well know."

Even before the gathering at Bourges, Pope Eugenius had issued a papal bull addressed to King Louis and urging everyone to take up arms to defend the Holy Land, though Louis did not receive it until his return to Paris. He sent a letter to Eleanor describing its effectiveness. It would add strength to his call for his vassals to take the cross, for it promised something Louis himself could not grant—the remission of sins and eternal life for those who took up their swords against the infidels. It challenged "the greater men and the nobles" to "gird themselves manfully" so that Christianity could be spread and the valor of the crusaders would be praised throughout the world. It was a powerful argument that would surely appeal to the knightly mentality. Eleanor was certain that Abbot Bernard's silver tongue would make the call hard to resist.

As the months back in Poitiers passed, Eleanor missed her sister. Her ladies surrounded her, of course, but she had learned her lesson well and no longer confided her innermost thoughts to them. However, she had made a decision she wanted to talk over with her most trusted vassal. One evening, as she sat before the fire in the great hall, surrounded by various courtiers and friends, she raised the question with Geoffrey de Rancon.

"Will you go with Louis on his expedition?" she asked him.

"It will require a great deal of time and effort to raise the funds, *Domna*," he said, addressing her in the *langue d'oc's* version of *ma dame*. "But like everyone else, I shall decide before Eastertide."

"I would like you to go as my escort," she said. "You and your troops, of course. Not just to Vézelay but to the Holy Land. I can't think of anyone I would trust more."

"You, my lady? You are thinking of going? Is such a trip advisable for a woman?"

"Perhaps not, Geoffrey, but when have I always done what is advisable?" She laughed. "It would give me a chance to visit my uncle Raymond, whom I haven't seen since I was eleven—two years before my marriage to Louis. I would give much to see him again."

Her father's brother, Raymond de Poitiers, only nine years older than she, had teased her unmercifully as a child, but she had adored him nonetheless. He had left France when he was twenty years old to marry Constance of Antioch and become ruler of the principality that had been governed by his bride's late father. Eleanor recalled fond memories of her uncle who felt more like an older brother to her, and she was eager to meet his wife and family. She was also worried about him, for the county in which Edessa was located lay adjacent to the principality of Antioch. The fall of Edessa could threaten Raymond's lands as well.

Geoffrey nodded. "I'm sure your uncle would be delighted to welcome you."

"Besides," she said, "I would also like to visit Jerusalem. Why should men be the only ones to have adventures?"

"It could be a dangerous trip, my lady," he said, a warning in his voice.

"But far less dangerous if you and your men were my escorts."

"Of course, my lady. If you go, my men and I would be honored to accompany you—with the king's permission, of course."

"I'd rather you not mention my intentions to anyone until I have had a chance to inform my husband. I wouldn't want him to hear it from someone else."

"As you wish, *Midons.*"

The more she thought about it, the more excited she became and the more she convinced herself that the crusade was not only justified, but essential. Not only did the fall of Edessa threaten her uncle's lands, it was possible that, without western intervention, all of the other territories held by Christians—Tripoli and the kingdom of Jerusalem—were also vulnerable.

A rescue of Edessa, she suspected, was not Louis's only goal, but more likely a convenient excuse to undertake a pilgrimage to Jerusalem for the sake of his soul. She'd listened to Geoffrey's warnings about the dangers of the trip, but the more she thought about it, the more exciting it sounded. *Why not? Why should I not take the cross as well as Louis? It will be an adventure.* And the thought of staying behind in that cold Capetian court, answering to Abbot Suger or Louis's mother or anyone else he decided to leave in charge, sounded like a nightmare. It would be the trip of a lifetime.

She thought for a moment of her daughter. They would, of course, have to leave her behind. It would be unthinkable to take such a tiny child, not yet trained to wipe her own bottom, on such a trip. She felt a tiny pang of guilt, but then thought *Claudine is more a mother to her than I am, and Marie's grandmother will be nearby. In any case, we won't be leaving for a while. I'll see her take her first steps and perhaps even hear her first words. Besides, we'll be back before she scarcely knows we're gone.*

CHAPTER 5

By the time Eleanor was beginning her preparations to leave for the Easter assembly at Vézelay, Marie was sitting alone, trying to crawl, and babbling at anyone who would listen. As she sat on Claudine's lap in the garden, she clapped her hands with joy whenever she heard birds singing or a lute playing. Eleanor smiled as she watched her daughter lean forward and reach out for the bright flowers that climbed the tower walls. Capturing two of them in her tiny fist, she tried to put them in her mouth, where two small pearls of teeth adorned her lower gum.

"She's a bright little thing, isn't she?" Eleanor said, smiling as she watched the nursemaid bouncing the baby on her knee and trying to keep the flowers out of her mouth at the same time.

"Indeed she is, my lady," Claudine replied, pride in her voice as though the child were her own.

The queen reached out to take Marie in her own arms, and the child reached back, warming her mother's heart. Eleanor loved the softness of her daughter's skin against her own cheek and her sweet, milky, baby smell. There was a joy in these moments she had not known before. *But they could become a lure*, she thought, *to keep a woman from the world.*

"What shall I pack Marie for the trip, *ma dame*?" Claudine asked, as Eleanor looked over the coffers her ladies had been filling with garments suitable for the Easter event.

"I've decided not to take her after all, Claudine," Eleanor said. "I think she would fare better here. We'll come back for her after the assembly." Eleanor could see Claudine's disappointment, for she knew the nursemaid had looked forward to the trip. But the woman merely nodded and curtsied before she left the chamber.

Although Eleanor would miss the sweetness of daily moments with her daughter, things would be so much simpler without her in tow. She knew that Louis would be annoyed when she arrived once again without Marie—not because he so longed to see his daughter, but because he expected Eleanor to return with him to Paris, and he knew she would not go without the child. In fact, she had other plans.

Springtime travel was glorious. Eleanor always felt safe with Geoffrey de Rancon at her side, as well as Arveo, her steward, who was always there to see to her needs. As she gazed about the greening woods at the profusion of wildflowers lining the roadway and the occasional splash of color of blooming wild pear or cherry trees, she laughed aloud.

"You are amused, *Midons*?" Geoffrey asked.

"Just happy," she said. "How good it feels not to be cooped up in a dreary castle, but rather outside surrounded by all this beauty of nature."

She let go of her palfrey's reins for a moment and stretched her arms wide. *How exciting the voyage to the Holy Land will be*, she thought. She had never been outside of France and Aquitaine before, and now she would see exotic worlds, hear foreign tongues, and meet many new people. She felt only satisfaction with her decision to accompany Louis and hoped he would not be too hard to persuade.

When Eleanor and her entourage reached Vézelay, Geoffrey's men pitched their tents in the valley below. She planned to be waiting for the king like a dutiful wife when he arrived.

Louis arrived the next day, accompanied by the most important members of his court, including his chaplain Odo, and his seneschal

Raoul. Eleanor was disappointed to learn that Aelith and her children had remained behind in Paris.

Louis smiled when he caught sight of Eleanor and approached her, his arms outstretched.

"How fare you, wife? It is good to see you again."

"And you, my lord," she curtsied, before giving him a chaste kiss of welcome.

"Where is the child?"

"I did not bring her, my lord," she said, watching his eyes begin to gather thunderclouds.

"Does this mean you don't wish to return to Paris with me?" he asked, his voice angry.

"Not at all, husband," she said, her tone warm and light. "I thought that, after Easter, we might travel about Aquitaine to consolidate support in the region and encourage our vassals to prepare to join this holy effort. We could finish the tour in Poitiers, gather up our daughter, and return to Paris all together."

She was relieved to see his anger subside somewhat, but he said, "You should have given me notice."

"I only thought of it lately. Is it not possible, husband?" She pretended disappointment at his reaction, though it was precisely what she had expected.

"Possible, I suppose, but I would like to have had an opportunity to plan for such a voyage." She could see already that he was on the verge of accepting her proposal. It would be all right. But she decided not to mention her desire to accompany him to the Holy Land until the next evening after he had rested.

She waited for just the right moment, when they were alone together in the king's tent sharing a glass of spiced wine, as shadows and candlelight danced slowly against the heavy fabric of the walls.

"I hope all your plans for the upcoming expedition are going well, my lord."

"As well as possible at this stage. We won't really know until Easter Sunday how well we have succeeded in building enthusiasm for the venture."

"When will Abbot Bernard arrive?" she asked.

"Any day now. We had hoped the Pope himself might be able to join us, but he seems to be detained in Rome. Not willingly, I gather."

"I'm sure Abbot Bernard will serve well in his stead. You've done an excellent job in organizing this Easter gathering." She paused for an instant, letting him absorb her flattery. He took another sip of wine, and she offered him a sweetmeat.

"Louis, there is something I must tell you before the abbot comes. He may not approve, but I hope I will have your support."

His pleased expression gave way to a frown, and he looked at her with suspicion. "What is on your mind now?"

"I want to go to Jerusalem with you," she said. "I plan to take the cross."

"What?" He almost spilled his wine, as he sat upright suddenly from his relaxed position. "This will be no trip for a woman. The travel will be hard, and you would not likely have the luxuries you are accustomed to. Besides, you need to stay here to look after my lands and our daughter. Absolutely not. Your place is at home."

"Louis, this opportunity may never come again, and I too want to see the Holy Land and the sites where our Lord walked."

"It is out of the question." He was adamant. She refilled his goblet before she spoke again.

"Think about it, my lord. You might be gone for years. It would be a long separation for us. I would like to be with you." She paused, seeing no immediate softening in his face. "… But let us speak of it no more tonight. There is time to talk about it later." She made certain it would be a night in which he would remember only sweet and undemanding caresses.

As the week went on, Louis's resolve weakened. Every argument he could think of, Eleanor was able to counter.

"Who would be in charge of the royal domain?"

"Abbot Suger would be the ideal regent in your absence," she told him. "He would be far more effective than I—a mere woman." She tried to make her voice sound demure. She was playing to his views about "the weaker sex," which she felt certain he had never expected to hear from her lips.

"He isn't even in favor of the holy war. He worries about my absence from the kingdom for such a long time."

"All the better. If he is concerned, clearly he would be happier and complain less if he were in charge, rather than having to endure someone else's incompetence."

"And what about our daughter?" he asked. "How can you abandon her for such a long time?"

"I won't be abandoning her," she protested. "She'll be well cared for. Claudine will remain, and Aelith can care for her with her own children. Besides, your mother will be nearby. Perhaps she would be willing to watch over Marie in our absence." The dowager queen, Adelaide de Maurienne, had established her own court at Compiègne, but she was frequently in Paris with her new husband, Mathieu de Montmorency, who served as the king's constable. She would no doubt be willing to look after the welfare of her granddaughter, though Eleanor intended to leave the child with her sister, who had children she could play with.

Little by little, Eleanor urged her husband to consider the benefits the shared experience of the crusade might bring to their marriage. "And my presence will encourage my vassals to commit more readily to joining you," she argued.

"I'm surely not the first woman to want to go on such an adventure. Some noble ladies accompanied their husbands in the first holy war, and I doubt I'll be the only one who wants to go this time." Actually, the only ones she could recall were Florine of Burgundy and Ida of Formbach-Ratelnberg, the margravine of Austria, who were both killed in battles or massacres during the journey. But the thought gave her pause for only a moment. *They must have been foolish in their actions*, she thought. Certainly she did not intend to put herself in such danger.

"And perhaps God will be pleased enough with our religious fervor to grant us the son we need. There is more opportunity if we are together." In the end, her arguments wore him down, and he actually began to think her going might be a good thing after all.

"I hope you will be willing to help Abbot Bernard understand," she said.

A shroud of uncertainty crossed his face. "I will do my best."

But his best was not good enough. Bernard did not understand. A deep frown creased his forehead when Louis, with Eleanor at his side, informed the abbot of her intentions.

"Women have no place in a holy war of this sort," he argued. "Women in an army campsite are no better than those harlots who follow the soldiers."

Eleanor gasped at his audacity.

"The only women necessary on a military expedition are the servants who prepare food and wash the clothes. Others can only bring disaster," he added.

His words infuriated Eleanor, who tried to hold her temper. "What nonsense! I'll be a pilgrim like everyone else."

"The men will not be mere pilgrims but soldiers… holy warriors. Having to protect women will be a distraction from their just cause," he argued.

In the end, he had little choice, for she indicated that, only if she were allowed to go would she be willing to rally the nobles of Aquitaine to the cause. With both Eleanor and Louis united, the abbot finally conceded.

Bernard's mood seemed to lighten throughout the rest of Holy Week, as unprecedented crowds of noblemen arrived in Vézelay. The crusade promised to be a success. He had recently returned from a speaking tour in Germany, where he had been able to convince King Conrad to join in the venture with the French king. Now he needed only to persuade Louis's vassals.

They came from all directions—the flower of French nobility. If they did not come in person, they sent their sons. The countryside around the hilltop town of Vézelay was dappled with bright-colored tents and heraldic banners flapping in the breeze. When the numbers grew so large that it became obvious they could not all fit inside the basilica of Saint-Madeleine for the Easter gathering, Bernard ordered a sturdy platform to be constructed outside the church on the slope of the Burgundian hill where Vézelay was located. There, in the view of all, he would preach.

Easter Sunday dawned, a glorious day filled with brightness and the joy of Resurrection. The gathered knights could see the abbot, his face lifted toward heaven, reflecting the sunlight, as the magnificent basilica of Mary Magdalene loomed behind him to form the perfect backdrop. His voice echoed over the valley, like the voice of God itself as he read the pope's call and promise of salvation to crusaders. Then he began to describe once again the calamity of Edessa's fall. In words that captured the imagination, he told all those gathered on the hillside and in the valley how the people of Edessa cried out for their help and how the kingdom of Christ needed them. They must form a powerful army to march against the Saracens who had defiled the sanctuaries and spit on their holy relics.

He told them nothing they did not already know, for Saracen atrocities, often highly exaggerated, had been told and retold for months throughout the kingdom. But Abbot Bernard painted such vivid pictures that they felt they could hear the Holy Spirit speaking through him, like an "orator from heaven," as Odo de Deuil would describe him, as he "spread the dew of the divine word." Throughout the sunlit afternoon the abbot spoke, inspiring their zeal and their energy, to a fevered pitch. Like the others, Queen Eleanor listened, moved and amazed as always by the power of the abbot's words. Finally, he raised his arms to bless the gathering and call out for all those present to take the cross and become soldiers of Christ.

The crowd was already cheering when King Louis took the first step forward. The cheers became a roar. It died to an astonished ripple as Queen Eleanor stepped forward to receive the second cross. A woman on crusade! If she could do it, then why not they? Once again the crowd roared its approval, and the voices of men reverberated throughout the valley, "Crosses! Crosses!" until Abbot Bernard literally had to strew the prepared crosses to their outstretched hands. There were not enough of them to go around, and he was compelled to cut up his own vestment to make more. It was a heady experience—one Eleanor would not have missed for anything. She knew she was unlikely ever to encounter such a moment again.

Clutching her cross to her breast, she gazed about the crowd, some young and some not so young, clamoring for crosses. One man in particular caught her eye. He appeared to be about eighteen to twenty years old. It was Henri de Champagne, the oldest son of Count Thibaut.

At his side were his comrades-in-arms, Anseau and Garnier de Traînel. Though she did not know their names, she recognized Henri, who had attended earlier meetings in Paris with his father. Their eager young faces shone with zeal and exhilaration.

"Where is Count Thibaut?" Eleanor asked Louis, who put his hand to his ear in order to hear her over the noisy crowd.

"Thibaut is getting old. I hear he's not well, so he won't be going, but he's sending his oldest son, a worthy young man. He came to call on me when he first arrived to bring his father's greetings and regrets."

The queen nodded and gazed about the fervent crowd, filled with such enthusiastic young men in their bright livery. There was no question about it. This was a day to remember, and she was sure this voyage to the Holy Land would be a trip she would never forget.

True to his word, when the festivities and fervor of Vézelay came to an end, Louis joined Eleanor in an amiable excursion to visit some of her most prominent vassals, thank them for their support, and bolster their commitment to his crusade. When they finally returned to Poitiers, Claudine brought Marie to the solar to visit her parents. The little girl smiled when she saw her mother, but when her father, who to her was a stranger, reached out to hold her, she shrank toward her nursemaid's breast. Safe in Claudine's arms, she gazed at Louis with curiosity, then reached out to touch his beard, which made him laugh.

"Time to take you home, little girl, and let you get to know your father," Louis said, patting her arm, before he lost interest and turned to Eleanor once again.

The queen nodded for Claudine to take Marie back to the nursery. "Pack her things, Claudine. We'll be leaving in two days' time to return to Paris."

CHAPTER 6

Paris, November 1146

Geoffrey, count of Anjou, sat chatting with King Louis in the great hall as they shared a goblet of wine and waited for the queen to make her appearance. Geoffrey's fourteen-year-old son Henry stood by his side. They had arrived in late afternoon, when shadows were already lengthening in the courtyard. Geoffrey had a serious proposal to make, and he wanted to do so before the king got too deeply into his crusade plans. He had requested the audience several times, but the king had refused until finally, as cooler weather set in, he invited the count to court.

"There is so much to do to prepare for this venture," Louis was saying, "so many people to consult, decisions to make. I'm sure it will be late spring or summer before we are ready to depart. I do wish you were going with us." The count had declined on the grounds that his absence would place his lands and the rights of his family in serious peril.

"I do as well, my lord, but it is impossible, as I'm sure you understand. You can imagine what might happen in my absence."

"I do understand, but you would have been a great asset."

"Thank you, my lord." Geoffrey's wife, Matilda, daughter of the late king Henry I of England, was still in a ferocious struggle for the throne of England with her cousin Stephen, the brother of Thibaut de

Champagne. It had been going on since 1135, when King Henry died quite suddenly after eating a plate of lampreys. By this time Matilda had all but given up hope of obtaining the throne for herself, but she and Geoffrey were still fighting to secure its inheritance for their firstborn son, Henry, now standing impatiently beside his father.

Their conversation was interrupted, and Geoffrey rose quickly to his feet, as Queen Eleanor swept into the room. Around her neck she wore a magnificent Byzantine cross of gold encrusted with rubies and pearls, which the emperor of Constantinople, Manuel Komnenos, had sent to her as part of his effort to woo her husband and his crusaders across the land route through Constantinople as they made their way to the Holy Land. The cross rested on her breast where it drew considerable attention as it gleamed in reflected light.

Even though Geoffrey wore his most charming smile, the thought of Bernard de Clairvaux suddenly flashed through his mind. The old abbot would no doubt frown on such a splendid adornment, even though it was a cross. Anything of man-made beauty seemed suspect in his eyes, but the count thanked God that Bernard wasn't present this evening. Rumors suggested that he didn't like the queen any more than he liked the Plantagenets, and Geoffrey sincerely hoped the negotiations that brought him to court could be completed before the abbot learned of them.

King Louis stepped forward to greet his wife, and Geoffrey watched with interest the interplay between the two. *Polite at best*, he thought, as the queen directed her eyes to the floor, dipping in a slight curtsey to acknowledge her husband's presence.

"Your majesty," Geoffrey said as he bowed deeply before the queen and then looked up to meet her startling blue eyes. He smiled broadly as he appraised the fine-looking woman before him. It was not the first time they had met, but tonight, in the glow of the huge fire, the candles and torches that blazed throughout the great hall, she seemed more radiant than ever.

Eleanor was rapidly becoming a legend in France. She had made her mark that Easter Sunday at Vézelay. Even though he was not present, Geoffrey had heard all about it. No one had been surprised when the king moved forward to take the first cross. But the count had learned how the crowd gasped as Queen Eleanor strode to the platform and knelt before the abbot to receive the second cross. Some said the abbot had even hesitated a moment before making the sign of the cross over the royal figure and presenting her with the crusader's emblem. Was that true? He had no idea. He wished he could have been present. After that, he'd heard, it was pandemonium. It must have been something to see.

Geoffrey glanced at the king, who was leading his wife toward the dais. He was hardly the glorious figure a woman like Queen Eleanor deserved. Everyone knew why he was undertaking this crusade. He was so contrite about the burning of Vitry that he had eagerly seized on the pope's promise of absolution for his sins and a guaranteed place in Heaven if he would lead the crusade. Louis wasn't much of a soldier, Geoffrey knew, but he had to give the man credit. He was willing to try, and if the king were willing, then many knights and foot soldiers would follow him. They too could earn a place in Heaven—and bring home some of the spoils of war, as well. The count was envious of the adventure, but he had his hands full at home, trying to keep the Norman barons in line to make certain it was his son, and not that of Stephen, who would inherit the throne of England.

Geoffrey had thought through the situation quite thoroughly before deciding to make his petition at court. Although Louis may not have been the image of the ideal king, he nonetheless held the considerable power of the French throne. A close alliance with him, closer even than vassal to lord, could be very beneficial to the future of the Plantagenets. Geoffrey felt certain that the king's more sensible advisor, Abbot Suger, would see the practicality and wisdom of the arrangement he wished to propose—a marriage contract between his son Henry and the king's daughter, Marie. Geoffrey believed that the queen could also be easily persuaded. He was less sure about the king.

"He's a fine-looking lad, Lord Geoffrey," Eleanor murmured, as she cast her eyes appraisingly over the boy standing beside his father. He suspected she'd already guessed the purpose of the visit. "Much like his father," she added. Geoffrey smiled with appreciation. His nickname was Geoffrey le Bel, Geoffrey the Handsome, and he felt full worthy of the name.

The boy's eyes darted around the court, his boredom all too obvious, once he had paid his respects to the queen. His complexion was ruddy from hours in the sun, hunting and learning to joust. His sandy hair was bleached to a fair reddish hue. He was well built and tall for a boy of fourteen, almost the height of his father. As he shifted his weight from foot to foot, his gaze came to rest defiantly upon the queen. She seemed amused by his bold stare. His self-confidence was palpable and unsurprising for a boy who believed he would one day be king of England. Fortunately, Geoffrey thought, his son had inherited his mother's courage and tenacity, and at least a modicum of his father's good looks. The count was pleased by the queen's reaction. She had much influence with the king.

King Louis frowned thoughtfully. "You wrote that you were coming with a proposal of some sort. What did you have in mind?" he asked.

Geoffrey glanced at the queen before he gave his response. "I have come most humbly with a betrothal offer—your daughter to my son—the future king of England. I thought that, perhaps, before you left on crusade you might want the matter settled."

"But she's only a baby," Louis said. Such betrothals often took place, but the marriage was supposed to wait until both parties were at an age of consent. "Your son will be in his mid-twenties before he could take her to wife."

"Nevertheless," said Geoffrey, "what better match could there be than the king of England for the daughter of the king of France? One day their offspring might rule both kingdoms."

"True, that's a possibility," Louis said, "but it's by no means a certainty."

Geoffrey watched with apprehension as King Louis looked the boy over. Surely he could see nothing objectionable. Henry appeared quite presentable in the short green cloak that gave him the nickname Court Mantel. He was an intelligent lad with good posture, almost as tall as the king, and he conducted himself courteously. There was nothing amiss in such a match for the king's daughter. Louis looked at his young wife as though to gauge her reaction. She was smiling at the boy.

"Would it be possible for us to meet the young princess?" Geoffrey asked the king when he had finished his inspection.

"Of course," Louis replied, motioning to his steward to have the child brought to the great hall.

As they waited, the cup-bearer stepped smartly forward to pour another serving of wine for the count of Anjou and for the king. Eleanor refused the goblet held out to her and turned instead to Geoffrey with a bright smile.

"And how fares your wife, the Lady Matilda?"

"Quite well, *ma dame*. She sends her greetings to your majesty."

"She is a woman I quite admire," Eleanor said with frankness. "She has fought with great courage for her throne. She deserves it."

"I thank you on her behalf." The count bent his head in gratitude, suspecting that there were not many women the queen *did* admire. He himself did not share the queen's fondness for Matilda, though fondness and admiration were of no importance in marriage compared to the glory and land one could gain from it.

The queen turned to young Henry. "Tell me about yourself, boy," she said. "Can you read and write?"

"I read tolerably well, my lady, and I am learning to write, though we have clerks for that sort of thing," the boy replied, his voice cracking a bit on the word *clerks*.

The queen laughed, and young Henry's face flamed with embarrassment. "So you do, lad. So you do."

At that moment the huge oak door at the end of the hall opened, and Claudine, wearing a Flemish wool *chainse* and a white wimple, came into the room carrying the young princess, still in the chemise she slept in. The child yawned, as though she had just been awakened.

Eleanor rose and moved in their direction, "Put her down, Claudine."

As the nurse bent to set the child on the floor, the queen stepped down from the dais, leaned toward her daughter, and opened her arms as the little girl toddled toward her mother.

"*Bonsoir, ma petite*," she said, kissing her daughter's cheek as she gathered her into her arms. The queen looked up at Geoffrey and his son and said, "This, gentlemen, is Marie Capet, heiress of Aquitaine and the only child of the king of France." She included young Henry in her word *gentlemen* to make up for her spontaneous, but thoughtless, laughter at this inability to control his voice just yet. He understood and managed a smile for the queen.

It was obvious to Geoffrey le Bel that the child Marie had not inherited her mother's renowned beauty. Unfortunately, she resembled her father instead. Her thin hair was a mousy brown, her eyes were a nondescript color somewhere between gray and a dull blue, and her cheeks were fat like her father's. But her looks were of no importance. Geoffrey scarcely glanced at the child before extolling her adorable face to her beaming mother. It was not entirely a lie. Little Marie had the sweet appeal of all babies. And perhaps it was too soon to tell what the toddler would look like as she grew up. In any case, Geoffrey knew that all mothers liked to hear compliments about their children.

His son Henry stared indifferently at the little girl. His father had told him not to react, no matter what the child looked like, and not to show surprise at anything anyone might say. He had also reminded the boy that the little girl's looks, intelligence, or demeanor had nothing to do with whether she was marriageable or not. He could avail himself of physical beauty anywhere. It was her father's rank and her inheritance that were of importance.

"She will be a fine match for the next king of England," Geoffrey reminded the king and queen.

"But just how certain is the boy's future?" the king asked cautiously. "I know that King Stephen has several living sons. They say that the oldest, Eustace, has his heart set on inheriting the throne." He was skeptical that his claim could be denied.

Geoffrey made every effort to appear more confident than he actually was. "It will do him little good, I think. The barons of England and Normandy are quite ready to recognize Henry as their lord and heir to the throne."

"But as you know, my friend, many things can happen before that occurs."

"It's true that many things can happen, but, as you also know, my wife Matilda's armies were strong enough to capture Stephen in the earlier conflict, and her armies are even stronger now. You remember surely that she refused to let him out of prison until he had sworn to turn over to us the duchy of Normandy, which had already been given to Eustace. Eustace had no choice but to relinquish it. Even then he was powerless to do otherwise. Now that we control Normandy, our armies are even stronger. I don't think the barons would dare deny the throne to the direct heir of Henry I a second time."

The queen nodded, impressed with his vehemence and all that Matilda had accomplished, but the king remained silent. He had no intention of agreeing to the proposal tonight, as Geoffrey had hoped.

"I will, of course, need to consult my counselors about the matter of the betrothal," said the king. "They are assembling tomorrow afternoon in the council chamber."

Geoffrey's heart sank a bit, for he feared that the word "counselors" might include the abbot of Clairvaux, though he knew Bernard was not now at court and hoped he would not arrive in time to be a part of the decision-making.

"We'll plan to meet again tomorrow at dusk to discuss the matter further and to have any documents we might agree to drawn up and signed."

Geoffrey took the king's words to be a positive sign that he was in favor of the betrothal. With that, he watched the queen kiss her daughter and hand her back to the nurse, who hurried out of the room to put her back to bed.

The next morning a flurry of horses rode into the courtyard just before the hour of sext and the midday meal that would follow. The abbot of Clairvaux dismounted with help from two of the young novices in his entourage. Usually the old abbot traveled in a litter, which was easier on his tired bones than the palfrey he rode today. But the horse moved faster, and he had learned of the count's intentions only four days ago, even before the king knew of them. He had immediately written a letter to the king, urging him not to consider the proposal. He read it over after it was written, hoping to persuade the king that his sacrifice in going on the crusade would be useless if he were to approve this marriage agreement. Although the letter focused on the argument of incest or consanguinity, there were other reasons, more important ones he'd chosen not to reveal just yet to the king.

... I have heard that the count of Anjou is pressing for a sworn agreement to the proposed marriage between his son and your daughter. This is something not merely inadvisable but also unlawful because . . . it is prohibited by the impediment of consanguinity. I have learned on trustworthy evidence that the queen's mother and this boy, the Count of Anjou's son, are related in the third degree. Thus, I strongly advise you not to take part in this matter, but to fear God and turn away from evil.

Could he persuade the king to take his advice? To strengthen his argument, he had suggested that it would make his crusade a useless venture:

Do not think that after this your sacrifice would be acceptable to God since it would be incomplete. While trying to save another kingdom, you would be sacrificing your own by aligning it against God, against what is right and just and against all that is expedient and honorable.

It was a strong letter, but was it strong enough? He continued to fret over it even after it was dispatched. No. It was not sufficient. He must go himself to argue the case. It was urgent enough, he believed, that he would have to endure the rough roads on horseback to prevent this terrible marriage of Princess Marie that was being proposed by Geoffrey of Anjou, whom he considered a Plantagenet upstart.

How could the king even consider such a marriage? There was a legend that the Plantagenets were descended from a demon countess. The story was well known throughout France of the beautiful woman of unknown origin who had married Geoffrey Greygown of Anjou, an ancestor of young Henry, a woman who seldom went to mass, they said, and, when she did, always left before the Eucharist. When suspicious courtiers tried to restrain her, she changed her comely shape, revealed her demon self, and flew out the window. *Obvious nonsense*, the abbot thought, but it should at least serve to make the king cautious in considering such an alliance. Surely he had heard the legend.

Whether it was true or not was unimportant. There were many factors to consider. The abbot thought little of Geoffrey Plantagenet, whom he considered an opportunist of the first order. This would not be a good marriage—that he saw clearly. And he was ready with his arguments against it as soon as the meeting was convened. God had granted his petition for Princess Marie to be born, and surely He would grant this favor as well. Bernard had no intention of letting his miracle child be wed to the offspring of a wastrel like Geoffrey Plantagenet—not if he could help it.

The meeting convened as the bells rang for the hour of none. The sun, midway down the sky, cast against the pale wall the shadows of the abbots, Bernard and Suger, seated at opposite ends of the long table where the king's most trusted advisors, including his seneschal Raoul, had gathered.

King Louis did not hesitate to broach the subject of the betrothal agreement at once. "As most of you already know, the count of Anjou has come to our court to propose a betrothal of marriage between the Princess Marie and his son, Henry. I'm sure I need not point out that such an alliance would help keep peace on the kingdom's western front in my absence, and it promises a good future for my daughter." The night before the meeting he had discussed the betrothal with Eleanor in private. She was convinced that the boy had a very promising future and that her daughter would do well to be married to the future king of England. She thought the boy quite comely as well, which mattered not a whit to him, though it might to their daughter when she was older. The queen's opinion was important to him, but he must also hear the advice of his counselors.

The men around the table, Suger included, were already nodding their acquiescence before he finished his comments—all but one. Abbot Bernard rose to his feet and directed his narrowed eyes to Suger at the other end of the table.

"I won't allow it," he stated simply.

"And why not?" Suger asked in a patronizing voice.

"The boy is no good. He will never be any good."

"Such a marriage would doubtless lead to a fine future for the princess—one that would in all probability make her queen of England one day," Suger pointed out. "The boy obviously has good prospects. He seems courteous and well bred."

Bernard said nothing in reply for the moment. He sat down again at his end of the table and glowered at Suger.

"I agree. It seems a good match to me," said the king, nodding first at Suger and then turning in appeal to Bernard. Louis had read the abbot's letter the evening before, but he hoped to change the old abbot's mind with his logic and approval from the other counselors. He should have known better.

Abbot Bernard leaned forward, his eyes sternly fixed on the king.

"I won't allow it," he repeated dryly. "It is a marriage that violates holy law."

"Indeed? And why is that?" Suger asked.

"The boy and the princess are related to a forbidden degree. It would be consanguineous." This would be his first and primary argument. He hoped he would not have to remind these foolish men of the demon legend.

Now he leaned toward Louis, his eyes still riveted on the king, who was stiff with apprehension. "Why would you even consider such a sinful thing, especially when you are on the verge of such great holiness? You have made a commitment to God, but agreeing to this union would undermine anything you might accomplish with the army you've promised to lead."

"Now, be reasonable, my lord abbot." Suger's mellifluous voice cut through the tensions around the table. "He's a good boy. And we can always seek a dispensation from the pope. I think the marriage could go a long way to ease tensions between England and France."

"It is forbidden by holy law," Abbot Bernard said, as though Suger had not spoken.

"But, my lord abbot," the king appealed, "would it not be a good thing to have the future of the Princess Marie settled before I depart?"

"Perhaps, but not in alliance with this boy. She has plenty of time."

"Do you not approve of him?" Suger leaned forward and stared at Bernard.

"I do not," he said, emphasizing all three words. His voice rose as he made his final pronouncement. "He came from the devil, and he will go to the devil."

With those words Bernard rose to leave the room. His judgment was final. If the king chose to sign this marriage alliance, then he would do it without the approval of the abbot of Clairvaux.

Abbot Bernard and his fellow white monks rode away from the still-dark castle on the Île-de-la-Cité the following morning just after prime. The abbot was angry over Louis's hesitation in the matter of the marriage. Angry that he had not immediately given in to wise counsel but had decided instead to delay the decision for a month rather than reject the offer outright, *probably at the queen's urging*, thought Bernard. No doubt Geoffrey was equally disappointed at not getting a clear answer to his proposal. That at least was a small satisfaction, but as soon as the abbot arrived back at Clairvaux, he intended to reiterate his objections to the king in writing once more.

The abbot had other ideas for the princess's marriage. It was much too soon and the peace was much too fragile to broach them to the king just yet. But he would do all in his power to thwart the Plantagenet's plans. This betrothal must not take place.

CHAPTER 7

Crusade preparations were going on furiously throughout the kingdom. Every knight who planned to go had to make certain that he and his men had sufficient swords, coats of mail, tents, wagons, horses, and adequate provisions to sustain them for at least part of the venture, which would probably take a year or perhaps more to complete. But the greatest burden to raise funds lay on the king, who announced additional taxes on the common people and raided church and abbey coffers insofar as he was able. The pope, as well, did all he could to encourage Christians to open their purse strings—promising salvation and releasing all crusaders from interest on loans they had obtained from Jewish moneylenders. He even agreed to come to France to aid in the efforts.

Finally, overwhelmed by the task and weary of Abbot Bernard's constant wheedling against the betrothal of Princess Marie to Henry Plantagenet, Louis sent a letter to the count of Anjou announcing that he had decided to reject the marriage offer and that he was far too busy at the moment to worry any more about such matters. He would rather endure the fury of the count than that of the abbot.

On the other hand, he thought, the betrothal would have solved the problem of what to do about the little princess during his and his wife's long absence. If he had agreed, the count would no doubt have taken Marie back to his lands to be raised by his own family, rather than leave her at the royal court where the king might change his mind. It was a practice not uncommon in noble families.

Louis informed Queen Eleanor of his decision only after he had already dispatched the message to Geoffrey of Anjou. He did not want to risk her persuasive powers to change his mind. As he expected, she frowned her disapproval.

"The boy will be king of England one day, mark my words. You've let a fine opportunity for our daughter slip through your fingers." She paused only briefly before adding with a wry smile, "He will become a powerful man. One can see it already in his demeanor, and he would make an important ally."

"Bah! He's far too young for such predictions, and King Stephen's son Eustace is equally determined to follow his father as king. We can't possibly know the future. There will be other and better offers."

"Others, yes. Better, I doubt it. We should have seized this opportunity for Marie's future." But it was obvious that the king had made up his mind. "Ah, well. What's done is done," she said with resignation, turning with feigned indifference back to the book she'd been reading.

Louis let the matter quickly slip from his mind, for he had more important things to consider than the fate of a mere daughter. He was, in fact, feeling a bit overwhelmed by the monumental task he had undertaken, all the decisions to be made, supplies to be gathered, and funds to be raised.

He held meetings to discuss the matter at both Châlons-sur-Marne, where German ambassadors were present, and at Étampes with French leaders only. One of the most important decisions to be made was whether to follow the land route or the sea route. Although Bishop Godfrey argued vehemently for the sea route, and Roger of Sicily even sent ambassadors to express his support, in the end crusade leaders chose the land route, which they hoped would be less costly.

They selected Bishop Suger to serve as regent in the king's absence. And when Guillaume de Nevers, whom the nobles chose as his aid, declined in order to take holy orders instead, the king selected his seneschal and brother-in-law, Raoul de Vermandois.

From Étampes, Louis made his way to Dijon, where he had agreed to meet Pope Eugenius at the end of March and accompany him to France to help with crusade preparations. Waiting with the pope were the abbot of Cluny, Peter the Venerable, and seventeen cardinals.

"Your Holiness, I am unworthy," Louis said with reverence, as he knelt to kiss his papal ring.

"My son, anyone who vowed to lead an army to the Holy Land is indeed worthy."

As they rode toward Paris, they made a stopover at the Abbey of Clairvaux, where Eugenius had once been a monk. As they approached in the late afternoon, smiling monks poured into the courtyard to greet them.

"Welcome, Your Holiness and my lord king," Abbot Bernard proclaimed in his most mellifluous voice. When he bent to kiss the pope's ring, Eugenius raised him up and gave him a kiss of peace on the lips instead. He assumed the role of beloved brother, now the most holy father, coming home to where he had been a monk only nine years earlier.

Abbot Bernard led his guests through the cloister to the refectory on the south side of the garden. Since it was Sunday, a day when Christians were permitted to break the Lenten fast, the abbot had made special provisions. Even when they were not in Lent, suppers at the abbey were sparse, consisting of little more than eggs, cheese, and bread. During Lent, they were required to forego even the eggs and cheese. This evening, however, novices brought in dishes of poached salmon, stewed pork ribs, and roasted chunks of venison called *nombles*, with ample ale and wine to wet the parched tongues of the travelers.

Louis was surprised at the relative lavishness of the meal, for Bernard was widely known for his austerity. He had once been criticized for serving Pope Innocent II only coarse bread, vegetables, herbs, and one small fish during Lent. Nor had he served him wine. Louis presumed it had been a day of fasting, unlike Sunday. But even so, this present fare was highly unusual for the monks of Clairvaux, who did not speak a word as they ate. Instead they listened to the lector readings from the writings of St. Benedict, relishing what for them was a rare feast in honor of their guests.

After two nights at Clairvaux, Louis was eager to push on to Paris, but the pope was clearly enjoying himself. When he and the abbot were not at prayer, they were closeted in the abbot's hall discussing scriptural interpretations, political matters involving the Church, or the *De consideratione*, as Bernard was calling the treatise on the papacy that Eugenius had asked him to write. But the king was growing increasingly anxious. He reminded the pope that, if they were to arrive before Easter, they had only twelve days to reach their destination.

"Ah yes," said Eugenius with affable reluctance. He turned to Abbot Bernard. "As much as I am enjoying this visit, King Louis is right."

The abbot nodded. "Even this brief visit has been an extraordinary honor." He paused and turned to the king. "I hope you do not object, but I have taken the liberty of notifying Count Thibaut that you would be passing through his lands. He has sent a most gracious invitation, offering you the hospitality of his palaces on your route. He himself will be waiting in Troyes, and his son Henri will accompany you to Provins, Meaux, and Lagny-sur-Marne and then on to his border."

Louis greeted the news with mixed feelings. He and Thibaut had not met since they had agreed to the peace in the presence of Abbots Suger and Bernard at St. Denis in October 1144. Although the king had spent a small amount of time with the count's eldest son at Vézelay, he was not sure how Thibaut would react at providing him hospitality. But Bernard, always eager to bring the two of them together, had obviously gone to some effort to make the arrangements, and Louis felt loathe to complain. Besides, the arrangement was practical, for all the count's castles were located with a day-or-two ride of one another—all located along the best route to Paris.

"It is a most generous offer," Louis said. "I shall express my gratitude to the count."

CHAPTER 8

Louis need not have worried. When the royal and papal parties passed through the Porte de Croncels and rode into the city of Troyes two days later, they were clearly expected. Colorful silk banners hung in welcome from windows along the Rue du Temple as they made their way toward the count's residence.

The castle stood in the northwest corner next to the ancient Roman wall in the oldest part of the city. Some of its buildings were as much as two hundred years old, and it had been constructed primarily for strength and defense, though parts of it were now crumbling. The buildings, including a small *donjon* and tower at the center, were dark and rather decrepit, making the castle look more like a prison than a palace. Even so, it had a hall for public meetings, a private residence for the count and his family, and a small chapel for their worship. Since the burning of Vitry, it had served more often as the comital residence. Louis hoped fervently that the subject of Vitry would not be raised. The matter had been settled once and for all, at least so he hoped. Nevertheless, he felt tense at meeting the count again face to face. But Thibaut, his three oldest sons at his side, was smiling broadly as he waited in the inner courtyard to greet their arrival.

"Welcome, Your Holiness," he said, as he genuflected and kissed the pope's ring. Louis did not notice any change of tone when the count turned toward him with a courteous bow. "And to you as well, my lord king. This is indeed a rare honor."

Thibaut has aged since our last meeting, Louis thought. The count was not yet sixty years old, but already there was a stoop to his shoulders the king had not noticed before, and his eyes had clouded over a bit. No wonder he decided not to go on the crusade, but rather to send his firstborn instead. *Firstborn only if one doesn't count the bastard,* thought Louis. A son, Hugh, born before Thibaut's marriage to his wife Mathilde of Carinthia, was now tucked away as a monk at St. Benet of Holme in East Anglia.

"I would like to present my sons, Henri, Thibaut, and Étienne." The three boys, well-built and dressed like young princes in silk *bliauts, chausses,* and short mantles, stood like stairsteps. Louis knew that Henri, the oldest, was nineteen, and the other two boys appeared to be separated by only a few years. Each bowed as he was introduced.

"You have kept them all at home, I see," the king said. He was wondering whether Thibaut's parade of sons was a subtle way of calling attention to his own lack of a male heir.

"Yes, they serve as squires in my household—all except Guillaume, my youngest, who is destined for life in the Church. He lives in England, in the household of my brother, the bishop of Winchester."

The pope nodded in approval. It was customary for at least one of the sons of noblemen to spend his life in the service of the Church, and it was usually the youngest son who had the honor, as the pope saw it, to be educated either in a monastery or by an ecclesiastic. *Four legitimate sons,* Louis thought. *One to spare for the Church.* Louis made every effort to brush away his envy, feeling that God had cursed *him.*

"I regret that my wife and our daughters are away visiting Abbess Héloïse and her nuns at the Paraclete." The pope smiled his approval, as the count gestured toward the castle door and bade them enter. Thibaut had done his best to make the dim and musty hall look festive. Colorful banners bearing his coat of arms hung along the walls, and the floors were strewn with fresh rushes and herbs to sweeten the air. Torches burned at intervals along the wall to provide more light than the small, high windows allowed into the room.

"This is indeed a special event," the count said, beaming at them both and urging them toward large chairs that had been drawn up around the fireplace in the center of the room. It blazed with only a small fire intended more for cheeriness than warmth. "You do me great honor with your presence," he said, addressing them both as they sat facing him. Louis nodded amiably and began to relax at Thibaut's friendly demeanor.

His host signaled to his son Henri, waiting, like a good squire, against the wall, for his lord's command. The young man disappeared and quickly returned with flagons of spiced wine for the guests and the count. It felt good, Louis thought, to be sitting somewhere besides his saddle. He was weary of all the days of travel, and he had enjoyed their brief respite at Clairvaux. Now in Troyes, they would spend two nights before continuing their journey. After this, their stops at Thibaut's castles would be only for overnight—a bed and a hot meal—for time was growing short. If all went well, that should let them arrive in Paris by the Wednesday of Holy Week.

"And how are preparations for your holy expedition coming along?" Thibaut asked the king.

"Quite well, I think. We plan to depart at Pentecost."

"So soon? Then we must hasten our plans," the count replied, glancing at his son.

As they spoke of the coming crusade, Louis noticed that young Henri was listening avidly to every word. The young man had impressed him favorably at Vézelay. He appeared to have grown even stronger and more mature since that time.

"Henri will most likely pass his twentieth birthday, though not his twenty-first, by the time you reach the Holy Land. I was hoping that, even so, he might be knighted in time to participate in the fighting, should it be necessary. With the king's approval, of course." Thibaut seemed unusually obsequious toward the king in the presence of the pope.

"I'm sure he will make a fine knight, and I will be pleased to have him in my army," Louis replied.

Dinner was a lavish affair for a fast day during Lent, but it followed the rules, which allowed fish but no meat, though each fish—baked trout stuffed with mushrooms and onions, stewed lampreys, and roasted pike in a wine and ginger sauce—was elaborately prepared and served. A dried fig concoction called *figues de carême* and dates rolled in crushed almonds replaced the usual tarts made with eggs and butter.

"I commend your cook," the pope said in a jovial tone, "for such cleverness in making even the Lenten fast into a feast."

"Nevertheless," Thibaut replied in a quiet tone, "it is served in your honor with the greatest reverence for this season of preparation. I assure you that no frivolity is intended, Your Holiness." Pope Eugenius nodded and raised his goblet to take another sip of the good red wine of the region. Louis remained impassive as he listened to the count's proclamation of piety. No doubt the pope was well aware of it, having spent so much recent time with Abbot Bernard, who had very likely informed him of the count's professed intent to be buried as a Cistercian monk. Louis knew well that the count would do anything to please Bernard.

After a good night's sleep, Louis was in a more amiable state of mind. He had been tired the day before and suspicious of any remark or gesture the count made. This morning he felt refreshed and in a surprisingly good mood.

He arose and broke his fast with bread and wine before the pope appeared. Thibaut joined him as he stood in the bailey watching Henri and his brothers practicing their horsemanship. Henri, who had more years of experience, was clearly the better rider, and his tilting at the *quintain* with his lance was unusually accurate.

"Your son Henri will make a good knight," Louis said.

"He's a fine lad," the count replied, pausing briefly before adding, "and not yet betrothed. His entire focus is on becoming a knight."

"You did not go through with the betrothal to Laurette of Flanders?" Louis asked, knowing full well the answer.

"Of course not, my lord. That was a condition of our meeting at St. Denis. Assuring the peace was far more important than the betrothal."

"Indeed," said Louis, biting his tongue to keep from noting aloud that there had been a time when peace had seemed less important to the count.

"I understand from Abbot Bernard that your daughter, Marie, is still not betrothed."

"She is only two years old. There is plenty of time. As you may know, we rejected an offer from the count of Anjou at the abbot's advice."

"I think Abbot Bernard is secretly hoping for an alliance between our two families, between your daughter Marie and my son Henri."

"That doesn't surprise me," Louis said, "but your son Henri is quite a bit older than Marie."

"What does that matter? Many marriages involve even greater age differences."

"I have decided to wait until after I return from Outremer to concern myself with such matters—again on the abbot's advice. Any such considerations will have to wait."

"I look forward to your safe return," Thibaut replied.

From that moment on, the king watched Henri carefully, weighing his virtues and his shortcomings. Once the travelers were finally on the road again, Louis found that he enjoyed the company of the young man, their escort through the count's lands. He was easy in conversation, always respectful and solicitous of both the king and the pope. He was also efficient in serving as host and organizing appropriate hospitality in his father's castles in Provins, Meaux, and Lagny-sur-Marne.

No doubt Thibaut told him what we discussed and he is on his best behavior. I'll reserve my opinion of his true worth until we are in the Holy Land, Louis thought.

Nevertheless, the seed had been planted.

St. Denis, Easter Sunday, 1147

The parvis in front of the church teemed with people, pushing and shoving one another to get a glimpse of both the pope and the king, as well as the other notables in attendance. The sermon, delivered by Peter the Venerable, reminded the crusaders of Christ's sacrifice on their behalf, urging them to be Christ-like and willing to give their lives, if need be, for their own salvation. On this day of celebration of the Resurrection, he reminded them that they would assure their own redemption by their service and sacrifice to God in the Holy Land.

Louis, like others in the congregation, was moved and felt inspired to march forth that very day, but he knew there was still much to do before their departure.

"Are you sure you have all you need?" Eleanor asked Aelith. Together they were looking over everything in the nursery of the castle on the Île de la Cité, for Aelith and her husband would spend much of their time there while the king and queen were away. Their presence would better enable Raoul to assist Abbot Suger in keeping order in the kingdom.

"Quite sure. I have children too, you know. Marie will be quite well taken care of, my dear sister. Please don't fret. It's the least Raoul and I can do while you are away."

"I'm excited about the trip, but I do hate to miss watching her grow up during these years."

"She certainly won't be grown by the time you return. And besides, she's already walking and beginning to talk, so you won't have missed all that."

Eleanor thought of the occasions she came to the royal nursery and saw her daughter's delight as she entered the room. The child's eyes would light up with joy, and her little mouth would widen into a grin that exposed all her pearly new teeth. When Eleanor held her on her lap, Marie would repeat the words she said and sometimes even remembered them on her own when she pointed to objects. She could not only walk, she loved to dance and wave her tiny arms whenever she heard the sound of the lute. Eleanor loved to hear her say *Maman*, knowing it was the name reserved for her alone.

Now the little girl was giving her full attention to her very active cousins and the unfamiliar playthings they had brought to the nursery.

"She won't remember me when I return, will she?" Eleanor asked, her voice wistful.

"I don't know," said Aelith, "but I'll tell her about you while you're away and remind her what you look like. Perhaps she'll remember something of her beautiful mother."

"Oh, Aelith, how I wish you were coming with me."

Aelith pointed to her growing womb. "Wouldn't I scare the Saracens in my condition? Can't you see me with a lance resting on my belly?"

Eleanor laughed. "I assure you I won't be carrying any lances."

Suddenly Aelith's face took on a dark and serious cast. "You do know that there were women killed in the first war against the Saracens, don't you?"

"Of course, silly, but I don't plan to get close to any fighting. The Saracens won't bother me."

"But what if they attack as you are traveling?"

Eleanor patted her sister's arm. "I assure you I'll be quite all right. Don't worry. Now I must go and make certain all my traveling chests have been properly loaded and secured." Eleanor and her maids had been packing for days. She wanted to be sure that she had sufficient gowns and jewels elegant enough to dazzle her uncle Raymond in Antioch. And she certainly had no intention of looking less than her best at the court in Constantinople.

Eleanor picked up her daughter once more and gave her a firm kiss on the cheek.

"Mommy's going away for a while, my darling."

The child, who had often heard that phrase before, hugged her neck and then wriggled to get down and play with her cousins.

"But I'll be back," Eleanor said, setting her squirming daughter down. "I'll bring you some presents," she added. Marie paid no notice. She was already squealing and toddling after the leather ball her cousin had rolled past her. Eleanor took one last, long look at her daughter, embraced her sister, and quietly left the nursery.

The day fixed for the crusaders' rendezvous and departure from Metz was Pentecost in June 1147. But first, there were to be glorious ceremonies and blessings at St. Denis to send the crusaders on their way. The king and his entourage set out from Paris on the day that marked the beginning of the Lendit Fair, guaranteeing that there would be throngs of people lining the roadways in and around St. Denis.

King Louis stopped along the way at a leprosarium to dine with the lepers, a gesture of his faith in God and his own good will. He would then continue on to St. Denis, where he would spend the night in prayer with the monks.

Eleanor and the king's mother, Adelaide de Maurienne, rode on ahead with their retinues. The queen certainly had no foolish intention of entering a leper house. Instead she would arrive at St. Denis before her husband and settle into the abbey's *domus hospitum*, the guest house, which was not luxurious but at least adequate for their needs. Louis himself would stay in the monks' dormitory, if he slept at all. She knew that he planned to spend most of the night in prayer in the abbey church.

The queen slept as well as she could, considering the hard mattress on the narrow bed of the guest house. Not long after sunrise, she was awakened by the noise of an enormous crowd already gathering before the abbey church and hoping for a glimpse of the pope and the king. In spite of the walls that surrounded the abbey, she could hear the clamor of the excited mob. Whenever such a crowd gathered, vendors hawked their wares and haggled over prices with their customers, money-changers set up their tables nearby, and acrobats and jugglers performed, hoping for a *denier* or two—all adding to the noise—not to mention the beggars, who were not always quiet at their begging.

The church would never hold all the people who gathered, hoping to see the king accept the *besace*, the sack carried by pilgrims, and take from the altar the *oriflamme*, St. Denis's vermillion banner, said to be carried into battle by successful kings. But most of all, they wanted to see the pope bestow his blessing on the king and his undertaking.

After Eleanor and the dowager queen arrived in the church and took their places near the front to watch the ceremony, the crowd became so great, with bodies pressing in from all sides, and the day so hot, that they could barely breathe. But soon Eleanor was so caught up in the service, the glorious words of the pope, and the beauty of the ceremony and gravity of their undertaking that she was moved to tears.

When the service ended, Louis, weary from his vigil of the night before, hurried from the abbey church to take refuge once again in the monks' dormitory and escape the suffocating crowd. It was all the queen's attendants could do to bore their way through the throng toward a side entrance and extricate the two women from the church. Eleanor clung to her mother-in-law's arm, as much to steady herself as the older woman. She thought she would faint before she reached the open air. Despite the warmth of the day, it felt cool and refreshing when she was able at last to draw a fresh breath beyond the heavy odors and oppressive heat of the teeming crowd.

One of the squires who helped to make way for the queen and the dowager queen to escape was a young man Eleanor recognized as Henri de Champagne, the oldest son of Count Thibaut. She remembered him from Vézelay. Neither his father, who was growing old, nor his younger brothers, who were only seventeen and fourteen, had taken the cross, but young Henri's face shone with enthusiasm. She paused to thank him.

Abbot Bernard, who, along with Abbot Suger and Pope Eugenius, had taken part in the ceremony, approached the three of them.

"It is good to see you both, my ladies. I take it you two know young Henri de Champagne," Bernard said, turning to the squire at his side.

Adelaide nodded, and Eleanor said to the squire, "We met at Vézelay. I'm glad you will be joining us on this venture."

"Thank you, my lady. I hope to be of service to my king and my Church. And I hope to return a knight."

"Oh?" she said.

"Yes," Abbot Bernard said. "I am sending a letter to the emperor of Constantinople to request that he dub him a knight before the young man sets out for battle. I trust he will agree."

"How wonderful," Eleanor said. "We shall all be present at the ceremony, no doubt."

"I hope so, my lady," Henri said with a bow in her direction.

"We must go now to take a rest before our departure. The service was quite inspiring, but also exhausting," Eleanor said, as her mother-in-law took her arm and they made their way back toward the guest dormitory.

The abbot and the squire watched them go, each with a glorious vision of the future in his mind, along with a sense of apprehension about what lay head.

CHAPTER 9

As the long procession of crusaders wound its way out of St. Denis and toward Metz, Henri de Champagne carried in his saddlebag the letter that Abbot Bernard had written to the emperor of Constantinople. It was the most valuable item in his possession. Although he had no first-hand knowledge of its wording, he knew that, if nothing else, the abbot would praise him as the son of Thibaut, whom he viewed as honorable, noble, and upright. Whatever it said, he could only hope that the emperor would agree to knight him.

At Henri's side rode his good friends, brothers Anseau and Garnier de Traînel, who had taken the cross with him at Vézelay. He felt closer to them than to anyone else in the world except for his own brothers, who were too young to accompany him. He hardly knew his brother Guillaume, who was ten years his junior and who had been sent to England when he was only six.

Anseau leaned over in his saddle, "You must be proud today, my friend, to be leading such a large group of Champenois knights."

Henri grinned, as he looked back at the number of men from his region, many of them young, like himself, but others, men of maturity, like Geoffrey de Joinville. He *was* pleased that his father had trusted him to lead the Champenois forces and proud that the king had given him and his men the honor of riding first behind the royal troops. The two groups together consisted of about two hundred mounted men, all on horseback, not to mention the multitudes of foot soldiers that followed them. But he was also a little envious of the young men whose fathers were accompanying them—men like Gautier de Brienne and his son Érard—and of those who were traveling as brothers, like Anseau and Garnier or Renaud and Odo de Pougy.

Pride and Envy, he thought, *two of the seven deadly sins*. Not a good way to begin the crusade. Quickly, he thought of reasons to humble himself. He knew full well that some of the older men like Milo de Nogent-sur-Seine rode behind him only out of respect for his father, and that they knew far more about such expeditions than he did. He was young and inexperienced. Although his father had filled him with all sorts of advice before he left and sent his chaplain Martin to keep him on the right spiritual path, he still felt uncertain in the task. He could only trust that such men would keep him from making foolish mistakes.

Anseau's comment had made him more self-conscious, and he tried to take on an air of confidence, sitting taller in his saddle, copying the stance of other leaders of high rank. But inside he felt only eagerness and anxiety.

"How far is it to Metz?" Anseau asked.

"At least a week's ride, I think," Henri replied.

"That far? And here I am, already longing for a mug of ale. This dust is parching my throat."

"You drink too much, my friend," Henri said in a teasing tone. "A day of sobriety will do you good."

Anseau's face took on a comical look of despair, and he clutched at his throat as both Henri and Garnier burst simultaneously into laughter. Anseau's antics made Henri relax, but they all knew that there was a long journey before them and many days in the saddle ahead.

People lined the roadway on both sides, cheering as they rode past. The June sun poured down on the bright-colored banners that identified the various nobles. Henri could barely make out in the distance the red *oriflamme*, for all the dust from the hundreds of riders ahead of them clouded the air. He gave only a passing thought to those in the rear and those who marched on foot, too poor to afford a horse, yet willing to give up whatever livelihood they had to serve God on this crusade. He was excited to be a part of it. What a glorious beginning his knighthood would have!

The excitement of their departure quickly wore off, and the slow plodding of the horses became monotonous and frustrating to the young men eager to reach their destination. They did not travel many miles each day, for the mounted soldiers could not leave those on foot too far behind. Whenever carts broke down or horses died, they all had to stop. Squabbles erupted among the crusaders, and sometime arguments and even fights broke out with residents of areas they passed through. The crusaders complained that high prices and profiteering were unfair to the soldiers of God. Many of them lacked discipline and the will to sacrifice that such a long and difficult trip required. One was even killed as a result of a quarrel with townspeople.

"I thought men on a holy mission would conduct themselves better," said Garnier, after Henri had just finished settling a dispute between two tradesmen from Provins.

"As did I," Henri answered. "But with so many different people, I suppose it's impossible."

The crusaders marched for months. The trip seemed endless. It was early October—the Sunday before the feast day of St. Denis. Milo de Nogent-sur-Seine was riding beside Henri, who had requested his advice on a disciplinary matter. Milo had been at his side whenever he needed support or counsel throughout the trip.

"Why are you so helpful to me, Lord Milo? I know you and my father have not always gotten along well in years past."

"True. There is little affection between us, but I do respect him, and I have found you to be a most amiable young man, who will become a fine leader for our region, I think. In any case, I believe it is my Christian duty to be of help whenever I can."

"I really appreciate your—"

Suddenly a great shout erupted from marchers up ahead. The two men strained to see what the shouters were pointing at. They could see the domes and spires of Constantinople barely visible through the haze on the horizon. The men were wild with excitement, knowing they would soon be able to stop for a while. They were eager to enjoy themselves in this legendary city.

"At last!" Milo said. "*Mon Dieu*, I thought we'd never get here."

Henri could only gaze in awe. He had never seen a city so large, though he had heard tales about it from old men who took part in the first crusade. They had reported a magnificent city, filled with wonders like nothing they'd ever seen before. Hundreds of thousands of people lived there, they said. And it was surrounded by the wall of Theodosius guarding it on the west side, with the rest protected by the Marmara Sea, the Golden Horn, and the Arm of St. George, as they called the Bosporus Strait. Henri could hardly wait to enter and present Abbot Bernard's letter to the emperor. He could only hope the emperor would agree. Men in his region were not usually knighted until they were twenty-one, and he wouldn't turn twenty for another two months.

As they approached the city, the nearest gate opened, and people poured out to meet them—noblemen and townspeople, all of them clearly wealthy—clerics and laymen alike. The one who seemed to be in charge greeted King Louis.

"We bid you welcome in the name of the emperor."

Once the inevitable formalities came to an end, the leader of the Greek delegation announced to the king, "Our emperor has asked us to escort you to the imperial palace, where he will welcome you in person."

Along with the queen and two of her ladies, Louis selected a few of the men in his company and some of his more prominent vassals, taking care to include Henri de Champagne, to accompany him. They followed the imperial delegation, riding two abreast, through an elaborate gate to the Blachernae Palace in the northwest corner of the city overlooking the waters of the Golden Horn. Emperor Manuel and his empress were waiting for them in the portico.

"Welcome, my friends," Manuel greeted them, his arms open wide.

The emperor and the king embraced and exchanged the kiss of peace. Henri looked on, elated to be part of this auspicious moment, as he admired Manuel's imperial robe of blue silk, pinned at the side with a large brooch of gold encrusted with sapphires. The fine garment, embroidered along the borders of the sleeves and hem with golden threads, put the Frenchmen's dusty traveling garb to shame. Manuel was younger than Henri had expected, still in his twenties, about the same size and age as the king of France. Beside him stood his new bride Bertha of Sulzbach, whom the Greeks had renamed Irene. They made a fine-looking couple. Garbed in splendor equal to her husband's, the empress greeted Queen Eleanor and her ladies with warmth and invited them to take refreshments while the men talked.

When the women disappeared toward the empress's quarters, the emperor invited the king and his men into the reception hall, where he sat on his throne, while Louis was offered only a simple chair. As the two men began to chat, Henri, like the other noblemen, stood back, not participating in the conversation. Manuel did not speak French, and Louis knew no Greek, so the two men required interpreters.

Henri studied the grandeur of the palace. He had never seen so much gold outside a cathedral before, and the marble floors were worked into intricate patterns. He was admiring the magnificence around him, when he suddenly heard the king say his name.

"I believe that one of our nobles, Henri de Champagne, has a letter for you."

"Indeed? From whom?" asked Manuel, as Henri stepped forward with a bow.

"From the abbot of Clairvaux," Louis answered.

"Bring me the letter." He gestured for Henri to approach and hand over the sealed parchment to his translator, who was also his scribe. "Read the letter to me," he commanded.

Once the emperor had heard the abbot's words, he said to Henri, "Clearly Abbot Bernard thinks highly of you, young man, to go to so much trouble. Read that part again," he said to the scribe, "I recommend to you above all others…"

The scribe repeated, "I recommend to you above all others the son of the illustrious prince, Count Thibaut. He is young, noble, and of fine character, and he has devoted his first year under arms to the pursuit of justice rather than maliciousness. He is the son of a man whose love of truth, kindness, and justice has made him honored among princes."

"A commendable recommendation. And he asks me to do the honor of making you a knight—an honor which I accept with pleasure."

"I thank you, your Imperial Highness," Henri bowed to the emperor.

"Now, enough of this, your king and I have much to discuss." The emperor dismissed him, and Henri stepped back to join the other men.

When the interview was coming to an end, the emperor sent for the ladies and said to the king, "My men will escort you to your lodging at the Philopation palace. I hope you and your nobles will find it comfortable."

The palace in question was located outside the city walls not far from the Golden Horn. As they followed their guide, Henri noted all the other weary-looking crusaders camped not far from the city walls.

"And where will they be quartered?" he asked the emperor's ambassador.

"They will remain camped outside the city gates, where they can do no harm. Only people of high rank, like yourself, will find available lodging. I can assure you the Philopation palace will allow the king, queen, and highest nobility to enjoy all the luxury Constantinople can provide."

It was true that the unruly mob of crusaders lacked discipline and sometimes stole, raided towns, and even killed along the way, when they could find provisions no other way. And Henri had heard about the destructiveness of the German army, which had preceded them. *Still,* he thought, *to come all this distance and never be admitted to the city....* He could only thank God for his noble rank.

After the king's party had enjoyed the welcome pleasures of a relaxing bath, a good meal, and a night's rest, messengers from the emperor arrived the following morning to escort them once again to the Blachernae Palace. There, the emperor himself waited to conduct them on a visit to the holy shrines of the city.

Henri had never seen anything so grand. He was amazed by the grandeur of the Orthodox basilica, the Hagia Sophia, as the Greeks called it, with its many mosaics and soaring domes. So many reminders of ancient days, like the acropolis, the column of Justinian, and the hippodrome, still stood. Most of the Great Palace, where Constantine once lived, also remained. Above all, he was overwhelmed by the

Church of the Virgin of the Pharos. There, before the most amazing collection of Christian relics, including the Holy Lance, a part of the True Cross, the sandals of Christ, and even the crown of thorns, he knelt on the hard stone floor and prayed until his knees were sore.

In mid-afternoon, the emperor announced, "Enough for one day. Now we will go to my palace for a fine feast."

The news was welcome to Henri. He was hungry, for in France they were accustomed to dining much earlier in the day. Today's banquet was far more lavish than their supper of the previous evening. And Manuel's great hall was festive with mosaics and fine woven rugs. Henri was astounded by the array of sumptuous dishes and strange customs, as well as by the musicians and dancers. The fragrance of spices he had never smelled before filled the air, and he was surprised to see the emperor and other members of his court reclining on sofas during the meal.

They ate with strange, pronged instruments to spear their meat, and spoons were set at every place. The French, accustomed to dining with only their fingers and their knives, watched with interest. Some of them tried out the new utensils but found their fingers far more efficient. The Greeks looked at them with expressions of distaste but were cordial nonetheless. The food, though strange, was delicious. Servants brought out platter after platter of meats—roast kid stuffed with garlic, leeks, and onions, and dressed with a fish sauce called *garos*, rabbit cooked with red wine and spikenard, and a dish that consisted of many types of fish, shrimp, and scallops, seasoned with thyme, fennel, and white wine.

"What do you call this?" Henri asked.

"*Kakavia*," the Greek nobleman lounging next to him replied. "We are blessed to live so close to the sea, don't you think?"

"I do indeed."

He could not say as much for the wine, some of which was flavored with anise, some with pitch and resin. Henri, accustomed to the wines in Champagne, found these undrinkable. Only one, spiced with cinnamon, cloves, black pepper, laurel, and saffron, which his fellow diner called *konditon*, was he able to consume. The sweets, on the other hand, he found most delightful—delicious honey cakes and syrupy sweetmeats. Some of them contained rice, unknown to Henri, but quite tasty when mixed with thyme honey and goat's milk.

At one point during the meal, the emperor sent for Henri, who approached his couch and bowed.

"You sent for me, your Imperial Highness?" Henri asked.

"Yes, I should like for you to spend the night here at the palace to prepare for your ceremony of knighthood tomorrow."

"Tomorrow? But all of my clothing is at the Philopation."

"We shall provide all you need. As custom dictates, you will do your ritual bathing in the palace baths, and you will be brought with a clean body to my chapel where you will cleanse your heart as you pray throughout the night. We will begin the ceremony at the hour of terce."

"But my garments—"

"You will be provided with all the things tradition requires. Then tomorrow morning, after mass, I will fulfill the abbot's request and bestow the arms of knighthood on you in my chapel."

"I am honored, sir," Henri replied with another bow. "Will anyone from my own lands be present?" he asked.

"You may invite whomever you wish," Manuel answered.

"Thank you, my lord," Henri said as he was dismissed.

Henri bowed to King Louis, seated beside the emperor, and said, "I hope you and the queen will come for the ceremony, my lord. It would be my great honor."

"Certainly, my boy. We will both be there."

Henri wished he had not eaten so much, since he would spend the entire night kneeling in prayer and meditation in the chapel next to the palace. But thank God he had drunk little wine. As he returned to his place at the table, he paused here and there to ask several of the Champenois nobles to be present, so that they could report the event to his father.

"And please make sure my chaplain, Martin, and my good friends, Garnier and Anseau, will in attendance," he asked Milo de Nogent.

"I will indeed. We shall look forward to it," Milo replied with a fatherly nod.

When dinner ended, attendants guided Henri across the courtyard to the palace bath. They washed him in warm water, until he felt thoroughly cleansed and renewed. Another attendant appeared, carrying the ritual garments he was to wear for the ceremony—a white tunic to symbolize purity and a red mantle to represent nobility and the blood he was willing to shed as a knight. Henri felt almost like a newborn as they led him to the emperor's chapel.

When dawn came and time for the ceremony drew near, the candles that softly lit the little chapel were extinguished. Servants lit fresh candles on the altar just before the emperor entered, side by side with King Louis, followed by the queen and the empress, Henri's friends Garnier and Anseau, the Pougy brothers, Geoffrey de Joinville, and all the others he had invited. He caught sight of Milo, who was beaming with pride as though he were the young man's father himself.

As the sun poured through the windows, the wall between the nave and altar was studded with icons of holy saints and gleamed with gold. It was Henri's own chaplain, Martin, who said the mass and preached a blessedly brief sermon, before the giving of arms ceremony began.

Then it was all over so quickly that Henri hardly felt the transformation to manhood he had expected. He knelt before Manuel and swore the oath of knighthood. Manuel then murmured the necessary words, "I dub thee, Sir Henri," and touched him lightly with a sword blade, first on the right shoulder, then on the left. When Henri arose, Manuel placed a kiss on his left cheek and girded on his sword. That, as well as a helmet, chain mail, and spurs had been blessed on the altar during the mass.

Most important of all, at the very end, Manuel said to Henri, "I have a very special gift for you—one I present to you with affection and honor." He held out a small golden reliquary and placed it in the young man's hands.

"It is a piece of the True Cross," Manuel said solemnly. Henri fell to his knees before the emperor, his eyes glistening with tears of gratitude.

"My lord," he said. "There is no way I can express my thanks. I shall protect and honor this holy relic for all the days of my life."

"May it protect you in the days ahead," Manuel replied.

King Louis watched the young man carefully throughout the service, pondering Count Thibaut's proposed betrothal of his son to Princess Marie. *He conducts himself well in peacetime. We shall see what kind of knight he will be in battle*, the king thought, as he took Eleanor's arm and they moved once again toward the great hall for yet another feast.

CHAPTER 10

"You cannot trust the Greeks," the bishop of Langres reminded the king almost daily, as they lingered in Constantinople.

"Why do you say that? I have seen nothing to make me distrust them," said Henri de Champagne. "The emperor has been only kind to me." Now that Henri was officially a knight, he took a more vigorous part in the leadership discussions.

The king's chaplain, Odo de Deuil, gave a dismissive laugh. "It cost him little effort to fulfill Abbot Bernard's request on your behalf. I support the suspicions of Bishop Godefrey."

"I think we should capture the city, while we can," said the bishop.

Louis looked with consternation from one to the other. "I agree with Sir Henri," he said. Henri smiled with gratitude to hear the king acknowledge his knightly status. "We have not come to plunder and destroy our fellow Christians."

"But are they really Christians like us?" the bishop asked. "They refuse to be subject to the will of our pope. As far as I can tell, they are heretics."

"We shall be wary, but I will hear no more about attacking Constantinople," Louis said in a firm voice.

The bishop muttered something under his breath to Odo as the two men left the room together.

The French army had already exceeded its intended stay of two weeks, as they waited for another group of crusaders led by Roger of Apulia, son of King Roger of Sicily and brother-in-law to Henri de Champagne. As they lingered five days more, the Greeks grew increasingly uneasy. King Roger was an avowed enemy of the Greeks and made them fear the very thing the bishop of Langres was proposing—an attack on their city by reinforced crusaders.

Finally, the emperor persuaded Louis to cross to the other side of the strait that separated the Black Sea from the Marmara Sea and wait there. Greek merchants and money-changers followed them, eager for more profits. As another five days passed, tempers flared. Frustrated by high prices and seeing French gold and silver piled higher in the merchants' stalls, a Flemish soldier began to yell and snatch whatever merchants' wares he wanted. Angry crusaders rushed into the mêlée. Soon there was a full-scale riot, as terrified merchants fled for their lives, leaving behind most of their merchandise.

King Louis had the man who incited the incident hanged and returned the stolen items to the merchants. But despite his efforts to keep the peace, Manuel was furious, and there was endless grumbling in the crusaders' camp. As matters grew increasingly tense, the king decided to break camp and depart without the Apulians. But, before Manuel would provide them a guide, he demanded homage from the French noblemen.

"I'll be damned before I'll pay homage to that heretic," muttered Thierry of Flanders.

"But we need the guide," said the king.

"My lord, how can you ask these men to pay homage to Manuel? It would be a disgrace. How can they promise loyalty to an infidel?" the bishop of Langres argued.

"Men often have several lords," Henri de Champagne pointed out, "for they hold some lands from one and some from another." He knew his father did.

"He's right," said Milo. "Paying homage does not necessarily mean fidelity if two liege lords are in conflict. One sometimes has to choose which obligation to honor."

"In any case, our loyalty to God would carry more weight than any feudal homage. I don't see what harm it would do," added another knight.

Although clergymen and nobles grumbled, eventually they agreed and grudgingly performed the act of homage. Even so, the promised guide never appeared. Finally, the crusaders set out toward Nicaea on their own without a Greek guide.

Once they reached the city, King Louis was compelled to choose one of three routes to follow across Asia Minor to Antioch. He made inquiries of the local people and listened to rumors and advice—unsure whether he could trust any of it. Finally, he decided on the middle of the three routes, the only one the Germans, who had split into two different groups, had not taken, hoping that they might find more food along roads that had not been plundered before their arrival.

The day before they were to leave, however, a messenger, disheveled and bloody, galloped into their camp, practically falling from his horse as he tried to dismount.

"I've come to warn you and to ask for your help." His French was halting and weighed down with a heavy German accent. "King Conrad's army was besieged by the Turks as we crossed the mountains. It was awful. They were everywhere. Our men were hungry, weak, totally unprepared. So many dead—" His voice broke and he began to weep. Someone brought him a goblet of wine, and he drank as though he were dying of thirst.

"Did King Conrad survive?" asked Louis, not knowing what to expect, for they had heard only good news back in Constantinople about the success of the German army.

"He's alive, but wounded and disheartened. Thousands are dead. The survivors are on their way back to Nicaea. The duke of Swabia sent me on ahead when he heard a rumor that you were about to depart. He wanted you to know before you set out."

In the days that followed, remnants of the German army limped back into Nicaea, bloodied and starving, their king among them. Louis had awaited his arrival and his counsel. Conrad urged him to take the coastal road. It was longer than the first route Louis had chosen, but the German king assured him that they would find more provisions that way. He decided to heed Conrad's advice, and the French crusaders finally set out once more, with even greater trepidation.

As the line of crusaders stretched for miles along the coastline, their route led them through the ancient city of Ephesus, now in ruin. They paused briefly to worship at the tomb of St. John. From there they passed through a verdant valley, where they pitched their tents on Christmas Eve.

During the night Henri was awakened by the whinny of their horses grazing nearby. Rushing from his tent, sword in hand, he caught sight of a group of mounted Turkish raiders harassing the tethered horses. The sentries were already sounding the alarm.

There were only a few Turks, and the French troops, determined not to meet the fate of the Germans, quickly drove them away, killing several in the process. Pleased by the ease with which they had routed the enemy, the French army spent the next few days of Christmas celebrating, relaxing, and letting their horses rest. So far the weather had been good, but clouds were gathering on the horizon.

After several days of incessant rain, when the sun finally broke through again, the king gave orders to break camp, concerned that the waters from nearby mountain streams would soon flood the valley. Three days after Christmas, members of the advance guard scouted the banks of the Maeander River, looking for a place to cross. Louis was eager to get to the other side before the waters became more swollen than they already were. He could see that higher country awaited them on the other side.

At Henri's advice, the vanguard leaders selected a ford they considered to be the least dangerous. It had a gentle bank to enter the river, though a steeper exit on the other side. Only Milo de Nogent-sur-Seine urged caution.

"The river is quite swollen, and the current swift," he said to Henri. "Do you think it's safe to cross?"

"It will be even more swollen tomorrow as the mountain creeks flow into the river," Henri answered.

Thierry of Flanders agreed. "The sooner the better. This looks like the best ford we've seen. The bank on the other side isn't that steep, and our horses are fresh. It shouldn't be a problem." And so it was decided.

Henri led the way carefully into the river, alongside two older and more experienced knights, Thierry and Guillaume de Mâcon. They passed the halfway mark, where their horses could no longer touch the sandy bottom. As they began to draw near the other side of the river, suddenly a small group of Turkish archers stepped from behind trees where they had been hiding. Henri heard the buzz of an arrow rush by his head. He could see the archers up ahead.

There was only one thing to do. Instinctively and ignoring caution, Henri spurred his horse forward, scrambling up the bank. He shouted as he drew his sword and raised it high. Thierry, seeing the young knight's quick reaction, did the same, with Guillaume on his heels. The three knights scurried up the bank with all the speed their horses could muster.

Yelling at the top of their lungs, they raced toward the Turkish archers.

"*Pass'avant li meillor!*" Henri, leading the charge, issued the *cri de guerre* his father had taught him as a young squire—Let the best pass first! He could hear Thierry's calling out in Flemish "*Vlaenderen die leu*," which he knew meant Flanders the Lion. And Guillaume was yelling "*Deus vult*," God wills it, the war cry he had learned from men who fought in the first crusade.

With all three men shouting at once and charging at full speed toward the archers, the Turks looked startled, then confused and frightened. They leapt on their horses and galloped away as the knights pursued them until they were out of sight. Clearly, they had not expected such a vehement response. But the French *destriers*, well fed and refreshed from their days of grazing in the valley, were strong and eager to run. And the knights were equally eager to fight. As they routed the Turkish archers, the rest of the crusaders cheered.

Guillaume de Mâcon, who was well over fifty, yet still vigorous, rode over to congratulate Henri. "Well done, young man. You inspired us all—even this graybeard," he said.

"Thank you, sir," Henri replied with a grin, exhilarated by the exuberance of his fellow crusaders.

As Henri trotted back toward those marchers who had by now completed their river crossing, he noticed that they were no longer cheering, but rather had gathered solemnly around something lying on the ground. It looked like a body.

Garnier was riding quickly toward him.

"*Bien fait*, well done, my friend. Now you are truly a knight," he said, slapping Henri on the back as soon as he was close enough. Then his face became somber. "But I'm afraid I have some bad news."

Henri frowned. "Was someone hit by one of the arrows?"

"No, but you've lost one of your men. It's Lord Milo. He's dead."

"Oh, no!" Henri moaned and bent forward in his saddle as though someone had driven a dagger through his heart. Only recently had he come to know Milo well, and they had formed a strong bond during the journey. *How could this be?*

"How did he die?" He asked in a quiet voice, once he had regained his composure.

"I didn't see it happen, but the men closest to him said he was so excited at what you had done that he was eager to be one of the first to congratulate you. He was in mid-stream and apparently tried to spur his horse to go faster. They said the horse struggled to obey and apparently lost its footing. They both fell, and the waters swept them downstream before anyone could reach him. They found his body just a few moments ago. The horse managed to survive."

"It's all my fault," he said. "He thought the current too swift, but I insisted." He felt a pang of guilt when he recalled how he had argued for the crossing. He remembered how well Milo had counseled him along the way, almost like his own father. It was the one time he had paid no attention. The young knight spurred his own destrier and rode slowly back to the river bank, where Milo lay.

"We couldn't save him, sir," said one of the bystanders.

Henri dismounted, made the sign of the cross, knelt beside his friend's body, and took his hand.

"I will have a mass said for you in Jerusalem," he said with tears in his eyes. "Thank you for your loyalty, my friend."

He felt a gentle touch on his shoulder and looked up into the sympathetic face of Geoffrey de Joinville. The man said nothing, but the touch told Henri that he had others among his men who would serve him loyally as Milo had done. And he was grateful for the reassuring moment.

Despite Milo's death, there was general jubilation in the camp that evening.

"I shall write about your exploit today," said Odo de Deuil, who usually sat in his tent most evenings, preparing his long chronicle of the journey for Abbot Suger. Tonight he joined Henri by the camp's roaring fire. "You three rushed into that rain of arrows like whirlwinds. It was thrilling. The abbot will want to know about it."

"We did only what any knight would do," Henri replied.

"Hardly, my boy. What you did was quite dangerous and daring. But you were a wonder to see. I'm only sorry we lost Lord Milo in the crossing."

"His death was a great loss to me, but I thank God for his company thus far along the way."

"You are going to be a fine knight. I congratulate you on your beginnings."

King Louis too approached him later in the evening.

"You were magnificent today, I hear from Odo. I wish I had been close enough to see, but we were fighting off those Turkish devils in the rear. I plan to send a letter to your father to tell him how heroic and fearless you were."

"Thank you, my lord. That is most kind of you." He was eager for his father to know that he had upheld the family honor and learned well his lessons on the practice field.

"Come by my tent tomorrow evening, Henri. We have things to discuss."

Henri felt honored by the invitation from the king, and the following evening, after they had set up camp, he made his way to Louis's tent. The king greeted him warmly and ordered wine for them both. Once the servants had brought the wine, he dismissed them, lifted his cup to Henri, and sat down, face to face, on an equal level with the young knight.

"Henri, while the pope and I were in Troyes, your father suggested that we consider a betrothal between you and my daughter, Marie."

The young man nodded, not knowing what to say.

When he made no answer, Louis asked, "What do you think of the idea?"

"It would be a great honor for me," Henri said, "to have the princess as my betrothed and eventually as my wife."

"You've never met her, of course. She's still a babe, not yet three years old—far too young to be wed. But I want to be sure she finds a good husband—one who will provide well for her and treat her with respect."

"Of course, my lord."

"Your father and I haven't spoken of any details, and I was unwilling to consider a treaty until I saw what kind of knight you would be. As you well know, I am very pleased at what I've seen so far."

"Thank you, my lord." Henri felt warmed by the king's compliments.

"You conduct yourself well both as a courtier and a warrior. You've made your courage and commitment to our holy cause quite evident. And I have found your counsel to be both sound and practical… unlike some others in our midst." The king chuckled.

Henri smiled his appreciation. "I hope so, my lord."

"Your father will, of course, inquire about her dowry," the king continued. "As you well know, Marie is heiress of Aquitaine. I will settle a few other small properties on her, to be sure, but her royal blood and her promised inheritance should be adequate."

"Yes, my lord."

"Would such a betrothal be acceptable to you?"

"Whatever you and my father agree on will be acceptable to me," Henri said, knowing full well that he would really have no say in the matter as long as his father lived. But he felt honored that the king would consult with him man to man. Louis wasn't that much older than himself—less than a decade surely. Still, he *was* the king.

"Courageous, devout, respectful, and obedient to your father. Who could want more in a son-in-law?" Louis said heartily. "Only one more challenge. The queen also wants to see whether she thinks you would be suitable as our daughter's future husband. I'll be the one to make the final decision, of course, but sometimes a man must indulge his wife in small matters. The queen has requested that she and her ladies be allowed to ride with you in the vanguard, so that she can know you better and see your fine qualities for herself. I plan to ask Geoffrey de Rancon, the man who leads the Aquitanian troops and who is in charge of protecting Queen Eleanor and her attendants, to lead the vanguard as we cross the mountains. And I am asking you to ride with them. Are you willing?"

"Indeed, my lord. I'm happy to serve in what whatever capacity I'm needed."

Louis raised his cup. "Then it's settled. You and Geoffrey, along with my uncle, Amédée de Maurienne, will all be in the vanguard, while my royal guard and I will remain among those who protect the rear."

By early January, they reached the city of Laodicea, where they hoped to replenish their supplies. In Biblical times Laodicea had been one of the wealthiest cities in the world, and the crusaders gaped at the ruined splendor the Romans had left there—a great stadium, temples, baths. They had been led to believe it was still a bustling city. However, upon their arrival, they discovered it empty of both people and food.

They had hoped for abundance, even in this winter month, for the land along the Lycus River, where the city was located, was said to be fertile. There was evidence that the city had been recently occupied, and they concluded that, given the reputation of the Germans for violence and looting, the approach of more crusaders frightened the population so that everyone had left, taking with them any supplies that would have benefited the French army.

They spent a day looking for the residents of Laodicea, hoping to find food. But all they found were terrified people, who seemed to have nothing themselves. So they pushed on toward Mount Cadmus, which they had to cross before they reached the next city of Adalia.

Henri thought the whole venture looked dubious, for already they were encountering on their road rotting corpses from the section of the German army that had been led by Otto of Freising. The ladies turned their heads away and held to their noses sprigs of dried lavender from their trunks to ward off the odor as they passed by the dead bodies, half-eaten by scavengers, and carrion crows still pecking at their eyes.

As they approached Mount Cadmus, Henri rode not far from the queen and her special knight and friend, Geoffrey de Rancon. In the past, Louis had insisted that she and her ladies ride with the mid-section of the crusading army, where he thought she would be safer. But the queen, eager to be at the forefront of whatever was happening, had grown weary of being part of what she laughingly called "the baggage guard." She had not been frightened by what happened at the Maeander River, she said, but rather exhilarated that there was "finally some action."

She's as beautiful and daring as her reputation, Henri thought, admiring her large blue eyes and the long blond braid that fell across her right breast. He hoped her daughter was equally as beautiful. Eager to push on, the queen rode beside Geoffrey to the mountain summit, where the king had instructed them to wait for the rest of the army, which moved more slowly. There they planned to camp for the night and make their way down the other side the next day. But the sun was still high when they arrived at the crest.

"Oh, let's go on a bit farther," the queen urged. "I see no good camping spot here, and it's much too early to stop."

"But, my lady, the king commanded us to wait here," Geoffrey said.

"*Mordieu*, Geoffrey. Don't be such a lapdog. You're the leader of this vanguard. No one pays much attention to Louis's orders, so why should you? Let's find a better spot, out of all this icy wind."

"As you wish, my lady," Geoffrey replied with a roguish grin. He sent a scout to ride on ahead to find a more comfortable campsite.

"Is that a wise decision?" Henri asked the king's uncle, the count of Maurienne, riding beside him.

"I don't see any harm in it. We've not encountered any resistance, and this cold wind won't do anyone any good."

The scout soon returned to announce that there was a grassy slope sheltered from the wind only a few miles ahead. It was still daylight when they arrived and made camp. Once the tents were pitched and the flagons of wine brought out to warm the innards, Jaufre Rudel, the Prince of Blaye, a troubadour who always seemed to stay as close to Queen Eleanor as he dared, took out his lute and began to sing a song with a plaintive melody.

Lanquand li jorn son lonc en mai
M'es bels douz chans d'auzels de loing,
E quand me sui partiz de lai
Remembra•m d'un'amor de loing

The song, sung in the *langue d'oc*, the language of the south, was unknown to Henri, but it appeared that the crusaders from that region, as well as the queen, were familiar with it. Henri could catch a few words here and there, but not enough to understand its meaning. He leaned toward one of the young men from Aquitaine.

"What's the song about?" he asked.

"What most of Jaufre's songs are about," he replied. "His love from afar for the countess of Tripoli."

"Love from afar?"

"He claims he fell in love on hearing of her beauty and reputation."

"You mean he's never even met her?" Henri was incredulous.

"No, and I suspect he never will. But he sings about it all the time. I think it's why he's come with the army—to prove himself worthy. I suppose he hopes to meet her when we pass through Tripoli—if we do."

Henri was not particularly fond of love songs, and he found the idea of "love from afar" bizarre and amusing—even a bit silly. But when he looked around to see the reaction of the others, they were all smiling with appreciation. As they listened, they lounged languidly on the grass and enjoyed their goblets of wine. Servants had spread blankets on the ground for the ladies, almost as though they were on a spring outing, despite their woolen fur-lined cloaks and the chill in the air.

As the song drew to a close, the young knight leaned over to explain. "He sings that for her sake he would be willing even to be captured by the Saracens."

Henri laughed. "Well, for his sake, let's hope it doesn't come to that."

When darkness fell, and the rest of the army had not yet arrived, the revelers became apprehensive. As the hours passed with no news, those in charge truly began to worry.

"What could have happened to the others?"

"I think we should send someone back to look for them," Henri said. "I'm really concerned."

"It would be far too dangerous on this dark mountain. I think we can only wait," said Geoffrey.

But the night dragged on, and no one came. A thick darkness settled like a pall over the camp, where no one slept.

CHAPTER 11

Henri, fearing the worst, sat silently beside his friends, Anseau and Garnier, staring into the embers of the campfire. He could barely make out the grim faces of Geoffrey and Amédée, who stood in the distance, outside their tents, talking quietly. Men paced anxiously, muttering to each other and cursing the darkness.

Hours passed. Nothing. Then, finally, from the dark path, they heard a sound, a voice from several hundred yards away, calling, "Help us." Every man in the camp leapt to his feet and rushed in the direction of the voice. Women flung open their tent flaps to peer out in search of missing loved ones.

A trail of broken men stumbled out of the black night, and members of the vanguard hurried to lend an arm or a shoulder to the wounded—some with their heads or limbs wrapped in bloody rags, others limping painfully with the help of a stick—ten of them at first, then six more—one leading a horse with two Turkish arrows still in its right flank. It struggled to stay upright with its burden—the body of an adolescent. Henri recognized the straggler as a man from Flanders that Thierry had called Joseph. The body lying face down across the horse's back, Henri saw with a shock, was that of the man's only son.

"I couldn't leave him," Joseph said, as he collapsed to his knees, dirty streaks of tears lining his face now visible in the dim light of the dying fire.

"There were too many bodies to bury or bring with us," said another man, his face smudged with dried blood.

Noblewomen and servants alike, some openly weeping, rushed about to find clean bandages and food for the stragglers, as the men helped them toward the camp. Henri went back to the edges of the dark road, where he anxiously watched for the king, praying that he still lived. He had almost given up hope when, finally, he caught sight of a group of men surrounding a single horse, on which King Louis slouched.

"I'm so relieved to see you, my lord," Henri said, hurrying forward to greet him.

Louis responded with only a grunt and a face like a thundercloud.

He was clearly exhausted, but appeared not to be wounded, except for scratches on his hands and arms, his clothes torn and dirty. He dismounted with difficulty but found the energy to locate Geoffrey de Rancon in the crowd and confront him with rage.

"You bastard!" Louis growled. "We've had to make our way all these miles in the dark, with the few men we have left… Bodies of our men are literally piled up back at the pass, where you were *supposed* to be waiting. I'll have you hanged for disobeying my orders." He was almost screaming at Geoffrey, who stood staunchly, eyes on the ground, as he received the king's attack.

Henri was shocked by the vehemence of Louis's words and horrified at what had happened. As he watched in silence, the king's uncle stepped forward, his head bowed.

"I, too, approved the new site, Louis," he said quietly. "Geoffrey does not bear all the blame."

The king glared at his uncle. Surely, Henri thought, he wouldn't hang his own kinsman. But if he didn't, in fairness, he couldn't hang Geoffrey either. Then, to his surprise, the queen, looking boldly into her husband's eyes, also stepped forward.

"And it was all done at my request, my lord. Please show mercy to these men who were only trying to find us a more comfortable spot. If not, you'll have to hang me as well."

The king, still seething, looked at her with speechless fury, then turned sharply on his heel and walked away, his fists clenched.

"We lost almost everything," said one of the survivors, his voice shaking. "Men and horses slaughtered… it was… a nightmare. The

Turks came out of nowhere and attacked us in a narrow pass—with arrows and those curved swords of theirs, those scimitars… slashing at everything in sight. It was horrible—so many bodies—so many dead." The man, overcome with emotion, sunk his face into his bloody hands and began to sob.

"How on earth did the king get away?" one of the ladies asked in a horrified tone.

"He survived," said a voice out of the darkness, "only because he was dressed as a common crusader and wore no emblem of office. He managed to scramble up a rock, where he was hard to reach. The Turks had no idea who he was and left him there to find easier prey."

"That was a blessing," the lady said.

"A blessing," the man echoed with a bitter laugh. "I don't know how any of us got away."

"I wonder why the heathens didn't attack us in the vanguard. We passed along the same route," Amédée said, truly puzzled.

"Perhaps they had heard what happened at the Maeander River," one man suggested.

"Or perhaps they were not yet in position," another added. "Who knows?"

Throughout the night, men who had been in the baggage train or the rearguard continued to stagger into the camp, a few at a time to tend their wounds and tell their tales.

When they grew silent, Henri could still hear the sounds of weeping and prayers for the souls of the lost as the crusaders tried to sleep. So many friends he would never see again. So many dead. So many noble lives lost. *The only comfort,* Henri thought, *is that having died in this holy cause, they're guaranteed salvation by the pope.*

As the sun rose over the battered camp the next day, Henri awoke, the horror of all that had happened washing over him once more. *Surely,* he thought, *the rest of the campaign will go better. Things can hardly get worse.*

But they did not get better. The discouraged and weary king turned over command of his army to the Templars who traveled with them. Discipline became stricter and the troops more orderly and able to turn back occasional Turkish skirmishes. Still, people continued to die along the way, from wounds, illness, and hunger. Soon the crusaders—

even the wealthiest among them—were reduced to eating their dead horses. By late January, three months after leaving Constantinople, they finally reached Adalia, a port city on the Mediterranean, where they found food to buy, but at exorbitant prices that many could not afford. Some of the men had hoped to replace their horses, but there were few suitable steeds to be found.

Although the city was in the hand of the Greeks, Turks controlled the surrounding area, and Turkish soldiers still harassed the crusaders with random killings of those who weren't already dying of starvation and disease. Weeks passed, as the crusaders recovered from their ordeal, dreading the forty-day march to Antioch that lay ahead.

As they sat idle, Henri gathered what information he could and waited with impatience for someone to make a decision. Finally, he approached the king himself.

"I've been asking about the road ahead, and the locals say we could sail from here to Antioch in a matter of days," Henri told the king, whose anger had finally calmed sufficiently to be approached once more. "It would be costly, but there, where the queen's uncle rules, we will surely find a more amicable welcome."

"Others have made the same suggestion," Louis replied. "And I've already spoken to Greek authorities who have promised to try to locate ships for the entire army, but we'll still need to await good weather to sail."

As they waited, winter unleashed its worst—snow, rain, and violent storms. Finally, when the ships arrived, they were insufficient to carry everyone, and the weather was still not suitable for sailing. The king tried to make provisions for those who would still have to endure the forty-days' march—paying five hundred marks to local authorities to provide them safe passage to Tarsus. He could only pray they would survive. Their fate was in God's hands.

After waiting for favorable winds, those who could afford the passage took to the sea, Henri among them. He was aboard the same ship as the king's household. At first the winds were brisk, but on the morning of the second day, a storm blew the vessel off course. It rolled and creaked, causing misery among its passengers, Jaufre Rudel among them. The ladies had been delighted that he was aboard and looked forward to his entertaining them during the trip.

Once on the ship, however, he fell ill. At first everyone thought he was merely seasick, but he had a fever that grew worse as the voyage continued. On the fourth day at sea, he asked to see Queen Eleanor, who came at once to the place where he lay.

"*Domna*," he greeted her in their mutual *langue d'oc*.

"My lord, Jaufre, I hope you will soon feel better." Her voice was gentle.

"I wish it were so, my queen, but you and I both know that I am near death. And I have a favor to ask of you." His eyes were cloudy and feverish.

"Anything at all, Jaufre," she answered, remembering how his songs had provided some of the few pleasurable moments of the crusade. "But you must get well to sing to me again."

"Alas, my lady, I fear I will never sing again."

"What can I do for you, my friend?" she asked, taking his clammy hand.

"I will not make it to Tripoli, but when you pass through that land, would you take greetings to the Countess Hodierne on my behalf? And deliver to her a copy of my songs?" It took all the strength he could muster to reach inside the pilgrim's sack beside him and pull out a rolled manuscript. He breathed heavily from the effort.

"It has been my life's goal to behold her beautiful face," he said.

"I know, my lord," she said with tenderness. "And I will see that she receives the manuscript of your excellent songs—which I know you have written to honor her and express your love. But you must do your best to get well so that you can present them to her yourself."

He gave her a weak smile. His eyes seemed to grow calmer as she took the manuscript from his hand.

"Thank you, *Domna*. I am grateful."

Jaufre died the next day, and the ship put in at the port of Kyrenia on the island of Cyprus, where the king ordered his body to be buried.

While in port, they restocked food supplies, and waited out the storm before setting sail again for the principality of Antioch. The king's uncle, Amédée, who was also ill, asked to be put ashore as well. He was taken to the nearby city of Nicosia, where, they later learned, he died the following month.

Finally, despite all the misfortunes, on a fine day in mid-March, the king's ship arrived at the mouth of the Orontes River and the port of St. Symeon. Raymond de Toulouse awaited eagerly to greet them with great honor. He was a handsome man in his thirties, with a straight nose, intense blue eyes, and a fine head of brown hair that hung to his shoulders. He was splendidly dressed in a gold brocade *bliaut* that reflected the sunlight.

No one was happier to see him than Queen Eleanor, who fell into the arms of her father's younger brother, greeting him without ceremony. Henri smiled at her enthusiasm, knowing that the two had not seen one another since she was a child.

"Thanks be to God we are finally here. I have waited so long to see you again, Uncle Raymond," she said, tears of joy on her cheeks.

"And I you, *Bela*. How beautiful you have become! Your father would be proud."

Raymond and Louis exchanged the kiss of peace, and the royal entourage was escorted with joyous ceremony to the palace in nearby Antioch.

What a contrast Antioch was to the Byzantine lands they had left. People were warm and hospitable. Raymond in particular was pleased to welcome the king's army, or the shreds of it that remained, and provided all his court could offer to make their visit memorable. Henri had never seen the queen so happy and relaxed. She was obviously overjoyed to be at a court where she felt safe and comfortable and could speak her native tongue freely once more.

One March afternoon, while the king and Prince Raymond were closeted in a private discussion, the queen and Sir Henri strolled in one of the palace's fragrant gardens. She had taken a liking to the young knight and decided that he would indeed make a fine husband for Marie, even if he was the son of her old enemy. If Marie could not be the queen of England, at least she could become countess of Champagne.

Henri watched with pleasure as Eleanor breathed deeply in the fragrant air, her eyes closed in rapture, and he wondered once again if her daughter would be as beautiful as her mother.

"Antioch in the spring reminds me of Aquitaine," Eleanor said with a relaxed smile. My uncle Raymond's court is so like my father's—musicians, exquisite food, and fine silk cushions everywhere. It's like coming home."

"It's very pleasant, my lady, and I can see that you are enjoying yourself."

"For a change," she laughed. "It's wonderful to have a place to bathe and a chance to wear silk gowns once more. Raymond is so like my father. I couldn't be happier."

Antioch was more familiar than Constantinople, to be sure, and he wished he shared her enthusiasm for the place. But it was nothing like home to Henri, who was beginning to feel a nostalgia for his own lands and family. Despite the lavish banquets and the soft couches throughout the palace, he missed Champagne and the accent of his own homeland. He was well aware, however, of the queen's delight at being here. She and Prince Raymond sat up late at night, laughing, talking, and exchanging stories of their homeland, long after Raymond's wife, Princess Constance, had retired for the night.

At such moments, Louis would turn to his wife and say, "Shall we retire as well?"

But more times than not, she would respond, "You go ahead. I'm enjoying myself," turning back to Raymond without a second glance. Already French crusaders were whispering among themselves, speculating as to what happened when she and the prince were alone. Henri had heard from Odo de Deuil rumors about an "improper dalliance" between them.

"That is one thing I will not report to Abbot Suger," he would say as he retired to work on his chronicle. "He has enough to worry about."

Although gossip spread throughout the noble ranks of the army, Henri put little stock in it. He knew first-hand how delighted the queen was to be with her kinsman again and how much she professed to love him, but not in the way the rumors implied. He would never believe that she would be improper in such a way with her father's brother.

As they turned a corner of the garden path, Henri caught sight of a tense-faced Raymond, his jaw firmly set, striding toward them. When the prince saw Eleanor, he let his face relax a bit.

"Hello, *Bela*. I hope you're having a pleasant day."

"Indeed I am, Uncle Raymond. And I always enjoy the company

of a handsome young knight like Sir Henri." Her voice was light and teasing, almost flirtatious. Then she looked at her uncle more carefully and perceived his intensity. "But you don't look as though you're having a very good day yourself."

They were speaking in their *langue d'oc*, but Henri had by now spent enough days in the presence of the Aquitanians in the vanguard and heard enough of the language to understand the gist of their conversation.

"*Bela*, your husband is a stubborn man."

"What has he done now?"

"He refuses to listen to reason. I laid out a perfectly logical plan to recapture Edessa, as I understood you came here to do. But he's determined to move on to Jerusalem to visit the holy places."

"But he's as close to Edessa here as he ever will be," she said.

"*Oc*, I know. But I cannot persuade him."

"Perhaps you should call a meeting of all the French noblemen. They can often convince him of more reasonable tactics," she suggested.

"What do you think, young man?" Raymond said, switching to the *langue d'oïl* of the north so that Henri could understand.

"This is Henri de Champagne, the son of Count Thibaut," Eleanor interjected.

Raymond nodded. "Yes, I know. What do you think, Sir Henri?"

"A council meeting is always a good idea, my lord. We need to find consensus in matters in which we all risk our lives."

"A good answer," Raymond said. "I'll arrange a meeting first thing tomorrow. I hope you will attend."

Henri nodded, and Raymond kissed the hand of Eleanor before he turned and strode back toward the palace door from which he had come.

The meeting of the Antiochene and French noblemen, all seated in the council chamber, took place the following day, and once again, Raymond was his charming and optimistic self. Henri was eager to hear his proposal, but even before the Poitevin prince began to speak, the king had a sour look on his face.

Raymond stood and spoke in a self-assured voice. "I am here to propose to you what I think will be a most logical and relatively easy way to meet the goals of your campaign, the recapture of Edessa, for which you have come so far and suffered such hardship."

The men around the table nodded in agreement.

"I propose that, as soon as you are all rested and strong again, my men will join you in moving toward the Saracen cities that stand between us and Edessa. The first city we must capture is Aleppo. That taken, the rest should be easy," Raymond said, then paused to wait for their reactions.

Henri watched the King Louis, who scowled, but made no comment.

"What would be the advantage of such a move," Thierry of Flanders asked.

"Antioch is the closest city to Edessa you will come to and still be in Christian lands and on your way to Jerusalem, which I know you all want to visit. But the loss of Edessa to the Saracens was the whole focus of this crusade. It seems best to launch your attack from here. But the cities in between, like Aleppo and Shaizar, must be captured first—before we reach Edessa, for they will fight us along the way, and we don't want the enemy at our backs. You know, of course, that Zengi, who first captured the city, was murdered in September a year ago. Nur-ad-Din is now emir of Aleppo."

"Do you think all that's really necessary before we recapture Edessa?" Henri asked.

"I do. Both are Saracen strongholds that block your way. Once we capture them, then Edessa should be easy to take, if you still think it's worth taking. But I must tell you, the city has been under siege, captured and recaptured so many times that there is not much left, I fear. It's virtually deserted."

"But if we don't take Edessa, why should we bother to attack Aleppo and the other Syrian cities that stand in our way?" Thierry asked. He paused for a long moment. When Raymond did not respond at once, Thierry spoke again. "I do wonder at the motive of your proposal, for I have heard that you have done homage to Manuel."

"As you have, my lords," Raymond answered with a quick smile.

"Yes, but ours was secondary to the homage to our king. You have made no homage to King Louis. I also understand that you made a prior agreement with emperor Manuel's late father to yield Antioch to the Greeks, if it is they who capture the cities that stand between here and Edessa. But they have agreed to turn those cities over to you. Is that true?"

Raymond's face reddened. "That is true, but if I were forced to weaken my powers here by yielding Antioch, it would also weaken both the French and the Catholic presence in the area and strengthen the Byzantines. If we could destroy Nur-ad-Din ourselves, we will strengthen the Latin kingdoms for all time to come and secure them for our children."

"And *you* will get to keep Antioch," Thierry added, "as well as have those other cities added to your domain." Raymond could not deny it.

To this point the glowering king had said nothing. Now he presented his own arguments.

"We should go on to Jerusalem to pray for God's help in the holy places. And we should consult with some of the other leaders of the Latin kingdoms before we commit ourselves to a plan that would accomplish the personal goals of the prince of Antioch." There was mumbling around the room.

"He may be right," Thierry finally said to Raymond. "Right now our army is weak, and we could find fresh horses near Jerusalem and meet with what's left of the Germans to help in any military activities."

"I can find you fresh horses here, and my men will march with you," Raymond said.

The noblemen turned to each other once again to exchange their opinions. Henri could certainly see both sides of the issue, but he was reluctant to counter the arguments of the king, whom he now anticipated as his future father-in-law.

Finally, as the hubbub died down, King Louis announced, "My men would like a chance to think it over and discuss it more fully among themselves. We will announce our decision in due time."

Raymond nodded. He had no choice. And Henri knew that it was more than he had gotten from the king the day before. Now he could only wait and see.

The wait brought him nothing. The crusaders, weary of violence, decided to heed their king's advice and continue on to Jerusalem.

None of them was sure it was the right thing to do, but they remained united in their opposition to Raymond's plan. Queen Eleanor, who had decided her uncle could do no wrong, was furious with Louis. She had looked forward to lingering in Antioch, while the men went to Aleppo and then on to Edessa to accomplish what the crusade had set out to do. But she could not persuade her husband to change his mind.

Only a few days later, after another great feast and as the courtiers were enjoying goblets of wine and entertainment in the great hall of Raymond's palace, Louis stood to make an announcement. Raising his goblet to the prince and princess, he said, "I would like to thank you for your hospitality, but the time has come when we must continue our march to Jerusalem. We shall depart within the week."

Raymond, still angry at the king's refusal to help him, did not rise to accept the Louis's thanks. Instead, it was Queen Eleanor who stood up—defiantly facing her husband.

"I shan't go with you," she announced to the amazement of all the French nobles in the room. "I'll stay here with Uncle Raymond until you return."

"You *will* go," the king said. "And I'll hear no more about it."

Her eyes widened. "How dare you order me about like that?" her voice rose, and all other conversation in the room ceased as all eyes turned toward Queen Eleanor and King Louis.

"You are my wife, and you will do as I say."

Henri saw her raise her chin and tighten her jaw before she spoke again. This time her voice was louder, obviously intended for all to hear.

"Your wife in a consanguineous marriage." The words that followed were almost drowned out by the gasps of astonishment in the hall. "You know very well that we are related by blood to a forbidden degree. Our marriage is not legitimate, and it should be dissolved," she announced to the king and to the court.

"I'll hear no more such nonsense," Louis replied angrily, his face flaming. He turned abruptly and strode from the hall. Henri, watching the scene in disbelief, saw the king's fury and feared Queen Eleanor would pay dearly for her impertinence.

CHAPTER 12

"We're leaving for Jerusalem tonight," King Louis confided to the most trusted noblemen in his company.

"Why are we leaving by night, my lord?" asked Odo.

"It's a precaution. I expect I will be taking the queen against her will, and it must be done with some stealth—or else Raymond may try to prevent it, which could lead to violence. At least so I fear."

Odo nodded.

"I'm going to need some men willing to bring the queen and her attendant with us."

No one volunteered for what would clearly be an unpleasant task.

"I am reluctant to appoint anyone from my own court, for no doubt the queen will take it ill if she is forced to come." Finally, when no one stepped forth to offer his own courtiers or servants, Louis turned to his brother, Robert de Dreux.

"Robert, would you be willing to appoint some of your men to do the deed?"

Robert's jaw clenched, and he frowned with distaste, as he brushed back a shock of dark hair from his forehead and replied without enthusiasm, "As you wish, Louis. How many men will you need?"

"For Eleanor and her companion, probably at least four, though perhaps there should be others standing by."

Robert nodded. "I shall see to it."

That night, after everyone in the Antiochene court had retired, Robert's men made their way stealthily down the palace corridor that led to Queen Eleanor's bedchamber. Count Robert had made certain that two of his men had been placed on guard outside her room, while four others, dressed in dark robes like monks, waited for them to open the door. The queen never bolted it from the inside. Some whispered that it was because she expected a lover, but no guards had ever reported such an entry.

Quietly, the door opened, and the men peered into the darkness of the chamber. In a large bed centered against the back wall of the room, the queen slept, her long blond hair unbraided and splayed out across her pillow. Her maid, snoring lightly, slept against the far wall. As they crept into the room, the maid turned over, and the men paused, afraid of waking her, even though Count Robert had made certain that the ladies' evening goblets of warm wine were laced with a tincture of opium. When the maid seemed to settle down again, they tiptoed in groups of two toward the beds.

The queen roused as they wrapped her in a blanket, but she only mumbled incoherently as two of the men carried her toward the waiting litter. In similar fashion, her maid was borne unceremoniously by two other men. With the still-sleeping women tucked inside the curtained litter and their coffers quickly loaded onto a waiting wagon, the king and his entourage made their way as quietly as possible toward the city gate. They had no difficulty convincing the gatekeeper to open them, for his main duty was to prevent unwanted people from entering the city, not leaving it. Thus, in the dark of night, King Louis left Antioch, not the way he had entered, with welcome and glory, but like a thief in the night, stealing away his unwilling wife.

It was Henri who now rode beside the queen's litter as dawn broke over the horizon. Her Aquitanian protector, Geoffrey de Rancon, whom Louis still blamed for the debacle on Mount Cadmus, was no longer with the crusading army. Given the king's wrath and the death on the island of Cyprus of his uncle Amédée, who had stood between him and the noose, he had decided it best to return to France without further delay.

By late morning, a sleepy face pulled aside the curtain of the litter and peered out.

"Where are we?" the queen asked Henri.

"Almost to the kingdom of Tripoli, my lady, on our way to Jerusalem," he replied, exaggerating the distance they had covered, as he had been instructed to do, though he dreaded her reaction.

"What?" her eyes, still red from her drugged sleep. "Stop this litter," she screamed to the driver. "Turn it around."

Henri had never seen her so angry, her face contorted in hatred and frustration.

The driver glanced back but did not slow his pace. Eleanor turned her wrath toward Henri.

"How could you do this? How could you be part of this? I hate you! I hate you!" she shrieked.

"I'm sorry, my lady. I had no part in it, but the king asked me to ride beside you for your protection."

"Protection from what? *He's* what I need protection from!" Her voice grew more and more shrill, until knights and foot soldiers within hearing distance strained to see what the uproar was about. Everyone knew that the queen would be angry, but no one had anticipated such a public outburst.

"I'm getting out. I'll walk back to Antioch," she said, dangling her legs over the side. She made an effort to leap from the litter, but her maid, who was now awake as well, held her back.

"*Ma dame*, what are you doing? You'll hurt yourself." The maid held on desperately and tried to pull the curtains shut.

Henri could hear the commotion from inside the litter. Queen Eleanor was in a fury like no one had ever seen. "He can't do this! I will not be held prisoner by him or any other man." He could tell she was crying now, but he knew there was nothing she could do. The king had made up his mind, and Prince Raymond had not pursued them to come to her aid.

In time, the queen calmed, but Henri, painfully aware of the rupture in the relationship of Louis and Eleanor, hoped it would not affect his chances for a betrothal to Princess Marie. He also hoped that the princess would *not* be like her mother in temperament. Eleanor rode beside him in silence for a long time. Little by little, however, she began to speak to him again. She clearly needed a friend to talk to, and he was convenient and sympathetic, as least so far as he dared to be. Finally, she told him of the promise she had made to Jaufre Rudel.

"Perhaps it worked out for the best," he suggested. "Now you will be able to keep your word."

She groaned. "Yes. … But at what cost?"

"I'm sorry, my lady. I know how happy you were in Antioch, but now you will also get to visit the holy city where our Lord was crucified."

"Yes, Henri, I know." She sighed without enthusiasm.

They arrived in Jerusalem in early June, after a brief stopover in Tripoli, where in a private chamber the queen delivered Jaufre's manuscript to Countess Hodierne. Eleanor never revealed the countess's reaction or spoke of the conversation that went on in that room, but Henri always wondered about it and whether the countess, who was not as beautiful as he expected, was worthy in character of Jaufre's devotion.

Jerusalem was the only highlight left in the crusade. But the French crusaders hardly had time to visit the holy sites before they were summoned to a general assembly in Palmarea, near the city of Acre, to be held on the feast day of John the Baptist. There they met with noble survivors of the regrouped German army and the ruling families of the Kingdom of Jerusalem to determine a course of action.

The meeting was hot and packed almost beyond capacity with the most prominent men from each of the kingdoms. The three kings, Louis, Conrad, and Baldwin III of Jerusalem, along with his mother, Queen Melisende, sat on a dais facing the throng. Henri had never seen a gathering of so many powerful and distinguished nobles in a single place—French, German, leaders of the Latin kingdoms, Templars and Hospitallers, but he noticed that neither Antioch nor Tripoli was represented. He knew that the decision would inevitably swing toward what was in the best interest of the kingdom of Jerusalem. In fact, there was a rumor among the French that Conrad and King Baldwin had already agreed that the best tactic would be to march on the Muslim city of Damascus, but they needed the agreement of the French.

Queen Melisende was one of the few who favored the original idea of attacking Aleppo and recapturing Edessa, which her father had once ruled and where she had lived until she was thirteen. But her advice was ignored in the hubbub of discussion, as they reached a general consensus that Damascus should be their new target.

A month later the siege began. It did not last long. The Christian army set out in high spirits and managed to fight its way through the narrow paths among the orchards and canals. Saracen archers lurked on every side and were able to pick them off one by one in the narrow line of marchers, but these were the only paths available.

The Christian forces finally fought their way to the city gates. They seemed on the verge of breaking through, when some local lords suddenly advised them to abandon their positions and move to the other side of the city where, supposedly, there was little defense and low walls, and victory would be easy. The entire army shifted its position. But there, they discovered only a barren plain with no water for the army and enemy defenses that were by no means weak, as they had been led to believe. By the time they realized their mistake, they could not return to their original site, because the Damascenes had quickly mounted substantial obstacles and set their defenders in place. In addition, rumor had it that the troops of Nur-ad-Din were arriving with reinforcements.

Parched from the July heat and the dust of their efforts, weary, and disheartened by the slaughter of so many, the Christian troops began to withdraw, retreating in humiliation and defeat after only a four-day siege.

The crusade was over. There had been no major battles, no epic victories or losses. Just constant hardship and harassment and a new wedge driven between the king and queen.

We have accomplished nothing for the entire time—nothing but loss of life, a dispirited Henri thought as he rode back among his men along the dusty road toward Jerusalem. His small exploit at the Maeander River was all he had to show for almost two years of privation, weariness, and the stench of rotting corpses. It was, in fact, about all the entire French army had to boast about—the driving off of a few archers who tried to block their exit from the river.

Inevitably, rumors circulated as to why they had failed so miserably in Damascus. Some blamed poor decisions by the military commanders. Others argued that there had been treachery, possibly even bribery, in the ranks of the local nobility. And, of course, they had all learned that the city was better defended than they had expected, especially as Saracen reinforcements began arriving. Henri and most of the other French nobles, who had lost men, horses, and much personal wealth in this fruitless endeavor, were fed up and eager to go home.

Anseau de Traînel approached Henri as soon as they were back in Jerusalem.

"Garnier and I want to return home. When do you plan to sail, my friend? Should we wait for you and all travel together?"

"Please don't feel obliged to wait until I'm ready to return. There are things I want to do here before I head back to Champagne. And on my way, I plan to stop for a while in Sicily to visit my sister Isabelle."

"The one who married Roger of Apulia, King Roger's son? Of course, it would be a good opportunity for you to see her again. But we are eager to get back. If you have no objections, we'll travel on our own to Acre and set sail from there."

"God be with you, my friends. Thank you for your companionship and loyalty during this long and fruitless trip. I'll see you back in Troyes." He embraced each of them warmly and bid them farewell.

The entire venture seemed pointless and incomplete. He wanted to do something to make it worthwhile. At least he could turn it into a true pilgrimage. He would spend a few more weeks in Jerusalem to buy gifts for his family, then visit the town of Sebastia, where the bones of John the Baptist had recently been discovered. He wanted to explore sites made famous in the Bible. And he wanted to make certain that he was still in good favor with the king and queen, despite all that had happened.

The royal couple had seemed preoccupied of late, carefully avoiding one another. The queen kept to herself, not participating in public assemblies, spending time only with the widowed Queen Melisende and the ladies who had accompanied her from France. Eleanor and Melisende found a common bond in both queenship and determination. For Eleanor, Melisende's company was also a good excuse to keep as far away from Louis as possible.

"I know you must miss your husband," Eleanor said, aware that Melisende's late husband, Foulques d'Anjou, had died in 1143.

"Indeed," Melisende answered, "But our son Baldwin is like him in many ways. His father died when he was only thirteen."

"I know Foulques's son, Count Geoffrey, and I have met his grandson, Henry. Are you not his grandmother?"

"No, that was Foulques's first wife, Ermengarde of Maine. She died three years before our marriage. I've never met the boy, but I hear he is a comely lad."

"Indeed he is, though not so much as his father. I think he has a bright future before him," Eleanor said with a thoughtful smile before their talk turned to other matters.

After less than two months Henri was ready to depart. Many of the nobles had already left for home, and the sailing season was growing short. In late September, he announced his intentions to King Louis.

"My lord," Henri said, "if you have no further need of my service, I would like to sail home as soon as I can book passage."

"I understand, Henri. It has been a long voyage. And we have all suffered much. I plan to stay here with my household until next Easter. I can think of nothing I would enjoy more than Easter in Jerusalem—where it all took place—the Crucifixion and the Resurrection." Henri suspected that he also wanted more time before he took Queen Eleanor back to France, where he had to face the utter failure of his crusade.

"Then I have your permission to go?"

"You don't need my permission, but you have my blessing."

When Louis said nothing more, Henri leaned forward. "I don't want to seem impertinent, but you once mentioned that you would send a letter to my father, expressing your satisfaction in my performance."

"I did indeed, and I have not yet done so. Before your departure, I shall have the letter drawn up, and you can take it with you. That way I know it will be in safe hands."

"Thank you, my lord. I would be grateful."

"And you can tell your father when you arrive that when I am home again and things settle down, we can discuss that betrothal."

Henri smiled broadly, relieved at this reassurance.

True to his word, Louis had the letter drawn up within the week and summoned Henri to his lodging in King Baldwin's palace.

The king held the parchment in his hand, but, as yet, it bore no seal. "Allow me to read to you what I have written to your father." He read the usual greetings before getting to the heart of the letter:

The close friendship which I feel in my heart for your loyal son Henri has compelled me, in these remote parts, to write to you of his reputation. The devotion which he has shown me at all times and his loyal service have earned my ever-increasing gratitude and have deepened my affection for him. For that, I thank you and I point it out so that you may be even more proud of him yourself.

Henri felt a pang of disappointment that the king had not praised his courage as a knight nor did it mention a pending betrothal. But he was certain his father had already heard about the battle at the Maeander River, and this letter surely expressed the king's favor, which would pave the way for a formal agreement.

"Thank you, my lord," he said.

The king sealed the document and handed it to Henri.

"I thank you for your loyalty. And we shall see one another again back in France. May you have a safe trip home."

It was the last time Henri saw the king before his departure.

The young man found passage to Sicily in early October. He would not travel alone. His chaplain, Martin, had remained with him. And the Pougy brothers—Odo and Renaud—would also accompany him on the return trip.

The voyage was rough. He had waited too late in the season, and autumn weather was treacherous for sea travel. In the worst of the storms, as violent winds tossed the vessel, causing it to take on water from the crashing waves, the four men feared for their lives.

Henri clung to a spar and prayed aloud. "I pray you, Lord God, and to you, St. Nicholas, patron saint of sailors. Spare us." Even bargaining with God, he swore even louder, so that the Pougy brothers would hear him and hold him accountable, that "if we live past this night and arrive safely, I will fund three canons in the church at Pougy." Several times before dawn, the ship seemed near foundering, but eventually the storm subsided.

The rocky coast of Sicily was a welcome sight, the mountains rising in the background, with Monte Pellegrino looming over the city. Henri could make out the rooftops of Palermo as they approached the harbor. He had never been so glad to set foot on land. King Roger, hearing of his arrival, had him brought at once to the palace, where he greeted him warmly and expressed his sympathy for the horrors the crusaders had suffered.

"Most of those misfortunes could have been avoided had King Louis taken advantage of the sea route and my offer to provide ships," he reminded Henri.

"True, my lord. But what's done is done. I lost many men on the journey—including a special friend—Count Milo de Nogent-sur-Seine. He had been like a father to me throughout the campaign, always ready with helpful counsel."

"And how did he die?"

"He drowned crossing the Maeander River."

"The place where I heard you were such a hero? How sad."

"Yes, it was one of the saddest moments of the entire campaign for me."

Roger rested his hand on the young man's back. "I am happy that *you* made it home without wounds or worse."

"As am I, my lord. Now that I am here, I would like to see my sister

Isabelle as soon as possible. It has been more than eight years since we were together," he said. "Do she and her husband know I am here?"

Roger's face darkened. "Then you have not heard?"

"Heard what, my lord?"

"Of my son's death."

"Good heavens, no! I am sorry to hear of your loss, Lord Roger. And here you are commiserating with me, when it is I who should be consoling you. How did he die?"

"It was a freak accident on the tilting field in May. It has been nearly half a year since his death. His wife, the countess, is still mourning, as I fear we all are. She is living in the palace now."

It explained her husband's failure to join them in Constantinople, and Henri knew now why God had sent him here. He must take his sister home. They had been close growing up, but Isabelle had wed Duke Roger when she was only twelve years old. The couple had no children, though Henri had heard it rumored that the duke had fathered two children by a mistress, as he waited for his bride to mature. Henri remembered well the day the two Cistercian monks, on behalf of Roger of Sicily, had come to take her away, her gray eyes large with fear, and her slight frame looking so vulnerable. As the monks led her through the city gates of Troyes, mounted on a palfrey, he had wanted to run after her and bring her back. But he was just thirteen and could only stand there, fighting his unwanted tears.

Henri expressed his condolences and added, "I'd also like to console my sister."

Roger snapped his fingers toward a squire standing nearby. "Fetch the duchess of Apulia."

As they awaited her arrival, King Roger took him on a tour of his Cappella Palatina—his new chapel. It was actually attached to the palace, making it more practical for morning mass and easier for interactions between the king and the clergy. Roger was clearly proud of its architectural splendor, which managed to blend traces of Norman, Byzantine, and Muslim architecture into a magnificent whole. Henri was gazing in admiration when the door burst open and Isabelle came running in.

She threw herself into her brother's arms. "Oh, Henri, how glad I am to see you again." Despite their closeness as children, he wasn't sure he would have recognized her. At eighteen, she was no longer the thin little girl he had last seen. Her gray eyes were weeping, just as they had been the last time he saw her, but her lank honey-colored hair was now brushed to shining perfection, and her breasts were those not of a child, but of a woman. Her face had lengthened to a perfect oval, and he was amazed at how pretty she had become.

"Oh, Henri, do you know about my Roger?" Isabelle asked.

He nodded, "His father told me. I am so sorry, *ma petite*. I know it has been hard."

"I loved him, you know. It has been a nightmare. I couldn't believe it when they came to tell me." She glanced at her father-in-law, who stood quietly aside as the brother and sister greeted each other. "But I'm so glad you are here," she said eagerly. "Tell me all the news from Champagne. How is *Papa*?"

"I haven't seen him for many months—nearly two years now," Henri suddenly felt in his heart and bones how long he had been away. "When I left, he was beginning to show signs of age. He's almost sixty, you know."

"Yes, I know. How I would like to go home again!" Isabelle said, a catch in her voice.

"And you shall, *ma soeur*. You shall. I will take you home with me."

Isabelle looked at Roger of Sicily, her eyes holding a question. He nodded.

"It is best, I think, daughter. You are too young to remain a widow. And your father will find another husband for you in due time."

"*Merci, mon beau-père*. I have been happy here."

"I know. And Sicily has been happy to have you. But your brother's arrival is a sign from God. It is time for you to return to your family."

She took Roger's hand and knelt before him. "I can't thank you enough for all your kindness. I shall never forget."

Henri and Isabelle remained in Sicily for another ten days, while she said goodbye to her friends and Roger showed Henri around Palermo. He questioned him about the crusade and suggested so often that the sea route would have been much easier until Henri was glad to finally depart.

They paused during their trip to visit Pope Eugenius, whom Henri remembered fondly from his visit to Troyes in preparation for the crusade. But their stay at the papal palace in Viterbo was brief, for Isabelle was eager to go home and see her family again.

It was early March by the time they arrived in Champagne. The woods on the outskirts of Troyes were just beginning to show tinges of green. Impatient to reach their destination, they quickened the pace of their horses. Isabelle was returning home a woman, a widow, and a daughter excited to see her parents again. Henri, who had spent nearly two years of his life on crusade, was also eager to reach Troyes. He had left as a squire. Now he was coming back a knight and a mature man, older and wiser, his prowess tested on the battlefield. Despite the crusade's failure, he felt a sense of triumph—with gifts for everyone, his widowed sister riding beside him, a letter from the king, and an offer of betrothal to the king's daughter—all to brighten his father's final years.

CHAPTER 13

Paris, November 1149

"Marie," the child's Aunt Aelith called up the curved stone stairwell that led down to the solar. The little girl roused as her nursemaid Claudine tickled her awake from her nap. "Wake up, little one. We have visitors!"

The four-year-old sat up and rubbed her still sleepy eyes, as Claudine scurried about, laying out a fresh tunic and dampening a rag in the basin beside the bed to wash the child's face and hands.

"That's cold," Marie grumbled at the touch of the rag.

"I'm sorry, *ma petite*, but you have to be alert. Some very special people have arrived. Here, you can't go down in your chemise," the nurse said, sliding a dark green tunic over the child's head.

"I don't want to go down. I want to play with *ma poupée*," Marie complained, clinging to the rag doll that had slept in her arms.

"You may take it with you, but you must go to the solar to see who's here. It's a surprise," Claudine said, sliding the child's feet into her leather shoes. "It's someone very special."

"Who?"

"You'll see soon enough." The nurse took Marie's hand, led her toward the narrow stairwell and down the curved stone steps. When they reached the bottom, the child could hear loud voices and laughter from the hallway that led to the solar. She entered, happy to see the other children already there. With squeals of delight, her cousins Elisabeth and Raoul were opening chests she had never seen before.

"Well, look who's here!" Aelith said, picking her up and handing her to the tall woman with shiny blond hair visible through her gauzy wimple.

"Marie, *ma chérie.*" The woman reached out to embrace the child and give her a kiss. She was pretty, and her voice sounded familiar. She even gave off a familiar fragrance like something Marie had known before. But she didn't recognize the woman or the man standing next to her, stroking his light brown beard, and smiling in her direction.

"I don't think she remembers me," Eleanor said sadly, as Marie stretched her arms back toward her aunt.

"Marie… these are your parents, back home again after so many adventures," Aelith reminded the child. "Don't you remember, we talked about their voyage?" Aelith turned again toward her sister. "I told her all… well, most of the stories we heard from your trip."

Marie's index finger hung from her bottom lip as she clung to her aunt and looked at her mother—the stranger-woman facing her.

"Marie," the man said. "I'm your *papa*. One of these chests is for you. Come and see." Her eyes lit up.

The child squirmed until Aelith put her down. She ran with excitement over to the wooden coffer he pointed to. He helped her lift the lid, and she began to rummage inside. She pulled out a small wooden horse on four wheels.

"Look, *Tatie*!" She held it up to her aunt before she began to roll it around on the floor. But soon she lost interest and began to delve once more into the coffer. There was a carved dog that would open and close its mouth to reveal a red tongue if she manipulated the lever attached to its chest. And she chortled with delight as she pulled out a doll, much finer than the one she already owned—its brown eyes and red mouth stitched in shiny silk threads. Its black hair was made of thin cords, piled on top of its head and fixed with a silver clasp. It wore a beautiful gown elegantly embroidered with gold and silver threads. Marie hugged it for a moment—then set it gently aside to turn once again to examine the contents of the chest.

She found a box containing a small gold cross, encrusted with rubies and sapphires. Her mother stooped to fasten it around her neck. There was a fine wool rug the length of her own body, woven with bright, intricate patterns, and underneath, at the bottom of the chest, she found yards and yards of a luminous red silk woven interwoven with fine gold threads.

"What lovely red samite," Aelith said, running her fingers over the material.

"She can have it made into a splendid *bliaut* when she's a bit older," Eleanor said.

All the other children were equally busy playing with their own toys and gifts, while the adults stood by, smiling indulgently and sipping goblets of warm red wine. Before long, the two men drifted toward the window ledges and began to talk quietly. The women moved closer to the fire, leaving the children under the watchful eye of Claudine.

"Are you quite all right," Aelith asked her sister. "We heard about your capture by pirates. It sounded frightening."

"Frightening, yes, but exciting too. They weren't really pirates, but Greek sailors stopping Sicilian ships. It was the Sicilians who rescued us," Eleanor answered.

"How did Louis fare on the trip?"

"I haven't the faintest idea," she said with indifference. "We traveled on different ships, and the ships got separated. I didn't care a whit. I certainly had no intention of spending any time with him in close quarters. Then I got sick. I can't tell you all I went through during that time, but I finally made it to Palermo, where I stopped to recover. Nobody knew where Louis was, until he finally showed up in Italy—Calabria—and sat there waiting for me to come to him."

"Didn't he know you were ill?"

"I don't know. We really haven't discussed it. There were more important things. I had some terrible news in Palermo. I heard from Roger of Sicily that Uncle Raymond had been killed—beheaded—in June, trying to capture Aleppo on his own. … It wouldn't have happened if Louis had agreed to help him. I was so furious, I never wanted to see Louis again. I wept for a week."

"Oh, Eleanor, poor Uncle Raymond."

"I stayed in Palermo for another three weeks, until I could control my fury and felt I could stand the sight of Louis once again. I finally joined him in Calabria. From there, Louis and I traveled, more or less together, to spend a few days at King Roger's court in Potenza."

"It must all have been a terrible ordeal," Aelith said.

"You have no idea," Eleanor said, with disgust. "And I haven't even told you about our visit to the pope in Tusculum."

"Why was he in Tusculum?"

"He had fled Viterbo, where there was trouble, and taken refuge at Count Ptolemy's fortress there."

"How dreadful. He should be living in Rome. But I hope you had a good visit."

Eleanor laughed bitterly. "Aelith, Louis and I… oh, how can I tell you? Until we reached Tusculum, we hadn't slept together since we left Antioch. I was still furious with him for refusing to help Uncle Raymond. And he had me literally dragged from Antioch. By the time we got to Italy, I wanted a divorce more than ever. I knew that Abbot Bernard had long wanted to see this marriage dissolved, and I thought perhaps Pope Eugenius would agree, so I talked Louis into visiting the pope. But the holy father had other ideas. Instead, he tried to help us reconcile. He counseled us. And in the end, he almost threw us into bed together."

She paused for a long time, sighed deeply, then added solemnly, "Aelith, I'm pregnant again."

"That's wonderful!" Aelith said, but when she looked at Eleanor's frowning face, she could see her sister did not agree.

"It's the worst thing that could possibly happen." Eleanor's voice was angry. "I hope I have another daughter. Then Louis may finally agree to dissolve our marriage."

"But, sister, what of me? What of *my* marriage to Raoul?" She said in a plaintive voice, frowning with worry. "What would that mean for us?"

"I don't know, Aelith. Why should it change anything?"

"Sometimes I think Raoul stays with me only because I'm the sister of the queen, and he doesn't want to lose royal favor."

"That can't be true. Look what he went through to marry you. Excommunication! What could be greater proof of his love?"

"But things change. He's no longer excommunicated. I think he's grown tired of me."

"But you just gave him another child."

"Only a girl… named for you, by the way. He wanted another son. I might as well have birthed a dog or a cat for all he cared."

"Oh, Aelith. It can't be as bad as all that."

"Yes, it can. The problem is, I still love him, but he finds his satisfaction elsewhere."

"What irony! You want your marriage to survive, and I want mine to end. But both our husbands seem to have opposite ideas."

"What do you plan to do?" Aelith asked.

"Nothing for the moment—at least not until this child is born. Louis doesn't want to let me go, but I don't think I can survive in this marriage for the rest of my life."

"Let's not think of it now. See to Marie. She has missed you, I'm sure. And she's a sweet child."

"She doesn't even know me. Now would be the best time to leave, before she can become attached to me again."

"But you won't. You can't."

"No, I can't. I love her too much," the queen said in a miserable tone, as she watched her happy daughter playing with her cousins and new toys. "If only I could, it would save heartache for us both."

Little by little Marie learned to call the queen *Maman* again. And her face began once more to light up with joy when she saw her mother coming into the nursery, especially now that her cousins had returned with their parents to their own home in Vermandois. As soon as Eleanor and Louis were well settled once more in the castle on the Île de la Cité, and after Raoul and Louis had exchanged all the information they needed to make the transition back to royal rule as easy as possible, the unhappy couple and their children were gone.

The months passed slowly, and Eleanor watched her belly swell with new life. She had told Marie that there was to be another baby, and the little girl was excited and eager—far more eager than her mother. She cuddled her old rag doll like a baby, while the new doll from Constantinople, her eyes staring aimlessly ahead, sat idly on a wooden chest by the window.

This time, Eleanor decided, she would have her baby in Paris. She felt no excitement, no determination that the child should be born in her own lands. And she prayed fervently it would be a girl.

CHAPTER 14

Paris, 1150

On an early morning in mid-June Queen Eleanor gave birth to her second daughter. She was exultant. Despite the "holy guidance" of Pope Eugenius, his plan had come to nothing. God had played a little joke on the pope.

"*Mordieu*, another girl," Louis cursed when he learned the newborn's gender. His face moved progressively from irritation to what Eleanor took for despair, before he turned away and left the room without a second glance at the child.

Eleanor smiled. "Aelith," she said, handing the baby to her sister who was standing by. "I'm going to name her for you to repay the honor you did me in naming your last daughter."

"I'm indeed delighted, *ma soeur*," Aelith replied, snuggling the baby girl in her arms and touching the blond hair of her tiny head. "Will Louis mind? Perhaps he wants to name her for his mother."

"Louis won't care what she's called. I am going to name her Aelith, though I suppose here she will be called Alix—the northern version of your name."

Aelith showed only the tiniest frown before she said, "I understand." She paused for a moment. "I think she looks more like you."

Eleanor glanced with indifference at the child. Then a sudden smile burst across her face. "Do you realize what this means?"

Aelith shook her head, "I'm not sure."

"Surely now I can persuade Louis to let me go. Two daughters after more than thirteen years of marriage… It's a blessing."

Aelith looked dejected. "For you, perhaps. But I think Raoul will take it as an opportunity to put me aside. I understand he's already been making overtures to Thierry of Flanders for his daughter Laurette."

"I can't believe he would do such a thing—not again. He is still married to you. He may find himself excommunicated once more if he tries to take her as his wife. Besides, isn't she already married?"

"Yes, to the duke of Limburg. But such things don't seem to matter anymore. If her father thinks Raoul has more to offer, he will arrange for an annulment."

Eleanor's heart went out to her sister, but she also saw the irony of the situation. She remembered how Raoul had put aside his first wife to marry her. Now it was her sister's heart he intended to break. *Aelith truly loves him,* Eleanor thought, though for the life of her, she couldn't understand why. He was so much older and had a missing eye, but he could also be charming and a bit devilish with his jaunty eye patch. The queen remembered how, with his one good eye, he used to look at her sister with hunger. Now she wondered whether that hunger was for the woman herself or for the prestige and connections she could bring as the sister of the queen. Evidently, he could already foresee what she hoped was the inevitable end of her marriage to the king.

I'm sorry if it makes my sister unhappy, but I can't give up my own freedom for something that might or might not happen to her, Eleanor thought.

She believed she could now persuade Louis that she was unable to bear him the son he so desperately wanted and that his only recourse was to put her aside and take another wife. Abbot Suger, she knew, would do everything in his power to stop it. He would argue that she was still young enough to have more children and that, above all, Aquitaine should be reserved for the crown. He was the practical advisor to the king, and convincing him could be a problem.

For once, however, she was happy to have Abbot Bernard as her enemy. He would be the primary force to argue for the dissolution of the marriage, which he had long ago pronounced as consanguineous. His voice would be very powerful against the abbot of St. Denis, and she knew there were many others in the kingdom who would agree with him and be happy to see her go.

Now, glancing at her new daughter lying in her sister's arms, she knew she would pay the child no mind. She would simply refuse to get attached to her. She would turn all the mothering responsibilities over to the nurse.

Aelith held out the baby to hand her to her mother.

"Give her to Claudine. That's all the mother she'll have," the queen said, turning away. Unfortunately, it was too late to spare Marie. The attachment was already there. She loved her too much to ignore her. She knew she was going to break the child's heart, but there was no help for it. She would have no choice but to leave her here. The children belonged to the crown, not to her. Even though they were girls, Louis could use them to seal a pact, or a peace treaty, or in exchange for some desirable property, as he saw fit. She assumed that he would keep his promise and marry Marie to Henri de Champagne, though as yet, there had been no official betrothal. Eleanor liked the young man well enough, though she thought his future did not look nearly so promising as that of the son of Geoffrey of Anjou, whose offer Louis had spurned. Henri's future was more certain, perhaps—but not nearly so grand. Marie would become only the countess of Champagne, instead of queen of England. *That honor is reserved for someone else.* She smiled a secret smile. *Perhaps it's for the best,* she thought, *if Henri proves to be as good a man as he promised to be in the struggle in Outremer.*

Of late, however, Abbot Bernard, who had originally pushed for the princess's marriage to Thibaut's son, was beginning to question the young man's attitude, or so she'd heard. He had complained about it to Abbot Suger while Louis was still in Jerusalem. Henri had become friends with Louis's brother, Robert de Dreux, who'd left Jerusalem in a surly mood after the defeat at Damascus. The two had joined forces and arranged for a series of what Bernard referred to as "those accursed tournaments," and he feared they would cause a disturbance in the kingdom during the king's absence. *Just a way,* she thought, *for frustrated warriors to try to wipe out the bitter memories of rotting bodies and disease and hunger and try to earn some self-respect after the humiliation of Damascus and the failure of the entire effort.* Henri was still a young man—in his early twenties. Abbot Suger had understood that youth was prone to reckless behavior and let the tournaments continue harmlessly, despite Bernard's complaints.

Unlike her mother, five-year-old Marie was delighted with her baby sister Alix, except when she cried or dirtied her swaddling. But she loved to watch the baby at the breast of the wet-nurse as she made funny little sounds of satisfaction. She loved to tickle her rosy-cheeks and help Claudine dress her each morning. And as Alix learned to crawl, Marie would play with her on a blanket on the floor, teasing her with toys just out of her reach to make her creep toward them.

Her mother came to the nursery less often now. Instead, she would send for Marie to walk with her in the garden. Together they watched twittering sparrows sparring on the stone bench, where the two of them had spread a few crumbs of dry bread. Eleanor could smell the sweetness of her daughter's youth. She reached out to touch her light brown hair, which had grown thicker and longer and taken on a chestnut color that reminded Eleanor of her Uncle Raymond's hair. She remembered those wonderful days in Antioch, and she longed for Aquitaine with its warmth and graceful pleasures.

Here in Paris, even in summertime, any nighttime chill seemed to be absorbed by the very stones of the palace. She had brought from Outremer some fine wool carpets, woven in the bright colors and patterns that had grown familiar to her in Antioch. They helped mitigate the cold of the limestone floors, but they seemed so out of place here in this dreary Capetian court.

I would like to show my lands to Marie, Eleanor thought. *She would blossom there, learn grace and joy.* Whenever she had such thoughts, Eleanor would send the child back to the nursery and try to harden herself against the pain she already felt forming inside her at the inevitable loss of her daughter.

January 13, 1151

When the bells of St. Denis began to toll mournfully, and as the news spread throughout the countryside, the belfries in Paris, began to echo them. Queen Eleanor rushed from her bedchamber.

"Why are all the bells ringing?" Eleanor asked as she appeared in the doorway of the solar, where wintry sunlight slanted through the narrow windows. Louis was standing before the fire, his head bowed.

"Abbot Suger is dead," Louis said. "I've just received word. It's a great loss to the kingdom."

He looks morose, she thought, as she said, "I'm sorry to hear that."

In part she truly meant it. Eleanor had always liked the old abbot. They had seen eye to eye on many sensible matters. But at the moment she felt only a flood of relief. His was the strongest voice in the kingdom against her divorce from Louis. Now Louis would hear only one side of the issue from his other spiritual counselor—Bernard of Clairvaux.

By the next morning, courtiers and prelates were all speculating about the implications of the abbot's death. One of the queen's most trusted ladies confided to her that people were already making assumptions that the royal marriage would finally be declared invalid and that Aquitaine would be lost to France. Eleanor suspected that most of the king's inner circle would not be sorry to see *her* go. They would grieve far more the loss of Aquitaine, which had been the young king's most important acquisition, than for the departure of their queen. She was not so sure about her husband. He wore a grim face most of the time of late, as though mourning the past and dreading the inevitable future.

Months passed before Louis was finally compelled to come to grips with his wife's failure to produce an heir. As much as he had loved Eleanor and desired her wealth, he felt he had no choice but to take a new wife. People were urging him on all sides, but he delayed for every reason he could think of. There was much to do before all arrangements could be made and archbishops found who would agree to nullify the marriage. Louis seemed to be in no hurry, while Eleanor waited impatiently.

By September he had finally accepted the situation. Leaving Marie and Alix in Paris, the couple made a final trip together to Aquitaine in an effort to ensure a smooth and peaceful transition. They spent Christmas in Limoges and then, in January, went on to Bordeaux ostensibly to deal with a minor squabble there, but in reality, to discuss the matter with the bishop of Bordeaux, who would be one of the prelates involved in the annulment. While they were there, a weary messenger who had obviously ridden hard for several weeks and was still coated with dust, arrived with a message for the king. He carried a letter from Henri de Champagne announcing the death of his father, Count Thibaut, on January 10—slightly less than a year since the requiem masses had been held for Abbot Suger.

Although Louis knew the count was not in good health, the news came as a shock. He had been far too preoccupied with his own marital problems to concern himself overmuch about the future of his daughters. Although he and Thibaut had briefly discussed the matter, there had still been no official betrothal between Marie and Henri, who was now the count of Champagne. He would take as the formal title on his new seal and in his documents "Count Palatine of Troyes." The news of Thibaut's death spurred Louis to act in greater haste so that he might get on with his plans for his daughter's future.

Finally, by the end of February, everything was in place, and the king and queen returned briefly to Paris. Eleanor wanted to say goodbye to her daughters and collect her sister Aelith, who would return with her to Poitiers. The judgment for dissolution of the marriage was to be given shortly before Easter, which fell early that year—on March 30. Eleanor did not want the separation to take place in Paris, but rather somewhere farther south, where she could escape more easily into Aquitaine. Knowing how women could be sometimes be kidnapped and even married against their will, she took every precaution. She had her own plans for her future, and they did not include being captured as a trophy for some lesser nobleman in need of added wealth. She wanted only a man of her own choosing. Thus, preparations were underway for the trip to Beaugency. That city had been a compromise. Eleanor had wanted the dissolution to occur even farther south, but Louis refused to go any farther. It was Beaugency or nothing.

"Aelith, are you nearly packed?" Eleanor asked, the color high in her cheeks.

Aelith had wept the entire time her servants were packing their clothes and other belongings. She had wept off and on for months now, for as soon as Raoul learned of Suger's death, he had sent Aelith back to her sister and moved forward with his own divorce from her and his marriage arrangements with Laurette of Flanders.

"Aelith, stop your crying. It will do no good. Soon we'll be home in Aquitaine. Doesn't that cheer you up?" Eleanor asked.

"No. And you will soon know what it's like to be without your husband and your children."

"My husband I can well do without. As for my children, I have prepared the situation as well as I can. I confess that I will miss Marie, but I have explained to her what I have to do, as best a child her age can understand."

"What have you told her?"

"That women, as she will know when she grows up, do not always control their own lives and destinies, but that I am trying to set a good example for her by doing what I must do to try to control my own."

"Have you told her you will be going away and not coming back?" Aelith's voice sounded worried.

"Yes. She wept, of course, and begged me to stay. I almost fell to pieces. I cannot tell you how it tore at my heart to see her so unhappy and to know that I was the one causing her misery. But I held myself together and told her that she is a big girl now and that she must try to understand."

Aelith only looked at her sister dolefully. Her own children had been wrenched from her arms when Raoul sent her back to Paris without them. Eleanor understood her grief, but she was growing tired of her self-pity. *What happened to her has happened to many women, and she must learn to cope. I can find her another husband, if she likes.* At the moment, Aelith wouldn't even talk about the future, which seemed to her only a gaping void.

Preparations for departure went on for days. When the packing was finally complete and the carts were loaded, the royal party would begin its long ride toward Beaugency in the Loire Valley. There a council of archbishops waited to pronounce the royal marriage invalid. One of them was Geoffrey de Lauroux, archbishop of Bordeaux, who was once Eleanor's guardian, and who had performed the royal marriage in his city fifteen years before. The other archbishops were coming from Rouen, Sens, and Reims.

Before mounting her palfrey, the queen made one final trip to the nursery to say goodbye to Marie and Alix. It was harder than she had imagined. Even though Eleanor thought she had prepared both herself and her oldest daughter for this moment, Marie clung to her skirt, "Please don't go, *Maman.*" Tears were running down her cheeks. "Please don't go."

Eleanor knelt, as her skirt and cloak billowed around her, to look her daughter in the eye. "Marie, we have talked about this before. You must be brave for your little sister. She's too young to understand, but you are older, and you must show her how to be brave. I know what you are feeling, for I lost my own mother at about your age. It was very hard. But you will survive… as I did."

The child was sobbing now, burying her face in her mother's embrace.

"Marie, you are six years old now… almost seven. You must be strong." Eleanor was only hoping that she herself could remain strong until this farewell was over. She quickly brushed back the tears springing into her own eyes before the child could see them. *All this crying seems to be contagious*, she thought, as she struggled to regain control of what she disdained as her "womanly emotions."

"What will happen to me?" Marie asked.

Eleanor held her daughter close for one final moment. "*Ma chérie*, you will grow up to be a fine woman. If you were a boy, you would become king one day, but you are a girl. You will become the wife of the count of Champagne and a mother most likely. Your only alternative is to be a nun, and I daresay that would not interest you. Like me, you belong in the world, not tucked away in a cloister." She held Marie at arm's length now and tried to look her in the eye.

"A woman does not often control her own destiny in this world. But we must try. We have talked about that. Do you remember?" The child nodded and wiped her nose with the back of her hand.

"Always be aware that women are more capable than most people think. Study your letters. Knowing how to read and even write can give you greater power than most women have. Learn all you can and keep a watchful eye. Listen to what the men say, for their words will surely affect your life. Obey your father but remember also that you are the daughter of a king and the duchess of Aquitaine. Hold your head high. Be proud of your heritage. And one day, when you are older, perhaps… perhaps… we will see one another again. Be strong and make me proud of you." She gave her daughter one more long hug, kissed her cheek, then rose quickly. She blew a kiss to a sleepy-eyed Alix and said to Claudine, "I must be gone."

Then she turned quickly and disappeared from the nursery with a swirl of her green wool cloak.

"*Maman*?" Marie whispered and held out her arms. But there was no one there to respond. The doorway stood empty.

Claudine took the sobbing child by the hand and led her to a narrow window where she could see her mother mount her palfrey and watch her parents ride together for the last time beyond the walls of the Cité Palace into their unknown futures.

CHAPTER 15

Paris, late May 1152

Marie held her sister's hand as Claudine led the two children down the stone stairs and into the solar for their brief, daily visit with their father. Alix was almost two years old now. She could walk with fair confidence and even run, though somewhat unsteadily, on her chubby legs. And she was beginning to talk. Already she could say "Marie" and "*Papa*" and "Mine!" She could make small sentences to order Claudine about and communicate her desires—baby sentences like "I want that!" and "I hungry."

Louis, his eyes looking haggard, as though he had not slept for days, leaned forward from the chair he had been slouching in to receive their perfunctory greetings. Marie was first to approach her father with an obligatory kiss on the cheek, a quick curtsey, and a "*Bonjour, Papa.*"

Alix followed suit with "'*jour, Papa.*"

He waved them away. "Go and play. I'll watch you," he said absently, taking a swallow of red wine from his goblet—his third for the afternoon—as he gazed absently toward the children.

The girls, sensing their dismissal, quickly began a half-hearted game of chase, which continued until Alix fell down on the hard stone floor and began to cry.

"Claudine!" Louis bellowed. The nurse had been standing just outside the door to give the king and his daughters some privacy. She rushed in and picked Alix up in her arms. The child was crying loudly now, more so than the tiny scrape on her knee warranted—as much for attention as hurt.

Claudine put the child on her shoulder and patted her bottom. "Now, now," she said. "It's not as bad as all that. Did you hurt your knee?"

Twisting around in Claudine's arms, Alix pointed tearfully to her wounded knee and looked at Claudine with soulful eyes, "*Oui, j'ai un bobo.*"

"Oh, I'm so sorry," Claudine was saying in a comforting voice, when a squire entered the room to announce the arrival of a rider with an "urgent message" for the king.

"Send him in," Louis said, standing to greet him.

A tall, thin man, who had clearly been riding hard, burst into the room and knelt quickly at the king's feet. "I bring a dispatch, sir, from the archbishop of Poitiers. He sent it to Abbot Bernard, who instructed me to bring it to you at once." The king took the letter, unrolled it, and dismissed the messenger. As he read silently, his eyes widened and his face blanched.

"*Mordieu,*" he said breathlessly, plopping back into his chair as his legs gave way. As soon as he caught his breath, he ordered Claudine, "Fetch my brother." Robert was in Paris, staying at the Cité Palace, while he worked out the property details of his upcoming marriage, his third, to Agnès de Baudemont.

Marie watched her father carefully, but said nothing until Claudine, still carrying Alix, was out of the room.

"What's wrong, *Papa*?" asked Marie.

"I've just had news of your mother," he said, his face contorted.

"Is she all right?"

"She has committed a very wicked deed."

"What has she done, *Papa*?" Marie's brow furrowed with worry.

"Never you mind, Marie. This is not a subject for children."

At that moment, Robert de Dreux strode into the room and, brushing past Marie, faced the king.

"What's happened, Louis?" he asked. "Why do you look so pale? Are you ill?" Louis handed the letter to his brother, who read it carefully.

"My God! How could she do this?"

"What has she done, *Papa*?" asked Marie again. Both men ignored the child.

"How *could* she do this, Robert? Even though I'm no longer her husband, I'm still her overlord, and she's my vassal. And so is he. This is a crime, not just against me, but against the kingdom, against feudal law. She has to seek my permission before she remarries." It was true. A female fief-holder was obliged to have her lord's permission to marry—or else forfeit her fief. "She cannot do this."

"But, Louis, it's already done," Robert pointed out. "According to this dispatch they were married on May 18. Apparently, she thought it safer *not* to ask permission."

"*Putain*! Less than two months since our marriage was dissolved. She didn't waste any time, did she? She'd hounded me about our kinship, our consanguinity, ever since we left Antioch. *Morbleu*, he's of closer relation to her than I am," he fumed.

That was the main point the Abbot of Clairvaux had argued in his opposition to betrothing Marie to this man her mother had married—Henry Plantagenet. He'd been adamant that they were of too close kinship, that it was against the laws of God. But Henry and Eleanor were even closer. Louis's grim expression echoed his thoughts, even before he voiced them.

"Abbot Bernard was right. The man came from the devil, and he'll go to the devil. She's a decade older than he is. What could she see in a stripling like him?" He knew what Henry saw in her—Aquitaine. And no doubt *she* was counting on becoming queen of England after the death of King Stephen—despite the existence of Prince Eustace, the king's own living son. *She thinks she can trade one crown for another. Well, they'll pay for this. I won't tolerate it.*

"Get me my chancellor." Louis ordered, his voice quivering with rage. "No, I'll find him myself," he muttered with impatience, flinging the letter aside. "I'm going to summon them to court to answer for this."

He strode from the room, followed by his brother. The forgotten letter lay on the floor. Marie picked it up and looked at it, but she could not read, and the scratches on the parchment meant nothing to her. Left alone in the solar, the bewildered child, weeping now in frustration, found her way alone back through the castle's dark passages to the nursery.

The formal summons did no good. When Louis convened his court of justice, Henry and Eleanor simply failed to appear, which enraged the French king all the more. He had come to prefer courts of law to outright war in settling disputes—a lesson he had learned from his earlier quarrel with Thibaut de Champagne. But he could not ignore this—a complete disregard of a summons from their overlord. He could see them in his mind, laughing at him, as they amused themselves in Poitiers or London or wherever they were. *They are mocking me*, he thought.

"They give me no choice," he said to Robert, who had remained at the palace during these difficult days. The king's face was red with fury. "All they seem to understand is force, and I have no alternative but to go to war against these *felons*, these traitors. Are you with me, Robert?"

"Of course, *mon frère*. And you are not the only one with a grievance against the Plantagenet. Prince Eustace would no doubt be happy to join you, as would the brother counts—Henri and Thibaut. Even Henry's own younger sibling—Geoffrey of Anjou—hates him. And there are others. They would all love the chance to attack his lands."

Louis had heard rumors that both Geoffrey and Thibaut, now count of Blois since his father's death, had lain in wait in hopes of capturing Queen Eleanor and marrying her by force after the annulment, but she had eluded them both, traveling to Aquitaine dressed as a man. Those two were probably as angry with her as they were with Henry. But they also had their reasons to despise Henry Plantagenet. Geoffrey felt shortchanged by his meager inheritance and resented his brother's lands and his power. Thibaut was angry with Henry for his refusal to do homage for the city of Tours, which he held in fief from the count of Blois. *And Count Henri will help*, Louis thought, *out of family solidarity and perhaps because he feels compelled to show loyalty to his future father-in-law*. Surely with such an alliance, they could whip the stripling into submission.

The war against the Plantagenet began in late June, just after St. John's Day, with a united invasion of Normandy. Henry had been poised at Barfleur, ready to depart for England when he heard news of the invasion. Despite his youth, he had learned much about military strategy while fighting for his mother's crown, and he knew the men who served the king would scatter if the fighting did not also serve their own interests. Thus, he bypassed the royal troops to attack the strongholds of the king's allies, laying waste some of the lands of Robert de Dreux, taking one of the few castles that had been part of his brother Geoffrey's inheritance, and capturing the Touraine, where the city for which he had refused to do homage to young Count Thibaut was located. When they heard of their losses, coalition members began to splinter, feeling they should be protecting their own lands rather than fighting the king's battle.

By August, it was over. Louis was defeated, and once again, Henry Plantagenet had triumphed. The king returned to Paris, dejected, disheartened, and feeling like a fool.

Early October 1152

In the courtyard of the Cité Palace, a pale and feeble Abbot Bernard was helped from the litter in which he had traveled. He had come in the capacity of the king's spiritual and political advisor and with the belief that he did not have long to live.

"Welcome, Father Abbot," Louis greeted him warmly and ushered him into the great hall, where they took chairs before the fire. "Have you come to console me or to castigate me for my foolishness?" He tried to say it with levity, but it came from a bitter place inside.

"Neither, my son. I have come on behalf of your daughters. May I see them?"

The two little girls were quickly summoned and appeared in the great hall, curtseying before their father and the abbot.

"They have grown much in body since I last saw them," the abbot said. He patted Marie on the head. "And I hope they have grown equally in spirit." His hand was heavy on her head, and she wanted to shy away from the old man. She had no idea why she and Alix had been summoned so suddenly, but, sensing the seriousness of the conversation, she stood quietly, saying nothing, holding Alix's hand, and listening as the two men talked.

"Louis, I haven't much time, so let's get directly to the point. You need a new wife, but your first priority must be to settle the future of your daughters. I know you have discussed the matter from time to time with Henri de Champagne. I think you should formalize this agreement as quickly as possible. I want to live to see this happen."

"Why do you take such an interest, Father? And you still favor Henri? I thought he and my brother had upset you with their tournaments after their return from the Holy Land."

"They should have known better, and they acted foolishly. But they were both young men—headstrong and filled with energy. Sometimes we must make allowances for the behavior of the young. Since his father's death, Henri has come to me for advice and shown a new maturity in his role as count. I think he will be a fine match for Marie."

"But why do you care so much?"

"There are two reasons, my son. First of all, Marie is my spiritual daughter," Bernard said, smiling benevolently at the child. "As you recall, my prayers and intervention on her mother's behalf are responsible for her very existence. And a marriage between your daughter and the son of Thibaut would go far to assure continued peace."

"Are those the only reasons?"

"Are they not enough? I have loved both the young count's father and you as my sons, and nothing would make me feel more content than to see your bloodlines joined. Besides, the girls need female guidance at their young age. Henri's mother, Mathilde of Carinthia, still lives. She is a good woman, not yet sixty, I believe, and she will see to their training. And as I said, you need to think of finding a new wife as soon as possible."

Marie heard enough to understand the gist of the conversation. The old abbot was trying to persuade their father to start a new family. She'd understood her obligation to marry the man of his choosing, but she did not expect it so soon. She held Alix's hand a little tighter, fearful of losing her sister as she had lost her cousins, her aunt, and her mother. *What will become of me?* It was the same question she had asked her mother. Now here was her answer.

But the abbot had not finished. "I think you should also betroth Alix to Henri's brother Thibaut, and he is willing. I have spoken to him as well." Marie listened, wide-eyed.

"But she's just two years old," Louis protested.

"All the more reason she needs a mother's influence. And it will leave you free to make another marriage without complications." He talked as though the two little girls were not in the room or were invisible. Although Alix was more interested in the large ring on the abbot's finger than in the conversation, Marie listened attentively, knowing that their words would affect the direction of both hers and her sister's lives. No one asked her opinion, and no one cared. She was just a little girl, expected to do whatever she was told, as though she had no mind of her own.

Abbot Bernard had no trouble convincing her father that it was time to take action, and Louis began at once to make plans. Within a matter of weeks, the young counts and the king came to an agreement. His two daughters were to be betrothed to the two oldest sons of the late Count Thibaut, with the ceremonies to take place at Count Henri's palace in Provins in the spring of 1153. Located halfway between Troyes and Paris, Provins was an agreeable city and a fairly easy three-day ride away, but its convenient location was not its only virtue. A more compelling reason for setting Provins as the betrothal site was its status as a city that Count Henri held in fief from the king. For Troyes, on the other hand, he did homage to the Duke of Burgundy.

As Claudine packed the girls' coffers, she was careful to include not just their clothes, but their toys and dolls as well. By the time she was done, the room was nearly bare, except for the furnishings and linens.

"Why are you packing everything, Claudine?" Marie asked.

"Because you will not be coming back. Once you are betrothed, the king will leave you with the count's family."

"Forever?" Marie asked. Her voice was shaky. "But why? I won't be married, only betrothed."

"It is the custom," Claudine explained.

"Alix too?"

"Yes, Alix too."

"Then at least we will be together. Will you stay with us?" The child's voice was plaintive.

"If the count wishes it."

Marie threw her arms around the woman's waist. "He must wish it. He must." She had lost her mother, her aunt, her cousins, and now her father as well would vanish from her life. To lose Claudine was too much.

The nursemaid stroked the girl's hair. "Let us hope so, my dear" was all she said.

Until now, Marie had not dreaded the betrothal, which she knew was only a prelude to marriage. But with this new information, the days passed too quickly until they were ready to leave for Champagne. As they were summoned to go down to the inner bailey to join the procession, Marie ran once more to the only window in the familiar room she shared with Alix. She looked down at the courtyard, where wagons were piled with their belongings and the equipment they would need for the three-day journey. This was where she had last seen her mother riding beside her father out the courtyard gates. She stood there for a moment and tried to recapture the image, but it had vanished.

CHAPTER 16

Early April 1153

The voyage from Paris to Provins was the first time in her memory that Marie had ever been on such a trip. Despite her uncertainty about the future, it was exciting to lodge in a tent, where she could hear the night sounds as though she were bedded among the creatures of the wild. Claudine and the two girls had their own tent, but voices from the men's tents also drifted through the canvas walls that did little to keep out the sound. Marie could not understand what they were saying, but the hum of voices, mixed with the sound of crickets and frogs, lulled her to sleep.

On the last morning of their journey, as the royal party crossed the plateau to the west of Provins, Marie rode quietly in the litter alongside her sleeping sister, who in two months would be three years old. Claudine's palfrey walked beside them. As they neared the town, the girl pulled aside the curtain and peered out. She could see from a distance a great tower looming on the hill and dominating the fortifications of Provins.

"That tower is called the Tour César," said Claudine, pointing up the hill. "I once visited here as a child." It looked rather forbidding to Marie as she rode into this new and unknown world.

The hill was in reality but a small rise, appearing greater only by contrast to the flat terrain they had crossed. But the horses climbed with ease and the caravan soon entered the city walls, passing through the Porte Saint-Jean. They wound through the narrow street leading to the Place du Châtel where the count's palace nestled just behind the old basilica of Saint-Quiriace.

Two small rivers, the Voulzie and the Durtain, cut through the city. The land in the area was fertile, and trade brisk. Provins had, in fact, grown well beyond its ancient boundaries. The original walls enclosed only portions of what was now known as the *ville haute*, the high town, which rested on the western plateau and which the royal party entered so grandly. But in the valley to the east, Marie could see new fortifications being built to protect the houses and shops that were springing up around the church of Saint-Ayoul in the lower part of the city, the *ville basse*. Claudine had told her that Provins was well known, along with Troyes, Lagny, and Bar-Sur-Aube, as one of the cities that hosted fairs for which Champagne had become famous. There in the autumn, merchants from many countries and regions flocked to the fair of Saint-Martin, and in the spring they displayed their wares at the May fair, which had been established not too many years before by Count Henri's father.

As the king's retinue passed along the narrow streets, Marie opened the curtains even wider to get a better look at the town where she had never been before. They were passing by a market site, which lay between the forked streets that led out of Provins to the west toward Paris and to the northwest toward Jouy. She could see spring flowers in abundance and early fruits and vegetables displayed in the stalls. People lined the street—peasants, merchants, burghers—to catch a glimpse of the king and the little princess who would one day be their new countess. Shouts of "the king… the king… Look, the king!" came from all sides, and people bowed as they passed. Marie could hear murmurs of "Welcome, my lord" from voices in the crowd, as faces peered with curiosity at the children in the litter.

A little girl about her age, standing to the side as the procession passed, lifted her hand and waved to Marie. She waved back with a shy, tentative smile. These would be her people, and she wanted them to like her. She hoped they were nice.

When the royal party finally reached the newly constructed palace, two men stood in the bailey to greet them. Marie assumed they were the counts Henri and Thibaut, though she couldn't be sure. But the little girls were whisked inside the castle so quickly that she barely had time to look them over. The two men only nodded at the children as they passed but stepped forward to greet their father effusively. Once inside, the girls were welcomed by a smiling older woman, who introduced herself as the mother of the two counts—Mathilde of Carinthia. She had a kind face, wrinkled around the eyes and mouth, and she was dressed in white and wearing a white veil, which, even at seven, Marie recognized as a sign of widowhood. The dowager countess took both girls by the hand and led them to the chamber they would share with Claudine.

The room was cheerful and sunny, with colorful pillows on the beds and an intricately designed wool carpet that Henri had brought back from the crusade. Waiting there on a table by the window was a tray of dried fruits and sweetmeats, with a small bowl of red cherries for each of them.

"I hope you will be comfortable," Countess Mathilde said. "Someone will come for you later in the afternoon when the ceremony is about to begin."

Once she had gone, Claudine suggested that they might want to rest, but neither of the girls was sleepy, and they were too tempted by the sweetmeats even to think of lying down. As they sat munching on candied fruit and mince tarts, Claudine said, "The countess seems very nice, don't you think?"

Both girls nodded but said nothing.

"She will be your mother now—teaching you what you need to know as young women to run a household." It sounded daunting, though rather dull, to Marie. Alix simply had no idea what she was talking about.

"But I don't want to run a household. I would rather be a jongleur," Marie countered, remembering their bright-colored costumes and lively songs when they entertained in the great hall and how they had always made her mother happy.

"My child, you have no choice. You are a girl. A girl of the nobility has but two choices in life. She becomes a wife and mother. Or she becomes a nun. You already know that, for you are wiser than your years, my child," Claudine said in a soothing tone. If that were true, it was because Marie had heeded her mother's counsel—to learn all she could and listen well. Although she already knew her choices, she still felt defiant against them.

"Then I would rather be a nun," Marie said, though she wasn't sure she really meant it. She liked wearing pretty garments, whether she could be a jongleur or not. Even a court lady could wear bright colors, whereas nuns could not.

"But you are a firstborn princess—about to be betrothed to a powerful lord. As I said, you have no choice. Your father has already decided."

"I wish I were a boy. Then I could grow up to be a king and do anything I want."

"Your father has wished many times that you were a boy, my dear, but he is doing the best he can for his motherless daughters."

"I *have* a mother." A fleeting image of her beautiful, young mother flitted through her head before it vanished like a dream.

"But she has abandoned you for another family in Normandy." Her voice was gentle, despite her words.

"She has no other family," Marie said, refusing to believe the garbled stories she had overheard about her mother's new marriage.

"Ah, but she has, and rumor has it that she is with child again."

"It's not true," Marie insisted, though in her heart she feared it was.

As the afternoon wore on, Claudine scrubbed the girls and dressed them in garments specially made for the occasion—matching indigo silk tunics over their linen chemises. They wore circlets of spring flowers like little crowns on their heads, and bright-colored ribbons that dangled down their backs. Alix gazed at herself in the glass with silent awe.

"You look like little princesses," Claudine exclaimed.

"We *are* little princesses," Marie reminded her. "Do we look all right?" she asked, wishing she were old enough to wear a *bliaut*. The tunics were not laced, but at least they were belted.

"You look quite charming."

There was a knock on the door, and Countess Mathilde entered.

"Are they ready?" she asked Claudine. "Yes, I see they are. You look very nice—both of you."

Alix's smile dimpled her cheek, and she curtsied, as she had been taught to do. Mathilde took her hand, leaving Marie to follow behind. "Let's go then."

At the door of the great hall, she told the girls to smile and walk side by side. They had been thoroughly coached ahead of time by their father that they should answer yes to all questions they were asked and do as they were told during the brief ceremony.

Finally, the door opened and Marie was able to have her first real look at the man who would someday be her husband. To the seven-year-old princess he looked old. He was a grown man of twenty-six, only six years younger than her father. In the fashion of the day, he was even dressed like her father. He wore a long, burgundy mantle and a beard, which curled like his dark umber hair, but made him look even older than he was. On his head he wore the ducal coronet of Champagne, made of gold and encrusted with precious stones. She had been told that he was a man of great dignity and with fine prospects, as the ruler of one of the most important domains in France, larger even than the king's lands, and she knew she was supposed to be impressed.

She tried to smile, as Countess Mathilde had instructed, but her face felt frozen. She sensed Henri looking her over with his curious blue eyes, and she tried to imagine what he saw—a thin, nondescript waif of a girl, with big gray-blue eyes, and brown hair that fell to her waist. She wished she was beautiful like her mother and had golden hair like her sister.

Nevertheless, he smiled reassuringly at her, and she noticed that his eyes looked kind, but he said nothing. Although Marie had been told what to expect, she still felt uncertain as she stood beside him. She was aware of the warmth of his body next to hers. Even though she was tall for a seven-year-old, she only stood a little higher than Henri's belt buckle. Her little sister was hardly taller than her own count's knee. The two little girls, side by side and still holding hands, were flanked by the brothers who would someday become their husbands.

Abbot Bernard was there as well, eager to bless the promised unions. King Louis stood beside him, facing them, preparing literally to give his daughters away to take their places in their new home of Champagne—in exchange, of course, for the brother counts' goodwill and loyalty and a suitable dower for his daughters.

The betrothal ceremonies were brief. Marie was pledged to Count Henri, as her sister was to the count of Blois, in the presence of her father, the barons of Champagne, and before holy relics, which included the piece of the True Cross that Emperor Manuel had given Henri when he was knighted in Constantinople. Marie heard Henri repeat the words he was told to say.

"I will take Marie, daughter of King Louis of France, to be my future wife."

The betrothal vows were much like marriage vows, only in the future tense. Once the necessary pledges were made, the count placed the betrothal ring on the third finger of Marie's right hand, and Count Thibaut did the same with her sister. Then, proper words spoken, property exchanges agreed to, it was all over. She had done her duty as the daughter of the king, and she and Alix were quickly forgotten in the feasting and business that followed.

There was a great deal of talk, none of which concerned Marie, and although she was allowed to attend the feast, while Alix was taken back to their bedchamber for a nap, she was painfully aware of being ignored. Her only value for these men, she knew, was in being the daughter of the king.

Every now and then, the count, seated between her and her father on the dais, would offer her a tidbit of choice meat from his trencher, though for the most part he ignored her and talked to the king. Marie felt self-conscious, seated for the first time at the table on the dais. At one point a drop of meat sauce spilled onto the bodice of her tunic. She looked around fearfully, sure that everyone was looking at her and waiting for her to do something inappropriate. But as she gazed around the noisy hall, it was apparent that those at the feast were so busy talking to one another they scarcely noticed her at all. She wiped the spot as well as she could and tried to enjoy her meal. But she was so nervous that she was scarcely aware of what she was eating.

She could hear only snatches of the conversation between Henri and her father, which seemed to be about adventures they had shared in the holy land. Then she heard the word "seneschal," but Henri shook his head and said something about "responsibilities in Champagne." The king sat quietly for a moment, as though contemplating something important, before turning to Thibaut on his other side to begin a new conversation. Marie's uncle Raoul had died quite suddenly the previous October, not long after his divorce from her aunt Aelith and his new marriage, and she knew that, at the moment, the kingdom had no seneschal. Perhaps that was what the discussions were about. But she didn't dare ask.

Henri turned to Marie. "I think you will enjoy the peacock," he said, offering her a morsel on the tip of his knife. She opened her mouth dutifully, feeling in part like a lady and in part like a baby bird being fed by its mother. She only nodded as she chewed. It tasted rather like a cross between chicken and pigeon, which she often ate in Paris. "I hope you will be happy in Champagne," he said.

"I hope so too, my lord," she replied. And she also hoped he was satisfied with what she feared was her small marriage portion—she being the primary property for their particular agreement. She did not understand the value of what her father had provided for her dowry—or, for that matter, what a dowry really was. But she had overheard a courtier complaining about its paucity. Her father had told her that, if her mother had no son, she would inherit Aquitaine. And Claudine had told her that, if her father had no son, Marie's own son would become king of France. It seemed that her whole life was tainted by the fact that she was a girl and that, if a boy was born to either one of her parents, her right to Aquitaine and her son's chance for a royal crown was voided. It didn't seem fair.

She had been told many times that both she and Alix had been a disappointment to their father, and Claudine had reminded her of it that very afternoon. He made no attempt to hide it, but she was expected to be satisfied with whatever crumbs were left, if there were any at all. Her only real worth, it seemed, was as a bargaining chip for the king and her potential as a breeder.

Abbot Bernard, also seated on the dais, on the other side of Count Thibaut, beamed his approval throughout the meal, though he ate little. For Marie, the best part of the feast was the entertainment. It took her mind off herself, and she loved the songs of the jongleur and the musicians, admiring the colorful extravagance of their garments and their smiling faces. As the evening wore on and she began to grow weary, she was grateful when Claudine came to take her back to her bedchamber, leaving the adults to continue in their merriment. She had completed her duty.

Seeing the betrothals of Thibaut's two eldest sons to the daughters of the king brought only joy to Bernard de Clairvaux, as he remembered with such affection his spiritual son, Thibaut de Champagne, who had died piously, wearing, as he requested, the white robes of a Cistercian monk. Bernard felt certain that Marie, this child for whose birth he knew his prayers were responsible, would fare well in a world with Henri de Champagne at her side. She was certainly better off, he reasoned, than she would have been with Henry Plantagenet, who, as far as he could see, was already well on his way to going to the devil, as he had predicted, and for whom her mother had abandoned her.

Count Henri, on the other hand, had passed beyond his impetuous youth, and Bernard believed he would become a peacemaker, not a warmonger. He and the princess would be a good match, and their marriage would be symbolic of the healed wounds between the monarch and the late count, just as Marie's birth had been. Despite her mother, whose recent actions, in Bernard's mind, only confirmed her wickedness, he felt that he had done what was right for the child. He saw her betrothal to Count Thibaut's son as her father's final recompense for the burning of Vitry. Thus, with the assurance that he had wielded his influence for the best in the temporal as well as the spiritual world, on the following August 20, Abbot Bernard laid down his burden of flesh and, surrounded by his weeping Cistercian followers, closed his eyes forever to this world.

CHAPTER 17

Paris, 1154

King Louis sat alone and morose in his solar. In only a few short years, so much had changed that his world seemed to have spun out of control. Nothing, he learned, was permanent, and death had begun to haunt almost every aspect of his life. His family had vanished—his wife now married to another man and his daughters gone as well. The pillars of his court had collapsed with the deaths of his most trusted and familiar counselors, Abbots Suger and Bernard, and that of his seneschal of many years, replaced now by his future son-in-law, Thibaut de Blois.

The whirlwind of change took place, not just in his domain, but in the wider world as well. His old adversaries, Geoffrey of Anjou and Thibaut de Champagne, were gone, as was his old ally in the crusade, King Conrad—all dying within a few months of each other in the fall and winter months of 1151 and 1152. Now Frederick of Swabia, known as Barbarossa, sat on the German throne. To make matters worse, the son of the English king, Eustace of Boulogne, had conveniently choked to death on a plate of eels the previous August, thus eliminating Henry Plantagenet's rival as heir to the English throne. Louis secretly suspected he had been poisoned, but no one dared to accuse the future King Henry of such treachery. And certainly there was no proof.

Even in the Church, which was supposed to be a rock of stability, there was a new pope to contend with. Pope Eugenius, who had tried so desperately to salvage his marriage to Eleanor, died not long after Abbot Bernard and was replaced by Anastasius IV, an old man in his eighties, whom Louis had never met. Learning about new popes and their ways was always troublesome.

The king had not yet fully come to terms with all the changes, when everyone in his court began to urge him to find himself another bride to give him a son. They were right, of course, and he began to cast about for possibilities. He had heard of a daughter of Alfonso VII of León and Castile, who styled himself emperor of all Spain. Sixteen-year-old Constanza of Castile was of marriageable age, a distant relative of Queen Eleanor and, like her, a descendant of Charlemagne. Perhaps it was time he took a pilgrimage to Santiago, during which he could arrange a stopover in Castile to meet the girl and her father. It was time to think of himself and his future.

As they rode through the countryside, Marie, sidesaddle on her own palfrey now, gazed about the landscape bathed in the tender green of early spring. The terrain flowed gently as they crossed the Marne River at Mareuil and approached the little town of Avenay to the north. She was nervous about the trip, for she knew no one at all, except Countess Mathilde, who was riding beside her. Marie had still not made up her mind whether she should admire or fear the countess, who was kind but could be stern at times. The child hoped the countess did not resent her for having to leave behind her quiet life at her dower castle at Chantemerle, where she had retired after her husband's death. She had, of necessity, come out of retirement to assist her sons with the upbringing of the young princesses.

While Claudine remained behind with Alix, Marie, escorted by Countess Mathilde and her knights, was on her way to a convent school, where she would receive an education befitting her rank. Before their departure, Claudine had told Marie all she knew of the old countess's blameless reputation and the piety of her late husband's court. No hint of scandal had ever touched her life. She was said to have raised her children to be respectful of others and mindful of their responsibilities and of God's law. She seemed friendly enough, though as they traveled her face sagged more and more with fatigue, and she looked older than she had before the trip.

"Are you well, my lady?" Marie asked, trying to show concern.

"As well as can be, with these aging and aching bones," the countess replied. "Pay me no mind, child. I am not accustomed to riding so far, but I wanted to accompany you to Avenay to get you settled and to visit my daughter Adèle. Perhaps I should have come in a litter."

"You have a daughter at Avenay?" Marie asked.

"Yes, I thought I had already told you, but sometimes I forget what I have actually said and what I have only thought. She's named for her grandmother, the daughter of the man known as William the Conqueror. She's only a year or so older than you, and she's a pupil at the convent of St. Pierre d'Avenay, where you will live and study for a few years."

"What will happen after that?" Marie asked.

"You will come to the court in Troyes, where you'll be tutored in the ways and duties necessary for the wife of the count."

"When will I be married?"

"It is our custom to wait until a girl is at least fourteen before she becomes a bride."

To Marie that seemed an eternity away, but she was glad. The idea of taking over the responsibilities of a court was terrifying and seemed completely alien to the child, who had learned nothing about such duties from her mother.

"But you will still be there?" Marie asked hopefully. A life supervising a court seemed overwhelming to her.

"God willing, for a short while at least, but only until you feel comfortable in your tasks." She laughed. "I have learned that having two mistresses in a household is never a good idea. But don't worry. I won't abandon you as long as you need me." Marie felt reassured by her words and only wished she could stay with the countess and go straightaway to the court.

"What will you do then?" Marie asked.

"Oh, depending on my health, I'll either retire back to my dower lands or go to a convent, possibly Fontevrault, where my daughter Marguerite is a nun, or to the abbey of La Pommeraye, which I founded. I haven't fully decided."

They were nearing the convent walls now. As a black-robed nun opened the gates, Marie and the countess rode inside the courtyard. A dozen or so holy sisters scurried into place to welcome them. As they lined up in their dark robes, they reminded Marie of a flock of blackbirds settling on a clothesline. Countess Mathilde greeted them warmly as one of her escorts helped her to dismount.

A girl about Marie's age rushed forward and threw her arms around the countess. When she drew back, Mathilde introduced them. "Marie, this is Henri's younger sister, Adèle." Then she turned to her daughter. "Marie is the betrothed of Count Henri, and she will be your new sister. I hope the two of you will be friends."

"Welcome, sister," Adèle smiled broadly and reached out to hug Marie, who had been terrified at what she might expect at the convent. She had never been away for a long time from the palace in Paris, and the nuns in their stiff-looking habits looked austere and rigid, despite their efforts to smile hospitably. Tears of gratitude welled in Marie's eyes at Adèle's embrace. It the first time she had felt arms about her since she had been forced to say goodbye to Claudine and her little sister, Alix.

After Countess Mathilde presented Marie to the gathered nuns, she paused to chat with the abbess, Adelise de Joinville. Eight-year-old Adèle stepped forward and took Marie's hand.

"Come. I will show you around the convent and introduce you to some of the other girls."

Marie smiled at her in gratitude. It was all new to her, and she had been nervous about coming to a convent for the first time. It was a whole different world for her, a world of women, while the court in Paris, ever since the departure of her mother and her ladies-in-waiting, had been almost entirely a world of men—except for Claudine and Alix, of course.

Adèle paused to present Marie to a tall, thin girl with large teeth and a cluster of freckles on her nose. Girls of all ages gathered around to get a glimpse of the new student. When they had satisfied their curiosity, Adèle and Marie broke away from the chattering group, and Adèle led her into the cloister to see the convent's impressive gardens. As they walked, Marie's new sister told her what little she knew of the abbey's history.

"It was founded ever so long ago by St. Berthe and her husband St. Gombert. The nuns say they died together—a most awful death." She leaned forward and whispered, "Murdered in their beds by the children of St. Gombert's first marriage."

Marie's eyes grew wide with astonishment. "Why would they do that?"

"Viciousness and greed. The nuns say the founders are martyrs, killed because they left all their property to the Church instead of to his children. They are buried together here in the church of St. Pierre. It's a kind of love story, I guess."

Marie was wide-eyed with interest. "Tell me more," she said.

"That's about all I know," Adèle said with a shrug.

"Oh," Marie was disappointed, for she loved a good story. "Is the convent very rich?" she asked after a moment.

"The sisters live quite well. I think the counts of Champagne, like my *papa*, have favored it for a long time. Many young noblewomen, even some of the students, become nuns here."

Marie nodded. "The gardens are beautiful," she said, reveling in the array of color and the fragrance of roses and lilies that surrounded them.

"Yes, the abbess is very proud of them."

"Do you like it here?"

"Most of the time. The nuns are very good to us if we are obedient and do our lessons well, but they can be quite cross if we misbehave—especially Abbess Adelise. She's very strong-willed."

"Which one was she?"

"The tall one on the left, at the head of the line of nuns."

"Oh, yes," said Marie, "I remember her." She smiled, remembering the stern look the abbess gave to the young nun who scurried last into place.

"She oversees both the convent and the school," Adèle commented.

"What do you study here?"

"Well, of course we all have to know things like the *credo*, the *ave*, and the *pater noster*, but you probably know those already. Best of all, they teach us to read—mostly in Latin, but once you learn the sounds, you can pretty well make out words in other languages you know.

Mostly we use a psalter as our text. But there are books in French in the convent library. I can read those better than the Latin manuscripts. They're also decorated with more interesting illuminations."

"My mother said that knowing how to read can give girls power."

"Well, I don't know about that, but I do know I'll be able to learn more if I can read. All my older sisters and brothers know how to read," Adèle said. She hesitated for a moment, then added, "*Maman* said you were betrothed to my brother Henri."

"Yes, and my little sister is betrothed to your brother Thibaut."

"How old is she?"

"Almost three." Marie paused, then asked, "Is Henri nice?"

"Oh, yes. Very nice. He's kind to us younger ones, but he's all grown up now, and when *Papa* died he became count."

"Yes, I know."

"I think he will be a good count. You're lucky."

"Are you betrothed?" Marie asked.

"No, not yet. An old man named Pierre de Jully once told my mother that I would grow up to be a queen." She laughed.

"You can't just grow up to be a queen. You have to marry a king," Marie told her. "Even though I'm my father's oldest daughter, I won't be queen unless I marry a king, and your brother is only a count. If I had been a boy, I could have been king."

"Then maybe we could have married each other," Adèle giggled. "Then I could be your queen."

"That would have been nice," Marie replied with a conspiratorial smile. "But boys have all the choices."

"Oh well, I prefer being a girl. That way I don't have to go and fight all the time."

"But girls can't do much of anything except have babies."

"That does sound scary, doesn't it?" Adèle said. "Mother Adelise would like me to stay here and become a nun. But I enjoy being at court too much to close myself in here forever. Have you ever thought about being a nun?"

"Well, I can't now that I'm betrothed."

"You're not married yet," Adèle reminded her.

"But I'm promised. My father says it's just as binding. Are you a good pupil?" Marie asked.

"The nuns say I talk too much, that girls should be silent as much as possible. They say I ask too many questions."

"I think it's important to ask questions about things you don't understand. I ask a lot of questions too, but people don't always answer them. I guess there are just things we have to learn by ourselves."

"Adèle, Marie!" They heard Countess Mathilde calling them.

"Here we are, *Maman*," Adèle answered, as she ran up the path toward her mother.

"Come with me. I'd like for Marie to meet the sister who will be her special tutor." With her stood a round-faced, young nun with clear skin and rosy cheeks. Her long black scapula was crisp and well pressed. The white wimple and black veil that covered her head only emphasized the creamy whiteness of her face. Except for the habit, Marie thought she would have looked quite comfortable in the great hall of a castle.

"Marie," Countess Mathilde said, "This is Sister Alix. She comes from a family in Mareuil, the village we passed through when we crossed the river."

The nun curtsied slightly and held out her hand. "Welcome, Princess. I am pleased that you will be with us for a few years. Please always let me know if I can be of help."

Marie wasn't sure whether she was supposed to curtsey to the nun or not. She had met many abbots and bishops at the palace, but no nuns at all. She curtsied anyhow, then said. "You have the same name as my little sister."

"Then I shall be your big sister," the young nun said with a gentle laugh. "I look forward to our studies together."

Marie's trepidation about her brush with monastic life was eased considerably by the friendliness of both Adèle and Sister Alix, and she was less fearful than she expected when Countess Mathilde said her final goodbyes and rode away with her escorts two days later.

Still, she had some difficulty adjusting to life in a dormitory and all the new rules she had to follow. She was excited, however, to begin her lessons and learn to read the familiar psalms on her own. Her favorite classes were music and reading, even though she found the Latin in unfamiliar texts difficult—not the pronunciation but the meaning. All the various endings of nouns and verbs confused her. She was not much better at needlework—at least at first. The nuns found her embroidery rather clumsy, but she quickly learned to make better stitches, and within a few months, she was doing well at her geometric designs before they allowed her to move on to more intricate forms.

Marie sometimes longed to be back at court where discipline was less strict and where there were jongleurs and musicians to entertain during the evening meal instead of sisters reading from holy books. Since her mother left, however, the courtly music had mostly ceased, except for the gloomy lament of a passing *trouvère*, as troubadours were called in the north, whom her father would occasionally allow. Now at St. Pierre d'Avenay, the only songs she heard were those of the liturgy chanted by the nuns and their hymns of praise to God. She missed the livelier songs her mother had enjoyed and all the laughter, bawdy as it sometimes was, at the court. Even when she was not in the great hall, she could often hear the sounds of lutes, lyres, and singing voices drifting throughout the castle.

Marie's years at the convent school passed quickly. Whenever she felt a momentary longing to be back with her sister Alix in the familiar nursery in Paris, she would remind herself that she was lucky to be a pupil at Avenay. Most girls never had the opportunity to go to school and were able to learn only what their mothers could teach them. She kept remembering her own mother's words that learning was power, and she made every effort to pay attention and try to absorb all she could.

The months passed, sometimes slowly, sometimes quickly, but with consistent monotony. She could hardly remember one day from the next, for they were all so alike, arising at dawn, attending morning prayer, breaking her fast in the refectory, classes, hours of study, prayers again and again and bedtime when night fell. Only when there was an unexpected visitor at the convent or some special occasion did the daily routine vary.

Marie's friendship with Adèle grew stronger through the years, until she felt even closer to her new friend than she had with her little sister. She could share secrets and thoughts with Adèle that Alix would never have understood. The two girls would sometimes lie awake at night, their beds side by side, whispering to each other in the dark.

"How did you feel when your *papa* died?" Marie asked softly one such evening.

Adèle was quiet, and Marie wondered if she had already gone to sleep. Then, out of the darkness, she heard a whisper. "I just wanted to die… at least for a while. I was so sad."

"I felt the same way when my mother left our court and married someone else," Marie answered quietly.

"How awful!" Adèle was horrified. "Why did she do that?"

"I don't think she and my father got on well together," Marie replied as honestly as she could.

"That shouldn't make any difference. My mother says that a wife has to pretend to be happy, whether she is or not." Without realizing it, she had let her voice rise above a whisper, causing the girl in the bed on her other side to rouse.

"Please be quiet," came a voice from the darkness. Neither girl said anything more, but Marie pondered Adèle's words and wondered whether she, unlike her mother, could pretend to be happy if she were so miserable. Perhaps someday, she feared, she would find out.

Two weeks before her thirteenth birthday, when Marie went to the privy, she was horrified to see a stain on the back of her chemise. She touched herself and her fingers came away red with blood. Although she already knew that some of the other older girls bled from time to time, she was nonetheless frightened by this sudden onset. She wiped herself with sphagnum moss from the shelf as best she could, then hurried to tell Sister Alix and ask her what she should do. The young sister showed her where to find the linen rags the nuns and older girls used, how to wrap them around the blood moss, as they sometimes called it, and to tie linen bands around her body to hold them in place.

"It won't last more than a week," Sister Alix said, "but it can be uncomfortable. You might want to lie down for a while this afternoon."

That night, after all the girls had fallen asleep, Marie whispered the news to Adèle.

"Now you are nubile," Adèle whispered back. "You are almost ready for marriage. Now you could have a baby."

"What do you mean?"

"Well, my mother says it's not a good idea to start having babies until you're older. And you have to be married first. But at least you're betrothed."

Marie said nothing, trying to absorb all this information and surprised at the terror it struck in her heart.

"All the girls think you are lucky to be betrothed to my brother," Adèle said.

"Why?"

"Well, the ones who've seen him think he is quite handsome," Adèle said. "And *Papa* trained him to be count for many years before his death, so he knows what counts have to do, and he's always nice to ladies."

"But he's so old," Marie said, glad that Adèle couldn't see her wrinkled brow in the darkness.

"Not as old as some of the men my friends are betrothed to. One of them is going to marry a man almost sixty next year when she turns fourteen."

"Almost sixty? How awful. Henri will only be over thirty when we marry."

"That's a lot better than marrying someone in his sixties, but I guess we would all prefer someone closer to our own age," Adèle agreed.

"But we don't get a choice."

"Well, I heard of one woman who made a choice. She cut off her nose so she wouldn't have to marry," Adèle said.

"Eww, I don't think I'd want to go that far. And you're right, your brother is handsome. I'll try to make him a good wife," the princess said with determination. That ended the whispered conversation, but Marie did not fall asleep for a long time.

As Count Henri went about the business of the court, he too found himself wishing that he and his betrothed were closer in age. He was not eager to have a child in his bed, and although he knew that some men were attracted to young virgins, barely nubile, he wasn't one of them. He was impatient, now that he was a count over thirty, to have a son to guarantee his lineage. But his mother had cautioned him against forcing Marie to give birth at so young an age.

"It's better," his mother had told him, "to give a girl long enough to mature a little before she becomes a mother. I would certainly not have wanted to have such responsibility at fourteen or fifteen." She had been nineteen when Henri was born, and his father already thirty-five. Henri had no doubt that his father had been impatient as well, but he hadn't needed to hold back in his conjugal demands, because Mathilde was already eighteen when they married. But King Louis was pushing for the wedding to take place as soon as Marie was fourteen. Fathers always seemed eager to get their daughters safely wed. His new wife, Queen Constance, had recently given birth to another girl. Perhaps he was at least hoping for a grandson to inherit the throne, in the event he had no son of his own.

There were so many demands on a firstborn son of a king or count. One was to produce an heir, and, like the king, Henri was eager to have his own son. But the girl was so young. He supposed he would at least have to deflower her on their wedding night, for it was the consummation of the marriage that made it really official, and he knew there would be people checking the bed sheets the next morning to verify that she had been a virgin and that they had performed the act. But to him it seemed unfair.

He would have to be content, he supposed, to satisfy his needs for the most part with other willing women, whose virginity was long past, until Marie was more mature. In the meantime, he was doing all he could to prepare for the marriage when the girl turned fourteen, which was only a year away.

Only a year away! He suddenly realized it was time to bring her to court for her domestic training. Thank God, his mother still lived.

CHAPTER 18

Troyes, April 1158

Workers were completing the final touches on Henri's new palace and chapel of St. Étienne in Troyes, when Marie and Adèle were summoned from the convent at Avenay and brought to the court. It was quite a sudden change, but both girls were delighted.

On their first day back, Count Henri proudly showed them around his new chapel, explaining that he had it built in the modern style of St. Étienne de Sens and the remodeled church at St. Denis, with vaulted ceilings, pointed arches, splendid carvings, and light—above all, light. It didn't look much like a chapel to Marie, for it was huge—much larger than the palace itself. It seemed to her more like a cathedral.

"But I also liked the plan of the *cappella palatina* of King Roger of Sicily," Henri said. "I saw it when I was on my way home from the Holy Land and brought our sister Isabelle back from Palermo." He was speaking more directly to Adèle than to her, Marie thought, but she listened intently nonetheless.

"What did you like about King Roger's church," Adèle asked.

"It was quite splendid, built in a mixture of styles—Greek, Arab, and Norman all together, and it's filled with excellent mosaics, but the main thing I admired about it was the way it adjoined his palace. The king could enter his chapel without going outside. I liked the convenience, where one could come and go at any time. I'm particularly fond of the music of the Church, and, as you see, I've included a special gallery, where I can enter, sit, and listen to the songs and chants of the canons whenever I like."

"It's a fine church," Marie said, though *she* would not likely search out sacred music for entertainment.

Henri smiled. "I hope so. I hired the best stonemasons and the finest glassworkers in the region." He pointed out the fine gold cross, studded with enamels and gems, gracing the altar. "We display that only on special occasions," he said.

"And is this a special occasion?" Marie asked. He was talking to her now.

"Of course, it's my betrothed's first glimpse of my new church," he said with a smile. She could feel her face redden with pleasure.

He seemed especially proud of the carving on the tympanum over the north portal of the church, commemorating his role as builder and benefactor of St. Étienne. It contained a stone portrait of himself, kneeling and offering to God a small replica of the church.

This is where the count and I will celebrate our nuptial mass, Marie thought, with a little *frisson*, not quite sure whether it was one of anticipation or fear. But the idea of marriage and all it entailed seemed at the moment overwhelming, as did the church itself. It took her breath away in its magnificence. Marie particularly admired how its height and soaring arches compelled her eyes to look upwards toward God. *The wedding will have to be quite grand to be worthy of such a church*, she thought.

The adjoining new palace seemed almost small by comparison, though it too was bathed in light from windows much larger than those she remembered in the Cité palace. Even after Abbot Suger had overseen efforts to refurbish the old castle while her father and mother were away on crusade, it had still seemed dark and gloomy to the little girl. By comparison, the new palace of the count seemed bright, and it was easy to find her way around its relatively simple design. She no longer had to pass through dark corridors or go down curved stone stairs, for the living quarters were on the same level as the great hall. One entered from the outside by a large staircase that opened into the courtyard to the east.

"Oh look, Adèle!" Marie said, peering out the window when they reached the bedchamber they were to share.

They could see the city laid out before them. Their room on the castle's west side overlooked the Rû Cordé, a canal that had been created from a tributary of the Seine River, on the banks of which Troyes was built.

"How charming it all is!" Marie exclaimed as she looked out over the teeming city. "What are those buildings?" she asked.

"That's the convent of Notre-Dame-aux-Nonnains, just on the other side of the canal. And that," she pointed toward a steeple to the right, "that's the church of St. Jacques." The window even provided a view up the narrow streets that led toward the market place at St. Jean-du-Marché.

"Henri says he's made Troyes his capital city in Champagne," Adèle announced. "I think it's a good idea. All the roads from the Mediterranean come through here, and during fair times, merchants come from all over to sell their goods."

"From all over where?"

"Oh, you know, Italy, Germany, Flanders, Spain. You'll see all sorts of people here, And I think all this new construction will probably bring even more merchants and money to the city."

They had seen St. Étienne and the castle, as well as a *domus dei*, the new hospital he was building next door to St. Étienne, and a row of houses for the church's canons. Overall, it was an impressive undertaking.

"Remember when Henri said this afternoon he was determined to have it all completed before your marriage?" Adèle asked. Marie blushed slightly as she nodded. Perhaps she too had noticed that he smiled only at her when he said it.

"I guess the time is drawing near," Adèle said with a grin, squeezing her friend's hand.

The dowager Countess Mathilde's instructions to Marie in her future duties as countess of Troyes occupied each morning. Adèle joined them in the lessons, for she too would need to know these things when she was married.

"Your primary duty," the countess told Marie, "will be to bear the count a son when you are old enough and wise enough to be a mother. I was nineteen when my first son was born, so there will be no rush at first. Still, always bear that duty in mind.

"You will, of course, be responsible for your children—even the boys until they are old enough to begin their knightly training, and the girls until their betrothal or marriage or entry into a convent. And as countess, you'll be required to oversee the servants and the household to make sure things are done properly. Whenever there is a feast, you will approve the menu and entertainment," Mathilde told her.

"What about some of the court officers like the butler and the seneschal? Will they help?" Marie asked.

"Oh, I'm sure they will, insofar as they can—but they are all men," the dowager countess laughed and added, "inevitably ignorant about certain domestic details. It is you who must have the final say about such things as linens, suitable Lenten meals, and what to select from the variety of dishes available for a feast."

"Do you think that, as countess, I can have my own seal?" Marie asked. "My mother had one."

"I don't see why not. Whenever the count is away, he frequently takes the primary court officers with him, and it is sometimes up to the countess to manage necessary affairs—and even occasionally hold court."

The idea of presiding over a court seemed daunting to Marie, but perhaps Henri would let her observe the courts he held and the justice he meted out so that she would know what should be done.

"The countess must always be a model of conduct for others in the court," Mathilde went on. "She must be courteous, well-spoken when it is time for her to speak, loyal to God, and to her husband. And she must oversee the well-being of her subjects."

"Rather like a queen," Marie said.

"Exactly. The countess is responsible for the moral well-being of her husband, her children, her household, and her husband's people. She's often expected to give alms and must know what is fitting in all circumstances."

"There's so much to learn," Marie said, a hint of discouragement in her voice. Adèle nodded in sympathy.

Mathilde smiled. "Some of it you will learn from experience and even from your mistakes, as I did. A good husband never hesitates to point out to his wife her shortcomings. And a good wife must be receptive to hearing them and correcting them."

"A husband sounds just like the nuns," Marie said with a laugh and a sidelong glance to Adèle, who tried to hide her giggle behind her hand.

Mathilde too laughed softly. "In some ways, perhaps. But there are also considerable differences," she said. Her enigmatic smile made Marie wonder what she meant.

The list of duties was staggering, as Countess Mathilde kept adding more and more responsibilities—appropriate attire for each occasion, good manners, how to smooth the rough edges of a court with gentleness, soft words, and seemly entertainment.

Will I ever learn all I need to know? Marie wondered.

"She's a quick learner," Countess Mathilde told Henri after a few months. "I think we could begin to plan for the marriage sometime next year—as soon as she turns fourteen." She hoped so, for she felt herself growing old and tired. She suspected she did not have long to live, and she was eager to retire from court and devote the rest of her life to prayer and contemplation.

For the moment, however, she still had the responsibility of Marie and her daughter Adèle to consider. All her other daughters were safely wed, including Marguerite, who had chosen the role of *sponsa Christi*, a bride of Christ, at Fontevrault Abbey. Thibaut had arranged a second marriage for the widowed Isabelle to Guillaume IV Gouët, lord of Alluyes and Montmirail, shortly after her return from Sicily. Only Adèle, the youngest, was still unwed at her father's death. The responsibility for her future would fall to her brother Henri, but as yet, he had taken no steps toward finding her a husband.

Whenever his mother mentioned it, he merely said, "Don't worry, *Maman*. I'll see to it that she makes a good marriage."

Mathilde wasn't really worried, for in addition to Adèle's noble blood and keen mind, she was the most beautiful of all the daughters. With her honey-colored hair, lively blue eyes, and sweet smile, she would have no trouble attracting a husband.

"I'm sure you will, my son, and I will see to it that she's ready," his mother answered. It was Mathilde who had insisted that Adèle return to Troyes with Princess Marie, for she would need a friend there. Besides, training the two girls at once made her task much easier.

Thibaut will have to make other arrangements for his betrothed's domestic training. Mathilde thought of the little girl and her nurse, currently living at his court. *I will no longer be up to the task when she is old enough.*

When they were not at their domestic lessons, Marie's new life in Troyes seemed liberating after such a long time at the convent. Her favorite times were whenever there was a fair.

"Our fairs in Champagne and Brie are famous," Adèle boasted. "My father encouraged them and made special efforts to protect the caravans of merchants that came here. There are also large fairs in Provins in May and November, and smaller ones in Lagny and Bar-sur-Aube." Marie looked forward to attending them all.

The important fairs in Troyes were the "hot fair," beginning on the feast day of St. John the Baptist, June 24, and lasting throughout July, and the "cold fair" of St. Rémi, which took place in November and December. Although the palace was some distance from the main market at the Place St. Jean, during those larger fairs, the merchants' stalls sprawled through the center of town, stretching from the wheat market on the west end of the city all the way down the Rue Moyenne to the canal behind the palace.

Marie could watch from her window as merchants streamed into the city, setting up stalls to display their wares amidst the colorful confusion of the marketplace. By night she could see their campfires. Well-dressed burghers wandered through the streets with heavy money pouches strapped to their belts. She could imagine them fingering the fine woolen fabrics offered by Flemish cloth merchants, weighing the value of the gleaming treasures of Italian goldsmiths, and tasting the wines, some from Champagne, some from as far away as Germany and Italy. She could hear mercers and furriers loudly hawking their wares and the sound of haggling voices of merchants and money-changers drifting up from the streets. Jews and Christians alike, even a few who looked almost like Saracens in their strange clothes, mingled in the streets of Troyes. Marie loved fair time because it was exciting and exotic.

Merchants would sometimes even come to the court at the count's request to display their samples of fine fabrics, perfumes, ivory combs, and jewels for the ladies. Henri would allow Marie and Adèle to select one or two items for themselves, though nothing too extravagant. At fair time the count would also replenish supplies for the wine cellar and the storerooms on the ground floor of the palace. Wherever there were merchants and burghers with money, there were acrobats, jugglers and minstrels wandering the streets, always ready to perform for a gathered crowd and adding to the commotion and color. Sometimes the girls were allowed to ride through the market place and view it all first hand, but only in the protective company of a well-trusted knight. Henri had assigned such a knight to Marie, Nevelon of Ramerupt, a married man in his forties with children of his own.

"What do you think of Troyes so far?" Henri asked Marie one afternoon as they strolled in the garden after the summer fair had ended.

She smiled. "I love it, my lord. In Paris I rarely saw anything beyond the castle walls. It's so different here, where I can observe the life of the town going on all around me."

He smiled his approval. "You enjoy the fairs?"

"Oh, yes. That's the most exciting part, but I like the calmer times as well." Without all those people and stalls, it seemed more spacious. With fewer distractions, she noticed more easily the gardens and vineyards in the area. "I especially enjoy it when you invite Adèle and me to join your hawking parties."

Although they were not yet allowed to handle the hawks, the girls could watch all the activity of more experienced courtiers and enjoy the picnics in the open fields and orchards along the river where the hawks swooped to seize their prey. When there was an impromptu tourney in the region, Henri sometimes allowed them to tag along to watch the jousting. Both girls were beginning to feel quite grown up.

CHAPTER 19

Troyes, September 1159

Advent, Lent, Easter, and the three-week period from Rogation Sunday to Trinity Sunday, when weddings were forbidden, were all well past, and Henri, consulting with the priest and canons of St. Étienne, had finally decided on the date for his wedding to Princess Marie. It was to occur on the feast day of the Nativity of the Blessed Virgin, for whom the princess was named, and which fell on the second Tuesday in September. Although the *vendange* would be just beginning, and many of the grapes from this year's harvest would be still on the vine, last year's best wines of Champagne were already stored in the cool cellar of the palace and ready for the celebration, as were remaining bottles from previous years. Best of all, the princess would by then be well past her fourteenth birthday. It seemed an auspicious day.

Preparations were already under way for the ceremony and the feast that would follow. Henri had invited King Louis to attend the wedding with Queen Constance. He also sent word to his brothers and sisters about the event. He had no idea how many of them would come, though he counted especially on his brothers Thibaut and Étienne. Adèle and his mother would be there, of course.

"Isn't this exciting?" Adèle asked Marie. "You're so lucky to be getting married."

Marie was filled more with trepidation than excitement. Had she learned her lessons well enough from Adèle's mother? What would the wedding night be like? That part of it frightened her most of all—the bawdy bedding process almost as much as the physical act. The dowager countess had tried to tell her what to expect, but it had been a difficult conversation for them both. Finally, Mathilde said, "I'm sure Henri will show you what to do," and they left it at that.

Two days before the wedding, King Louis and his new wife, Queen Constance, arrived at Henri's palace, along with their two-year-old daughter, Marguerite. Marie had never met her stepmother or her new little sister before, nor had she seen her father for several years. They spent the evening in the great hall getting to know one another again. Marie was surprised to see that her stepmother was so young—just nineteen, not too many years older than Marie herself.

She and Adèle ushered Constance back to their bedchamber to show her Marie's wedding gown. She had finally pulled from her coffer the beautiful, red samite fabric her parents had brought back from the crusade to have it fashioned for the wedding by the court seamstress into a splendid *bliaut* with grand, wide sleeves. Constance spoke French with a decided Spanish accent, and there were words she did not know, but she tried to be friendly, and Marie liked her. The queen brought little Marguerite with her to the bedchamber and allowed the child to toddle about the room and entertain them.

"She's adorable, Constance," Marie said. "I know she was a disappointment to my father—as I was—but she will be a comfort to you."

"Ah," the queen answered. "But for how long? The king of England has already proposed a betrothal of his four-year-old son Henry to our daughter."

Marie considered the situation for a moment, then said in what she hoped was a steady voice, "I would think she was too young, if my sister Alix hadn't been betrothed when she was only three. Such an alliance would make our family rather complicated, wouldn't it? My father's daughter betrothed to my mother's son. Has *Papa* agreed?"

"Not yet," Constance said, "but he is thinking that if he has no son, at least our daughter would one day become queen of England and his grandson would rule over both England and France."

Marie thought fleetingly of the betrothal offer her father had once received from the count of Anjou for *her* to become the wife of the man who was now king of England and her mother's husband. Claudine had told her all about it when she was old enough to understand. It all seemed so improbable. But if it had happened, how different her life would now be.

Suddenly the candle at the window flickered, and little Marguerite reached out toward the flame. Her mother quickly snatched her away and called for her nurse, who took her for a nap.

When they returned to the great hall, Henri, Louis, and Countess Mathilde interrupted their conversation and looked up.

"Ah," King Louis said appraisingly as he looked over the young women, "The three graces," he said, raising his goblet in salute. Constance and Adèle laughed and curtseyed with poise. Only after seeing their gesture did Marie follow suit, her face flaming with self-consciousness. Countess Mathilde looked at her with raised eyebrows, followed by an indulgent smile. *She will learn to be more graceful as time goes on. Fourteen is such an awkward age*, she thought.

On the morning of the wedding, Marie's maid awakened her at dawn to prepare for the ceremony, which would take place at the hour of terce. She lay abed for a few moments, once again admiring her new gown as it hung on a peg in her chamber. *It turned out splendidly*, she thought, suddenly recalling that afternoon in the solar in Paris when she had opened the exotic coffer from Jerusalem, an afternoon when both her parents were there. She quickly brushed away the memory when Adèle, who had already broken her fast, danced into the room.

"Today's the day," she said, teasing Marie, who was laughing at her antics. "Time to get up and make ready!"

Marie rose and splashed her face with the cool water that stood in a nearby basin. Suddenly she realized that she was very nervous. *Today. Her wedding day.* It was not something she had looked forward to.

The maid brushed her hair until it shone, helped her into her *bliaut*, tightened its fine, silk lacings, and pinched her cheeks until they took on a rosy hue. Marie gazed at herself in the small mirror and felt, in spite of her plainness, almost pretty. It was not that she was ugly. Her features were regular enough, but there was just nothing special about them—not the brilliant blue and perfectly arched brows of her mother's eyes, nor her thick, golden hair and the natural rosiness of her cheeks and lips. Marie's lashes did not sweep her cheeks if she looked down demurely, nor did her skin have that perfection she longed for. There were still a few freckles on her nose, and her face still reddened unbecomingly when she felt embarrassed. Her eyes were blue, but not the startling blue of her mother's. They had a grayer cast. And her hair, though it was no longer thin and wispy, was still, she thought, an uninteresting shade of brown. She lacked the chiseled contours of her mother's oval face. She was just—plain.

People often complimented her good manners and her "charming" demeanor, though no one had ever told her she was pretty. But today, as she gazed at herself in the mirror, she was making every effort to look her best. The red samite was a flattering color that reflected delicately on her skin, and her maid had arranged her long hair in a particularly becoming way to enhance the circlet of flowers that would later be replaced by the crown of the countess. This was the last time, she knew, that she would wear her long hair loose and flowing in public like this. Married women were expected to cover their hair with a wimple or veil.

Before the ceremony she would again pinch her cheeks and bite her lips to redden them a bit and give herself what she hoped was a becoming flush. At her neck she fastened a lovely ruby brooch that had been a gift from the count to honor their wedding.

"You look very nice," the countess Mathilde told her as she waited with her ladies in the great hall. When everyone was assembled, the processional began. It stopped at the church door, where the count stood to the right and Marie to the left as they faced the smiling bishop of Troyes, who waited there. The bishop was Henri's uncle, his mother's brother Henry of Carinthia, whom the count had invited to bless the marriage and officiate at the nuptial mass. Although it was not essential for a priest to preside over the wedding itself, it was the custom for noble weddings, and the bishop took on the role with enthusiasm, standing before the couple at the church door to verify that the marriage was taking place according to canon law.

"Do you enter into this marriage willingly and without coercion?" he asked.

Although everyone knew the answer, for these matters had already been decided, they must once again publicly declare their intent. With the repeated assurance that both were willing, King Louis, who stood between the couple, placed Marie's hand in the hand of the count, literally handing over his daughter to be Henri's wife. It was the first time Marie and Henri had touched since the day of their betrothal, and Marie felt a rush of blood to her face, which receded only as the bishop began to bless the gold ring Henri was holding in his right hand.

"*Benedic, Domine, anulum hunc...*" the bishop began. Bless this ring, O Lord.

Then it was Henri's turn. "*De isto anulo te sponso, et de isto auro te honoro...*" With this ring I thee wed, and with this gold I honor thee...

Marie felt as though she were floating up from her body and viewing the scene from far away. She could see Count Henri's brothers and court officers standing behind him, all dressed in their best garments. The count had chosen to wear a belted tunic in red silk brocade that reflected the color of Marie's *bliaut*. His beard was neatly trimmed, and he was smiling. He looked quite splendid, she thought.

A group of women, most of them wives of court officials, who would be Marie's ladies stood behind the princess, along with Adèle, Countess Mathilde, and Henri's other sisters, who were nearby, watching.

Once the little ceremony ended and the priest had blessed the new couple, the church doors opened and, holding hands, they entered the bright splendor of the nave, bathed in morning light, for the nuptial mass.

Marie listened carefully to the service, wishing her Latin were better, but she did recognize Psalm 127, one verse of which emphasized the bearing of sons. *Sons, always sons*, she thought. *What about daughters? There would be no sons without daughters to bear them.*

Lo, sons are a heritage from the Lord,
the fruits of the womb a reward.
Like arrows in the hands of a warrior
are the sons of one's youth.
Happy is the man who
has his quiver full of them.
He will not be put to shame
when he speaks with his enemies
at the gate.

As the mass ended, a red canopy of gold-embroidered silk was held over the couple at the altar to signify the indissolubility of the marriage bond and the posterity of the blood. Next came the celebration. The great hall was crowded with guests and performers. The crowd even spilled into the courtyard before the feasting began. There were acrobats and tumblers, jongleurs and musicians with flutes, *vielles*, pipes, drums, lutes, and tambourines, all playing as the day wore on. Henri had spared no expense for the wedding feast. Every kind of meat imaginable, copious amounts of wine, bread, sweetmeats, and all that went with them were abundant. The squires ceremoniously paraded before the guests dishes of wild boar and roasted swan and peacock, their feathers replaced to look as though they could fly away at any moment, even an elaborate cake, perfectly molded in the form of the count's new castle and St. Étienne. Marie was dazzled by the splendor and variety of the dishes. The count was generous in rewarding the entertainers, the jongleurs in particular, knowing how much his new wife enjoyed their performances—bestowing lavish gifts of mantles lined with *vair* or rabbit fur, silk *bliauts*, and to one, even a fine palfrey.

Marie was happy to get to know Henri's sisters and their husbands: Mathilde, whom they called Mahaut, recently wed to Rotrou du Perche; Agnès and Renaud de Bar; Isabelle and Guillaume Gouët. Even the nun, Marguerite, who, with her abbess's permission, had come all the way from Fontevrault and was trying to persuade her mother to return with her, at least for a lengthy visit.

Marie had been fearful that tension might still exist between her father and Henri's brother Thibaut, for even though Thibaut was now Louis's seneschal, the count had joined King Henry of England in the spring of that year in an unsuccessful siege against Toulouse. It was the same effort Louis had made so many years earlier in an effort to claim that city as part of Queen Eleanor's birthright. Since then, King Louis's sister, Constance, following the death of her first husband, Prince Eustace, had married the count of Toulouse. Now, wanting to keep Eleanor from gaining that birthright, Louis rode swiftly south to help his new brother-in-law—putting the French king and his seneschal on opposite sides of the battle.

Although they had patched up their differences before the wedding, Marie was concerned that ill feelings might linger on. However, the two men seemed to be getting along well enough, raising their goblets side-by-side to toast Count Henri and his bride. It always amazed Marie how men could put aside their differences or allegiances whenever it was convenient—enemies one moment and allies the next.

There was only one moment of tension—when Henri's brother, Étienne de Sancerre, tried to speak to Anseau de Traînel, usually an affable courtier. This time, however, Anseau turned his back rudely and walked away. After Henri spoke to him in private, he made an effort to be more civil. But Marie did not know what to make of his uncharacteristic behavior.

"What is the problem between Anseau and Étienne?" Marie asked.

"I'll tell you about it later. Nothing to worry about now, thank God."

Since Henri seemed to have it under control, she gave it no more thought. Étienne was now talking and laughing with Thibaut, and Anseau had sought out his recent bride, Hermesende de Bar-sur-Seine, who would be part of Marie's entourage of ladies. The couple seemed to be chatting merrily. In any case, too much else was going on for her to worry about it further. She was expected to smile and greet the guests. She was now, as Countess Mathilde reminded her with a kiss after the ceremony, the countess of Troyes. It was difficult at first, for she was by nature a bit shy, but it became easier as the day wore on.

The sun did not set until well into the evening, and the guests spent a long afternoon of feasting and entertainment, during which they consumed much fine wine and enormous quantities of food. Many of them were clearly drunk, and their voices, especially those of the men, grew louder as the evening progressed, almost drowning out the sounds of the musical instruments.

When there was full darkness outside, well after the hour of compline, Henri whispered to Marie, seated beside him on the dais, "I don't think we can avoid the bedding ritual much longer, *ma chère*. Else they might come and carry us to the bedchamber."

He took her hand and led her down from the dais and toward the count's chambers. She could hear the crowd's roar of approval behind them and the sound of benches scraping across the stone floor as eager guests rose to follow.

This was the moment she'd dreaded most. She had heard nightmare stories about it from other ladies in the court, how the tipsy, raucous crowd would join the couple in their bedchamber to cheer them on. Marie thought it a rather barbaric custom, but the groom's bedding of the bride seemed to be what made the marriage finally official and beyond all question.

The bishop, who, like the others, had clearly consumed his share of the wine, joined them, sprinkling a generous amount of holy water as he blessed the marriage bed, which was strewn with rose petals. Then he stepped aside, leaving the bystanders to do their worst. As they cheered and joked, the ladies drew the young countess behind a screen to undress and prepare her. When she reappeared only in her chemise, her hands held protectively in front of her breasts, the ladies tucked her into bed, as the count reappeared, naked, from the next room and slipped in beside her.

"May your quiver be full of arrows, Henri!" one of the men shouted in a drunken voice.

"Hear! Hear!" Several bystanders, who could barely stand, cheered and hooted, adding their own ribald taunts. They meant it to be all in fun, to encourage the couple to forget their inhibitions and enjoy a night of frolic, though it did not always have that effect.

Henri gave the crowd a dismissive wave and a final grin before he reached over and closed the bed curtains. It was the prearranged signal for his brother, Count Thibaut, who had tried to maintain a sufficient level of sobriety, to begin urging the bawdy crowd to leave the room. Finally, after much persuasion, countered by good-natured grumbling from the would-be observers, the couple heard the door of the chamber close.

"Thank God they've gone," said Henri. "I was afraid they'd stay to observe the act. They sometimes do, you know."

Marie made no response but tried to prepare herself for what she knew came next. Lying stiffly next to her new husband, she was keenly aware of his naked body beside her.

"I know you're very young," Henri said, "but I think we have to perform our duty—at least this once—for now." He gave her a tender kiss, and she tried to kiss him back, but she had never been kissed before, except for their ritual embrace during the ceremony, and she wasn't sure she was doing it right.

She was not surprised by his words. She too knew it was her duty, but she felt a sense of shame, as he lifted her chemise over her head to remove it and his hands began to explore her body. Her first thought was to push him away. The nuns had always taught her to protect her virtue, but Countess Mathilde had told her she must allow him to do whatever he wished, so she lay as still as she could. He seemed as eager to get it over with as she was. Yet despite her mind's resistance, she was surprised when her body reacted as though it had a will of its own. When his hands and then his lips played around her small breasts, she felt her nipples rise up under his touch. She began to tremble.

"Just try to relax," he coaxed her, as he moved his hands slowly and deliberately, caressing her private parts in an effort to arouse her. But relaxing was impossible. She was tense and fearful, when he lifted the weight of his body over her, that he might crush her. She held her breath, breathing only when she could hold it no more, as he finally invaded her body. After a few painful thrusts, it was over. His duty was done, and so was hers.

As he pulled back, she could feel tears beginning to run down her cheeks.

"Please don't cry, my dear," he urged. "It's all done now. I suppose it's always like this for a young woman the first time."

He smoothed her hair and wiped a tear from her cheek with the back of his fingers, trying to comfort her. "I won't do it again. Not right away, at least—not until you are ready to bear children."

She covered her face with her hands so that he could not see her weep. Then he put his arms around her and pulled her close, holding her like Claudine used to do to comfort her.

"There now," he said, kissing her hand. "Did it really hurt so much?"

"No," her voice sounded like a wail, and she felt like a foolish child. There had been a sharp pain and some discomfort, but she was crying now more from humiliation than from pain. She was sure that he had taken no pleasure in what he had done, nor had she. She had merely endured it. That too made her feel ashamed.

"I hope that someday you might even enjoy the act," he said in a quiet voice, almost as though he were reading her mind while he stroked her hair, now spread across the pillow.

Was he mocking her? But she was beginning to feel calmer now, as he held her, her head resting on his shoulder, and patted her until her tears ended. Then he sat up and reached out for a flagon of wine that had been left on the bedside table. As she wiped her eyes on the skirt of her discarded chemise, he poured himself a goblet full and one for her.

"Here, my sweet, this will make you feel better, and we'll have the appropriate bloody sheets to show the busybodies tomorrow morning." His voice was almost playful now, as she sat up and reached out to take the wine.

It was the first time she realized that she was bleeding. "Oh, but it will stain…"

"No, *ma petite*, let it go. It's what they want to see. It proves you were a virgin and that our marriage was consummated. We've done our duty. It's all part of the ritual."

Countess Mathilde had told her that the first time would be hard, but that she would get used to it. Count Henri—her husband—she would have to grow accustomed to the word, said he wanted her to enjoy it. Would she ever be able to enjoy such a thing? Could she? She sat up quietly in the bed and sipped the wine, thinking about his hands exploring her body and how it had reacted in such unexpected ways. She supposed she was truly a woman now, part of a sisterhood that knew secrets no little girl should know. The worst thing had been letting a man see her naked and touch her in such private places. A grown man. But he was her husband. It would take some getting used to. She hoped he wouldn't repeat it too often. At least now she knew what to expect.

"Feeling better now?" Henri asked in a voice of concern. He had set his goblet aside and was propped on his elbow, looking at her.

She nodded with a weak smile.

"You asked me earlier today about the tensions between Count Étienne and Anseau de Traînel," he reminded her. "This might be a good time to tell you what happened."

How could he be so casual? Why would he want to talk about that now? she wondered. Perhaps he just wanted to take her mind off what they had done.

"It all started six years ago," he said, "on the wedding day of Anseau and Alix, the daughter of Geoffrey de Donzy. The wedding vows had been made, and the wedding feast was under way when a false messenger sent by Étienne informed Anseau of an attack on his lands. Anseau kissed his bride, armed quickly, and rode away. Once he was gone, Étienne swooped suddenly into the town and literally stole the girl. He rode with her to another church, married her in haste, and forthwith consummated the marriage—apparently all with her father's full knowledge and approval. Evidently Geoffrey decided at the last moment that my brother might be a better match than Anseau." He sat up again and took a swallow of wine.

"Unbelievable!" she answered. "I see why Anseau was so angry."

"Ah, but it didn't end there," he told her. "I was present for my friend's wedding, and when Anseau returned and discovered what had happened, he appealed to me. It was clear that Étienne was in the wrong. Anseau and I rode together to the castle where the wedding feast was still under way. I informed my brother that he had to give up his bride to her rightful husband, but he refused, telling me that *he* was the rightful husband because they had already consummated the marriage—even before the wedding feast—if you can imagine such a thing."

"Then what happened?"

"Your father, the king, intervened as well. And my brother Thibaut joined us in an assault against Étienne at Saint-Aignan. There was nothing we could do about the marriage. Since that one had been consummated and the other had not, it was legally binding. But we did require Étienne to relinquish to Anseau the dowry he had stolen. Needless to say, he wasn't happy about it, but he complied."

"I can see why there is animosity on both sides. I'm amazed that you were able to keep them peaceful today."

"They've avoided each other since then, but thank God there was no violence. You'd think that, after six years, they'd be willing to put the past behind them."

"Was Étienne's wife here today?"

"No, she avoids going anywhere she might encounter Anseau."

"I can understand that."

"But you see why it was so important that we consummate our marriage tonight. I didn't want to risk anyone stealing you away tomorrow morning."

Marie smiled, as warmth flooded her body. She looked up to see him smiling as well, as he played with a lock of her hair.

"Was Étienne angry with you?" she asked.

"Of course he was, but we're brothers. He knew from the outset that Anseau was not only a member of my court, but also my friend, and that I would defend his rights. I think he's forgiven me," Henri answered.

"I'm glad Anseau found someone else," Marie said. "I like his new wife. Hermesende is a lovely addition to the court."

"Yes, she is. I'm happy for him too," he replied.

The goblet of wine and Marie's exertion from crying were starting to make her drowsy. She lay down on her pillow, realizing that she felt a sense of safety with the warmth of Henri's body next to hers. She dreamed of him in the night, feeling his arms around her, protecting her. They had done their duty.

CHAPTER 20

True to his word, Henri did not trouble her in bed again. Instead, he provided her a chamber of her own, adjacent to his. But she knew that he often took other women to his bed. She could hear them through the closed doors and open windows, and she had occasionally seen them leaving his room late at night or early in the morning.

There were different ones wherever they traveled. Whenever they were in Provins one woman in particular came fairly often, a pretty woman with long, red hair. She appeared to be in her twenties. Her name, Marie learned, was Anne Musnier, and she was the wife of a local merchant, Gérard de Langres. Marie knew that it was common for noble husbands to have mistresses. But it was rarer for any husband to be so permissive as to allow his wife to share another man's bed with impunity. She assumed that Henri must reward Gérard generously for the privilege of bedding his wife. Still, it angered Marie, who considered it most disagreeable that he chose to do it under her very nose. One day she found the temerity to mention it to her husband.

"I know that you bring other women to your bedchamber," she said quietly one morning as they broke their fast together.

"Only until you are old enough to be a responsible mother, *ma chère*," he answered with a casual air. "In the meantime, a man has needs."

"And when will I be old enough?" she asked.

"When you're sixteen perhaps?" he suggested in a tentative tone. "It's up to you."

"I hope you go to confession whenever you've been with another woman. It's against God's law, you know."

"God made men's flesh weak, *ma petite*, and of course, I always confess and receive absolution. The priests understand because they too are often guilty of sins of the flesh."

Marie knew it was true. The Church tolerated and forgave many such sins. She had heard the story of the infamous love affair between Héloïse and her teacher, Abelard—the very Héloïse who was a friend of Henri's mother and who had joined her in founding the convent of La Pommeraye. Héloïse still lived and was abbess at the Paraclete, a convent that Abelard had founded for her. He had also written the rule by which her nuns lived. Abelard himself was now dead, but this man, who had seduced the young Héloïse, had become an abbot. Certainly, for both of them to rise to such positions in the Church, *their* sins must have been forgiven. Marie knew that the famous couple had married by the time their son, Astrolabe, was born, but he had been conceived out of wedlock when Abelard was still Héloïse's tutor. She knew too that there were many priests and even bishops who took mistresses. It was not an uncommon practice. Still, lust was supposed to be a mortal sin.

"I worry for your soul," Marie said, reminding him of her wifely duty to try to keep her household sinless. And she was annoyed by her husband's blatant unfaithfulness.

"All sins can be forgiven," Henri reminded her. "Christ died for our sins."

She wondered whether Henri would be so tolerant if she were the one to commit such sins of the flesh. She was certain he would not, for women were expected to be the moral compass of the household, to remain pure and faithful, while men did whatever they wanted. She bit her tongue at the injustice of it all but said no more.

Troyes, 1160

It was mid-May, almost time for the hot fair, when Henri's brother Thibaut, who was nearby on the king's business, rode into Troyes for a brief visit. He brought news from Paris that Queen Constance was pregnant again.

"The king is hoping for a boy this time," Thibaut added.

"Well, that's good news," Henri said, making an effort to greet the information in a cheerful manner. He could not deny, however, that both he and Marie were happy that Constance's first baby had been a girl, who did not threaten Marie's standing as the oldest child and her father's heir. As things stood now, their son, when they had one, would inherit the crown. That would change of course if the queen gave birth to a living son. Nevertheless, he felt compelled to express pleasure about this new pregnancy.

As for inheriting Aquitaine, that hope was long since gone. The August after Marie's betrothal to Henri, her mother had given birth to a son, William. Although the boy died before his third birthday, Eleanor had by now borne three more sons. Clearly Aquitaine was lost to Marie. The only remaining hope of a significant inheritance was the possibility that Marie might bear a son to inherit the royal crown.

"There's more news, Henri," said Thibaut. "King Louis met only last week with King Henry of England in Rouen. It was an important conference with the presence of some high-ranking bishops and noblemen. I believe the bishops of Durham, Evreux, Lisieux, and Bayeux were there, and the counts of Flanders, Beaumont, and Soissons. Maybe a few others."

"I too was invited to the meeting but was unable to attend. And what did the gathering accomplish?" Henri asked.

"They signed a betrothal agreement between Princess Marguerite and Prince Henry."

Marie gasped. So her father had really accepted a marriage agreement between Queen Eleanor's son and his own daughter. She'd never thought he would agree, given his resentment toward her and his hatred of the English king.

"Did he turn the princess over to the king of England?" she asked. That was what he had done with her and her sister—given them over to be raised by the family of the intended husband.

"He did, Marie," Thibaut replied with a nod.

"But why? It's not as it was for Alix and me. Her mother is still there."

"The king didn't want the queen to have any worries while she was pregnant. He didn't want her tripping over a toddler or trying to pick her up. This time he seems sure it will be a boy, and he wants no problems."

"Then *my* mother will raise her?" Marie asked in amazement.

"King Louis wasn't willing to go that far," Thibaut replied. "She is being placed in Normandy in the household of Robert of Newburgh for the moment."

Constance must be heart-broken, Marie thought. *She loved her daughter so much. Poor little Marguerite.* But mothers had no say in such matters.

Troyes, October 10, 1160

There was a crispness in the air, and the bright leaves of autumn were floating to the ground in colorful profusion, when another unexpected messenger rode into the castle courtyard. Count Henri and Countess Marie were still at Sunday mass. As soon as it was over, a squire greeted them just outside the door to St. Étienne with the news that an emissary from the king had arrived. Henri and Marie hurried together into the great hall to greet him.

The messenger wore a grim face as he bowed before them. "My lord and lady, the king has a new daughter," he announced.

It was clearly not intended as good news, but Marie felt a surge of pleasure despite herself and tried to keep from smiling—until she heard the envoy's next words.

"But I also bring you the sad news that the queen has died in childbirth." His voice was grave.

The shock was profound, and the announcement met with stunning silence.

Finally, Marie, choking back tears, managed to say, "Poor *Papa*. He must be deeply grieved to lose his wife so suddenly. Her daughters are both so young that they won't even remember her." *Constance dead—not yet twenty-one.* It wouldn't surprise Marie if she had died of a broken heart after losing one daughter and giving birth to yet another. She felt a fierce guilt at her tinge of relief that there was still no prince.

"What is the child's name?" Marie asked.

"*Alais*, my lady."

Count Henri shook his head in dismay. "Another daughter and a dead wife." It was indeed a misfortune for the king. Henri could only imagine his sorrow and disappointment.

But the messenger was not yet finished. He pulled from his pack a letter from the king to the count.

"What? There's more?" Henri asked. The young man shrugged with uncertainty. Clearly he had no idea what the parchment might contain.

Henri unrolled it and read it carefully. His brow creased at first. Then his eyes widened in astonishment.

"What is it?" Marie asked. Henri glanced at her with the slightest shake of his head, but he gave no answer. Instead he turned to the messenger.

"Thank you. That will be all. My squire will see to it that you have a cup of ale and food to refresh you." The count dismissed the young rider and turned to lead his wife to their private chambers where they could talk alone. Only then did he hand her the letter from her father.

"Here. I want you to read this."

Marie paled with shock as she untangled the Latin of the letter.

"Good heavens." She had never known her father to show such poor taste. He might have waited at least a month before he wrote such a missive, but the letter made the matter sound urgent.

"What do you plan to do?" she asked her husband.

"I would like to think it over before I decide. It is a rather unexpected request, and I must consider whether it is in the best interest of all involved."

She nodded with understanding. "That seems a good plan, my lord."

Three days passed before Henri sat down to dictate a reply. He and Marie had discussed the matter thoroughly, and he'd consulted his sister Adèle, who remained at the court in Troyes while her mother was away. She was willing.

"It is my destiny, after all," Adèle said. "Remember the prediction Pierre de Jully made to my mother before I was born?" Henri looked puzzled until she reminded him of the old man's words to their mother.

"That I would marry a king."

"Ah, yes, I remember now." He smiled.

Then she turned to Marie, "One part I didn't tell you. He predicted not only that I would become a queen, but that I would become queen of France."

"Well," Marie answered. "It was an amazing prediction."

When Henri spoke alone with Marie, although she was startled by the proposal, she did not oppose it. "He will marry someone anyhow. At least if it's Adèle who gives him a son, it will be your nephew who becomes king. And she is not already promised, so I doubt there's any honorable and peaceful way to prevent such a marriage."

King Louis had obviously been quite taken with Adèle at the wedding of Marie and Henri. Marie remembered how he had labeled her one of the three "graces," along with his wife and daughter, and she recalled how his eyes had lingered on Adèle. He had even commented at the time to Count Henri on her beauty, saying, "She will surely make a fine marriage someday soon."

Marie's only reservation was the timing. To offer such a proposal only days after his wife's death was unseemly, she thought. But it was what it was, and she had no choice but to accept it. She and Adèle giggled together at the thought that Marie would become her friend's step-daughter.

"And I will be the grandmother of your children!" Adèle laughed. "Just don't have any babies too soon. I'm far too young to be a grandmother."

It was all so strange. Henri's father-in-law would also be his brother-in-law. And Marie would be her father's sister-in-law as well as his daughter. Nevertheless, given the king's impatience and the inevitable humor of the situation, the days of mourning for Queen Constance were brief. Only five weeks after her death, on November 13, the feast day of St. Brice, the king would marry his daughter's best friend, Adèle de Champagne, and as an old man had predicted so long ago, she would become queen of France.

The only event that spoiled the wedding was the news that on November 2, King Henry of England actually had the marriage performed between his six-year-old son Prince Henry and Princess Marguerite, still a toddler of only three, in order to claim her dowry.

King Louis had placed her dowry, the Vexin, in the hands of the Templars, to be held by them until her marriage. It was a territory on his borders that the king of England had long coveted and to which he now laid claim. Although the wedding was not canonically legal, for the two children were not of an age to consent or to consummate a marriage, prelates were reluctant to speak out against the king of England.

King Louis was too busy preparing for his own new wedding to fight back as aggressively as he might normally have done. At his behest, Henri and Thibaut did make the menacing gesture of fortifying the castle of Chaumont-sur-Loire in the county of Blois, near the border of King Henry's lands. However, when the English king pushed back, Louis's forces withdrew. *Was it really worth a war just before the king's wedding to protest a marriage that would take place sooner or later anyhow?* Henry II had timed it well. He'd wanted the Vexin badly, and he usually got what he wanted.

The wedding of Louis and Adèle and the crowning of the new queen were celebrated at the old cathedral of Notre-Dame in Paris. The king and the canons were already casting envious eyes on the rebuilt cathedral at St. Denis and longing to duplicate such grandeur in Paris. But the present church had served as the site of many royal weddings, as it would for the wedding of King Louis and his new bride.

It was a grand and festive event on a beautiful November day, with a large number of important clerics in attendance. Archbishop Hugh of Sens performed the mass, while others read the scriptures and led the great processional. Only Samson, archbishop of Reims, refused to participate, contending that the bride and groom were too closely related.

With his marriage to the young and beautiful Adèle, the king felt certain that his relations were solid on all sides with the house of Blois-Champagne. All their previous quarrels seemed settled once and for all, and the multiple family ties looked absolutely solid. Yet even then, seemingly unrelated events were unfolding that would reveal that no bonds, however carefully forged, were unbreakable.

At the wedding feast, the recent death of the pope and the crisis that followed were the source of much conversation and debate. After the unexpected death of Pope Adrian IV in September the previous year, the Sacred College of Cardinals met in Rome to choose his replacement. This time the selection, traditionally made by consensus, proved to be neither simple nor peaceful.

The papal states lay between the Holy Roman Empire to the north and Sicilian lands controlled by the Normans to the south, and the cardinals were deeply divided in their loyalties. Over time they had formed factions—and each faction favored its own candidate. They met for three days without coming to an agreement. Finally, the Sicilian faction lost patience, gave up on the idea of electing a pope by consensus, and declared their own candidate—a cardinal named Rolando of Siena—pope by majority vote. He took the name of Alexander III. The imperialist faction objected vociferously, and the meeting erupted in chaos. Conflicting reports of what happened next spread quickly throughout the continent. All anyone knew for certain was that now there were two popes.

Once the obligatory nuptial toasts at the wedding feast were done, noisy conversations and even a few arguments about the papal situation erupted throughout the hall. The more wine the courtiers consumed, the louder the discussions became.

"How do you think it all happened?" asked a young knight.

"I heard that when the Sicilians proclaimed Rolando the new pope, there was shouting and yelling and even swords drawn in the basilica. They say the imperialist cardinals were literally frothing with rage." Thibaut's voice was forceful as he raised his cup after a fourth serving of wine.

"Can you imagine such an uproar? It must have been something to see—all those quarreling cardinals—red feathers flying." His brother, Étienne, well inebriated by now, laughed and waved his goblet about, sloshing some of the red liquid onto his brother Guillaume's priestly garments.

"I was told by a good source," Thibaut went on, "that when Alexander's supporters tried to put the purple mantle of pope on his shoulders, one of the imperialist cardinals snatched it away and threw it on the ground."

"Is that so?" This time it was Philip of Flanders who had joined the conversation.

"I don't know if it's so, but it's what I heard. Then they opened the doors to the basilica and drove out the Sicilians." Thibaut gestured widely as though to open the doors himself, managing to strike his brother-in-law, Eudes, the duke of Burgundy, with unintended force in the face.

The duke took his arm gently and forced him to sit down, while he picked up the story. "The version I heard said they opened the door to let in armed men who chased away the pro-Sicilians at sword point. Then the cardinals who were still inside—the imperialists—took another vote and elected their own candidate."

"What's his name?" the young knight asked.

"Octaviano of St. Cecilia. He decided on the papal name of Victor IV," someone added.

The voices in the room began to compete. "So I guess this one was unanimous!" shouted a drunken voice. Everyone laughed.

"With more than half the cardinals missing? Does that count?" another voice asked.

"Who was finally consecrated?" asked Étienne de Sancerre. He knew the answer full well, but he wanted to hear the whole story again.

"Both of them, but neither one in Rome," said Eudes.

"Now I hear they've excommunicated each other," Guillaume said, rising to his feet again. The crowd guffawed.

"So now we have two excommunicated popes." Étienne shook his head in disgust.

"That's right," Guillaume answered. "There are so many different rumors that I guess we'll never know for sure exactly how it happened."

"It doesn't matter how it happened. All that matters is that now we have rival popes," added Count Henri, who had been listening attentively.

"That could get complicated. Who do you think the king favors?"

Eudes asked.

"Alexander," said Thibaut, the king's seneschal. "He says most of the cardinals preferred him."

"But that vote was not unanimous," another voice said. "Victor's vote was unanimous."

"Most of the cardinals were no longer in the basilica. How can that be legal?" Philip asked.

"It fulfills the letter of the law," someone said.

"Legal or not, it has to be one or the other—not both," Henri added. "I really hate these conflicts within the Church."

"So do I," another voice chimed in. "Let's hope it all gets settled soon. I may decide to marry my sister, and I have to know where to go for a papal dispensation."

Everyone laughed, and the conversation ended abruptly when the king's brother rose and lifted his goblet to make another toast.

At the wedding feast, the dowager countess Mathilde focused less on the question of the two popes than on her family. Even though she had not been feeling well, she had left the quiet surroundings of Fontevrault, determined not to miss her youngest daughter's royal wedding and see the prophecy of Pierre de Jully fulfilled. It had seemed improbable at a time when the king was married to the richest woman in France, and he and Thibaut had been arch-enemies. Now it seemed foreordained.

Mathilde was pleased that so many of her family members were present, for she suspected it might be her last opportunity to see many of her children. As she surveyed the room, watching her sons and daughters all enjoy themselves with such abandon, she felt blessed. Her daughters were all married now, one of them to God, her sons all in positions of power, three of them counts, and the youngest now a provost at the cathedral of Sens and well on his way to becoming a bishop. Or so she hoped. She smiled with satisfaction, seeing only blessings ahead. She and Thibaut had done well by their children.

When the celebration ended, she planned to embrace her family one last time and depart with her attendants for the abbey of La Pommeraye. There, in the convent that she and Abbess Héloïse had founded together, she would spend her final days. She planned to take holy vows and devote herself to prayer and devotion to God.

Only three weeks after Adèle's wedding, Henri received news that his mother was near death. He rushed to her bedside at La Pommeraye. There, on December 13, Henri and his brother Guillaume were kneeling beside her bed at the moment of her death. Tears glinted in Henri's eyes, as he held her hand against his cheek one last time. He had always respected and admired his father, but he loved his mother with a special tenderness.

The burial of Mathilde, revered as the convent's founder and benefactor, took place the next day. It was a mournful affair attended by all the nuns, with both the archbishop of Sens and Mathilde's brother, the bishop of Troyes, participating. Dark skies that reflected Henri's grief held back the rain until the service ended.

When Henri returned to Troyes after the funeral, Marie greeted him with genuine sympathy. She too loved her husband's mother and would remember her fondly for all her lessons on how to be a good wife to her son and a good countess to her people.

"She had a peaceful death," he told her. "It's as though she knew her duty to her family was done and she no longer felt needed here."

"But it was a joyous thing in a way. She felt finally free to turn her thoughts to God and to her soul, without having to worry about others," Marie added.

Mathilde's death marked the end of an era for all her children. They were the ones who must now bear all responsibility for their world.

For a while, in the wake of his mother's death, Henri was able to banish the papal situation from his thoughts. He had no strong feelings about it one way or the other. He knew King Louis thought it logical to accept Alexander as the new pope, since he was favored by a majority of the cardinals. Although the count was not surprised to learn that Emperor Frederick Barbarossa was one of Victor's staunchest champions, it was not good news.

They rarely agree on anything, he thought. *But surely there is some way to work it out.* Henri was concerned, for both of them were his liege lords. *It could even lead to war, and Champagne is caught between the two realms.* He hoped to find a way to resolve the matter. The situation threatened far more than he knew.

CHAPTER 21

"What's wrong, my lord?" Marie asked her husband, as he paced the floor of the solar, his face clouded with worry.

"I am concerned about the inability of the Church to settle the papal issue. It threatens the peace between two of my liege lords."

"My father and the German emperor?" she asked.

"Do you know about it?" he asked, stopping to look at her.

"I listen, my lord. It is difficult *not* to know about it. Everyone seems to be taking sides. I also hear that the pope they call Victor is one of your kinsmen. Is that right?" she asked.

"So I'm told—on my mother's side, but I can't let that influence me. I don't know which is the better candidate."

"Does it matter? I doubt you'll have any say about it," she said.

"That's true, but I would like to keep peace between my overlords. If there's tension between them, we are caught in the middle." Henri started to pace again.

"I don't know all the reasons, but I hear my father favors Alexander, while the emperor prefers Victor, since he has German kinsmen."

"That's right," he replied.

"But what can *you* do?" she asked.

"I don't know," he said, looking at her intently. "Perhaps I can mediate between them, get them to talk it over and come to some kind of agreement."

He had learned, from observing the war between King Louis and his father, that an intermediary can sometimes be beneficial when parties are in a hostile deadlock. Observing Abbot Bernard's persistent efforts to bring peace between the two men all those years ago, he had seen that mediation could be more effective than violence. And before his death, Bernard had encouraged him as well to be a peacemaker. Perhaps he could help.

"At least I can try," he said.

"What will happen if you don't succeed?" she asked, genuinely curious.

"I don't know, my dear. I just don't know."

Months passed, without resolution to the matter, as tensions between the two parties increased. Most of Europe seemed to favor Alexander, but the Holy Roman emperor, as well as the kings of Denmark and Poland, supported Victor. Neither side seemed willing to compromise.

"This can't go on forever," Henri announced to his wife. "It's tearing the Church apart."

Marie was more concerned for her husband's distress than she was for the Church. In the past two years, her marriage to Henri had become more a friendship than a real marriage. By the time she reached sixteen, Marie was beginning to wonder if her husband was ever again going to approach her in bed. She felt ready, but she had no idea how to go about luring him to her bedchamber. *Perhaps he considers me undesirable*, she worried. He certainly seemed more preoccupied now with the papal schism than he did with her or with starting a family. She resented the fact that he frequently bedded other women. It was not uncommon among men, she knew, but she hated it when she could smell another woman's scent upon him.

For the moment, however, she would not press him, for she knew his deep concern about the papal quarrel. She could only wait until they were both ready. But as soon as this matter of the papacy was settled, she would find a way to urge him to do his conjugal duty. She hoped he would have a willing, even eager, heart.

May 1162

As it turned out, Henri did not have to volunteer to mediate between the king and the emperor. King Louis sent Bishop Manassès d'Orléans to ask him to do so. It was a significant change of heart for Louis. His support for Alexander had cooled when he sent emissaries to the pope, who received them with a haughty and uncordial welcome. Annoyed by the pontiff's apparent indifference toward his representatives, Louis decided he himself was now willing to subject the matter to arbitration. He was prepared to meet with the emperor and discuss how they might bring about a settlement.

At Manassès's urging, Henri agreed to the task, and together the bishop and the count traveled to Pavia to find Frederick and try to arrange for the negotiation. The emperor listened to their request and agreed. The meeting was to take place on August 19 at St.-Jean-de-Losne, a Burgundian border town on the Saône River, which separated the imperial Franche-Comté from the French duchy of Burgundy. Although Frederick set some harsh terms, he was at least open to the meeting and even sent back a letter to Louis praising Count Henri for his efforts to foster good relations between the two monarchs.

The arrangements Frederick and Henri agreed upon required each ruler to appear with his papal candidate, as well as bishops, abbots, and barons for both sides. There the matter would be discussed and decided by arbitration, and if either side did not meet these terms, it would automatically lose by default. As a surety, Frederick demanded that, unless these terms were met, Count Henri would be required to take an oath of fealty to the emperor for whatever lands he held in fief from the king.

King Louis was horrified when he heard the news. It was a serious matter, for it would mean that Henri would owe aid and counsel only to Frederick, while in truth he held the lands in fief from the king.

"How could you do such a thing? I did not agree to those terms,"

Louis said when Henri and the bishop returned to Paris with word of Frederick's agreement.

"Bishop Manassès informed me that you gave your authorization for me to arrange the conference. He said it was urgent and that you did not specify any restrictions. I made the best arrangement I could. The emperor would agree to nothing less," Henri replied.

"Well, it isn't fair. Pope Alexander has already refused to go to the meeting. He claims he was elected and consecrated and that he has no reasons to submit to such arbitration."

"But as things stand, he isn't even able to live in Rome, while Victor occupies the Lateran palace. As you know, Alexander has fled to France for fear of hostility. You must try to persuade him to come to the meeting. It's the only way the matter can be settled. We must fulfill the terms I have arranged. It was the best I could do."

Louis was enraged, and his tone was harsh. "The terms are unacceptable. I will ask the pope again, but I give no guarantees. You should never have made such an agreement without my consent. It was foolish."

Henri gritted his teeth and tried to remain as calm as he could, but the king's reprimand, particularly in front of so many courtiers, was a major insult. He could see his sister Adèle's distress clearly etched on her face, as she stood in the background, wringing her hands. Henri tried to unclench his fists, but his whole body was tense. He remembered Bernard's words, "Always be a peacemaker." *But it's hard, Reverend Father, when one is dealing with such stubborn men*, he thought.

"I did what I could, my lord," he said to the king. "I have taken many weeks from my own lands to do your bidding. If you don't like the arrangement, perhaps you should go yourself next time." He made every effort to keep his voice calm and steady, but he could feel the redness rising in his face. "The meeting is set for August 29. I hope to see you there. I shall be waiting in Dijon."

At that point he made a curt bow, turned on his heel, and strode from the hall before the king could reply. He went directly to the bailey, where he summoned his men and ordered his steed saddled. He would not stay the night at the royal court in Paris as he had planned.

Marie knew that something was terribly wrong as soon as her husband returned to Troyes. He hardly spoke to her when he entered the great hall. When she tried to question him, he was curt.

"This is between your father and me. It's not your business."

She felt as though he had slapped her. Even though they had yet not come together again as man and wife in bed, they'd always been courteous to one another and talked freely about matters that concerned each of them. But this time he was shutting her out completely.

It was times like this when she especially missed Adèle. But Anseau's wife, Hermesende, who had become one of her ladies and a good friend, saw her look of dismay and followed her as she hurriedly escaped to the solar.

"Are you all right, my lady?" she asked softly.

"Only bewildered," Marie answered. "If you learn what has happened to put him in such a mood, please tell me. Now I think I'd like to be alone for a while." She found her psalter lying on a nearby table and began to read, hoping to find a familiar psalm that would quiet her feelings of utter rejection. Wasn't it when a husband was upset that a wife could be most valuable? Wasn't it her role to soothe him and reassure him? She could only hope his demeanor would soon soften.

It didn't. Hermesende, who learned from her husband, Anseau, what had occurred, told Marie that the king had insulted Count Henri in open court. Marie was astonished. *How could my father do such a thing? And how could Henri hold me responsible?* Yet a public insult from the king, his own father-in-law, was no doubt a hard blow to a man of his standing. She understood that, and she tried repeatedly to talk with him, but he ignored her. As the months went by, they hardly spoke to each other, and Marie became despondent.

As he was departing for the August meeting, she had tears in her eyes as she followed him down the great stone steps of the palace to the courtyard to say goodbye. He was leaving early in order to spend time with his sister Marie and her husband, Duke Eudes of Burgundy. At their court in Dijon Henri planned to await the arrival of the king and his papal candidate. He turned to face his wife as she approached him.

Seeing her tears, he said, "I'm sorry if I've treated you badly," though his voice carried little warmth. "It's just that you remind me so much of your father."

"I'm sorry that he was so disagreeable to you," she said sincerely, grateful for even a half-hearted apology. "May you travel in safety."

He nodded in response, dutifully kissed her fingertips, and quickly mounted his horse.

The weather was good as Henri made his way over the well-worn road to Dijon, accompanied by his uncle, the bishop of Troyes, and some of his own courtiers, among them his scribe, his notary, two chaplains, and his friend and butler Anseau who was almost always at his side. The mornings were cool for mid-August. But during the middle of the day the warmth of late summer poured down its sweltering heat. Pear and apple trees along the way were heavy with fruit, and here and there peasants were already beginning to clear their fields of dried stalks and leftover vines from the summer harvest.

When Henri finally reached Dijon, his sister Marie was pleased to see him. She looked pale, he thought. He noticed new wrinkles around her eyes, though he considered her still young—for she was a year younger than himself.

"Are you well, my dear?" Henri asked, holding her close in a brotherly embrace.

"I am well. It's my husband who is ill," she said. He could see the worry on his sister's drawn face. "He regrets he could not greet you."

"I'm sorry to hear that," Henri said, recognizing the responsibility she had on her shoulders at the moment. "I hope it's nothing serious and that he will soon improve."

His sister and her husband still had three minor children, all as yet unwed. Their son, Hugh, was fourteen. Their oldest daughter Alix was sixteen, and Mahaut, the youngest, not yet of marriageable age.

"The doctors don't think he will get better," she said. "It is a wasting sickness." Her voice caught in her throat.

Henri reached for her hand. "I'll help any way, I can," he promised. "You know that."

"Yes, I do, my dear brother, and that is one of my greatest comforts."

"Perhaps the doctors are wrong." He squeezed her hand. "I just hope my visit doesn't add to your burden."

"On the contrary. It's good to have someone to lean on just now," she replied with a sad smile.

The king and the bishop of Orléans with their entourage of prelates and nobles arrived three days later—*without* their papal contender. Henri was dismayed.

"Alexander refused to come," Louis announced bitterly. "I knew he would. But I am here to negotiate on his behalf."

"I think it will do little good, my lord. You recall that one of the stipulations was that if one party did not appear, he would forfeit the election," Henri reminded him. "As a consequence, I am bound by oath to join Frederick and swear fealty to him for the fiefs I hold from you."

"What made you think you had the right to make such an agreement without consulting me?" the king stormed at the count.

"You yourself gave me the power through Manassès, bishop of Orléans."

They both looked at Manassès, who stood nearby, looking sheepish, realizing that he had overstepped his bounds in trying to persuade Count Henri to undertake the negotiations. But the deed was done. They must try to work out a solution.

On the appointed day, King Louis watched from a safe distance as the emperor arrived, accompanied by his own candidate, Victor. When Frederick reached the bridge that spanned the Saône, which separated the empire from the duchy, he found waiting for him only Count Henri and his party, which included the archbishop of Tours, the bishop of Paris, and the abbot of Vézelay. The emperor smiled.

"Well," he said, "since neither King Louis nor the would-be pope, Alexander, is here, I can only conclude that I may safely proclaim Victor to be the rightful pope."

"My lord, may we discuss this further? My king seems to have misunderstood."

"I think the matter is settled. I am returning now to my castle at Dôle. If there is anything further to discuss, we can do it there. I shall await your arrival and your pledge of homage." He turned his horse abruptly and rode dramatically back across the bridge where the meeting was to have taken place.

By the time Henri reached Dijon, the king was already there, warming himself before the large fire in the great hall.

"What did he say?" Louis asked.

"He considers the matter settled with Victor as pope, and I am to go to Dôle to pay homage for the lands I hold from you."

"Nonsense. You must go and persuade him to agree to another meeting in three weeks' time."

"What will that change?"

"I will try once more to persuade Pope Alexander to cooperate," Louis said. "I don't think he understands the seriousness of the situation."

"Then I will do what I can, my lord," Henri said. "But I can promise nothing."

The next morning a disgruntled Henri set out with his men for the Franche-Comté and the imperial palace in the city of Dôle. How did he get caught in the middle of this papal fiasco? He didn't much care which candidate was finally chosen. He only wanted the matter settled so that he could return to his own lands in peace—with no war between the empire and the kingdom, since Champagne lay between the two.

To his surprise, the emperor, after some persuasion, agreed to another meeting to be held in three weeks. The terms were the same, only this time the emperor demanded as guarantors the counts of Flanders and Nevers, who would become his prisoners if the king failed to comply. He wanted the duke of Burgundy as well, but when Henri told him of the count's illness, he agreed to settle for Count Henri in his stead.

The second meeting, set for September 22, would, like the first, prove to be a fiasco. Once again, despite King Louis's efforts, Alexander stubbornly refused to come. Louis came without him, arriving on the bridge of St.-Jean-de-Losne on the morning of the appointed day. He waited until midday, but the emperor did not appear. Instead, Frederick sent his chancellor and the archbishop of Cologne. Louis triumphantly indicated that he had met his obligation, but that the emperor had failed to come, and turned back toward Dijon. The emperor's ambassadors followed him, urging him to come back, assuring him that the emperor was on his way and would arrive shortly. But the king refused, declaring that he had met his obligation.

In the evening, at sunset, the emperor appeared and, seeing no French king present, he sent his ambassadors once again to Dijon to announce his presence, but the king refused to return, at which point, Frederick declared his obligations fulfilled and, once again, proclaimed Victor to be the rightful pope. Upon threat of war against the French king, he called on the three guarantors to deliver themselves into captivity.

Henri, furious at the stubbornness of both Alexander and now of the king, prepared to leave once more to ride to Frederick's court and put himself in the emperor's hands.

"What foolishness," Louis said, "Why would you feel required to become a prisoner or to do homage when the emperor himself did not meet the requirements? The anti-pope was not even with him, I'm told."

"Neither was your candidate present, my lord. But when the emperor appeared, I was honor-bound to make certain you did so as well."

"I *did* appear, and the emperor did not."

"There was no appointed hour, only an appointed date."

"And I was there," the king sputtered.

"But you did not wait," Henri reminded him. "And you refused to return."

"Why should I be obliged to be at his disposal whenever he feels like showing up?"

"Nonetheless, my lord, I gave my word. And the emperor has twice met his commitment without finding you there. I feel honor-bound to keep *my* word, even if you don't," the count said.

"Are you implying that I have not acted honorably?" The king's voice was louder now, more menacing.

Henri's jaw tightened. "I cannot speak for you," he replied. "I can only say that *I* am bound by *my* word."

"I will not be insulted by you or anyone else," Louis said, turning abruptly toward his squire. "Make arrangements for our departure tomorrow morning," he said to the young man as he marched toward the door.

"Yes, my lord," the lad replied.

The king turned around only once to say to Henri in a gruff voice, "And don't expect me to pay any ransom for you."

Henri, infuriated by his words, started to speak once more. But King Louis was already slamming the door behind him.

As the sound of the heavy door echoed throughout the cavernous room, Henri gritted his teeth, turned to the squire, and said, "You may also inform your lord that he should pass through Troyes on his way back to Paris to reclaim his daughter. I will no longer honor this marriage if such stubborn blood runs in her veins."

Even as he said it, he regretted the unfairness of it all. It was not Marie's fault, he knew. She was the innocent victim in all this. But she was the only weapon he had to use against her father—the one punishment he had the power to inflict. He remembered the tears brimming in her eyes at his departure and knew that this cruel rejection would hurt her. But so be it. It would also hurt the king to see his daughter so ill-treated. The future looked bleak for them all.

CHAPTER 22

Paris, November 1162

By now Marie had wept all she intended to weep. Nevertheless, she could still recall vividly how shocked she had been that September afternoon her father and his companions swept into Troyes and demanded that she prepare to return with them to Paris.

"But why?" she asked.

"Your husband has put you aside. He doesn't want you anymore. Besides, he won't be back for a while," King Louis said.

"What do you mean? What happened? Where is he?"

"In the emperor's dungeon, for all I know... or care." He told her what had happened, how Henri had defied him and gone to do homage to Frederick Barbarossa. He and the other guarantors were now captives, he assumed, at one of the imperial castles.

"But surely there will be a ransom. Perhaps you can negotiate his release," she said.

"And why should I?" he asked bluntly.

"Because he is my husband."

"Not any more. Not as far as I'm concerned." Louis's voice was uncompromising.

"But Father, you can't have our marriage annulled. It's been consummated!" She remembered her discussion with Henri on their wedding night and how that made it legal.

"Then we'll find other grounds. It was his choice, not mine." He was adamant.

When they arrived in Paris, Adèle was surprised to see Marie, but she greeted her warmly. After she heard what had happened, she took Marie in her arms and stroked her hair.

"I'm so sorry, my dearest. I can't imagine Henri being so cruel. But I'm sure Louis must have hurt his pride terribly. My brother was only trying to help keep the peace. But to treat you so badly, it's uncalled for and so unlike him. They were both in the wrong—both Louis and Henri."

Marie needed the comfort of Adèle's embrace, just as she had the day they first met at the convent. Her father, the king, had shown her little affection and had hardly spoken to her on their return to Paris. And he'd not *asked* her to accompany him to Paris. He'd *ordered* her.

Marie wept for days, but finally she had decided she would weep no more. Instead, she let anger consume her. *I am so weary of having men control my life*, she thought. *First, my father and Abbot Bernard. Now my husband. Will I never have a say in my own destiny?* She could understand her mother better now and her need to leave her claustrophobic marriage and make decisions for herself.

In time, even Marie's anger dissipated, replaced only by a desire to go home. Home now meant Troyes. This old castle, where she had spent much of her childhood, now felt alien to her. In the two years she and Henri had been together, she had come to like, even to admire, her husband, but only Adèle seemed to understand.

"I want to go home," she said. "I enjoy being with you, but…" Her voice trailed off with a sigh.

"All this is so unlike Henri," Adèle said.

"I know. He's usually a charitable and generous man—too generous, my father thinks," Marie said wistfully. "Whatever passed between them must have been harsh indeed."

"I know it will be hard to forgive him for sending you back to Louis," Adèle's voice was sympathetic.

"He isn't asking for forgiveness," Marie said. "I only wish he would."

In fact, she'd heard nothing at all from her husband since he'd gone to the emperor. She knew that her father had negotiated the release of both of the other captives, who were now home again. But his anger with Henri was too strong. He would do nothing to help him.

One of Henri's knights, a man named Girard Eventat, had even ridden as a messenger to Paris to ask for the king's help, but Louis refused. Marie managed to seize a moment alone with the man in the bailey before he left for the emperor's court to take the unwelcome news back to Count Henri.

"How does he fare, Sir Girard?" she asked, genuinely concerned about her husband's well-being.

"Well enough, my lady. He's not being kept in some rat-infested prison, if that is what you're concerned about, but rather treated as a guest at the imperial court. Of course, he won't be released without negotiation, and he refuses to do homage for castles he holds from your father. But I feel certain Count Henri will find a way—even if he has to turn over to the emperor some of his own castles to pay his ransom."

"Please tell him I asked about him and that I'm concerned for his welfare. I doubt that I can change my father's mind, but I'll keep trying."

He nodded and mounted his horse to ride away.

Marie was making an effort to be the kind, forgiving person she had always thought Henri was—though now she had her doubts. But perhaps she could persuade him to take her back. While she still felt hurt and resentful, she did not want to spend the rest of her life at her father's court. She would rather think of herself now as Henri's wife than Louis's daughter. Her mother had always said there were ways to persuade men to do things, but Queen Eleanor had never taught her how. She would have to figure it out for herself.

Before the end of the year, Sir Girard arrived once more at the royal court with the news that Count Henri was free.

"Thank God," said Marie. "What were the terms?"

"The count did homage to the emperor for nine of his own castles in Champagne in return for his liberty."

"And the lands he holds from the king?" she asked.

"He still refused to swear fealty to the emperor for lands he held from another."

Grâce à Dieu, thought Marie. *In spite of everything, he remained loyal to my father.* She hoped the king would be grateful for that at least. *Surely he will come soon.* But she heard nothing more. He made no effort to contact her, and she spent most of her anxious days in the solar, sewing with the queen and her ladies, waiting for a visit that did not come.

Henri ignored the cold February weather, still seething with indignation as he rode hard from Provins to Meaux. Shortly before his departure, a letter had arrived from Pope Alexander, commanding him to come to Sens for a face-to-face meeting. Henri scoffed, still bitter at the pope's lack of cooperation at St.-Jean-de-Losne.

"What shall I tell His Holiness?" the young messenger, confused by the count's response, waited for an answer.

"What is the purpose of this meeting?" Henri asked.

"I don't know, my lord."

"Then tell His Holiness," he spat out the word with disdain, "that I am not available. I have other matters to attend to."

"Shall I wait for a written response, my lord?" the messenger asked.

"No, just tell him I won't be coming."

Henri had not forgotten the pope's role in causing the rift between himself and the king, and he had no intention of being at his beck and call.

But Alexander did not give up. As the first shoots of spring were beginning to peek through the soil of Champagne, the same messenger arrived once more. This time he bore not a summons, but an invitation, carefully and diplomatically worded, to ask Henri to join him in Châlons to help him plan a Church council to be held in the city of Tours at Pentecost. "Your friend, Hugh of Toucy, will be here as well," the letter said. How could he turn down the request when it involved such a polite plea for help to the Church? And he would enjoy seeing his old friend, the archbishop of Sens.

Still somewhat reluctant, but willing, Henri summoned his chancellor Guillaume, who took out his quill to draft the count's letter of acceptance.

When Henri rode into Châlons on that sunny day in late March, he was surprised to see royal knights gathered in the courtyard. They looked at him without surprise but said nothing. Suddenly he realized what this meeting was really about, and he knew he would find King Louis inside the court.

Mordieu! he thought. *The pope is trying to undo the damage he did when he refused to come to St.-Jean-de-Losne.* Bile rose in his throat as he dismounted and climbed the stone steps into the palace.

It would be the first time Henri and Louis had seen one another since that last contentious meeting at Dijon. Both men stood stiffly, ignoring one another, as they waited for Alexander.

"Welcome, welcome to you both." Pope Alexander greeted them with a smile and open arms as he strode into the great hall with the archbishop.

Henri and Louis both knelt to kiss the pope's ring. Although Henri had not yet declared in favor of Alexander, he felt obliged to show him the courtesy due a pope. He would have done the same for Victor.

Standing up to face Louis, however, Henri merely nodded, refusing to bow. Louis, his eyes steely, nodded back, choosing to ignore the slight.

The meeting was tense. Both the pope and the archbishop mustered all their diplomatic skills, plied the king and count with good wine and a bit of flattery, and reminded them of their family ties. Soon, they had the two men at least speaking to one another. Alexander also extracted promises from both of them that they would encourage the clergy of their regions to attend the council at Tours. But the real purpose of the meeting was clear.

"It's not good to have such bitterness between fathers, brothers, and sons—all of which you became by your vows of marriage," the pope reminded them. Henri's jaw tightened at the mention of marriage vows, but he said nothing.

Alexander was unusually genial in his efforts to mend their relationship.

"What can I do to help restore good will, Count Henri?" he asked in a cordial tone.

"What did you have in mind, Your Holiness?" Henri asked in turn, a hint of coolness still in his voice.

"I know you've had many problems with the abbot at Lagny. Isn't that where your father is buried?" asked the pope. "That must be vexing."

Henri nodded cautiously, wondering what the pope had in mind.

"Well, I've been thinking about that problem, and I've come up with an idea I hope you will find agreeable, assuming, of course, that the king concurs." Alexander was being uncharacteristically diplomatic but also candid. He was trying to placate them both, in hopes of healing their quarrel and bringing Count Henri, still uncommitted to either pope, to his side.

Henri cocked his eyebrow with a silent question, and Louis leaned forward.

"I would like to appoint your half-brother, Hugh, to be abbot of Lagny. That should solve your problems at the abbey and bring your family closer together. Family is so important, don't you think?" The pope's eyes were fixed on Henri. He glanced away only once to gauge the king's reaction. "Would that be agreeable to you both?"

"I have no objection," Louis said.

Henri hardly knew his half-brother, but no doubt he would support the interests of his father's family at Lagny. "I'm sure my brother would be pleased, Your Holiness," Henri said.

The pope merely nodded. "It shall be done."

Despite all their efforts, nothing he or Archbishop Hugh did that afternoon moved either man to make a friendly gesture toward the other.

"Both of you are stubborn men," he said finally, throwing up his hands in surrender. Then, he stood, and dismissed them with a blessing, "May God forgive you, and may his grace shine upon you and place charity in your hearts." The three men at the table all made the sign of the cross, but Louis and Henri did not look at each other as they rose to leave.

With Anseau de Traînel at his side, Henri rode away from the meeting, feeling a bit more favorable toward the pope, but with none of his rancor toward Louis dissipated.

"How did it go?" Anseau asked.

"Well enough with the pope, I suppose, but the king did nothing to make amends. And I'll be damned before I make the first move."

Once Louis was back in Paris, Adèle constantly reminded him of the misery he was causing his daughter—not to mention the tension she felt personally at having her own husband and brother at odds.

"It was not my fault," Louis said. "It was he who sent her away."

"But it's you who made him so angry that he would do so," Adèle reminded him. "Some gesture of reconciliation would go a long way toward healing the wounds. You know it's not like Henri to hold grudges. You must make some effort. After all, it was your failure to meet the agreement that caused all this."

"Not my failure—the pope's refusal."

"Can't you find in your heart the magnanimity a king should have?" Adèle asked.

He would sulk for a while after such conversations, but little by little, she knew she was wearing him down.

Following the council of Tours, the pope kept his word and had Henri's half-brother, Hugh, consecrated as abbot of Lagny. Henri took the occasion to surround himself with family members, inviting all his brothers to the abbey, which was located not far from his castle at Meaux. Only Étienne refused to come, which surprised no one, irascible as he was. He had only met his father's bastard son once or twice and had no intention of starting a relationship with him now. But Henri, Thibaut, and Guillaume, now dean at the cathedral in Meaux, all came. Many of Henri's usual courtiers also accompanied him—among them Anseau, Pierre Bursaud, and Guillaume the marshal—and witnessed the charter of privilege Henri gave to the new abbot and his abbey church in celebration.

Thibaut seized the occasion to make his own efforts, as Louis's seneschal, to reconcile his brother and the king. He was deeply concerned about the ruptured marriage between Henri and Marie, which was tearing the family apart.

"Henri, Marie's sister Alix will be fourteen next year, and I plan to marry her then. I'd like to have you and Marie, as well, and King Louis and Adèle, at the wedding. Any chance of that?" Thibaut asked.

"I doubt it," Henri replied.

"This has gone on long enough, Henri," Thibaut chided him. "It's time to bring your wife home. She is totally innocent in all this, and you have made your point with Louis."

"I'm aware of that, Thibaut, but I see no honorable way to do it. It is he who was in the wrong."

"He was at the mercy of the pope," Thibaut answered.

"But he refused to help once I was captured by Frederick."

"It was you who agreed to go into captivity."

"I had no choice, if I was to honor my part of the agreement," Henri said.

"But Marie is the one who suffered most—and she had nothing to do with any of it. Alix is very worried about her sister," Thibaut told him.

"I know," Henri conceded. But what was he to do? He wanted the king to take the first step.

Even Henri's courtiers tried to persuade him. Anseau in particular saw how unhappy he was. He knew that Henri hated such conflict and that it was against his nature.

"Hermesende really misses the countess," he said to Henri during the ride from Lagny back to Troyes. "She and the other ladies at court don't know what to do with themselves."

Henri listened, but said nothing. In fact, he too missed Marie. He missed their lively conversations, her presence in the solar and at his table. Even though they still slept apart, chaste as brother and sister, she was his companion, and he had not forgotten the warm innocence of her body beside him that first night. He'd made no effort to find grounds for annulment, nor had the king. But neither of them saw an honorable way to reconcile their differences and still maintain their dignity.

Henri kept himself busy for the rest of that year, moving his peripatetic court restlessly throughout the county of Champagne, judging cases, resolving disputes, and granting privileges to abbeys and churches. He stopped only once at his childhood home of Vitry, the village now rebuilt on the ashes of the great fire. As he stood on the windy hilltop looking down at the new structures, he smiled to think of all the happy boyhood hours spent with his family at this now-ruined castle. How many summer afternoons he and his brothers had played at knighthood, slashing at each other with wooden swords, riding their ponies, and aiming their toy spears at the *quintain*. He could still hear Thibaut, wailing with outrage and surprise the time his older brother split his lip with his sword. He could even hear his mother's cross voice scolding them both. It had been a shock to discover how heavy a real spear was when, at fourteen, he'd first tried to hold it level to ride toward the *quintain*. Then he thought of the fire.

Considering how much his family and the townspeople had lost on that terrible day when the king burned the town, his jaw tightened as he considered his father's quarrel with Louis and the devastation it had caused. Only the intervention of Abbot Bernard resolved that matter. If the abbot were alive today, Henri suspected, he would try to move heaven and earth to reunite his miracle daughter and Count Thibaut's son, to preserve this marriage he had helped to arrange. But Bernard was gone now.

At least, Henri thought bleakly, *Louis and I are not at war. The damage involves only myself and my marriage—not my people's safety.* Still, he wished it were over. But the year ended and another began, the matter still unresolved.

Early May 1164

Henri and his retinue milled about in the courtyard, as their squires fastened on their leather gauntlets for a hunt, while the keepers and trainers stood by with hawks and falcons recently brought from the mews and hounds from the kennels. Hunting was a favorite pastime of Henri and his knights when they were not at war. It seemed to satisfy their knightly training and hold their more bellicose instincts in check. Their frequent hunts kept the kitchen larder well stocked with game birds and venison throughout the spring. The hunt was also a distraction for the count when he felt morose, which seemed to be more and more often these days.

When he'd mounted his courser, Henri held out his left arm to allow the keeper to fasten his bird of choice, a peregrine falcon, to his left wrist. The bird suddenly flapped his wings and the dogs began to bark as a young unknown knight galloped into the courtyard.

"I come from the emperor, my lord," he announced to Henri.

"And what news do you bring?" the count asked.

"I was sent to tell you that Pope Victor is dead, my lord."

"When?"

"On April 20. He died in Lucca, Italy."

"May he rest in peace," Henri said aloud to the messenger as he made the sign of the cross. *And thanks be to God*, he muttered under his breath, emitting a sigh of relief at the news. *The antipope is no more.* He felt a sudden lightness, as the ghost of the conflict and his failure at St.-Jean-de-Losne seemed to vanish.

His horse pawed at the ground.

"The hounds and horses are eager," he called to the young messenger as he spurred his courser forward. "My servants will see that you are fed and rested." There was little doubt that Emperor Frederick would probably support another pro-German pope in Victor's stead, but Henri felt no obligation to intervene any further. He'd done his duty. It was enough.

"Will you now acknowledge Alexander as the rightful pope?" Anseau asked, riding by his side as they approached the open field near the river where they frequently hunted. "It seems that God has chosen."

Henri hesitated. "I suppose I should. In any case, Frederick and Louis can take responsibility for any further quarrel. I'll have nothing more to do with the matter." Spotting a gray partridge pecking at the ground not far from a nearby hedgerow and seeing his falcon take notice of it as well, he released the raptor and watched it swoop down on the startled creature as it tried to fly away.

"But I feel free as a bird now," Henri said.

"Which one, my lord?" Anseau asked, watching the two birds before cocking his head to look at Henri. "There's still the quarrel with the king and the matter of your wife to consider."

Henri said nothing as he gazed at the soaring wings of the returning falcon, the frantic partridge still alive but bleeding in its claws. *Which one indeed?* he wondered.

When the marriage of Thibaut and Alix took place as planned in late September, Henri did not attend. Instead, on that bright, breezy day in early autumn, he sat alone, sulking in the dark emptiness of the great hall, consuming a large flagon of wine, and remembering his own September wedding day five years earlier, when the hall had been filled with friends and family, all celebrating as he should be doing with his brother today.

"No doubt Louis and my sister, maybe even Marie, are in Blois enjoying themselves at Thibaut's wedding," he muttered to himself, taking another deep draught of wine. He'd wanted to be there, but his unwillingness to be congenial with the king had kept him in Troyes.

"I've let my brother down," he said to his cup of wine.

A letter from Thibaut that arrived later that same month only made him feel worse.

I was deeply disappointed that neither you nor the king and Adèle chose to attend my wedding to Alix, presumably both for the same reason—to avoid each other. However, another matter has arisen concerning our younger brother Guillaume that will, I hope, move you to less selfish action.

The letter outlined an unfortunate and hotly contested election, still unresolved, to the bishopric at Chartres. Their brother Guillaume was one of the two candidates, "and clearly," Thibaut wrote, "the most deserving."

I have written to the king in support of our brother, and I beseech you to lay aside your quarrel with the king to intercede on his behalf as well. Surely you can do this, if for no other reason than to honor the memory of our mother.

Thibaut knew exactly what would move his older brother to action. His words, "to honor the memory of our mother," struck Henri to the heart. He was well aware that this was a squabble Louis might be able to resolve, and he agreed with Thibaut that it was a matter too important to let his personal pride get in the way. His brother's whole future might depend on it, and for Guillaume to be bishop of such an important diocese as Chartres would be the fulfillment of his mother's dream for her youngest son. But it would require Henri to put aside his anger against Louis and make an effort to help his brother become the undisputed bishop.

"I can do this," Henri said to himself. "I must go to Louis myself and ask for his help, even if I have to humble myself." *Why have I allowed it to go on so long and cause such anguish?* he wondered. *Why have I hurt my wife so cruelly?*

"Ready my horse and prepare for a trip to Paris," he said to his squire. "And notify Anseau, as well as my marshal and the chancellor and all those who usually accompany me. You know who they are. We leave tomorrow at prime."

The count and his knights rode out of Troyes at the earliest light, without sending riders in advance to announce their impending arrival. They rode hard for the three chilly days it took to reach the Île de la Cité. Henri worried that the king might refuse to receive him, but when he announced his presence at the castle gates, they opened at once—almost as though he were expected.

By the time Henri and his men dismounted, King Louis had already rushed to the bailey to greet them. He opened his arms and stepped forward to give Count Henri an unexpected warm embrace, his heart filled with gratitude and relief that his son-in-law had taken the first step.

"You've come at last, my son," he said. "Have you come to forgive a stubborn old fool?"

"I've come to speak to my king, in hopes of seeking his forgiveness—

and to ask a boon." The words flowed out, unplanned. Suddenly the entire quarrel seemed ridiculous, and they were once again father and son and brothers by marriage.

Louis kissed him on both cheeks and threw his arm around his son-in-law's shoulders. "Come in where the fire is warm and the wine is flowing, and where, I suspect, your wife is waiting anxiously."

"I shall be happy to see her again, my lord," Henri answered, grateful to the king for making all this so easy. It was almost as though there had never been a rift, and a current of pent-up goodwill seemed to overflow between them.

Word of his arrival spread quickly throughout the castle. By the time they reached the great hall, where a huge fire roared, a large number of people were already gathered—courtiers, the queen, and, on the edge of the crowd, Henri saw Marie, pale as a lily, wearing a white robe as though she were in mourning, watching him intently.

With Queen Adèle smiling nearby, King Louis reached out for Marie's hand and placed it once again in the hand of the count. Marie stood there, anxious, waiting to see how her husband would greet her. He was looking at her with such intensity that it was almost frightening, but neither of them seemed able to move for a moment as they gazed into each other's eyes.

Finally, Henri reached out to embrace her. "I have wronged you," he whispered in her ear. "I hope you will be able to forgive me."

Tears of joy spilled over her lower lids and ran down her cheeks. "Of course, I forgive you, my lord. Will you—" Her voice trembled slightly. "Will you now take me home?"

A flood of warmth closed out any chill that may have remained in his heart with her use of the word "home" when she referred to Troyes.

"We'll leave first thing tomorrow, my dearest." He whispered again, words intended for her ears only. "After all, I think it's time for us to start a family."

She blushed as she smiled and nodded. The entire court was beaming. Queen Adèle wept openly and even the king had tears in his eyes, but their lips displayed true joy.

When Henri finally submitted his petition to the king on behalf of his brother, Louis assured him without hesitation that he would never uphold the other candidate's irregular election at Chartres—which had been performed even before the old bishop's burial and without the presence of the dean and some of the canons. He would submit the matter to the pope with his recommendation, promising to support the election of Guillaume, the brother of his sons-in-law and his own by marriage, with every fiber of his being.

"Now, let us rejoice," the king announced to the court. He ordered torches and tapers lit, musicians called in, and acrobats and story-tellers summoned. Food was quickly prepared, and an evening of feasting and merriment filled the great hall with an aura of celebration.

When dawn came, it was not the bleak autumn morning of earlier days, but rather a crisp, sunny day that promised only gladness. After breaking their fast with bread and ale, Henri and Marie bid farewell to Louis and Adèle and, with a cheerful party of knights and squires, set out eagerly to return to their own court in Troyes and whatever future awaited them there.

CHAPTER 23

Henri, his wife at his side, chose to enter the city of Troyes not through the most direct gate, but through the Porte du Beffroi, which led to the street where the largest number of people would likely be gathered. When his horse trotted through the city gate toward the crowded marketplace along the Grand'Rue and people saw the countess on her own palfrey beside him, they began to gather by the roadway's edge to cheer.

"The countess!" they called out, attracting others to the roadside. "The countess is back!" Every face seemed to wear a broad smile as they shouted in welcome. The riders slowed their horses to a walk to give the people ample time to see their count and countess, smiling and waving, together again after two years of separation.

Henri and Marie had prepared for just such a greeting and were dressed in their very best travel clothes. Henri had sent a page on ahead to announce the arrival of the count and his men, but he'd kept the return of the countess a secret until now. In anticipation, he and Marie had even paused before they reached the city gate to put on their gold comtal crowns, studded with gemstones, gleaming in the autumn sun. As men and women lined the street and laughing children played along the edge, all looked delighted to see them together and hopeful that the trouble was behind them.

The joy of the townspeople was not unexpected. It was always in their best interest to have a happy count and, with any luck, an heir.

That way future disputes or wars were less likely. One thing no people wanted was to be caught up in battles over who should be the rightful count. It was always best for a count and countess to produce a son—several if possible, for life was uncertain, and death always lurked at the edges of knightly training and activity.

"The harvest looks fruitful this year, my lord," Marie said to Henri as they rode past the church of St. Jean and the marketplace. He acknowledged her observation with a nod and a grin, gazing about at all the baskets of apples, melons, and grapes that splashed the market stalls with a variety of colors.

"Indeed," he called back with an impudent grin. "Let's hope the season continues to yield good fruit."

The innuendo of his words was not lost on her. She blushed slightly, as she lowered her head and let a smile play about her lips. "Let's hope so indeed, my lord."

News of their arrival preceded them throughout the town. By the time they had crossed the Rû Cordé and passed through the Artaud Gate to reach the palace courtyard, any of Marie's ladies who lived nearby were already there, awaiting the return of the countess. They greeted her enthusiastically with warm words and welcoming faces. After she dismounted, a few of them, including her closest confidante, Hermesende, even dared to give her hugs.

"It is so good to have you back, my lady." Hermesende, her face shining, curtsied to the countess after her less-formal embrace.

"My thanks to all of you," Marie said. She found herself looking forward to assuming once more all the duties her late mother-in-law had drilled into her before her marriage. In fact, to her surprise, she had taken to the role of countess with relative ease, despite her youth. Mathilde had taught her well, and she found that she enjoyed the responsibilities as well as the choices and decisions she was required to make as countess. They were small, perhaps, in comparison to the choices men had, but at least they gave her a modicum of authority over her life.

With short notice, the kitchen staff managed to assemble a fine feast for their homecoming meal. Although it was less copious than their nuptial dinner, it reminded Marie in some ways of their wedding day. This time, thank God, there would be no bedding ceremony, so she felt none of the dread she had felt on that occasion, only anticipation. She and the count had still not slept together since their reconciliation. At the castle in Paris she had remained for that one night of Henri's return in the small bed in her old room that was once the nursery, while Henri and his men, whose arrival was completely unexpected, were provided other accommodations. During the trip back, there had been very little privacy. Marie found herself looking forward to their first night together again back in their own bedchamber. This time, she promised herself, she would not be afraid.

Once they had left the feast to retire to their private apartment, Henri took her in his arms and kissed her eagerly even before they were bedded.

"Let us never be apart again for such a long time," he said. "I have missed you."

Marie was pleased by his words, and she echoed, "I missed you too."

He kissed the top of her head, and released her, turning to the flagon of red wine and two goblets that sat, as before, on a table near the bed. Henri poured her a goblet and handed it to her, as he raised his own.

"Let us drink once more to celebrate our marriage. And may it be fruitful," he said in a solemn voice. They both drank deeply of the full rich wine. Then Henri set down the goblet, took her hand, and pulled her toward him once again.

"This time, no ladies. *I* get to undress you instead," he murmured, his lips brushing the nape of her neck. She felt a shiver of anticipation as he reached for the laces of her *bliaut*.

Once they were finally in bed, he held her close, and this time she did not resist. Her body was not rigid as before, but pliant and receptive to his caresses. She was no longer surprised when her breasts, now fuller, responded so readily to his touch, and she found herself nestling safely in his arms. She let her reactions carry her where they would, feeling his hands touching her so gently at first, then with greater urgency as he explored her body.

So often since their first night together, she had remembered his touch and let her eager imagination do the rest, wondering why she had been so afraid that first time. Now she opened herself to him willingly, and when she felt his firm member penetrate her body, this time there was no pain. She welcomed the moment with a quick intake of breath, feeling the need to be even closer to him—a part of him, inside him as he was inside her. This time he did not hurry, but she could feel his tension mounting, his need to move, to thrust more and more rapidly, as she felt her own body beginning to throb with desire and respond with its own receptive movements.

When it was over, he whispered in her ear, "That was good."

She smiled at the darkness and murmured, "Yes."

His warm breath made her body tingle, and she snuggled closer. She didn't want him to pull away, but to hold her as he had that first night, this time not to comfort her, but just to let her feel his body close and his arms around her, to reassure her of his presence and let her breathe in his now-familiar scent. *Was this love?* she wondered. Was this what all the troubadours from the south and their counterparts from the north, the *trouvères*, wrote about? Was this what the girls whispered and wondered about at the convent? Was this the meaning of the dowager countess's secret smile? Or was this what the church warned young maidens about? How could it be a sin? Didn't God command them to be fruitful? It was like the apple from Eden's tree.

Marie was sure that, after such an evening and others like it, she must be pregnant. But when her usual blood flow began later in the month, she was disappointed. The nuns had led her to believe that was all it took—that if she let a man touch her like Henri had done, even once, she would find herself with child. But now it had happened several times, and there was still no pregnancy.

Why am I surprised? she wondered. Her mother and father were married almost eight years before she was born. And Adèle and her father had been married now four years, and there was still no child. Perhaps they too had waited, but she doubted it. Adèle was older than she had been at her marriage, and Marie knew that her father, the king, was impatient for an heir.

I must be patient, she told herself, determined to settle back into court life as the true mistress of the household. Her knight and protector, Nevelon de Ramerupt, was at her side once again whenever she ventured from the palace. She had been overjoyed upon her return to see his welcoming face, and he had greeted her with a fatherly smile.

And now she had her own chaplain, a priest named Drogo, and her personal scribe, Laurent, who penned her letters.

Henri had even allowed her to have her own seal now, which identified her not only as the countess of Troyes, but also, as she requested, as daughter of the king. She ran her fingers over the seal attached to a letter that still lay on her writing table, feeling its waxy, oval form pointed at both ends. It was a shape frequently used by both women and clerics, while her husband's seal was round, with his knightly image on horseback, a raised sword in his hand. Although the image didn't look much like her, with its blank eyes and tiny waist, she recognized the garments. She was depicted standing, wearing a flowing *bliaut*, tightly laced on both sides, and a mantle fastened at the neck. Her outstretched arms emphasized her wide sleeves, which reached to the hem of her garment, *only a bit of an exaggeration*, she thought. In her right hand, she held a *fleur de lis*, which she'd insisted on as a symbol of her royal blood. Her left wrist held a bird, her sparrow hawk, her favorite bird in the hunt. A veil, secured by a small coronet, flowed around her head.

Marie loved her new seal and was eager to use it. Seeing her official imprint, she felt herself to be truly the countess of Champagne. She had been pleased and honored by the way in which she had been greeted upon her return to Troyes, both by the common people and those at court. Now she savored the status of her station as a mature woman with her own staff, basking in her new role.

Paris, December 1164

The Christmas court in Paris that year was especially festive, celebrating along with the birth of Jesus, the marriage of Thibaut and Alix and the reunion of Henri and Marie—all of whom were together for the first time in a very long while. The king's enthusiastic smiles showed Marie a side of her father she had rarely seen before. He seemed truly happy, and she could hear excitement in his voice, as he led them all to his work table.

"Come, let me show you the plans for the rebuilding of Notre-

Dame. It will be a new cathedral in the modern style, something Paris will be proud of." The building had been begun the previous year, and Marie had watched the stones being fitted one by one when she was an exile in Paris. She wondered then if her marriage could ever be rebuilt, and if so, would it be as slow to accomplish as this cathedral? Now secure once more, she was able to admire the magnificent plans for what Notre-Dame would become.

She was delighted to have the opportunity to see Adèle once more and to enjoy the company of her sister, Alix. They had seen one another only rarely for the past eleven years, and both of them were very different people now. Alix seemed more grown up at fourteen than Marie had felt at that age.

"I so wanted to attend your wedding," Marie said.

"I wish you could have been there. Just think, we're not only sisters, we're also sisters-in-law now," Alix said.

"I know. Our family is so complicated. Our sister-in-law is also our step-mother," Marie suggested, making both Alix and Adèle laugh.

"And your brother will be your nephew," Adèle pointed out.

"Oh?" Marie asked. "Is there to be a brother?"

"I'm not sure yet," the queen confided, "and so far I haven't told Louis. But I have missed my monthly bleeding. Please don't mention it even to your husbands until I know for sure."

"Well," Alix pointed out, "our sister could be our niece just as well. That's been our father's luck so far."

Adèle chose to ignore the remark and change the subject.

"I suppose you've both heard the rumors about the recent quarrels between the English king and the archbishop of Canterbury," she said. Marie and Alix both nodded. "Did you know that Thomas Becket has now fled England and gone into exile?"

Marie *did* know, since Becket's exile was in Champagne. The dispute between the English king and the archbishop of Canterbury over royal versus ecclesiastical power had come to a head the week before Christmas. When Henry Plantagenet had appointed his friend and chancellor Thomas Becket to be archbishop, it was with the belief that he would always be sympathetic to royal interests. Henry was wrong. His former friend proved to be more loyal to God than to the crown. Now Henry's infuriated threats were so menacing that the archbishop had fled England, fearing for his life, and taken refuge at the Cistercian abbey of Pontigny, located in the southern part of Champagne.

Except for that one bit of gloomy news, the court was gay, and for once the old stone castle glittered with light and song and merriment. Even the king linked hands to dance with his wife in the *carole* ring after the great feast. Everyone was at peace with everyone else, and all seemed almost right with the world.

Troyes, May 1165

The count and countess were sharing a quiet supper alone in the great hall, when Henri leaned forward and said, "I think we should invite the archbishop of Canterbury to our court for a visit. He's an interesting man to know."

Marie nodded thoughtfully. "I agree. But I find your proposed hospitality rather surprising, considering that you have the same quarrels with prelates in your own lands as King Henry does with Becket."

"My concerns are totally different from theirs," he argued. "Besides, I'm in the right, whereas the king of England, as usual, is in the wrong."

"Your concerns are as much about the bounds of secular and ecclesiastical authority as his. I don't see much difference. You're just not as menacing," she teased.

"If you're talking about my disagreement with the pope, who wants my brother Guillaume to resign as provost at St. Étienne and St. Quiriace now that he's a bishop, it's ridiculous. Surely you can understand why I want to keep my brother close. We spent ten years apart while he was in England living with our uncle, the bishop of Winchester. We've just begun to know one another again," he said.

She laughed softly. "And besides, your brother always seems to agree with you on any issue," she said, her voice tinged with gentle mockery. "But is the pope really so wrong in thinking Guillaume should focus his attention on Chartres. Won't he be there most of the time?" she asked in a more serious tone. "How can he do his duties here?"

Henri ignored her questions. "He wants to appoint an English prelate to replace Guillaume. He's proposed Becket's friend, Herbert of Bosham. I don't think that would work very well, do you?"

"I suppose there could be disagreements."

"Anyhow," he said, "I think the pope has decided to accept the situation since I agreed to provide refuge for Becket. He doesn't want to lose my support for him and the Church, as I've informed him he would, if he presses the matter."

"What about your… conflicts with the bishops of Langres and Meaux?" She tried to keep her tone light, but they both knew the questions were weighty.

"They're complicated matters," Henri replied defensively. "And I'm taking care of them. The bishop of Langres has made unfounded accusations."

Marie wasn't so sure. Bishop Gautier de Langres had accused Henri of attacking and pillaging his lands and also of having received an oath of homage from one of Gautier's own liegemen. The bishop appealed to King Louis, who summoned Henri to a meeting at Gisors on April 11, hoping to settle things. Henri refused to go, making up an excuse about needing to consult his barons. Nothing had been resolved.

"As for the matter concerning Étienne de Meaux, I confessed I was wrong, and I've sworn on holy relics never to do it again. It was foolish and unnecessary, I know," Henri said.

The bishop of Meaux had accused Henri of counterfeiting his coinage and trying to undermine its value by copying it in base metals. Marie knew full well that the accusation was true. Her husband was trying to enhance the value of his own coins, the *deniers provinois*, which were already gaining wide acceptance as the currency of choice at most markets. Henri was embarrassed at having been found out, and Marie well remembered his public confession and his oath on holy relics that he would never do it again. His best friends, Anseau, Eudes de Pougy, and Hugh de Plancy, swore that he would abide by this agreement, thus ending the matter. Still, she saw little difference between his own determination to control affairs in Champagne and King Henry's to control affairs in England.

"Why make enemies of bishops and archbishops?" Marie asked.

"Because they sometimes overstep their powers. But I admit," he went on, "that was a foolish and hotheaded thing to do. I can assure you it won't happen again."

"You never did such things when Abbot Bernard was alive. He was always so sure you would be a peacemaker," she reminded him.

"Marie, I have admitted my mistake and made amends. Let's not discuss it any further."

Marie sensed that she had overstepped her bounds and that he was becoming irritated. She certainly didn't want to rile him, though it was her duty as a wife to worry about her husband's soul and moral behavior.

That summer nobles and clerics throughout France set aside any quarrels to rejoice at long last in the birth of a prince. On August 21, Queen Adèle had finally given the king his longed-for son. He was considered *Dieudonné*, the God-given, believed by many to be the result of Louis's fervent prayers for an heir "of the better sex." Louis named him Philippe for his grandfather—a king who had sat on the throne of France for almost fifty years.

Beside himself with joy, the king freed serfs and prisoners, and strewed donations to churches and monastic houses all over Paris, as the kingdom celebrated with pealing bells and songs of celebration. Count Henri's gifts for the child, one poet proclaimed, surpassed all others. Marie's father, who had occasionally derided Henri for his excessive generosity, now accepted it without complaint. At last, after three wives and four daughters, he finally had a son. Like everyone else in the kingdom, Marie expressed happiness for her father and Adèle at the birth of a son, but she felt a shadow in her heart that she couldn't quite explain.

CHAPTER 24

Troyes, July 29, 1166

Eleven months after the new prince was born and just as morning was beginning to lighten the sky over Troyes, Countess Marie gave birth to her own son. The child came quickly once she went into labor. When it was over and the scene was well prepared, Count Henri was invited to enter the birthing chamber and see his son for the first time. Only Hermesende was still there, keeping a watchful eye on the countess and the baby lying in his mother's arms. Count Henri was beaming.

"My dear," he said proudly. "Do you know what you have managed to accomplish?"

"I've had a baby. It wasn't unexpected, you know," she teased, feeling tired, but relieved that it was over.

"Not just a baby. A son. And a son born on a very special day in Troyes."

She could hear the bells of St. Étienne beginning to clamor the news.

"What day is that?" she asked.

"Today is the feast day of St. Loup, who was once bishop of Troyes. He saved the city from destruction at the hands of Attila the Hun," Henri told her. "The townspeople will be most impressed, I think. It's an auspicious beginning."

"I'm happy I was able to accommodate," she said. "He's a fine-looking boy, don't you think?"

"He's perfect," Henri said, inspecting the child from head to toe and assessing his blue eyes and his sparse, golden strands of hair. He smiled as the baby wound his tiny hand around his father's forefinger. "Little Henri," he murmured, touching the baby's cheek with his other hand.

"Little Henri," she echoes with a smile. "It's perfect. He looks like you," she said with a smile. "However will I tell you apart?"

He laughed. "We'll figure it out. You get some rest now, my dear. You deserve it. May God give you happy dreams." He touched the child's cheek one last time before Hermesende shooed him from the bedchamber.

The local folk made much of the coincidence of the child's birth on the saint's day, and eager to commemorate the connection, Count Henri commissioned for the Abbey of St.-Loup an *Evangéliaire*, a book containing the Gospel of John. To show that it honored the birth of their son, the gem-studded cover contained a silver engraving depicting the image of the child offering the book to St. Loup.

Marie was pleased that so soon after her reunion with her husband, she had accomplished what Countess Mathilde had told her was her primary duty as countess—to give him an heir. She knew that he was eager to assure his lineage, for he was now nearing the age of forty. *Adèle and I will be able to share this new experience of motherhood*, she thought. Everything seemed almost perfect, were it not for the disagreements that still lingered between Henri and some of the clergymen in Champagne.

Troyes, late November 1166

Ironically, Henri remained sympathetic to Thomas Becket, who had occasionally stopped in Troyes when he was living in Pontigny, but he had never come just for a pleasant visit. The archbishop had left Pontigny, when the English king threatened the entire Cistercian order for sheltering him there, and was now living at St. Colombe in Sens. Henri invited him and, at Marie's suggestion, his friend and former secretary, John of Salisbury, also living in exile in Reims, to come for a visit. She had always wanted to meet John, who was well known for his writings, and she knew that all three men shared a love of books. *They should get along well,* she thought. But she also had personal reasons for wanting to meet him.

To honor their guests, Marie organized a splendid feast to welcome them. At the high table, Henri was seated with the archbishop to his right, while Marie, to her husband's left, sat beside John of Salisbury. Musicians were playing a lively tune on their *vielles* and *gitterns*, as the guests waited for the squires to deliver the next dish to the table.

"We are so pleased to have both you and the archbishop living so nearby," Marie said, leaning toward John to speak above the music, "but I do regret for you the circumstances that bring you here from England."

John took a sip of the fine red wine and nodded, "As do I. You probably know, I earned the wrath of King Henry even before Archbishop Thomas did, but I fear Thomas is in much greater disfavor than I."

"I am concerned for you both. You are living in Reims, I hear," she observed.

"Yes, at St. Rémi with my old and very dear friend Pierre de Celle, who is abbot there. I'd spent time with him in 1148 while I was still in France during my studies and when he was abbot of Moutiers-la-Celle. Abbot Pierre was kind enough to offer me refuge once more," John told her.

"The abbot is a good friend of Count Henri as well. He visits us quite often," she told him. Then she added, "I hear that you once studied with Pierre Abelard."

"Yes, I was one of his fortunate pupils. I came to France in 1136, while he was still in Paris, but I studied with many other masters as well after his… unfortunate departure from Paris." Marie had heard of that "unfortunate departure." It happened after Abbess Héloïse's uncle, a canon at Notre-Dame named Fulbert, furious at Abelard's seduction of his niece, had had him castrated. She shuddered and thought it best to change the subject.

"You must come from a wealthy family to have been able to continue your studies in France for such a long time," Marie surmised, motioning to a squire to serve more wine to the guests.

"Actually, *ma dame*, I come from a family of quite limited means. We were not from the ruling class of Normans. I supported myself by tutoring young men from noble families in France."

"Then I suspect you have many admirers among the nobility," she said. "My husband is very fond of his old tutor, Master Étienne de Provins, who also studied with Abelard."

"One can only hope to be remembered fondly, my lady," he said. The musicians ended their tune and began another, this time adding the beat of a *tambour* to keep the time.

John was a small and unpretentious man with dark hair. He was at an age where his hairline was receding or, as he had joked earlier in the evening, all the learning he'd crammed into his head had caused his forehead to stretch a bit. Marie knew his reputation as a brilliant and witty man. Her husband avidly read his works, which contained some not very flattering observations about the nobility in such manuscripts as the *Policraticus*. To Henri they provided valuable lessons on how a prince should or should not behave.

"Please tell me all the news about my mother, Queen Eleanor," Marie asked John, knowing that he'd had first-hand observations of the English court.

"Well," he hesitated. "I have not been in England for some time now. I know only what I hear from others."

"Surely the archbishop is well familiar with recent events."

"Indeed he is, my lady, but I can only share with you the news he brought with him when he fled England and what I have heard from other English visitors since his arrival. Nothing from my own recent experience."

"I am eager to know everything."

"I suppose you've heard that Queen Eleanor gave birth in Anjou last October to another female child they call Joanna," he said.

"Yes, I am aware of her many children. And what of the king? I heard he didn't join her for Christmas. Why was that?"

John looked evasive. "He had been away for a while fighting the Welsh."

"But wasn't that all over by then?" Marie asked.

"True, my lady, but he apparently remained in England for the rest of the year."

"Has he seen the child?"

"Yes, I think so. Rumors say he spent Easter with Queen Eleanor in Angers and that there may be another child on the way," John said.

"Then is the gossip I have heard about some love affair of the king unfounded?" she asked hopefully.

John lowered his head and speared from his trencher a morsel of the roasted venison a squire had just set before him. He chewed thoughtfully and wiped his lips before he answered.

"I know little about the king's personal life, *ma dame*," he said quietly taking another swallow of wine.

"Surely you have heard the stories?"

"Yes, I've heard the gossip," he admitted.

"Do you think it's true?"

"Some say all kings have mistresses, my lady," John said, not looking into her eyes.

"And I say there is something you're not telling me, John. Please. I am her daughter. I have a right to know," Marie said anxiously. "Is there more?"

"Only rumors. I have no personal knowledge of the king's affairs."

"But you know more than you are saying," she said, watching him intently. "Tell me."

John brushed his thumb thoughtfully across his lips and took yet another sip of wine before he replied. "There are rumors, my lady, that the king is smitten with a young noblewoman called Rosamund Clifford. Her father is a Norman knight who guards the Welsh border. I know little else, except… people say it is more than a casual bedding of a mistress and that the king makes no secret of it. I'm told that he's brought her to live in the queen's chambers at Woodstock. But these are only rumors. I know nothing for a fact."

Marie nodded, keeping her face calm, her inner turmoil hidden. But she knew that her mother must be furious to be carrying the child of a man who made no secret that his devotion belonged to someone else. It must be humiliating for her. She thought of her own relationship with Count Henri. Although she was fairly certain that he still occasionally bedded other women, he no longer did so in such a blatant way as before. And none of them was ever the daughter or wife of another nobleman.

"Tell me about your life in Reims. Are you enjoying it there?" she said with a quick smile, steering the conversation in other directions now that she had confirmed her fears.

She wondered if Eleanor ever thought about the daughters she had left behind in France, now that she had so many other children. Certainly Marie had never forgotten her—her beautiful face and flowing hair, her exotic smell, and that final morning when she had knelt beside her in the nursery and gazed into her eyes to say goodbye. *Someday*, she thought, *someday I will see her again*. She was determined to make it happen.

When Thomas Becket and John of Salisbury returned to their places of refuge three days later, the halls seemed emptier after all the stimulating conversations.

"I really enjoyed their visit," Marie said thoughtfully to her husband the evening after their departure.

"I did as well," he said. "They probably won't come often, but we've promised to exchange books, and I will, of course, contact them with my questions."

Both Henri and Marie thrived on lively discourse and enjoyed conversing together on many topics. However, when he wished to debate philosophical and scriptural matters, he usually turned to his chaplain Nicholas of Montiéramey, prior of nearby St. Ayoul.

Marie rarely talked with Prior Nicholas. He was charming to be sure, always ready with a clever remark and a flattering phrase. He had once been in the service of Abbot Bernard, but he'd left Clairvaux under somewhat questionable circumstances, accused of theft and forging documents in the abbot's name. In spite of that, Henri had welcomed him to Troyes. He was well read and intelligent, and above all, a good conversationalist with a talent for flattery. Henri seemed to bask in being called a "princely philosopher" and a "philosopher prince," as the silver-tongued prior sometimes referred to him.

Marie, aware of the man's past, did not fully trust him, though she had to admit that he was an accomplished scribe and had copied many manuscripts for Henri, among them Josephus's *Antiquitates Judaicae* and the *Bellum Judaicum*, both of which contained important historical information about Jews, who were a significant portion of Troyes's population. Henri was interested in history in general and wanted to know more about the Jewish people—indeed, about almost everything, it seemed. Sometimes Marie found her husband so engrossed in his books that he would return to practical matters only grudgingly.

His preference ran to history, theology, and philosophy—while she preferred poetry and romance, including recent vernacular adaptations of classical works like the *Roman d'Énéas*, based on Virgil's *Aeneid*, and the more recent *Roman de Troie* by a writer named Benoît de Sainte-Maure. She was fascinated by Benoît's accounts of Paris's abduction of Helen and the love story of Troilus and Briseida.

"I think you come by your literary tastes quite naturally, my dear," Henri once suggested in a joking manner. "It's no doubt a heritage from that naughty great-grandfather of yours—the one who abducted his vassal's wife… what was her name—something bizarre?"

"*Dangereuse*," Marie said, blushing a bit. He was referring to her mother's grandfather, Guilhem de Poitou, the duke of Aquitaine, who had a rather flamboyant reputation as far as women were concerned and was known for his love poetry, composed in the *langue d'oc* of the south.

She recalled one afternoon when Henri entered the solar and saw his wife sitting beside one of the tall windows, engrossed in a manuscript.

"What are you reading, my dear?" he asked.

"A story about a knight named Tristan. I borrowed it from the scriptorium at Notre-Dame-aux-Nonnains, where it was being copied. It was written in the common language by a local poet named Chrétien. Have you heard of him?"

"No, and I can't imagine why you waste your time reading such trifles. Works not written in Latin will never survive. They're just frivolous entertainment."

"Perhaps you're right, Henri," she said, "but I enjoy them and find them quite delightful." She saw her husband's brow wrinkle in distaste. She had long known that their literary tastes were quite different. Henri preferred the writings of Boethius and Jerome to what he dismissively referred to as "fairy tales." Even when he commissioned retellings or condensations of classical works like the *Ylias*, based on Virgil's *Aeneid*, which Simon Aurea Capra, a canon of St. Victor in Paris, had composed for him before their wedding, he wanted them only in Latin.

I wish I were allowed to commission works to my own taste, Marie thought wistfully. But she knew that the count had no intention of making room in his library for such "trifles."

"Well," he said, his frown vanishing. "Even though you aren't a very discriminating reader, you *are* a wonderful hostess. The visit of Archbishop Becket and John of Salisbury was a delight. You had everything planned so marvelously." He leaned down and kissed her on the forehead. "I'm proud of you," he said with a grin.

Marie smiled at his words. She worked hard to entertain all their visitors, and she had become quite accomplished at doing so. Once she was past her adolescent awkwardness and self-consciousness, she began to observe how other women behaved and how people responded. Good manners, cleanliness, and a cheerful demeanor were, of course, essential, but there were other factors as well. Women who talked too much were not well received, she'd noticed, but those who listened to others with rapt attention seemed to garner favor on all sides. Such women also asked leading questions and focused their attention entirely on the person to whom they were talking. She'd watched others whose eyes darted about, even when they were in conversation, to see who else might be in the hall and whether there might be someone more interesting or more influential to talk with. That, she concluded, was a mistake. One's eyes should rest appreciatively on the person with whom one was conversing. *It isn't that difficult*, she thought, but it took practice to learn that kind of focus.

She had also learned the art of sincere praise, but never the excessive or insincere kind. She made an effort to find something good about everyone and call it to their attention—their looks, their manner of dress, their fine horse, their gentle words. There was always something, no matter how unappealing a person might be overall.

Whenever she entertained, she always took great pains to assure that the food and diversions at her court were equal to, if not more impressive than, those at the royal court. *Adèle need not worry so much about charm and hospitality*, Marie thought. *She will always be well regarded for her beauty and her status as queen*. But Marie wanted to be certain that her husband was never sorry or ashamed he had married her. As a result of her efforts, she was earning a reputation for incomparable hospitality and charm. She intended it to enhance her husband's reputation. *I want my mother to be proud of me as well*, she thought.

Only a few days later, Marie found Henri standing beside a window of their bedchamber, perusing a document in his hand.

"Now what are *you* reading?" she asked.

"A letter from John of Salisbury that a courier delivered this afternoon. It's a response to the list of questions about Biblical matters I sent him. Here," he handed it to her. "You should read it too. It may make you appreciate your husband more." He laughed.

Marie took the parchment page and read it painstakingly. It praised Henri as the finest son of Thibaut the Great, whom John had known well when he was a student near Troyes. Of all the count's sons, John wrote, "the eldest received gifts twice as great as the others. He … surpasses them, both by the extent of his wealth and by the splendor of his excellent virtues. Among these virtues two shine above all others: a remarkable generosity that everyone speaks well of and a humility that I have experienced myself amidst the anguish of my exile."

"How delightful," Marie said, handing back the letter after she had completed her reading. "Better not let your brothers read that," she said with a smile. *John too knows the art of flattery*, she thought, *and he has the fine language with which to weave it*. Although his letter gave the entire credit to Henri for the success of their visit, she was content. As long as their court was perceived as gracious and hospitable, she had succeeded in her goal.

CHAPTER 25

Troyes, December 1166

Marie stood in the doorway of the great hall, watching two maids on their knees, vigorously scrubbing the stone floor for the second time this week.

"Pay special attention to the wine stains," she cautioned them.

For two weeks the servants had been at work, scrubbing, preparing clean linens, gathering fresh straw for the floors and all the necessary supplies they would need for their guests at the Christmas court. When the time came, Marie intended to be ready.

Remembering her husband's praise, she felt more assured than ever in her role as countess. Now a grown woman past her twenty-first birthday, she had given her husband a son and learned to fulfill her courtly duties with confidence. She participated fully now in court proceedings. Henri had even included her recently as a witness to one of his charters. What's more, now that she had her own seal, she had granted her first charter in her own name. It had been witnessed, of course, by her husband, who gave his "permission, agreement, and praise." Still, it was *her* official act.

Now she was readying her household for Christmas with a greater sense of excitement than usual. Alix and Thibaut would both be in attendance, and Marie was determined to make it a great celebration to honor Henri's and Thibaut's joint efforts to settle a dispute between the abbey of Vézelay and their cousin Guillaume de Nevers. Instead of being caught up in another quarrel with the clergy, this time Henri had played the role of intermediary and peacemaker. She was proud of him.

Christmas was always a time of great merriment, but this year it would be special with the matter of Vézelay behind them. She knew Henri had a great fondness for the place where he had taken the cross. "The holy war itself didn't turn out to be so glorious," Henri had said more than once. "But that day at Vézelay was worth it—almost."

Marie listened, but made no comment. She did not think of the crusade with any fondness at all, for it had disrupted her life and driven her parents apart.

"I'm only glad you made it home safely," Marie said. "Let's just make this Christmas court a memorable one. Things are settled with Vézelay, and we have a son. It's much to be thankful for."

"And thankful I am," he said, putting an arm around her shoulder to give it a squeeze.

When Thibaut and Alix finally arrived for Christmas, Marie took her sister by the hand and led her to the nursery. "I want you to be the first to see my son," Marie told her. As they entered the small room, six-month-old Henri was just waking up from a nap.

"Oh, Marie, he's adorable," Alix exclaimed when she saw the child in his cradle.

"He's getting his first tooth," Marie said proudly.

"Where? I don't see it," Alix said.

Marie pulled back his lower lip and pointed to the tiny white tooth barely peeking through his lower gum.

"Isn't it beautiful?" his mother said. "Like a little pearl."

"I see it now. I'm sure it will be a most lovely tooth," Alix said in a jovial tone.

"You wait and see. You'll be just like me when you have your first baby." She picked up her son and snuggled him to her breast, loving the sweet, sleepy smell of his young skin.

"We'll soon find out," Alix said softly, placing both her hands on her belly.

"What? You're pregnant?" Marie asked.

"Only a few months," Alix said. "Thibaut is sure it will be a boy."

"Alix, that's wonderful. Our children can play together and be friends." Marie felt closer to her sister at that moment than she ever had.

As the Christmas season continued, the great hall of the palace filled with laughter and conversation, with everyone in a celebratory mood. The feasts were succulent, and the hall fragrant with the aroma of spiced meats and mulled wine. The castle's bakers had been working for days to prepare the sumptuous cakes, pies, and tarts that accompanied these repasts.

Marie had even sent for the poet Chrétien to come to court and recite some of his shorter works between the lively music and dances that entertained them all. She had not actually met him before, but she liked him at once. He was young and affable, about her age, she guessed, and he wore no beard. His warm brown eyes seemed to take in everything that went on. And his voice, as he performed some of his translations of Ovid's tales, was rich and mellow.

"A most talented fellow," she observed to Alix, who sat beside her on the dais. Marie's eyes sparkled as she listened to the rhythmic retelling of the ancient story of Philomena.

Henri listened only half-heartedly. She knew he only tolerated these light amusements of the court, preferring the more serious discussions he had with Nicholas de Montiéramey or John of Salisbury. But he was willing to indulge his wife's tastes at such celebrations, saving his own debates for another time. Certainly the visitors seemed to enjoy Marie's choice of entertainment, listening to Chrétien's stories with rapt attention and laughing loudly at the fool who amused them with his antics between the various performances throughout the feast.

The court festivities and the religious services to celebrate the birth of Christ ended all too soon, and the guests began to return to their own lands and households. The court grew quiet and empty again, but at least Marie had the rest of her son's first year to fill her days.

Then, in late January Henri informed Marie that he intended to make a trip to visit some of his various castles located strategically throughout Champagne.

"I want you to come with me," he told her.

"Why?" she asked, thinking of her young son.

"It's important for the people we rule to see us together from time to time," he said. "Besides, there are some court issues in Meaux and Provins that must be resolved before spring. You need to attend some of these courts and learn about the matters that come before them."

Marie enjoyed travel when it was for a very special reason, such as a wedding or a family visit, but the dead of winter was hardly her favorite time. And she knew it would not be possible to take her baby on such a trip this time of year. But Henri was insistent. Most of all, she hated leaving her little son behind, but he was far too young to be jostled about in a cold litter for days on end.

"Jeanne will care for him as though he were her own," Henri reminded her when he saw her hesitation.

She knew it was true. Little Henri's middle-aged nursemaid was the widow of a local wool merchant and had much experience with raising six children of her own, all now grown. Widow Jeanne's gentle manner reminded Marie somewhat of her own nursemaid, Claudine. Although her ample body was nothing like Claudine's slender frame and she was some years older, she had the same soothing tone of voice. Two of Jeanne's sons had taken over their father's wool trade, and she was no longer needed by her children. As a consequence, she'd been delighted to move into the palace nursery to care for little Henri. Her presence allowed his mother greater freedom to accompany her husband on such trips.

"And, besides, I want you by my side," Henri said. "You know when spring comes, I will likely be off fighting alongside your father." He knew well how to win her over.

"Yes, I know," she said sadly. All too often in the pleasant days of spring and summer, the fighting season, Henri was away fulfilling his vassal's duty of forty days of military service to his lord. She knew that then there would be many lonely hours to fill. Thank God, this time she would have her son to occupy her time.

"Of course, I'll go," Marie said. What choice did she have, after all?

The morning of their departure, she stood in the bailey and kissed her baby for the last time for several months, knowing that he would have changed a great deal by the time she returned. Handing him over to Jeanne and mounting her palfrey was even harder than leaving her father and sister behind after her betrothal. She could only imagine how painful it must have been for her mother to leave her two daughters, knowing that she might never see them again.

The trip itself was not unpleasant, except for the cold, rainy days and occasional snows, but they avoided such days for travel. Wherever they went, they were fêted, while leaving behind a trail of goodwill. Henri encouraged Marie to attend all his courts of judgment.

"One never knows when you might be called upon to decide such cases yourself," he told her. She listened and learned, but she doubted that any decisions she made as a woman would be treated with the same respect the people showed her husband.

Summer 1167

When summer came, as he had predicted, Henri was gone, serving the king in one of the endless border skirmishes where Louis's lands adjoined those of Henry Plantagenet. They seemed to fight constantly over territorial disputes and questions of homage.

"The king of England is also still furious with Louis, and probably with me, about the refuge we've provided to Thomas Becket. That's part of what it's all about," Henri told her as he departed.

Marie devoted these months largely to her son, delighting in his accomplishments as he took his first steps and began to repeat the sounds his mother made. Left in charge as she was, she found herself compelled to listen from time to time to petitions brought before the court, and she was glad for the experience of the winter trip. Even so, she made every effort to defer judgments until her husband returned.

When he finally came back in late summer, he brought what she thought at first was good news. He led her to the solar where they could be more comfortable before he told her what had happened. As they sat together, he took her hand.

"There's a truce," he told her, "from now until next Easter."

"Thank God," she said.

"But your father has called me into service again. He says he's tired of this constant fighting with Henry Plantagenet, and he wants me to help bring about a more lasting peace."

"And did you agree?" She rose, poured two goblets of wine, and handed one to her husband.

"I asked him if he was giving me a choice in the matter. I'd rather not be the one responsible, considering what happened after I tried to negotiate on his behalf with the emperor." He grinned wryly.

She too smiled, remembering all that had happened. "And his answer?"

"He said, 'Not really, my son.' But then he laughed and said 'No more feuds between us, I promise. But this time, don't make any promises without my signed consent.' What could I do but agree? Of course, it means I'll be away more often on diplomatic missions."

"Oh, no!" Marie sighed deeply, setting her goblet on a window ledge. She wanted another child, but since her husband seemed never to be at the court, it was not going to happen any time soon.

Seeing her dismay, he added, "But I did ask one concession—that someone else be involved to help."

"And did he concur?" she asked.

"He did and asked my advice about whom I would like."

"What did you say?"

"Well, I was tempted to ask for Thibaut, but I know Alix is pregnant now, almost ready to give birth, and that he would prefer to be at home. I suggested Philip of Flanders. He's a good man, and I think we would work well together."

"And did *Papa* approve?" she asked.

"He did. And Count Philip accepted."

"He's a good choice, I think. When do you set out?" she asked, dreading his answer.

"As soon as possible. It would be good to settle the matter before the bad weather begins and before the truce expires."

For a long time, Henri's efforts seemed pointless. King Henry was more interested in rebellious Welsh lords than in making peace with Louis. The summer ended without any agreement being reached. Then, news of unrest among Henry's vassals in Aquitaine opened an unexpected door. With fires burning on several borders of his kingdom, he finally decided to pay attention to the entreaties of Henri and Philip. After considerable negotiation, by the fall, they came to terms—terms Henri felt were almost too good to be true.

The king of England agreed to pay homage once again to the king of France and fulfill his feudal duties as the duke of Normandy. As for Anjou and Maine, which he also held from King Louis, he would cede them, in name at least, to his oldest living son, also named Henry, who would, in turn, do homage for them to the French monarch, promising to fulfill his feudal duties. The agreement also included a betrothal between Louis's fourth daughter, Alais, and Prince Richard, to whom his father would cede Aquitaine on the same conditions. The third son, Geoffrey, was to be heir to Brittany and likewise swear homage and fealty for it to the king of France. In addition, the treaty called for the release of all prisoners each king had captured from the other. It brought the requested homage, while all it asked of Louis was his daughter and the release of the prisoners.

"It's a virtual miracle," Henri said, raising his mug, as he shared a pitcher of ale with Philip of Flanders at a tavern where they stopped for the night, as they rode together back toward their own lands for a well-needed rest.

"Indeed. King Louis will surely be satisfied with the agreement," Count Philip said, lifting his mug to touch his companion's with a light tap.

"I just wish King Henry had signed it on the spot. It would have saved us another trip. I had hoped to have all this done before cold weather sets in," Henri grumbled.

"It's unfortunate, I agree. But we have to have Louis's agreement anyhow, and I can understand why he insisted on Louis's approval before he would sign, given what's happened in the past."

"Fortunately, we have plenty of time before the truce expires. Shall we plan to spend Christmas with our families before we arrange a rendezvous with Louis? As long as we meet with him before Easter and allow ourselves time to get back to the English king before the truce expires, we could avoid traveling in the worst of winter weather," Henri suggested.

"Agreed," said Philip.

King Louis, they learned, was celebrating Easter not at his own court, but in Soissons at the court of Yves II de Nesle, an old friend who had accompanied him on his crusade, and his wife, Yolande. Henri and Philip arranged to meet him there several weeks before Easter.

As a rule, Marie did not accompany her husband on diplomatic missions for the king. He did not invite her along, nor did she ask. However, this time she was determined to make an exception.

When they had settled in their chamber for the night, Henri, propped against the bed pillows, told his wife all that had happened.

"Will this meeting settle the matter and end the war?" Marie asked, leaning on her elbow.

"If your father agrees, and I think he will at least for the time being, for the treaty is definitely favorable to the French. But I will still have to go back to Normandy to have it ratified by the king of England."

"I thought he already knew the terms," she said.

"He does, but he didn't know whether Louis would agree and wouldn't sign it until he did."

"Will you go directly from Soissons to Normandy?" she asked.

"I will. By the time I get to Soissons, I'll already be halfway to the castle at Argentan, where Henry said he would be," he told her.

"Then I want to go with you," she said, suddenly sitting upright in bed.

"Why?"

"I've heard that my mother is there, and I want to see her again. This may be my only chance, and I don't want to miss it." She set her chin in determination.

"It's a foolish idea. I will take you as far as Soissons to see your father, but the rest of the trip will be long and hard, and the weather is still uncertain."

"You didn't mind the bad weather when I accompanied you last winter."

"That was different. We were staying along the way at our own castles. It's a foolish idea," he repeated, fluffing his pillow so that he could sit up at her level.

"Foolish or not, I am going with you to Argentan," she said firmly, "even if I have to follow behind on a mule."

"Don't be stubborn, Marie. You will slow us down." His tone of voice showed his annoyance.

"You will still arrive in plenty of time," she said calmly, folding her arms over her chemise.

"We sometimes stay in monasteries that don't permit women," he argued. He sat up on the edge of the bed with his feet on the floor, gazing about for the flagon of wine that was usually at their bedside.

"Then we shall seek shelter in convents, where men are allowed to stay," she responded in a firm tone.

"You were so reluctant last time to leave our son behind," he pointed out. "You definitely can't take him on this hard trip." He stood up and walked to a table across the room, where the flagon sat beside a goblet that still held the dregs of wine from earlier in the evening.

"You showed me that I could survive without him for a few months. At least I will not miss his first steps, because he's already walking now. He learned while you were away." She smiled, realizing that she was wearing him down. He frowned as he took a gulp of his newly poured wine.

Short of commanding her, which he was reluctant to do, he had nothing more to argue, but he was clearly not convinced. Having a woman along on such trips not only slowed them down, it would inevitably cause more trouble. During the crusade he'd seen what it was like traveling with women. They had needs men didn't have. They were temperamental. They wanted luxuries that were no part of such travel. They were unaccustomed to sleeping in freezing tents or strange castles. He pointed out all these problems, but she was adamant.

"But you will have to travel the entire distance on horseback instead of in a litter, which would make the trip even slower."

"Fine," she agreed. "I will see more that way."

When they reached the court of Yves de Nesle in Soissons, Count Philip and the king had already arrived. Philip was there with his wife, who was Marie's cousin Elisabeth, the daughter of her aunt Aelith. The two women had once been playmates at the royal court, though they had not seen one another since they were children. Philip and Elisabeth had married the same year as Henri and Marie.

"It is such a joy to see you again, Elisabeth," Marie said, embracing her warmly.

"For me as well," Elisabeth said. "I believe you already know my husband, Count Philip."

For the first time, Marie took real notice of Count Philip. She had never paid him much attention before when they had been in large groups at such places as her father's wedding to Adèle. Now that she assumed they would be traveling together, she took the time to observe him more closely. He was much younger than Henri and, she had to admit, more handsome. In the style of the day's younger men, he wore no beard, and his sun-bleached hair and stunning blue eyes gave him a boyish look. Unlike Philip, her husband and father wore the beards of their generation, making them look, Marie thought, even older than they were. Philip's glorious reputation for his many victories at the tourneys here and there also added to the luster of his presence.

Henri, on the other hand, had taken relatively little interest in jousting since his youth and the time, long ago, when he and the king's brother Robert had been chastised by Abbot Bernard for organizing a tournament following the crusade. Now he considered such events no more than dangerous courtly games that could destroy valuable resources like horses and lances and sometimes even the knights themselves. But to younger men and women, they still seemed quite festive and exciting. Marie had attended only one or two tourneys after she left the convent and in the early days of her marriage. Henri had tired of them, preferring to spend his time with his books and in his conversations with Nicholas. Marie thought Elisabeth quite lucky to be married to such a gallant and handsome man.

The three young women, Marie, Elisabeth, and Adèle, all so nearly the same age, found pleasure in one another's company, as their older hostess, Yolande, bustled about the castle making sure that all went well. When Marie and Adèle exchanged stories of their two young sons, Marie noticed that Elisabeth remained silent.

"Do you have children?" Marie asked gently.

"Philip and I have not been so lucky. We're still childless," Elisabeth answered, sadness in her voice.

"Oh, my dear, you are still very young. There's plenty of time," Marie said, aware that Elisabeth was only a bit older than herself. "And it's such a joy to look forward to."

"I hope so," Elisabeth answered with a smile. "I hope so."

As Henri had predicted, King Louis was pleased with the agreement and signed it at once. But when the discussion of returning to Argentan for King Henry's ratification, Philip turned to Henri, reluctance in his voice.

"Must we both go?" he asked. "I have urgent business back in Flanders. And now that the matter is settled, I see no need for my presence."

"I suppose not, though I had hoped we'd see this through together." His annoyance showed in his voice, but it did not change Philip's mind.

Thus, before Easter, Henri, Marie, and their usual travel companions set out in a fine early-morning mist for Argentan to find King Henry and Queen Eleanor. Marie was both eager and a bit fearful about seeing her mother again. *Has she changed? Does she still have golden hair and the most beautiful face on earth?* Marie wondered, for Eleanor was now forty-five at least. *How surprised she will be to see me again*, she thought. She could only hope Eleanor would be as happy to see her as she would be to see her mother.

Travel was harder than Marie expected, for the spring rains had set in early. They had been only two days on the road, spending nights in castles along the way rather than pitching tents, which would have made the trip even harder. Although she was not fully prepared for the chill, damp weather and shivered a bit in her light wool cape, she refused to complain. Instead, as the horses, muddy from puddles left by last night's rain, plodded along the road toward Pontoise, she rode beside her knight, Nevelon, planning what she might say to her mother when they met.

Suddenly, she heard the approaching hoofbeats of galloping horses. She raised herself in her saddle to see who was coming. A group of Norman knights was riding toward them. Henri's hand, she noticed, was resting on the hilt of his sword as he awaited their approach.

"Are you the count of Champagne?" the man clearly in charge of the detail called as soon as they were in hearing distance.

"I am, as you can see by my standard," he said, pointing to the small azure banner with silver bend cotised with gold held aloft by one of his knights.

"Yes, my lord. I just wanted to be sure. We bring news from the king of England." His horse pawed impatiently at the ground.

"What news?"

"The king has left Argentan and is escorting his wife to Aquitaine," he said, trying to control his mount.

"But why? He knew I was coming and that we had an important matter to attend to," Henri said.

"I'm sorry, my lord, but he thought this was more important."

"And when will he return?"

"I don't know, my lord. But he wanted you to know before you had come all that way," said the knight in charge, his voice growing impatient.

"Thank you. You've done your duty," Henri said. He was clearly annoyed, as he turned his horse back toward the rest of the riders.

Marie knew what he was coming to tell them, for she too had heard the knight's clear voice. Now he would inform her that she would not see her mother again after all—not this time and perhaps never. Tears of disappointment welled in her eyes.

With no peace agreement ratified, the truce ended at Easter, and border skirmishes between the two kings broke out again and continued throughout the summer. Only a few months after the fighting season ended, Marie realized, to her joy, that she was pregnant again. However, it did not keep her from attending on December 22 the consecration of her brother-in-law Guillaume as archbishop of Sens. Her husband was delighted, believing that his intervention in the earlier election at Chartres had helped to smooth the path of his brother's career and prepare his rise in the Church. Being archbishop of Sens was far more important than being bishop of Chartres. The cathedral there, St.-Étienne-de-Sens, was one of the first built in the new style with soaring vaults and pointed arched windows that allowed the light to pour in. It was even larger than St. Denis. And its construction, begun before 1140, would continue under Bishop Guillaume.

Henri was proud of his youngest brother. "Perhaps he will be a cardinal one day."

"Or even pope," Marie added. There had been few French popes. Most were Italian. Certainly, Guillaume's splendid consecration, with its magnificent processional, the fine liturgical garments, gold and jewel-studded crosses, and mellifluous chants that echoed throughout the service, seemed to her worthy of that of a pope.

After the ceremony, Henri and Marie stayed at the king's court in Sens to celebrate Christmas with the rest of their family. Shortly after the festivities ended, Henri and Louis, with a large retinue of attendants, rode out to make their way together to Montmirail, where an Epiphany meeting had been arranged to fulfill the treaty terms, which had finally been agreed upon between the two kings.

Marie, who felt queasy most mornings, stayed behind with Adèle. Their little boys, walking and trying to talk, though Philippe was almost a year older, amused them. The women spent most of the time in the solar, chatting and doing needlework, but their brief times with their babies were the highlight of their days together.

"Aren't they fun?" Adèle said.

"It's like rediscovering the world. I can't imagine loving another baby as much as I love Henri."

"But you will, I'll bet," said Adèle. "You're so lucky to be pregnant again. Louis worries himself sick every time Philippe has a cold or cough. If we had a second son, he might relax a bit."

"You shouldn't worry. Philippe is a healthy child," Marie said.

"I know. It's just that life is so uncertain," Adèle said sadly.

When the men returned from Montmirail, both the king and the count were in a jolly mood.

"It went well," said Louis, as he described the king of England kneeling before him, bare-headed, and without a sword. "It all happened just as it should. He placed his hands in mine and swore the oath to become my true and faithful man in all that regards Normandy. I leaned forward and gave him the kiss of peace. I swear I could smell the ale on his breath."

Everyone laughed.

"It was indeed quite a show King Henry put on there," Henri said. "All his sons looked splendid and healthy, wearing bright-colored garments and the finest fur-lined capes. He wanted to impress all of us, that was certain. And the young men played their roles quite well."

"What of Alais?" Queen Adèle asked about her step-daughter, who was promised to King Henry's oldest son.

"She too played her role well and went with the king and his entourage without complaint. They had, of course, brought ladies to attend her."

"Thank God for that," Adèle breathed. Both the women had worried over the nine-year-old girl who was to be betrothed to Prince Richard. But before their departure, Alais had seemed to feel herself lucky to be promised to a boy only a few years older than herself and said to be comely, a boy second in line to be king of England.

"And what of the archbishop of Canterbury? Was he reconciled with the king?" Marie asked.

"More or less," Henri replied, "though if I had to guess, I would predict that there is more trouble ahead between them."

When they were finally alone, Marie asked her husband, "What are they like—my brothers?"

"Well, young Henry is obviously everyone's favorite. He's a handsome lad, blond and blue-eyed like his mother, though rather arrogant. About fourteen, I'd say, and extremely sure of himself. Richard, who's a couple of years younger, is already as tall as his older brother. He has darker reddish hair and intense eyes. I had the impression that, even at twelve, he had a more serious temperament than Henry."

Marie listened avidly to every detail. "And Geoffrey?" she asked.

"He's only a year or so younger than Richard but he seems much less certain of himself. He lacks the height of his brothers, and I'd say he's even short for his age. He reminded me in some ways of my own brother Étienne. I think he knows that he's the least doted on of the Plantagenet boys, and he seems a little combative sometimes."

"What about the youngest one—John?" she asked.

"He wasn't there at all. He's still only a baby. I assume Henry left him at court."

"Perhaps he's with his mother."

"No, they say she didn't take him with her to Poitiers for some reason."

"That's strange," she said.

"Maybe it's because he was born right after she found out about Rosamund Clifford," Henri speculated.

"Still, he's her son. I can't imagine not wanting to raise one's own child—at least during his boyhood. He's only five or six months older than our little Henri."

So much about her mother's life, and her brothers, remained a mystery to her—one she longed, more than anything, to untangle and understand.

CHAPTER 26

Troyes, June 1169

This birth was more difficult than Henri's, and after sixteen hours of labor, Marie, exhausted and wet with perspiration, had prayed to every saint whose name she could remember. But the baby had still not come.

"Perhaps it's twins," said one of the ladies as she hovered over Marie, wiping her damp forehead. "Maybe that's why it is so difficult."

"Pray to St. Scholastica," said Hermesende, who sat behind her, holding Marie steady on the birthing stool. "She's the twin sister of Saint Benedict. Maybe that will help."

Marie gritted her teeth and began to pray fervently—anything for this to be over. Then, as she pushed with all her might once more, feeling as though her body were being torn apart, suddenly the top of the baby's head began to emerge. "It's coming," the midwife said with excitement.

The excruciating pain intensified beyond imagining until Marie thought she would faint. Then, suddenly, the baby slid into the midwife's waiting hands.

"It's a girl," she said. "A beautiful little girl!"

Marie looked at the child that had emerged from her womb and was still attached to her body by its umbilical cord. She was hardly beautiful at the moment. Her head was a bit pointed, and her skin was covered with a white, greasy substance. Her eyes were pinched shut and her face wrinkled as she screamed in outrage at her birth trauma. The women were laughing with relief. The midwife handed the baby to one of the attendants as she cut the cord and waited for the afterbirth.

Once it was finally all over and Marie realized she wasn't going to die in childbirth after all—at least not this time—she too relaxed and smiled wearily. The ladies cleaned the child and swaddled her in the waiting bands of white cloth before handing her to her mother.

"She looks much better now," Marie said with a laugh.

"I think she resembles you, my lady," the midwife said. The only resemblance Marie could see was her few strands of damp, brownish hair.

"Perhaps you should let my husband know that he has a daughter. I'm sure he'll be disappointed it's not another son."

But if he was disappointed, he didn't show it. When he was finally allowed into the room, he grinned with pride, as he let the baby hold his index finger. "What shall we name her?" he asked.

"Scholastique," Marie said without hesitation. "It was St. Scholastica who finally brought her into the world. We'll consider it a tribute to the nuns at Avenay." Her voice was growing weary, as she vaguely recalled her days at the Benedictine convent.

"Then Scholastique it will be," he said.

A boy he would insist on naming himself, but a girl? That a mother could decide, Marie thought.

A little girl, Marie discovered in the months to come, was quite different from a little boy. While young Henri, at two, was already prancing around the nursery on his stick horse, Scholastique watched him with fascination, but there was a delicacy about her that had never been characteristic of Henri. He was aggressive and demanding from birth, it seemed, while his little sister was calm and observant. *Perhaps it's the difference in their ages*, Marie thought. But she could never remember Henri so silently watching what was going on about him. He was always reaching out and wanting to be part of the action. When his father set the child before him in the saddle, the little boy chortled with delight, already eager to be a horseman himself.

Before she was a year old, little Scholastique was cuddling a rag doll she would not sleep without, while Henri preferred his wooden soldiers. He had virtually taken command of the nursery, now that he knew enough words to order everyone about. Jeanne indulged him for the most part, encouraging him to act like a little count, and his father found it all very amusing. Marie tolerated it as long as he was kind to his sister.

Their family life was lively, with frequent trips to Provins, Meaux, and Lagny, where Henri delighted in showing off his young family. Marie too was enjoying her children—both of them, but little Henri was still her favorite.

Only one shadow loomed over the entire court. Once again Count Henri had found reason to quarrel with prelates and the church hierarchy. *Will these disagreements never cease?* Marie thought. *Will Henri never stop putting his soul at risk?*

The new controversy had begun with the death of the count's uncle, Henry of Carinthia, bishop of Troyes, on January 30, 1169, bringing to an end more than two decades of tranquil coexistence between the bishop and the counts of Champagne. Henri was worried about who might take his place and confided his concerns to his brother, the bishop of Sens.

"Matters were so easily decided between Uncle Henry and me. It will be different with another bishop in Troyes, I fear," he said.

"Not necessarily. It depends on the bishop. Have you considered Mathieu Burda of Provins? You know him and his family well, and his brother Gautier is your marshal."

"What an excellent idea. I had not thought of him, but you're right. I know him well. He's currently the dean of secular canons at St. Quiriace in Provins. We meet frequently when I'm there, and we seem to get along well enough."

"Then, if you approve, I'll recommend him to the pope and you should indicate your consent," Guillaume said.

"A recommendation from you is tantamount to an appointment, I'd wager," said Henri. And so it was done.

With the consecration of the new bishop, however, an issue arose that had not been questioned as long as Henri's uncle served in the role—authority over the church of St. Étienne.

When Henri had built the church and attached it to his castle, he had done so of his own volition and without the command or support of the pope or the bishop of Troyes. He assumed as a consequence that, since he considered it his palace chapel, he had complete authority over it. It was he who selected the canons and chaplains. His uncle, Bishop Henry, had never meddled in his affairs. Bishop Mathieu, however, assuming he would have the usual episcopal authority over it, included it in a clause of his appointment.

Henri was furious. "Why have you done this?" he asked the new bishop. "It has never been this way, and now you have called it to the special attention of the pope."

"I assumed it was the way things were always done. No one told me otherwise," Mathieu replied in his own defense.

"You should have asked," Henri said emphatically. "St. Étienne is my palace chapel. I built it and paid for it, and it is I who have authority over it." Henri was well aware that the so-called chapel was grander and more magnificent than the older cathedral in Troyes. He had endowed it generously and given all that he could to embellish it.

"I intended no harm, my lord," said the new bishop.

"I know, but the pope is now trying to assert his powers over *my* church. I can only protest."

"If you do so and the pope agrees, I will not oppose you," Mathieu promised. His voice held no hint of guile.

With that assurance, Henri sent an appeal to Pope Alexander that included a threat to withdraw his support from both the pope and the Church, if ecclesiastical authority were imposed on his chapel. Under such pressure from the count, Alexander granted the church a seven-year exemption from clerical oversight. But that would not end the matter.

It was almost a year later when Henri stamped into the solar, red-faced and angry, a parchment letter in his hand. Marie could see that it bore the seal of the pope.

"What's wrong, Henri," Marie asked, after she had handed Scholastique to Widow Jeanne and sent her with the children back to the nursery.

"That cursed Alexander has rescinded his exemption of ecclesiastical authority for my church."

"But why?"

"It was that son of a whore—Thomas Becket—who persuaded him. After all we did for him—offering him refuge and hospitality, even friendship, when he was on the run—he has dared to act against me."

"What has he done?" she asked.

"He persuaded the pope not to allow the exemption he previously promised. I begin to understand King Henry's complaints about him. How dare he butt in where he has no authority—and in Champagne, of all places? What business is it of his?"

Marie tried to calm him, but he fumed for days, until Bishop Mathieu, who hated confrontations, finally found the courage to seek him out at the palace. She was surprised when Henri led him to the solar, where he knew she waited and where they rarely admitted anyone outside the family household. *It's probably best for this meeting to take place in private*, she thought, for she was not sure her husband would be able to hold his temper in check.

"May I speak openly in the countess's presence?" the bishop asked.

"Of course," Henri replied brusquely. "She is privy to my business, since I never know when she will be required to settle a case in my absence."

Marie looked at him, surprised by his comment, for although she sometimes heard cases in his absence, he had never encouraged her to settle them before his return. How many times had he reminded her that she was only a woman, after all? Was he changing his views? She doubted it, but one could always hope.

"Count Henri," the new bishop began, nodding to the countess as well, "we have long been friends and I trust you to do what is right for your church. I can assure you that I will not interfere in your affairs, but rather approve whatever you recommend to me. I shall have plenty to occupy my time with all the other churches in my diocese. But for now, I think it best that we leave it nominally at least in the hands of the pope. Any future matters we can settle between ourselves."

"I worry less about you, Mathieu, than about any future bishop that might be appointed," Henri said. "My anger is not with you."

"I am a fairly young man and have no taste for war. I am likely to live as long as you," the bishop answered. "Perhaps even longer."

"Then my son will have to fight the battle all over again," Henri replied curtly.

"Perhaps your son will not mind so much as you. The church is, after all, *your* gift to God—not his."

Before he could answer, Marie interceded. "I think he's right, Henri. Why stir up more trouble unnecessarily? Why not just let the matter rest?"

He started to protest, for he liked things settled in law, but Marie said, "Why don't you consider it for a day or two before you decide?" She wanted an opportunity to talk to Henri alone. She had begun to learn on her own that there were indeed ways to persuade men, but they needed to be used in private.

"That seems reasonable. Shall we meet again two days hence?" Henri asked. The bishop nodded with relief.

"Thank you, my lord," he said, nodding again to the countess as he departed.

When he was gone, Marie turned to her husband again. "I like the new bishop," she said softly. "And I suspect he is as trustworthy as his brother Gautier."

"That remains to be seen."

She poured him a goblet of wine and led him toward a pair of armchairs near the fireplace. He sat down, and she began to rub the back of his neck and between his shoulder blades, which always made him feel better in stressful situations or after a long ride.

"Why not trust him until he proves false? Then, if need be, you can take action," she said, her voice soothing. "I doubt that Bishop Mathieu will make any effort to impose his will on the church of St. Étienne, knowing now how much it means to you."

He leaned back and closed his eyes. "That feels good," he said, his voice softer than before.

"Even though he has nominal authority, he seems diplomatic enough not to impose it."

"Hmmm," he murmured with contentment, as she leaned over to whisper in his ear.

"And if he does, you can always take action then," she reminded him softly. "Why add to your worries?"

"I suppose so," he murmured, reaching out for her hand and pulling her onto his lap to kiss her. "You're probably right."

Provins, late June 1170

In the summer months, when he was not at war on behalf of the king, Count Henri traveled about his territories, spending weeks at Meaux and Provins, and taking Marie and the children with him when the weather was good. They were all in the city of Provins for the May Fair, which had recently ended. Henri was quite pleased with the revenues it had brought in.

He had just returned from the counting house to the solar, after a lengthy meeting with his treasurer, when a messenger arrived from the royal court. Henri went out to the courtyard, to greet a freckled-faced squire in his late teens. His flaxen hair hung to his shoulders, as he waited patiently, still holding the reins of his chestnut palfrey.

"You bring news from the king?" the count asked, leading the young man up the stone staircase after he had called a groom to see to the squire's steed.

"The king thought you would want to know that Henry of England has just crowned his oldest son king. King Louis thinks it's the first time it's ever been done in England during the lifetime of a living king."

"Perhaps he didn't want his son to have to fight for the throne the way he did. This way he can be sure of the succession. But I wonder if the Young King's father will grant him the power to go with the title. Do you know who crowned him, since the archbishop of Canterbury is still in France?" Henri asked.

"The archbishop of York, my lord. The prince was crowned at Westminster."

"That will not sit well with Thomas Becket, I fear. It has always been the archbishop of Canterbury who crowns the king of England." They were in the great hall now, and Henri bade the young man to sit beside him in one of the carved, oak armchairs that lined the wall.

"Perhaps not, my lord, but it is well to remember that the sister of your wife is now queen of England," the messenger said with a boyish grin that seemed incongruous with his effort to speak with a tone of authority.

"Was she crowned as well?"

The young man frowned, thinking before he spoke. "I think not, my lord. Not officially."

"I suspect King Louis is not happy about that. Will he protest?" Henri asked.

"The king has told me nothing of his intentions, my lord."

Henri liked the boy and his sincere manner. "You must join us for the evening meal and spend the night here before you return to Paris," he offered. "The countess will be eager to hear the news from her father."

"I am grateful, sir." Henri could tell the boy was delighted. It was not often a squire was invited to dine with a count. Usually, the closest he got during the meal was to serve at the high table.

Henri signaled to his chamberlain to find the young man a place to sleep for the night.

When Henri told Marie about the coronation of the Young King, she laughed. "Now," she said, "my half-brother is king of England and my half-sister, sweet Marguerite, is his queen. Did I ever tell you that King Henry's father once tried to betroth me to his son?"

"Oh, a few times," Henri replied with a laugh. "A good thing he didn't, or you might have borne him eight children by now, as your mother has."

She laughed as well. "God forbid! I'm only twenty-five. That would have been a feat."

"But not impossible," he teased. "I hope you're not sorry that betrothal didn't work out," he said, furrowing his eyebrows in a semi-serious expression.

"Certainly not. I wouldn't want to be put through the humiliation my mother has faced with that whore of his."

Henri said nothing, but he wondered if she knew about the women he himself occasionally took to bed. Of course, his little encounters were by no means serious like the English king's attachment to Rosamund Clifford, who by now had become the widespread topic of songs and stories, with Queen Eleanor cast in the role of a jealous spouse. It must indeed be humiliating for her.

His mind turned briefly to Anne Musnier. He had rewarded her well for her services over the years, and it was convenient to have such a mistress when his wife was too pregnant to meet his needs or had her monthly bleeding. Anne was not the only one, of course. There were others in Troyes and Meaux, but Anne always made herself available whenever he was in Provins and whenever he sent for her. And she had told him she provided no such service to anyone else, except her husband, of course. *She's still a comely wench*, he thought, *despite her more than thirty years.*

Troyes, Early August 1170

Before Assumption Day Marie knew that she was pregnant yet again. It was not a happy thought as she recalled the difficulty she'd had with the birth of Scholastique. She knew it was a good thing to bear children for her husband—the Church said so. But every childbirth risked death for the mother, and there was always a conflict within her at the thought of another pregnancy. Henri was delighted of course.

"When is the baby due?" he asked.

"Sometime in mid-winter, I think," she said, without excitement.

"Surely it will be a boy this time," he said with a grin.

Troyes, mid-January 1171

Not long after the new year, the same freckled squire of the king appeared once more. Acelin was his name, as Henri had learned during his previous trip. He had clearly ridden hard. His horse was lathered, his boots and *chausses* mud-spattered, and his nose red from the cold. The news he brought would spread like wildfire across Europe.

"Thomas Becket has been murdered," he told the count the moment he dismounted.

"Are you sure?" Henri asked. "He just returned to England in late

November."

"Yes, my lord. I'm sure."

"When did it happen? And how?"

"On December 29 at Canterbury Cathedral. They say he was killed in front of the altar."

"In the church itself? *Mordieu*! Who would do such a deed?"

"There were four knights from King Henry's court," Hervé said. "I forget their names, but they claimed they were doing it for the king. He denies it, of course. At least he denies sending them."

While Acelin warmed himself by the fire in the great hall, Henri made his way to the solar to relay the news to Marie.

"Why did he even go back to England?" she asked.

"I think it was because of the coronation of the Young King by the archbishop of York. It stung his pride and offended his sense of justice. He went back and excommunicated the bishop of York for doing the king's bidding. No doubt, that infuriated King Henry."

"Henry Plantagenet really is a terrible man, isn't he? I can see why my mother spends as much time away from him as possible."

"He has his problems now. There's no question about it, and he well deserves them. His sons, I hear, are all growing increasingly restless, bearing their titles without any power. They're bound to be frustrated lads. And Louis is taking full advantage of that to stir a troubled pot."

"What do you mean?" Marie asked.

"He welcomes the Young King to his court as often as possible, and they say he encourages him in his displeasure with his father's dominance. Louis seems delighted to have his son-in-law at odds with his father."

"I'm sure Marguerite must be pleased to see her father and her husband on the same side for once," Marie said.

"But I fear it will lead to warfare sooner rather than later. And your father will call me into service if there's another war against the English king, one on behalf of his son-in-law."

Henri was not as outraged by the murder of Thomas Becket as he might have been earlier. He no longer felt great affection for the man who had sided against him concerning the question of jurisdiction over the church of St.-Étienne-de-Troyes.

However, Henri's brother Guillaume, archbishop of Sens, was so moved by the act that he began the process of seeking canonization for the slain archbishop. Guillaume had been a far greater friend to Thomas than Henri had. He had known him better, serving as his advisor on many occasions and sometimes as his intermediary with the kings of both France and England. Most people believed that Becket was murdered at King Henry's behest, which created greater sympathy for his sons and, in some, even an eagerness to see them wrest power from their sinful father. And rumor had it that Queen Eleanor encouraged them in such desires.

Even in the taverns of Troyes, the townspeople gossiped about Becket's murder and expressed their disdain for the English king.

"I'd like to see the bastard kicked off his throne for good," the town's bailiff announced loudly.

"I'd rather see those stripling sons of his rule in his stead," the blacksmith answered, raising his flagon of ale to the bailiff.

"He's damned himself, if you ask me. He'll be excommunicated for sure," echoed the wool merchant, Widow Jeanne's oldest son.

"I hear the mother of those boys, the old queen, favors the sons over the father," a barmaid said, as she meandered through the crowd to serve three mugs of ale to a nearby table.

"Can't say I blame her, what with that whore he keeps. If he were my husband, I'd cut it off," the bailiff's wife said, giving her husband a meaningful look and kicking him under the table when he pinched the bottom of the barmaid as she passed by. The entire tavern roared with laughter.

CHAPTER 27

Troyes, February 1171

Marie gave birth to a second daughter in late winter. This was an easier birth. The baby was smaller than her sister had been, and she appeared delicate, but determined. *She looks like my mother*, Marie thought, remembering Queen Eleanor's straight nose, wide-spaced eyes, and delicate bones. She could no longer recall the color of her eyes, only how they'd gazed at her with such intensity, as though they could see inside her and the rest of the world did not exist. And she remembered the full but well-defined lips that could turn up in an easy smile or show displeasure when they were pressed together. Sometimes they had shown no expression at all. Marie wished she could control her facial reactions as her mother did.

Her first thought was to name the child for her mother, but she knew that it would make her father furious, and there was no real need to stir up his rancor again, particularly at a time when he was making a point to befriend the Young King of England. Thus, she decided to name the child Marie for herself, without consulting her husband. She knew he would not care one way or the other. They would call her Mariette.

I wish Maman could see my new baby, who looks so much like she must have looked as an infant. If only that were possible, she thought.

Queen Adèle would also bear her second child in the spring—a little girl named Agnès—*a playmate for Mariette*, Marie was delighted.

At the end of May, as petitioners gathered at the count's tribunal, Henri asked his wife, now well recovered from childbirth, to join him in the courtroom. Having seen the docket, he knew that there were Jewish petitioners today, and he thought she needed to know more about that population in their city in order to better judge their cases should the need arrive during his absences. Having read so much of their history, he had come to have genuine respect for the Jews of Troyes.

When he and Marie entered the tribunal, it was easy to recognize the Jewish petitioners. They stood clumped together in a tight group, separate from the other supplicants, all dressed in fine dark robes, some torn in what Henri recognized as a ritual gesture of grief. Their spokesman was a man he knew well, a rabbi named Jacob Tam and a grandson of Solomon ben Isaac, an eminent rabbi and Talmudic scholar known as Rashi, who had lived in Troyes many years ago. He'd created a *yeshiva*, a highly respected school that taught the Torah and Talmud, and his teachings were widely known in the European Jewish community. He'd died before Henri was born, but he knew his reputation—and his grandson.

Rabbi Jacob was very old—too old, he suggested to the count, to undertake this leadership for his people. "But," he said, "the Jews of the community were insistent, for my family has been here for generations, and we are known to the count."

Henri nodded, acknowledging his statement. It was unusual for the Jews to come before his court. Most often they settled any disputes among themselves, unless it involved someone outside their community. Unsure why they were in court today, the count received them cordially and introduced the countess, knowing it must involve a matter of great importance.

"My lord," Jacob began, his voice quavering with age. "We have come to report a terrible incident that has occurred in your brother's land of Blois and which threatens our community as well."

Henri knew that there were many Jewish citizens in Troyes and that they contributed a great deal to the economy and the vitality of the city. Rashi's family had been vintners, producing some of the finest wines in the area. Other Jews served as money-changers, lenders, and artisans, and their presence was highly valued at the fairs of Troyes. Although they tended to live in predominantly Jewish quarters, they were active in commercial life throughout the city. It was in the count's best economic interest to make them feel safe.

"What has happened there, Rabbi? Does it involve my brother?"

"I fear so, my lord, and many Jews are fleeing his lands."

"Pray tell, what has occurred?"

"I hate to report the incident, my lord, but it concerns us all." He paused for a moment as though trying to gather his strength to go on. "More than thirty innocent Jews have been burned at the stake in the city of Blois." Marie gasped.

"Good heavens, how could such a thing have happened?" Henri asked, glancing at his wife, whose face had grown pale.

"There are many Christians, as you know, who hate the Jews," the rabbi said. "Many more in Blois than here—even the Countess Alix, I fear." Marie's eyes grew wide with disbelief.

"That surprises me, for I have never heard her express such views," Henri answered,

"Nor have I," said Marie, "and she is my sister."

"I beg your pardon, my lady. I had forgotten she was your sister," Jacob said.

"May I question this man, my lord?" she asked Henri. He nodded.

She turned to face the rabbi. "What evidence do you have against my sister?" she asked. "And why would she be in any way responsible for such an atrocity?"

"We do not believe she is responsible, *ma dame*. But we think her jealousy may have contributed to the incident."

"Jealousy? Of what?" Marie asked.

"Of Lord Thibaut's mistress, my lady. There is a Jewish woman named Pulcelina, who, through no fault of her own, has been summoned many times to the court in Blois for the count's pleasure. As you know, she did not have the liberty to refuse. We fear that Lady Alix may hold her accountable and, because of her, hate all Jews." Marie thought of Henri's own mistresses, and she understood why her sister may have felt resentful. But toward a whole people? It made no sense.

"Was it she who ordered the burning?"

"No, my lady, but we think she may have encouraged it, for Pulcelina was one of those who met death in the conflagration."

"What caused the burning, if it wasn't her order? Surely Thibaut wouldn't want a woman he favored to be burned alive," Henri said, not meeting the eyes of his wife, who was listening intently to his words.

"A rumor was circulating in Blois that Jews in that city had drowned a Christian child in the Loire. It was not so, my lord. What happened, or so we've heard, is that a Jewish man was watering his horse on the riverbank, when a stable hand brought his master's horse to the river for a drink. It was a dark evening, and when they came upon the Jewish man unexpectedly, the servant's horse startled, broke free, and ran away. The servant was very angry, and it is he who is said to have started the rumor," Jacob said. He tottered a bit and reached out for the arm of a man who stood close by.

"My lord," another man stepped forward from the Jewish assembly. "May he be permitted to sit? He is in his eighties, and I fear he is growing weary."

"Of course," Henri gestured to a waiting squire, who fetched the man a stool.

"Thank you, sir," Jacob said, sitting heavily, clearly too weak to stand much longer.

"Then what happened?" Henri wanted him to get on with the story.

"People seemed eager to believe the rumor, and though no child's body was ever found, and no child seemed to be missing from the town, a large crowd of Christians assembled at the palace and demanded the harsh punishment. Local priests and canons joined in the demand."

Tears were welling up in Marie's eyes. "How awful," she murmured.

Henri, leaning his elbow on the arm of his chair, lowered his head into his hand and rubbed his forehead for a moment. "And Thibaut gave in," he said in a quiet voice.

"Yes, my lord."

The count raised his head. "And why have you come to me?"

"We seek your protection, my lord. A statement issued by you expressing disbelief in the rumor could go far in keeping the anger and violence from spreading here. Yesterday we heard that the falsehood has spread as far as Épernay."

"Rabbi Jacob, I seem to recall that you yourself were once attacked by Christians when you lived in Ramerupt?"

"Yes, my lord, I was attacked by soldiers returning from the war against the Saracens. They broke into my home and robbed me, beat me, and took me to an open field to kill me, until a good nobleman passed by and saved my life." Jacob paused briefly at the memory and took a deep breath before continuing. "It is one of the reasons I moved to Troyes, where my family had lived for many years and where I knew we had a good count. We are here seeking your protection from atrocities such as the one in Blois."

Henri sat silent for a long moment, gazing thoughtfully at the men who stood before him. The Jews began to stir with discomfort at his silence. One of them whispered to the seated Rabbi, who nodded.

"My lord," Jacob said, drawing a pouch from a pocket in his garment. "We have gathered a thousand *livres* that we are willing to pay for your protection." The men all looked at the count with anxious faces.

"Of course, you shall have my protection and support," Henri said. "I will issue a statement at once to be posted and read aloud in all the churches throughout my lands."

The Jewish men heaved a collective sigh of relief. And Marie's look of worry faded a bit.

"But you should not have worried, my friends. Hasn't the count of Troyes always protected you from such harm? And I will protect you as my father did. We need you in our community," Henri said warmly, as his bursar stepped forward to accept the proffered heavy pouch of coins. "We thank you for this tribute, but fear no more."

The men, their faces showing relief, all bowed several times, each one saying "*merci*" in his own quiet voice. Then they shuffled out of the courtroom. Two of the men walked on each side of Rabbi Jacob, supporting him.

Henri called his scribe at once and dictated a statement of tolerance and forbearance. He began, "We do not find in the teachings of the Jews that it is permitted to kill a Christian. Yesterday on the day before Passover, such a rumor was spread about Épernay, but I do not believe it," he dictated. "Make it clear," he said to the scribe, "that we will not tolerate such unfounded violence against the Jews."

After the eight-day Passover celebration ended, word reached the count on June 9 that Rabbi Jacob Tam had died in his sleep, his face wearing a look of contentment. His last act on behalf of his people had been his appeal to the count of Champagne. Little by little, the matter seemed forgotten by all in the palace except Countess Marie, who only hoped her sister had not encouraged the terrible act. Surely Alix would not want innocent people put to death in such a way. Marie was troubled by the atrocity and determined to see that such a thing never happened in her husband's court.

As a result of the incident, there was grumbling throughout the town and region about Henri's tolerance of the Jews. Many Christians regarded them as the killers of Christ and would have rid the county of the entire lot of them if it were in their power. Marie heard the rumors and worried that such a terrible thing could happen anywhere—even here. Only a visit from Count Philip of Flanders in mid-June drove the terrible event from her mind. Philip and Henri had formed a fast friendship during their negotiations with the king of England. Now he had come to Troyes to propose an alliance between their two families.

Henri and Marie welcomed him into the great hall with a goblet of spiced new wine. He was as attractive as Marie remembered—clean-shaven and blond, tanned from his hours in the sun, broad-shouldered and keen-eyed as an eagle. Once they had exchanged the usual pleasantries, Philip got to the reason for his visit.

"I have heard of the birth of your new daughter, and I have a nephew, also born this past year. He was born in fact the day of the great fire in Valenciennes."

"Yes, I heard about that. Terrible. So many homes burned," Henri said.

"Four thousand, I'm told. As for the boy, he'll be my heir for the county of Flanders," he told Henri, "and I would like to suggest a betrothal between the two of them."

"But I can't let Mariette leave our care so young," Marie protested. "We can discuss a betrothal, but I would like to be her mother a while longer."

"As you wish, my lady, but nonetheless, we could perhaps come to an agreement to be ratified later," Philip suggested affably, with a courteous bow toward Marie.

"And what if you later have a son of your own?" Henri asked.

Philip's laugh had a bitter undertone. "Elisabeth and I have been married eleven years. I think it's quite unlikely at this point," he said.

"But you might marry again someday. It could happen."

Philip frowned. "I plan to keep my wife, Henri, and have no intention of putting her aside to marry someone else. No, my heir will be young Baudouin, my sister's new son—Beau, we call him. His father is the next count of Hainaut, as you probably know. His grandfather, who's known as Baudouin the Builder, is ill at Mons and could die any day now. His son and I formed a strong alliance when he married my sister Marguerite, and I think you could be proud to betroth your daughter to his grandson."

"I know the boy's father. He quite enjoys the tournaments, I hear," Henri replied.

"True. And he's quite good at them, I might add. He tries to find a tournament wherever he goes. We've fought together at various times. At a recent tourney at Trazegnies, he defeated Godefroy de Louvain despite overwhelming odds. Brought him a lot of profit. Even though he's not yet count, he's already a wealthy man, with hundreds of knights at his court." He brushed back his blond hair. "I think it's fortuitous that he has a son born so nearly the same time as your daughter. It seems a good omen, and I hear that she is exceedingly fair," he said.

"It's probably much too soon to tell what she will look like when she is grown. All babies are adorable, Count Philip," Marie said, with a smile.

"Elisabeth told me that she had heard a rumor that the child looked like Queen Eleanor," he answered. "If that's true, she should be quite beautiful."

"She has some features that resemble my mother, it's true. But babies change as they grow."

"I wouldn't know," he said dryly. "May I see her?"

"She's napping at the moment, I believe. Jeanne, the nursemaid, will bring the children to the great hall when they awaken. You can see her then."

"Doesn't your sister also have a daughter?" Henri asked Philip.

"Yes—a daughter, named for my wife—Elisabeth. We call her Isabelle. She was born a year ago this past April. And she's a charmer. I was going to bring that up. She would make an excellent bride for your son and namesake," Philip suggested.

"Are you willing to be as generous in her dowry as you are to her brother's inheritance?" Henri's question was not unexpected, for it was Count Philip, after all, who initiated this meeting.

"I'm willing to offer the county of Artois as her dowry," Philip said solemnly. "Will that do?"

"That's quite a liberal dowry, my lord," said Marie with surprise.

"Well, she's worth it. And she will be an excellent match, worthy of any prince in the realm."

"I think your offers are most generous, my friend. Countess Marie and I will discuss the matter overnight and give you our answer tomorrow morning, if that is satisfactory," Henri offered.

"Indeed it is, my friend."

"And we shall have a room prepared for you at once. Would you care to share another goblet of wine as we await the children?" Henri said, gesturing toward the two armchairs in front of the fireplace.

"I'll excuse myself to visit the nursery and see to it that they're soon ready," Marie said with a graceful curtsey and a warm smile for their visitor.

Later that evening, once Philip had seen six-year-old Henri and baby Marie and said all the complimentary things a mother liked to hear, the three adults shared a light supper of cheese, bread, cold chicken, and wine before retiring to their respective bedchambers.

"What did you think of the count's offer?" Henri asked his wife once they were alone.

"Quite generous," she said. "But what of Scholastique? Shouldn't we plan her betrothal first? She is the older daughter, after all."

"I don't think we need to worry about her. Several counts have already approached me about a possible betrothal between her and their sons. In any case, both the girls are still babies. And my sisters weren't betrothed in any special order. It's the marriages that matter most."

"But Adèle, the youngest, was betrothed last," Marie pointed out, as she loosened her hair and let it tumble over her shoulders.

"That's true, but I think my mother was holding out for the prophecy to come true, not that any of us ever really believed it—until it happened. But she did think Adèle was special and didn't want her married to some minor lord of no consequence."

"Well, I have no objection, if you don't. I like the count very much, and his wife is my cousin. That shouldn't be an impediment since she's not the children's mother, but only their aunt. It would be a very good marriage, I think." She knew full well that, even when kinship was an impediment, such things were often ignored, unless one wanted to be rid of a spouse.

Henri laughed. "Good. We'll tell Philip in the morning, but their father, the count of Hainaut, will have to come to Troyes to ratify the agreement. I don't think there's any particular hurry, as long as we have a verbal commitment."

"But I insist on keeping Mariette at home and not turning her over to the count and countess of Hainaut at such a young age. Remember what happened to my sister Marguerite? King Henry married her to his oldest son when she was still a small child so that he could take over her dowry lands. I think a girl should be raised by her mother—at least for her first years."

"You came to Champagne after our betrothal," he reminded her.

"But that was different. I was seven, and I had no mother at home to take care of me. Your mother became my mother. She trained me."

"And I must say, she did a fine job," he said, kissing her softly on the lips.

CHAPTER 28

Troyes, summer 1171

Marie was pleased that the peace Henri had made with the prelates of Champagne, uneasy as it was, appeared to be holding. He seemed to be trying his best to get along with them. And when word reached the court of Troyes that soldiers of the Archbishop of Reims had attacked and overcome a group of bandits holed up in a fortress at Sampigny, Henri was pleased. The outlaws had been hiding in the woods along the roads of Champagne, robbing and even killing merchants on their way to and from the region's fairs. Henri was eager to put a stop to it and keep the roads safe from all the thieves who waylaid travelers and cut into his profits at the fairs.

"What provoked the archbishop to act?" he asked the messenger who had brought the news.

"The bandits robbed and murdered one of his tenants," the man said. "He wanted them out of the woods and out of his bishopric." Although Reims was not a part of the county of Champagne, it was all but surrounded by the count's lands. The archbishop's actions could only help.

Henri was delighted that the attack justified the punishment. He even wrote to the archbishop, who was brother of the king and Marie's uncle, to commend his efforts. Although he did not like the man very much, he had always tried, for the sake of family harmony, to get along with him. Archbishop Henry was a rigid and contentious man. In earlier years, the townspeople of Reims had risen up against him and his heavy-handed ways. They had come to Count Henri for aid. Although he listened to their complaints, in the end, he was unwilling to intervene and sent them back to work it out with their lord. The family relationship put him in an awkward position. For that reason alone, he wanted to keep the peace, but also because the archbishop was, for some of his lands, his liege lord.

The fairs of Champagne were becoming more and more widely known, and that same year, for the first time, merchants from Milan were coming to Troyes. Although they did not have to pass through the archbishop's territories, Henri welcomed his support in helping to keep the roads safe for others. A week later, however, a small group of the count's serfs arrived in Troyes to report that some of the bishop's soldiers had wandered onto the lands they worked and killed some of the count's own people. This time Henri was outraged.

"Who does he think he is?" he ranted. "Killing bandits is one thing, but invading my territory and attacking my people is something else indeed." He armed himself that very afternoon, still in an angry mood, and rode out with his own troops to exact his retaliation and lead them in a series of raids on the archbishop's lands.

Ten days later, the men returned, not in a triumphant procession, but looking grim and downcast.

"What happened?" Marie asked.

"We rode to Sept-Saulx to investigate the problems there," he told her, as though it were merely an ordinary *chevauchée*.

"And what did you find?" she asked.

"Not a pretty sight. The archbishop's men had driven the canons out of the church and torn it down. They built a watchtower from the stones, cut down trees in the abbey's wood, and left the area in a mess."

His report did not ring entirely true to Marie. At best, she thought it was not complete, for some of his men had returned with wounds and battle-scars. She knew there must be more to it than what he was telling her. Other knights were less discreet and confided to their wives what had occurred. Marie learned the truth from some of her ladies.

As Henri was returning from the confessional at St. Étienne, Marie confronted him in the solar. She made no effort to conceal her outrage.

"It's one thing to try to protect your lands from Uncle Henry's men," she said, "but I hear it didn't stop there. This time, my lord husband, you've gone too far." Her voice was quiet but seething, and there were tears in her eyes. It was impossible to tell whether they were tears of sorrow, fury, or frustration.

"What are you talking about?" he asked, hoping it was not what he feared.

"I hear that you've burned a church with more than thirty people inside, some of them children—a church where they had taken refuge. How could you do such a thing?" She was weeping openly now and ready to lash out at the count.

"It wasn't my fault, Marie. I didn't give the order. Some of my men did it of their own volition," he said in his defense. His men had been in high spirit, eager for a kill, almost as though they were on a hunt, but they had met with little resistance. "The people just barred themselves inside the church, and my men torched it to drive them out, but they didn't come out."

"But you didn't stop them, did you? Why must you always pick these quarrels with the Church?" she said in frustration. "Do you never fear for your soul? Don't you remember the horror of Vitry?"

"You take care of your own soul, and I'll tend to mine," he said angrily. "I've been to confession and received absolution. Besides, my men didn't nail the door shut as your father's did. I'm tired of your judging me when you know nothing about the situation. You're only a woman. Leave these things to men who understand them."

His words infuriated Marie all the more.

"You know Uncle Henry will excommunicate you."

"It will do him no good. I expected that, and I've already sent an appeal to the pope. As you well know, excommunication under appeal isn't valid. For once you need to look at my side of the situation. Your uncle's men damaged my lands and killed some of my people. He deserved what he got."

"I'm not talking about what they did, Henri. I'm talking about what you did," she said in a frustrated voice. "I've admired you—at least most of the time—but burning a church with innocent people inside, using it for sanctuary? You're no better than all the others."

"No better than your father, you mean?" he asked, his voice sardonic. "You might never have been born, my dear, if your father hadn't burned Vitry. He might never have bedded your mother if he hadn't been ordered to do so by Abbot Bernard."

She stared at him in disbelief. "I can't believe you said that. Sometimes I fear that God has cursed you," she said, lifting her chin, marching out of the solar, and slamming the heavy door behind her. Once outside, her bravura collapsed and she sank to the floor, her face in her hands, weeping inconsolably. Would there never be peace in this world? Even in her own household?

Over time and after a week or so of silence, the count and countess mended their quarrel as best they could, but Marie was still wary, as she thought about her husband and the shifting currents of their marriage. *He is in so many ways a contradiction*, she thought. *How can one who gives such generous donations to monks and canons that they call him Henri the Liberal be so ungenerous in sharing power with prelates?* Nevertheless, he was her husband, and she would try to see his side of such disputes. It would not do to have such rancor in the household. But in truth, she did not understand the thirst for blood that seemed to take hold of men at times of war.

The countess was not the only person disturbed by the count's act of hostility. While the nobility might have seen the peasants as inevitable victims of war, the common people had quite a different view. The rumor of the church burning spread quickly throughout the county. In Troyes, Provins, Bar-sur-Aube, and throughout the region, people were horrified at the brutality. By autumn, when the count and his household traveled to Provins for the autumn fair that began on the feast day of St. Ayoul, gossip about the incident was rampant in the town and marketplace. But it was in the taverns, where tongues were loosened by too many pitchers of ale, that the most strident voices could be heard.

The crowded Boule d'Or on the rue St. Jean, located not far from the old marketplace, was no exception. A great diversity of people gathered there once daylight had vanished. The pockmarked tavern keeper welcomed them all and kept the ale flowing as long as they had a few coins to pay for it. But he served no one on credit.

"That count of ours. What do you think? He protects Jews and burns Christians instead," a man said loudly so that his voice carried throughout the noisy room.

Anne Musnier, who came almost nightly to the tavern with her husband, Girard, to share a pitcher of ale at the end of a long day, looked up sharply. The man, who had a sun-hardened face and unkempt red hair, was a visitor to Provins. He was unknown to her. They were accustomed to strangers in Provins, for during fair time, the city was overrun with people from all over Europe. But she could tell from his voice that he lived somewhere in Champagne, and she could see many people around the room nodding in agreement.

"He's right. The Jews think they can do anything in this town," a portly merchant's wife said to those at her table, but she intended for all to hear.

"He's a Jew-lover," another voice rang out.

"Burning a church with good Christians inside? It's a mortal sin," said the farrier standing near the ale keg.

Several men sitting at the table next to that of the Musniers grunted their approval and muttered in clear harmony with the general anger. They were trying to talk softly, but with all the hubbub in the tavern, they were forced to raise their voices just enough so that, given the proximity of their table, Anne could hear them clearly, even though her back was turned.

"Somebody should teach him a lesson," one of the men said in a gravelly voice.

"Got any ideas?" another asked.

"I say we cut off his balls," the man with the gruff voice said.

"You're drunk, man," another said. "You can't be serious."

"No drunker than usual—and I swear by God's bones that I am ready to do whatever it takes. I hate that count. That whoreson once had me flogged for stealing a pittance from an old Jew who was rich as Croesus."

"What'd you steal?" one of the men asked.

"Some kind of heathen candlestick. Solid gold—and he didn't light the cursed thing but once a week." The thief laughed bitterly. "He didn't even need it."

"What were you going to do with it? All the Jews here about know each other. You couldn't've sold it to them. And no good Christian would buy such a thing."

"Yeah. The Jews use 'em for some kind of pagan ritual they have on Saturdays, maybe tryin' to figure out a way to murder another Christian child."

The first man scoffed. "You don't know nothing, you fool. There's rich Jews everywhere. I could've sold it for ten *livres*—not in Provins, maybe, but in Bar-sur-Aube or Lagny."

"Don't call me a fool. You're the one who's a fool—stupid enough to steal from Jews in this town. The count always looks after 'em."

"I say let's get rid of the Jew-lover once and for all."

"What have you got in mind?"

"I say we cut his throat."

"A scullery maid I know at the palace says he doesn't keep guards at his chamber door," the first man confided.

"Could we get in?" another asked.

"Why not? I hear the palace guards are always asleep at night."

"I've got a sharp dagger, ready to go," the third man said, as he slammed his mug down on the table. "Let's do it tonight."

Anne had seen the two local men many times before at the tavern. One was a ruffian named Frobert, the ne'er-do-well son of a serf. The other one was the bastard son of a local priest. They were always up to no good and spent most of their time at the Boule d'Or whenever they had enough money for a pint. Both were unmarried, and they clung together like leeches.

Surely they can't be serious, Anne thought.

Suddenly she spotted another man just entering the tavern. He looked as though he had already been drinking, as he lurched toward the table behind her to join the others.

"God's blood, Simon. You look awful," the gravelly voiced man greeted him with a hearty laugh. "How would you like to help us send that Jew-loving count to hell?"

Anne had heard enough. She was growing alarmed now. How could she get word to the count? Sending a written message was impossible. Even if she had a scrap of parchment, she didn't know how to write.

And it would do no good to go to the palace, for no one would let her in. Nobody in the town, outside of a few of Henri's most trusted knights, knew of her nocturnal visits to the court. The count always sent for her, but she had no way to contact him.

"I must warn him," she whispered to her husband, who looked baffled by her words.

"Warn who?" Girard asked. She put her finger to her lips to quickly shush him, in case the men at the next table might hear. Sitting on the other side of the table, he had not heard their words.

"Come on, let's go," she said, standing up and turning toward the door.

"Let me finish my ale first," her husband answered.

"Hurry up." She patted her foot as he guzzled the remaining quarter of a mug. Wiping his mouth with the back of his hand, he lumbered to his feet to follow her.

Once they were outside, she told him what she had heard.

"*Pardieu*!" he exclaimed. "You're right. You have to warn the count." Count Henri paid him well for his wife's service. Even though the summons and the sums were becoming less frequent, he'd kept himself out of debt with the extra occasional income.

"Do you have any ideas?" she asked.

"No," he said. "Do you know when they'll act?"

"They were talking about tonight. I think they'll want to do it while everyone is so agitated about the church burning. But I'm not sure."

"Let's go home," he said. "We'll think of something."

But when they entered their small cottage, Anne's husband, who was logy from all the ale, went straight to bed, leaving her to consider the matter alone. As the only candle in the room burned lower, she thought furiously. *What should I do? I can't just sit here and let them murder the count without somehow warning him.* Finally, realizing that too much time was passing, she decided to act alone. She put on her dark cape, took a carving knife from the kitchen to protect herself, and unlatched the door to let herself out into the dark street.

The night was more than half over, but they would still have four or five hours of darkness left to do their wicked deed. The town was quiet. Only a few mewling cats skulked about in the dark corners of the narrow streets or jumped out of nowhere, startling her. It was not the first time she had been on the streets before prime, returning from bed sport with the count, but he always provided an escort for her. Now she was alone and vulnerable. She gripped the hilt of her knife tightly, not sure what she could do if she encountered the ruffians or some other night prowler. She was only a woman, and they were three, possibly even four men. She was apprehensive as she wound through the dark streets that led toward St. Quiriace and the count's castle. If nothing else, she could keep watch. If only she could find someone she knew at the palace.

There were fortifications around the palace and the church, and, as she approached, she saw two guards, sleeping at the gates. *Perhaps if I wake the guards up and tell them—*

Suddenly she heard the faint sound of scuffling, but she could see nothing. Quietly slipping around the side of the wall, she saw the three men farther along, where portions of the wall had crumbled. One of them, his foot held by another, had climbed to the top and was about to jump to the other side. The third man held a rope, preparing to toss it over the wall.

Anne did not think. She gripped the handle of her knife, threw her dark cape over her head, and headed for the men, who were only about ten feet away. As she raised her knife she screamed, loud enough to wake the two guards. She lunged toward the startled men, her knife plunging into the back of the one who was helping his companion over the wall. He fell to the ground with a thud. The man on the wall watched, frozen in horror, as the third dropped the rope, grabbed Anne around the throat, and wrenched the knife from her hands. Holding her in his murderous clutch, he managed to get his dagger free. As he did, the two guards rushed noisily around the corner.

"Let her go," one of them yelled, his sword raised in threat. The noise had alerted other guards at the front door of the palace, and they too were running toward the sound of the commotion.

"*Putain*. Bitch," the man growled in Anne's ear. She could smell his liquored breath as he raised his dagger to thrust it into her body, but she was struggling and twisting in his grasp, trying to free herself so that she could breathe. The dagger managed to pierce only her upper arm. At the same time, the older and more experienced guard gouged his sword deeply into the left side of her attacker, who crumpled to the ground, moaning.

The man on the wall had nowhere to go, for guards now stood on both sides. Finally grabbing his feet, they forced him to fall over into the courtyard, where the palace guards seized him. The other two men were both lying on the ground, wounded or dead.

"Are you badly hurt?" the younger gate guard asked Anne. She was bleeding badly and fainted without answering his question. He picked her up and carried her to the palace kitchen, where he laid her on a large table. The other guard summoned one of the kitchen maids. The woman, arriving disheveled and sleepy-eyed, sprinkled the wound with ground yarrow to staunch the bleeding, then smeared it with honey and bound it in clean rags.

"The wound is deep," the maid said. "But she will live, unless it festers."

"I recognize this woman," the youngest guard said. "She's been here before. In fact, I escorted her home once, so I know where she lives. Perhaps we should take her there.

"But what was she doing here?"

"Perhaps she'd been summoned by the count," someone offered.

"At this time of night? I don't think so."

By this time the noise and uproar had awakened the entire palace. Henri strode out of his chamber, "What's going on?" he asked a guard who was returning to his post.

"Three men were apprehended trying to get into the palace, my lord," one of the palace door guards told him. "They stabbed a woman in the process, but she managed to kill one of them first. We've taken the other two into custody."

"Where is the woman?" he asked.

"They've taken her to the kitchen to tend her wounds, my lord."

"Bring her up to one of the bedchambers. We'll look after her."

As two of the soldiers carried Anne's still-unconscious body up the stone stairs, Marie, who had taken the time to cover her chemise, came out to see what was happening. When she saw them carrying Anne Musnier, she recognized her at once.

"What is *she* doing here?" she asked. "What happened to her?"

"She's been stabbed, *ma dame*, but not by us. Some men trying to climb over the palace wall. She killed one of them."

By the time they had carried Anne to a bedchamber, she was waking up. Marie went into the room. Anne's red hair had come loose and was splayed across the pillow.

"Were you here at my husband's request?" she asked, suspicion in her voice.

"No, *ma dame*," Anne said, trying to avoid the countess's fearsome gaze.

"Don't lie to me. I know who you are. I've seen you before."

Anne, still dazed, murmured, "No, *ma dame*. I was only here to warn him."

"Warn him of what?" Marie asked

"Of the men. Bad men. I heard them in the tavern. There were four of them. They planned to kill him."

"Why?"

"Because of the church burning and his protection of the Jews."

Marie pressed her lips together and frowned.

"I see someone has already tended to that cut on your arm," Marie said, "but I think the bandage already needs changing." A combination of blood and honey oozed through the rags. The countess sent her maid to the kitchen for more yarrow and clean rags to wrap around the bleeding arm.

"You were brave to come here," Marie said, as she unwrapped the bloody bandage from Anne's arm. "You may have saved the count's life. Why had the guards not stopped them?"

Anne, more alert now, did not want to tell her that the guards had been sleeping. If she did, they would be punished and perhaps even dismissed.

"I don't know, *ma dame*. Perhaps they were too far away to hear them."

"They were probably sound asleep," Marie said, annoyance in her voice.

"I wouldn't know, my lady," Anne answered. "But they came at once to save me and capture the men." In fact, Anne remembered little about the scuffle. Her last clear memory was plunging her own carving knife into the back of the man helping his fellow rogue over the wall.

"You rest now, and we'll deal with the intruders."

"There were four of them, *ma dame*. Tell the count there were four of them in the tavern planning to kill him," Anne said. "But I saw only three. Someone must find the fourth man."

"I have no doubt that the others will be eager to tell us his name. We'll find him, Anne. And thank you for saving my husband's life."

Marie blew out the candle and left the room, closing the door gently to let Anne sleep. She was amazed at the rush of affection she suddenly felt for this woman—her husband's mistress—who had risked her life to save his.

She went to find Henri, who was outside in the bailey questioning the two men still on their feet, though one was bent double with pain. The third man's body had been dragged inside the wall and lay about thirty feet away.

"There was a fourth man," Marie told her husband.

"How do you know?" Henri asked.

"She told me. May I speak with you alone?" she said.

Henri looked annoyed, but said to the guards, "Lock them up. I'll talk to them later. Question them about the fourth man."

Once they were back inside the hall, Marie turned to Henri. "It was Anne Musnier—the woman," she told him.

"Anne Musnier?" he was startled that she knew the name.

"She saved your life," Marie said.

"Good heavens! Where is she now?"

"She's resting in one of our bedchambers. She's wounded, but we've tended to her. I think she will be all right."

"You know her?" Henri asked.

"I know about her, Henri. I have known for a long time. But I'm grateful for her courage. You should reward her," Marie said.

"Of course," he answered quietly. "I'll find an appropriate way."

"Should we send a messenger to her husband to tell him that she is safe at the castle?"

"I'll send someone at the hour of prime," he said. "Now I must return to my guards to find out what happened and why."

"There's one more thing, Henri. She told me that the men were angry because you protected the Jews and burned the Christians in that church."

She saw a look of aggravation cross his face. "I said I would have the men questioned. Now go back to your bed," he ordered.

She obeyed, returning to the bedchamber, but sleep was no longer possible that night.

The two frightened prisoners did not hesitate to identify the fourth man, who swore he had refused to participate in such an act. Anne could not contradict his story, for she had left the tavern before she heard his reply. But with her testimony, court officials found the two other men guilty, and the count ordered them hanged in public as an example to others. The fourth man involved was given his freedom with only a warning to mind the company he kept. Henri wanted to appear strict, but also benevolent.

As for Anne, the count rewarded her with a sum he never revealed to Marie.

"I am grateful to you for saving my life," he told Anne, "and I will reward you in a more lasting way. Give me time to think of a suitable compensation." With that, the matter ended, though it would not be soon forgotten. The story spread throughout Provins, and as it spread, it grew in the telling. The three men were transformed into rebellious knights, and over time, Anne became the greatest heroine and the most beautiful woman the city had ever seen.

CHAPTER 29

The attempt on Count Henri's life quickly sobered the people of Provins. Despite his protection of the Jews, most of them believed that Henri was a good count. He made fair judgments and did not tax them as unmercifully as some lords did. In fact, they decided it was a good thing that he calmed the waters between Jews and Christians in the area, for they did not want to be guilty of the same sort of atrocities that had taken place in Blois. Although Henri had become warier than before, he was eager to put the matter behind him and soon returned to Troyes with his young family.

Upon their return, Marie tried to forget what had happened in Provins and resume a calm life. But it would not be long before it would be disrupted again by events that, at first, seemed to have little to do with her. She learned that King Henry had crowned his oldest son, the so-called Young King of England, a second time, along with his wife Marguerite. The second crowning, in Winchester Cathedral on August 27, 1172, was an effort to placate Marie's father, angry that his daughter had not been crowned with her husband in the first place. But the new coronation changed nothing, for the king of England still refused to give up any power to his son, who, he argued, was too young to have such responsibility.

The Young King, fed up with his father's tight fist, managed to escape his close watch and make his way instead to the court of his father-in-law, who was sympathetic to his cause and willing to defy the

English king. Under Louis's protection, the Young King made a quick trip to his mother's court to elicit the help of his brothers Richard and Geoffrey, who were with her in Poitiers. In the early spring of 1173, he returned to Paris with his wife, Marguerite, to plan an outright war against their father.

Troyes, March 1173

"We've been summoned to the royal court for Easter," said Marie, who was already waiting in the courtyard as her husband and Anseau rode in from an early-morning hunting trip. There was excitement in her voice as she reported the visit from the messenger, who was enjoying a glass of ale in the great hall as he waited for Henri's response.

"When does Easter fall this year?" Henri asked, as he handed his peregrine to the falconer and peeled off his gauntlet.

"The eighth day of April," she said. "It promises to be a most festive court. The courier tells me that Philip and Elisabeth are invited, as well as Thibaut and Alix. He says even Étienne is coming, and Young King Henry and Marguerite are already there. I do hope we'll go."

"Of course we will," he said, quaffing a swallow of the wine she now handed him.

The countess looked forward to nothing else for the rest of the month. It was rare to be able to see so many of her siblings in one place. She spent days packing and choosing just the right garments to take—her finest, of course—and all must be matched with just the proper accessories. Her jeweled gold belt and shoulder clasps must be included, the silver bracelet presented to her as a tribute by Count Philip during his recent trip to Troyes to propose the betrothals, and of course, the ruby brooch Henri had given her at their marriage. She wanted to look her best, as she knew the other ladies would.

She and Henri, their three children, Widow Jeanne, and a well-attired retinue of courtiers and attendants arrived in Paris the Wednesday of Holy Week. The court was already teeming with people, but Thibaut and Alix had not arrived yet.

"They will be here tomorrow, I hope," said Queen Adèle, as she greeted her brother and his wife with a warm smile and arms open wide.

"Goodness," Marie wondered, "where will they all sleep?" She knew they would bring a retinue of servants and knights with them as well.

"Oh, we'll find a place," said the queen airily. "Louis and Philip have taken little Philippe out for a ride. Count Philip has shown quite an interest in the boy and offered to train him in his duties of knighthood. It's such a shame he and Elisabeth have no sons of their own. He'd be such a good father."

"Philippe could have no better teacher," said Marie, remembering the count of Flanders's renowned prowess on the tourney fields. "Then Elisabeth is here?" she asked.

"In the garden with Henry and Marguerite. I think they're playing Hoodman's Blind or some such game."

"The day is splendid," said Marie, gazing out the window at the sun glinting off the paving stones of the courtyard. "We should all be in the garden, including the children." She looked pointedly at Widow Jeanne, who nodded her understanding. There was a separate play area for the children, where they could visit the ducks and sail their tiny boats in a small, shallow pond.

"I'm so glad you brought your children. Mariette and Agnès can get acquainted." Both little girls were walking and beginning to talk. "And Philippe will have little Henri for a comrade-in-arms," Adèle said with a cheerful laugh.

"Or for an adversary," Marie countered, as she observed the competitive nature of the two boys. At seven and almost seven, they were of an age to enjoy playing at knighthood and even to begin their knightly training.

The day passed most agreeably, with the arrival of Thibaut and Alix, but by evening the seriousness of the occasion came upon them all as they partook of a light Lenten supper. Afterwards, the guests filed out of the great hall and made their way to the old basilica of Notre-Dame. There they observed the ritual stripping and washing of the altar and the snuffing of the candles, extinguishing the light of the world and leaving the church even darker than usual. The priests blessed the host and stored it in the tabernacle for the mass to be said on Good Friday. It was a somber occasion, reminding them of what was to come—the arrest, trial, flogging, and crucifixion of Jesus. Good Friday was a day of penance and fasting, with only a single service, involving the veneration of the Cross and the Eucharist, using the host that had been blessed the day before.

They all knew that these quiet days of contemplation and repentance would come to a joyful end on Easter morning—the day of Resurrection and celebration. Marie spent these tenebrous days walking alone in the garden, reading her psalter, and talking quietly with her sisters, her cousin, and the queen. But like everyone else, she looked forward to the Easter celebration. It was one of the most joyous feast days of the year, and certainly the most welcome, for it brought an end to the forty days of Lenten fasting.

The courtiers, who'd had their fill of fish, bread, and lentils for more than a month, were hungry for the roasted venison and baked swan prepared to look like the live bird, the stewed beef and pork pies, which were served in such abundance. The exquisite fare served at the Easter court disappointed no one. The great hall was festooned with the bright banners of the visiting knights, and sweet-smelling flowers perfumed the air until their scent was overwhelmed by that of roasted meats being carried into the hall. Feasting went on for hours, interrupted by lively chatter and the entertainment of jongleurs, acrobats, and musicians.

It was a gay gathering indeed, and Marie basked in the family warmth that surrounded her. Such occasions, with so many of them together, were rare. Alix and Adèle she knew well, and she delighted in the opportunity to renew her acquaintance with Marguerite and to deepen her friendship with Elisabeth.

"Do you remember the days we spent here together, when my parents were in the Holy Land?" Marie asked her cousin as they sat side by side at one of the trestle tables.

"Not well, but I do remember the day they returned, bringing all those wonderful gifts," Elisabeth answered with a smile.

Marie could still recall the occasional merry gatherings at the court while her mother was there, but after Queen Eleanor left, all joy seemed to vanish from the Cité palace. No doubt it was Adèle who had planned this feast, for Marie knew that her father had rarely taken much interest in such revelry. It continued on into the night—as festive as a great wedding.

The next day would prove to be quite different. Marie slept late, and it was raining when she awoke. She peered out the window. It appeared to be one of those spring rains that come suddenly out of nowhere, soon to be replaced by a sunny day with trees still silvered with shining droplets. The dripping leaves and the wet grass would soon dry, she expected, and leave a day washed clean by the morning rain. Henri had already arisen and was no longer in the chamber.

"Do you know where my lord has gone," she asked one of her ladies, as she sat on the edge of the bed in her chemise.

"All the men were summoned by the king at prime, my lady. I do not know why."

"Well, let's leave that to the men. I'll dress now and find my sisters." How sweet it was to say those words. She loved having the pleasure of the female company of her kin. While she was always grateful for her female companions at court, it was not the same thing as having her sisters—who shared her blood and her lineage. And her ladies, like Hermesende, returned to their own homes when their husbands were not at court.

By the time Marie finished dressing, the rain had stopped and the bright sun was peeking from behind the passing clouds. She soon made her way down the old stone stairs toward the great hall, where she assumed everyone was assembled.

She was wrong. It was empty, except for a few servants bustling here and there, still cleaning from the previous night's feast. She could hear the rumble of men's voices coming from behind the closed doors of the king's council chamber, but the women were nowhere in sight. She found them instead in the solar, huddled together, their heads bent silently over their needlework.

"Why are you not in the garden on this beautiful day?" the countess asked.

"It's still too wet," Adèle said as she raised her head to greet Marie. All the other ladies smiled their welcome.

"I suppose you're right. Do you know what the men are discussing and why they are huddled behind closed doors on such an occasion?"

Adèle and Marguerite exchanged glances.

"Sit down, Marie," said Adèle. "I have something to tell you all. The celebration of Easter was not the only reason the king wanted to invite you here together. There is something far more serious on his mind." Marguerite nodded nervously, trying to keep her attention focused on the linen altar cloth she was working on. Alix and Elisabeth, following the conversation, looked as bewildered as Marie felt.

"What is it?" Marie asked, seating herself on the only vacant chair left in the room.

"Tell them first about Richard and Geoffrey," Marguerite interjected.

"Richard and Geoffrey rode in last night," Adèle said.

"Richard and Geoffrey? My brothers?" Marie asked.

"Yes. They've come from Poitiers."

"They rode here during the Easter season?" Marie was astounded. "Why were they not somewhere commemorating our Lord's death and resurrection?"

"They thought they were less likely to be detected if they rode during the holy days, when most other Christians, including the English and the Normans, were at their prayers."

"What is the purpose of their trip?" Marie asked. She detected an uneasiness in Adèle's voice she did not like. At the same time, she felt a sense of eager anticipation. She had never met these two brothers before, and she was delighted to be able to spend a few days in their company—at least until she heard the queen's next words.

"The Young King has decided to challenge his father for the throne, and Richard and Geoffrey plan to fight for their rights as well. Louis is taking the side of Henry's sons. I think we are about to be at war again with the English king," Adèle answered solemnly. "A very serious war this time—not just a few skirmishes."

"Whose side does my mother take?" Marie asked, her voice worried.

"She sides with her sons, of course," Marguerite said without hesitation. "I have been with her recently in Poitiers, and though she won't come here, there is no question that she will support their rebellion against their father. Ever since he took up with Rosamund Clifford—" She frowned and bit her lower lip but said no more.

"And my father wants to enlist the military service of Henri, Thibaut, and Philip in this rebellion," Marie concluded grimly, not sure how she felt about the whole thing.

"Wouldn't it be wonderful if they could just overthrow their father and my Henry could take his place on the throne?" Marguerite said with excitement. "He's already been crowned, you know, but that old pinchfist won't give up a tittle of power."

"Do you think they have a chance?" Marie asked.

"I hope so," Adèle said.

"How can he fail with the help of all your husbands?" Marguerite asked, her earlier discomfort giving way to youthful optimism.

"When is all this to begin?" Marie asked.

"This summer or sooner, if Louis has his way. He'd much rather have his son-in-law on the throne of England than that stubborn old Plantagenet," Adèle replied.

"I guess all we can do is wait and see what they decide," Marie said. Elisabeth and Alix nodded in agreement and turned nervously back to their embroidery.

The hours passed slowly as the men continued their discussion. Finally, in mid-afternoon they all emerged from the council chamber and Count Henri found the ladies still in the solar.

"Well, dear sister," he said to Adèle, "it looks as though you may have to host all our wives and children far longer than you anticipated."

"Does that mean you have decided to support my husband and his brothers?" Marguerite asked hopefully.

"We have. Thibaut, Philip, and I have already made arrangements to dispatch messengers back to our courts to summon our men. We'll set out as soon as they're all assembled. That will take a while."

"Oh, Henri, another summer at war? How awful!" said Marie.

"But you ladies are free to frolic to your heart's content. Ah, the easy life of a lady." Henri's tone was gently mocking.

"Humph. Little do you know," his wife responded. "But at least I'll have some companions this time."

"Well, I'll leave you ladies to your pastimes, while we men get on to more serious business."

Once he had closed the door, Adèle said, "Wet or not, let's go to the garden. I need a breath of fresh air. Perhaps we can find one of the lute players from yesterday's feast to entertain us." The ladies left their needlework on their abandoned chairs and benches, and followed the queen into the garden, where diamonds of water drops still sparkled on the spring leaves. They hoped, like the queen, to conceal their worry under a guise of good cheer.

The days passed, as the men began preparations and waited for their vassals and other knights to join them. God's truce, which forbade fighting during Lent, had ended at Easter. But it would take time to assemble all the men and plan their attacks.

"What on earth will we do all this time?" Elisabeth asked. "I have no courtly duties here—only a need to entertain myself. It's too much."

"Well," Marie said. "I guess we can pray and read our psalters." Her voice was playful. "At least I have the responsibility for my children," she added.

"Yes, at least you have that," Elisabeth said. Her voice bore the sorrow of her childlessness, and Marie immediately regretted reminding her of it.

"I have an idea," said Adèle. "When the men leave, why don't we go on an excursion together? A short pilgrimage, perhaps?" Pilgrimages were serious undertakings, but they also allowed pilgrims to see the sights along the way and enjoy stories and songs as they rode through forests and fields. It would be better than spending the spring in this dreary castle.

"What a splendid idea," Marie agreed. "Where shall we go?"

"Well, obviously faraway places like Jerusalem and Santiago are out of the question," Adèle said. "Can anyone suggest something closer?"

"We need to go someplace to the south or east," Elisabeth suggested, "away from any fighting."

Richard and Geoffrey were sitting nearby in an idle game of chess, listening half-heartedly to the ladies' conversation.

"Why don't you go and visit our mother at Poitiers instead?" Richard suggested. "She would no doubt be delighted to see all of you, and especially Marie and Alix. After all, she hasn't seen you since you were children. I know it's not exactly a pilgrimage, but—" He groaned as Geoffrey gleefully captured his bishop.

"That's a splendid idea," said Marguerite. "Her court is always gay this time of year, and she often invites noble ladies from places like

Gascony and Narbonne."

Marie's heart leapt. She smiled warmly at the half-brother she had met only a few days earlier. He was tall for his age and a handsome lad, not yet seventeen, with a shock of dark hair and penetrating eyes, like she remembered their mother's. Geoffrey was younger and seemed less sure of himself. He was fair and looked a bit like his handsome grandfather and namesake. She liked them both, but Richard had made the greater impression on her.

The idea of going to Poitiers was like a dream. It was hardly more than a week's journey if they took advantage of the waterways. A barge was easier and faster than travel on horseback, and her mother would be at the end of the journey. She had never dared even hope for such a voyage, and she held her breath to see the other ladies' reaction.

Alix's answer surprised her. "I don't think I ever want to see her again. Claudine told me that she refused even to hold me when I was born. I don't think she cares about us one way or the other."

"I don't remember her that way at all. On the day she said goodbye, there were tears in her eyes," Marie said. In fact, she didn't really recall tears—except her own—just Eleanor's intense gaze and the passion in her voice. But she felt compelled to defend her mother.

"Well, I don't remember her at all," said Alix. "Go if you like. I will travel with you as far as Blois, and you are welcome to a stopover there, but I have no desire to waste my time going to Poitiers. I'm needed at home anyhow."

Richard shrugged and said nothing, until he later encountered Marie in the garden.

"Thank you for the way you defended our mother this morning. Alix is wrong, you know. I think she loved you both very much, but she was miserable with your father. She told me once how difficult it was for her to leave you behind. She said you were crying when she left."

"I'm sure I was. She was so beautiful, and I was afraid I would never see her again. I'm not going to pass up this opportunity, if the others will come."

"You should send a messenger at once so that she can prepare for your visit. Who will you take with you, aside from the other ladies?"

"Well, we'll have to have protection along the way, so I expect each of us will have a few knights. I'll take Nevelon, and perhaps Henri will allow Girard Evantat to accompany us. My chaplain Drogo, for sure. Other than that, I'm not certain. I wish you could be there as well. It has been such a joy getting to know you and Henry and Geoffrey. What is John like?"

"My little brother? He's still a child—not yet seven—about the age of your son. The few times I've been with him, he seemed to be a sullen boy. Papa sent him away to school at Fontevrault, and I don't really know him all that well, but what I know I don't much like."

"Can you blame him? Your father has given all of you land and titles and left nothing for John," Marie reminded him. "And our mother apparently took no interest in him at all—just like Alix."

"That's true. But Papa is fond of him, and I'm sure he will make it up to him somehow—probably take something from us to give to John—unless we succeed in wresting power from him. Then he'll have no say in the matter. Still, I wouldn't want my brother to have nothing. Perhaps he can go into the Church," Richard suggested.

"Mayhap that's what your father had in mind for him," she said.

"Who knows, but given the child's ornery nature, I'm not sure he'd have much of a calling for the Church. But come to think of it, he might fit in quite well."

"You seem so mature for your age, Richard—more so than Henry and Geoffrey. There is a seriousness about you I don't see in them." Despite his youth, he had the presence of a man, a quality she did not see in his brothers.

"When you're the son of Henry Plantagenet, you have to grow up quickly. I just hope my brother Henry has the maturity to be king. It's harder than he thinks. He sees glory and power, but not so much the responsibility. I think that's what worries my father. He doesn't think we're old enough or wise enough to rule. But it's frustrating to have the title of king or duke but no authority to go with it."

"I'm so sorry we never knew each other before. Has our mother been good to you?"

"She's wonderful. Henry, Geoff, and I spend as much time at her court as we can. She's convinced us all that we can do anything we set our mind to. She's an amazing and determined woman, Marie—yet one who still fosters joy and gaiety in life. My father, on the other hand, never relaxes. He's exhausting to be around."

"Which one are you most like?" Marie asked.

"A little of both, I think. But it's my mother I admire most."

"*Our* mother," she reminded him. "Oh, Richard, I can't believe I'm really going to have the chance to see her again. I've missed her so much."

"Your visit will gladden her heart more than anything I can think of. I only wish I could go with you."

"As do I," his sister added. But she would not be sorry to have as much of her mother's attention as possible. "We leave in three days' time," she said with a joyful smile.

CHAPTER 30

Loire Valley, May 1173

The party of more than thirty people traveled by horseback for three days, stopping before dark each evening for the servants to pitch their tents. Although these first days were the hardest part of the trip, the women's hearts were light. The spring woods teemed with life, as the sun reflected off the dewy new-green grass and tender leaves. Chestnut trees were in blossom, columbine and hawthorn bloomed along the wayside, and birds darted through the trees building their nests. Rabbits scurried across the path ahead of the horses, and butterflies flitted through the fields. The travelers were in a holiday mood, singing, posing riddles, and telling stories as they rode.

Marie, more than anyone else, mounted her palfrey each morning with joyous anticipation, looking forward to the day's ride, knowing that it would bring her closer to the goal of her journey—to see her mother again—the beautiful Eleanor of Aquitaine. At night, weary as she might be, Marie lay contented in her tent, trying to imagine their first meeting and listening to the gentle night sounds of crickets and the occasional hoot of an owl. Each night she slept and each morning she awoke with a smile on her lips.

When the group reached Orléans, they boarded two royal barges, which the king kept at the ready to ease his journeys when he visited his vassals to the south. Fresh horses would be waiting for them at the end of the river portion of their trip, and the ones they had ridden from Paris would be rested and ready to ride when they returned. As oarsmen bent their backs to the oars, the courtiers glided in relative comfort, watching the verdant countryside of the Loire valley unfold its fresh spring glory. Waterfowl with their young paddled by or honked at them from the riverbank. Water lapped gently in a steady rhythm against the sides of the boat.

It was good to be off the horses, after three days of riding, and resting leisurely on the deck of the royal vessel. Deer and an occasional fox peered at them from the banks. Peasants working in the fields looked up from their work as they drifted past. The noble ladies and their close attendants, among them their knights and chaplains, and of course, their talented jongleur, Roland, traveled on one of the barges, while the servants occupied the other. The cook had packed ample baskets of food and wine for them to consume along the way. They relaxed with goblets of wine and listened to the songs Roland sang to entertain them. He strummed his lute and, in anticipation of their destination, would sometimes sing *cansos* composed by well-known troubadours like Cercamon and Bernard de Ventadorn.

"You will no doubt hear many of these songs at the court of Queen Eleanor. You might even meet Bernard there. Although he's now in the service of the count of Toulouse, I hear he's occasionally invited to her court. He composed this song," Roland told them. "It's one of my favorites." He began to sing.

Can vei la flor, l'erba vert et la folh
Et au lo chan des auzels pel boschatge...

His voice rang out, clear and strong over the water, turning the heads of fishermen along the banks and children playing in the shallows beside the river. Although Marie couldn't understand every word, for he was singing in the *langue d'oc*, there was enough similarity to her own language, the *langue d'oïl*, that she could at least tell that he was singing about flowers, grass, and the birdsong that filled each spring day. The song seemed perfect for the occasion.

"In case you grow tired of this jongleur," Alix had promised at the beginning of the trip, "I can recommend another one when you reach

Blois." But Roland's pleasant voice, his abundant repertoire of stories and songs, and his versatile abilities had so far proved praiseworthy. He could even juggle a bit, though not more than three wooden balls at a time. He told stories in such a compelling manner that the ladies hung on to every word. Besides, he was a ruddy-faced, cheerful man they had all come to like.

The knights joined in the revelry when they weren't playing chess or tric-trac. Some of the younger ones spent their time grumbling about having to accompany the ladies, rather than riding out with their lords as part of king's army against Henry Plantagenet. It would no doubt be June or even July before the troops finally went on the attack. The ladies planned to be away for many weeks and not to return until the fighting ended. The trip provided a much-needed distraction from the constant anxiety they felt when their husbands or sons were putting their lives in danger. Wartime was usually only a somber time of waiting and worry. Now they could try to forget for just a little while the dangers their men were facing.

Elisabeth of Flanders had selected as one of her two knights a young man named Gautier de Fontaine. He was the son of a household knight of the Count of Hainaut, Philip's brother-in-law. The young man's father was widely admired and considered to be "handsome and wise," and young Gautier, who had been one of Count Philip's squires before he was knighted, had certainly inherited his father's good looks. Marie noticed that he and Elisabeth spent a good deal of time with their heads together in quiet conversation, but they were all in such close quarters now that it was difficult to avoid one's own knights, not to mention everyone else's, so she thought little of it. Besides, when he was not talking with Elisabeth, Gautier spent much of his time with the queen's chaplain, Andreas, and Drogo, chaplain to Countess Marie, who assumed they were discussing matters of theology, as her husband would have done.

The ladies and knights sampled the regional wines along the way and made merry throughout the journey. It was a trip unlike any they had ever taken. And the famous court in Poitiers, Queen Eleanor's court, was their destination—at least for everyone except Alix, who still refused to go.

When they reached Blois, they stopped for two days to enjoy Alix's hospitality. Marie continued to urge her sister to continue on with them to visit their mother.

"I've made my decision," Alix was adamant. "I don't want to see her."

"I'm sorry you have hardened your heart so against her," Marie said sadly. But she embraced her sister. "We will miss you." *She never felt our mother's love*, Marie thought. *She never really knew her at all. Not as I did.*

After two days of revelry at Blois, where the travelers were entertained with the most lavish feasts Alix could arrange on short notice, the diminished group—Marie, Adèle, Elisabeth, Marguerite, and their attendants—continued their river journey as far as Tours, where they were compelled once again to mount steeds for another two days' ride to Poitiers. But after their relaxing trip by barge, they were eager for this final stage of their journey.

On the last morning of their travels, twelve days after they had left Paris, Marie dressed carefully in her best riding clothes and soft leather boots. She wanted to make a good impression on her mother, and her heart was beating with anticipation. As they approached Poitiers, Nevelon, Gérard, and Gautier rode on ahead to announce their arrival. When the larger party finally reached the Maubergeonne Tower, where the queen resided, Eleanor and her ladies were waiting in the courtyard with open arms and beaming smiles. Servants stood by with trays filled with goblets of hippocras to welcome the visitors.

Marie and Eleanor recognized each other at once. As Nevelon helped the countess to dismount, Eleanor stood waiting to take her first child in her arms.

"Marie, is it really you?" she whispered in her daughter's ear as she embraced her. "You still resemble your father, but in a feminine way, of course." She drew back and held Marie at arm's length looking her over. "You still have those wonderful, alert eyes, I see. You have grown into a fine young woman. We have so much to talk about." Her eyes glistened with joy.

Marie could feel tears running down her own cheeks, and words were hard.

"*Maman*," she said, her voice breathless. "*Maman*." It seemed to be the only word she could utter at the moment. Her mother was still beautiful, although Marie could see lines of age and experience around her eyes and lips. But she was still tall, slim, and stately.

Eleanor smiled and kissed her. "I have always loved you," she murmured softly. Then she backed away to greet her other guests and give Marie time to collect herself.

"How wonderful of you all to come," she said warmly. "And give my thanks to your men for their aid to my sons. I pray for their success."

The women uttered their agreement.

"I see that my daughter Alix decided not to accompany you," Eleanor observed, with sadness in her voice.

"She had much to attend to at her court with Thibaut away," Marie said, wanting to spare her mother's feelings.

"No need to sweeten the snub, my dear. I have heard for years that she resents me, and I probably deserve it. But I am so pleased to see my first daughter again that I will allow nothing to mar this day." She put her arm around Marie once more and kissed her damp cheek before she led her by the hand into the great hall. It was festooned with bright colored tapestries and the red banners that bore the gold lion passant of Aquitaine.

"We shall have such fun getting to know one another again," she said to Marie. "And ladies, please know that you are all welcome here. We shall have a court ruled by women, without all the rough talk and rude behavior of men." She laughed. "I have most of the young men here and a few of the older ones well trained to be courteous. You must let me know if they step out of line in any way." Her voice was merry.

Four squires, not yet twenty, stood in attendance at intervals around the room, and Marie noticed that they followed the ladies' conversations with interest, all grinning good-naturedly at Queen Eleanor's words. Although they trained in their knightly skills with one of her noblemen, they served at her behest.

"Tomorrow, regrettably, is court day, and I have necessary duties to attend to." Her voice held a warm apology. "But I suspect you all could use a day of rest from your journey, and I want you to relax and enjoy yourselves. After tomorrow, however, I will devote myself entirely to your visit." She summoned one of the court officials standing by. "Now let my chamberlain show you to your rooms."

Marie's bedchamber, which she shared with Adèle, overlooked a small garden, abloom with fragrant roses and lilies of the valley. A yellow wagtail splashed in the birdbath near a garden bench. *Surely Maman must have chosen this room for us herself. It's so perfect.* The wall above the bed was painted in soft colors with a scene that depicted a lady and her lover on a ship, goblets in their hand. She recognized Tristan and Iseult drinking the love potion brewed by Iseult's mother. She had heard the poet Béroul's story read aloud in court, and Chrétien, a poet from Troyes, had retold a version of the tale in one of his manuscripts.

A nightingale sang gaily in the garden, as Marie leaned on the windowsill and gazed out on the dying afternoon. She was tired, but she had never felt quite so content and so calm. Here she was in her mother's palace, preparing to spend a month or two, perhaps even more, in Queen Eleanor's presence. She had no duties, no responsibilities, no obligations. She felt free as a cloud floating high above the war-torn earth.

Marie awoke eagerly the next morning. When she had washed her face in cold water, and her maid had braided her hair, helped her dress, and attached her wimple, she descended the stairs to join the others in the sunny hall. Bread, cheese, and dried figs were laid out on the trestle tables for any who wanted to break their fast. Baskets of oranges which she rarely saw in Troyes, strawberries, and spring flowers brightened the array of food. All the women had brought their needlework and found a quiet spot in the castle gardens, where they were dutifully stitching with silken threads on altar cloths or liturgical vestments.

The night before, Eleanor had announced, "Tomorrow you must rest and spend your time in useful work if you wish. But the next day we begin our frolics with an all-day excursion to the River Clain. There we will enjoy a picnic and amuse ourselves with games and dancing and story-telling. I have a surprise for you. We have two troubadours, Bernard de Ventadorn and Rigaud de Barbezieux, who will join us and treat us to some of their songs. Your jongleur, Roland, must come as well and bring his instrument. We shall have a delightful time. So prepare yourselves for an adventure."

Every day would not be so carefree, of course, for Queen Eleanor still had court duties to attend to on occasion. She waited anxiously each week for reports of her sons, as her guests awaited news from their husbands. They all hoped that King Henry did not suspect the coming attack, but more likely his spies had already informed him, and he too was preparing for battle. However, with three of the king's sons and so many French barons ranged against him, along with soldiers from Eleanor's lands and a few disgruntled vassals from England, Normandy, and other territories to which her sons held titles, their chances looked good. All those noblemen would rather see her sons, young and inexperienced as they were, as their overlords or allies, than her husband, whom they neither trusted nor liked.

When her court duties ended that first day, Queen Eleanor sought out her daughter, who was in the garden reading a book she had borrowed from her mother's collection.

"Am I interrupting?" her mother asked before she sat down.

"Not at all! I came here to see you, after all. But I know you have responsibilities, while we're all utterly carefree at the moment. Or better, let's say we have left our cares behind for a while."

"One must do that from time to time to maintain one's sanity," Eleanor laughed, joining her daughter on the long stone bench. "I think that today I completed enough court work to spare me a few weeks to get reacquainted with my daughter."

"Just being in your presence is enough for me. I never thought this day would come," Marie said, her voice wistful.

"I too feared it would never come, but I hoped that, when I sent my sons to Louis, he might ask your husband for help. I suggested to Richard that he should encourage such a trip. I hadn't initially expected all the other women to come, but I'm glad they did. We'll have a most amazing spring and summer together. It's truly exciting that we're all here—my first daughter, my first daughter-in-law, my first niece—and my second replacement in your father's bed." She laughed softly.

"I hope you don't mind. Adèle is my best friend. We grew up together in the convent, and we've become very close over the years. She's more a sister to me than Alix."

"She seems to be a delightful young woman, and she's finally given Louis what he wants. I hope she's happy with him." She hesitated for a moment then said, "I don't hate your father, Marie. I never did. We just weren't right together. We wanted different things and had such different needs and desires."

"I understand. But he and Adèle seem to get along well enough," Marie said.

"And you? Are you happy in your marriage to Count Henri?" Eleanor asked, arching her brow.

"He's good to me, and I am as content as most women, I suppose." She closed her book now, hoping for a long talk with her mother.

"Are you? I heard about your separation," her mother said.

"That was before we had children. I don't think it's likely to happen again, and it was really a quarrel between Henri and *Papa* that had little to do with me."

"But you were the pawn in the game nonetheless."

"Yes, I suppose I was," Marie answered. She rarely thought of it anymore.

"Women always are," her mother said. "We have to fight to have any control at all over our lives."

"You seem to have succeeded quite well at that," Marie said, not sure whether her tone sounded admiring or reproving.

"Only because I have left Henry to rule my own court. Heaven help me if I ever have to live under his roof again."

Eleanor clapped her hands to catch the attention of a servant. "Fetch us some wine," she ordered in her most regal voice. Then she turned back to Marie and said in a more intimate tone, "Tell me about my grandchildren."

Marie spent the next half hour relating to her mother stories about little Henri, Scholastique, and Marie. How they looked, their various personalities, likes and dislikes, and recounting anecdotes of their early years. Eleanor listened intently to her daughter's words, laughing now and then at the stories and taking an occasional sip of wine.

"My baby, Mariette, looks like you, *Maman*," Marie told her mother.

"I wish you had brought them with you," she said, a touch of sadness in her voice.

"We thought about bringing the children, but we all knew that the trip would be hard with little ones in tow. Henri wanted to come, and I suppose that he and Philippe are both old enough to make the trip, but we didn't want to bring them and leave the others behind. I just wanted to spend time with you alone. Besides, both Marguerite and Elisabeth are still childless, and Adèle and I felt that our children would only be a painful reminder to them."

"That was thoughtful," Eleanor said. "Marguerite is still young, and I'm sure she will bear my son Henry a child soon enough, but Elisabeth has been married to the Count of Flanders for a very long time. I suppose she must be barren. That always diminishes a woman in the eyes of the world, as you well know. She reminds me of her mother in so many ways."

"I was sorry to hear about Aunt Aelith's death."

"She was never herself after Raoul put her aside to marry Laurette of Flanders. When he died so soon afterward, she saw it as God's retribution. Still, like a widow, she grieved herself to death. I miss her very much."

Marie nodded. "I'm sure you do. She was very good to me while you and *Papa* were in the Holy Land."

Eleanor reached out for her hand and squeezed it before she stood up.

"I must go and make certain the squires and cooks are all ready for this day's feast. They are preparing some very special dishes to make up for last night's meager fare."

"It was more than enough. I was so excited to be here, I didn't care whether I ate anything or not. But now I'm ravenous," said Marie, draining her wine goblet.

"Good." Eleanor smiled at her daughter. "I have enjoyed our talk. And I look forward to many more."

The next day's excursion to the river was delightful. The sky was cloudy when Marie woke up that morning, but by the time the courtiers began the ride toward their destination, the sun had scattered the clouds and begun to gild the world with its warmth. They descended the gentle slope from the palace to the nearby river, the scent of honeysuckle wafting in the air along the roadway, and little dogs trailing along beside their horses. Mules pulling carts filled with food, trestle tables, and benches plodded behind. Bernard and Rigaud took turns singing as they rode, their voices ringing out as they followed the path along the riverbank.

Marie rode beside her mother, with the two troubadours on palfreys behind them. Next came Adèle and Marguerite, followed by two of Eleanor's knights, who teased the ladies along the way. Elisabeth and her knight, Gautier de Fontaine, brought up the rear of the picnickers, except for several squires whose steeds ambled behind with the packhorses and carts. Two more knights served as an informal rear guard to ward off any trouble should it occur. But it was the last thing on anyone's mind on such a festive day.

"I hope you will encourage Rigaud," Eleanor confided to Marie, as they rode side by side. "He is a handsome young man, but not wealthy. Although he sings quite well, he seems rather unsure of himself. He comes from Barbezieux, a small town near Saintes, where you were born."

"He seems quite talented, and I like his songs very much," Marie replied, glancing back at the young, clear-eyed troubadour, who was gazing with such admiration at the older, bearded man singing beside him as they rode. "I'll do my best."

When they had gone a short distance downstream, the courtiers dismounted, and servants began to bustle about, setting up the trestle tables and benches. As squires tethered the horses, the knights and ladies strolled along the riverbank, stopping now and then to pick a wildflower or examine an unfurling fern they had not seen before. The River Clain was a narrow, gentle river, compared to the Seine. Willow trees dipped their branches toward the flowing water, and blossoms from an occasional apple tree gave off their sweet scent, as sparrows and robins darted from limb to limb. The nobles could hear the servants behind them unfolding snowy-white linen tablecloths with a billow and snap. Birdsong filled any silence, and a mother duck fluttered to get all her ducklings in the water before the strollers reached their nest. On the other side of the river, a pair of swans drifted lazily in the current.

When the courtiers returned from their walk, baskets and bowls of food were spread out on the tables, and squires were standing by with flagons of wine.

"Shall I sing while you dine, my lady?" the troubadour Bernard asked Queen Eleanor.

"No, you and Rigaud must join us at the table. I'm sure Roland would be willing to grace us with some music as we enjoy this lovely repast. He can eat later with the squires. You don't mind, do you, Roland?"

"It would be an honor, *ma dame*," Roland said with a courteous bow. He retrieved his lute, still in the leather pouch attached to his palfrey, and began to strum, as the knights and ladies took their places at the tables. Some chose to sit on blankets that had been spread on the ground for their leisure. Servants passed among them serving savory meat pies and mushroom tarts, as they filled their wooden trenchers and goblets. There were ample bottles of wine, loaves of bread, cheese, bowls of shiny red cherries, and sweetmeats galore. Marie, Elisabeth, and Adèle, accustomed to a more formal atmosphere in their northern courts, joined in the chatter as everyone began to dine. The melodious voice of Roland, singing the songs they had heard as they floated on the Loire, echoed across the river and through the woodlands that surrounded them.

Marie thought as she listened, seated beside her mother on one of the wood benches, *I have never been happier*. While she knew that such earthly joys never endured for long, she was determined to absorb this memory to warm the rest of her life.

CHAPTER 31

Each evening Bernard and Rigaud sang their *cansos*, while Roland made the courtiers laugh with his lively *pastourelles*. Eleanor showed such favoritism toward Bernard that Marie was not surprised that Rigaud might feel less than worthy in her presence. It was to be expected, she supposed, for the queen and her favored troubadour were old friends. As a consequence, Marie made a special effort to compliment Rigaud on his performances, and he began to end his *cansos* with a shy smile in her direction.

"Your songs truly touch my heart, Sir Rigaud," she told him one evening, meaning it sincerely. "They also help me to understand better your beautiful language here in the south. Perhaps someday you will come to my court in Champagne and sing them there."

"It would give me great pleasure, *Midons*," he said with a shy smile.

"Whether you come or not, I can promise that your songs will be sung there."

He knelt to kiss her hand, which was for him a bold gesture. "I am grateful, my lady."

Both troubadours sang of love, Bernard expressing great joy at the coming of spring and in the reciprocal love of his lady, but abject sorrow at the lady's absence. Marie had heard from other ladies of the court that he had once loved her mother and perhaps still did, though he saw her only rarely now that he was in the service of the count of Toulouse. Rigaud's songs, on the other hand, emphasized the lover's suffering from unrequited love and the ennoblement he gained from loyalty and his efforts to find satisfaction in the mere presence and contemplation of the beloved. The lady of Rigaud's songs, Marie's mother had confided to her, was rumored to be the daughter of Jaufre Rudel, the troubadour who had died on the last crusade.

The chaplains, Andreas and Drogo, sat with the courtiers together in the great hall most evenings, watching and chatting with one another over a goblet of wine, while knights like Nevelon and Gautier joined in the fun and laughter, as they interacted with the countess of Narbonne, Ermengarde, who had arrived to great fanfare only a few days after the visitors from the French court in Paris.

Ermengarde in her mid-forties was still an attractive and stately woman, perhaps not the great beauty Marie had expected from the love songs the troubadour Peire Rogier had written for her, but beautiful nonetheless. Peire, once a cathedral canon, had left the Church to become a troubadour and had been a favorite for a time at Ermengarde's court. Gossip about their relationship had caused her to send him away, but not before the rumors spread. Like Eleanor, she was well known and ruled her own lands, and the two women enjoyed exchanging stories of what it was like to be a female ruler in a world dominated by men. Some men, they agreed, were quite unwilling to accept the judgments of women, but not all. They had shared many of the same experiences and were able to laugh at them now when they were together, although at the time they happened, they'd been quite irritating.

"Women need practice at making judgments," said Ermengarde one evening, "for many of you will need to do it at one time or another."

"Do I sense a call for a court of love?" Eleanor laughed.

"Well, it's one harmless way to practice looking at all sides of an issue before making a judgment," Ermengarde said. "And it's a pastime we all enjoy."

"What's a court of love?" asked Elisabeth.

"It's a game we play that gives courtiers an opportunity to ask a question about matters of love to the judge, who is always a woman. She must make a decision based on precedents and logic," said Eleanor.

"Women always make better judges in such cases than men, who know little of matters of the heart or of courteous behavior for that matter," Ermengarde said with a lofty smile. "We women of the south, where, thank God, we don't live under that detestable Salic law that keeps women from inheriting and ruling in their own right, are making an effort to civilize men. It's an effort we'd like to spread throughout Europe."

Marie and Adèle both laughed. "Is it working?" Marie asked, directing her question to the young squires standing around the room. They all grinned and nodded.

"It had better work," said Eleanor. "I won't tolerate boorish behavior at my court. I saw enough of that in northern France and Norman England." Her voice was light, but Marie sensed a seriousness of tone underneath. She'd noticed in fact that the knights and squires at Eleanor's court did seem extremely courteous, always addressing the noble women with respect and eagerness to serve.

"There are rules to follow and limits that must be observed in matters between men and women—especially matters of love and courtesy," Eleanor said, her voice growing more serious now.

"What are some of those rules?" her daughter asked.

"For example, we tell them that for any man to be worthy of love, he must be loyal to his lady and generous in giving gifts and alms. Avarice has no place in an honorable man. He must be able to practice self-control, for an excess of passion is not so much a sign of true love as of lust. He must be discreet, for the love must be kept secret. When it is revealed, it loses its power. That sort of thing."

"Well, those are certainly worthy goals," Marie agreed with a smile.

"Oh, that's only a few of the rules," her mother said. "Lovers must learn to be obedient to their ladies. Given the unruly youth of today, it is important for them to understand that any man worthy of a woman's love must be of good character. It's a way we have of teaching them what is admired by all of society, but especially by a woman if one hopes to have his love returned. It's completely consistent with the code of chivalry."

"Except that it puts women in charge." Marie laughed.

"Indeed," said Queen Eleanor with a smile.

"Tell us more about these courts of love," Adèle said, sounding intrigued.

"They work this way: someone sets forth a question, and the lady assigned to be judge must give a logical and appropriate response. It cannot be based on her personal feelings or biases, but rather on the rules—just like any court of law. Ermengarde, you've done this before," Queen Eleanor said. "Why don't you go first and show them how it's done."

"*Avec plaisir*," Ermengarde said with a curtsey. She mounted the dais regally and sat on the throne-like chair where Queen Eleanor gave her court judgments. "Now, who has a question?" she asked.

There was silence in the room. Then people began to murmur among themselves. Many of them had never done this before, and everyone seemed reluctant to pose the first question. Finally, Marie whispered in Nevelon's ear. He nodded, thought for a moment, and then stepped forward. She knew he was a man of good character, happily married, and she thought he might provide an interesting challenge for the countess of Narbonne.

"*Midons*," he said, using the term of address to a lady in Aquitaine. "Let me ask the first question. I want to know which you think is the greater: marital love or that of lovers."

It was just the sort of question Marie had expected him to ask. Most of the ladies present were married, and they all leaned forward to hear Ermengarde's answer. She sat quietly for almost a minute, her chin resting on her hand and a tiny frown on her forehead, as though in great contemplation. Everyone waited quietly. Finally she looked up and smiled at Nevelon.

"The two have nothing to do with one another, sir knight," she said. "Marital affection and the true love of lovers are completely different and derive from different sources. Love is a matter of the heart, while marriage is an institution based on social and economic benefit. They can't be compared. I agree that the nature of the word 'love' is rather ambiguous and that we commonly use it in both instances, which is unfortunate. But they belong in totally different categories. I would prefer to think of one as '*amor*' and the other as 'affection,' which can grow from proximity and interdependence."

Nevelon bowed his appreciation, and everyone applauded the judgment. One of Queen Eleanor's knights then stepped forward and glanced at his duchess. There was irony in his voice when he posed his question.

"Suppose there is a woman who has been married but was set aside by her husband, and suppose that former husband once again seeks her love, how should she respond?"

Marie was shocked by the knight's audacity, for she knew that for several years, even after he had married again, King Louis had pined away for her mother. She had seen it in his behavior until he wed Adèle, who seemed to have made him truly happy again. But Queen Eleanor did not react. She merely waited, her chin raised in anticipation, for Ermengarde's answer. *How I wish I could be as inscrutable and unfazed as my mother*, Marie thought.

Once again Countess Ermengarde became pensive as she considered the question. This one seemed to take a bit longer, and Eleanor motioned for the squires to refill everyone's goblet with sweet red wine as they waited. Finally Ermengarde lifted her head to make her pronouncement.

"It is difficult to envisage such a situation," she replied, "and I can't imagine any woman who would encourage such attentions. Either she has found him unlikeable in the first place or he has put her away of his own accord. In any case, if two people have been married and separated for any reason, we consider love between them totally unthinkable and appalling."

Eleanor laughed and nodded knowingly. The other courtiers applauded once more.

"Now you see how it works—this court of love," said Queen Eleanor. "We'd like to give some of the other ladies here a chance to practice their skills of logic and judgment—some of you who have never done it before."

"Oh, but we shall need far more time with our judgments than Countess Ermengarde, for she is well practiced in such matters. Would it be possible to assign the questions in advance and let us give our rulings at a later time?" asked Adèle. None of them wanted to embarrass herself before the more practiced court.

"That seems a perfectly reasonable request. We'll listen to some more of Bernard's *cansos* to inspire everyone. Please tell me any questions you might have before we retire for the evening, and I'll assign them to certain noble ladies present," said Eleanor.

When Marie returned to her bedchamber for the evening, she

pondered the questions that had been assigned to her. One involved a knight who loved a lady. She granted her embraces but did not love him with her whole heart. Yet when he tried to leave her, she insisted that he stay. Was she acting properly? The second question, which would keep her awake much of the night as she considered a suitable answer was whether love can even exist between husband and wife. After the answer she had heard the countess of Narbonne give that evening, she was unsure of what she should say. There was no question that in their wedding vows women promised to love and cherish their husbands. But could the first one really be fulfilled when marriages were made for reasons of property and status and had nothing to do with love? Many couples, like Henri and herself, had not even met before they committed themselves to marriage. How could one say it was a matter of love? When she fell asleep that night, she dreamed of a duel between the demands of love and marriage. By the time she awoke the next morning, she had forgotten the dream, but she had an answer ready for the evening's court of love.

By the time the courtiers had finished another of the lavish feasts Queen Eleanor provided to her guests, Marie was ready. She'd sat quietly throughout the meal organizing her thoughts and looking forward to the evening's entertainment. Another of the guests, a woman who also bore the name Marie, had agreed to sing one of her *lais* to start the evening. She was a poet, one of Marguerite's ladies and her special friend. Apparently, she was also a great admirer of Marguerite's husband, Young King Henry, and his friend William Marshal. It promised to be a very special evening.

After a long dinner, courtiers strolled in the garden, breathing in the early evening air and watching the fireflies begin to appear in the grassy areas. Torches lit the walkways that wound among the flowerbeds beside the castle. The air was filled with the sweet scent of the eglantine that climbed on the garden wall. It promised to be a perfect night. Queen Eleanor gathered everyone together there in the garden to listen to Dame Marie sing in the Anglo-Norman dialect spoken at the English courts since the conquest a century earlier. She called her song the "*Lai du Chevrefoil,*" the *Lai* of the Honeysuckle.

It was a tale of the famous lovers, Tristan and the wife of King Marc, whose name remained unspoken by the poet, though everyone knew who she was. The *lai*, a brief, rhymed narrative, revealed how the lovers communicated in secret even when compelled to live apart. Dame Marie's voice was clear and lyrical, just right to sing the delicate *lai* depicting a rare episode of joy when the lovers are able to find precious moments together. It ended with the lover, Tristan, composing a *lai* of his own to commemorate their tryst, leaving the listeners in just the right mood for one of Bernard's *cansos*. Everyone applauded with enthusiasm, as the squires passed among them refilling their goblets.

As Bernard began to sing, his deep, rich tones echoed through the garden.

Can vei la lauzeta mover
De joi sas alas contral rai...

As he sang in his native *langue d'oc*, Eleanor whispered to her daughter that the song was about the joy of a lark in the morning and the lonely lover's envy of such happiness. When his *canso* came to an end and the applause died away, Marie called for a song from Rigaud to end the entertainment. He smiled his gratitude to her, picked up his lute, and began to strum. His dulcet tenor voice was vibrant and filled with emotion, as he sang of the lover, who, like Perceval overcome by the sight of the Holy Grail, is stunned by the beauty of his lady. When it ended with a soft final plucking of the lute's strings and an enthusiastic response from the listeners, the moment seemed perfect for the queen to lead everyone into the great hall to begin the court of love. There was much laughter and excitement among the courtiers, who were eager to hear the judgments of the ladies to whom the questions had been given.

"Who will judge first?" Eleanor asked.

"Countess Marie," Nevelon called out, grinning as he put her on the spot as she had done to him the day before.

"You rascal!" Marie whispered in a teasing voice. He grinned.

"Are you ready, my lady?" a voice called out.

"I am," she said as she mounted the dais. "First, I wish to hear once more the question, which was asked by Gautier de Fontaine. Would you pose it again for the court, Sir Gautier?"

"*Avec plaisir, ma dame*," he said. "My question was this. We all heard the judgment of Countess Ermengarde yesterday concerning the nature of love in marriage and between lovers. Here is my question, to which I am sure that a woman of your wisdom can provide the correct answer. Can love even exist between a husband and wife?"

The entire court erupted with laughter.

"That's a provocative question if I've ever heard one," said Adèle, with a coy smile. "We're eager to hear your response, Marie," she teased.

"Then you shall hear it. And bear in mind that this is my first judgment in such a court. I hope you will consider that I am not so wise as Gautier suggests. But I have listened well, and I consider yesterday's judgments as precedents. Here is my decision." The countess paused and took a deep breath before continuing.

"I have carefully considered Countess Ermengarde's ruling that the so-called love in marriage and that of lovers are completely different. I agree with her that marriage is a state where duty and obedience of the wife to the husband are required and where each must pay the marriage debt as requested by the other. It is, thus, a situation, as the countess of Narbonne has proclaimed, in which affection may exist, but love or *fine amor*, as we are speaking of it here, has no place. Lovers must give everything to each other under no compulsion, but freely. A lady's love should increase the honor and worth of her lover, but how can it ennoble a husband if his wife grants him her embraces, for she is required to do so by the laws of marriage? From all I have gathered here, a lady can truly wear the crown of love only outside of wedlock, and no woman can love two men. Therefore, I rule that *fine amor*, by its very nature, cannot exist within the bonds of marriage." Sounds of both approval and dismay erupted among a few in the crowd, but Marie raised her hand for silence and went on.

"There is one more reason. Jealousy has no place in marriage, but it is one of the things, I have been told, that is expected of lovers. As you all know, a jealous husband is the butt of many jokes. Jealousy only makes him appear weak and ridiculous. However, jealousy is not only common, it is even essential in a lover, if he suspects anyone else of courting his lady. Thus, I hope that my verdict will find favor with the ladies, as well as with the noblemen. I repeat, love, as we speak of it here, cannot exist between two people who are married to one another."

She was almost breathless at the end of her pronouncement and looked about her for the court's reaction. Some courtiers began to applaud once more, while a few of the single young knights even cheered. Most of the ladies merely smiled or pretended to be shocked by her answer.

"Well done, daughter," Eleanor said with a smile, approving her answer.

"You have inherited the wisdom of your mother," Ermengarde added. Marie flushed with pleasure at the reaction to her judgment.

"You must put that judgment into writing," Eleanor added. "Send it by letter so that it becomes one of the firm precepts of the love court."

The two chaplains, Andreas and Drogo, sat to one side, frowning in mock disapproval. Even though they were men of God, they believed it was all in fun.

"In fact," Queen Eleanor added. "I think the rules of love should be written down so that there is no future misunderstanding. We can then base judgments more easily on rules and precedents." She turned toward the two chaplains. "Andreas, would you be willing to record these matters for posterity? I am told that you write well and while you are here, you can gather all the information you will require. I'm sure Queen Adèle will give you leisure and support for this project."

Adèle nodded, laughing.

"I will do my best, my lady," Andreas said with a bow. "But I must say in advance that, given my position as a priest, I must also represent the Church's point of view." The queen nodded. He went on to add, "I should like to address this little treatise on love to one among you, if someone is willing."

"Yes, indeed. Who will it be?" the queen asked.

"Address it to me, for I shall be asking many questions about these matters of love, which I am not yet sure I fully understand. I confess that I am a new recruit of love, and there are many questions you can answer with such a work." The speaker was Gautier de Fontaine, who glanced toward the lady Elisabeth. She was blushing slightly and smiling demurely at her folded hands.

"Then it will be addressed to my new friend, Gautier. I shall do my best," Andreas said, bowing to the court.

After Marie had given her second judgment of the evening, Eleanor asked, "Queen Adèle, are you prepared to give your ruling to the question posed by Gérard?"

"I am," she said, mounting the dais. "State your question once more, Gérard."

"I asked the lady whether it was preferable to love a young man or one advanced in age. I look forward to the answer." He was a young knight, only twenty-two, and in competition with an older and more experienced man.

"My answer is this," said Adèle, who, as everyone knew, was married to the king, a man old enough to be her father. "Age should have nothing to do with it. Love is based on the wound of the heart, on knowledge, good character, and admirable manners. It is interesting to note, however, that young men seem to prefer older women, while older men prefer young ones. I have also observed that most women, certainly not all, seem to prefer the embraces of younger men, though again, I say, age should not be a factor."

The court applauded its approval, and Marie wondered if Adèle herself would have preferred a younger husband. Then, remembering her own judgment, she thought, *but a husband's age is not relevant to this question—only a lover's.* To her knowledge, the queen, her stepmother, sister-in-law, and friend, had not taken a lover. She knew that Adèle was fond of her father and was good to him, and that was really all that mattered.

The judgments went on until a late hour, when Queen Eleanor finally announced that the court session had come to an end for the evening. Several courtiers, who had by now had far too many goblets of wine, groaned their disappointment. Nevertheless, they all left the hall to find their places of rest, their minds filled with thoughts of love and how it might be obtained and kept.

CHAPTER 32

A few days later, Marie and Eleanor sat in the garden, playing a game of chess and sharing their innermost thoughts. Marie had grown closer to her mother than she'd ever thought possible in such a short time. It was as though they had never been apart.

"You know, Mother, you are still so very beautiful. I've always wanted to look like you, to have that golden hair and those startling blue eyes," Marie said, capturing one of Eleanor's pawns. *How could I ever have forgotten their color?* she wondered.

"Your eyes *are* blue," Eleanor reminded her.

"Not really. A smoky gray-blue maybe. But not like yours," Marie answered.

"As for my golden hair, much of it is now turning gray, my dear. Beauty is a gift from God that is ephemeral. It doesn't last forever. He has given you things far more valuable—wisdom and intelligence, a good and forgiving heart. Those are the things that will endure. I had feared that you felt like your sister and would never forgive me for deserting you so young. Thank God I was wrong. You do realize I had no choice?" Her mother looked at her intently, her hand resting on her one remaining bishop.

"Of course I do. There was no way you could have taken me with you. I saw what happened to Aunt Aelith. She did not leave of her own will, but she was still not allowed to take her children. It must have broken her heart."

"Her heart and her spirit, my dear. But you must know I have prayed for you and your sister every day of my life, and I have always longed to see you again," Eleanor said, sliding her bishop horizontally across the board to capture her daughter's knight.

Marie wrinkled her forehead at her loss, then looked up at her mother, smiled, and said softly, "You can't imagine how much these days together mean to me. I'll never forget them."

"I think I *can* imagine, Marie, for I feel the same way." She reached across the small table to touch her daughter's hand.

"But I still wish I looked like you," Marie said wistfully.

"Pah," Eleanor's tone was dismissive. "Looks can always be enhanced. You don't think I don't do everything possible to enhance my own, do you? Now let's see—" She looked her daughter over with a critical eye, turning her head this way and that. "There is nothing about your looks that a few herbs and roots can't improve. If you're willing, we can get right to work while you're here. Chamomile rinses will brighten your hair. Ground angelica leaves or safflower petals can add color to your cheeks—"

"I thought only harlots used such things. Aren't they forbidden by the Church?"

"Most pleasurable things are, my dear. But don't assume that noble ladies don't use them anyhow. We just don't talk about it. If someone comments on a rosy cheek, you can always claim that you are flushed from being in the open air or from excitement or some such. Good heavens, if we did nothing that the Church forbids, it would be a gloomy world indeed." Eleanor laughed.

"How naughty you are, *Maman*!" Marie laughed too, as she made a desultory move of her own bishop. It was such fun to be with her mother, who obeyed whatever rules she chose whenever she chose. She made her own way through life with such joy and exuberance. *How could Henry Plantagenet possibly ever prefer another woman to my mother?* Marie wondered.

Suddenly, Eleanor swept her queen across the board. "Checkmate."

Marie looked at the board in surprise "Do you always defeat kings so easily?" she asked.

"If only I did, my dear," her mother answered quietly. "If only I did."

The very next day Eleanor set her maids to grinding lily and cyclamen roots to powder her daughter's face, and she had them wash Marie's hair weekly and rinse it with chamomile. Eleanor herself applied tiny amounts of safflower mixed with rosewater to her daughter's cheeks from time to time and touched her lips with berry-stained suet to add color and make them shine. It was hardly enough to notice, but when Marie looked in the small silver mirror her mother handed her, she could see the difference. These small touches brought a new light and life to her face.

Rigaud was the first to notice. "You are fresh as a garden rose this morning, *ma dame*," he said with a voice of admiration. Marie rewarded him with a smile.

When even her chaplain Drogo began to remark on the changes, he commented, "It is good for you to be here, my lady. I can see from your appearance that you are thriving in your mother's presence."

She wasn't sure whether he perceived the truth or not, but she chose to accept the remark at face value, saying merely, "It has brought me great joy to see my mother again."

She felt her heart lighten as well, as she continued to enjoy the sounds of the lute and the *vielle*, the songs and dances that surrounded her here and filled her mother's court. Every day seemed to bring a new delight as Eleanor was determined to show the visitors her beautiful city of Poitiers. They worshiped at the splendid old-style church of Notre-Dame, which, although it was dark inside, was brightened by its painted columns and façade.

"But wait until you see the new cathedral of Saint-Pierre we are building. It's in the new style, of course, and will be filled with light and magnificent stained-glass windows like St. Denis." As they wound through the narrow streets toward the cathedral, Marie could already see the new church rising upward toward heaven. Here in Poitiers she was learning how to find more pleasure in life and to shut out, at least for a little while, all the cares of the world.

"Life mustn't be all worry and sorrow," her mother said. "We must enjoy the moment and let the morrow care for itself." She knew that men dominated the world outside, but at her court and in matters of love, it was the woman who must be obeyed and served as *domna*. It was a whole new experience for Marie, Adèle, and Elisabeth. Less so for Marguerite, who had spent many months at the court in Poitiers.

Even so, despite Eleanor's carefree attitude, Marie could see that she felt moments of deep anxiety. As spring turned into summer, with the fighting season well under way, she saw her mother waiting impatiently for news of her sons and their struggle against their father. She had confided to Marie that she worried less about their lives than their freedom. Henry would never harm his sons. She knew that. But he would have little compunction about restricting their movements if he were to capture them.

There was no way to shut out the world entirely. Marie was equally concerned about Henri and her father, but these moments in Poitiers, snatched out of time, had become very precious to her, and she was determined, like her mother, to relish them to the fullest. Stark reality would confront her soon enough.

At first, news from the fighting seemed good, as the troops of the Young King and his allies invaded Normandy. Rumors reached Poitiers that King Henry had been caught off guard by the number of nobles in Normandy, Brittany, and Anjou rising up against him to join his rebellious sons and that his defense seemed ineffective. Even on the basis of such slim information, the court rejoiced.

Then, late one evening, an official messenger arrived. The court was in the midst of one of its weekly courts of love. Elisabeth of Flanders sat on the dais poised to make a judgment on a question posed by a young knight from Narbonne, when the weary-looking messenger entered the hall. Everyone fell silent in anticipation of what he had to say.

"I am happy to report," he began, and Marie could see Eleanor visibly relax at his words, "that all is going well. When I left the troops, they were settled safely in camp around the city of Verneuil in Le Perche, prepared, if necessary, for a long siege. In the meantime, Count Philip and his men have captured Aumale, Drincourt, and Châteauneuf. Unfortunately, the count's brother, Mathieu de Boulogne, was wounded in the knee at the battle of Châteauneuf, but the wound is not thought to be life-threatening. Overall, the Young King is elated and feels that our men are on the road to victory."

Everyone was heartened by the news. Countess Elisabeth was

particularly delighted to hear of the exploits of her husband, Philip. For the moment, the entire assembly forgot about questions of love as the courtiers lifted their goblets in celebration. If the Young King and his allies were victorious, it would mean renewed peace between the rulers of the two kingdoms and release the women from worry during the summer fighting season. Queen Eleanor called for her servants to provide the messenger with food and drink. He settled at one of the trestle tables to watch as the court of love resumed with renewed enthusiasm.

As summer settled in, another messenger arrived with less cheerful news. Count Philip's brother, Mathieu, was dead from the festered knee wound at Châteauneuf. Andreas and Drogo quietly agreed that it was surely God's judgment against Mathieu for an earlier scandalous abduction and forced marriage of a nun, the abbess of Romsey, daughter of the late King Stephen. But whatever sins his brother may have committed, Philip loved him and was deeply grieved by his death. He left the battlefield to return at once to Flanders to bury him. Mathieu's marriage had been annulled by the Church three years earlier and the children born from it were all too young to take on that responsibility.

Nor did the siege of Verneuil bring happy news. King Louis had sent his brother Robert, along with Henri, Thibaut, and Archbishop Guillaume, to negotiate a three-day truce with the people of the city. But the French had violated the truce, attacked the unsuspecting town, and killed many of its citizens, to the outrage of Henry Plantagenet, who had by now assembled a sizeable army of mercenaries and loyal men. When Louis learned that Henry was riding hard to attack, he abandoned the cause and ordered a rapid retreat. As the bad news trickled in, the noble ladies who had come from Paris realized that the time had come for them to return home as well.

On their last day as their feast ended, the troubadour Rigaud approached the queen. "I request permission to present a song I have written to honor the Countess Marie, whose presence will be greatly missed," he said, for he had very much appreciated her friendship and encouragement during her time in Poitiers.

"Of course," Queen Eleanor said, and everyone turned to Rigaud with great interest.

"I call it, 'Everyone asks what has become of Love,'" he announced, as he picked up his lute. It seemed an appropriate topic, considering all they had discussed and the rulings Marie and the other women had made in the courts of love. The song described the demands that *fine amor* made of a lover—sense, wisdom, generosity, loyalty, valor, and humility—all to make him a better man. And for these reasons, the lyrics declared, he wanted to meet its requirements, to do his lady's will, and even to suffer love's inevitable but ennobling woes. As he neared the end of his lyrics, he praised the lady Marie, expressing his love and admiration for her and his sorrow at her departure.

Pros comtess'e gaia, ab pretz valen,
Que tot'avetz Campaign'enluminat,
....

Wise and joyful countess, of noble worth
You who have illuminated all of Champagne,
I want you to know the love and friendship
I bear you, for I leave my soul and my sad heart.
Bel Paradis, all the sweet realms
Would benefit from your teaching.

Marie was moved by Rigaud's words, which brought tears to her eyes and a smile to her lips. It was the only song that anyone had ever composed for her, and she would never forget it. It praised her and her judgments and called her "*Bel Paradis,*" bestowing on her a special *senhal*, a code name that troubadours sometimes used to conceal the identity of their ladies. She knew the love he expressed was formulaic, but it touched her heart, this earnest tribute to her kindness. She stretched out her hand to thank him, as he knelt before her.

She would, of course, have Nevelon reward him well on her behalf and ask him to make a copy of the song for her. It was the perfect conclusion for her visit to Poitiers, a moving farewell from a poet she had encouraged, as her mother had encouraged Bernard in his youth. The older poet was well aware of his talents now and had little need of such reassurance, but Rigaud's song made her realize how much young poets needed approval and admiration. He was still forging his path and making his reputation as a troubadour, and her support clearly meant a great deal to him. His was a song she would always carry in her heart.

The next morning, as they all stood in the courtyard to say goodbye, Marie saw Rigaud, a sad look on his face, standing among the gathered courtiers. She gave him a smile of gratitude. It was difficult for her to leave, for she had longed for this visit her entire life, and she couldn't believe it was coming to an end. Tears stood in her eyes as she said goodbye to all her new friends and especially to her mother. A squire was already holding the stirrup for her, prepared to help her mount her palfrey.

"I shall never forget this time together, *Maman*," she said, as her mother held her in her arms.

"Nor I, my dearest. Please know that you will always be in my heart and that I hope you will take a bit of me home with you."

"I will take not only memories of you, but of all those wonderful love courts and dances and happy moments we have shared—the picnics and the games. Perhaps one day I shall even be good enough to beat you at chess."

Eleanor laughed. "Richard has tried for years. When he was younger, I let him win, but now he needs to learn strategy, as we all do, my darling."

"And I'll teach all my ladies the rules of love. Maybe we'll even hold such courts in Troyes and Provins. We'll take your teachings north with us to make our courts less stodgy."

"They're your teachings too now. You'll find that they help to while away those days when the men are away fighting, and they'll brighten the dark days of winter as well. They're harmless fun, unless one takes them too seriously, and they certainly help teach good manners and courtly behavior to those ill-mannered, adolescent squires who show up at our courts."

"I hope Henri will agree," Marie said. "Let him and his knights instruct the young men in how to fight, and we ladies will polish their manners and teach them the other rules of chivalry."

Eleanor laughed. "Well said, Marie. Put it in the context of love to lusty young men, and they'll pay attention to matters of good behavior. Otherwise it's just words."

When they had all said their goodbyes, Marie turned to the waiting squire and quickly mounted her horse. She was fighting tears as the knights, ladies, and all their attendants rode through the palace gates and set out toward the north. The travelers were all quieter than they had been during their voyage south, and their faces were more somber. As hard as it was for Marie to leave her mother behind, she looked forward to seeing her children, who would be waiting for her at the end of the journey.

Once back in Paris, Marie and Adèle rushed to the nursery. Both Henri and Scholastique skipped toward their mother, shouting, "*Maman, Maman!*" Mariette toddled along behind, her arms raised in greeting. Marie knelt to scoop them all into a warm embrace, loving their very smell. It was good to be back with them.

When Count Henri saw his wife again for the first time, he gazed at her for a long moment. "You look… different," he said, smiling at what he saw.

"It was the relaxation and the lovely weather in the south. It's rejuvenating," she said. "It brings back health and vigor." She gazed at him expectantly, but he said nothing more about it.

Although Henri had been waiting impatiently for his wife's return. Philip had already gone back to Flanders to bury his brother, leaving instructions for Gautier to escort Elisabeth home. Marie could see that Gautier didn't mind in the least, for he was clearly smitten with his lady, willing to obey her every command and trying to live up to the rules. Whether Elisabeth returned his affections she couldn't say. If so, she was hiding it far better than her swain. He still had much to learn.

As Marie and Henri prepared to return to Troyes with their children and their entourage, Marie sought out the chaplain Andreas.

"You have been a delightful companion for Drogo," she said, "indeed, for us all. Should you ever wish to leave the court in Paris, I would welcome you to my own court in Champagne."

"*Merci, ma dame*," he replied. "I have kinsmen in Ramerupt, and such an opportunity would allow me to return home and see my family more frequently. Perhaps one day, God willing, I will appear on your doorstep. Godspeed in your voyage, my lady."

She said goodbye to Adèle and Marguerite reluctantly. When would she see them again? It had been a rare opportunity to spend time together, and they had grown close during the trip. Even as they embraced, Marie knew that Marguerite was eager to get back to her dejected husband. The Young King had been in a foul and petulant mood when the ladies arrived back in Paris, his efforts to overthrow his father having come to a disappointing end. Now the brothers would have to begin all over again the following summer or else make peace and accept whatever terms Henry was willing to offer. They were frustrated, but they would have to make the best of it. King Louis was trying to persuade the brothers to call a truce and meet with their father to see whether he might be ready to relent and share power with his sons.

The Young King was still thinking it over when Marie and Henri departed for Champagne. They planned brief stops in Lagny, Meaux, and Provins as they made their way back to Troyes. Henri's brother Étienne would accompany them as far as Provins, where he had business to attend to before he headed back to his own lands in Sancerre. Most of the time the two brothers rode side by side. As they traveled, Marie on horseback and the two youngest children with Jeanne in the litter, young Henri rode a small palfrey beside her. His mother watched him, proudly upright in the saddle, and smiled. He looked very grown up. She so wished Eleanor could see him.

In one of the rare moments when Count Henri dropped back to ride beside his wife, he observed, "You're very quiet."

"I've just been thinking," she said softly. She was contemplating not only her son, but also how her own life had expanded in recent months to include her mother, her English brothers, and an entirely new attitude about life. Her mother had shown her ways to keep her court occupied in the winter months and her ladies amused during those long summer months while their husbands were away. She was already considering how and where she might hold her courts of love. She wasn't sure what Henri would make of them, but he wasn't always there.

"Thinking about what?" he asked.

"About the many things I learned at my mother's court in Poitiers."

"Such as?"

"Well, she's trying a whole new way to civilize the young men who come to her court, ways to teach them courteous behavior and restraint, many of the things they should learn about chivalry," she said, trying to couch the matter in a way that would be acceptable to her husband.

"You're not talking about those silly courts of love, are you? I've heard about them. They're an utter waste of time, if you ask me, and they can lead young men in paths they should not go."

"I disagree. They're a distraction from warfare. That's all you men ever talk about. Warfare. All you teach the squires is behavior on the battlefield, and they sometimes bring that roughness and belligerence into the great hall. The only other activity they seem to care about is jousting, which is basically the same thing, just with more rules."

"Those rules are important and may save their lives someday."

"I'm not questioning their value. I'm just suggesting that there are other rules that might civilize them and make them good courtiers as well as good soldiers. There is more to life than fighting," she said. "They need to have good manners and know how to treat ladies."

"From what I hear, those courts teach men to seduce women," Henri replied in a grumpy voice.

"Not at all. In fact, it's the lady who controls these matters," she said.

"Well, don't expect me to participate if you ever try such a thing," he said, ending the conversation as he spurred his horse and trotted ahead to speak to Anseau, who was leading the group of riders.

As daily life resumed in Troyes, neither Marie nor Henri mentioned courts of love for a long while. But Marie had not forgotten. She spent her spare time scribbling on a piece of parchment her answer to the question about love and marriage that she had promised to send to her mother.

Before the letter was finished, however, a nobleman from Aquitaine, passing through Troyes on his way to Reims, requested hospitality for a night at the castle. Marie greeted him eagerly.

"Have you news of Queen Eleanor?" she asked him with a warm smile as they sat at dinner. Her reputation for hospitality was still a matter of great concern to her, and she always tried to show visitors the courtesy she would hope for at another's court. "I visited her in the spring and summer," she added.

The man, whose name was Imbert, took a sip of the wine a squire had just served. "You do, know, *ma dame*, that she is no longer in Aquitaine?" he asked.

"Where is she now?" Marie asked eagerly. She had assumed that her brothers would rejoin their mother's court in Poitiers after meeting with their father at Gisors. She'd heard that the young men had not accepted their father's terms and that things stood just where they had been before the summer battles began.

"No one knows, my lady," Imbert said. "The gossip is that she heard King Henry's men were on their way to her court to capture her. They say she sneaked away dressed in men's clothes to try to make it to Paris, but I heard she was betrayed by some of her own vassals—treacherous dogs. That Plantagenet must have paid them well, for she has been good to us all."

"What do you mean—no one knows where she is? He hasn't harmed her, has he?" Marie was alarmed.

"We don't know, my lady. No one has heard news of her since she was taken."

"Why would King Henry do such a thing?"

She was immediately sorry she had asked the question. Of course he didn't know, but *she* did. *He thought she had encouraged her sons in their rebellion. And he was right.* Eleanor was furious with her husband, not just because he was swiving that Rosamund Clifford, but because he was doing it so publicly, openly flaunting his mistress in the queen's place. *He deserved the rebellion*, she thought. Although she worried for her mother's safety, she did not believe that even King Henry would have the audacity to kill her.

Her mother's capture made Marie more determined than ever to honor her teachings. If King Henry would do such a thing and try to stifle Queen Eleanor, then she would be her mother's voice and carry on her efforts to civilize young knights and squires. She would make it her personal rebellion against men who sought to control everything in the lives of women. She recalled how easily her own husband had cast her aside over a quarrel with her father. If he ever did such a thing again, it would be because she was trying to have some say over her own life, as her mother had done. She refused to concede that everything in her life would be determined by men. She would hold her first court of love during the Christmas season, when many women would attend the festivities. She could hardly wait.

CHAPTER 33

Marie reminded him a few days before their guests arrived that she intended to hold a court of love sometime during the Christmas season. He objected, but she was adamant.

"Well, don't expect me to participate," he said firmly.

As the courtiers arrived for Christmas, she eagerly gathered the women together to tell them about the new game and the rules she had learned at Poitiers. The younger ones seemed particularly interested and enthusiastic about participating.

"I wish our husbands treated us that way," said Félicité de Brienne, wife of Henri's seneschal, Geoffrey de Joinville.

"Oh, but you miss the point. The relationship between husbands and wives is totally different. They are usually arranged by our fathers and are not our choice. We grant our favors to our husbands because we must. Church law requires it. But this new kind of love is of our choosing. It has nothing to do with marriage," Marie told her.

"Are you recommending adultery?" Félicité asked, shocked.

"Of course not," Marie said. "In fact, the ideal of *fine amor*, as it is called, is a love that is noble and ideal, usually even chaste. Only in the most extreme cases does it come to the physical act. Restraint and decorum are an important part of the goal. Besides, it's only a game—something to help us teach the young men how to behave in the presence of ladies if they seek our favor."

"What is the lady's role exactly?"

"It's rather like that of lord and vassal, but it's the lady who is the lord and the lover who is her vassal. She teaches him appropriate refinement. Sometimes she puts him to the test to see if he understands his role."

"It sounds rather cruel," Hermesende observed.

"No more cruel than that of the usual male and female relationship, only the roles of *fine amor* are reversed from the usual. In this noble love, the lady controls the relationship."

"What a grand idea," said Hodierne, the wife of Artaud.

Your marriage may be the exception, Marie thought, for, unlike most women, Hodierne had a degree of control over her husband. Artaud had been a poor man, born a serf, fortunate enough to marry a rich woman. Although marriage might raise a woman's rank, it did not do the same for a man. Despite the airs he took on and the roles he played at court, he was still a serf. His marriage to a woman of higher rank and greater wealth had saved him, but she could put him in his place from time to time and exact her due. Had they both been noble, even if the wife were richer, it was the husband who controlled the purse strings, but the precariousness of Artaud's position made their relationship different. Nevertheless, Hodierne seemed quite interested in the new courtly pastime Marie was proposing.

"Do you think any of the men will agree to take part?" asked Hermesende.

"They've all heard rumors about these new ideas from the south. I think they'll come just out of curiosity—some of them anyhow," Marie said. *Not Henri, perhaps, for he's stubborn, but perhaps the others*, she hoped. "I'm sure you can persuade some of your knights and squires to participate."

During the forty days of Advent, the court had been subdued with fasting and preparing for the Nativity. But with the Christmas season, fasting ended. Feasting began and lasted for the twelve days that led to Epiphany. The gathering for the Christmas court was always festive, and Marie planned to make this one even more memorable. She had instructed the ladies at the court how to prepare for the questions they might receive, and on the evening when she planned to launch her first court of love, she invited the usual jongleurs and acrobats to entertain during the feast itself. Only afterwards would the male courtiers learn the new game.

"It's a waste of time," Henri muttered. He could imagine what his brother Archbishop Guillaume would have to say about such an undertaking.

"Well, I think the ladies will enjoy it. And it will be instructive to the young knights."

He said no more, though his face wore a definite look of disapproval. He certainly didn't plan to take part, but he would keep an eye out to make sure these so-called courts of love didn't get out of hand.

On the day after Christmas, as the feasting came to an end, the ladies all gathered together, laughing and talking, excited at what was about to happen. At Marie's instruction, the servants quickly removed the trestle table from the dais and replaced it with a stately chair from the tribunal chamber. Marie herself mounted the dais and stood in front of the chair.

"Fill your goblets and prepare for a courtroom where ladies will be the judges," she announced.

The men groaned in mockery and muttered a few incomprehensible comments, but nonetheless they summoned squires to fill their goblets and waited for her to continue.

"Anyone may pose a question or present a case that involves matters of love and courtship. That petitioner may select the lady to give a judgment. Now, who would like to begin?" she asked. "Ladies may take their time to consider their answer."

She was still a bit unsure how the court was going to work out here in Champagne. Courtiers from the north seemed more reticent and less candid about such matters than those at her mother's court in Aquitaine. She could only hope for the best. There was a long silence in the room, as everyone waited expectantly for the first question. Finally, Nevelon, who had posed the first question at Queen Eleanor's court, stepped forward.

"How should a young knight demonstrate his love for a lady? I address my question to Countess Marie."

Marie, already on the dais, sat down to ponder the question. She was quiet for a moment before she replied. "He should seek to be the best of knights, striving in all things to be courteous, honest, generous, and always ready to obey his lady's commands. He should be sensitive to actions, manners, ways of speaking, and dress that seem to please her, and he should keep only the best of company, always avoiding the presence of evil-doers. He should listen to her every word and be prepared to praise her good qualities, but only to her, not in the presence of others. A lover is worthy who shows restraint and respect and who is always prepared to serve the lady in her time of need."

Her answer done, she stood up.

"In other words, he must be a saint," the archbishop called out. His tone was mocking, but Marie was unperturbed.

"He should strive to be one, my lord," she said with a curtsey, "as should we all. Certainly he should be prepared to serve God as well as his lady. But we all know that men are human—at least most of them," she said. The court laughed. "We can only do our best as human beings to be kind and generous and gracious." The archbishop found nothing to argue about in her answer. He simply remained silent.

"Thank you, my lady. A very thorough answer," said Nevelon.

"Now I cede the dais to another lady and another question."

Most of the married men seemed reluctant to speak up, but Anseau, prompted by his wife, said, "I have a question. What is the lady's obligation in all this?"

"And whom do you choose to answer the question?"

"I choose Hermesende, my wife," he said quickly, to the laughter of everyone in the courtroom.

"Is that appropriate?" a voice called out.

"There is no rule against it," the countess said.

Hermesende's face was flushed, but she bravely stepped up onto the dais and sat down in the armchair, as Marie had done. "Please repeat your question," she said to her husband.

"My question is this: Does the lady have no responsibility in this relationship? Is her role only to make demands and judge a man's behavior?"

After a few moments of thought, Hermesende raised her head to reply. "The lady has the obligation to help anyone seeking her love to understand that he must be prepared to follow the rules Countess Marie has mentioned. If he is a young knight, not yet trained in courtesy, then she must do her best to instruct him. As he learns, she should put him to the test—to make sure he can show the restraint and obedience she requires." She paused for a moment and raised her hand for silence, as people began to mumble to each other. Then she continued.

"But she has other obligations as well. She too must strive always to be worthy of his love, living with honor and honesty. She must not deceive him by accepting his gifts if she has no interest in his love. She should encourage him no further. But he has lost nothing, for whatever efforts he has put into his training in proper behavior, he will surely gain favor elsewhere and benefit from his experience in seeking the love of other ladies."

"Well said," Marie complimented her, and the other women applauded her answer. Anseau nodded, looking impressed, as he gave his hand to Hermesende to help her down from the dais. It was an excellent answer, especially for one being asked her first question.

As the evening wore on, questions came more easily, men seemed more relaxed and their reactions more lively. All the ladies were called upon at one time or another, and each of them made efforts to give clear answers, some more successfully than others.

Marie wanted to end the court while people were still interested. "We shall have only one more question," she announced.

"May I pose a question, my lady?" asked a squire who stood beside a door away from the crowd.

"How old are you, lad?" she asked.

"I'm eighteen, my lady," he said.

"Then you are old enough to be involved in the game of love," she said. "A man must be at least eighteen before he is mature enough to consider these matters. It is young people like you who can benefit most from this instruction. It can complete your noble training—helping you to understand that there is more to being a knight than merely clashing on a battlefield. One must also learn how to behave within the court itself."

"Thank you, my lady. Here is my question. How does one know if he is in love?" The older men laughed, but the countess raised her hand to silence them.

"That is a fine question. And whom do you choose to answer?"

"I choose you, my lady, if you are willing. You seem to know more about these matters than anyone present."

"Only because I had practice at my mother's court in Poitiers," she said. "But I shall be happy to answer your question. Once more she mounted the steps to the dais and took her place as judge. She paused only a few moments to consider her answer.

"The lover recognizes the signs of love by its symptoms. It's like an illness. When he finds himself suddenly in the presence of a lady and feels his heart begin to palpitate, he will know. When he feels himself grow pale in her presence, he will know. And if he can eat and sleep but little for thoughts of her, he will know. In fact, his every act will be imbued with thoughts of her."

The young man grinned and bowed as he accepted her answer. "*Merci, ma dame.*"

"And so, are you in love, my boy?" asked one of the older knights, slapping him on the back with a hearty laugh.

"I have learned this evening that it is never wise to reveal one's love, my lord," the boy said smoothly. The entire court cheered his reply, and he blushed as he moved back to his position by the door.

And so the first court of love in Troyes ended. Marie thought it a triumph. Henri did not agree, as he informed her when they were alone later in their bedchamber.

"It was a silly game, and I think many people were embarrassed by it. My brother Guillaume disapproved—that I know." He poured himself a goblet of wine from the flagon by the bed.

"It's not a game designed for the clergy, but the chaplain Andreas and even Drogo seemed to enjoy it at the court in Poitiers," she said. "Would you pour me one as well?"

"I expect they were just being polite. Guillaume thought you were encouraging adultery." The goblet he handed her was only half full.

"Nonsense. Things like that go on, as you well know, but we certainly don't promote them. We're just trying to civilize court behavior."

"You can say that all you want, but you're inspiring dangerous flirtations," he argued.

"We're just trying to teach young men that they can't treat a lady as they would a scullery maid or a peasant. If they want a noble lady to pay attention to them, they must treat her almost as though she were the Madonna herself," she said, sipping on her wine.

"That sounds blasphemous to me, Marie. It can only lead to trouble."

"We'll see. But I'm doing this for my mother, Henri, and I'll continue to do it because she can't, thanks to her brute of a husband. In the meantime, I'll make sure not to hold courts of love when you are here. I certainly don't want them to trouble you." Her voice was defiant.

"They might trouble me more when I'm not here."

"Are you forbidding them?" she asked curtly.

"I'm considering it," he replied.

"That's not a good idea." Setting her goblet on the table with a thud, she flung back the coverlet and blew out the candle on her side of the bedstead.

Henri did the same and said no more. They lay in bed back-to-back, not touching, as they waited for sleep.

During the summer of 1174, Marie and her children waited in Provins while Henri and his men were away once more, fighting beside Louis and Eleanor's sons, who had renewed their challenge to King Henry for power. Once again they failed. In the end, they had no choice but to accept the terms their father dictated, which were far less generous than they had been a year earlier—a few castles and a set income. They met at Montlouis between Tours and Amboise on September 21 to settle the matter. The following May, the Young King did homage to his father at Winchester and promised him henceforth only good conduct, offering Louis, Henri, and Thibaut as his pledges. Thus the matter ended, at least for now, without further bloodshed.

During Henri's absence, at the time of the fair of St. John, which began in late June, the countess once again held a court of love. Many of the same ladies as before were present, along with those few knights and squires who remained at court. This time they varied the game with mock conversations between a lady and her potential lover. His role was to explain why she should return his love, and hers was to argue why, in her view, it would not be suitable—good practice in reasoning for them both.

Although she didn't mention these diversions to Henri when he returned, he learned of them anyhow. The court was always full of gossips. She could tell he was displeased, and she decided to end them, at least for now, to keep him happy. But she could not help but resent the fact that he was curtailing even her leisure activities.

The count and countess returned with their family to Troyes well before the cold fair, which began on All Saint's Day. One afternoon in the midst of the fair, Henri returned from buying two new horses brought from Spain. She could tell immediately that he was upset.

"What's wrong?" she asked, as he entered the solar, his face like a thundercloud.

"I told you those silly courts of yours would only lead to trouble."

"What do you mean?" Marie asked.

"One of the merchants from Flanders has told me that Count Philip found his wife in adultery."

"Elisabeth? *Mordieu*. What happened?"

"Philip heard rumors and set a trap for his wife. He pretended to go on a hunt but returned without warning and found his wife in *flagrante delicto* with that knight, Gautier de Fontaine. I guess they were practicing that *fine amor* you talk about." He spat out the word with disgust.

"You mean… they were caught in an act of love?"

"If that's what you want to call it," he said in a bitter voice. "Love… humph," he muttered. "An act of fornication."

"What did Philip do?" she asked, alarmed for her cousin.

"He did what he should have done. He locked up his wife and now keeps her under close surveillance. He had Gautier whipped and hung head down over a sewage pit. The merchant told me the wretch died there. Good riddance," Henri said with a sense of satisfaction.

Marie was horrified. "Poor Gautier," she said in a breathless voice. "And poor Elisabeth." Tears welled in her eyes as she remembered their interaction during the trip to Poitiers. It had seemed so harmless. And now this.

"Poor Elisabeth?" Henri's voice rose in anger. "What of the humiliation of the count of Flanders? What of him? What of their marriage?"

Marie just shook her head and said no more. What could she say?

She had grown very fond of Elisabeth during their travels together. Even then, Marie suspected that her cousin was unhappy because she remained childless after such a long marriage and felt she'd failed in her role as a woman. She also suspected that Philip's motive for not putting her aside had less to do with his "great love" for her than for his desire to keep her land—the Vermandois. Marie had noticed in Poitiers that Gautier was obviously smitten. Perhaps Elisabeth needed consolation. Gautier had no doubt made her feel valued in a way that Philip had not. Who could ever say why anyone took such risks? She could only imagine Elisabeth's grief and misery at seeing her lover so brutally killed. How could they have been so foolish and so careless?

Marie wondered how the chaplain Andreas would react to the news. He had already sent the first few pages of his little treatise on love to Marie, pages he had addressed, as promised, to Gautier. It was written in Latin—*the language of priests*, she thought. But she had read it, making a few suggestions when she returned it, and urged him to continue his work, as Queen Eleanor and the other ladies would want.

For a time Marie's enthusiasm for the courts of love diminished. Perhaps Henri was right that they encouraged illicit liaisons. But during the next summer season, when the men were away fighting their endless battles, the ladies left behind clamored for another one. Everyone had been shocked at the news of Gautier's death and Elisabeth's dishonor, realizing the dangers their game could bring. But to many of them, it seemed even more exciting because of the danger. Some of the tales told by jongleurs included jealous husbands as comic and ignominious characters, but the women at Marie's court knew that they could also be vindictive and cruel.

"It seems so unfair," one of the ladies pointed out, "that men can have all the mistresses they want without consequence. Even the Church turns a blind eye—with a few Hail Marys for penance." The others nodded, thinking of poor Elisabeth, condemned by the clergy and probably confined to her room for the rest of her life. Or worse.

It was true that men engaged in such actions with impunity. Marie thought of Anne Musnier, that mistress of Henri who may have saved his life. She'd reminded him during the May fair in Provins, which began the day before Ascension, that he had not yet provided for her and her family the lasting reward he had promised. As a consequence, he had granted her husband, Girard de Langres, along with their family and heirs, exemption from all taxes and exactions and from any type of military service or expedition. Along with that, he gave them the right to be brought to court only before the count himself. Their only obligation in return was to make a small annual donation of ten *sous* paid to his almoner, to be distributed to the poor. It was quite a concession and one that would last in perpetuity. As a rule, only nobles were exempt from taxes, but he felt that Anne deserved it by her courage.

However, her bravery had also caused her name to be linked publicly to his. As a consequence, he had stopped sending for Anne to meet his personal needs. There were always others he could call on, and she *was* growing older.

At least, Marie thought, *she's no longer part of our lives.*

Several months later, the court of Troyes received news of the death on November 13 of Archbishop Henry of Reims. Henri met the news with outward regret, though in his heart he was relieved.

"I'm sorry for his death," he told his wife. "I know he was your uncle, but perhaps the new archbishop will be easier to get along with." Relations between the two of them had never ceased to be contentious.

Marie remembered the time Pierre de Celle had sent his own emissary, a fellow abbot from Reims, Bernerède de Saint Crispin, to try to patch up relations between Archbishop Henry and her husband. Pierre had later informed her how effective her diversions had been.

"He came back to Reims feeling completely bedazzled by your hospitality, dragging a long tail of glory behind him from all the attentions you gave him in Troyes. He was so charmed that I gather he completely forgot why he had come and merely relaxed and enjoyed himself," he told her.

She laughed. "I do my best to provide gracious hospitality, my lord."

"I'm well aware of that, having been its recipient from time to time. There's no denying it. You do hold an excellent court, my lady," said

Pierre.

At least Archbishop Henry's death had put an end to the conflict between him and the count. There would be no more need for such emissaries.

"Wouldn't it be wonderful if my brother Guillaume could be archbishop of Reims instead of archbishop of Sens?" Henri suggested.

"Why couldn't he be?" Marie asked

"It would be extremely unusual to have someone trade one archbishopric for another. I don't know if it can be done," he said.

But the idea was planted. Why not indeed? It was worth a try to urge the pope to appoint his brother to the post.

When Henri and Marie attended the Christmas court of Louis and Adèle that year, he broached the idea. The king was immediately enthusiastic. Having his wife's brother as archbishop of Reims would benefit him almost as much as having his brother as bishop, and certainly Guillaume was not averse to the idea. "But it might be difficult to convince the pope," he said.

"It's worth a try," Henri urged. "I believe Pierre de Celle will support the idea, and I think the pope will value his opinion."

To their surprise, Pope Alexander did not resist, and in 1176 he named forty-year-old Guillaume de Champagne as archbishop of Reims, with the consecration taking place August 8.

"People have taken to calling him Guillaume aux Blanches-Mains. I'm not sure why," Henri told Marie.

"Perhaps they're proclaiming his purity," she suggested.

"Or maybe his hands are just whiter than most," her husband laughed. "Who knows? Who cares? I'm just delighted with the appointment. I've lost an adversary and gained an ally."

This promised to be a new era.

CHAPTER 34

It was a new era indeed, but not the time of tranquility the countess had hoped for. While the new archbishop in Reims might ensure greater peace in the county, increasingly bad news was arriving from the Holy Land. The crusader states were being threatened by a new Muslim leader named Salah-ad-Din, called Saladin in France.

Since the death of Nur-ad-Din in 1174, various factions had struggled for power among the Muslims, but Saladin had finally emerged as their clear leader. Christian leaders were alarmed by his ease and success in consolidating his power. He had captured Damascus in 1174, and the Muslims in the Levant were growing stronger and beginning to threaten the Christian kingdoms there. The pope was calling for a new crusade.

It had been thirty years since such an undertaking. Although some of the veterans of the last crusade hesitated, others had all but forgotten the hardships, choosing to remember only the adventure, but convinced that this time, they would do things differently. It was an opportunity to correct the failure of their youth. For younger men, who had become knights more recently, it would be their first great exploit. Thus, by mid-1177, crusading fever was beginning to take hold once again.

The kings of France and England met on September 25, 1177, to draw up a peace treaty, each pledging at that time that he would take the cross and go to Jerusalem. It promised to be the beginning of a massive new crusade.

"I'm going to take the cross at Christmastide," Henri announced one evening as he and Marie were preparing for bed.

"Must you?" she asked. "You've done it before. Must you go again?"

"I feel God's call in my heart," he said. "And I would like to see the holy places once more. When I was there before, I was young and eager for battle, but also eager to get home again and make my mark on the world. I walked where Christ had walked and went to the holy sites, but more as a sightseer than as a true pilgrim. I didn't really appreciate the spiritual fulfillment I should have felt. Now I'd like to go back."

"Just don't go there and do what Étienne did," she said. Henri's brother Étienne had gone to the Holy Land in 1170 shortly after the death of his wife, Alix de Donzy, hoping to marry Sybilla, the daughter of the king of Jerusalem. But the marriage had not worked out. While he was there, the bishop of Jerusalem complained that he had led a "disgracefully licentious life."

"Of course I won't," he said. "You know me better than that."

"And what did it gain him? On his way back, he lost everything to those Armenian bandits, except for that wretched horse they left him with."

"I'll be careful," he promised.

"I suppose it's useless to ask you not to go or else to take me with you," she said, climbing into bed. She had heard him speak many times of the problems women caused on the last crusade.

"I wouldn't think of taking you. You have three children to care for, and the last such venture destroyed your parents' marriage. Frankly, I'm surprised that you would even bring it up."

"Women want excitement and spiritual fulfillment in their lives just as men do."

"Perhaps, but such a journey is not the place to seek it."

"Who will rule the county in your absence?" she asked. "Our son Henri is much too young."

"You will, I hope. That's one of the reasons I've wanted you at court occasionally—to see how it's done. Whatever decisions you can postpone until my return can wait. But I trust your judgment in *most* things, and I will ask for the pope's protection for my lands while I'm away." He blew out his candle as though that ended the conversation.

Marie lay staring into the darkness and thinking about being left in control of all of Champagne and its almost two thousand knights. It seemed overwhelming. And for how long? It could be years. She had watched Henri conduct court sessions often enough, and presiding over courts of love, however frivolous some might view them, had helped her gain self-confidence in leading discussions and maintaining order. But this was serious. *Could she do it?* she wondered. *Surely Henri will leave some able advisors behind.*

Henri was expecting to join the two kings in their expedition. By the beginning of the next year, it became apparent that they would not be going after all. Louis's health was failing, and he would be unable to make the trip. King Henry had no intention of leaving the king of France behind to plot against him. So it would not be a full-fledged crusade led by two kings after all.

"Must you go, now that the kings will not go?" Marie asked. "Is the situation in the East as dire as all that?"

"I have taken an oath," he replied. "And I want to see the holy places again."

Perhaps, then, it will be primarily a pilgrimage, Marie thought. She was relieved that both her husband and father would not be away at the same time. *At least I will have* Papa *nearby if I need him*, she thought. She knew that many men had little respect for women in positions of power, for she had heard her mother and Countess Ermengarde talk about the difficulties of ruling as a woman. It was wise to be wary of men's efforts to cheat or trick her in any way, for she had little doubt they would try.

Henri spent the entire following year preparing for his journey and dealing with matters of importance that he wanted to accomplish before he left. He had his new chancellor conduct a thorough inventory of all his fiefs and make a written record for the benefit of the countess in his absence. It would be known as the *Feoda Campanie* and would, he thought, provide an important document for years to come.

He also wanted to make certain that all was well with those to whom he owed homage. King Louis, he felt sure, would make no effort to take advantage of his absence while his daughter was in charge. He was less certain of the German emperor. Thus, as a precaution, he visited Frederick Barbarossa to be sure that all was in order on that front. He also wanted to be certain that the emperor was sincere in his agreement in a recent Treaty of Venice finally to recognize Pope Alexander as the rightful pope and abandon his efforts to support the current anti-pope, Calixtus III. His assurance would put Henri's mind at rest that there would be no future troubles from that controversy.

One late fall evening as he and Marie sat before the fire in the solar, Henri, who had been staring into the blaze, said unexpectedly, "You know, Marie, I could die on this journey."

"Then don't go," she replied.

"You know I must. I took the cross. But I wanted to discuss the possibilities before I leave, and it occurs to me that death is one of them."

"Don't say such a thing. You're barely fifty. I'm sure you have many years left."

"But this is a hard trip. One never knows what to expect. I want you prepared just in case."

"Oh, Henri, please don't talk that way," she said, turning her head away so that he could not see the anxiety that clouded her eyes.

"I want to discuss the plans for my tomb," he went on. "I want my sarcophagus to rest in the very center of my chapel, and I want the tomb to reflect the splendor of the chapel itself. I've already discussed the design with a tomb-maker. Promise me that you'll follow through with this if I should die on the journey." He was looking at her earnestly now.

"Of course, Henri, I'll do whatever you want. I just wish you wouldn't think of such matters right now, because I have some good news to share with you," she said.

"Yes? What is it? I can always use good news," he said, his expression brightening.

"I am expecting another child. Perhaps it will be a second son."

"That is good news indeed, my dear. Are you sure?" he asked with a broad smile.

"I waited long enough so that I could be sure before I told you. I think the baby will come in the spring—most likely late April or May," she said. She was feeling sick in the mornings and had missed her last two monthly bleedings, though Henri did not seem to have noticed. When her breasts began to swell, she'd called in a midwife, who confirmed her suspicions. She'd waited for the right moment to tell Henri, but hearing him talk about his possible death made her reluctant to keep it from him any longer. It would give him reason to try harder to return safely from his journey.

"Please don't leave before this child is born. I can't conduct a court until then," she said.

Henri was planning his departure for mid-March to take advantage of the longest possible stretch of good weather. The delay would cost him and his men valuable travel time, especially if the child didn't come before May. Nevertheless, for once, he acceded to her wishes and postponed his trip accordingly.

As it turned out, he needed more planning time, given the influx of visitors that appeared in Troyes during the winter months—some of them bishops on their way to a meeting in Rome for the Third Lateran Council, which Pope Alexander had called for the second and third weeks of March. One of its purposes was to confirm the agreement with Frederick Barbarossa to end the papal schism.

Among the winter visitors who stopped at the court of Champagne en route to the council meeting was a secular clerk from the court of England named Walter Map. Marie was delighted by news of his impending arrival. She knew him by reputation as a well-known raconteur, said to be collecting tales about King Arthur and his court, which she was eager to hear. But more important, if he came from the English court, he might also have news of her mother.

Walter Map rode hard into the courtyard one afternoon in mid-January, accompanied by his scribe and a single servant. They were soaking wet from a sudden torrential downpour. The icy rain was still sheeting down, as Henri greeted them, and Walter's teeth were chattering.

"Come in. Come in and dry yourselves," Henri said, rushing them into the great hall before the warm fire and having his squire pour a glass of mulled wine for Walter and his scribe, as the servant was sent off to the kitchen.

"Welcome, my lord." Marie curtsied, gave the new guest her most hospitable smile, and turned to instruct the chamberlain. "Have the maids make rooms ready and find them some dry clothes. They're both soaked to the skin."

"Yes, my lady," Artaud said with a bow and scurried off to do her bidding.

While Henri was making every effort to make the two men comfortable, Marie began to consider what they might have on hand to prepare as a feast. Time was short, and it would not be as elaborate on such short notice as she would have liked. But perhaps Walter would visit for a few days and entertain them with his stories.

"I would be delighted to stay a while," he agreed, "as long as I can make it to Rome on time for the council. It's at least a month-long journey—maybe more. I don't look forward to the trip in the middle of winter."

His presence at the Lateran Council was not required by the pope, unlike that of the nearly three hundred bishops who would attend, but King Henry wanted him there to observe the events and report back to him. He did not always trust clergymen's accounts.

"I'm so pleased, and I hope you will tell us some of the Arthurian stories you have collected," Marie said.

"Of course, I would especially like to share my latest interest—a story of a knight called Lancelot, who was the lover of Guinevere, King Arthur's queen." Walter smiled with pleasure at her interest.

The countess nodded in appreciation. "Then we shall hold a large feast two days hence, where you can tell the story to our court."

Despite her pregnancy, she made elaborate plans for the feast, inviting, along with various jongleurs and minstrels, the writer Chrétien, who had recently completed an Arthurian romance of his own about a couple named Erec and Enide. She liked the story very much, for one reason because the heroine, Enide, was a clever woman who helped to direct the actions of her husband. Erec always did best when he listened to his wife's advice, which pleased the countess. Perhaps, she thought, Chrétien could learn from Walter and gather material for other tales to write. No doubt the two men would enjoy knowing one another.

Marie had heard no news of her mother for many months, and as far as she knew, she was still held captive by the English king. As they took their evening meal, Marie broached the subject.

"I have not seen her of late, *ma dame*," he replied to her question. "As far as I know she is still in confinement at the castle on Salisbury Plain. However, I hear that she is being treated in a most queenly manner, with all the luxuries she's accustomed to. She even has visitors from time to time. All she's deprived of is her liberty," he assured her.

All? Marie thought. *To deprive such an independent woman of her freedom of movement is a cruel punishment indeed.* But she was relieved to know that her mother was at least able to maintain a dignified life style. *Even though she must be intensely unhappy.*

"I have heard also that Rosamund Clifford is dead. Is that true?"

"Yes, my lady, for several years now."

"But still he keeps my mother prisoner," she said. At least she felt a sense of satisfaction that Rosamund was no longer in the king's bed.

The mention of Rosamund clearly made Walter uncomfortable, and he seemed eager to change the subject. He took a swallow of wine and said to Marie, "I have heard about these courts of love you have conducted. I know for a fact that Queen Eleanor has been told of them. I've been told that she is quite pleased that you carry on one of her favorite pastimes. Tell me how they work."

Marie smiled, pleased to know that her mother had heard about them. She would understand that her daughter was holding her courts with fond remembrance of their time together in Poitiers. As she began to explain the purpose of the game to Walter and how the courts of love worked, she informed him that they had added a new component.

"Sometimes we vary it with lively dialogues between a man and a woman, posing as members of various social classes."

"You mean like a lady and a rich merchant?" he asked.

"Yes, that's the idea—or like a man of the high nobility and a lady of lower rank, or even a commoner," she said. "Perhaps even a lady and a clergyman."

"A clergyman? That's interesting. I should most like to observe such a conversation," he said. "You are no doubt aware the Church urges priests to forego such love affairs and even marriage. The pope is not happy with the news that some of them are leaving their worldly goods not to the Church, but to their sons at death." Walter laughed. "I wouldn't even be surprised if the issue were brought up at the council meeting."

At the large feast in Walter's honor, Marie watched Chrétien as he sat at one of the lower tables, listening with rapt attention to the clerk's stories of Arthur's court. She had also seen the two men in animated discussion earlier in the evening. *Perhaps*, she thought, *I could persuade Chrétien to write a story about Lancelot, one in which the knight is, above all, obedient to his lady. A story of* fine amor. *Perhaps I could commission such a work while Henri is away.* It was an idea worth considering, and it would give her something to occupy her thoughts during Henri's absence in Outremer.

In addition to his story-telling skills, she discovered during the feast that Walter was a lively conversationalist. He could discuss literature and philosophy, and overflowed with anecdotes that delighted both the count and countess. Although Walter had never visited their court before, he seemed like an old friend, interested and curious about their lives, and Henri spoke freely with him.

At one point in the evening, Walter was telling Count Henri about meeting one of his kinsmen. Henri, who had by now consumed three goblets of wine, leaned over to Walter, and Marie heard him say, "He's a fine young man—except for one thing."

"And what is that?" Walter asked.

"He's far too generous—verging on extravagance," Henri replied.

Walter looked startled. Marie too was surprised. She knew well that her father had more than once chastised Henri for enriching what he called "effeminate churchmen" at the expense of his son's inheritance. Walter too was well familiar with the count's reputation as unstinting in his own generosity.

"I can hardly believe you would criticize a kinsman for being overly generous," he said, "when you yourself are called Henri the Liberal for your own, almost prodigal, largesse. What, may I ask, are the limits of generosity, in your opinion?"

"The limit comes when one has no more to give. I don't find it admirable to acquire and use ill-gotten gains just to be able to appear generous. That's not honorable, in my view," Count Henri replied.

Walter nodded, impressed by his answer.

Marie said nothing, but Henri's own liberality did worry her at times, for thanks to his constant gifts, their coffers were far from overflowing, and she had begun to find it necessary to keep a strict accounting of her household expenditures. Although he had constructed his household and his chapel lavishly and spent freely on books and hospitality, which he considered essential, he was not overly indulgent in luxuries to his family. While Henri denied Marie nothing she truly needed, he was rarely extravagant in his gifts to her. Growing up in the royal household, her mother had taught her as a child to love beautiful things—a taste that had been reinforced at the court in Poitiers. In Paris Eleanor's small indulgences—silken pillows, jewels, fine garments—had also helped to brighten the gloomy atmosphere. Here in Troyes, Marie was surrounded with the splendor of the new palace and St. Étienne, but she missed the personal luxuries. There was always enough, but never a great abundance, for Henri gave away such a large portion of their income to monasteries and churches. Now, with this crusade of his, he was stripping his own wealth once more to fund the voyage. Like her father, Marie was concerned that he might be impoverishing his heirs to enrich priests and canons. But whenever she commented, Henri tried to soothe her by saying, "God will provide." She certainly hoped so.

Walter's visit ended all too soon, as far as Marie was concerned. She had delighted in his stories and interaction with the members of her court, and she gathered from his comments that he and Chrétien had become mutual admirers in their short time together. Nevertheless, he bade goodbye on a cold but sunny morning, soon enough to give himself ample travel time to reach Rome before the council meeting began.

Several months remained before the expected birth of Marie's baby. Henri used the time to make more donations to churches, endow another chapter of canons, increase various endowments, and exempt the Hospitallers from taxes. He even granted a communal charter to the city of Meaux, exempting its citizens from taxes, even the *taille*, which only commoners paid, in exchange for 140 *livres* a year. It was the first time he had ever granted a communal charter and such relative independence to one of his cities.

One day in early March, Marie looked up from her needlework as her husband entered the solar. "Henri," she said, "I've been thinking about the future. Since you are taking care of so many details before your departure, don't you think we should ask the count of Hainaut to ratify the betrothal agreement between his children and ours? At this point we have only Count Philip's agreement. Don't we need that of the children's father as well?"

"You're right," he said. "We've put that off long enough. I'll send an invitation at once to Count Baudouin to visit Troyes to ratify the agreement.

Troyes, May 13, 1179

Count Baudouin arrived in early May. In his party was a young poet named Gautier d'Arras, a man eager to meet the countess, who was becoming well known for her love of poetry. But Marie was already in her confinement and unavailable to greet them. Thus, with the help of Artaud and Anseau, Henri did the best he could to provide for his visitors' needs. But he keenly felt the absence of his wife's legendary charm and hospitality. Gautier was obviously disappointed, but made the best of things by entertaining the court for several nights with readings of his tale of *Ille et Galeron*.

Now it was Sunday, and the two counts had attended mass together at St. Étienne and were enjoying a leisurely walk in the castle garden and discussing Henri's upcoming trip to the Holy Land. Their primary business was behind them. The marriage agreement was ratified and settled to everyone's satisfaction. It was their last day together, for Baudouin and his retinue planned to depart the following morning, all except Gautier, who wished to remain until the countess was free of her confinement.

Suddenly a young page came running into the garden, grinning broadly.

"What is it, my boy?" asked Henri. He'd been informed at prime that Marie was in labor. It had begun the night before, but by the time mass began, the baby had still not come.

"My lord." The boy was breathless from excitement. "You have another son."

A smile broke across Henri's face. "Thank you, lad," he said, dismissing the page.

"Congratulations, my friend," Baudouin said, offering his hand to Henri. "What name will you give him?"

"Thibaut, for my father," Henri answered without hesitation.

When he made no move to return to the palace, Baudouin said, "Please feel free to go. I'm sure you'd like to see your son."

"Not until I'm summoned. You know how these things are. As men, we're not welcome anywhere near the birthing room until we're invited." Henri had never dared to approach the birthing room during his wife's labor, nor did he want to. Such rooms had a stifling, dark atmosphere, for ladies did all they could to make it seem womblike—covering the windows to keep out the light and chill. All a father could do was try to keep himself occupied and wait for news of the child's birth. Most men's greatest desire was for it to be over so that they might have another son to carry on their name and a wife who would return to their bed as soon as she was churched, usually about forty days after the birth—though Henri doubted he would wait that long before he set out on his voyage. The good travel season was passing rapidly.

Near the end of May, as Henri and his soldiers prepared to begin their journey, the courtyard was filled with commotion—men saying last-minute goodbyes to their wives and children, squires talking excitedly to each other, and horses pawing impatiently at the ground. Dogs barked at the servants who scurried about on last-minute errands. Hélie wept openly and clung to her husband, Milon de Provins, while Pierre Bristaud was saying a reluctant goodbye to his new wife, Héloïse. Even Hodierne had come all the way to Troyes to see Artaud on his way. Already mounted beside Henri were his chaplain Nicholas and his former tutor, now his chancellor, Étienne de Provins. This time, his old friend Anseau was not going along, for he had been ill and was not yet able to travel such a long distance. He stood with the others in the courtyard, looking forlorn as he watched them mount their steeds and prepare to depart.

Their leave-taking was not so grand as the splendid and ceremonial departure from St. Denis had been back in 1147. As the men spurred their horses and rode two abreast out of the courtyard, Marie, her new baby in her arms, stood beside her other three children at the top of the palace steps to be able to watch the departing knights as far as possible. She could see the people of Troyes lining the streets to wave farewell.

Henri had no intention of repeating the mistakes of the earlier crusade. Instead of taking the land route, he planned to march his men south through Dijon and debark by ship at the port city of Marseille.

In the early weeks and months after their departure, news of their whereabouts trickled back to Troyes. Their ships docked for a time at Brindisi, where Henri encountered the archbishop of Tyre, returning from the Lateran Council. It was a fortuitous meeting, for the archbishop was able to inform him of all the most recent events in the Holy Land.

Once the count and the Champenois forces sailed on for Acre, Marie heard nothing else for quite a while. She had her hands full with her court responsibilities and a newborn son. She also felt a sense of liberty she had never felt before. She was in charge, able to make her own decisions and undertake a new venture she had in mind. For now, she continued to enjoy the visit of Gautier d'Arras, encouraging him to finish a work he had begun even before he wrote *Ille et Galeron*—a work he called *Eracle.*

"It will do great honor to Count Thibaut, who asked you to write it. And I will look forward to it as well."

"But you too have given me encouragement, as has the count of Hainaut. Before the work is ended, I assure you, I shall acknowledge you both," Gautier assured her.

She nodded and smiled. At the same time, she thought with pleasure, *Soon I will commission a work on my own.*

When Gautier departed at the end of the first week of June, Marie stood once again on the palace steps to wave goodbye. His visit had been delightful, making her more than ever determined to serve as patron to a great poet. As she watched him leave, she took a deep breath, then turned to one of the younger squires who had not accompanied Henri on his journey.

"Go to the home of Chrétien de Troyes, the writer, and ask him to come and see me tomorrow morning just after terce," she commanded in a self-assured voice.

"*Oïl, ma dame,*" he said with a bow. She watched him with a shiver of excitement, as he scurried out the gate and disappeared on his errand.

CHAPTER 35

Troyes, Tuesday, June 8, 1179

The poet Chrétien approached the palace gate with his usual awe. He was seldom invited to court unless it was for the purpose of reading his work at a feast or listening to the words of another poet the countess wanted him to meet. This time he had no idea why she had summoned him, for he knew Gautier had departed. He mounted the stone steps accompanied by a guard, who informed a squire of his presence.

When he entered the great hall, Chrétien was amazed by how large the room seemed when it was empty. Whenever he had been there before, it had been crowded with courtiers and alive with color, activity, and the mingled sounds of music and conversation. His footsteps echoed as he approached the dais, where the countess now waited, seated in an elegant armchair flanked by two squires ready to do her bidding. She was dressed in a blue silk *bliaut,* her wide sleeves almost touching the floor as her hands rested on the arms of the chair. A small gold coronet atop her wimple added to her regal appearance. He could see that she was smiling with welcome as he drew near.

"Chrétien de Troyes, at your service," he said with a bow. Then, straightening up so that he could look at her face, he asked, "You sent for me, *ma dame*?"

"I did," she said. "I want you to know that I enjoyed reading your *roman* about Erec and Enide. It's good of you to come. May I suppose that you are, like most poets, in need of patronage?"

"Poets always need patronage, my lady. It's how we make our living," he said with a grin. "And we are always grateful when a person of the high nobility like yourself appreciates our work." She was looking at him with interest, as though she were assessing him in some way.

"Then I may have an idea for a story that I would like you to write for me."

"I should be most happy to oblige, my lady," he said, adding a flourish to another bow. When he looked up to face her once more, he was smiling broadly, his warm, brown eyes dancing with delight. It would be his first paid commission, for she was promising what all poets hoped for. It was through such patronage that a poet could best support himself and a family if he had one—unless, of course, he was also a court officer or a priest or chaplain or even a monk. As for Chrétien, he had no interest in devoting his life to religion, even though he believed himself a good Christian who tried to follow Church teachings. But the idea of living such a confined life had never appealed to him. He preferred to work, like his friend Guiot de Provins, as a scribe to supplement his income and travel when he could to learn more of the world.

"As you surely recall," Marie said, "I invited you not long ago to a feast to honor our visitor from the court of England—Walter Map. I hoped you might find it an evening of pleasure and inspiration."

He nodded with enthusiasm. "I did indeed, my lady, and I thank you for including me at such times to meet him—and Gautier d'Arras as well," he said, growing more and more curious about what she had in mind.

"It was one of Walter's tales that set me to thinking. Do you recall the one he told about the knight Lancelot?" she asked.

"I do, *ma dame*."

"Good. It occurred to me that a story of Lancelot and his lady, the queen, for example, the tale of her abduction and his heroic rescue, might well serve as a good example to some of our young knights," she said.

He looked puzzled but said nothing, waiting for her to continue. His own impression of the story was that it depicted a wife's unfaithfulness and a knight deceiving his lord. How could such a tale possibly serve as a good example to young knights? A negative one perhaps? A cautionary tale of what one should not do? But as she continued, he could clearly see that she had a very different idea about the value of the story.

"I thought it might be useful in helping me teach young knights about their duties to a lady whose love they seek," she said. Her eyes were watching him carefully, and he could feel himself growing a bit uncomfortable under the intensity of her gaze. It was not unfriendly, just penetrating.

"But my lady, the tale—is it not one of betrayal and adultery?" he asked.

"I suppose one could choose to interpret it in that way, but I'm not asking you to emphasize that aspect of the story, but rather the knight's devotion to the queen, his willingness to undergo any sort of hardship to rescue her. I would like you to write of a Lancelot who honors and even worships his lady and seeks her love, one who would do anything to please her, even risk his life and dignity to do so."

Chrétien waited quietly as she explained her request. He had no problem with a young knight setting out to rescue his queen, but in his view, a man not her husband should never expect such carnal rewards, even if he is successful. Although Chrétien was not married himself, for he could not afford a wife, he was a firm believer in marriage and faithful love. He certainly saw how love could enrich a man's life, but he had also explored in his first work the dangers of an obsessive love, how, even within marriage, it can interfere with duty. A knight needed to keep his mind on his own honor and prowess as well. The hero of his story of Erec was so deeply in love with his bride that he was interested only in her. As a consequence, his reputation was called into question, until his wife insisted that he go out and prove his courage to others. In the course of his adventures, the hero found a proper balance between love and knightly prowess and became, in the end, worthy to be a king.

In his next book, Chrétien had planned to explore the other side of the equation—that of a knight who abandons his wife to seek a life of adventure, who cares more for his reputation for prowess than his love and responsibility for his wife, a knight interested only in proving his courage and earning a heroic reputation. Like Erec, he would have to find the balance between love and knightly duty, but from a very different direction. He had already begun the work, though he was not yet far into it. It was to be about a knight named Yvain. But even so, how could he refuse the commission of the countess? It was his first real offer of patronage, he reminded himself.

The countess continued to speak. "The duties I am referring to are those we talk about in the courts of love. In your version of the tale, Lancelot should have all the symptoms of one in love and be thoroughly absorbed in thoughts of his lady. And he should be willing to obey her every command, no matter what. In other words, you should depict him as the perfect lover."

"I shall no doubt need your guidance," he said. "for I'm sure I have no such understanding on my own." She looked both pleased and amused by his response.

"Of course," she said. "Since you have translated Ovid, I assume you are well versed in Latin."

"Yes, my lady." Even though Chrétien's family was not of the nobility, he had been well tutored by the young priest at his parish church, who had noticed him when he was only seven and thought him very bright. Father Albéric had asked his parents if he could teach the boy, and they agreed. Thus, for many years the priest and the child spent three afternoons each week poring over the two books Albéric owned and those they managed borrow from the library of Montier-la-Celle, where Chrétien's cousin Jean was a monk.

Thus, as a boy, he learned first to read and then to write, which seemed to come easily to him and for which the priest thought he had a special talent. When Père Albéric had taught him all he could, he continued to learn on his own by talking and debating with other educated people and by continuing to read everything he could get his hands on, thanks to the help of his cousin, who had tried to convince him to become a novice. That he had refused to do.

"Then," the countess said, "if you are willing to undertake the task, I shall lend you the first part of a little book that is being written by the chaplain Andreas, who serves at the court of Queen Adèle. In this section of the treatise, you can learn the art and rules of this courtly type of love we call *fine amor*."

"You say he is a chaplain?" he asked.

"It may sound rather odd that a chaplain would undertake such a work, but how could he refuse, when all the ladies in Poitiers begged him to do it? He himself had observed some of the courts of love held there by Queen Eleanor, and he seemed to understand what it was all about. The ladies were eager to have their ideas committed to writing. The little book, even though it is still incomplete, could no doubt be of help to you," she said.

He nodded gratefully. "I should like that very much."

Are you willing?" she asked. "I can promise to reward you well." She leaned forward, her eyes wide with anticipation, waiting for his answer.

There was no way out of it. He could not refuse the request of his countess. Besides, he was sorely in need of the patronage she promised. "Of course, *ma dame*," he replied.

With a well-known patron like Countess Marie, he could no doubt attract others. He knew of poets who had occasionally written about her, perhaps in hope of reward, but none, as far as he knew, had ever received a direct commission from her.

"I would like you to begin work as soon as possible," she said, smiling her approval. "You must come to the court once a month or so to share with us what you have written. It will be a splendid undertaking, I have no doubt. Perhaps you would even like to attend one of the courts of love."

He nodded. "That might be very helpful," he said. Chrétien was reminded at that moment why she was considered so charming. Her voice was gentle and reassuring, and her smile was captivating. He couldn't call her beautiful, but she had a natural warmth and charm that attracted people, and she was renowned for her hospitality.

"I thank you for coming. I shall see that you are well provided with parchment and any quills and inks you may require. If you have other needs, please inform my scribe Laurent," the countess said. And with that he was dismissed.

And so it was done. Countess Marie had commissioned her first literary work—her first indulgence without Henri's permission. She felt a deep sense of pride and satisfaction. Now if only Chrétien could carry out the task to her satisfaction, she would be delighted. And she would be the sole judge of his talent and ability to fulfill her wishes.

It was late summer before he was summoned to the palace once again for his first reading. He had attended a court of love, which the countess had assembled with her ladies the previous month. Now to hear his reading, Marie invited the ladies whose husbands had gone to the Holy Land with her husband, as well as those few court officials who remained behind to attend a feast and hear the beginning of Chrétien's new story.

The hall was brightly lit with candles and torches, and the sound of music and conversation echoed throughout the room. Chrétien, a sheaf of parchment pages in his hand, stood against the wall alongside the musicians, waiting to read. Once the remains of the meal and the trestle tables had been cleared away, Marie signaled the musicians to cease their playing. The courtiers arranged themselves in informal groups around the hearth at the end of the room, while the squires poured everyone fresh goblets of red wine. It was time for Chrétien to share what he had written so far. The countess nodded for him to come forward.

"You may begin," she said to the poet, as she leaned back on a purple, silken pillow in a carved armchair to listen.

Chrétien stood in front of the great fireplace and looked about nervously. This was the first time he had been compelled to do a public reading for the patron who had commissioned it. Marie smiled at him with encouragement and nodded once again. He began to read.

Puisque ma dame de Champaigne
Viault que romans a feire anpeigne…

His voice was warm and mellow, and his words fell on welcoming ears.

Since my lady of Champagne
Wants me to undertake a romance
I will do so most willingly
As one who is entirely hers.

Then his words became more playful, as his verses went on.

But another might begin
by wishing to flatter her.
He might say, and I would concur with it,
That she is the lady who surpasses
All women who are living.

People began to smile as Chrétien went on in his backhanded way to pay compliments to the countess.

Certainly I am not one
Intent upon flattering his lady.
Will I say, "As the polished diamond
Eclipses the pearl and the sard,
So the countess eclipses queens"?
Indeed not. I'll say nothing of the sort,
Though it be true in spite of me.

By now Marie could hear a soft ripple of laughter making its way throughout the audience. When Chrétien paused in his reading to take a sip of wine, Marie turned to Anseau, who was seated nearby. "I don't understand why they are laughing so," she said. "His words are clever, but not humorous to that extent, I think."

"They are amused by the way he is mocking Gautier d'Arras for the effusive language *he* used to describe his own patron. While you were in confinement, he arrived with the count of Hainaut and read to us his *Ille et Galeron*. Master Chrétien attended his readings. Like everyone else, he must have thought Gautier was excessive in his praise of the emperor's wife. He claimed she was the best woman ever born, and his praise went on and on and on."

"Oh, I see." She smiled and settled back to enjoy the rest of the reading, now that she understood. She knew that the mockery was good-natured, just the kind of teasing one poet gave another, but nonetheless she was enjoying his indirect praise.

His next lines went on to say how little he was responsible for the tale he was about to tell, giving all the credit to Countess Marie.

I will say that her command

Has more importance in this work
Than any thought or effort I might put into it.
Concerning the book that Chrétien is beginning
About the Knight of the Cart,
The plot and meaning are provided to him
By the countess, and he is undertaking
To add nothing to it
But his effort and his diligence.

And so he began his tale. The courtiers listened avidly, soon caught up in the first part of the story that told of Queen Guinevere's abduction. The dual quest to find her contrasted two knights—Lancelot, the knight who loved the queen and served only her, and Gauvain, who was more concerned with his own prowess and served the king. The poet intrigued his audience by concealing the identity of the first knight in the beginning.

When Chrétien finished his reading for the evening, there was applause and hearty praise from the various knights and ladies present. The story was captivating, they assured him, and cleverly written.

"We will eagerly await your next reading," the countess said, rewarding him, as she had promised, with thirty silver *solidi* for the work he had put in so far.

Chrétien left the court a happy man—happy for the handsome reward, which was enough to pay the rent on his small cottage for nearly a year, happy to know now that he would be amply rewarded for his work, but happiest of all to get this first part over with. He had worked hard to make it lighthearted, yet pay tribute to the countess. And he thought he had found a way to disavow any and all responsibility for the content of the work, which he deemed sinful. His friends among the clergy could hardly blame him for its adulterous content, for he had informed his listeners that he was, after all, merely following the command of the countess. The blame or praise, whichever the work evoked, was entirely hers.

Chrétien attended court more often now and became aware that this courtly love, this secular *fine amor*, was not the only type of love that was being discussed at Marie's court. In fact, there were constant debates about the nature of true love. They were most lively when a monk named Adam de Pontigny came to Troyes. His monastic life had begun as a Benedictine, but he had been persuaded to join the Cistercian order, which was especially popular in Champagne where he was born and where he spent his youth. Count Henri's entire family was quite fond of him, and he often counseled various ones of them, especially the women—Queen Adèle and her sisters. He had been present at the marriage of Count Henri and Countess Marie, and he often came to Troyes at the invitation of the countess, whom he sometimes served as a confessor.

He chided her occasionally about her courts of love. "What you speak of at these courts is not true love," Adam told the countess. "The only true love, the real *fine amor*, must grow within the love of Christ."

He was well armed with language and quotations from scripture, as well as from other ecclesiastical writers. The priests, chaplains, and canons at the court, who also jumped into the debate, were ready at a moment's notice to cite the famous sermons on the *Song of Songs* of Bernard de Clairvaux. Bernard depicted the Savior and the soul as lovers, but not just lovers. They joined together as man and wife, loving each other with faithful, fruitful, and ever ardent love. Christ, Bernard once claimed, is the bridegroom whose very kiss is so potent "that no sooner has the bride received it than she conceives and her breasts grow rounded with the fruitfulness of conception." In his interpretation there was no question that love and marriage were not only compatible, but inevitable.

"There is also the work of Aelred de Rievaulx, of blessed memory," Adam would point out. The older courtiers nodded. They recognized the name of the English abbot who had once preached a sermon in Troyes as he passed through on his way to a meeting at Cîteaux, the motherhouse of the Cistercian order. He had died more than a decade before, but left behind a book called *De spirituali amicitia*, a treatise on spiritual love and friendship, where he defined love as "a certain 'affection' of the rational soul whereby it seeks and eagerly strives after some object to possess it and enjoy it." But like Adam, he argued that true love and friendship "cannot exist among those who live without Christ."

"There is something dangerous and heretical about these new ideas on love you are promoting," Adam cautioned Marie and the rest of the court. "They are imbued with ideas of Muslim philosophers."

Marie usually listened to him with docility and tolerance, but she was shocked by this suggestion. "What Muslim philosophers?" she asked.

"A man named Ibn Hazm, in particular. He was a theologian and a poet, who lived in Andalusia in the last century. Some of his ideas are heretical to us and others merely peculiar," he said.

"I've never even heard of him," the countess said.

"Perhaps not, my lady," Adam said, "but the influence of his writings has crept into areas like Aquitaine and Toulouse and Narbonne. This whole idea of serving the lady, of seeking to love her wholly, even chastely, comes from their culture. Some of these ideas have influenced that new Cathar heresy in the south. A group of bishops, along with a cardinal and an abbot, traveled recently to the region to investigate and judged their so-called religion to be heresy. It was condemned at the last meeting of the Lateran Council."

"Nonsense," Marie laughed. "You know I'm not a heretic. Some of these ideas have been around since my great-grandfather's generation," she argued. "He wrote some of the first songs of love in all of France. My mother told me all that, and I have heard some of his songs."

"I am aware of them. Many of them are quite bawdy," Adam said with a disagreeable smirk.

"But not all," Marie countered. "There is a beauty and purity to the love we discuss in the courts of love. It is not the unseemly concept you seem to think. We do not believe that carnal rewards are the goal of *fine amor*. On the contrary. It is something that raises a man to a higher plane, something refined and almost spiritual."

"Almost," retorted Adam. "But not truly spiritual, for it always contains carnal thoughts—even if they are not acted on. And it certainly has nothing to do with the love of Christ."

Whenever he visited, he would suggest books in the library of St. Étienne for Marie to read. She would try to read them, but they were all in dense Latin, and she found them boring in comparison to the writings of the poets, who wrote in the common language that everyone could understand. Still, she found the debate about love, the *fine amor* of her courts versus the spiritual love Adam spoke of, to be stimulating, but she had no intention of sacrificing one for the other. They fulfilled different needs in life in her view.

As word spread of her interests in poetry, *trouvères* began to flock to her court and seek her patronage. Just as Chrétien regularly attended her court in Troyes, so Guiot de Provins and Gace Brulé were frequent visitors in Meaux or Provins. She enjoyed their company, though Gace always seemed downhearted. He was fair-haired and handsome, except for his slightly crooked nose, but he was constantly melancholy. He claimed he was too broken-hearted to sing, for the lady he loved paid him no mind.

"Nonsense," the countess said. "She would no doubt notice you more if you sang than if you did not. I insist that you sing."

Marie gave him no choice, and for her he began a new song.

Bien cuidai toute ma vie
Joie et chanson oublier…

I thought for the rest of my life
I would forget joy and song.
But the countess of Brie
Whose command I dare not refuse
Has commanded me to sing…

"You called me countess of Brie," she said, with a laugh. "I hear that so rarely."

"And yet it is true, *ma dame*. I could have used Troyes or Champagne, but Brie best suits my rhyme," Gace replied, echoing her laughter.

"I'm glad you're active again and not so dejected. Surely your lady will see your worth if you continue to serve her faithfully."

"I can only hope so, *ma dame*," he said wistfully.

He repeatedly sang of his misery at being ignored by the woman he adored but proclaimed his true love and loyal service to her. Only rarely did a shaft of sunlight shine through his lyrics, when his lady, whose name he never revealed, would occasionally show him favor.

Although, as her mother had taught her, Marie chose to brighten her days during Henri's absence with light-hearted tales and the songs of poets, she could not help but let worry creep in from time to time. There was a somber and practical side to being left in charge. As she had anticipated, some of the men she had to cope with did not deal with her as they had the count. At one point she wrote to her father, complaining of the difficulty she was having collecting tolls that had always been freely paid when her husband was present. But her father was little help, especially since his own men were part of the problem.

His health was also fragile, and he was preoccupied with having his son, Philippe, crowned during his lifetime, as was the Capetian custom. King Louis was too busy planning his son's coronation, which he had set for Assumption Day—August 15—to pay much attention to her petty worries, as he no doubt thought them. It was, of course, no real surprise to her since sons always came first. *I suppose I'm lucky to have no major matters to deal with, for apparently I can count on him for nothing,* she thought, grateful that Henri had made such a great effort to put things in order before his departure. The pope had also agreed to take her lands under his protection during her husband's absence, which freed her from worry about preparing military defenses, for she assumed the pope's protection inviolable.

At least she was free to enjoy her increasing fame as an admirer and prospective patron of the poets who frequented her court in growing numbers, counting on her hospitality and generosity for their performances. If only such good times could last forever.

CHAPTER 36

Troyes, August 8, 1179

Marie looked forward to her trip to Reims for the coronation of her brother and was already packing for it when the royal messenger rode into the courtyard. The event was to take place one week before the prince's fourteenth birthday, and everyone expected it to be a glorious event. Her brother-in-law Guillaume, archbishop of Reims, was to place the royal crown on the boy's head, as his predecessors had done for centuries. All Henri's brothers planned to be there for the coronation of their nephew. Marie only regretted that Henri himself could not be present to enjoy it.

She recognized the young messenger at once. It was the freckled squire, Acelin, who had delivered news to the court in Troyes on several previous occasions. This time, when the guard ushered him into the great hall, he wore a distressed look on his face, and Marie knew the moment she saw him that the news he brought was not good.

"What has happened?" she asked at once.

"I've come to inform you that the coronation of Prince Philippe has been postponed."

"Why?" It was most unusual to postpone such long-announced plans. Something dire must have happened.

"The prince took ill," he replied.

"Is it serious?" She was worried of course but couldn't stop her fleeting thought that if something should happen to Philippe, her own son was next in line for the throne.

"He has recovered now, but he suffered an ordeal," Acelin reported.

"What kind of ordeal?"

"He and his father were already on their way to Reims, when they paused to rest at Compiègne. The prince and his friends went boar hunting, but when he didn't return from the hunt with the others, the king was frantic."

"Good heavens! What had happened to him?" Marie asked.

"The boy lost his way in the woods and took refuge in the hut of a peasant. They finally found him after two days and brought him back to his father, but he was ill—something he must have caught from the peasant."

Or ill from fear, Marie speculated, thinking of her own son and what a terrifying experience it must have been for the boy.

"But you say he's recovered?"

"He has, my lady, but his father doesn't know yet."

"Why not?"

"Fearing the worst, the king cancelled the coronation and rushed to England to pray for the prince's life at the tomb of Thomas Becket."

"He's gone to England?" She was surprised. To her knowledge, he had never been to England before.

"He had dreams that, if he prayed at St. Thomas's tomb, the saint would make his son well again. He left at once for Canterbury and has not yet returned."

"I wish him a safe journey, and I'm pleased to hear that the prince is well again." She would have to wait for her father's homecoming to learn when the coronation would be rescheduled. Thanking the friendly messenger, she sent him to the kitchen to be fed.

It was early September by the time the king returned from his hurried pilgrimage and learned the good news. He was overjoyed and immediately rescheduled the coronation for All Saints Day, November 1. Once again, Marie, in the company of her oldest son and her husband's family, planned to attend—until she received the letter from Adèle in late October.

I am sorry to send you such bad news of your father. Not long after his return from England, he had an attack that has left him paralyzed. We kept hoping he would recover and that his condition would improve in time to attend our son's coronation. The doctors have done all they can. He has been bled and given their concoctions to drink. We have prayed to the Holy Virgin, and we keep a candle lit for him in the cathedral. But so far nothing has helped. In fact, the doctors are not certain that he will recover at all. If you want to see your father alive, please come soon. I am concerned for his life."

Marie left at once for Paris. Of course she wanted to see him alive and would do whatever was in her power to help him recover. When she arrived, Thibaut was already there with her sister Alix at his side.

"How is he?" she asked.

"Not well," Alix replied. "He's not able to speak. Philippe may become king in more than name sooner than we had expected. He is now the one making the final preparations for the coronation. You may not like them," she said somberly. "Adèle is with our father."

Together the sisters made their way toward their father's bedchamber and knelt beside his bed.

"*Bonjour, mon père,*" Marie said softly as she had when she was a child. Alix echoed her words.

The king cut his eyes toward his daughters. A semblance of a smile moved his withered cheeks and his lips trembled as though he were trying to speak. *He looks like an old, old man*, Marie thought, though he was only fifty-nine. Her father's appearance brought tears to her eyes, but she did not want him to see her cry and quickly brushed them away. She was determined to stay with him as long as she possibly could. The coronation would go on without her, she knew.

It also went on without the presence of Henri's brothers. Thibaut, King Louis's former seneschal, was furious when he learned that Prince Philippe had chosen the count of Flanders to carry his sword in the ceremony and Henry, the Young King of England, who had now replaced him as seneschal, to carry the crown. The young prince, who had taken charge in his father's stead, seemed intent upon rejecting any advice from his mother's brothers, who, he seemed to think, were trying to control him. Only Guillaume would fulfill his traditional role as archbishop to crown the king.

By the time the coronation was over and Philippe returned to Paris, Thibaut and Alix, in disgust, had already left for Blois. Marie, who still remained with Adèle, heard from returning courtiers many tales about the ceremony—how splendid it had been—and about the tournament at Lagny that followed. Philippe boasted that the Angevin and Flemish nobility shone brightly, and that he and his mentor, Philip of Flanders, had done the honors to the winners. But she paid little mind. All that concerned her at the moment was her father's illness. He lingered on in his paralytic state, but getting no worse, and it seemed for a time that he might rally somewhat. His color was better, and he had begun to try to speak though not coherently.

With hope for his recovery, Marie returned to Troyes, but the news that continued to arrive from Adèle in Paris was not good. Philippe began almost immediately to show his immaturity by rebelling against everything his father had embraced, especially the family of his mother. He allowed his mother no part in his decision-making, despite his young age. And while King Louis had turned to his brothers-in-law for advice and military aid, Philippe completely rejected them in favor of Philip of Flanders.

He also began to mistreat the Jews, whom his father had allowed to live in peace, given their economic importance in the city. A Jewish man named Simon, who had lived in Paris in a fine house on the Île de la Cité, came in desperation to Marie's court seeking refuge. He wept as he told her all that had happened. "King Philippe sent soldiers with swords to seize our synagogues and terrify our women and children. Then they came without warning to ransack our homes and drive us out."

"Why is he doing such things?" she asked. "King Louis always set an example of tolerance and protected the Jews. Have your people done something to anger the new king?"

"No, my lady. We don't know why he is taking these actions. He has also canceled all debts that Christians owe to the Jews. We can no longer survive in Paris, and many of us are seeking your permission to resettle here in Champagne or other friendly territories."

"You are welcome here," she assured him, "as long as you obey our laws."

When he had gone away, her son Henri, now fourteen, who had sat with her at court and heard the man's story, confided in her later that afternoon. "I think I may know what has caused Philippe to hate the Jews so much, *Maman*," he said. "I remember that when we were little boys, the young squires used to tell us all sorts of dreadful tales about Jews murdering Christian children and drinking their blood."

"How awful," she said.

"I think they invented all sorts of gory details just to scare him and watch him react. I heard a few of their stories, but I knew that *Papa* never took those rumors seriously. I tried to tell Philippe that they were just silly stories, but he didn't believe me. The squires were older, and he thought they knew more than I did. He was really upset by what he heard. I think they were just trying to tease him because he was so gullible."

"And to think of the damage they did to so many people. Never listen to rumors and tales that can't be verified, son. Prejudice against one's fellow man is a terrible thing, and Philippe is too young to have sound judgment."

The worst news came in early May, when a messenger Marie did not recognize arrived from the royal court. She wondered what had happened to Acelin. This new young man looked uncomfortable in his task.

"King Philippe has taken a wife, my lady," he announced in an uncertain voice.

"Oh? When did this take place?" she asked in surprise, for she had heard nothing of this from Adèle.

"The 28th day of April at Bapaume."

"And whom did he choose?" Marie asked, thinking Bapaume, a town in Artois, an odd location for a royal marriage.

The messenger's face reddened. "The new queen is Isabelle de Hainaut. She will be crowned by the archbishop of Sens at Pentecost." He expected her to be angry at the news that the archbishop of Sens, not the archbishop of Reims, was to crown the queen. He'd been told that she would consider it an insult to her husband's family. But her reaction was not what he expected. Her face blanched.

"What?" How can that be? She's betrothed to my son Henri, and she's only ten years old." Now she understood the location, for the

Artois was Isabelle's promised dowry.

The messenger began to back cautiously toward the door, not knowing what to expect. He'd heard of messengers who brought bad news being punished for it. But she dismissed him and turned to Anseau.

"How could he do this? My own brother! What treachery!" Marie rarely showed her anger, but now she was too furious to control it. Her voice rose, startling her two oldest children, who were playing a board game called *merelles* at the other end of the room.

"I fear he is ill advised, my lady," Anseau answered in a grave voice.

"It's that deceitful Philip of Flanders, isn't it?" she fumed, drawing her own conclusions. "He saw a greater reward in marrying his niece to the king than to my son. What a betrayal! He's clearly a man never to be trusted." She could envisage him dangling the dowry of Artois under the boy king's nose, knowing that Philippe was completely under his spell and anticipating the influence such a marriage would give him at court.

It had been less than a year since the girl's father, Count Baudouin, had come to Troyes to ratify the betrothal agreement. It was easy to understand why the naïve king could be so easily influenced by Count Philip. He no doubt seemed like a great hero to the fifteen-year-old boy, for he was a handsome and skilled knight, with a fine reputation. He looked splendid in his armor and consistently performed with great prowess at the tournaments, personifying all that a young boy of noble blood might aspire to. And he had begun to train young Philippe in the skills of knighthood.

"He's taken advantage of my father's trust and my brother's youth and immaturity. And he's waited until my husband was away. He and Philippe both obviously consider me, as a woman, weak and afraid to take vengeance. Well, they're wrong!"

"I would advise you not to take action until Count Henri returns," Anseau counseled.

"I'm beginning to understand why the English king denied his sons any power when they were too young to have good judgment. Philippe needs a strong guiding hand, but not that of Count Philip. God forbid!"

With all that on her mind, she prayed nightly for her father's recovery and help, knowing it was unlikely. Nevertheless, she prayed.

It did little good.

Her son Henri had looked forward to his marriage to Isabelle and to gaining control over the Artois himself when he was old enough. *I can't simply stand by and let my brother steal my son's promised bride and her dowry*, Marie thought. But she was reluctant to act while her father still lived.

The irony of the situation was that Marie had always counted on a harmonious relationship with her brother when he became king. He and her own son had played together, albeit with frequent rivalry, and his mother was her best friend. She'd naturally assumed that Philippe would turn for support and advice, as his father had done, to his maternal uncles. Instead, he seemed to be doing everything in his power to alienate them and to break free of any relationship with his mother's family. Marie was mystified by his attitude.

The dreaded announcement did not come until late September.

"King Louis is dead," the same messenger said in a somber voice.

Marie made the sign of the cross, and the messenger echoed her gesture. "God rest his soul," she said, tears welling in her eyes. Although his death had at first seemed imminent, he'd survived for many months, and she had continued to pray for his recovery in the hope that he could exert some control over his son. Now that hope was gone.

He was buried, the messenger said, not at St. Denis like his father, but at the abbey church of Notre-Dame de Barbeau. It was a Cistercian monastery that he himself had founded in 1147, when Marie was only two years old and just before he left on his crusade. The death of Bishop Mathieu de Troyes that same month, and his eventual replacement by her husband's old friend, Manassès de Pougy, though normally a huge event in the life of the county, caused barely a ripple to Marie, as she grieved for her father.

I should go to Paris at once to be with Adèle, she thought.

But it was not necessary. For it was Adèle who came to her.

Queen Adèle's tears gave Marie even more reason to be angry with her brother. He had driven his mother from the royal castle and seized her dower lands. *What an ungrateful child!* Marie thought, as she held Adèle in her arms to comfort her.

"How could he do such a thing?" Adèle sobbed. "And he's already sent his little sister away to be married in Constantinople!" She was distraught. Marie couldn't imagine her son Henri ever doing such things. He'd always shown respect for his parents, and she loved him beyond all measure. He was her firstborn, and there was nothing she wouldn't do to keep him safe and encourage his advancement in life. She felt sure that he would always protect her as well.

Out of respect for her father, she had refused to act against her brother, but now that he was gone, she began to think what she might do to show Philippe that she would not be trampled on in such a way. A military alliance perhaps with others he had offended? She wished her husband were here.

Only a few months later, she learned that Henri had already returned to France. He'd gone first to the king's Christmas court in Sens, for Philippe had sent for him. Although Marie was pleased to know he was safe, it concerned her that he did not come home straightaway, for she could only imagine the distorted version of events he might be hearing from Philippe.

She eagerly looked forward to her husband's return to Troyes, where he could learn the true story of her brother's reign—not what he'd probably been hearing at the king's court. She wondered how he had reacted to learning of Philippe's marriage and that his sister was being deprived of her dower lands. Marie was furious with her brother, and she couldn't imagine why Henri would spend time at his court, unless it was to negotiate some kind of settlement.

Rumor had it that Philippe had summoned some of his vassals to discuss a possible war against the emperor. She felt sure that Henri would advise the boy-king against it. For some reason, unlike his brothers, her husband still seemed to have the king's ear. But Marie felt certain that Henri would not want to be drawn into another war so soon after his return.

It was not until March 8 that Henri returned to Troyes, and he was not astride as he had left, but in a litter. She was shocked by his appearance. He looked old and sick and haggard. How could he have changed so much in so short a time? His friends Anseau and Garnier were both there to greet him, and the two men helped him to his bedchamber. They looked as shaken by his demeanor as Marie felt.

"What on earth happened to you?" she asked.

"I was captured by Saracens in Anatolia and spent many days in their prison," he said. His voice was weak, but he seemed eager to tell her all about it. "It was Manuel of Constantinople who paid my ransom—the emperor who knighted me."

"Yes, I know."

"I was on my way to his court for the wedding of his son Alexios and Adèle's daughter, Princess Agnès, when we were captured. So many of my men, so many close friends, were killed or died in captivity—Nicholas, Daimbert, Pierre Bristaud, Guillaume Rex…" His face was gray, his eyes filled with tears, and his voice broke. When he recovered, he said, "I've been so sick. God has let me come home to die."

"Oh, Henri. Don't say such things. We'll have you well and on your feet soon," she said bravely, but her voice trembled with uncertainty. She had never seen him so sick before.

"No, my dearest. It's true. I am dying. But there are things I must do first."

"More than anything, you need rest. I'll call for a physician. He'll come and bleed you of the bad humors. We'll make you well again."

"It's far too late for that." His voice was resigned. "But there are matters I must tend to at once."

"I can help with those. What are they?"

"Donations to the cathedral chapter and a few others. I made a vow to Saint Mammès that if he would save us from the Saracens and bring us home, I would…"

Marie waited patiently for him to continue.

"I would give an annual donation of thirty *livres* to his church in Langres."

"An annual donation? So much?" she asked, realizing that she might be the one to have to find the funds. But she would worry about that later. For now, she must help him meet those obligations.

"I'll send for your chancellor, Étienne..." she began.

"He too is dead. My old tutor and friend... gone," Henri said, a sob catching in his throat. "Send instead for Haice de Plancy. He's a good penman. I'll instruct him to draft a letter to Bishop Manassès."

For several days, Haice, a canon of St. Étienne, sat by the count's bedside, trying to keep track of all the benefactions Henri wanted to leave to various churches and abbeys. The final donation to St. Étienne he gave with the consent of Marie, whom he described as "*karissima uxore mea,*" my dearest wife, and "*dilectissimo filio meo Henrio,*" my most beloved son. These were superlatives Henri had never used before in speaking of his wife and son, certainly not in legal documents. He was not a man who easily showed tenderness, and he was struggling now to express what was in his heart. Marie understood. He was trying to tell her and the world through these official documents how much she meant to him. Their relationship had always been on a more formal level. And for the first time in her life, Marie fully realized how deep her affection was for Henri, how much her trust in him had increased over the years, and how she had looked forward to his return.

When he left for the Holy Land, he had sought to leave things in good order for her so that there would be little to worry about in his absence. As a consequence, she'd been required to conduct relatively little official business—just to make an effort to maintain the status quo. Any decision she felt compelled to make was always done conditionally, "until the return of the count who will decide once more." She had indulged herself to a great extent in her love of poetry and stories, in what Walter Map might have described as "courtiers' trifles."

Now she knew that she was going to have to deal with serious and practical issues on her own and not burden her husband with them. Reality surged in upon her as she watched Henri's health grow worse each day. She was at his side most of the time, bathing his forehead with a cool cloth, whispering prayers or words of comfort, or just holding his hand. On the seventh day after his return, a Sunday, he asked for a priest. She left the room as he made his confession, but she returned for his last rites.

"You've been a good wife," he whispered, squeezing her hand with the little strength he had left.

"And you a good husband," she whispered back. "I love you." Was it the first time she had ever said those words to him? *Surely not,* she thought. But these were words they didn't commonly exchange, words she had even belied in a court of love.

All the children, except her youngest, Thibaut, who was not yet two, knelt at their father's bedside. Tears poured down the cheeks of the two daughters, Scholastique, almost twelve, and Mariette, just two months away from her tenth birthday. Henri, the eldest at fourteen, knelt silently, his lips quivering as he blinked his eyes to keep his own tears from falling. Widow Jeanne stood by, holding little Thibaut, asleep on her shoulder.

As vesper bells were ringing the next day, March 16, Henri took his last breath. Marie held his hand for a long time unwilling to let go, feeling his fingertips grow cooler to her touch. Her heart ached with grief. It was over. Henri was dead. Marie's world seemed to be crumbling about her. She clung to her children as they all wept together.

CHAPTER 37

The funeral was grand. Marie saw to that. A crucifer led the long procession of priests and monks, followed by Count Henri's court officials and knights carrying his sword and shield and the banner of Champagne before and after the funeral cart pulled by two white Spanish horses.

Countess Marie and Queen Adèle, both in their white widow's veils and accompanied by several of their ladies, walked behind the cart-borne casket, covered with an elaborate purple pall. Church bells throughout the city tolled in mourning, as the slow procession wound through the old city. The cortège wove through the narrow streets, past the cathedral of St. Pierre and the Abbey of St. Loup, to give the people of Troyes an opportunity to pay their respects to the late count, eventually returning again to where it had started at the door of St. Étienne.

Mourners filled the church, where countless candles lit the walls of the nave. The body of Count Henri was placed in the center of the church, and knights laid his sword and shield on his coffin. As the dean of St. Étienne delivered the lengthy funeral oration, Marie felt numb and exhausted. But when a scribe began to read the completed portion of a *planctus* or lament called *Omnis in lacrimas*, written in her husband's memory at her request, she had to struggle to hold back her tears.

Only after the day ended and she was alone in her bedchamber did she allow herself to give way to her emotions and weep, as much for herself as for her dead husband. She would miss him—the certainty of his strength, his fearlessness, his firm hand governing the lands, and even that unexpected surge of love she'd felt for him toward the end, when she realized that they had been happy together. It was not the passion and desire that troubadours expressed in their songs, but a steady certainty, a familiarity, and a sense of comfort and grace. All that was gone now, and she felt overwhelmed by what lay ahead.

She went through the following weeks in a daze, doing what had to be done. She sent for the tomb maker to whom Henri had entrusted the plans for his elaborate sarcophagus. It was to be made of metal rather than the usual stone—gilded, studded with silver, and bronze, encrusted with rubies and gemstones, and ornamented with colored enamel plaques. It would partially enclose a gilded bronze effigy of the count, depicting him not in his armor, but in a simple tunic and mantle, his eyes open in awareness, his hands joined in prayer over his chest. The effigy would be visible through a series of double arches that pierced the walls of the sarcophagus. Together the countess and the craftsman reviewed the plans for the monument, adding a few details here and there.

"The plans look fine. I would like you to allow space here for an appropriate epitaph, which I've commissioned from Simon Aurea Capra. Henri admired his Latin poetry, and I think he would be pleased," Marie said, pointing to the spot on his sketch where it would be placed.

"Of course, *ma dame*," he replied with a bow.

Having agreed upon that, Marie sent the man off to begin his work and set herself to the necessary administrative tasks and all the decisions she had to make when people sought her favor as they once had the count's, now that he was gone for good. There were also Henri's last-minute wishes to fulfill, among them his vow to St. Mammès and the large distribution of alms to the poor that he had ordered to be given following his funeral. For the time being, there was no question of returning to the pleasing pastimes she'd learned at her mother's court.

"Shall we play for you tonight, my lady?" musicians began to ask after a few weeks.

"No, not tonight," she would answer.

Their love songs seemed inappropriate given the circumstances. She had little time for anything but official matters. Although she might allow a minstrel to sing an occasional lament, by the end of day she was too exhausted to appreciate even these.

One thing, however, weighed on her mind—the romance she had commissioned from Chrétien. He had made great progress on his story of Lancelot and the queen during Henri's absence, and it had delighted her for the most part. Occasionally when he'd come to court to read, Marie had wondered whether he might be teasing her a bit and even mocking Lancelot, for there were times he made him appear ridiculous.

When she had pointed out these passages, he merely said, "But my lady, he is always in the service of love. At various times the queen even bids him to be ridiculous. He must follow her commands, mustn't he?"

She could not argue his point, for it was consistent with the orders she'd given him. Still, *were all those scenes really necessary?* She thought of Chrétien's Lancelot, lost in reverie over the queen, being knocked off his horse in a most undignified manner to fall flat on his back in a creek. In another scene, he found strands of the queen's hair caught in an abandoned comb and literally swooned. A damsel had to rush to his side to keep him from falling off his horse again. Once Chrétien even depicted Lancelot fighting on foot with his back turned to his adversary during a one-on-one combat, so that he could gaze constantly at this lady. At such moments in the readings, she had noticed, the courtiers laughed, the men in particular.

"It will all come to a good end and to his glory, my lady," Chrétien said to her expressions of concern. "Do not fear."

But now, with Henri dead, she felt it inappropriate to go on sponsoring a work that included a married lady's unfaithfulness. Even though that was not what she had asked Chrétien to emphasize, she knew that it could be misunderstood and considered trivial and insensitive at such a time.

"Summon Chrétien to my court," she ordered a young squire a few weeks after Henri's death.

When the poet arrived the next afternoon, he was nonplused. "My lady," he said, "I have written little more since I read to the court a short time ago. I need more time to write between readings."

"That is not why I've sent for you," she replied. "You know that my husband has died."

"I do, my lady, and I am deeply sorry for your loss. May God keep his soul," he said, crossing himself. She echoed his gesture.

"Under the circumstances, I do not want you to continue your work," she said.

"But my lady, it's two-thirds finished… perhaps more. How can I abandon it now?" he asked.

"It is not seemly for me to be the patron of such a work on love given the state of affairs," she replied.

"Perhaps if I just put it away for a while until your period of mourning has ended…"

"I want you to end your work," she said emphatically. "I will reward you for what you have done, but for nothing more." She was doing her best to control her emotions. Although she too would ordinarily be reluctant to end the work, her chaplains had advised her to turn her thoughts to God and put away such frivolous matters. Her sometimes confessor and advisor, Adam, a longtime friend of the house of Champagne, had come from Pontigny to attend Henri's funeral. He had taken the occasion to remind her that she was a widow now with many responsibilities and that she should set aside these courts of love and frivolous pursuits and focus more on the life of the spirit.

She echoed his words to Chrétien. "I must concern myself with more seemly matters." She could see the poet's stricken face and then the annoyed set of his jaw. "Don't worry. I shall reward you for the work you have done." She sought to reassure him.

But he had come to expect a steady income for many months from this commissioned tale—one he did not himself conceive or believe in. But he had done his best, even though the work ran counter to his own beliefs about marriage. He was well aware that he made Lancelot appear foolish at times, and truth be told, he did so intentionally. He did not find adultery a palatable topic and was convinced he could better write of knights who loved their ladies within the context of marriage. But he was trying to obey the countess's command. Now, to have worked so hard and have it ended before completion was extremely annoying.

"If you continue to write, and I hope you will, write something that will celebrate the count and his virtues," the countess suggested.

"Are you suggesting a new commission, my lady?" he asked hopefully.

"No. At least not now. I must turn to my duties as the count's widow and regent, as mother of the next count. You must no longer consider me your patron. Surely there are others."

"Were you not pleased with my work, *ma dame*?"

"It's not that. I was indeed, but as I have already told you, I must turn my attentions to serving as regent for my son, who is not yet old enough to assume the responsibilities of count."

She was well aware of the implications of her words. The new king, her brother, was not much older than young Henri, yet he had been in charge of a kingdom for more than a year now. *But he's doing a poor job of it,* she thought bitterly. She'd learned that a young man needed greater maturity to rule—or else sound advisors. Instead, Philippe had turned away from his father's wise counselors and toward his own mentor, Philip of Flanders, who seemed to be advising the king to make moves that would benefit the kingdom less than himself. The king's marriage to Isabelle de Hainaut was a case in point. With his niece Isabelle as queen, the count of Flanders no doubt expected to garner favors from the crown. It was not hard to see his efforts behind the scenes. It infuriated Marie. Her brothers-in-law were equally upset, in part because they had clearly fallen from favor, but also because of his ill treatment of his mother, their sister Queen Adèle. It was an insult to the entire family.

As for Chrétien, the countess kept her promise, rewarding him well for his efforts. Still, he went away dejected. As he trudged home, he tried to consider the event in a more positive light. *Now I'm free,* he thought, t*o return to my work on the story of Yvain, who'll serve as a contrast to my earlier hero Erec.* It was important, he thought, because they were, in a sense, a matched pair. While Erec was drawn away from his knightly duties by passion for his wife, Yvain would be so caught up in the need to prove his knightly prowess that he left his beloved wife behind. After many trials and adventures, both of them would learn that love and prowess could coexist within the stable relationship of marriage.

But first, he mumbled to himself, *there's something else I must do.* He wanted to cleanse himself of that work on adultery he had been writing for the countess. *I'll write a defense of marriage.* The more he thought about it, the more excited he became. He felt sure that such a work would find greater favor with monastic libraries than a work on adultery. He would likely sell more copies of such a work.

I think I'll set the story in Constantinople. It was a city some Champenois knights had recently visited. He would indirectly pay tribute to Count Henri and remind readers of his knighting there so many years ago. He would underscore in his characters the importance of generosity, for which the count was so well known. *It might even interest the royal court*, he thought, for after all, Princess Agnès, the king's sister, had recently wed in Constantinople. And it was Emperor Manuel who had paid the ransom to free Count Henri and his men from captivity. *I think such a work might be looked on with favor*, he thought, *certainly more so than the adulterous tale of Lancelot*. By the time he reached home, he was already feeling better.

As he set to work on the new romance, which he would call *Cligés*, he decided to make Queen Guenevere not an adulteress at all, but rather a veritable defender of marriage. He wrote quickly and gleefully as he had her say to a pair of would-be lovers, "Join yourselves in honorable marriage. Thus, it seems to me, your love will last long." Instead of making Guenevere and Lancelot his adulterers, he chose Tristan and Iseult, having his heroine Fénice say, "I would rather be torn limb from limb" than be like Iseult, whose love she considered "exceedingly base; for her body belonged to two masters and her heart entirely to one." Chrétien smiled to himself as he even allowed his hero, Cligés, to defeat Lancelot in a tournament.

When he wrote his prologue to *Cligés*, he called attention to his previous works, pointedly omitting any mention of the unfinished tale of Lancelot. *I wonder whether the countess will ever read this tale*, he thought. In a way, he hoped so, but it might be better if she didn't. He had tried to protect himself from her displeasure, in case she did, by suggesting to readers that those "who are being instructed in love" must follow the rules and grow pale in the presence of the beloved, as the chaplain Andreas had made clear in his little treatise.

Countess Marie was too busy with other matters to concern herself about Chrétien's new work. She needed to appoint court officers to replace those who had not come back from Henri's crusade. She appointed as her new chancellor Haice de Plancy, who had filled in so ably at her husband's deathbed. She knew him well and trusted him. As her new marshal she selected Érard d'Aulnay, kinsman to another of her favorite courtiers, the knight Geoffrey de Villehardouin, who loved history and often entertained the court with his stories of great deeds of various noblemen.

To replace the deceased chaplain Nicholas, she thought of Andreas Capellanus. Now was a good time to send for him, if he were still willing to come to Troyes. She obtained the bishop's approval and dispatched a messenger to Paris with the invitation. Andreas responded quickly, expressing his eagerness to accept and indicating that he would be in Troyes before the end of the year.

Fortunately, some of the court officials who had gone on crusade with the count *did* return, among them the almoner Guillaume, the treasurer Milon de Provins, and even Artaud, who was now ready to serve Marie as attentively as he had served her husband. But even with these old friends to advise her, she did not relish the task before her.

May 13, 1181

The first thing Marie felt compelled to do once her new court was assembled was to punish the treachery of her brother in stealing her son's betrothed. She had waited until after her father's death and had hoped her husband would return to deal with the matter. Now it was left to her alone. Less than two months after Henri's funeral, she summoned to her palace in Provins her brothers-in-law and Queen Adèle, along with their nephew Hugh, duke of Burgundy, all of whom had expressed various grievances against King Philippe. She chose Provins primarily for its convenient location for most of those who would attend the meeting, but also partly because it was a city better fortified and easier to defend than Troyes. Its Tour de César loomed on the brow of the western hillside, providing a good watchtower from where guards could see anyone coming from the direction of Paris long before they arrived.

It was late afternoon before the little group assembled briefly in the council room. The faces around the table were glum.

"All of you understand, I'm sure, why I called this meeting," Marie began. "I want to discuss what actions we might take against King Philippe, who has turned his back on our family, mistreated his mother, and usurped my son's marriage rights. I hope you will join me."

"Military action is all he understands," Étienne said.

"I cannot agree with that," Queen Adèle said quickly. "He is my son."

"But Adèle," Marie argued, "he seized your dower lands and forced you to take refuge elsewhere."

"I know, and I'm grateful for your hospitality at the time," the queen answered, "but thanks to King Henry, at least he's now agreed to provide me with an income instead. You must understand, Marie. Suppose it was your son."

Marie could not imagine her son Henri ever doing such a thing. He was loyal, handsome, intelligent, and responsible, a young man who, she felt sure, would one day be a good count, for he was learning quickly. She depended on him to be at her side in the coming years. They would help each other always. He was as furious with his cousin as she was, and although he was willing, even eager, she thought him too young to command an army.

"She may be right, Marie, a war against our own king and nephew is a serious matter," Guillaume said, using his sonorous archbishop's voice. "I don't see how I can involve God's army in such a revolt against the king."

"I agree," said Thibaut. "It's too strong an action."

Then Étienne spoke in an angry voice. "Well, I don't agree. King or not, he's an obstreperous boy, and if we don't teach him now to respect his vassals and his family, matters will only get worse. He's invaded my territories without any recognition of borders, and if the situation were reversed, he wouldn't hesitate to go to war against us."

"*Bien dit!*" the duke of Burgundy shouted his approval. Well said.

"I think you're right," Marie added, relieved that at least one of her brothers-in-law supported her. "Adèle, I understand your feelings as a mother, but Philippe is also our liege lord. He has responsibilities toward us as we do toward him, and he must learn to respect those boundaries."

Adèle looked down. Her eyes filled with tears, and despite her efforts to hold them back, they spilled over her lower lid and rolled down her cheek. Marie leaned over and put her arms around her friend. "Please try to understand. You don't have to take part or endorse our actions. And we won't harm Philippe, I promise. Not his person, at least." Clearly, emotions were running high, and she thought it best to end the meeting for now.

"We've all traveled quite a distance, and we're tired. Perhaps we should all get a good night's sleep, give everyone time to think a bit, and we'll resume this meeting tomorrow," Marie said, hoping that by then she could persuade Thibaut at least to change his mind.

The next morning, to Marie's surprise, a guard brought news that men carrying the banners of Flanders and Hainaut were approaching Provins.

"Do they have soldiers with them?" Marie asked.

"No, my lady, they seem to be only courtiers unprepared for combat. The counts of the two regions appear to be with them."

How do they have the temerity to come here? she wondered. She alerted the marshal to ready the troops, even if there were no soldiers in the incoming party.

"You may open the city gates to them, but I want them met by guards and allowed to approach the palace only with an armed escort."

By the time the two counts finally entered the great hall and knelt before her, Marie had taken her seat on the dais, where she could look down on them with cool hospitality. Her brothers-in-law stood at her side.

"Your arrival is something of a surprise, my lords," she said, her voice icy. "To what do we owe the dubious pleasure of such a visit?"

"We've come to beg your forgiveness, my lady." Philip's voice took on a humble tone. "You and your kinsmen undoubtedly hold us in justifiable contempt for our recent actions involving the king. We've heard rumors that you are here to consider taking up arms against him. First of all, we would both like to make our abject apologies for our poor judgment." Baudouin nodded in agreement. "And I would like to join you in your revolt against the king, if you'll have me," Philip added.

"I thought you were the king's chief advisor," she said. "Is this some trickery on your part? To learn our plans and betray us?" She gestured for them to rise.

"The king no longer looks to me for advice, my lady," he said, now standing and able to look into her eyes. "He made that clear at Gisors when he turned from me to the king of England for counsel."

Marie remembered the incident well, although she had not been present. Queen Adèle had called on the king of England to settle the dispute between her and her son. The meeting had taken place the previous June. It was King Henry who urged Philippe to provide a pension for his mother and to take her brothers back into his good graces. Thibaut seemed to be the only one who had benefited.

It was for this reason, Marie assumed, that Adèle and Thibaut were reluctant to participate in the war she was proposing. The meeting at Gisors had not, of course, addressed *her* grievance against Philippe—the violation of the marriage treaty. But it had served to alienate Count Philip from the crown, and the king was even threatening to set aside his new queen, Philip's niece. Now out of favor with the crown, Philip was seeking to redeem himself in the eyes of the countess and her brothers-in-law and to join their alliance against the king.

"I have brought with me the count of Hainaut, who wishes to express regret and ask forgiveness for breaking the betrothal agreement he made with your husband. It was an unfortunate mistake. He brought with him some of his most trustworthy men as guarantors that he will uphold whatever he swears to in the future. We hope, in your mercy, that you will agree to negotiate a new betrothal treaty between your son Henri and the count of Hainaut's younger daughter Yolande."

Marie did not hesitate to express her dismay and outrage. "Do you dare to think that you can change your loyalties so easily? Why should I trust either of you to negotiate a new betrothal after this betrayal?"

"I can understand your feelings, my lady," Baudouin said, "and I respect them. You have every right to be angry, and I regret my poor decision more than you can imagine. However, I would like to make a sincere apology and a new offer. In the interest of your daughter Marie and my son, who seem an excellent match, I hope we can renegotiate this treaty."

His words caught her attention. She was deeply concerned for the future happiness of her daughter. Mariette and young Baudouin had met only once, still children really, but they seemed instantly attracted to one another. It promised to be an excellent match, and Mariette would be broken-hearted if it never happened. Marie no longer worried about Scholastique, who was promised to the widowed son of Gérard, count of Mâcon. That had been one of the matters waiting for the count upon his return. But it had been Marie who finally negotiated the agreement. Now, if she were to agree to a new treaty with Count Baudouin, both of her daughters' futures would be settled.

She still hesitated. Then, remembering the joy in Mariette's eyes at the thought that this wonderful boy would one day be her husband, she finally said, "In the interest of my daughter, we will bring the matter before the assembled barons this afternoon. The meeting begins just after sext. You may bring three of your men with you."

When the council resumed, Queen Adèle chose not to attend. Marie understood. As a mother, she did not want to be involved in a discussion about her son's behavior. She had been obviously uncomfortable at the previous day's meeting, and Marie loved her too much to insist. Counts Philip and Baudouin, however, were both present, and she was surprised to see that one of the three courtiers the count of Hainaut had invited to accompany him to the meeting was Gautier de Fontaine, the father of the young man with the same name who had been executed for his indiscretion with the countess of Flanders. *How can he bear to be in the presence of Count Philip who had his son put to death in such a horrible way?* she wondered. She noticed that he sat as far away from Philip as he could, but still he was there as counselor to the count of Hainaut.

Marie had asked her own son Henri to attend this first part of the meeting, which would involve the matter of the renegotiated treaty. It would after all affect his life, and she thought he should be present for the debate. Besides, she wanted his approval in the matter.

The discussion began, with Count Baudouin offering to substitute his younger daughter, Yolande, as the bride in the new marriage treaty. "As you may recall in the old treaty," he said, "a younger sister was to be substituted in the event of the older one's death."

"This was hardly a death," Marie said coolly.

"Hardly," Étienne echoed.

As negotiations continued, Marie could see from her son's expression that he was not greatly pleased by the promise of Yolande, who was five years younger than her sister Isabelle—only a small child now—and whose dowry was far less important.

Finally, after they had discussed the various details of a new treaty, the countess asked the men from Hainaut and the count of Flanders to allow her and her allies to consider the matter in private.

"Of course," said Baudouin, and all the members of his group shuffled out of the room.

Marie turned to her son. "What do you think of the offer?" she asked. She knew she could make the agreement without his consent, but she was reluctant to do so.

"It's obviously a less desirable match," he said, "but I've thought about it, and in the interest of my sister's happiness, I will agree."

"And you?" she asked of her brothers-in-law, who all nodded their approval. While the arrangement may not be ideal, it would help to seal the peace and bring the counts of Flanders and Hainaut to their side against the king. With that assurance Marie had the other parties summoned back into the room.

"We have decided to accept your offer," she told them.

"Splendid," said Baudouin. "I will have my chancellor, Gislebert, draw up the agreement at once." He rose from the table, beaming. He had accomplished what he had intended—a new betrothal agreement—and he was eager to get the treaty signed before the countess could change her mind. He bowed to Marie and took his leave with all his men. The count of Flanders remained seated.

"You may go too, if you wish, Henri," his mother said, understanding that no boy his age would rather sit in a dreary council room, when he could be outside with his fellow squires. He smiled, jumped up at once, gave a quick bow, and followed the others out of the room.

Marie was proud of the mature way her son accepted the situation. Once his sister was safely married, she thought, he would no doubt do whatever he wanted.

"A fine-looking boy," Count Philip observed. "He does you proud, my lady."

"He is much like his father," she replied, pleased by the compliment to her son.

The matter of punishing King Philippe for his treachery was still before the council, and she was a bit unsure how she should proceed in the presence of Count Philip. He sensed her unease at his presence and quickly intervened.

"If I may speak, my lady, I would like to assure those present that I am sincere in wishing to join you in whatever action you plan to take against the king. I too have my grievances against him and I hope you will allow me to remain and take part."

"Why are you suddenly so willing to help us?" Étienne, by nature suspicious, wanted reassurance. "A year ago this time you were against us and on the king's side."

"I know. Since then, however, he has become as hostile to my family as he has been to yours, even threatening to put aside my niece, the queen, who is, of course, distraught, merely because he is angry with me. I agree that he's too young and immature to rule and that he should not be allowed to treat his vassals in such a disrespectful manner. Trust me, I am sincere."

Count Thibaut reluctantly agreed to provide strategic help to his brother Étienne, but nothing else, as they began their plans of attack. He didn't want to alienate the king again. Guillaume chose to remain neutral. Those who showed themselves eager to join Countess Marie in these hostilities included Étienne, Philip, and Hugh of Burgundy.

"Then it's settled," Marie said. "We shall unite forces and attack the lands of the king this summer."

When King Philippe heard of their planned attacks, as he inevitably did, he appealed for help to both the emperor and the king of England. The emperor urged him to make peace but offered no military support. But help came from England in the form of King Henry's three eldest sons, who were not only sympathetic to a young king trying to establish his authority but who were also his vassals, pledged to support their liege lord.

Thus, Countess Marie would soon find herself at war against four of her brothers.

CHAPTER 38

Planning battle strategy was a new and exciting experience for Marie, but it was daunting at the same time. She would be sending men she knew to fight and perhaps die for her son's honor. It was her right, of course, as regent of her lands, but she still wrestled with her decision. Her various allies had their own grievances against Philippe, but her main goal was to teach her brother that he could not trample on her son's rights with impunity. Just because she was a woman did not mean she would not fight back. Above all, she wanted him to know that. Still, she wanted to risk as few lives as possible.

A large map of France and the surrounding counties lay on the council table as they devised a plan of attack.

"I would suggest that we attack from my lands in the north. That's the shortest way to Paris," said Philip.

"But that would mean that my men would spend weeks just getting into position," Étienne complained.

"And mine," added Hugh of Burgundy. "Why not attack from the east? That would mean half the distance for each of us."

"Or," Marie suggested the thing that seemed most logical to her, though she was well aware of her inexperience, "why not attack from all three positions at once? Philip's men from the north, Étienne's and Thibaut's from the south, and Hugh's and mine from the east?"

The men glanced at her but said nothing. They went on discussing at length the advantages and disadvantages of the various options, until finally, Thibaut spoke up.

"I think we might consider a pincer movement—attacking from various directions at once and trying to catch the king in a trap."

"That's an excellent idea," Philip said. "That way the king would have to divide his forces, and they would be weaker."

"I agree," Étienne added. "And we wouldn't have to worry so much about troop movement for long distances. That way our troops wouldn't tire out so much before the battle even started."

Marie said nothing, but she wondered what was different about what she had suggested half an hour earlier. Perhaps they think it sounds better coming from a man, she thought. *Oh well, what difference does it make if it gets the job done?*

They went back to their own castles, understanding the role each was to play and eager to begin. There were almost two thousand knights Marie could call upon for help. Not all of them would be able to come, of course, but she could count on a large number of troops. And Hugh's men would be marching north to join hers in battle.

Philippe was determined to attack first. King Henry's sons arrived in late May to plan the attack. The four brothers of Countess Marie all agreed that their best defense was to go on the offense before the allied forces were ready. They were young, strong, and eager for battle. With their combined armies they rode under the bright June sun, avid to strike against the troops they considered most easily defeated—those of Étienne de Sancerre. Taken by surprise, Étienne's men made an effort to fight back but were quickly overwhelmed.

Before word of the attack could reach Champagne, the king's army turned eastward to confront the gathering soldiers of Marie and Hugh. The Champenois and Burgundian forces, not yet fully assembled, saw them coming from a distance and tried quickly to mount a defense. Hearing of the arrival of the king's army, Marie, her son Henri beside her, rode at once to the battlefield to encourage their men. The moment they arrived and saw the size of the attackers' combined forces, it was obvious that such a hasty defense would be useless. They were outnumbered, and they'd been caught off guard. It was too late, and there were too few of them to succeed. Marie and Henri watched grimly as the Champenois-Burgundian forces were soon routed and forced to surrender, easy prey to the united attack of the countess's four brothers.

After the surrender, only Richard sought out Marie. Sweating in his chain mail, he removed his helm as he approached her on horseback, greeting both her and Henri, with apology in his eyes. "I had never hoped to see you under such circumstances, sister. And I beg your forgiveness. Please understand that we had no choice, for we've done homage to Philippe for our lands."

"I understand, Richard, and I too regret that we meet in such circumstances. I hope it never has to happen again." Despite her disappointment, she knew that he was obliged to meet his feudal obligations. "I'm only relieved that so few men were killed. I'll see that the wounded are cared for." Richard nodded and gave her a weary smile.

As they watched him ride away, Henri said, "He was the best soldier on the battlefield. I hope that someday I'll be able to fight like that."

"I hope you never have to fight."

"But, *Maman*, it's what I'm being trained for. It's what I want. If I never fight, how can I prove I'm a man?"

She looked at him with tenderness. "How indeed?" she murmured, wondering if noblemen would ever find another measure of success in life.

The king's forces turned westward once again, knowing that by now Philip of Flanders had learned of the king's victories against his rebellious vassals and had set out to attack the kingdom's northern lands while Philippe was still busy elsewhere. It was true. The count of Flanders had already captured Dammartin and besieged Senlis. But when he realized that his allies had been easily defeated and that it was now his turn to confront the king's army, he scurried thirty miles farther north to safety at Crépy, taking refuge behind the castle walls and preparing for a siege. But it did not come. King Philippe and his allies knew that they had broken the coalition and that, for now, Count Philip on his own would be no problem. Besides, the forty days of military service the vassals owed to their lords were coming to an end, and the armies began to disperse. The count, relieved, decided that there was little he could do on his own and went home. Thus, the revolt against the young king of France came to an early end.

On April 4, 1182, Henry Plantagenet set out once again to be peacemaker, a role that ill-suited him. He summoned King Philippe and Count Philip for a meeting on an open plain near Gerberoy to hammer out a peace treaty. Since neither Marie nor Hugh were present, he convened a second meeting a week later on April 11 between Senlis and Crépy, to which he summoned all the other allies, including Countess Marie. There they would be compelled to ratify the peace treaty, which made it clear that King Philippe had soundly defeated his adversaries. At least peace was restored. Marie was more or less back in her brother's good graces, and Count Thibaut was back at his post as royal seneschal. The meeting was amiable enough, and Marie was glad to see her Plantagenet brothers again, this time in a peaceful mode.

"Whoever thought we would be adversaries in war, even briefly?" she said to Richard. "I'm sorry all this happened, but I wanted Philippe to see that he could not trample on my son's rights with impunity."

"If our mother had been in your shoes, she would have done the same thing," he answered. "I think Philippe understands what's at stake now. But as his vassals, we were obliged to help him."

"I understand. How is she, Richard?" Marie asked.

"Well enough, I suppose. I miss her at court, but, as you know, my father is not a forgiving sort—except for his sons."

"Are you happy?"

"Of course not. We're still restless and eager to assume our duties, but our tyrant father keeps a close eye on us all. We have little freedom. This war, except for having to be your adversary, was a nice respite."

She was not eager to hear any more about her defeat and deflected the subject away from the war itself. "He won't live forever, you know," she reminded him.

"Perhaps not, but he seems to have the stamina of three men. He can cover distances with his army in times that no one else could accomplish. It's like he's everywhere at once."

During the feast that followed, Philippe approached Marie. "I regret that you felt you had to go to war against me, dear sister," he said, his voice cool.

"You know perfectly well that you gave me no choice, Philippe. I will never stand by idly while you ignore your feudal obligations and refuse to honor such agreements as my son's betrothal to the girl who is now your wife. She was too young to marry in any case."

"It was that devil, Philip of Flanders, who tempted me into it. Then he turned on me. He was the serpent in the garden. He is the one you should blame, yet you allied yourself with him. I fail to understand that."

"He has apologized and seen the error of his ways, Philippe," she said. "Have you?"

"I see that she was too young to be married. And she's not a good wife. She's not even nubile yet and certainly not ready to give me a son."

"You knew that before you married her. You just wanted her dowry," she said.

"I won't deny it. It's my duty to expand the kingdom, and you would do well to stay on my good side, Marie." It sounded like a warning to her.

"I regret having to wage war against you, little brother, but you gave me no choice. I want your word that you will never interfere with my son's rights again. That way you have nothing to worry about from me."

"I swear to it, sister. And I want your word that you will never again take up a sword against me."

"I swear to that as well, provided you keep your word."

"Done," he said and reached out to give her the kiss of peace.

In early April of the following year, word reached Marie that her cousin Elisabeth had died on March 28. Apparently, she and Count Philip had never really reconciled after he'd killed her lover, Gautier. Marie wondered what Philip's reaction was to her death. Even though he had turned his back on her, he would not divorce her, for he feared the loss of Vermandois, which King Philippe also coveted.

Countess Marie was surprised when Count Philip showed up one afternoon in early June on the threshold of her castle in Meaux with a rather abrupt proposal of marriage.

"It would be a very beneficial union to us both, Marie. It would join our two lands, and we would have the weddings of your children and my niece and nephew as well to bind our two families together. I think it must be God's will, since he took both our spouses within such a short time of each other," he added by way of persuasion.

"It sounds very practical, Philip, but I will have to think about it. I'm not sure that I want to marry again. Or that the king will approve," she replied. She was weary of the practicality of such marriages.

"The king be damned," he said in an angry voice.

"He's my brother," she reminded him, "and my liege lord as well as yours."

"Perhaps you can persuade him. I doubt that I can. I am still not in his favor, despite the treaty. You, on the other hand, he seems to have forgiven completely."

Marie could not deny that she found Count Philip attractive. He was younger than Henri and far more handsome, with his fair hair and clean-shaven face. She also admired his reputation as a knight. It was no coincidence that both the young kings had been drawn to him because of his renowned valor and fighting skills. He had taken them both under his wing, first her brother Philippe whom he had trained as a knight, and now Henry, the Young King of England, who, with his friend William Marshal, had joined him in the tournament circuit.

Her chamberlain, Artaud, made the necessary household provisions for Philip and his men to stay for the rest of the week or longer, as they requested, allegedly to rest before they began their journey back to Flanders. With her usual hospitality, Marie arranged for fine feasts and entertainment during their sojourn. There was no question that Philip could be charming, though he was sometimes perceived as arrogant. *I suppose some people are just jealous*, Marie thought, for most considered him the flower of knighthood—brave, generous, and wise. And she enjoyed his company.

He seemed delighted by the musicians and singers she brought in once more to entertain them now that her period of mourning had ended. There were always nearby jongleurs and *trouvères*, ready to be called to court at a moment's notice. The reputation of the countess as an admirer of their songs had become widespread, and they were always delighted to perform for her and much relieved that she had begun to welcome them once more. The poets Guiot de Provins and Huon d'Oisy were among the most familiar faces at her court gatherings. Her husband Henri had never particularly cared for the secular poets or taken them seriously, but Philip seemed to enjoy them immensely.

As the first evening wore on and the count began to realize that his practical approach to a marriage agreement was not making much of an impression on the countess, he began to change his tactics.

"Has anyone ever told you what splendid gray eyes you have? They are the color of the sky just before dawn and equally full of promise," he said softly, leaning over to offer her a choice tidbit of his roasted peacock as they dined in the great hall. "They have such life and depth, like the sea on a stormy day."

Marie could feel herself blush a bit. No one had ever talked to her that way before. Only her mother had ever commented on her eyes. She smiled demurely and shook her head. "Not really," she said. He returned her smile and summoned a squire to refill their goblets.

Then, when the musicians with their pipe, drum, and flute began to play and dancers took their place for the *carole*, Philip turned to her. "Shall we join them?"

She could not imagine Henri ever being the one to suggest such a thing. She'd always had to coax him into dancing. Philip took her hand and led her around the trestle table and down to the floor of the hall as the music played. Marie loved to dance, but she had not done so since her husband's death. It felt good to be once more among the dancers in the circle, holding hands and singing as they went through the simple steps.

By the end of the evening, after the merriment had ended, and as Marie was preparing for bed, she confided in her maid. "The count of Flanders has asked for my hand in marriage," she said, smiling as Jeanette brushed her long hair. She did not normally reveal her secrets to her maid, but she was bursting to share this unexpected turn of events.

"And how did you reply, my lady?" Jeanette asked with a smile.

"I told him I would think about it," Marie replied.

"He is very handsome, *ma dame*," the maid said.

"Yes, I know. And we seem to have many common interests. But I'm not sure I want to marry again."

Jeanette caught her eye in the small mirror Marie was holding before she said, "Many ladies would find him quite desirable." She paused. "But whatever you decide, my lady, I'm sure it will be the right thing."

"I hope so," was Marie's answer.

Before the end of the week the countess found herself weakening in her resolve not to remarry. She liked the way Philip touched her elbow or took her arm to lead her into the feast each day. She liked the way he gazed at her when a *trouvère* sang his latest love song. They were nearly the same age. She was thirty-eight now, and he was only three years older—far younger than Henri had been. It seemed a logical match. And if she didn't marry Philip, she thought, perhaps her brother would insist on wedding her to someone else, someone distasteful. If she married Philip, at least it would be her own choice. But there were impediments.

First of all, she and Philip, as fourth cousins, were related in a forbidden degree. She wondered whether the fact that Philip had been married to her first cousin would also require a special papal dispensation. Then there was also the need to seek the king's permission. These were major obstacles. *Is it worth the effort?* she wondered.

Then, on the fourth night of Philip's visit, he insisted on walking her to her bedchamber as they retired for the evening. Once they were in the dark hallway, he caught her arm and turned her to face him. Gazing into her eyes, he pulled her to him and kissed her.

When she drew back, he said in a husky voice, "Forgive me, my lady, but I could no longer resist. Your kiss is sweeter than honey from the comb. I hope you will grant me another."

She was startled by his audacity, but she had to confess, at least to herself, that she'd enjoyed the kiss. It had been so long since anyone had put his arms around her in such a way. And she'd always felt that Henri did it more from duty than pleasure. This was entirely different. She yielded herself to a second kiss and felt Philip touch her left breast with his hand.

Once again, she pulled away, even though her action belied the sudden desire that flooded her body. "I must go in," she said. "We shall talk tomorrow."

"My dreams will be filled with you, my lady," he said, as he bowed before her and kissed her fingertips. "And may yours be as pleasant as mine." Then he was gone.

She stood before the door to her chamber for a moment, trembling. It had all happened so quickly. Thank God, she thought, he had not tried to enter, for she was not sure she would have been able to resist.

CHAPTER 39

For three nights he had walked her to her door, kissed her, and touched her in increasingly intimate ways, until she would finally push him away. He sensed she was weakening despite her efforts to resist. Now Philip stood alone in the dim hallway outside the closed door of Marie's bedchamber, smiling to himself. He had found her vulnerability. She longed to be touched, to be desired, and even though she was not beautiful, she had a sensual quality that made him want to fulfill that desire more and more. If he made love to her, she would have to marry him—or she would lose her honor and her reputation.

He knew she was weakening, for she did not pull away from his embrace as quickly as she did at first. He knew from much experience how to entice a woman and how skilled he was at lovemaking. It was a matter of practice and strategy—much like the tourney, where he had learned to join in the mêlée only toward the end after the other participants had grown weary. And he had become better at both over the years. Now he sensed his chance. He was almost there. She was resisting less and less, and if he controlled both Flanders and Champagne, he would be the most powerful baron in the realm.

Is this the kind of love the troubadours sing about? Marie wondered, as she prepared for bed. This ardent yearning of the flesh? If so, the noble thing was to resist and let them both burn with a desire increasingly refined, but never consummated. As a woman, she should let herself be worshiped instead. At least that was the picture Andreas painted. But he had written of *amor purus*, which did not include fleshly conjoining, as well as what he called *amor mixtus*, which did. And that seemed to be the goal, at least for the men, of most of those courtly dialogues he had invented. So a physical relationship was not ruled out in this *fine amor*, was it? This desire was something she had not experienced before with such intensity—not in all her years of marriage to Henri. Their lovemaking had always seemed dutiful and only when *he* felt the need. Philip, on the other hand, seemed ardent. He didn't write love songs himself, but he urged the minstrels at the court to sing of love and desire. She felt sure he was trying to express his longing for her through the songs of others.

But what of her children? She lived for them now. Perhaps she should set aside her own desires and needs for their sake. She was already planning the marriage of Scholastique to the son of Count Gérard de Mâcon. The young man was a widower and eager for their nuptials. His father was ill, and Marie expected the son would soon be count. There had been other offers, but none quite so desirable as this. It was a good match and one she knew her husband would have approved. Scholastique would soon be fourteen, old enough to be wed.

Little Marie—Mariette—would soon be ready for marriage as well, and she was most eager, but her mother once again was determined to wait until after her fourteenth birthday. Then there was her son Henri. He had never been happy with his betrothal to Yolande, and he still did not trust her father. Nevertheless, he was determined to see his sister wed to the boy she said she loved. He didn't want to spoil her happiness.

Life is so complicated, she thought. But she was finding Philip harder and harder to resist. He was pressing his suit now, trying to convince her to become his wife. *Suppose I agree*, she thought. *What would be the consequences?*

The next night as they stood outside her bedchamber door, Philip held her close and whispered heavily into her ear. "I want you, Marie. I need you. My whole body burns for love of you. Let me come in." His voice was urgent, and she could feel herself weakening.

For days now, she had not allowed any of her ladies or servants into her chamber at night, for fear that they might hear his murmurings outside the wooden door. The room was empty—except for that soft bed, luring the two of them. She knew that there were two wine glasses on the table beside the bed, as there had always been. She still insisted on that. They comforted her and made her feel her husband would return at any moment. A fresh flagon of wine was always put there for her in the evening. But she was not thinking of that now—only of Philip's hands caressing her breasts and his breath, hot on her neck. He did not lift her skirt, but she could feel his hand moving down her body to touch the spot between her legs, where his cock, straining in his *braies*, was already pressing. She did not push him away.

He reached around her to grasp the door handle. The door opened inward, and he pushed her gently into the room. She heard the closing of the wooden door and the click of the lock. Then he picked her up and carried her to the bed. Before she could protest, he took off her wimple and loosened her braided hair. Pinning her firmly with his own body as she struggled beneath him, he began to undo the lacings of her *bliaut* with one hand, while his other hand groped beneath her skirt to touch the nakedness between her legs. She gasped.

"Philip, no. Don't. Please. We can't."

"Yes, we can. There is no one about, and we shall soon be man and wife."

"Philip, you mustn't," she moaned as his fingers explored.

He flung her skirts up now, forgetting about the lacing, using his arms instead to hold her writhing body in place. In spite of her efforts toward reluctance, she could feel her body responding, already moist at his touch and her mouth opening eagerly to his kisses. There was no turning back now. Things had gone too far, and she could no longer deny her own desire. Instinctively, once he'd slipped off his *braies*, she opened her legs to let him enter. Quickly, he satisfied his desire with hasty thrusts as though he could contain himself no longer. Although Philip was soon spent, she longed for more.

He was not insensitive to her need and finished undressing her slowly and with great care. He took time to taste her nipples and explore them with his tongue, while continuing to stroke her longing parts with his hand. He wanted her satisfied, but not too much, so that she would beg for more, so that she would agree to marry him, just to have him in her bed again and often. Then, when he was able, he entered her once more, this time more slowly, making her arch her back in an effort to feel him deeper inside her, making her want him with the same intensity he had wanted her.

When they were both satisfied and exhausted from their lovemaking, Philip sat up to keep himself from falling asleep. "Would you like a goblet of wine?" he asked.

"Mmm..." she murmured. "Yes." She lay languidly on her pillow, watching him as he poured, feeling at the moment only pleasure from his presence. He was muscular and lean, looking younger than his forty-one years. His straight blond hair fell almost to his shoulders. She reached up to touch it, then let her hand slide down his naked back.

He smiled and held out the goblet and gave her a light kiss on her lips. She sat upright as she took the wine, remembering the image on the wall above her bed in Poitiers of Tristan and Iseult drinking the love potion on the ship. *But we are not adulterers*, she thought. *Neither Philip nor I is married.* Then why did she feel this tinge of guilt? *Because it's still a sin. Fornication is a sin.* She thought of her children sleeping at the other end of the long hallway. *What would they think,* she wondered, *to see their mother like this, lying here naked as a whore on what had been her marriage bed.*

"Philip, you must go," she urged as soon as he had drained his goblet. "You must go now, while the palace is still dark and quiet. And no one must see you."

"You have no guards at the door?"

"You know I don't," she said.

"Thank God for that," he laughed. "But you must tell me now. You *will* marry me, won't you?"

She hesitated only a moment before she said, "I will, under two conditions—that we can obtain permission from my brother, the king, and that you can get a papal dispensation."

"That will not be easy," he pointed out.

"I know, but I will have it no other way."

"Even though you have already defied God's law?"

"Even though *we* have defied God's law in our weakness of the flesh," she said. "God will forgive. I'm not sure the king would."

"Then you must be the one to approach him," Philip said firmly.

"I will—at the same time you send messengers to the pope."

"If that's all you will agree to," he replied with grudging acceptance.

"And I want you to leave tomorrow. Go home, for I can no longer run such risks as we have taken tonight."

"Must I?" he asked. He had hoped to remain long enough to make sure she was pregnant before he left. That would give her absolutely no choice, nor the king either for that matter. They would both do everything to make sure the child was born legitimate. But she was adamant.

"Tomorrow. For if you stay, I know we will sin again." Her voice brooked no defiance. She felt her strength returning.

As he departed from Meaux the next day, Philip began to consider whom he might send as an emissary to the pope to request the dispensation. There was a new pope, Lucius III, and no one was sure what to expect from him. He was still an enigma to many noblemen. All Philip knew about him was that they shared a common hatred of heretics. He was hopeful of the pope's approval, though it would undoubtedly take time, diplomacy, and gifts. But it was worth it. The widow-regent of Champagne, sister of the king, would be a fine asset. With her as his new bride, he would be able to rule for many years over both Flanders and Champagne, huge territories that dominated most of northern France. He would strengthen his army by commanding her two thousand knights. By the time he had reached the borders of his own lands, he had decided that he would send Pierre, abbot of Andres, a small Benedictine monastery not far from the Pas de Calais, a man reputed to be persuasive, to lead his emissaries to the pope. They would depart as soon as possible.

Although Marie had agreed to the marriage in the heat of the moment, in her heart she was not sure it was a good idea, and she was in no particular hurry to seek the king's approval. She knew it would take many months to obtain a papal dispensation, if the pope agreed at all. As she left Meaux and rode with her entourage back toward Troyes, young Henri at her side, she pondered the situation. Given the king's continued hostility toward Philip of Flanders, she did not expect it to be easy, and she thought it best to give her brother more time to forgive and forget their intentions in the recent war. Theoretically they had made peace, but she knew there was still mistrust between them. Perhaps her brother would see this marriage as a chance to make a more lasting peace, but she wasn't sure. She wanted to find him in a good mood when she approached him. She would bide her time.

Before Christmas, Count Philip sent her a message that good progress was being made with the pope and asking about the king's approval. Thus, when an invitation came to the king's court at Sens for Christmas, she accepted, knowing that this might present the best time to ask for Philippe's permission. She still had mixed feelings about the marriage. While she would welcome Philip's physical presence and she knew it would lift the burden on her as a woman trying to rule over two thousand obstreperous knights, she worried that she had consented for all the wrong reasons. Would such a marriage be in the best interest of her son, or even of herself? Was she simply running away from the responsibilities that had been thrust upon her? Had she simply given in to temptations of the flesh without any thought for her soul and her family's well-being?

As soon as she reached the court of Sens, she requested a meeting with her brother. He invited her to his solar for a cup of spiced wine. Once they had settled before the fire, with the wine poured and waiting, it was the king who spoke first.

"It's good to have you here on peaceful terms, sister."

"Thank you, Philippe. It's good to be here."

"May we never find ourselves at war against each other again. Now why did you need to see me alone?"

"Is it not enough that I wanted to speak to my brother to say that I too am glad we are friends again?"

"It would be, I suppose, but I daresay that's not the issue. You have a request." It was not a question, but a statement she could not deny.

"I come to seek your permission," she said. "Philip of Flanders has requested my hand in marriage." It seemed ludicrous to be asking permission from this boy of only sixteen summers, but he *was* the king and her liege lord, and she had no other choice.

Philippe said nothing for a moment. He merely stared into the flames. "Why do you think he wants this marriage?" he asked.

Marie thought for a moment. "He says he loves me. But I suppose he also wants the regency of Champagne."

"Precisely," Philippe said. "With him in control of both Flanders and Champagne, he would have far too much power. I can't possibly grant permission for such a marriage."

"You were very close to him once."

"Yes, I know, but he has shown himself to be a man I cannot trust. Why would you want to marry him?"

"I find him very attractive, and it would ease my burden. As you know, men sometimes do not respect women's judgments. Some of my vassals are already trying to move their cases into ecclesiastical courts as a way to avoid coming before my court for rulings."

"I can find you another suitable husband," Philippe offered.

"No. If you cannot consent to my marriage to Philip, then I will not marry again. I've come to you in good faith. But if you refuse to approve, then I want your promise that you will seek no other husband for me. I also want your support in my appeal to the pope to forbid laymen in my region to take their cases to a church court if it does not involve the clergy." She had already planned her strategy in the event that Philippe did not give his permission.

"You are a strong woman, Marie, and I have no doubt that you can rule your lands quite satisfactorily on your own. If you don't wish to marry again, I won't force you. But this marriage to Philip of Flanders is not acceptable to me. I cannot give my permission."

Marie felt no real sense of disappointment at her brother's words—but almost relief. Her son Henri was already fifteen, and she had already worried about conflicts between him and Philip as a stepfather. *It's better this way*, she thought. *I can control my desires.* As the memory of that night of love flitted through her mind, she felt a brief sense of loss that she quickly banished. *I should send a message at once to Count Philip so that he can recall his emissaries before they waste more time with the pope.* That way she would not be tempted further.

After he received the news, Philip rode immediately to Troyes. When he arrived, Marie could see that he was angry, though he was trying to keep his temper in check.

"What effort did you make to persuade him? The king is just a child. What does he know? And why should we allow him to control our lives in such a way?"

"He is my brother," Marie said, "and my liege lord."

"But he's not your only liege lord. There are the duke of Burgundy and the emperor. You hold lands from both of them, as well. Why not seek their approval instead?"

"Philip, above all, I want peace in my lands and in my family. Try to understand."

"Why don't we just do what your mother and King Henry did? Marry and then ignore the consequences?"

"Philip, I have told you my conditions. Without the king's permission and the pope's dispensation, I will not marry you."

"The pope is coming around. A few more gifts, and he will surely agree. If God's representative on earth is not sufficient for approval, I don't know what is."

"I'm sorry, Philip. But those are my conditions."

He could not believe that she was turning him down. After all his efforts.

"What of your reputation?" he scoffed.

"I trust you as a gentleman," she replied. "What happened occurred only once and will not happen again."

He laughed. "All women are alike, wanting only to satisfy their own lusty desires—just like my wife."

"I regret that I was weak, Philip, but you were very persuasive, even insistent. And why should the fault be only mine?" Her voice carried a challenge.

"Such things are expected of men. It's a noblewoman's duty to resist such temptations outside of marriage." He hesitated. "Unless, of course, she plans to marry the man."

"Then you must be like all men—wanting only power and your own satisfaction, with no thought about whom you might hurt in the process." She too was growing angry now. It was tiresome—this attitude that men were exempt from all moral responsibility. "Now I think you should leave. I'm certain you can find another wife to your satisfaction."

"And no doubt a more beautiful one," he sneered. "That I can easily do."

"Please go, Philip," Marie said, raising her chin in disgust at his intended cruelty. "I think the king is right. You are not a man to be trusted. I'm sure you will find someone more suitable." *And thank God I see you for what you really are*, she thought.

She turned her back and walked away, leaving him standing alone in the great hall. There had been no witnesses to their conversation, and she had no idea what stories he would spread about her, but she would not let him humiliate her. He was not worth it.

Philip's parting shot on his way out of Troyes was to stop briefly by the home of the poet Chrétien, whom the count took to be Marie's favorite, and invite him to his own court. "I have a commission for you," he said. "You should leave here and come to *my* court, for I think you will receive no more patronage from the countess."

Chrétien was flattered that Count Philip should seek him out in this way. Even though Countess Marie had disappointed and even angered him by reneging on her commission, she still invited him from time to time to her court to share his stories. She was especially fond of his translation of Ovid's tale of Philomela and she always paid him well. But she had not given him a new commission. Even so, since her dismissal he had been productive, almost finishing his *Cligés* and continuing his work on *Yvain*. Still, this was an opportunity that might never come again. How could he turn it down?

"Can you share with me the commission you have in mind?" Chrétien asked.

"There is a legend of the knight Perceval and his search for the Holy Grail I would like you to write about for me. Would that interest you?"

"Indeed it would, my lord. Give me time to finish my work already in progress, and I am your obedient servant," Chrétien told him.

"Fine. Come ahead to my court. You can complete your work there and then begin the one I have in mind. I'll expect you before the end of the year."

"I'll do my best, my lord." At last. A new noble patron. His future was assured.

Philip rode away, smirking in triumph, sure that he had punished Marie by stealing her best court poet. And he would make certain that the abbot of Andres, who had led his expedition, learned of her indiscretion. That was the reason he would give for breaking off the negotiations—that he did not want another wife with loose morals. He was not sure he had the nerve to tout it about in the courts. She was the king's sister after all. But he would not have the abbot think she had turned him down.

CHAPTER 40

Troyes, February 1183

Marie sat in the solar in the fading light of afternoon, contemplating the trap she had just avoided and the possible consequences of her actions. *In all probability, when the count recalls his emissaries from the pope, he won't tell them of my refusal but of my weakness. I suspect he would do anything to save his pride.* Even if he told only the abbot leading the expedition, there could be gossip. But she had no regrets. *Let him do his worst. I will hold my head high and not dignify such accusations with a response.*

She knew now that she would never marry again or give any man that much power over her. *What was I thinking?* As a widow with ample resources at her disposal, she could control her own life—insofar as a woman ever could. It was an enviable position, *one my mother would no doubt covet,* she thought. She felt certain she had made her brother, the king, understand that she would not be forced into another marriage. *Thank God I managed to escape the bondage in which lust almost ensnared me.*

Suddenly there was a soft knock on the door.

"*Entrez,*" Marie called.

As her son Henri came alone into the room, she felt a rush of love and pride. His dark hair, so like his father's, fell in unruly curls around his face, clean-shaven in the style of the day.

"May I speak with you for a moment, *ma mère*?"

"Of course, my son. Sit down."

She smiled at Henri, no longer a boy. At sixteen he already looked like a young man—tall and fit, his dark curls so like his father's. She loved him more than anything in the world. She loved all her children, of course, but there was something special about her firstborn son—who had fulfilled her married woman's primary duty—to give her husband an heir. Henri perched on the windowsill, looking somewhat nervous.

"I don't mean to speak out of turn," he began. "But I just wanted to tell you that I am glad you sent Count Philip away. I don't like him, and I don't trust him any more than I trust Baudouin de Hainaut. They both betrayed us with the king's marriage, and I didn't like the way the count looked at you or the way he treated me—as though I were in his way."

"Henri, I had no idea he did that."

"I was afraid for a while you were going to marry him. His squire, Arnoul, told me that's why he was here and that he had requested a papal dispensation for the marriage. Is that true?"

"It is true, my son, but thank God I realized in time it was not a good match, and King Philippe did not approve in any case. Put your mind at rest. I've refused him, and I do not plan ever to marry again. I have informed the king that I will have no unwanted husband thrust upon me." She put her hand on his cheek. "You are nearly a man now and will soon be able to be knighted and rule the county yourself. Until then, I plan to serve as regent and keep everything peaceful and under control."

He was smiling now. "I'm so proud of you, Mother, that you didn't let yourself be manipulated by that conniving count. I know you must be lonely sometimes."

Marie felt a wave of both guilt and relief rush over her, as she considered just how far she *had* allowed herself to be manipulated by Philip and how close she had come to marrying him.

"I know some of the problems you've had with various men in the county, but you've always shown good judgment and fairness. You're so dignified and honorable. I want to be just like you—except a man, of course." He smiled shyly.

She laughed. "Of course."

"*Ma mère*, I have a confession to make—to you alone."

"What is it, son?" Her smile vanished, and she was suddenly serious. A confession? What had he done?

"I did not enter my betrothal to Yolande in good faith. I did it only to guarantee the marriage of Mariette to Beau. The two are truly fond of one another, and I think it will be a good marriage. Would you think me dishonorable if I seek another bride after they are wed?"

"It's your life, son, and I can certainly understand your feelings. To break such a treaty would be breaking your word, though it's no more than what Philip and Baudouin did to you. I can't speak to the consequences, but it would be their just due, and I'd certainly support you."

It was good to be able to talk to her son this way—adult to adult. He was mature for his age, more so than his cousin, the king, she thought. His judgment of people was perceptive, and he was concerned for the honor of his family. She was sure that his uncles would not only understand, they would probably encourage it. In fact, they were still angry with Baudouin and Philip and were doing everything they could to urge the adolescent monarch to set aside his young wife Isabelle to eliminate any possibility of their future influence.

"But I would suggest that you speak to no one else of this, especially if you intend to wait until your sister is married. Rumors are so easily spread." She herself could hear the irony of her words.

"Of course, Mother. Thank you for understanding." He kissed her cheek.

"Henri, I want you to begin coming to court with me on a regular basis. There are so many things you need to learn before you become count. And there will be times when I might consult you on various issues. You can be one of my advisors."

His eyes sparkled, "Really? That would be wonderful." Like all boys his age, he was eager to grow up, and the invitation to advise her occasionally showed his mother's confidence in him. He had grown increasingly restless, now that he was in his teens, and he had in recent years begun to frequent tournaments with his other young friends, among them Arnoul de Guînes, one of Count Philip's squires. Now, if he were to assist his mother at court, he would begin to learn his duties as count, in addition to those of a knight. It was a big step.

"Well, I'll let you get back to your reading," he said with a broad smile, making a move to leave.

She put her hand on his arm. "No, stay for a while. There are matters I'd like to discuss with you. You may know that some of the men have been seeking to take their cases before ecclesiastical courts to avoid bringing them before a woman. What do you think I should do about it?" His eyes lit up, and they began to talk, exchanging ideas, as she occasionally pointed out the limitations of feudal law or gave heed to his suggestions as he reacted to hers. They talked on for a long time, mother-to-son, regent-to-future count, and friend-to-friend. The conversation brought them ever closer and assured Marie that Henri would soon be a fine count. When the pope eventually ruled in her favor regarding the ecclesiastical versus the secular courts, they rejoiced together.

For the first time in her life the countess felt that she was on the firm ground of self-assurance. She had always strived to please someone else, to be a good hostess, to be a good wife and mother, to be womanly for the sake of the men in her life. But now, although she still intended to do her duty and be a good hostess, she would do it on her own terms—pleasing herself and God and devoting her life to her children's happiness and wisdom.

This felt like a whole new phase of her life, where she was for the first time truly in control, where she alone could determine the people who surrounded her and those in whom she confided. Establishing her authority was not an easy task, and she knew that men would continue to try to take advantage of her, but they no longer intimidated her. She had once worried over the harsh actions her men had taken at Coulommiers when her father was still alive, seizing the king's men who tried to get by without paying the full tolls they had paid so readily when Count Henri was in charge. But she had no regrets about it, and she felt certain that King Philippe already understood that she did not intend to be treated in any way differently from a man in charge. He had seen that she would not shy away from asserting her rights and making justifiable demands. Even though his troops had won, it had cost him significant effort.

Her determination to become a strong ruler, however, in no way reduced her interest in the works of poets or even in the occasional courts of love she still held. She believed that they had already made a difference in the attitudes of at least some of the men in her region. The differences were subtle, perhaps, but they were there. Many of the courtiers were far more polite and attentive than they had ever been, and clearly the women who attended her courts were holding themselves in higher regard.

Her determination to rule wisely over her region made her better aware of what a good count her husband had been and more appreciative of his attempts to be fair and generous to a fault. It had given her a better understanding of his annoyance when bishops or anyone else had tried to undermine his authority. She'd learned not only from watching him, but also from presiding over her courts of love and their requirement to justify any decisions based on solid reasoning and precedent. And if she overstepped her bounds in any way, she was quick to acknowledge it and make amends, as she had recently done with the Cluny priory of Reuil-en-Brie, when she claimed the right to lodge there with her household on one of her travels. She'd suspected that she had no such right, but it was conveniently located and seemed a matter of necessity at the time. Afterwards, when the prior complained, she'd quickly admitted her wrong and mollified the monastery with the gift of a silver chalice. She had done the same thing when the abbot of St. Loup complained of a similar infraction, not by herself, but by some of her knights. This time she gave something more personal—her garnet ring—which the abbot attached to the volume that the count and countess had donated to the abbey to commemorate their son's birth on the feast day of St. Loup. It was always better, she believed, to head off any serious protests they might make than to let matters fester.

Although the feud between Philip of Flanders and her brother, the king, continued, she chose not to take sides. Instead, she busied herself preparing for Scholastique's wedding to Count Guillaume, for she turned fourteen that year. Marie and her children traveled to Mâcon, south of Dijon on the Saône River, where the marriage took place at the Cathedral of Saint-Vincent. Scholastique looked nervous but lovely. Mariette watched with envy as her older sister, splendidly garbed in her mother's red samite dress, wed the handsome knight, sixteen years her senior. Although she was only twelve, Mariette was already dreaming of her own wedding.

"My darling. You're not ready to be a wife," her mother said. "There's so much you still need to learn. You won't be fourteen for another two years. Don't be so eager to grow up." Mariette pouted for a while, but soon she was in the garden playing a hopscotch game with her little brother.

Thibaut, at five, was beginning to be aware of his own maleness, and although he still played with his sister from time to time, he preferred his boy games. He felt ready to start his lessons on the *quintain*, though Marie thought it too soon. He loved to ride his pony with his older brother, who made a miniature wooden spear and sword for him to play with. Marie took pleasure in seeing the boys together, with Henri helping his little brother as his father had helped him. Watching her children grow and learn was her greatest joy—even more so than her ladies' courts and the great feasts she still gave. But they were growing up much too fast.

Not long after Scholastique's wedding, Marie received the unhappy news that her brother Henry the Young King had died on Saint Barnaby's day, June 11, in a merchant's lodging in a village called Martel, just north of the Dordogne River. He had been fighting this time not against his father, but against his brother Richard in Poitou. His death was not the result of a battlefield wound, as one might have expected, but rather of fever and a flux of the bowels. Marie knew that both her mother and her sister Marguerite, widowed so young, must be heartbroken.

The following summer Marie and her entourage rode to Rouen to join Marguerite, along with Geoffrey and his wife, Constance, in commemorating the first anniversary of the Young King's death. There Marguerite funded a mass to be said for her husband each year on the anniversary of his death, while Geoffrey and Constance endowed a chaplaincy in his memory.

When it was over, Marguerite rode with Marie back to Troyes, where she planned to remain for an extended visit. Marie invited Queen Adèle to join them there for her Christmas court. She gladly accepted. Although Adèle's son, Philippe, tolerated his mother at his court, he seemed to prefer it when she was elsewhere. Marie always enjoyed her company—another woman in whom she could always trust and confide.

With her year of mourning now over, Marguerite took the occasion to set aside her widow's white garb, though she still wore her sadness like a cloak, with sorrow etched on her face. Marguerite was only twenty-six—more than a decade younger than the other two women, but her downcast look marred her beauty and made her seem far older than her years.

As they spent time together, Marie began to suspect that it was not only her husband's death that weighed her sister down. Disturbing rumors about Marguerite and William Marshal had widely circulated before Henry's death. Perhaps none of it was true, and Marguerite's misery indeed resulted only from the loss of her husband and the fact that she had no children. She had given birth only once seven years earlier, but the baby, a premature boy, had lived only a few days. Since then, nothing. Marie wondered whether, like Elisabeth of Vermandois, her sister may have turned to a lover for comfort.

Two nights after her early December arrival, Adèle complained of a headache and went to bed early, leaving Marie and Marguerite alone together in the solar. Marie ordered a flagon of wine for them to share. After the squire brought it in, the two women sat quietly gazing into the fire. Suddenly Marguerite turned to her sister.

"Marie, did you know that Henry and I were living apart at the time of his death?"

"I..." Marie began, but Marguerite, tears pooling in her eyes, interrupted her.

"It was because of his suspicions and foolish jealousy."

"Were his suspicions ill founded?"

"Of course! And he sent me back to *Papa*, just as Henri did to you—only for different reasons." Now her words were pouring out. "He accused me of taking William Marshal as my lover. But you know William. He would rather cut off his own arm than betray a friend." She paused, then added, "I cannot deny that I found him attractive. He was more mature and courteous than Henry and showed amazing skill and valor at the jousts."

"Was the attraction reciprocated?"

"I suspect it was," Marguerite confessed with a blush, "and occasionally he wore my tokens into the joust—a scarf or a ring. But there was never anything more. I swear it. He thought he was only doing honor to the lady of his lord. He was falsely accused."

"Would I know the accuser?" Marie asked.

"Probably not. It was a man named Adam of Iquebeuf, a regular member of the court. At first Henry didn't believe it. He couldn't imagine that the two people he loved most would betray him. But to convince him, Adam filled another young man with wine and flattery and persuaded him to lie and say that he had personally witnessed these acts."

"How awful!"

"Henry sent me back to *Pap*a immediately, but he didn't banish William. I suppose he loved him more." Marguerite's voice caught in a little sob.

"Oh, Marguerite, I'm so sorry." Marie took her sister's hand.

Marguerite was crying openly now. "William begged Henry to let him prove his innocence and mine in a trial by combat, but Henry refused. Finally, William left the court of his own accord."

"But they were eventually reconciled, weren't they?" Marie asked. "I recall that they were together last spring in my own lands, at Montmirail-en-Brie."

"Yes, and Henry welcomed him back. I think he would have eventually taken me back as well—but then he got sick..." Marguerite's voice trailed off. "Oh, Marie, he was only twenty-eight. He had so much to live for." She was sobbing on Marie's shoulder now.

Marie let her sister cry for a while before she asked, "What made the difference? What convinced him of William's innocence?"

Marguerite blew her nose on her handkerchief and tried to dry her tears. "That felon, the accuser, Adam, abandoned my husband and went over to his father's side. That convinced Henry that the man had been a liar all along. I just hope he didn't die still thinking I had betrayed him."

"I'm sure he would have recalled you as soon as he returned from the expedition he was on," Marie said. "Where is William now?"

"He's gone on a pilgrimage to the Holy Land, fulfilling a vow Henry had made. Oh, Marie. He's such a loyal man. Such a good man." Marguerite gave way to her anguish, which seemed as much for William as for the Young King.

Marie took Marguerite's hand and tried to soothe her. Then she refilled their goblets of wine, and they sat quietly before the fire, remembering happier times and watching as the burning logs slowly turned to embers.

It was hardly a merry court, at least not at first, though Marie did her best to cheer her friends with sumptuous foods and the songs and stories of the poets and jongleurs who still flocked to her feasts. Being the excellent hostess she was, she did not want gloom and sorrow to prevail at her Christmas court, and she began to summon more and more entertainers to liven their feasts. There were acrobats and jugglers, fools and jongleurs, who dispelled the heavy atmosphere with color and liveliness.

Instead of dwelling on their misfortunes, Marie tried to steer the women's conversations to more joyful recollections of Poitiers and the festive Christmas courts they had shared in the past. None of them was an old woman yet, and life still stretched before them with promise—for themselves and for their children. Marie tried to vary the entertainment and the adventures. Sometimes she organized hawking expeditions outside the wall of Troyes. At other times, she invited the ladies to watch the fun as little Thibaut struggled to impress them with his miniature lance and his brother's help.

"Your sons are marvelous, Marie, but I envy your having daughters as well. It must have been such a joy to see Scholastique so well married. And now, at fifteen, she's already a countess," Adèle said. Scholastique's father-in-law, Gérard, the count of Mâcon and Vienne, had died earlier that year, making Guillaume the new count.

"Yes, and I think she's well trained for the role," Marie said proudly.

"I have no doubt of that. She's learned from the best, as we did," Adèle said with a smile, remembering her mother's instructions with the two of them. Marie had been fortunate to keep both her daughters at home as long as she had, but once Scholastique's betrothal had become official, Guillaume's mother, Maurette, had insisted that she come to live at their court. Marie, accustomed to having all her children with her, missed her daughter terribly, but she consoled herself that at least Baudouin de Hainaut had not insisted that Mariette be raised in his household. She would not have allowed it, for she still did not trust him.

Little by little the dark cloud of sorrow lifted, and the three women were soon able to laugh like young girls together over their shared experiences. But Marie had not forgotten it was still Advent and had also planned more contemplative pastimes, like their brief visit to the Priory of Notre-Dame de Foissy—where a taking of the veil was scheduled on December 21. By the time they started on their excursion to the priory, their lightened hearts were more receptive to the moving experience of the two young sisters taking the veil together.

The village where the priory was located, St. Parres-aux-Tertres, was an easy ride, little more than a mile from Troyes. It was a double priory, housing both nuns and monks, and attached to the order of Fontevrault. Marie knew it well and supported it, for the mother of Anseau de Traînel had once been prioress there.

As the women watched the two novices take their final vows to become *sponsae Christi*, brides of Christ, they contemplated their choice to become nuns. To be a virgin was supposed to be the most valuable role a Christian woman could choose. It meant giving up marriage and motherhood, which was considered the third most valuable path for a woman's life. Some young women chose to become nuns because of this hierarchy of values, but also because marriage meant risking one's life in frequent childbearing and becoming the property of a man who might or might not treat them well. Marie, Adèle, and Marguerite, as widows assumed to engage no longer in carnal intimacy, stood on the second rung of that hierarchy.

"Has either of you ever thought of becoming a nun?" Marie asked the other two women as they rode back from Foissy.

"Of course," Adèle said. "Haven't you?"

"Eventually, perhaps, but I still have obligations I must fulfill, and quite frankly, I enjoy court life. What about you, Marguerite?"

"I don't think convent life is for me, but you never know what the future holds," she said with a laugh. "There are times when I think it would be a comfort."

"It would certainly be more peaceful," Marie agreed.

A few days after they returned from their expedition to Foissy, Marie announced, "I have a surprise—a translation into the common language of Psalm 44 that I requested just for our Christmas court from Adam de Pontigny, who has recently been named abbot of Perseigne. Adèle, I'm sure you know him. He's an old family friend and has been my confessor at times."

"How on earth did you get him to do it?" Adèle asked. "Like most clergymen, he doesn't approve of scriptural translations."

"Well, it's mostly commentary," she laughed. "He's managed to turn a psalm of seventeen verses into a poem of more than two thousand lines. But he's done it in an amazing way that I think will appeal to courtiers. He even depicts King David as a jongleur of God."

"That's certainly a novel idea," Adèle said.

"And he uses all the courtly language. He's often been involved here in debates with the court poets about the true meaning of *fine amor*. He argues that the term is better suited to spiritual love than worldly love. For Adam, the only true *fine amor* is love free from impurity—one that is sinless and noble. And he says it should never be used to describe such impure relationships as that of Lancelot and Guenevere. He even describes the love between Christ and the Church as *fine amor*."

She had found these dialogues between Adam and the court poets, including Chrétien when he was there, most interesting. And she thought it exciting to see the crosscurrents that flowed among the different writers and their topics, with the spiritual and the secular seeming to feed upon one another.

"By all means, let's hear it," Adèle said.

"Yes, let's," added Marguerite. "It sounds delightful."

The women listened with rapt attention as Marie's chaplain began, after a light supper, to read the work aloud. The poem, called by the Latin phrase *Eructavit cor meum*, "my heart overflows," began with both praise and a gentle criticism of the countess, depicting her as one whom the Lord God teaches and inspires with all good things, except for one. The poem contended that she was a little too generous—the very virtue for which her husband had been most admired. But the poet seemed to think that *her* generosity was prodigal. Marie exchanged a knowing smile with her friends at the remark, for they had often talked about the fact that what was considered a great virtue in men was often seen as a flaw in women. She had chosen to ignore Adam's criticism because of his other efforts to treat women with respect throughout the poem.

It celebrated the daughters of kings and depicted King David, author of the original psalm, singing at the wedding feast of Christ and the Church—a day in which courtiers celebrated the "joy of the court," which echoed a phrase from Chrétien's *Erec*. She smiled as she listened to Adam's words, clearly inspired by the secular poets of the day: "*Aime le roi,*" as he called King Jesus, "*par fine amor*." Love the king with love that is good and pure, and you will grow more beautiful from day to day, the poem promised.

Marie was delighted and intrigued by Adam's combination of translation and commentary on the chosen psalm. It was especially appropriate for the Christmas court for three noblewomen. Not only was it often used in Christmas services and at royal weddings, it also aimed to please ladies. The poet praised the queen in eight verses and the king in eight more—treating them equally, as he pointed out. It glorified the daughters of kings and exalted their sons. There seemed to be something special for each of them in Adam's words.

All in all, the secular entertainment and the spiritual nourishment at Marie's Christmas court provided the three women both consolation and joy, and strengthened their friendship. They all regretted Adèle's need to return to Paris when the festivities of the season ended, but at least Marguerite remained.

"You make me feel so welcome," she told her sister. "And I really have nowhere else to go, except to Philippe's court, and I think he tires of having me. King Henry never allowed my husband and me to establish our own court. And now, he won't give me my dower. I feel rootless."

"You can stay here for as long as you want, my dear."

"Even now, our brother Philippe is no doubt casting about for a new marriage for me—to get me off his hands and to benefit his own kingdom somehow," Marguerite said.

"Of that we can probably rest assured," Marie agreed, touching her sister's arm in sympathetic understanding.

CHAPTER 41

Sens, December 1185

Marguerite was still with Marie for the season of Advent the following year. Along with Marie and her children, she attended the king's court at Sens, where the countess had asked her brother Philippe to summon Count Baudouin de Hainaut to a meeting set for December 1. There she planned to confront him to insist on the wedding of Mariette to his son and namesake. Both children would be fourteen the following month, and they were exceedingly fond of one another. In fact, Marie had seen them kissing behind a rose trellis in the winter garden only a few hours after their arrival. Both Mariette and Beau were eager for the marriage to take place. But the boy's father was dragging his feet.

"If I allow this marriage between my son and your daughter," Count Baudouin said to Countess Marie, "what guarantee do I have that your son will then marry my daughter Yolande, who is not yet old enough to wed?"

"You have a signed treaty and my assurance, as well as that of his uncles, Archbishop Guillaume and Counts Thibaut and Étienne," she replied. The count could hardly argue the point, considering his own earlier perfidy, but he was wary. He was given little choice in the matter, however, for the king, Countess Marie, and her brothers-in-law all bore down on the man and insisted on the wedding. At the very least, he demanded, there must be a renewal of the earlier betrothal vows.

When Marie discussed the matter with her son Henri, he indicated his willingness to cooperate. "I promise I won't make any trouble about it, Mother," he told her. "I'll renew the vow, but I don't promise to keep it."

"I hope you have told no one else of your intentions," she cautioned.

"I trust no one but you in this matter," he said, "for I know you want Mariette's happiness as much as I do. Once she is safely married, I will decide what to do."

Baudouin finally agreed, but only if the renewed treaty were ratified before the wedding. "It must be guaranteed by the archbishop of Reims," he insisted, relying more on the word of an archbishop than that of a countess and mere counts like himself.

Once the agreement was made, Marie insisted on the wedding at once. She wanted no delays, for she did not trust the count of Hainaut any more than he trusted her. Finally, the date was set for them to meet on January 13 at Château-Thierry, where the wedding would take place. It was the soonest all arrangements could be made. Marie also insisted on that location, which stood more or less equidistant between Troyes and Baudouin's capital of Valenciennes, but it had the greater advantage of lying within her own borders.

Cold and snow flurries greeted Countess Marie when she arrived in Château-Thierry. Her distrust of Baudouin was such that her retinue included not only her family and usual knights, but also her new marshal, Geoffrey de Villehardouin, whom she brought along to keep order, should the need arise.

She spent time the evening before the wedding with her daughter, the bride, trying to prepare her for the ordeal, but Mariette merely blushed and laughed. "Don't worry, *Maman*," she said. "I know all about that. It'll be fun."

She was radiant as she prepared the next day for the ceremony and then stood with young Beau at the church door. Her face wore an eager smile, as she spoke her willingness to be his wife. Everyone present noticed how they gazed into each other's eyes, looking more like lovers than a pair who had been destined to become husband and wife since they were babies. They were beautiful to look at, both in the first flush of youth, with their fresh young faces, shining blond hair, and rosy color in their cheeks.

Henri and his mother stood behind the bride, facing the count of Hainaut, who was positioned beside his son and glaring at them with a sour face, still angry that he had found no way to delay the ceremony until Yolande was old enough to wed the future count of Champagne.

After the wedding and nuptial mass, Marie took her son Henri aside. "Please don't make any trouble for at least a year. Give them a little time in peace," she urged him. "I know your desire to avenge Baudouin's betrayal, but bide your time, and think carefully before you act."

"Rest easy, *ma mère*," he replied. "I have no new bride in mind at the moment," he assured her, "and I'll discuss it with you before I act. I promise." He kissed her on the cheek and hurried off to join his young friends as they were all preparing to ride to the marriage feast, which was to take place later at Valenciennes.

When Marie and Marguerite returned to Troyes, they were distracted once more by a summons to a joint assembly at Gisors held by the kings of France and England. One of the matters was the settlement of what was to be done about Marguerite's dower and dowry now that her husband was dead. Marie had been summoned as well since Philippe wanted as many of his vassals present as possible. To Marguerite, the dower was important, for this was her sole livelihood. But there were many other issues to be discussed as well, and it would be a large gathering. *Perhaps my English brothers will be there,* Marie thought, *and I can learn more recent news of my mother.*

The meeting was held the second week in March, and the weather, though sunny, remained cool. Courtiers, still dressed in their splendid furs and fine-woven wools, gathered in an open field near Gisors, where a large elm tree provided ample shade for those who arrived early. Latecomers were destined for a day of unrelieved sunshine.

Marie and Marguerite mingled with the other ladies, one of whom was the new wife of Philip of Flanders, a Portuguese princess named Teresa, who was still trying to accustom herself to her new name of Mathilde, as she was called in Flanders. She was the daughter of King Alfonso of Portugal and co-heir of the kingdom with her brother Sancho after their father's death the preceding year. Her marriage to Count Philip the year after Marie had rejected his proposal brought him a considerable dowry. The new countess of Flanders was a tall woman with coal black hair and eyes too close together to be considered truly beautiful in this culture where wide-spaced eyes were admired. She appeared to be rather haughty and aloof, but Marie suspected she was merely timid and uncomfortable around so many people she did not know.

It was the first time since Philip's angry departure from Troyes that Marie had seen him. He was as handsome as ever, but seemed even more arrogant than before, despite his inability to best the king. They had finally come to an agreement the preceding year known as the peace of Boves, which settled the fate of Vermandois, now partitioned between the king and the count. Marie greeted Philip and his new wife graciously, but he returned her greeting with a look of disdain. She made every effort to be polite, but soon excused herself, leaving Marguerite to chat with the new countess of Flanders, while she spoke with her English brothers.

They were all there, except John of course, the youngest, whom she had never met, and Marie was delighted to see them again. Geoffrey had now become Philippe's close friend and a favorite at the French court, which annoyed his father greatly. It was Richard, however, whom King Henry considered the more dangerous of the two. They both greeted Marie with affectionate embraces.

"Have you heard recently from our mother?" she asked.

"She feels like a caged animal," Richard said bitterly. "You know how much she likes to control her own life. Now she can't even control the kitchen cooks."

"But she's in good health," Geoffrey added more optimistically. "And she has ladies with her. And a minstrel who plays for her from time to time. I think he's teaching her to play the lute."

"How else does she spend her days?"

"Reading or doing occasional needlework if she's completely bored.

And worst of all, I hear that she's confined to her room, except for daily walks in the garden under a guard's observation," Richard replied in an angry tone.

"Good heavens. It sounds like a prison sentence," Marie observed.

"It is. At least she thinks so. Papa sees her only on the rare occasions when he allows her to come to court. I think she prays daily for his death." Marie could almost have sworn that she heard him add, "as do I," under his breath.

"If you get a chance to see her or send her messages, please tell her I think of her every day and that I pray to God for her freedom."

"She will be pleased to hear that." Richard gave a grim smile.

When it came time for Marguerite's case to be discussed, the two sisters moved closer to the front of the assembly. It was not Marguerite's dower, but rather her dowry, the Vexin, that was of greatest concern to the men. Although Philippe argued for its return, since her husband was dead, Henry was determined to keep it for himself. Finally, after a heated debate, the two men agreed that it should be transferred to Philippe's sister Alais as part of the dowry for her marriage to Richard. Philippe used it as a bargaining point to insist on an early date for their wedding. Alais was already in her mid-twenties, but King Henry continued to delay. The non-marriage had become a very sore point for Philippe, but Henry swore that the marriage would take place very soon, provided he be allowed to keep the Vexin. Marguerite felt forgotten and betrayed by her brother.

"What about my dower? How will I live?" she complained to Philippe.

"We'll get to that. You will receive a stipend to live on. Besides, I have already begun negotiations for a new marriage for you with King Béla of Hungary."

"A man I have never seen and know nothing about."

"He is, I assure you, a man of considerable wealth who holds a splendid court—not what you might expect in Hungary, for he grew up in Constantinople and brought back with him many of their luxuries, so I'm told." She found his description little consolation.

Marguerite told Marie about their brother's plans for her as they traveled back to Champagne in a shared litter. She had made inquiries about King Béla from some of the older knights who had met him. In

Constantinople, he'd been called Alexios. He had once been betrothed to the emperor's daughter but had married Agnes of Antioch instead. Her name had been changed to Anna when she was brought to Hungary as Béla's queen. But she had died two years before, and he was now looking for another wife.

"Do you suppose they'll change my name in Hungary?" Marguerite asked her sister.

"I doubt it. Yours is a name that exists in many countries. They might pronounce it a bit differently, but I doubt they'll change it."

"Why do you suppose he'd want to marry me?"

"Maybe it's love from afar like those poems of Jaufre Rudel we heard at *Maman*'s court," Marie said with a smile.

"When he's never even seen me?"

"Jaufre had never seen the countess of Tripoli either. I suspect the king of Hungary considers it a great honor to ally himself with the French king. Besides, you have a reputation for beauty and piety. How old is he?"

"I'm not sure, but I'm told he's in his mid to late thirties."

"Not too old then. Perhaps he'll also be handsome and elegant and rich and—"

Marguerite laughed. "Stop it. You'll get my hopes too high."

Marie laughed with her for a moment. Then her face grew serious. "When will they come for you?"

"Philippe told me that they are scheduled to arrive in late August."

"I hope you'll stay with me until then. I can help you prepare for your trip."

As the time for Marguerite's departure drew near, Marie agreed to accompany her to Paris, where her Hungarian escorts were to meet her. The Champenois entourage was already en route and only a day or two away from Paris when a messenger from the king galloped along the road to meet them.

Marie could hear him talking with her son Henri, who was riding at the head of the procession.

"I'm glad you have already come so far. The king wants to hasten your arrival."

"Why the rush?" She heard Henri ask, as she pulled back the curtain of the litter to see what was happening. The messenger had clearly ridden hard, for his horse was in a lather.

"I regret to bring the bad news that your uncle Geoffrey Plantagenet has been killed. The king is distraught and wants you present at the funeral."

Geoffrey? Dead? "What on earth happened?" Marie called out.

The messenger trotted closer to the litter. "I'm sorry to say, my lady, that he was trampled to death when he fell from his horse during the mêlée at a tournament in Paris. The other riders couldn't stop in time."

Oh no, Marie thought. *Geoffrey had everything to live for.* Even though he was not his father's heir to the throne, he had married Constance, duchess of Brittany, in 1181. They had two daughters already, and it was rumored that Constance was with child once more. Like his older brother, young Henry, he had loved the excitement of the tourney. But it had caused his death.

When Marie and Marguerite arrived in Paris at nightfall, they found Philippe lying in his chamber, his eyes red and swollen from weeping. He sat up and fell into Marie's arms and began to sob once more like the boy he still was.

"He was my dearest friend," Philippe managed to say. "I had planned to make him my seneschal. He was so young… too young."

"Philippe, calm yourself. You will grow ill," Marie said. "I too am grieved, for he was my brother. But you must calm yourself. We have a funeral to plan." She turned to a nearby servant. "Have some dill water prepared for him at once. It will soothe him." The king lay down again as his sister stroked his back. Marguerite stood by helplessly, relieved that Marie was there to take charge.

"Now try to get some sleep," Marie said, once Philippe had drunk the potion. "We will meet first thing in the morning to plan the funeral."

As the king began to relax from the effects of the dill water, she and Marguerite slipped quietly out of the room and made their way to the solar, where they ordered some cold chicken with fruit tarts and goblets of wine, and settled down to talk.

"The funeral must be soon," Marie observed. "The Hungarian delegates will arrive in less than a week, and there's much to do before then." The two women discussed the necessary steps to prepare.

Despite her outer composure, Marie grieved inside, not only for her dead brother, but also for her mother, who had to endure the loss of yet another child. She had lost three of her five sons so far—William, Henry, and now Geoffrey. This time she couldn't even attend the funeral. The news would hit her hard, Marie knew.

Philippe insisted that Geoffrey be buried in front of the main altar at Notre-Dame Cathedral, so Marie met with the bishop, Maurice de Sully, to make the necessary arrangements. When the burial took place, Philippe, still overcome with emotion, had to be held back from jumping into the grave that held the body of his friend. Once the service was finally over, as a tribute, Marie donated an annual fund to support a canon at Notre-Dame to pray for the repose of Geoffrey's soul on the anniversary of his death, something she felt sure Queen Eleanor would have wanted.

Only a few days after the funeral, the delegation from Hungary arrived, bearing rich gifts for King Philippe and for the bride-to-be of the Hungarian king. As she was preparing to depart, Marguerite turned once more to Marie.

"Thank you, dearest sister, for all you have done for me—for the hospitality, the comfort, the sympathy, and the love you have shown. You will always hold a special place in my heart." They were both crying now.

"You will always be welcome at my court, Marguerite. I'll miss you very much."

And she would. The return to Troyes was sad. Marie's companions, including her chaplain Andreas, tried to comfort her, but she was disconsolate, feeling that she had lost not just Geoffrey, but Marguerite as well. Her sister promised to write, but Marie knew full well that their letters would be few, for messengers passed between the two countries on such an irregular basis. Marguerite would be busy starting a new life, learning a new language and new customs, while Marie adjusted once more to a life increasingly depleted of those who had filled her world. Her husband was gone. Her two daughters now lived at the homes of their husbands. And now Marguerite, who had been with her for the past two years, was gone.

Thank God her two sons still remained at home, though Henri would be twenty on his next birthday—only a year away from knighthood and taking over the role of count. And Thibaut, now seven, was old enough to become a page at his brother's court. How quickly everything was changing. Soon, she felt, she would be no longer needed.

One morning, while Henri and Anseau, along with several other courtiers, had gone on a hunt, Marie settled into the solar to read the third and final book of Andreas's treatise on love, which he had presented to her that very morning. This book, he said, represented the part of the work he believed he had to write because he was a cleric and did not want the book condemned by the Church. Marie was relieved to see that there were fewer pages in this section, which he called *De reprobation amoris, The condemnation of love*, for her reading of Latin was still slow.

He'd begun this third part by once again addressing his "ami Gautier," even though the Gautier for whom it was allegedly written was now dead for love. The first book had focused on the nature of love and how to win it, while the topic of the second book was how to keep it. This one, however, was quite different, and the more she read, the more exasperated she felt.

"Now that you know the way to arouse women's love," Andreas wrote near the beginning of the third book, "by refraining from such actions, you will earn eternal rewards." She could understand why a cleric would make that statement. But when he wrote that "extremes of love and self-indulgence are tolerated in men because of the audaciousness of the sex, but in the case of a woman, it is considered a mortal sin, causing her to lose her good name, and every wise man sees her as a foul harlot and holds her in contempt," she began to lose patience. While she was well familiar with this hypocrisy of men and the Church, it never ceased to incite her indignation.

The text went on to accuse women of being greedy, envious, slanderous, disloyal, proud, and arrogant. It contended that they were misers, gluttons, drunkards, lechers, liars, and gossips, heaping insult after insult upon the sex. Andreas stopped short of calling them the "devil's gateway" or "bags of dung," as some earlier church fathers had done, but he came close. Marie had always believed that such writing encouraged the contempt some men showed toward women, but never had she expected such extremes of condemnation from Andreas.

The earlier sections of the book had mentioned her mother, herself, and others by name. Would people associate these vile insults with them? The whole point of Queen Eleanor's creation of these courts of love was to dispel such absurd claims and teach men to respect women. How could Andreas, who seemed so affable, kind, and sympathetic, write such things? Perhaps in going to such extremes in condemning women he was only mocking the foolishness and unfairness of it all. But whatever the reasons, it would be unseemly for him to remain at her court. If he did, it would appear that she endorsed such views.

Marie wanted to be fair to Andreas, and she thought about it for a week before she took action, but she could see only one solution. Finally, she summoned him to the council room to discuss the matter.

"You sent for me, *ma dame*?" Andreas asked as he entered the room where Marie was already seated, the book lying in front of her.

"I did, Andreas. Sit down," she said amiably.

"I see you have the third book of my manuscript. Have you read it?" he asked, his voice apprehensive.

"Yes, and I found it filled with all the Church's most negative teachings about women. To be honest, Andreas, I was disappointed. I know you said you had to write such a part in order not to have the book condemned by the Church, and I understood. But such terrible condemnations—did you have to go to such extremes? Do you find *me* guilty of all those dreadful sins and weaknesses you mention?"

"Certainly not, *ma dame*," he said, shaking his head vigorously. "You know I do not view you in such a manner. Nor, in fact, do I believe most women to be so evil. But in order for the book to survive and not be condemned and burned, I felt obliged to repeat such teachings. I thought perhaps if I exaggerated in such a way, clever readers like yourself would understand that I merely point out the excessiveness of such attitudes, for no man can judge his mother or sisters in such a manner, nor, in my case, the lady I serve."

"I understand what you are saying, Andreas, but we cannot count on all who might read this book to be 'clever readers.' I find it troubling to have my mother, myself, and the other women you mention by name associated with such a text."

"I beg your forgiveness, my lady, but I could conceive of no other way to allow the book to survive." She could see from his embarrassed expression that he was genuinely troubled.

"Even though I understand your intent," she said, "you must also realize that I cannot have such writings associated with my court. As distressed as I am about the matter and as much as I enjoy your presence among my chaplains, Andreas, I must send you away. I do so with regret, but there are many other courts you could serve, and there is always the option of the monastery."

"I think I should be stifled in such an atmosphere, my lady. The court is where I serve God best. I know that your daughter Mariette has recently wed young Baudouin de Hainaut. Perhaps she would consider providing me a place in her own court."

"Perhaps, but she is not yet countess. Her young husband, and no doubt his father, would have to approve. Or perhaps Queen Adèle would welcome you back. I'm truly sorry I must send you away. I have enjoyed having you here. But you must understand, I have no choice. Although I was pleased with the first two parts of this work, I must in my own way reject the third book."

"I understand, my lady, though I shall be sad to leave. I've found your court to be stimulating, especially the discussions between Abbot Adam and the court poets. While I am obliged by my calling to take the side of Adam, I have found the debates to stir the imagination and the intellect."

"Unfortunately," she said, sadly, "the abbot will be coming here less often now that he has moved from Pontigny to Perseigne. As abbot there, he will have fewer opportunities to travel to Champagne. I know he will still visit from time to time, for this is his homeland, and he will surely come if requested. He has long been a friend of this family, and I can always call on him in my time of need, but his visits will be rarer."

"You may do the same with me, my lady, call on me in your time of need. I am always at your service. When must I depart?"

"As soon as you can find your place elsewhere, Andreas. I shall miss you," she said earnestly.

"And I you, my lady countess." He put his two hands together as though in prayer and lowered his head to touch them to his chin in a slight bow. With that he left the room, leaving her with only sadness. He had been frequently at her side—both in the official court and in the courts of love—during his few short years in Champagne, and she held him in her affection. The time she had spent with Andreas brought back memories of their days at the court in Poitiers. She would truly miss him.

CHAPTER 42

October 1186

"*Ma mère*! I've found my bride!" Henri burst into his mother's chamber without even knocking. Her maid was arranging the wimple on her head.

"Henri, what on earth? … Please leave us alone for a while, Jeanette," Marie said to her maid, who quietly left the room. When the maid was safely out of hearing, the countess admonished her son. "Not in front of others, Henri, not even the servants."

"I'm sorry, Mother, but I just had to tell you the news. I've found the perfect way to pay back that perfidious old count Baudouin. I know I said I wouldn't do anything within a year of Mariette's marriage, and I won't, but I had to tell you what's happened. It may be a miracle."

"Calm down, son. I'm eager to hear your news, but miracles are very rare."

"People always said your birth was a miracle of Saint Bernard," he replied.

"Yes, I know." She shrugged with indifference. "But tell me what's happened?"

"Do you remember the old count of Namur—Henry, the one they sometimes call the Blind because his vision is so poor?"

"Yes, of course. Is he still alive? He must be nearly eighty by now."

"Seventy-six, I'm told," Henri replied. "But he's just become a father!"

"A father? At his age? Are you sure?"

"Well, his wife, Countess Agnès, has given birth, and he's certainly claiming paternity. It's a daughter, and I plan to arrange a betrothal with her." He was effervescent in his excitement. "She'll be his heir. I can't imagine that he'll father another child, can you? And I doubt he'll live too much longer. As you know, he's inherited a lot of territory over the years, the counties of La Roche, Durbuy, and Luxembourg, all from his cousins, and Namur from his father. It would allow me to expand our borders considerably. But that's not even the best part of it all."

"What is the best part?" his mother asked.

"Before her birth, his heir was his nephew—Baudouin de Hainaut!" He laughed aloud. "Isn't it perfect? Not only will I avenge myself for his breaking our earlier agreement, I'll also punish him by taking *his* inheritance."

"Well, it *would* serve him right, wouldn't it? But you know he'll fight to keep it," his mother reminded him.

"Yes, but he'll lose—even if she is a girl. It's perfect."

"Don't be too sure," she cautioned. "Does she have a name?"

"She does. Ermesinde, for her grandmother."

"That's a pretty name, but she's still a baby. You'd have to wait another twelve to fourteen years before you marry. That's a long time."

"I wouldn't be any older than my father was when he married you," he pointed out.

"That's true. I suppose the age difference would be about the same, wouldn't it?"

She could hardly argue against it, since she had already agreed to his breaking the marriage treaty—just asking him to wait at least a year before he did anything that would upset Baudouin.

As though he were reading her thoughts, he said, "Don't worry. I'll keep my word to you, Mother, and not make any agreement until next year. I won't start negotiations until I become officially count of Troyes, I promise. That way you won't have to break *your* word."

On his twentieth-first birthday, July 29, 1187, in a simple ceremony,

Henri assumed his role as count. Marie watched as the bishop placed the comital coronet on his head. Only then, with a proud smile, did she step forward to present him his first seal of office, which depicted him as count palatine of Troyes, astride, his sword raised. He grinned with boyish pride, though he was trying his best to look dignified. He had even managed to grow a short beard before the event, which he hoped would make him look older and more dignified.

True to his word, now that he was count, one of his first acts was to negotiate an official marriage agreement with the count of Namur, who was eager to see his daughter's future settled before his death. The fragile child, not yet a year old, was given over to the custody of one of Henri's men, a castellan named Manassès de Rethel, who happened to be a nephew of the count of Namur. When word of the agreement reached Hainaut, Baudouin was furious and appealed at once to the German emperor, his liege lord, who ruled that Baudouin should remain heir. Both Henry the Blind and Henri de Champagne chose to ignore the ruling, but Baudouin was determined to enforce it.

He appealed next to King Philippe, and Marie knew that Henri did indeed have a battle on his hands. Baudouin was, after all, Philippe's father-in-law. She supposed that, even if her brother thought her son justified, he didn't have any real choice in the matter. The situation threatened to disrupt family relations once again, and she could only pray that Philippe would keep his word and not march against Champagne on his father-in-law's behalf.

The king was momentarily distracted in August by the birth of his first son, whom he named Louis for the child's grandfather. Then, apparently losing patience with his father-in-law, the fickle king's loyalties shifted, and he took the side of Count Henri. In the end, however, he favored his father-in-law, Baudouin, and awarded him the entire inheritance, allowing Henri only two paltry lordships, should he marry Ermesinde. Although the young count did not declare the betrothal invalid and send the child back to her father, it certainly dimmed his enthusiasm for it.

Once the matter was settled, however unfavorably, and it was clear that Henri was well accustomed to his new role as count, Marie decided it would be best to give her son the freedom to run his court without her peering constantly over his shoulder. Now that she was no longer regent, she could take advantage of her new leisure to pursue her own interests. With these thoughts in mind, she planned to set up household in Meaux. There she could indulge more freely in her courtly pleasures and spend time with Adèle, who kept a frequent court at the royal residence there.

Henri was not happy with her decision to leave and begged her to stay.

"*Maman*, I wish you wouldn't go. I may need to turn to you for advice," the young count said, reverting to his childhood name for his mother.

"Son, you are a capable man now, able to rule on your own. You've always given me sound advice, and I see no reason why you won't do a fine job as count. I won't be too far way, and if you ever need me, I'll come back. But for now, I think you need to make your own decisions without my hovering about like a useless shadow."

First, she planned a retreat with the sisters at the priory of Fontaines-les-Nonnes, not far from Meaux, to enjoy a tranquil respite away from the distractions of the world for a little while. She thought that Thibaut might come with her, but he was not eager to leave his friends in Troyes, and the idea of spending any time at all in a nunnery sounded horribly dull to him.

"I'm seven years old now," he said with all the maturity he could muster, "and I want to stay in Troyes and be a page at my brother's court." His mother was not surprised. Little boys were always eager to grow up, and he was no different. He was certainly old enough to take on the role of page, and then, when he turned fourteen, he could become a squire and officially begin his knightly training. After much begging on his part, Marie decided to let him stay. His brother Henri had always been his mentor and pledged to undertake, with the help of other knights at his court, his training for manhood. For the first time in her life, Marie would be truly on her own.

"I will miss you both, and I promise to visit often," she said, giving them warm hugs on the morning of her departure. The winter sun was bright as she set out with her attendants for her convent retreat at Fontaines on the tranquil banks of the Thérouanne River. There, she could read, pray, walk in the gardens, and consider her future.

One evening shortly after her arrival, she and Prioress Edna were sharing a late-night glass of wine after compline in the prioress's private quarters. Marie enjoyed her company, for she embodied a feisty mix of intelligence and compassion. And she always spoke her mind.

"It is so good to have you here, Marie. You bring a whiff of the outside world into our quiet realm," Edna said. "When do you plan to retire here for good?"

"Soon enough, I suspect." Marie laughed. "But not quite yet. I still want to enjoy some of the pleasures of the court."

"I have read that treatise on love that the chaplain Andreas wrote. I suppose you plan to put away that sort of foolishness in your retirement."

"It's just a harmless pastime, Reverend Mother," Marie said.

"Not so much so for your cousin Elisabeth and her lover evidently," Edna observed wryly.

"Yes, that was most unfortunate," Marie agreed. "But Gautier worshipped her."

"When he should have worshipped God."

Marie took another sip of wine and decided to change the subject. "What books do you have in your library here that you would recommend to an aging widow?"

"Mostly saints' lives, my dear. You might find them dull reading after those romances you like to read. And I would hardly call you 'an aging widow.' You're barely in your forties."

Marie laughed. "Chrétien de Troyes writes the best ones. I'm sorry he left Troyes for Flanders, but his works are still widely read and recited. Do you know them?"

"No, but I hear that he is writing a story about Perceval and the Holy Grail for Count Philip. I shall certainly make an effort to read that one when it's finished."

At the end of her month-long retreat, a well-rested Marie traveled the short distance to Meaux to take up residence and establish her own independent court there. It was a pleasant city, tucked into a great bend in the Marne River, and it held various attractions for her, including friends among the clergy and the nobility. Not only was Adèle a frequent visitor, but Marie's niece Marguerite de Blois, the daughter of her sister Alix, also lived there. She was the recent bride of the local viscount, Huon d'Oisy, who held a relatively small but lively court in Meaux. Huon was a talented *trouvère* who had had often sung at Marie's court, and she was always made to feel welcome at his.

Huon liked to entertain his guests himself with his delightful songs and tales. His young cousin and protégé in the poetic arts, Conon de Béthune, often performed at Huon's court as well. Marie was fond of them both. Conon had a pleasant voice, though he was still a bit unsure of himself. But Marie introduced him to some of the troubadour music she had heard in Poitiers—songs of Bernard de Ventadorn, Rigaud de Barbezieux, and Bertran de Born—whose works he'd come to admire and even tried to copy, for he was still young and finding his own style. Marie recalled an embarrassing incident that had occurred the one and only time he had sung, at her encouragement, at the court of King Philippe in Paris. As the young man started to play his lute, everyone listened attentively, but when the king heard his Artois accent, he had burst out laughing. Even his mother had been obliged to hide her amusement by covering her mouth with her hand. Conon was humiliated, especially by the fact that it had happened in the presence of Countess Marie, whose reputation for poetic patronage had become widespread. His face turned bright red, and after that day, he had refused to sing ever again for the king. When he later wrote about the incident in one of his songs, he suggested that the king and his mother were "neither well taught nor courtly" in their manners. Since then, Marie had made it a point to invite Conon to her court only when Adèle was not there, but she was still quite fond of both him and Huon, and enjoyed hearing them perform together.

She was particularly delighted with a new work Huon had recently composed and which he called the *Tournament of Ladies*. As his guests sat before a roaring fire, goblets of sweet red wine in hand, Huon amused his listeners by describing in a playful tone the jousting exploits of well-known ladies as they took up arms against one another and displayed their prowess at a fictional tournament at Lagny. Many of his characters were the wives of prominent noblemen, several of whom were present at the gathering. Marie laughed with delight when she found herself among the combatants. She smiled proudly as Huon depicted her performing quite well, riding in on her Spanish horse and jousting successfully against a hundred other ladies. When she was finally captured by Aeliz de Montfort, who managed to grab her horse's reins during the *mêlée*, she moaned in mock dismay.

The other women responded with equally good cheer as ladies bearing their names entered the lists. And like Marie, they groaned if they were defeated. Her niece Marguerite clapped her hands with excitement when her husband described her charging into the fray shouting his family's battle cry, "Cambrai."

It was all in fun, Marie thought—at least at first.

She was delighted that he could imagine women, even in humor, fighting their own battles and not just passively watching men in action. It was, in some ways, not unlike the courts of love, where women took charge. But as she thought about it later, something in the work also made her uneasy. She suspected that Huon intended it as a goad to spur men to action in response to the troublesome news that had recently arrived from the Holy Land.

She had heard it not long after setting up her court at Meaux. As much as she would like to have put it out of her mind, it was impossible. A general malaise seemed to have seeped into the whole region, sparked by heresies, rampant superstitions, and dire predictions from eastern astrologers of storms, earthquakes, and general discord. A monk at St. Denis had summed it up by concluding that "the world is ill." The most disturbing stories were brought back by travelers to the Holy Land of an emerging new Muslim leader, Salâh ed-Dîn, called Saladin by the Franks, who was having great success in uniting the Muslim world against the Christians in Outremer.

The worst news arrived in the fall of 1187 of a devastating and humiliating defeat in July. Christian forces led by the king of Jerusalem, Guy de Lusignan, had been overwhelmed by Saladin's army at a place called Hattin. Following his victory, Saladin had marched across the Levant capturing one Christian city after another—Acre, Sidon, Beirut, and Ascalon—leaving the city of Jerusalem surrounded by lands in

Muslim control. Matters looked grim.

The new pope, Gregory VIII, who had been elected in October, had also begun to preach the need for another crusade. *Not again*, Marie thought, as the call for another holy war was growing ever louder. She was all too aware that her son Henri was of an age to go and that he would be eager to do so. Holy wars had been costly in her life, and she was appalled at the thought of another one that might involve her son.

Only three months later, on January 21, the kings of France and England began a two-day conference between Trie and Gisors, attended by many of their most important vassals. Those present took the cross and swore a truce that their ongoing conflicts would wait until their return from Jerusalem. Marie knew full well that her son was among them. He would never have missed this splendid gathering of the most important men of England and France, the first meeting under the famous Gisors elm since he became count.

She could feel the fragile peace of her own life beginning to crumble at the news. She had served as regent for nine years while her husband was on his personal crusade and since his death. And she was not surprised when a messenger arrived from Henri, requesting her to return to his court and informing her that he had indeed taken the cross on January 22. She would be needed to assist him in his preparations and to assume the regency once again at his departure. Her "retirement" had lasted less than a year.

Marie returned to Troyes in mid-May, well before the opening of the hot fair. While Henri was away giving his forty days of annual service to the king, leaving his mother in charge, emissaries from Henry the Blind rode into Troyes. They had come to request Champagne's aid against a feared attack on his lands from Baudouin de Hainaut, who was still furious about the new betrothal. There was little she could offer in the way of help, for the fighting men were all away with the count, and the emissaries were compelled to ride back to Namur in disappointment.

The hot fair, which lasted six weeks, opened on St. John's Day, June 24, with its usual ceremonies, as merchants and buyers began to pour in from all over Europe. The city was lively with activity during the day, and the sound of hawkers and haggling filled the streets. It seemed to have gone well all month, with local peasants and castellans from the countryside mingling with those from distant places.

Then, near midnight on Saturday, July 23, when the city was quiet and the countess was sleeping peacefully, Jeanette was suddenly at her lady's bedside, shaking her awake.

"*Ma dame.* Wake up. There is a fire. The town is burning!" Her voice sounded frantic.

"What?" Marie sat bolt upright in bed and smelled smoke drifting in through the glowing windows of her room. She jumped from her bed and peered out. Below, on the other side of the canal, she could see fire blazing along the merchants' stalls and the half-timbered houses that hung over the streets, some so narrow that two ox carts could barely pass one another. Flames were leaping easily from one roof to the next in the strong wind. The fire was spreading quickly, devouring the buildings on the west side of the Rû Cordé.

She gazed in horror at the flames already blazing in the convent buildings of Notre-Dame-aux-Nonnains, just east of the fairgrounds, where the fire had started. How had it begun? Caused by a merchants' campfire that got out of control perhaps? Or a lantern tipped over by a careless hand or foot? Marie could hear with horror the screaming of the nuns. *Oh, God*, she prayed. *May they escape in time.*

"We must get out, my lady," Jeanette said with fear in her voice. "The fire is spreading this way." Marie had taken her books and her other most valuable possessions with her when she had left for Meaux, but she thought of St. Étienne and the rich books and goldwork in the church and its library. She hoped that the canons were all awake and working hard to get the most valuable items to safety. The countess grabbed a cloak to cover her shift and followed Jeanette quickly out of the building.

Once outside in the midst of the chaos, Marie summoned the guards and ordered them to assemble whomever they could and make efforts to control the fire. Soon, long lines of townspeople, men and women alike, had gathered and were passing buckets of water from the canals to try to douse the fire. But the task looked hopeless

By daybreak, much of the city was black with smoking embers. The few blazes that continued to burn here and there looked less menacing. Bucket lines were still at work, even though the people looked weary and ready to collapse. Marie, exhausted from her efforts to help the canons save what they could, stood in the smoky air, holding Thibaut's hand, as much for her own reassurance as for his, and surveying the ruins of the town.

Most of the damage was on the west side of the Rû Cordé, where merchants' goods from all over western Europe lay in ashes. Many of the merchants and townspeople had been unable to escape in time, and bodies were being found one by one, piled on carts, and carried from the embers. The cathedral had been in the path of the fire. Its roof was badly burned and partially caving in.

Flames driven by the wind had even spread to the eastern side of the Rû Cordé as far as St. Étienne, burning a few of the manuscripts and melting some of the magnificent goldwork in the church. The castle too was damaged and black with soot and ashes that the wind had scattered throughout the town. Bereft townspeople stood here and there, weeping, trying to comfort one another, and mumbling prayers, while some of the men carried out the bodies of several nuns who had not escaped the fire in Notre-Dame-aux-Nonnains.

"What will we do, *Maman*?" Thibaut asked his mother.

"We will rebuild," she said. "We will open our coffers to help our people rebuild." But even as she said it in a firm tone, she knew it would not be easy. Earlier in the year, in March, King Philippe had declared in his own lands a heavy tax called the *Dîme Saladine*, the Saladin tithe, to raise money for the crusade to aid the land of Jerusalem. Count Henri had followed suit, imposing a similar tax on his own people. They grumbled of course, but now, perhaps, at least some of that revenue could be used to rebuild the city.

When Count Henri returned from his service to the king, looking forward to beginning his crusade preparations in earnest, he was shocked to find his capital city in embers and to see the mournful faces of his people.

"What in God's name shall we do?" He shook his head in dismay, sounding almost as young as Thibaut.

His mother smiled bravely and reassured him. "We shall restore our city, mourn our dead, and thank God for what he has spared." Her voice was brave. It had to be, for it was her strength they all counted on, even the young count, who had never had to face such a catastrophe before. It was the same message she had delivered to the people, whose disheartened faces she remembered. She was not as brave inside as she tried to sound, but everyone needed to believe that rebuilding what they had lost could be accomplished. She knew it would take much time and money, but it would have to be done. She also knew that much of the burden would fall to her, once her son left on crusade.

Even the fire did not dampen the crusading spirit among the men. The appeal was always the same—the anticipation of seeing far-off lands, the hope of glory and fortune in God's service—and should death come, a martyr's crown of salvation.

For the women who would be left behind, there was less enthusiasm, and their feelings were more mixed. Marie was no exception. Along with her fears and trepidations, she felt a sense of pride for her son, so admired among his peers, who were themselves much esteemed. Even as far away as England, one writer noted that "all of France shines by its taste for arms, but the knights of Champagne surpass those from other parts of the kingdom." Certainly a crusade would give Henri an opportunity to put his manhood to the test, despite his mother's apprehensions at the thought of another holy war.

She remembered the crusade of 1147, which had utterly destroyed her parents' marriage. They might have divorced anyhow, but Marie had heard the dreadful stories of all that happened on the journey, especially in Antioch, and how it was the breaking point of the royal union. Then, her husband Henri had died as a consequence of his own pilgrimage-crusade, his capture and imprisonment, and the difficulties of the trip. Now it was her son's turn. She could only pray that he would demonstrate his courage and prowess, and return safely. *Please protect him*, she beseeched God fervently every night as he began his preparations to depart. Although she was aware of the weighty responsibilities he would leave behind for her to resolve, her prayers were for him alone.

Oh, God, she prayed nightly, *bring him safely home.*

CHAPTER 43

Troyes, July 1189

Crusade preparations were well under way when a messenger appeared at the palace gates in Troyes, looking thirsty from his long ride in the hot afternoon sun.

"I must speak with the Countess Marie," he said to a guard, who recognized from his blue surcoat ornamented with gold *fleurs-de-lis* that he came from the king. The countess did not know this fresh-faced young man, who seemed so eager to convey his message. She greeted him without enthusiasm, for messengers from Philippe rarely brought good news.

"What's happened now?" she asked with a slight frown.

"King Philippe sends word on behalf of King Richard that Queen Eleanor is free. He thought you would want to know."

Marie's eyes suddenly brightened. "My mother free? *King* Richard? Tell me more. How did this come about?"

"King Henry died on July 6 at Chinon. Prince Richard was with the king of France when he heard the news. They had joined forces against King Henry."

Marie nodded, for she already knew about the alliance and the continuing struggle of her English brothers to extricate power from their father.

"Yes, yes," she said impatiently. "But how did King Henry die? Was he killed in battle?"

"The king was ill, and someone told him that his favorite son, John, was also involved in the plot against him and had taken his brother's side. They say it was the final blow and that the king just turned his face to the wall in his bedchamber at Chinon and died." The messenger seemed to savor his role as the bearer of important news, which he continued to embroider with gossip. "After the king's death, they say servants looted his room and even stole his clothes, leaving him there, dead, and naked as a worm."

"My word!" said Marie, not sure how to react to such shocking news. "And you say my mother is free?"

"*Oui, ma dame*, it was one of the first acts of King Richard. He sent word to Salisbury that the queen should be freed at once. He thought you'd want to know."

Marie smiled broadly and rewarded the messenger generously. "You bring me such good news." *My mother is free, and Richard is king. He will be a good king*, she thought. He was mature, already over thirty, his judgment sound, and he had been waiting impatiently for the throne since he was a boy of sixteen. She wanted nothing more than to rush to her mother's side, but she knew it was impossible, at least for now. She couldn't leave Troyes with her son preparing to set out on crusade. He'd requested her help, and she must be ready to serve as regent once he was gone. Eleanor, too, would have her hands full, helping Richard plan his coronation and take over his royal duties. *But someday*, she vowed, *I will see her again*. Her eyes danced and her heart was light as she thought of how jubilant her mother must be.

"When you return to your lord, please give him my utmost thanks. Tell him I greet the news with great joy." She smiled at the messenger and offered him a goblet of her very best wine.

Troyes, May 1190

Just as she had so many years ago when her husband left for the Holy Land, Marie stood on the stone steps of the comital palace to watch as her son led his men in a long procession from the courtyard, through the streets of Troyes and toward the Porte de Croncels. She had embraced him fervently, whispering her love and prayers in his ear, then watched him mount his steed, lift the banner of Champagne high, and wave farewell.

He looks so splendid. They all do, she thought, gazing with affection at those brave young faces as they rode out so eagerly. Her heart swelled with pride at the same time her breast was heavy with worry, for try as she might she could not dispel her fears of the future. So many things could happen—a deadly Saracen scimitar or Damascene sword. Capture and imprisonment. The scourge of illness that beset so many in the Holy Land. She tried to put such thoughts out of her mind, knowing that his uncles would be at his side protecting him. But the future was impenetrable as he rode into the distance.

The men headed south toward Marseille, where they planned to board ships and sail to Acre. Unfortunately, they would not be joined by royal troops. The main armies of the kings were delayed because of Richard's need to secure his kingdom before he left and because Philippe's young wife, Isabelle of Hainaut, had died on March 15 giving birth to stillborn twins. They postponed their departure until early July. Thus, Henri and his men, joining his troops with those of his uncles, Thibaut and Étienne, would form an advance guard. Their spirits were high.

Troyes, June 11, 1190

Marie returned to administrative duties with resignation, settling matters that Henri had left unfinished. As she sat alone in the council chamber, sorting through the rolls of parchment that littered the table, she sighed. Not unlike his father, Henri had engaged in a squabble with the church before he left. The canons of Notre-Dame de Reims had complained to the bishop that some of the men in Henri's service had done damage to their property at Vertus. Rather than delay his trip, the young count left the matter in the hands of his mother and uncle, Archbishop Guillaume. Marie hoped that such disputes would not become a pattern during his years as count. Hoping to head off future matters of this sort and show Henri that just because he was count, he could not condone such conduct in his men, Marie and Guillaume ruled in favor of the bishop and ordered Henri to pay the canons forty *solidi* a year to compensate for the damages his men left behind.

The remaining pile of parchment on the council table was not entirely Henri's fault. Many people had brought petitions when they learned he was leaving on crusade, and he had worked until the eve of his departure to take care of necessary court matters. But he was not so experienced, systematic, or efficient as his father had been, and despite his last-minute flurry of activity, he had left many affairs in the hands of his mother, who was now tallying up the many things that needed to be done.

There was a knock on the council room door. At her permission, a somber-faced squire entered.

"I regret to announce that the bishop of Troyes is dead, *ma dame*," the young man announced.

"Oh, no! Not now! What happened?"

"He had a sudden attack and just collapsed," the squire replied.

The death of the bishop, Manassès de Pougy, who had once accompanied her husband to Jerusalem and back, was a blow to Marie. She had known him ever since her arrival in Troyes when he was provost of St. Étienne, and she had worked with him throughout her earlier regency. He had always been supportive and sympathetic to her needs and requests. They had become friends who confided in one another from time to time, and she'd counted on him to be still at her side. It was a setback so soon into her renewed regency, for things were always uncertain when a new bishop was appointed, unless he too was a friend.

"Thank you, Simon," she said, refusing to show grief in his presence and thinking furiously who might replace the bishop.

She summoned her scribe, and they spent the afternoon preparing a hasty dispatch to Henri informing him of the situation. She'd kept track of his progress from the emissaries he sent back, bearing instructions and charters issued at stops along the way. Knowing that a single rider could travel far faster than an entire army, she hoped her message would reach him before he left Marseille. There was only one man who could replace Manassès to her satisfaction.

"Please allow Haice de Plancy to return to Troyes," she dictated in her message to her son. "I need his help. I hope you will appeal to the pope to name him bishop. We will miss him as chancellor, but a chancellor is easier to replace than a bishop. Out of consideration for the difficult task I face in your absence, I beg you to release him to come home." She added her own personal greetings and indications of her love, attached her seal, and had the scribe deliver it to the fastest messenger at the court.

She knew Henri was grateful for her efforts on his behalf and felt sure that if the message reached him in time, he would send Haice at once. She smiled as she glanced over her son's recent charters and letters, which usually referred to her as "*karissimam matrem meam*," my dearest mother. His father had never publicly stated such feelings, until just before his death. But she was sure of her son's love. They had always been close—mother and son. She felt free to ask this of him, and she knew he felt free to ask any sacrifice of her, for he trusted her.

She sighed with resignation. She was not to have the peaceful retirement she had hoped for. At least not yet. She had looked forward to her freedom—to encouraging the talent of young poets at her court in Meaux, listening to the *trouvères* sing their songs, and entertaining her courtiers with her superb hospitality. Toward the end of her life, she had planned to retreat from her court to the priory of Fontaine-les-Nonnes to spend the remainder of her days in prayer, as her mother-in-law had done. But all that would have to wait. Now she still had much to do in this world.

The messenger returned, accompanied by Haice, within two months. Henri had made the request of the pope, who, in consideration for Henri's sacrifice, approved Haice de Plancy at once as the new bishop of Troyes. Marie appointed Gautier de Chappes, who had also been on the second crusade with her husband, as the new chancellor.

By now her son and his men had set sail. She waited eagerly for news that he had safely reached Acre. It was a joyful day when the new bishop shared with her an account of their arrival he had received from one of the men in Henri's company, a cantor at the cathedral of Châlons-sur-Marne. The sail from Marseille to Acre had taken thirty-five days, he reported. His letter described the scene as the city came into view.

Occupied by the enemy, Acre was already under siege by our army. . . . Our helmets, our swords, our shields gleamed in the sunlight like flashes of lightning. The splendor of our arms, reflected by the waves, played on the breast of the sea. The breeze gently ruffled our silken banners.

As Marie listened to his words, she could feel the spirit of optimism and hope of glory. She could almost see the scene and hear the Champenois war cry, "*Pass'avant li meillor*" resounding outside the city walls. It all sounded so exciting, especially compared to the more somber situation here at home.

The ongoing rebuilding of the cathedral and the city of Troyes was the most pressing matter that at the moment confronted the countess and the new bishop. Private homes, markets, and churches had all been destroyed or damaged by the great fire. Even the castle had suffered. Every day the sound of hammers and workmen's voices echoed throughout the city from morning to night.

Marie was also kept busy by the seemingly endless stream of legal issues brought before her court. She was especially struck by how many of the petitioners were women. Some of them had evidently held back before—unsure of the young count's judgment. Now they came forth with their disputes, donations, and requests, noble ladies and commoners alike—Erembourg de Rouilly, Helisende du Croiset and her daughter-in-law Marguerite, Reine, the seedsman's daughter—one after another they came. Even nuns from convents like Notre-Dame-aux-Nonnains and the Paraclete appeared before Marie's court in increased numbers. Although she did not always rule in their favor, they knew they would receive from her a fair and well-reasoned decision. She was especially indignant in cases where women had been mistreated, and she was determined to set things right.

In one case a knight donated to the Templars property from his sister's inheritance and his wife's dower to which he had no claim. When the two women learned of it, they brought suit. It was a difficult case. Marie was reluctant to take property back from the Templars, who were so important to the crusaders, but she ruled nonetheless in favor of the women and required the Templars to pay them for the properties they had received.

She always tried to be even-handed, treating women with the same justice men could expect. As early as 1181, during her first regency, she had ruled against her own treasurer Milo de Provins, who sought to claim the full estate of his deceased and childless brother Jean. But Marie declared that Jean's widow was entitled to both her dower and half of anything the couple had acquired during their marriage. Milo was compelled to reimburse his sister-in-law.

The countess even found in favor of a group of reformed prostitutes in Provins, who had decided to leave the world to become nuns. They settled on land belonging to an abbot and his prior, who were horrified by their presence and sought to drive them out. Countess Marie intervened and, working with their overlord, the archbishop of Sens, persuaded the priory to let them stay and arranged for their rent payments until they could buy their own land. She missed her son at her side during such tribunals. They would have been excellent learning opportunities for a young man, she thought.

It was July when one of her guards brought her welcome news. "The kings have left France to go to the aid of the Holy Land, *ma dame*. A tradesman from Vézelay who came to the hot fair saw them ride out together."

Thank God, she thought. Her heart lifted at the news, for she knew that her son would need their help. To her frustration, however, she later learned that the kings of England and France did not go directly to Acre. Instead, a German knight passing through Troyes before Christmas brought the news that they had decided to spend the winter in Sicily. Marie had thought, by now, that they would be fighting beside Henri in the Holy Land. It was not a leisurely winter stay, the knight assured her, but an attempt to resolve problems that had to be dealt with.

"What exactly are those problems?" the countess asked, clearly annoyed.

"One was King Richard's sister, Queen Joanna of Sicily. She's a widow now, you know, since her husband died last November."

She's my sister too, Marie thought, *even though we've never met.* "What is the problem?" she asked again.

"Well, as I understand it, the illegitimate grandson of an earlier king, a man named Tancred, seized the throne of her dead husband and refused to hand over the queen's dower. King Richard is ready to go to war over the matter and wants it resolved before he goes on to Acre."

Marie's head was spinning, as she tried to absorb all the implications of the situation.

"But why didn't King Philippe continue to Acre?" she asked.

"From what I hear, he wants to settle a quarrel with King Richard before he goes. I think it concerns the betrothal to Princess Alais, the French king's sister. There's a rumor that Richard plans to marry somebody else, and Philippe is furious. At the very least, he wants the Vexin back if Richard doesn't plan to go through with the marriage. That was her dowry."

"It's always about property, isn't it, Haice?" Marie commented as she later discussed the situation with the new bishop, who had taken on the name of Bishop Bartholomé—though he would always be Haice to her.

"I'm afraid so, *ma dame*," he answered.

"Please call me Marie," she said. "We've known each other for more than thirty years now, and you have always been a loyal friend.

"*Merci, ma dame*… Marie." It was awkward on his tongue.

"I am so worried about Henri," she said. "I do wish the royal armies would settle all their squabbles and go on to the aid of Acre." But she could only worry and wait.

The information that trickled back to Troyes from the siege in Acre in the coming months was not good. In March, Marie learned that both her brothers-in-law Thibaut and Étienne had died of sickness raging in the Christian camp. She grieved for them and was especially distressed that their deaths had come in such an undignified manner—not as martyrs in a sacred battle, but as victims of fever and dysentery in a filthy tent that smelled of human waste and death.

They had been at her side as a young widow, supporting her when she needed it most. The messenger also informed her that her son had been wounded in November but that his wound had healed. At the same time she mourned for her brothers-in-law, she thanked God for Henri's recovery. She still had not received a letter directly from him since his arrival in Acre, which worried her, but she knew that, as the siege continued, he had little time to write, and messages were always uncertain. Still she prayed for news directly from him. Only a week would pass before her prayers were answered.

"*Maman*," Thibaut found her in the council chamber preparing for the next day's court session. "There's a messenger here who brings a letter from Acre." Marie's heart leapt with both fear and hope. A letter. Her heart pounding, she followed her son into the great hall to greet the young courier.

"You have a missive for me?" she asked.

"*Oui, ma dame.*" His voice was weary. His face wore no expression, other than fatigue from his long ride. He took the letter from his pouch, removed its leather wrapping, and held it out to her.

A smile burst across her face when she saw the seal of her son Henri.

"Thank you. Oh, thank you," she said to the messenger, wanting to throw her arms about him in gratitude. Instead, she instructed a nearby squire to see that he was well fed and given their very best wine to drink and a place to sleep for as long as he wanted to stay.

Together, she and Thibaut rushed to the solar to open the letter. It contained much of the news she had already heard from various travelers, but it didn't matter. It was written in his own steady hand.

You must have heard by now of the deaths from a terrible sickness of my uncles, Thibaut and Étienne. I miss them and their wise counsel terribly, and I send my condolences to their families. I too was sick for a while, but I have regained my health and resumed all my normal activities. We are still anxiously awaiting the arrival of Richard and Philippe. I pray to God that they will soon come. We need their help.

She noticed that he did not mention having been wounded—to keep her from worrying, she supposed, and she was grateful that she did not know of his sickness until he was well again. The letter was brief. He went on to explain that he was running short of funds to feed his troops and that he needed help, not only military, but also financial aid from his uncles to tide them over until the city was captured and the spoils divided.

"I know you've been worried about him, *Maman*," Thibaut said. "So have I."

She reached out to give him a warm hug. "I thank God for you every day, my dearest son. And I pray for your brother. I'm very lucky to have you both."

He accepted her kiss on the cheek although, like any boy his age, he was embarrassed by such a show of emotion. Returning her affection with only a bashful smile, he said, "I need to make sure the knights don't require my services," and slipped out of the room.

She thought about her sister Alix, who was still in mourning. She had taken her children and gone into solitude for a while at La Perche. Marie supposed that Alix too would be compelled to serve as regent for her minor son. So many women left in charge. Queen Adèle as well, along with her brother, the archbishop, was overseeing the kingdom. It made Marie feel less lonely when she thought about them all.

Less than a month later, a young squire interrupted Marie's work in the council chamber to announce yet another messenger, "An envoy has just arrived wearing the livery of the king of England. Shall I show him in?"

Marie was startled. *An English messenger. What on earth?* "I'll meet him in the great hall." Once again her heart thumped with anticipation.

He waited with a broad smile on his face, his complexion ruddy from his long ride in the March sun. "I bring what I hope will be happy news, my lady," he announced.

"I am glad to hear that. We can always use happy news. What is it?"

"Queen Eleanor sends this letter," he said, holding out a rolled parchment, with a dangling seal.

"A letter from my mother! How wonderful," Marie said. She took the letter and held it to her heart. She wanted to save it to read in private, as she always preferred to do.

"She sent it from Rome, where she stopped to meet the new pope," the messenger said.

"The new pope?" she asked. She had not heard yet of the death of the former pope, Clement III.

"Pope Celestine III was elected on March 30, the same day the queen arrived in Messina."

"What on earth was she doing in Messina? Was she with the English army? I hope she isn't planning to accompany them to the Holy Land again."

"No, my lady. She remained there only four days before heading north again. She says she will tell you all about it herself when she arrives."

"What? She's coming here?" This news was beyond all her hopes and dreams.

"*Oui, ma dame.* She will send a rider ahead to announce her arrival."

Marie, eager to read the letter, assigned a squire to see to the messenger's comfort and then hurried to the council chamber, where she quickly unrolled the parchment.

"*To my beloved daughter Marie from her mother, Eleanor, queen of England, duchess of Aquitaine and Normandy, countess of Anjou, greetings.*" The letter went on to inform Marie that she would be staying a short time in Rome and then sailing to the south of France, where she would take to the rivers Rhone and Saône and then the Seine to hasten her trip to Troyes. She hoped to arrive by the end of April and spend at least two weeks with her daughter before continuing her journey back to English lands. "*I have matters to discuss with you that concern our sons and I bring with me a proposal for you to consider,*" the letter said. "*But above all, I want to see my firstborn daughter again before age makes such travel impossible.*"

Her mother was coming! What joyful news! Marie began at once to plan for her visit. The palace was scrubbed from top to bottom. *Trouvères*, jongleurs, and musicians were notified to prepare, and the countess began to arrange for a sumptuous series of feasts. She hoped her mother would arrive in time for the first day of May—always a day of music and revelry when people cast off their drab winter garments and decked themselves in bright colors for the festivities that marked the coming of spring. Maidens would wear flowers in their hair and dance around beribboned poles. This year there would not be many young knights to join the celebration, but Marie would make sure it was festive nonetheless.

She could hardly believe it. Her mother was coming to Troyes!

CHAPTER 44

Troyes, late April 1191

True to her word, Queen Eleanor managed to arrive on the last day of April. Marie stood waiting for her in the courtyard, her arms open wide and a warm smile lighting her face.

"I can't believe you're actually here," she said, falling into her mother's embrace.

"Nor can I. Thank God for the rivers. They make the trip so much easier and faster. I don't know why more people don't use them—the river tolls, I suppose. But I'm far less exhausted than I might have been on horseback alone—ready for anything the first day of May brings. I trust there are plans."

"Indeed there are," Marie said, her arm around her mother as they walked into the castle. "And I'm so glad you arrived in time."

Marie had arranged for the most elaborate picnic she had ever held, in an open field on the banks of the Seine River. Bright-colored tents dotted the edges of the sunny field to provide resting places for ladies, especially her mother, who might need repose from time to time throughout the day. Musicians with a wide array of instruments played at the slightest invitation. People danced in lines or rings as an array of psalteries, flutes, *vielles*, drums, and bagpipes took turns making lively music to keep the merriment flowing. Tumblers and acrobats in vivid-colored costumes amazed onlookers with their nimble feats. Laughter and singing filled the air from every side. Maidens, circlets of flowers adorning their free-flowing hair, danced as they wove their multicolored ribbons around the pole in the center of the field.

Wines, ales, and ciders galore flowed as freely as the river waters throughout the day. Trestle tables groaned with tarts, meat pies, chunks of roasted lamb, pork, and beef, bowls of fruit, cheeses, platters of sweetmeats, and little spice cakes. The only thing missing from the celebration was the presence of the young knights, who were in Outremer with Count Henri. Only squires and older knights remained, but they tried to make up for the absence of the others by being particularly boisterous.

At mid-point in the afternoon, as people rested here and there, exhausted from the day's frolics, a jongleur entertained them first with his lute, then telling a tale of love and adventure about King Arthur and his knights. Marie could not help but note that he was a man of far lesser talent than Chrétien. Nonetheless, people gathered around to listen, sitting on benches or blankets and cloaks they had spread on the ground.

After many hours of gaiety and feasting, Queen Eleanor took refuge in one of the tents and stretched out on a cot with her eyes closed. Marie, who had hardly left her side all day, came to sit on a small stool so they could talk.

"What a lovely welcome, my dear," Eleanor said. "But I need a rest. At the age of almost seventy now, I can no longer dance with the young as I once did."

Marie laughed. "You have more energy than any woman I know, regardless of age. You're no doubt still weary from your trip to Messina and then to Rome before coming here. In your lifetime, you've crossed the Alps and many seas."

"And recently, the Pyrenees," Eleanor added.

"The Pyrenees? Have you been to Iberia?"

"I have… to fetch a bride for Richard, the oldest daughter of the king of Navarre. Her name is Berenguela. We call her Berengaria."

"But I thought he was betrothed to my half-sister Alais. I saw her only once as a baby and don't feel I know her at all, for she was taken so young by King Henry."

"Taken indeed." Queen Eleanor made a wry face. "Richard was her betrothed for many years. Then my dear late husband decided that she was a tasty little morsel, too tempting to resist, and took her to his own bed instead of letting her marry Richard. Some say she even bore him a child."

"Good heavens!" Few things shocked Marie anymore, but this was too much—having a father steal his son's betrothed for his own pleasure.

"A wretch to the very end," Eleanor said grimly. "Now Richard refuses to marry her, and I agree with his decision, but he needs a wife to bear him an heir as soon as possible, so I brought Berengaria to him in Sicily. I'll tell you more about it tomorrow when the revelry is all over and I am better rested. Now, I just want to lie here for a while."

Marie kissed her on the cheek and left the tent, looking forward to another precious day with her beloved mother.

The next morning dawned, warm and beautiful as the day before. Marie slept later than usual, and when she arose, Queen Eleanor had already broken her fast and gone for a brisk ride with one of her knights.

Marie waited for her in the solar.

"I take it you are well rested," she teased, when her mother returned.

"I am indeed, and I feel wonderful this morning—only a few achy bones, but they're always aching—not just after a trip or a ride. Yesterday was glorious, by the way. I see that you have learned not to worry constantly, but to take pleasure where you can in life. I'm proud of you. And I've heard about your courts of love and your efforts to put into practice some of my ideas about civilizing the noble youth."

"It seemed important since you were captive and couldn't do it, and it did help me forget some of the trials of the world. Unfortunately, I find this current war in Outremer hard not to think of constantly, but I do try. How do you stand it—with Richard away fighting so often?"

"I've grown quite accustomed to it, as you well know. But of course, I too am concerned. And with Richard heading off to Acre, I have to contend with his brother John—not a pleasant task. We've never been close. He was always Henry's child, and quite frankly, I don't trust him to have his brother's best interests at heart. I knew that God had kept me alive for some reason, and holding the throne for Richard while he's away may be my most difficult task."

"I'm so sorry, *Maman*, that you've had to deal with such matters all your life. At least I don't have to worry about Thibaut's intentions toward his brother. He adores him, and he's too young to make such troubles. He'll turn twelve while you're here. We can celebrate together," Marie said with a smile.

Eleanor returned her smile for a moment, but then her face took on a more serious look, and wrinkles settled around her eyes and mouth.

"It's Thibaut I wanted to talk with you about—one of the reasons I've come here." Then her face relaxed again. "My main reason, of course, was to see you. I had such a glorious time when you visited me in Poitiers that I couldn't let my life end without seeing you again."

"Oh, *Maman*, your life is not about to end. You have many years left, I'm sure."

"Too many perhaps," she said with a grimace, "but I'm glad our sons are together. I know Richard will do his best to look after Henri—not that he needs looking after. I hear that he's as fine a young knight as his father was, and I saw *him* in action during the last holy war."

"I'm glad to hear that my son's reputation is sound." Marie's voice was proud.

"It is indeed, and it precedes him on his mission," said his grandmother.

"What is it about Thibaut that concerns you?" Marie asked, curious.

"I hear that he is not yet betrothed. Is that right?"

"It's true. I've been so busy getting my daughters married and helping Henri deal with his plans to depart that Thibaut's future has not yet had the full attention it deserves," Marie confessed.

"Well, I have a proposal for you to consider. The father of Richard's bride, Berengaria, is Sancho de Navarre. They call him Sancho el Sabio, the Wise, and quite justly so. He has another daughter named Blanca, who is actually prettier than Berengaria and far more lively and intelligent. She's just two years older than Thibaut. It occurred to me that, with Richard married to Berengaria, if Thibaut should be betrothed to Blanca, they would eventually become brothers-in-law as well as nephew and uncle. I think she would be a fine bride for Thibaut.

I was quite impressed with her."

"But Navarre is so far away. It would be nice at least to know her family and see the child."

"I took the liberty of having a small portrait painted for you to see. It's in a coffer in my chamber. I'll fetch it," Eleanor said as she rose.

"I'll come with you." Marie followed her mother down the hall to the sunniest bedchamber in the castle.

Eleanor rooted around in the chest until she got to the bottom. "Here it is," she said, drawing out a miniature portrait of a girl, almost a young woman. "Isn't she lovely?"

Marie had to admit that, if the portrait portrayed her accurately, she was indeed very pretty. Her dark hair and large eyes were a deep rich brown. Her skin was fair, and her lips were full and well defined. She looked very mature for a girl of fourteen, and the image gave her a sense of poise and intelligence.

"Marie, if Thibaut marries a noblewoman, countess or duchess though she might be, wouldn't it be better for him to marry a princess and have his sons in line, however distantly, for a crown?"

Marie gazed at the portrait as she considered her mother's words. "I've thought about this a great deal," Eleanor said. "Your sons might have become kings of England, you know. King Stephen was the *younger* brother of Henri's father, Count Thibaut. Since the barons refused to accept Matilda as queen, it should have been Thibaut, not Stephen, who was crowned king—if only he'd had a faster steed. I doubt that the barons would have found *his* son, your husband Henri, lacking as they did Stephen's son Eustace. Another missed opportunity was that Geoffrey Plantagenet wanted originally to betroth his son to you, but Bernard de Clairvaux would have none of it. Your father gave in to the abbot's advice and refused." She gave a bitter laugh. "I married him instead. So that's twice your son Henri was denied the throne."

"Three times, now that you mention it. Had I been a boy, he would have become king of France instead of Philippe. How easily such matters can affect so many lives!" Marie said in a thoughtful tone. Then she smiled. "But if *Papa* had betrothed me to the son of Geoffrey Plantagenet, then I would have been tied to your tyrant of a husband."

Eleanor laughed. "I'm glad you were spared that at least. But I think your son Henri was destined to be a king. And that possibility was denied him. I would like to see your grandchildren—at least some of them—in line for a throne."

Marie looked once more at the portrait of young Blanca. "Why don't we show it to Thibaut. I'd like to get his reaction before I decide."

When Thibaut saw the portrait later in the afternoon, his eyes grew large. "Who is *she*?" he asked.

"Her name is Blanca de Navarra, or Blanche de Navarre in your language. She's a princess. Her father is the king of Navarre," his grandmother answered.

"She's prettier than any girl I know," he said, admiring the image once more.

"Would you like to keep the portrait?" Eleanor asked.

"May I?" His voice was eager. Then his face took on a more somber expression. "Why are you showing… giving… this to me?"

"Your grandmother has suggested that she might be a good match for you, since you're not yet betrothed," his mother said.

"Do you know her?" he asked Eleanor.

"Yes, I met her recently at her father's court. Her older sister is marrying my son, King Richard."

"What's she like? Other than pretty, I mean."

"Well, she's very smart. She can speak and read three languages, and she can do sums. She has good manners and a delightful laugh. She sings like a nightingale, plays the lute, and she's prettier than her sister." Eleanor hoped she wasn't praising the girl too highly, but she felt sure that all she was saying was true.

"What do you think, *Maman*?" Thibaut asked.

"I trust your grandmother's description. She would never have chosen Blanca's sister for King Richard if she did not approve highly of the family," Marie answered. "But I would like to make sure you are satisfied with my choice. You are of an age now to have an opinion of your own." After seeing the joy that Mariette had found in her marriage, Marie wanted her other children to find the same happiness and attraction in a mate.

"Then, if what you say is true and if she really looks like this, I think she would make an excellent wife… someday," he said with satisfaction.

"Thank you, Grandmother."

"You're most welcome," Eleanor said. Both women were smiling at the boy, who was almost as tall as his mother now.

"I'd better get back to my duties," he said, ducking out as quickly as he could, but Marie saw him glance once more at the small portrait and grin as he tucked it into the lining of his sleeve.

"That went well," Queen Eleanor said. "Do you agree?"

"I do, assuming her dowry is adequate," Marie answered.

"More than adequate," her mother said.

"Then how should I contact King Sancho?"

"Oh, there's no need for that. I took another liberty on the chance that both you and Henri might agree. I had a betrothal contract for Thibaut and Blanca drawn up while I was in Navarre. Richard and I both thought it would be a wonderful match. It's subject to Henri's approval, of course, and Richard will take care of that. All you need to do is look over the terms and sign, if you accept them. Sancho has already signed."

"And what would you have done if I refused?" Marie asked, lifting her eyebrows.

"I would leave the agreement in my coffer to be destroyed at a later date," her mother said. "But I'm sure you will accept when you see the terms. She will be a fine wife for Thibaut. And that's one less worry you'll have to contend with while your son is away."

Eleanor's visit would last another ten days before she planned to set out for Rouen, her son's chief city in Normandy. While she was there, Marie's ladies clamored for a court of love that would involve the famous Eleanor of Aquitaine, and Marie consented—to show her mother her new introduction of courtly debate between a lady and would-be lover.

"A very nice variation," Eleanor complimented her daughter when it was over. "I heard what happened to your cousin Elisabeth's lover. Perhaps learning to debate in this way will force people to think through their decisions and consider the risks more thoroughly before they rush into unwise relationships."

"Have you ever engaged in such a relationship?" Marie asked her mother with a sly smile. "I suppose that's an impertinent question to ask one's mother, but I've always wondered if the rumors were true."

Eleanor laughed. "You must know that you have asked a question I never plan to answer—not for you or anyone. I know there have been rumors and speculations, but I have always refused either to deny or confirm them. It's far better to remain a mystery to the world than to answer such questions and be seen as either boring or wicked. Let's just say that I am a Christian, who has always tried to be a good mother and a good queen."

"Whether the rumors are true or not, you could never be seen as boring," Marie said, echoing her mother's laugh. "*Au contraire*, you're the most exciting woman I know."

"You flatter me. I just believe that women should have some say in their own destinies, and I've tried to shape my own as best I could. You seem to be the daughter most like me. I have seen your efforts not to allow yourself to be taken advantage of by overbearing men. I'm proud of you for that. And I heard about your recent request to Adam de Perseigne to do a biblical translation into the common language. You must know that such translations are frowned on by the Church."

"I know, but you once told me that if we did nothing the Church disapproves of, it would be a dull life indeed. It wasn't easy to persuade Adam to do it, and of course, he insisted on adding commentary because, he says, the reason for the Church's concern is that laypeople shouldn't be able to interpret the scripture for themselves. He felt this might satisfy the critics."

"Well, at least you chose a psalm, which you are already permitted to read for yourself in Latin."

"I'm thinking of having the book of Genesis translated as well," Marie said.

"Now *that*, my dear, will be even more subject to criticism, and I suspect Adam will absolutely refuse to do it. You know that laypersons are allowed to read for themselves only devotional books—like the Psalter and the Book of Hours."

"I know it will be controversial, and you're right. I'll probably have to find another translator. Now that he's an abbot, he's probably too busy anyhow. But I also know that you've done controversial things in your own life, Mother, and I won't be deterred. I'm the sister of two kings and the sister-in-law of an archbishop and cardinal of the Church. I doubt that anyone will dare complain." Marie laughed. "I might as well use the men in my life for my advantage, just as men use women."

"You're a bold woman, Marie. And I'm proud of the way you have done your duty. They tell me that you have ruled the county of Champagne very well, that you've not lost a single hectare of land to unscrupulous nobles and churchmen who try to take advantage of female rulers."

"Not so far. It hasn't always been easy, as I'm sure you know. There are two thousand knights to govern here, many of them now in Outremer, of course. But I *am* my mother's daughter, after all." The two women looked with recognition into each other's eyes and at that moment felt a stronger bond than ever before—one that could not be broken despite distance and absence.

When the day came for Queen Eleanor to leave, Marie's heart was heavy. "I will miss you more than ever," she whispered to her mother as they embraced one last time in the courtyard.

"I will always be with you in spirit," Eleanor said. "It was such a joy to meet my grandson and have the opportunity to celebrate his twelfth birthday with you both. I think you made a wise decision concerning his betrothal. Has the treaty been dispatched?"

"I sent a messenger the very next day. I didn't want to give King Sancho time to favor another suitor. If what you say is true, and I assume it is, I'm sure there are many others."

"I suspect so as well, but he seemed quite pleased with the match," Eleanor assured her.

"I can't believe you missed Richard's wedding just to visit me. I can't thank you enough," Marie said.

"I couldn't do both. Richard wanted to delay the ceremony until he reached Cyprus, and I didn't want to make that trip. I just wanted him married. I left your sister Joanna in charge to help Berengaria prepare for the wedding."

"When you write to Richard, please ask him to keep an eye on Henri. I will be forever in his debt." There were so many more things she wanted to say, but the time had come for them to part, as she knew it must.

"Of course." Queen Eleanor kissed her daughter once more. "Well, … I'd best mount. I can see that both the horses and my knight escorts are growing impatient." One of the young knights was indeed trying to calm his restless horse.

"Will we ever see each other again, I wonder?" Marie said.

"Perhaps… or perhaps not, but you will always be in my heart."

"And you in mine, my dear *Maman*."

At that moment, Thibaut burst through the palace door, ran down the steps to his grandmother and threw his arms around her. "I just heard you were about to leave, and I wanted to say goodbye once more."

"You're a wonderful lad, Thibaut, and you'll make a fine knight one day. I'm so glad we got to know one another."

"So am I. *Maman* has talked about you so much. Thank you for coming," he said, then added with a whisper, "and for bringing me the portrait."

Eleanor smiled, leaning forward to give the boy a kiss on the forehead. "It was my pleasure. Learn all you can, and listen to your mother. She's very wise," his grandmother said. Then she gave Marie's hand one last squeeze and mounted her palfrey.

As Marie watched her ride out the gate, she remembered the last time she had seen her do that—from the window of the Cîté palace when she was seven years old. How different that departure had felt, leaving only a trail of despair in the courtyard dust. This time, her heart was full to overflowing. The tears she shed now were tears of happiness and hope. Although she was sad to see her mother leave, she knew that an important part of her stayed behind. She knew firmly in her heart that she was and would always be Eleanor's daughter.

CHAPTER 45

Her mother's visit had been a welcome respite from Marie's daily preoccupation of wondering what was happening in the Holy Land. She hoped that by now the kings had arrived and were providing the aid and assistance Henri needed. She only knew that her son was doing all he could and facing daily danger to serve God. It made her more determined than ever to do her part and support him as regent. Even though she still preferred a courtly romance, a *lai*, or even a bawdy tale like a *fabliau* to dreary court sessions, she understood the meaning of duty, and she was determined to be respected by her subjects. Thus, she carried out her function as ruling countess—maintaining order, dispensing justice, and settling disputes—with efficiency and without fanfare. Her competence and determination earned her the respect of both the women and the men around her. One chronicler even wrote that she ruled Champagne "vigorously and like a man," paying her the highest compliment he knew how.

The leaves were turning red and gold by the time Marie finally received a long dispatch from Henri. She took the rolled, sealed letter to the solar where she could read it in privacy and comfort. There she had a fire built and poured herself a goblet of cider before she settled down to read his words. The letter had been begun in May and was written over a long period of time.

Philippe arrived yesterday. I hoped he would provide the help I need, for I used up all my resources while the kings dawdled in Sicily. When I went to his tent this morning to discuss the matter, he made no effort to make me feel welcome. After I had explained my plight, he said only, with a sneer, that I should have been more frugal. When I begged for his help, he offered me a miserly loan of a hundred livres, in exchange for my pledging all of Champagne to him. Needless to say, I did not accept, and in my heart, I cursed him to hell—a sin that awaits my next confession.

Here there was a hiatus in the letter, and she could tell from his writing of the next part that he was using a different quill. It was clearly written much later.

Thank God, Richard arrived in mid-June, after stopping once more to conquer Cyprus. By this time, my men were beginning to fear starvation, and I had nothing left. We had hoped to have plunder from the city to carry us on, but that did not happen.

And thank God Richard is nothing like Philippe. With the heart of a real king, Richard did not even hesitate. 'Don't worry about your men,' he said. 'I can be of help. After two successful campaigns in both Sicily and Cyprus, I am well provisioned. Let me offer you four thousand measures of wheat, four thousand pounds of cured pork, and four thousand pounds of silver.' When I asked what he required in return, he replied, 'Only what you came here to accomplish. That we fight side-by-side and capture this city and everything else on our way to Jerusalem.'

News of King Richard's generosity spread quickly through the camp, and even the most untaught foot soldier could see the stark contrast between the two kings—one paltry and greedy, the other generous, more ready to give than to receive. It had the effect of making Richard the unquestioned leader of the expedition. Philippe had made a tactical error of the greatest proportions, and he hates Richard now more than ever.

I wanted to fight for my king, but clearly he has no use for me except for what is mine. I will now follow King Richard as my leader in this holy war.

Marie was shocked by Philippe's refusal to help her son. "Thank God for Richard," she said aloud. She remembered Queen Eleanor saying that she had instructed her son to look after Henri. "And for my mother as well," she added.

"What are you saying, *Maman*?" Thibaut was just entering the solar to join her.

"Only thanking God for his many blessings," she laughed. "I didn't realize I was saying it aloud."

"You spend too much time alone, I think," he teased. At twelve, he was tall for his age and his voice wavered uncertainly between that of a boy and that of a man. He seemed to have matured even since his grandmother's visit. It would not be long before he would become a squire and begin his knightly training.

"Sit down. I'm just reading a letter from your brother. Shall I read it aloud to you?"

"That would be wonderful," he said, pouring himself a goblet of cider and perching on the window sill to listen. She reread the part she had just completed and then went on.

With all our combined forces, we took the city of Acre with ease. It was a grand day—July 12, I believe—except for one event that rather spoiled the victory. The soldiers had placed three flags on the wall—French, English, and German. Then, one of Richard's soldiers, who hated the Germans and resented sharing the spoils with them, tore down their flag, and threw it to the ground. The incident created a great disturbance in the camp and infuriated Duke Leopold of Austria, who claimed it was done at Richard's orders. It had terrible repercussions and destroyed our united effort to defeat the infidels.

Now both the Germans and King Philippe have packed up and sailed away. Rumor has it that Philippe suspected Richard of trying to poison him, for he was quite ill. I don't believe it, for Richard was ill as well. But that was only one of Philippe's excuses. His pretexts disgusted all of us, and especially Richard, who worried what the king of France might do to harm English and Norman lands in his absence. But despite the dangers, he remains steadfast.

Marie paused in her reading and took a sip of cider.

Thibaut looked at her quizzically and asked. "Is that all?"

"No, no, there's more," she said, resuming her reading of the letter.

You might be interested to know that, shortly after King Philippe's departure, Philip of Flanders died of the same fever that killed Uncles Thibaut and Étienne. The two kings and I all recovered from our various illnesses, but Philip was not so lucky.

We waited for more than a month for Saladin to pay the ransom for the nearly three thousand prisoners we had taken at Acre. He kept promising to pay and to return the True Cross, which he had captured at Hattin. Finally, when it became clear that Saladin had no intention of keeping his word, Richard made the decision to execute the prisoners and had them all beheaded. He really had no choice. We could not feed all those extra people, and Richard wanted to show Saladin the consequences of not keeping his word.

"He executed three thousand prisoners?" Thibaut looked horrified. Marie too was sickened by the thought of such brutality, of so many deaths. She only hoped Henri had not participated in the executions. The letter went on to describe their march south along the coast and the battles along the way.

Now, after another great victory, we have settled for a time in Jaffa, where I am finishing this letter. I am hoping that we will soon capture Jerusalem from the Saracens. But it complicates matters that there are squabbles within the Christian leadership. You have probably heard of Guy de Lusignan. He was married to the queen of Jerusalem—Sybilla—who died a year ago, along with her children. In spite of that, Guy still claims the right to be king.

He's the one who lost the battle at Hattin, and most people don't want him as king. They prefer a man named Conrad de Montferrat, who became the husband of Sibylla's younger sister Isabella, the rightful queen now. She used to be married to Humphrey of Toron, but that marriage was annulled because the High Court thought he was too weak to be king. Conrad is certainly the best warrior and leader of the three.

While Guy lost most of the kingdom and allowed himself to be captured at Hattin, Conrad, on the other hand, showed strength and steadfastness by successfully defending Tyre—the one city in the kingdom of Jerusalem that Saladin never conquered. However, Richard is not fond of him and supports Guy, who is his vassal, instead. The High Court of the Kingdom of Jerusalem will meet to decide.

The future is in the hands of God. I will write again, I hope, from the recaptured city of Jerusalem.

The letter, which had begun with greetings to the people of Champagne and especially fond greetings to his mother and brother, came to an end with "God keep you and save you in peace and safety. Farewell."

"It all sounds rather chaotic, doesn't it, *Maman*. So many details," said Thibaut.

She smiled at him and said, "Indeed it does. And so many more details we'll probably never know, but it sounds as though they are succeeding. Please pray for your brother's safety," she said.

"Of course I will, and I do." He drained his goblet and hopped off the window ledge. "Thank you for sharing the letter." He bent to give her a quick kiss on the cheek, and then he was gone back to his duties.

The kiss surprised his mother. *He's growing up*, she thought with a smile. She sat alone for a while, contemplating all the news and thinking about her two brothers and how different they were. She hated the animosity between Philippe and her son. They had not liked each other much even as children. But she thanked God once more for Richard and his generosity.

Then her thoughts turned to another matter that Henri had passed over rather quickly—the death of Philip of Flanders. She remembered his touch, his skillful lovemaking, and his determination to make her his wife. And she recalled his anger when she refused. What a different man he seemed then. She wondered if he had ever forgiven her. He was only forty-eight when he died—still a very active man and quite capable, despite his arrogance. Queen Eleanor had told her how helpful he had been in negotiating the agreement that settled the matter between the two kings. It had released Richard from his betrothal to Princess Alais but allowed him to keep her dowry, the Vexin, in exchange for ten thousand pounds—thus freeing him to marry Berengaria.

It's ironic, she thought, *that Philip of Flanders survived so many battles and inspired an entire generation of young noblemen, including my brothers, Henry the Young King and King Philippe, only to die, not in a glorious battle, but like my brothers-in-law, of a foul disease in Outremer*. She could only imagine the dreadful conditions he had endured before his soul left his body. *Poor Philip. I hope he was happy in his new marriage.* She would pray for his soul and even harder for her son's safety.

Meaux, July 1192

Countess Marie took advantage of the warm weather to visit some of the episcopal cities in Champagne and deal with necessary matters. Now at her castle in Meaux, she was enjoying a quiet afternoon with Queen Adèle, chatting about this and that, when another letter from

Henri arrived. They came so seldom, and they took so long to arrive that she eagerly devoured the news from her absent son. His letters, written in the common language, were so much richer in detail and easier to read than the official dispatches, all composed in stiff, formal Latin.

"Forgive me," she said to Adèle, as she broke the seal at once and began to read in silence.

Adèle nodded and sat quietly until Marie looked up, her eyes wide with amazement. "Henri is married!" she said.

"Married? But isn't he betrothed to Ermesinde de Namur?"

"I suppose he no longer considers that betrothal valid since Philippe took away most of what was to be her dowry. In any case, he has been elected king of Jerusalem and has married Queen Isabella."

"How on earth did that happen?" Adèle asked.

"Let me read you the letter."

I told you I would write again after we had recaptured Jerusalem, but that has not happened. Yet so much else has occurred in so short a time that I can hardly believe it. I wish you could be here to meet my beautiful bride.

You will remember that I wrote you earlier about the High Court's preference for Conrad de Montferrat. I was even sent as one of the messengers to take the news to Conrad. Guy was rather bitter, but he is now living in Cyprus, which Richard sold him as his new domain, and for now he is out of the way.

All seemed more or less settled, when suddenly we learned that Conrad had been murdered. Two men sent by a Muslim lord they call the Old Man of the Mountain stabbed him to death as he was walking home from a visit to the bishop. The Old Man is the leader of a radical Muslim group known as Hashashins and apparently had some kind of grudge against Conrad. I was saddened for his beautiful widow, Isabella. She's been through so much. The next thing I knew people were talking about what a fine king I would be if I married Isabella.

I told them I was betrothed to Ermesinde de Namur, but no one seemed to take that seriously. Richard suggested that when Philippe stripped away her inheritance, it nullified the agreement, and before I knew it, the High Court had taken another vote. Suddenly, to my amazement, I was supposed to marry Isabella and become the new king. I thought she was an incredibly beautiful woman with much to offer, but I didn't want to do it unless she was willing. When I went to talk with her, she greeted me with the keys to the city of Tyre. She was evidently quite willing and did not seem to be mourning very much for Conrad. And so we were married as soon as possible. You would like her, I think, and I am immensely happy, my dear mother. There is one thing, however. She is pregnant with his child.

That sentence made Marie pause. She reread it. "She is pregnant with his child."

"Good heavens," Adèle said.

Marie was stunned. *What if it's a boy?* she thought. Will Henri then be reduced to the role of regent? Was this a wise thing to do? And what of Isabella's first husband? Is he sure that marriage has been officially annulled? How frustrating it was to be so far away and not to know all the facts. But he was a king now. King of Jerusalem. That was something special. Ruler of God's Holy Land.

"My mother once said that my sons were destined to be kings," Marie said, smiling. "And now Henri has achieved that goal. But he doesn't mention a coronation. I wonder why?"

"Read the rest of it," Adèle urged. "Perhaps he will explain." Marie began to read. Ten lines later, she found these words:

For now I use only the title of dominus or lord of Jerusalem. Although some refer to me as king, I wanted to wait until I could be crowned in Jerusalem itself to take that title. I think we could easily have captured the city last January, had so many other things not conspired against us. As you know, Philippe abandoned us and took his men back to France. And the Germans departed as well. We were fewer, but we might still have retaken Jerusalem, except for the dreadful winter weather. I hope we will try again during the summer. I know that Richard is becoming more and more anxious to go home since he heard rumors from England that his brother John is conspiring with Philippe to attack his lands.

Marie turned to Adèle. "Is that true?" she asked. "Are Philippe and John conspiring against Richard?" She could see that Adèle, hearing such comments about her son, was uncomfortable, but she answered honestly.

"You know that Philippe does not confide in me about such matters. But frankly I wouldn't be surprised. John is ambitious and would like to be king himself. I do know there have been communications between the two of them of late, but I don't know the contents."

"Aren't Richard's lands under the protection of the pope while he's in Outremer?" Marie asked.

"Ostensibly," Adèle replied. "But you must know as well as I do that the pope is not always obeyed, especially where money and land are at stake."

Suddenly Marie had a horrible thought. "I wonder if this marriage means that Henri doesn't plan to come home at all but will remain in Jerusalem." Tears sprang to her eyes at the possibility.

"Just praise God you have another son still at home."

"I do, of course, but it means I will have to continue to serve as regent—until Henri returns or until Thibaut is old enough to take on that role. He's only thirteen now."

"You mustn't worry, Marie. You're doing a fine job." Adèle reached out to take her hand.

"But I had truly hoped to retire and focus the rest of my life on poetry and prayers, as you are able to do."

Adèle laughed. "I read mostly saints' lives—not poetry. Except when I'm at your court. But you *will* serve as long as Henri needs you, won't you?"

"Of course," Marie said with a sigh. "Of course I will. I would do anything for my son. And I suppose one of the first things I must do is see that Ermesinde de Namur is returned to her father."

Marie was proud to think that her son had been *elected* king because the other barons admired him so much. It all sounded so glorious. She only wished that she could have been there. "You would like her, I think," he had written. She was pleased to see how Henri described his "beautiful bride." He seemed so happy. *How I would love to meet her*, she thought, *my new daughter-in-law*.

When Marie had finished her reading, her thoughts drifted to the psalm Abbot Adam de Perseigne, as he now was, had translated for her Christmas court the year that both Adèle and Marguerite were in attendance. She remembered how he had glorified the daughters of kings and suggested that their sons would become princes over all the earth. It seemed prophetic.

CHAPTER 46

Troyes, December 1192

Marie felt almost as though she were living two lives—one here in Troyes, dealing with all the problems and issues that arose during her regency and another vicariously with her son in the Holy Land. Here in Champagne, while she was managing to keep a steady hand over the county, it was not easy. The ongoing rebuilding of the burned city had been costly, and the St. Rémi fair, called the cold fair, now taking place in Troyes, was bringing in fewer buyers than it had before the crusade began. The Saladin tithe, imposed on everyone who had not taken the cross, had left many with less to spend than before. On top of that, Henri's letters had begun to include requests for money from the coffers of Champagne to pay the expenses of his little kingdom. Marie was looking for ways to manage it all. There appeared to be no end in sight to all the demands.

To make matters worse, the news from Outremer was not good. The crusaders had not recaptured Jerusalem and its riches, as Henri had hoped. Although they had come within twelve miles of the city a second time in August, Richard had decided once again not to risk a siege. Unlike the first occasion when hailstorms and freezing rains had kept them from attacking, this second time the weather had been hot and dry, too dry, and Saladin had made sure there was little food or water available to the Christians during any assault on the city. A letter from Henri described it all.

Richard did not want to risk another situation like that on the Horns of Hattin, where Christian troops were trapped without water. The Templars and others also convinced him that even if we took the city, it would be impossible to hold it, once all the remaining soldiers went home, as they have now done. Richard dared not stay longer, for fear that Philippe and John were doing all they could to undermine his kingdom. He departed for England October 9. We did not retake Jerusalem, and we are denied the riches we had hoped to gain.

Before he left, Richard negotiated a truce with Saladin. It is to last three years and eight months and allows Christians safe passage and access to the holy sites of Jerusalem. But it compelled us to dismantle recently rebuilt fortifications at Ascalon, Darum, and Gaza. I am left in control only of the coastal area from Tyre to Jaffa. Having declared I would be crowned only in Jerusalem, I must content myself for now to remain only dominus, lord of the region, and to depend on Champagne for financial help.

It is, of course, a disappointment, but Richard promised that, when the truce expires, he will return with a large army to retake all the land and see me crowned in Jerusalem. When he sailed for England, my last words to him were "Don't forget your promise."

Troyes, January 1193

But Richard did not make it back to England.

"Your uncle Richard has been captured and imprisoned by Duke Leopold in Austria," Marie, her face grave, informed her son Thibaut. She had received the news from her marshal, Geoffrey de Villehardouin, who had just returned from Acre and heard the news on his way home. Thibaut sat at his favorite perch in the solar—on a window ledge overlooking the canal. He was almost fourteen now, about to become a squire and begin his knightly training, and old enough to understand all the implications.

"How did that happen? I thought he was on his way home by sea," he replied.

"He was, but apparently bad weather forced him ashore at Corfu. Then, in disguise, he took passage on another ship. Rumors say it was a pirate ship. But that one wrecked on the Adriatic coast of Italy." She poured them both a cup of cider.

The boy listened, wide-eyed, to his uncle's adventure. "Then what?" he asked, reaching out to take the cup.

"Apparently he'd had enough of the sea and decided to continue on by land. He was evidently trying to reach the lands of King Béla and your aunt Marguerite, but someone recognized him as he passed through Austria, and he was captured. I gather that Duke Leopold is still bitter from having his banner torn down from the walls of Acre. Do you remember? Henri wrote to us about that. All I know is that Richard is now in Leopold's prison."

"Is there a charge against him?" Thibaut brushed his unruly sand-colored hair back from his forehead in a nervous gesture.

"The murder of Conrad de Montferrat."

"The man Henri replaced as king? I thought that was done by the one they call the Old Man of the Mountain. And I thought holy warriors were supposed to be under the protection of the pope," Thibaut said.

"So did I. And Pope Celestine might excommunicate Leopold… for what it's worth." Marie recalled her own naïveté, when she had once believed the pope's protection inviolable. But obviously, some were willing to defy him, regardless of the consequences. *Our mother must be frantic*, she thought.

Throughout the year, Marie waited for more news of Richard. There were rumors of all sorts, but nothing certain. Her son Henri had also learned of Richard's capture and was fearful that the man everyone was calling Lionheart might never be able to return to the Holy Land. Then, during the next hot fair she heard from a German merchant that Leopold had held Richard only about three months before he turning him over to his liege lord, Emperor Heinrich VI, who had set a ransom for his release.

In December a Parisian nobleman passing through Troyes informed Marie that Philippe, in alliance with John, was trying to persuade Heinrich to turn Richard over to him—for a sizeable fee, of course. If that happened, she knew that Richard would never again see the light of day, for the French king hated and feared the king of England above all men, and his brother John wanted only to rid himself of his brother and become king himself. All she knew for certain was that Richard was still in captivity. Once again, the countess discussed the matter with her son Thibaut, who avidly followed all the news involving the recent crusade, wishing he were there himself.

"Richard must be miserable," Marie said. "He's enough like your grandmother to despise his lack of freedom more than anything." She could only imagine how such captivity would constrain an active man like him.

"Is he in chains?" Thibaut asked with a frown.

"I doubt it… or that he's in any real danger just now. The German merchant claimed that he'd been released months ago from Trifels Castle, where he was kept prisoner for a while, and brought to Hagenau. He said the emperor, who sees him as a prize captive worth a fortune, treats him more as a guest than as a prisoner." She only hoped it was true, for Trifels was reputed to be stark and gloomy, located as it was on a rocky, wind-swept peak. Even so, Richard couldn't return home to deal with John and Philippe, as she knew he must want to.

"It's rumored that Heinrich has proposed to ransom him for 150,000 silver marks and two hundred noble hostages," she told her son. It was an enormous sum, even for the English crown.

"Oh, one more thing," she said. "The merchant also said that Duke Leopold has compelled Richard to agree to a betrothal between Eleanor of Brittany, the daughter of his dead brother Geoffrey, and Leopold's son."

"That's terrible. He must feel awful having to marry his niece to the son of such an awful man," Thibaut said. "I'm glad I'm not a girl who can be married off like that. I guess boys will be among the hostages, but that's not usually for life—like a marriage."

"Things like that happen all the time. Women are supposed to be peaceweavers. Men often use daughters, sisters, and nieces to help seal peace treaties or land transfers," she pointed out, remembering that such an agreement had been the reason for her own marriage. That was why Abbot Bernard had been so determined for her and her sister to be married to Henri and Thibaut—to make sure war would not break out again between the king and the count of Champagne. She had never mentioned that to her children, and she doubted that Thibaut realized she was speaking from personal experience.

"I'm just glad I'm not a girl," he said with a shudder.

"Remember that," Marie said, with a sad smile at her son, "when you're a father with daughters."

She knew that her mother would move heaven and earth to raise the ransom money for Richard. But when? It could take years.

On a dark, overcast morning only two weeks later, an unexpected courier arrived directly from Hagenau. Marie was apprehensive, hoping he did not bring news of Richard's death. She was relieved to discover that the rider was delivering a packet from Richard himself. Enclosed was a carefully constructed poem. She took it to her solar to read to herself aloud, as she thought a poem should be read. No doubt he'd set it to music, but she had only the words. They began...

Ja nus home prise ne dira sa reson
Adroitement, s'ensi com dolans non...

No captured man will ever speak his mind
With competence, unless he speaks with sorrow;
But he can find comfort in making it a song.
I have many friends, but their gifts are poor;
They will be shamed, if for lack of ransom
I remain these two years a captive.
My men and barons,
English, Norman, Poitevin, and Gascon,
Know that I've never had a companion so poor
That I would leave him in prison for lack of funds.
I am saying this with no reproach,
But still I am a captive.
...

By the time she'd finished reading all the rest of the poem, tears were rolling down her cheeks. Her brother clearly felt abandoned and feared that he might spend yet another winter in captivity. She read the poem carefully, admiring the effort it must have taken to write it. Every stanza starkly expressed his desperation and ended with the same bleak word—captive—all except the brief *envoi*, where he made it clear that this poem was written specifically for her—his "Countess sister," whose sovereign worth he asked God to guard and defend.

Once again, Marie sent for Thibaut to come to the solar so that she might read the poem with him. He listened intently, clearly touched by it.

"Is there anything we can do, *Maman*?" he asked.

"If only there were," she said. She had not previously revealed all her financial burdens to the boy, but she knew, given Henri's increasing requests, she would have little to spare for help with the ransom. Anything she could give would be but a pittance of the huge amount.

"He didn't ask for your help," Thibaut pointed out when he saw the sadness in her face.

"I know, but I'd still like to help. It's just that the ransom is so high. And given the demands of Henri's kingdom, the cost of rebuilding the city since the great fire, and meeting all the annual donations that your father and brother have so generously made," she admitted, "there just isn't much to spare." At times she felt almost overwhelmed. The demands were increasing, and it was up to her to find the funds to meet them.

"Are you all right, *Maman*?" Thibaut asked, seeing how distraught she looked.

"I'm fine," she said, trying to smile.

"Ruling is not easy, is it?" he asked.

"No, it isn't, my son, but it's an important responsibility."

She herself had ceased to make such generous donations as those she had given in the past to Fontaines-les-Nonnes and the other priories, convents, and churches she helped to support. She still hoped someday to be able to endow a lifetime income for the Prioress Edna, who had become a dear friend and whose priory held a special place in her heart. Someday, perhaps, she would retire there.

Her spirits lifted only a few weeks later when she learned that her mother was finally en route to Speyer, Germany. The rumor was that she had raised Richard's ransom—or at least had sufficient pledges for it! *I wish she could come here again for she will be so close,* Marie thought with longing, but she knew that Eleanor's top priority now had to be Richard. And once he was free, he would want to get back to his lands immediately. She doubted that Queen Eleanor would take time for a side trip to Troyes or Provins when so much was at stake in her son's lands. These were the realities of being a mother. She would never put her own desires first when her son was in need.

Garnier de Traînel was now bishop of Troyes. When Haice had died unexpectedly of a seizure earlier that year, she had urged her brother-in-law Guillaume to use his influence with the pope to request that the appointment be filled by Garnier who, along with his brother Anseau, had been among her husband's best friends. She trusted him implicitly and felt she could confide in him as she had in Haice, a needed relief in a time of such tension and worry. She particularly valued having a close friendship with the bishop, who often received news from various sources, news that Henri chose not to write about for fear of worrying his mother.

Except for the acknowledgment of his debts, Henri's letters to her were mostly filled with positive events. He wrote of his cordial relationship with Saladin, whom he viewed as a generous and honorable man—"*if only he were a Christian.*" He told her of gifts Saladin sent to him and how the sultan had returned to Isabella's stepfather, Balian d'Ibelin, some of the family lands his army had taken.

He also sent me a caba, which is an open-front tunic, and a sharbush, a type of fur-trimmed turban with a triangular plaque sometimes worn by Saladin's high-ranking officers. They are robes of honor. I have actually worn them here in Acre, and I must admit, they are quite comfortable. Some of my courtiers were shocked to see me so attired, but I wore them to show my good faith to Saladin, whom I have come to admire, despite his religion.

He sounded like a little boy, dressing up in someone else's clothes. She could remember when he used to try on his father's chainmail hauberk, which fell all the way to his feet and was so heavy the boy could hardly stand. It was a sweet memory.

I hope you are not shocked at the thought of my wearing Muslim garments, but you must understand the vulnerability of my little kingdom. Its survival depends not only on your financial support from Champagne, but also on keeping peace with the Saracens, who all but surround us. I try to be friendly with their leaders and have learned some of their customs and language. They respond well to my efforts and seem to view me as a tolerant and capable man.

The things he chose not to mention in his letters she learned from Bishop Garnier, whose clerical sources revealed tensions between Henri, as de facto king, and other Christians in the kingdom. When Eraclius, the patriarch of Jerusalem, died, Garnier learned that the canons elected the archbishop of Caesarea to replace him without first submitting his name to Count Henri for approval as was the custom with a king. Henri was angry that his prerogative was ignored.

"He went so far as to throw the canons briefly into prison and threaten to drown them all," Garnier said, stifling a chuckle.

"Good heavens!" Marie said, catching her breath.

"However," Garnier assured her with a smile, "cooler heads prevailed and calmed Henri's temper so that he freed the canons."

"Just like his father," Marie said softly, "squabbling with clerics."

Henri also didn't reveal to her that he had banished a group of disgruntled Pisans from the city of Acre and imprisoned his constable, Aimery de Lusignan, for coming to their defense. He believed they were all conspiring against him in support of Aimery's brother, Guy. Finally Balian, Henri's father-in-law, helped calm the waters by persuading Henri to release Aimery. Although he let him go, he dismissed him as constable and sent him to join his brother in Cyprus.

"I think, my lady Marie, it is a good thing he has an experienced man at his side like Balian, who knows the region well," Bishop Garnier assured her as they shared a goblet of wine in the solar and discussed matters in Outremer.

"Yes. Thank God for that," she agreed.

Unfortunately, however, as Marie and Garnier would later learn, that was the last matter in which Henri's father-in-law would ever be his support. Balian died not long thereafter, and Henri was left to make his own way. Fortunately, the young count seemed to be maturing, and after the death of Guy de Lusignan, when Aimery himself became lord of Cyprus, Henri eventually chose to make peace with him. In the end, Garnier informed her, Henri betrothed his two little girls, Marie and Alix, to Aimery's young sons.

"He's like his father in so many ways," she observed. "He too was impetuous as a young man, but he quickly learned when he had to take on responsibility. So, it seems, has Henri. He had no choice." Garnier nodded in agreement.

In the end, although her son never wrote of his quarrels with other Christians, he did write her of his daughters' eventual betrothals. *He has learned all too well,* Marie thought, *that his daughters, like his mother, can be useful in sealing a peace treaty.*

CHAPTER 47

Troyes, December 1193

The death of Balian was a blow to Henri in more ways than one. Not only had it deprived him of his father-in-law's wise counsel and experience, it also compelled him to increase his household expenses. Now acting as head of the family, he'd felt obliged to take into his household more people to feed and clothe without any increase in his income. It was Balian's young son, Jean d'Ibelin, who inherited his father's goods and lands, but he was still a squire in his teens, too young to take on all of his father's responsibilities. As a consequence, Henri accepted some of Balian's attendants and squires into his own court, only two of whom he described to his mother.

One of them is a squire name Ernoul, who is intelligent, well educated, and a quite likeable fellow. He has been writing a chronicle of events in the kingdom, which I have urged him to continue. There are several others as well, including a dwarf named Escarlate, one of those whom Balian saved when Saladin captured Jerusalem. I didn't have the heart to cast him out to fend for himself, and Isabella also interceded on his behalf. I'm glad he is here. He follows me wherever I go and is always ready to lighten my moods and entertain the children. He is delightful to have around, and I have grown quite fond of him. As happy as we are to have them, the expense of maintaining so large a household is sometimes overwhelming.

Henri's court and lands weren't the only ones suffering from a lack of resources. Matters were becoming increasingly difficult in Champagne, where people had begun to suffer from poor harvests. Marie felt she could tax them no further, especially when the heat and drought of the growing season promised ever smaller gains at the next fair. Even so, she sent her son everything he requested, cutting back as best she could at her own court to provide the assistance he required. More than anything she wanted to meet his needs. But his demands were increasing at a pace that was beginning to cause real hardship.

She had already taken to selling or pawning some of her household possessions—among them golden candlesticks and a few tapestries, even some of her jewels. Although she had learned from her mother to love beautiful things, she loved her son more. It soon became apparent that there was nothing left to do but try to borrow the money Henri needed.

The thought of taking loans from Jewish moneylenders was humiliating. At first, she had sent her seneschal to try to negotiate for her, but he came back empty-handed. Lenders wanted her to come in person so that she could sign and seal the note. There was nothing to be done except to go herself.

She dressed carefully for the outing, wearing nothing extravagant, and covering it all with a black woolen cloak. Only her old friend and knight Girard Evantat accompanied her, for she did not want to call attention to herself. As she set out, her chin held high and her wimple floating about her in the wind, she pulled up the hood of her cloak to block the chill. Mounted side-saddle on her palfrey, she and her knight rode slowly across the Rû Cordé and through the now quiet streets to the Rue de la Montée des Changes, not far from the Marché St. Jean. During fair season it was a busy, narrow lane lined with the stalls of moneychangers. Since the cold fair had not yet begun, the street was virtually empty.

The countess and her knight stopped in front of a shuttered house that had a small wooden sign with the painted likeness of a silver coin hanging above the door. It was the home and place of business of a wealthy Jew named Bernard de Conches, who was known to Girard. All moneylenders were Jewish, for Christians were forbidden to charge interest and had no incentive for making loans. The knight pulled the rope of the bell, which jangled loudly. A middle-aged gentleman with long sidelocks, whom Marie took for Bernard, opened the door. He was a friendly-looking man dressed in dark-colored, soft woolen garments, clearly costly ones. He recognized her at once and showed his surprise for only a moment.

"My lady," he said with a gracious bow. "And Sir Girard. Welcome to my humble home." A cheerful fire was blazing in the fireplace, and the familiar smell of burning wood permeated the room.

"Good day, sir. I have come on business," Marie said, as Girard returned his greeting with an amiable nod. She was not sure how one should behave in such circumstances, for she had never borrowed money before.

"Well, in that case, please come in and sit down." He gestured toward two armchairs on one side of a wooden table with several leather-bound ledgers placed on top. He himself went around to the other side of the table and took a simple chair facing them.

"I hope all is well with Lord Henri in the Holy Land," Bernard said in a friendly manner.

"Very well indeed," she replied, but she had no intention of making social talk nor of discussing the problems of Henri's small kingdom with this man, who did not pursue the matter further.

"Now, how may I help you?" Bernard asked.

"I have come to ask you to assist me with a loan until the closing of the hot fair, when I will repay you," she said, feeling her face flush. There would be sufficient revenue from the St. John's fair, she felt sure, to repay the loan in full at that time. It always brought in more than the cold fair, for travel was easier in the good weather.

"I see," he said. "And how much did you have in mind?" He asked quietly.

Marie found this discussion unpleasant and demeaning. Although Bernard was polite and mannerly in his behavior, she was unaccustomed to having to ask favors of a moneylender. This was a new role for her.

She looked down at her hands, which were clutching each other tensely. "Five hundred *livres.*"

Bernard raised his eyebrows. "That is a rather large amount, my lady. Do you have anything you wish to offer as surety for the loan?"

She wasn't sure just what he meant, and she looked pleadingly at Girard.

"He wishes to know that, if the loan cannot be repaid at that time, is there something of similar or greater value you could offer instead?" Girard explained.

"The loan will be repaid," she assured them both quite firmly, annoyed that her credibility was being questioned.

"It is merely customary in such transactions, my lady," Girard told her. "It is not an expression of doubt about your intention to repay the loan."

"Oh, I see," she said, trying to think of what she might own that had a value of five hundred *livres*. She had little knowledge of the relative value of many of the objects in her household. "Land perhaps? Vineyards? Livestock? What do you suggest?"

"Or perhaps some privilege?" Bernard suggested.

"Such as what?" she asked.

"Exemption from all levies and taxes for a period of ten years, for example," he offered.

She hesitated for a moment, calculating what might be at stake. But she intended to repay the loan, so what difference did it make? "That sounds quite reasonable to me, but only in the event that the loan is not repaid, which it will be," she said firmly once more.

Girard prompted her. "Perhaps you should inquire about the rate of interest Bernard will require before you agree."

"Interest?" she said with a slight frown. "Oh, yes." She turned to Bernard once more. "What is the amount you will charge for providing the loan?"

"My usual fee is thirty percent per annum, my lady. In your case, because I believe there is little risk, I will settle for twenty-five. If the loan is repaid as agreed, that would be only six hundred and twenty-five *livres* for a full year," he told her.

"Oh, I see." She was surprised that it was so much, but she was in no position to object. "Is there anything else?"

"No, *ma dame*," Bernard replied.

"Then I agree to your terms."

"Fine, my lady. Give me a few moments to record our transaction in my ledger here, and I will write a copy of our agreement for you as well." He opened one of the large ledgers and began to scribble.

"Do you read, my lady?" Bernard asked after a period of silence.

"Of course," she said, lifting her chin, "and I write as well." He smiled appreciatively and handed her a small piece of parchment on which he had neatly written the terms of the loan.

"Does this meet with your approval?"

She read it carefully to make certain it said precisely what they had agreed upon.

"It does," she said, handing it back. Bernard signed it and gave it back to her.

"You must sign it as well," he told her.

She looked at Girard, and again he nodded. She took the quill Bernard was holding out and signed her name—Marie, Countess of Troyes.

He smiled at her when she offered him back the parchment. "No," he said, "that is for you to keep. I have made a similar notation in my ledger and another copy here for us both to sign. This is the one I will keep. That way we both have a reminder of our agreement." Once they had both signed the second copy, Bernard asked, "Did you bring your seal, my lady?"

"I did," she replied, indicating the pouch attached to her belt.

He smiled, took a stick of red sealing wax from a drawer and melted a small amount of it on the bottom of the document, then pushed it toward her. She pressed her seal into it, leaving a clear impression.

When it was all done, with both documents signed, Bernard excused himself for a moment to count out the money. He returned shortly with a leather bag, which he opened and poured out on the table.

"Let me count it here in your presence." One coin at a time he counted out five hundred gold *livres*. She nodded, and he put the coins back in the leather bag and handed it over. "I hope it will help in your time of need," he said warmly.

It was heavy. Marie stuffed the bag into the pouch, which now bulged at her belt, and covered it with her cloak to make sure it was well hidden.

"I thank you for your courtesy," she said gracefully, as she rose to leave.

"It is my pleasure, *ma dame*, and good day to you both." He bowed once more, and she stood aside so that he might open the door.

The cold air felt good on her face this time. She knew it must be flushed—more from embarrassment than the heat, but she had gotten through it successfully. Girard helped her mount, and the two of them headed back to the castle at a faster pace than before. She would be glad to be home.

That was only the first time. By now she was well familiar with the process. And she had come to know most of the moneylenders in Troyes, Provins, and Meaux by name. Bertrand de Lames, Bernard Aufredi, Guillaume Giraud, Bernard l'Écrivain, Pierre Étienne, Arnaut Cap de Mall, and Raymond Raimondi. She chose to use various ones to make certain they never really understood the state of her affairs. Sometimes she would borrow from one to repay another, for it was important that each loan be paid when it was due to keep the interest from mounting and to make each one think that she had the debts under control. She did, as best she could. The clerics of the region, who didn't know her true circumstances, began to wonder why she had so suddenly become less generous. Perhaps, she thought, they would only think she was following the advice of Adam de Perseigne who had suggested that she should curtail her "excessive" largesse.

News of the death of King Sancho the Wise of Navarre in June of 1194 distracted her briefly from her financial worries, and she took the time to reconfirm the betrothal agreement of Thibaut and Blanca with the new king, Blanca's brother Sancho VII. Thibaut was sixteen now, growing stronger, maturing rapidly, and becoming more capable by the day. She was proud of him and thought he would soon be ready for marriage. When he was old enough, perhaps he would take over as Henri's regent and allow her to retire from public life. By then, she hoped, harvests would be better and the fairs more lucrative. She'd begun to discuss matters with him more openly as part of his training and even urged him to attend the judicial courts, as she had done with Henri. As much as she wanted him to learn, she had tried never to worry him by revealing the true state of the depleting treasury.

She kept hoping matters would improve, but they only grew worse. During the next growing season, exceptional heat dried up the fields, and a series of tornadoes, windstorms, and hail destroyed most of the surviving crops. Then, in March 1196, a terrible flood of the Seine submerged entire villages and swept away bridges, again severely damaging the newly planted crops and making food scarce. People believed that these calamities must be God's punishment. In Paris, the populace formed great processions and waded through the flooded streets, crying out to God to pardon their sins and displaying holy relics—a nail from the True Cross and the arm of St. Simeon. Marie, too, felt it must be the Lord's will.

God must surely be angry with us for some reason, she concluded, as she prayed on her knees with the canons in St. Étienne. *But what? Could I be the cause? Have I misjudged?*

She remembered how, several years ago, before the financial situation had become so dire, she had tried to follow Abbot Adam's advice and turn her thoughts and efforts to more spiritual endeavors. Toward that end, she had conceived the idea of sponsoring a translation of the Bible, beginning, of course, with the book of Genesis. She had decided to approach a young priest of the lady chapel at St. Étienne named Evrat, who showed a special talent in creating verses for meditation, about her translation project.

"Would you consider taking on a special task for me?" she had asked him one morning.

"With pleasure, my lady," he said.

"I would like you to undertake a translation into the common language of the book of Genesis. It could be the beginning of a translation of the whole Bible."

Evrat paled. "But, my lady countess, you know that the Church frowns on biblical translations. My superiors might even view it as a sinful effort."

"Nonsense. I know it's a bold request, but I hardly think it's a sin. I just want to be able to read God's word in my own language and make it more accessible to others. I believe that ordinary people—not just clerics—should be able to read the scripture. You can add some commentary if you think it would help," she suggested.

Unlike Adam de Perseigne, who was known and well respected in the Church, Evrat was only a canon, easily replaced and without any real power himself. He stood silently before the countess pondering the situation and its dangers.

"I could lose my prebend, *ma dame*. Then how would I live?"

"I hardly think so. You may be more likely to lose it, if you refuse," she said in a teasing tone. "Who do you think provides funds for the prebends?" She remembered that even Adam had resisted her request at first. "Do something original and daring for a change. People will notice."

Evidently that's what he feared. But she was the countess, and St. Étienne was the church founded by her husband and a dependence of the castle. It was she who must now make the count's annual donations. Surely, he didn't want to risk her disfavor for himself or the church. Thus, reluctantly, he had agreed. But Evrat worked slowly and deliberately, only occasionally bringing verses for her to review. He'd already been at it for several years now.

During those years, however, she had come to know him well and learned to trust him. He would tell her the truth. Now she sought him out at the lady chapel.

"Evrat, on what do the canons of St. Étienne blame the flood?"

He hesitated for a long time before he answered, then finally spoke without meeting her eyes. "Some of the clerics of the region are blaming the flood… on Count Henri's marriage to Isabella of Jerusalem, who still has a living husband," Evrat confided to her.

His answer shocked her. "They do not speak of it in my presence," she said. "Surely they know that marriage was annulled by the Church." It was important to her that they recognize the validity of annulment, for her mother too had remarried almost immediately after her own marriage was annulled.

Evrat spoke no more about it. And Marie asked no more questions. Still, it rankled.

She pondered the matter, which worried her greatly, but soon, when news arrived that her daughter, Mariette, along with another noble lady, planned a visit this very month, she chose to focus on preparations for that instead. Perhaps Evrat would even be willing to read portions of his translation for them. Even though he was progressing at the pace of a snail, Marie was overall pleased with his work.

When she asked him to present a portion of the text he might read to her visitors, he suggested a passage he had recently written concerning the fall in the Garden of Eden. It would cause the only serious disagreement they had about his commentary, for it contained lengthy passages describing Eve as the temptress who caused Adam's fall, portraying her with many of the usual sins the Church attributed to women. While it was not the excessive diatribe that Andreas's last book contained, it was enough to annoy her. She was more irritated than surprised by his words, but they would not do in a work she requested.

"Evrat, why do you write such negative things about women?"

"It is church doctrine, *ma dame*."

"Surely you can find other interpretations." She knew he had no reason to require the same kind of protection that Andreas had felt he needed when he wrote his third book of the *De amore*. Andreas's first two books concerned matters he knew the Church would condemn, but Evrat's work was a translation of holy scripture. It was not the same thing at all. If it were attacked, it would be because it was a translation, not because it was blasphemous. Besides, Andreas did not address his book to Marie, while this one would bear her name as its patron. She had no intention of letting him read these verses to her daughter.

Evrat nodded with dismay. All those hours of work to be discarded.

When he finally presented the revised version, too late to be read to the visitors, he had found a solution. He reminded the reader that Eve, who stood for all women, was created in Paradise, while man was created outside. And instead of dwelling upon the sins of Eve, his revision waxed eloquently upon the virtues of the Virgin Mary.

"Thank you for your revision, Evrat," she told him when he presented the new text. "I like it very much." After that, the writing went more smoothly. While his poetry may have lacked the eloquence and courtly echoes of the *Eructavit* by Adam de Perseigne, it was nonetheless competent and pleasing.

Although the work was still far from complete, one morning he presented to her a new beginning—one that contained high praise of her as its patron.

Tuit li bien venoient a li,
Ke riens tant ne li abeli
Com largece et honors a faire.
...

She was endowed with all good things,
For she enjoys nothing more
Than generosity and giving honors.
From her all ladies now living
Should take their example,
For in her all good things arose.

She has taken away the bad reputation
Of other ladies in the world
So that great honor abounds in them.

"You flatter me, Evrat, with your high praise," she said when he read the lines to her.

"Not at all, my lady. It's true. You are greatly admired in Champagne. The people are thankful for your help in rebuilding the city and for all the many benefactions you have done over the years. You have been our sovereign for a long time now, and you are the one they know best.

Marie was touched by his comments. "I'm not sure everyone would agree," she said with a smile. She was struck by the fact that his praise of her generosity contradicted Abbot Adam's comment that she was too generous. Instead of chastising her for excessive largesse, Evrat was encouraging it. Of course circumstances had changed since Adam wrote the *Eructavit*. She wished she could still be as generous as she had been—or as her husband had been, but now, with the demands of Henri's kingdom added to those of Champagne, there was little to spare.

Nevertheless, Evrat's words made her realize that she had, in the eyes of some at least, accomplished her goal of helping women to value themselves more and of increasing their status in the eyes of others. Ever since she had become aware as a small girl of how her own birth had disappointed her parents, and especially once she realized the prejudices of men against women, she had worked to dispel such attitudes. Her actions, making certain that both sexes were always treated fairly in her judicial courts and of encouraging courtesy and respect toward women in her courts of love, were among her efforts in that direction. If she could overcome, even in part, unfair judgments against women and help men to see them as human beings to be respected and even admired, she would feel her life worthwhile.

"I thank you from my heart for your kind words, Evrat."

The canon smiled his appreciation. "You have protected and governed our lands very well, my lady, with the heart of a man, and I give you no more honor than you deserve."

CHAPTER 48

Troyes, late March 1196

Although Evrat was not ready to share his revision of the story in the Garden of Eden with the visiting ladies, Marie was unperturbed. There would be other entertainment. She thought often of her mother's advice that life must not be all worry, but that one must always find pleasure regardless of circumstances. This would be Mariette's first visit since her daughter had become countess of Hainaut. Count Baudouin had died the previous December, and Mariette's husband, Beau, now ruled both Flanders, which his uncle Philip had left him, and Hainaut, which he inherited from his father.

To Marie, her daughter's life seemed golden. The rare, mutual love of the young couple had become virtually legendary, and Mariette, called Marie in her husband's lands, was young, beautiful, and relatively carefree. Now, along with another noblewoman, Mathilde de Louvain, she was undertaking a pilgrimage to the tomb of St. Gilles, located on the Via Tolosana, the road that led by way of Toulouse to Santiago de Compostella. Troyes would be a stopover along the way, and Marie was determined, despite her financial difficulties, to celebrate the visit.

"We must plan a fine feast," she informed her seneschal, Geoffrey de Joinville.

"It will be very costly, my lady."

"I'm well aware of that, Sir Geoffrey. We'll invite fewer people, but

I want to welcome my youngest daughter, whom I haven't seen now in quite a long time, with great honor."

He frowned in worry at the expense, but she would not be deterred. Her daughters were as important to her as her sons.

"As my husband used to say, 'God will provide.' I don't want her to realize the poor state of our coffers, even if we have to scrimp a bit more later on." Somehow she would find a way.

The two young women, with their retinue of knights and servants, arrived to a warm welcome on a sunny morning in late March, not long after the flood waters had receded.

"My dearest child," Marie said, embracing her daughter. "Let me look at you. What a splendid young woman you've become, and as beautiful as ever!" Mariette resembled her grandmother in her youth—with her blond hair braided in a long *trecheure*, partially covered by a wimple, and her blue eyes still bright and eager.

"It's wonderful to see you again, Mother. And this is Mathilde de Louvain, the wife of Duke Henry of Brabant." The smiling young woman with clear hazel eyes and the freshness of youth appeared to be about the same age as Mariette.

"*Bienvenue*, my dear." Marie held out her arms to welcome the duchess.

It was exciting to have the young women, both so full of life and eager for adventure, at her court. They reminded her of her younger self en route to her excursion to Poitiers.

"Beau… ," Mariette laughed, "he prefers Baudouin now… is doing homage to the king in June, and I hope you and Thibaut can be there.

"I wouldn't miss it for anything," Marie said, embracing her daughter once more. "You seem so happy, my dear."

"I couldn't be happier. Baudouin is the best husband on earth, and I can't bear to be without him. It's just that he's traveling now through his lands in Hainaut to get reacquainted with all his father's… *his* vassals," she corrected, "and Mathilde was free to travel, so we decided to make this brief pilgrimage. Spring is such a lovely time for an adventure, don't you think?"

"Indeed I do. It's a joy to have you both here."

Mathilde, as cheerful as she was, seemed almost subdued compared to the chatty Mariette, who was trying to ask all her questions at once.

"What have you heard from Henri? Is he safe in Acre? And where is Thibaut? He must be in his knight's training by now? I've heard he's betrothed to Blanche de Navarre. Is that true?"

Marie laughed. "One thing at a time, my dear. First of all, Thibaut is on a hunt, but he will be back for the feast later today. And you're right. He's no longer a page, but now a squire, eager, like all boys his age, to be knighted. And yes, he has a betrothal agreement with the princess of Navarre. As for Henri, well, as you might imagine, there are always difficulties in that region, but he seems very happy in his marriage."

Mariette frowned slightly. "Do you think the marriage is truly sanctified? I've heard that she still has a living husband."

"Oh, nonsense. Of course it is," Marie said, her voice firm. "That first marriage was long ago annulled. She was below the age of consent, and they claim it was never consummated." Mariette raised her eyebrows doubtfully as her mother spoke. "Henri and Isabella have two children now. The first one they named Marie. She is truly the child of Conrad, but Henri is raising her as his own."

"They named her for you? How sweet!"

"More probably for her real grandmother, Maria Komnena."

"And the second one? She's Henri's? And what's her name?"

"Alix. She's about three now."

"She's lucky to be so fertile," Mariette said with a slight frown, for as yet, she had no children.

"Don't worry, my dear. You're young. There's plenty of time, and you are free to travel," Marie reminded her.

"How many children does Scholastique have now?"

"Two sons so far. Do you plan to visit her during your trip?"

"Of course. We'll spend a few days at her court. I look forward to seeing her again."

"And I look forward to meeting her," Mathilde interjected with a soft smile.

The women chatted on, exchanging news until early afternoon, when Thibaut returned from his hunt. They could hear his hounds barking in the courtyard, as they protested their return to the kennel. Only a few minutes later, Thibaut burst into the solar.

"Mariette," he said, rushing to take his sister in his arms. "How good to see you! You look wonderful."

"My goodness, you've grown into a man in my absence. How did you do that?" He was taller than his older sister by a foot now, and she was compelled to look up at his face. "Let me introduce my good friend, Mathilde de Louvain. This big fellow is my baby brother, Thibaut." She laughed.

"The pleasure is mine," he said with a courtly bow. "You'll be happy to know that I've brought home almost a dozen quail and several partridges to add to the day's feast. Our hawks were quite avid today. It was a good hunt."

Marie had summoned several musicians and jongleurs, whose appearance at her court had grown rarer in these austere days, for she could not provide the generous patronage of earlier years. But she was determined that this feast would be bountiful and merry. *Thank God for Thibaut's hunt*, she thought, pleased to hear that there would be food that did not require payment. She had made arrangements for a suckling pig and a hindquarter of beef for the occasion. She hoped it would be enough to provide for feasts throughout the visit. Her cooks had been baking for days, and Marie was ready to empty the dwindling wine cellar if necessary to provide ample wine for her guests and their attendants.

Mariette sat between Mathilde and her mother at the high table, and Marie listened with delight to her stories of life in Flanders and Hainaut. She relished her daughter's pleasure at this opportunity to travel in the spring and her obvious friendship with Mathilde. Everything a young woman could ever want seemed to be hers—a husband she adored, friends, wealth, freedom to travel. It warmed Marie's heart to remember the efforts she had gone to in making sure her marriage to Baudouin took place.

Seeing the delight in Mariette's eyes when she spoke of her husband, Marie considered the possibility that she may have been wrong in her earlier decision in the court of love. *Fine amor*, although rare, did seem possible within marriage after all. The thought made her remember the works of Chrétien, who supported the conjunction of love and marriage. She had read them all, and she assumed he still lived in what was now her daughter's domain.

"Do you know anything about the poet Chrétien?" she asked her daughter. "Is he still working on the story of Perceval that Count Philip had commissioned?

"He is dead, I'm sorry to say. I should have let you know. And I'm also sorry to say he never finished it. Only a year or so after Count Philip's death, he stopped writing and became gravely ill. The doctors said he had a growth inside, and they couldn't save him. He lived on for a while but eventually died. We all miss his stories and readings at court. Did you know that the work you commissioned from him has now been completed?

"He finished it?" Marie was surprised, for she had given him specific orders not to do so.

"No, but just before his death another poet asked his permission to add to it. Chrétien apparently told him that he had been ordered not to add any more and that the other writer, a man from Namur named Godefroy de Lagny, could do as he wished."

"*Morbleu*! Have you read it?" Marie asked.

"I have, and all of Chrétien's other works as well. He was a fine writer."

"And the continuation?"

"Well, not as accomplished as Chrétien's own work, but I suppose it's satisfying as an ending. I was impressed with the praise Chrétien heaped on you as his patron."

"Rather backhanded praise, as I recall," Marie said with a laugh.

"But praise nonetheless. Your name will be remembered as long as anyone reads his work." Mariette covered her mother's hand with her own. "I'm very proud of you, you know. And I'll never forget how determined you were to make sure my marriage to Baudouin took place. I'm very grateful."

The four-day visit of Mariette and Mathilde seemed much too short, but Marie consoled herself with the knowledge that she would see her daughter again in June.

When June came, Marie rode eagerly to Paris, her son Thibaut by her side, to attend the ceremony of Count Baudouin's homage to King Philippe. At fifty-one, she had reached an age where such ceremonies symbolizing the continuity of life and lineage had taken on supreme importance. It also brought a flood of memories, for she'd witnessed the same act many times before. She watched as Baudouin folded his hands, which Philippe clasped inside his own, symbolizing the vassal's submission to his lord. The kiss of peace between the two men came next. As their lips touched, their friendship and concord were supposedly sealed. The ceremony was moving, but Marie was all too well aware that such oaths and gestures were often forgotten in the heat of dispute.

Only a year later, although Baudouin honored his oath to aid the king at a siege in Normandy during the following fighting season, he renounced his allegiance to King Philippe not long afterwards and formed an alliance with King Richard instead. Although she was still angry with Philippe for his refusal to help Henri, Marie was determined not to take sides in this constant struggle over the borderlands between their two realms. She'd heard that Richard had built a castle, with the saucy name of Château Gaillard, at a major bend in the Seine River, defiantly guarding the entrance to Normandy and serving as a challenge to Philippe. She could only be glad that Thibaut was not yet knighted or pledged to either of them. He was seventeen now, and she feared it would not be long before he too was dragged into their constant bickering. Would it never end? She was so weary of war. But already, talk of yet another crusade was in the air.

The three-year truce between the Saracens and the kingdom of Jerusalem had ended, and men both east and west of Champagne were stirring the air for yet another crusade. Saladin was dead now, and after a brief power struggle with the emir's sons, his brother al-Adil had emerged as the new Muslim leader. Not far from Paris, a holy man named Foulques de Neuilly, a simple curate of the village church, had become widely known for working miracles and for preaching the need for a new holy war. In Germany the idea had already taken hold, and Emperor Heinrich was now preparing his army.

The thought was chilling to Marie. Her son Thibaut was burning for knighthood and his turn at the challenging adventure, eager to follow in his father's and brother's footsteps. But Marie could think of nothing she dreaded more. Once again, she remembered that crusades had been the source of much of her life's misery—her parents' divorce, her husband's death, the departure, apparently for good, of her oldest son, even the near impoverishment of her own court. And now, she did not look forward to the possibility that Thibaut might soon follow that same path.

Then an unexpected letter arrived.

To my dearest sister Marie, countess of Troyes, from Marguerite, dowager queen of Hungary. Perhaps you have already heard that my husband, King Béla, died just before Easter. He was a good king and a good husband, but we had no children, and there is nothing left for me here in Hungary. I have decided to join the German emperor on his upcoming efforts in Outremer. This time, I pray to God, our men will retake the holy city of Jerusalem, and I would like to be among the first to enter the city when it is once more in Christian hands. I hope you do not think me foolish, but this opportunity to walk where Christ walked and share in his passion is an opportunity that will never come again. I am selling my dower to my husband's brother to raise the necessary funds for the trip. I do not expect to return, but rather to live out the rest of my life in the Holy Land.

I will, of course, take the opportunity to visit your dearest son Henri. If you have messages or goods you wish to send, I shall be happy to take them with me. I wish that you could accompany me on the journey, but I know that you have heavy responsibilities in Champagne. Be assured of my most sincere affection, and please pray for me. Farewell.

Marie had not seen her sister for more than ten years, but they had kept in contact by letter. She was saddened to hear that Marguerite had lost yet another husband but decided to take advantage of her sister's upcoming trip and entrust to her care letters to her son and the latest funds he had requested. That way she wouldn't have to pay a messenger to go all the way to Acre, when Hungary was so much closer. She chose as her emissary a man named Joscelin, abbot of Notre-Dame de La Charmoye, a Cistercian abbey near Épernay that her husband had founded in 1167, and a man she knew to be trustworthy.

Marie would like to have taken the trip with Marguerite, for she too longed to see the holy places, meet her grandchildren, and visit her son. But she knew it was impossible. She was needed in Champagne, serving the kingdom of Jerusalem in her own way—trying to hold together her son's lands here and helping him support his tiny kingdom of Jerusalem. He had been away for six years now and had become almost a stranger to his native Champagne, where many still did not accept his marriage to Queen Isabella and looked upon his daughters, those grandchildren Marie had never seen, as bastards. But whatever he did, he was her son, and she loved him with all her heart.

Troyes, late summer 1197

Marie's thoughts and best wishes, along with funds and a letter to Henri, accompanied her sister on her voyage. By early September, however, she began to have an uneasy feeling that would not go away.

"It's only natural," Bishop Gautier assured her. "A new holy war with its inherent dangers, Henri now ruler of a kingdom in turmoil, and your own beloved sister facing perils that have brought down many strong men. Anyone would feel uneasy in such times."

What he said was true, but she couldn't shake the darkness that invaded her spirit. She tried to think how happy Henri must be to welcome his aunt Marguerite, who'd spent so much time at their court in Troyes. She tried to imagine their joyful reunion, but the image would not come. If only God could transport her to the Holy Land to see for herself what was happening.

CHAPTER 49

Troyes, late October 1197

A dusty and exhausted messenger stood waiting in the great hall of the castle in Troyes. He had been fortunate to take a ship from Acre that had not encountered any of the autumn storms that often beset sailing vessels this time of year. Once he'd reached Marseille, he had ridden hard all the way, making time like the wind, even though he knew his visit would not be welcome.

"I can't believe the trip took you only six weeks. That's amazing." Girard Evantat stood beside the table where, at the time of the messenger's arrival, he had been, in a rare moment of leisure, playing chess with the seneschal. They had sent a squire to summon the countess, since the messenger had said he was told to deliver the news to her in person.

"I was fortunate to make good time, and I rode hard to beat the worst autumn rains and get here as quickly as possible."

"Do you want us to leave?" the seneschal Geoffrey de Joinville asked. "Should she receive this news alone?"

"I think it may be best if you remain, my lord. It is not good news."

Thibaut, now eighteen, escorted his mother into their presence. She had been ill and was taking a rest when he went to fetch her. Now she allowed herself the luxury of holding onto her son's arm as she entered the great hall. When he'd told her that a courier was newly arrived from the kingdom of Jerusalem with important news, she rose at once, her heart in her throat, hoping against hope that he brought only information about the arrival of another grandchild that she knew was on the way. Her expectant smile faded the moment she saw the grim expression on the face of the messenger.

"You bring news from my son?" she asked in a tense voice.

He knelt before her, his head lowered. "I regret to say that I bring the worst of news, my lady."

Her hands began to shake, and her face drained of color.

"Your son, Count Henri, is dead, my lady," he said bluntly. "He fell from a high window when a balustrade gave way. But he died at once and felt no pain." Thibaut was well aware that the man could not know whether the last information was true or not, but at least it spared his mother as much as possible.

At his words, Marie cried out. Her legs gave way, and she collapsed into the arms of Thibaut. He held her tightly, though he himself was shocked and distressed by the messenger's words.

"Was he pushed?" he asked.

"No, my lord, he fell. It was an accident. A dwarf tried to save him and fell with him. They're both dead. I hear that Queen Isabella had the dwarf buried at his feet."

Marie, wracked with sobs, was almost unable to breathe.

"There is more, my lord. Shall I go on?"

"I think that's enough for now," Thibaut said in a voice as authoritative as he could muster at eighteen. "Sir Geoffrey, please see that he is fed and given a place to sleep. We'll hear the rest later."

Thibaut, supporting his mother on one side, with her knight Girard on the other, helped her to her bedchamber, where her ladies fluttered about, trying to comfort her. She fell onto the bed, turned her face to her pillow, and began to weep inconsolably. Thibaut felt helpless. He leaned down and kissed her on the cheek. Then he knelt and put his arm around her.

"Try to rest, *Maman*. I'll be back soon. Try to rest." He hated to leave her side, but he wanted to know what other information the messenger brought so that he might help to prepare her. Surely it couldn't be news as bad as what she had already received.

"Please look after her until I return," he told the ladies as he arose.

Then he went to find the courier again.

"What other news do you bring?" he asked, joining the messenger seated at a trestle table in the great hall with a large mug of ale, a loaf of warm bread, a chunk of cheese, and a thick slice of roast beef before him. Thibaut listened, still in a state of shock, as though none of this were real, while the messenger delivered the remainder of his report.

"Your mother's sister, the queen of Hungary, is also dead. She died only a week after her arrival in Tyre. It was one of the fevers that strike down so many newcomers in Outremer."

"*Mordieu*, that news will be another blow to my mother. Next to Queen Adèle, Aunt Marguerite was probably her closest friend. She spent a lot of time here when I was a little boy, and my mother was very fond of her."

Thibaut sat quietly for a few moments, trying to sort through his own feelings. He loved and admired his brother very much, and he knew he would grieve for him for many months. He thought of Henri's wife, Isabella, and their little girls. What would become of them now?

"How is Queen Isabella? Has she had her baby yet?" he asked, just as the messenger stuffed a chunk of beef into his mouth.

The man nodded and chewed for a moment, glancing down at the meat still left on his trencher as he wiped his lips on his sleeve and said, "Another daughter… Philippa. They say the queen was distraught about her husband's death. But when I left, there was already talk of her marrying again. By now she should already be wed."

"Poor woman," said Thibaut. "This is the fourth time. They hardly give her time to bury one husband before they want her to marry another. Who is it this time?"

"Aimery de Lusignan," the young man said, taking a large gulp of ale.

"What? The king of Cyprus? I hope he's a better king than his brother was." Thibaut knew there had once been bad blood between Henri and the Lusignans, but Henri had written that they had patched up their differences and even betrothed their children to one another. Still, Thibaut was surprised. "Doesn't he already have a wife?"

"King Aimery was recently widowed," the messenger told him. "They say he's a good king in Cyprus. A better lord than his brother anyhow."

"That wouldn't take much, from what I hear. Wasn't his brother Guy the one who led his army to defeat in the battle of Hattin? What a disaster! He lost almost the entire kingdom."

The messenger nodded and lifted his mug for another swig of ale.

Thibaut sat quietly for a moment, thinking about everything that had happened. Then, all at once, it occurred to him that he had just become count of Champagne. He remembered how, before Henri's departure, he had required all his barons to swear to recognize his younger brother as count in the event of his death in the Holy Land. Thibaut himself had been only a boy at the time, but they readily knelt and made the vow, never believing that their handsome young lord would not return. Now it had happened. Henri was dead. Thibaut felt the sudden heavy weight of responsibility.

He left the weary messenger to finish his meal and sent a page to summon his mother's friend Garnier, bishop of Troyes. Returning to his mother's room, he dismissed her ladies, sat down beside her bed, and took her hand. Her eyes were closed, and he gently wiped away the tear tracks on both her cheeks.

She opened her red-rimmed eyes and said softly, as though to herself, "You know you have lived too long when you outlive your children." Her eyes closed once more, as new tears seeped out from beneath her eyelids.

Her anguish broke Thibaut's heart, and he wanted to do nothing more than bring her solace, but he did not know how. His own feelings were complicated. He loved his brother and was sickened by his death. He felt grief, but he also needed to be strong for his mother. He thanked God for all she had done to help him prepare, for confiding in him, asking his advice, giving him an opportunity to try out his ideas, just as she had done with his brother. Though she hadn't always agreed with Thibaut's suggestions, sometimes she did, and inevitably she always made the right decision, he thought. *All this time… all this time she has been preparing me for this moment, which both of us hoped would never come. But there is so much to do, so much more to learn. I'm not even knighted yet, he thought. Thank God* Maman *is still here to guide me.*

Marie kept to her bed for two days, never rising, weeping intermittently until she had exhausted herself. Both her son and the bishop worried for her health. Along with the chaplain Evrat, they took turns sitting for hours beside her bed. Thibaut made certain that food was brought to her at every mealtime, but she never touched it. He had seen her grieve for his father, but never like this.

He decided not to tell her yet about the death of her sister Marguerite. He remembered his aunt as a pretty young woman in her twenties, recently widowed, wan and in mourning for her husband, the Young King of England, but not in the depths of despair like his mother, who seemed to feel her life was over. At the time, he was only a little boy, and his aunt was visiting their court and waiting for the escort that would take her to Hungary and a new marriage. That was fourteen years ago. Now she too was gone. He dreaded telling his mother about her death, yet he knew he must.

He waited for several days until she was at least taking nourishment again and walking through her days with some awareness of the needs of daily life. Then finally, as they sat quietly together in the solar late one afternoon, it was she who raised the question.

"That messenger… he mentioned that there was more news. What was it? Has the new baby come?"

"Yes, *Maman*, it was another little girl. They named her Philippa."

"He left no son then. I wonder if I shall ever meet his daughters…" she said wistfully. There was no strength or determination in her voice, none of her vigor of old.

"There is more news, *Maman*, though I hate to have to tell you."

"More bad news?" She looked as though she were in pain. He nodded slightly.

"Aunt Marguerite is also dead of a fever," he said in a soft voice.

She looked at him in horror. Quiet tears spilled over the rims of her eyes, still red and swollen from her weeping of the last few days. She had thought there could be no more. She made no sound, for her chest still ached from the wracking sobs her body had already endured. She was worn out, weak, subdued, anguished.

"Marguerite," she whispered. "Sweet Marguerite."

Thibaut took her once more in his arms and held her until she seemed calm. Then she pulled away and said, "I think I'll rest now." She went to her bedchamber to lie down, and she took no supper again that night.

By early December, Marie had grown thin and listless. Her body, weakened by her illness, refused to recover. And despite the fact that she thought she'd never find the strength to make another decision in her life—she had finally made one, which she announced to Thibaut on December 6, the feast day of St. Nicholas.

"I have decided that I am retiring from court. You are stronger than I am now, and you are the new count, old enough and ready to rule."

"But what will I do without you? How can I rule on my own?"

"You'll do well, son. You're ready. Trust me. I'll be here for a while longer. Then I'm planning a retreat to regain my strength at the convent of Fontaines-les-Nonnes. I'll still be nearby."

"Do you intend to take the veil?" Thibaut asked, wondering if his mother, who had so loved the world and its joys, her musicians and poets, her hospitality to visitors, would long survive under the austerity and discipline of the nuns.

"I haven't decided yet. I must have time to think—away from the court and its distractions. For the time being, I will just be what they call a *grande pensionnaire*. They will let me bring a few servants as well. At least I'll be in a place where I can find solitude and pray."

"I understand, *Maman*, but I'll miss you."

"You can visit, and I hope you will. There are a few things you will need to take care of. I had not told you, but given your brother's financial needs in the Holy Land, I was compelled to borrow from moneylenders. The loans will need to be repaid. The chancellor has all the notes."

Thibaut was stunned. His mother dealing with moneylenders?

"Now that there is a new king in Acre," she began, her face drawn, for he had told her of the marriage of Isabella and Aimery de Lusignan, "those demands will cease, and you should have no difficulty in settling all the loans with the income from the next two fairs—three at the most. Please see to it for me. Girard knows all about it. He can help you."

"Of course, *Maman*."

Marie remained in Troyes through the Christmas season, despite her growing indifference to the feasts and festivities, far more subdued this year than usual. The sounds of the lute and the songs of the minstrels and *trouvères* did not bring her joy, and she could hardly stomach the rich foods without feeling ill or overfull. Instead, she spent most of her time in her bedchamber, praying and reading. After Epiphany, she began her preparations for her retirement at the Priory of Fontaines-les-Nonnes.

CHAPTER 50

Near Meaux, late January 1198

As the small retinue of Countess Marie rode north on the road that led from Meaux to Acy-en-Multien, they drew near the narrow valley where, in the distance, they could see, rising amidst the trees, rooftops of the refuge the countess sought—the priory of Fontaines-les-Nonnes. The rich fields all around, once considered a wasteland, but now cultivated, had been harvested, cleared, and lay in wait for spring plowing and planting. The riders caught occasional glimpses of the river Thérouanne, which ran along the borders of the priory's lands.

Fontaines, one of the earliest of the daughter-houses of Fontevrault Abbey, had been named for the many springs in the area. Marie knew the convent and its history well. She'd been told that, at its founding, her mother-in-law Countess Mathilde and Count Thibaut had both taken a strong interest in it, offering land and aid to these nuns sent from Fontevrault. Then, when the building of the priory church of Sainte-Marie had been compelled to cease for a lack of sufficient resources, Marie's father, King Louis, had come to its aid. Both she and Henri had also supported the priory with their gifts. She now welcomed the sight of its steeple rising among the trees, for the ride from Meaux had exhausted her.

During the brief period of her first retreat there, she had come to love the prioress, Edna. Two years earlier, despite her financial burdens, Marie had finally fulfilled her desire to endow her dear friend with a modest lifetime income, but only by selling a portion of her own dower, the sole support for her retirement. She looked forward to seeing her again and knew that she would find healing here, if it was to be found.

Fontaines, like Fontevrault, which her mother and three of Henri's sisters had chosen for their own retirement from the world, was a double monastery where both nuns and monks could live, but where the head nun, in this case the prioress, had authority over the men. It suited Marie's sense of justice. She had considered Fontevrault, but she wanted to be nearer her son Thibaut and remain in Champagne. While she had given serious thought to taking the veil, she had not yet decided on such a definitive step. First, she needed prayer and God's help to find peace and healing from this sorrow that had taken hold of her since her son's death. That was what she sought within these walls.

When they reached the priory, her knight Girard rang the bell. The old *portière*, keeper of the entrance, an older nun with keen eyesight, opened the small window of the wooden postern to peer out. When she saw Countess Marie, she smiled in welcome and at once opened wide the gate. Marie urged her palfrey inside the courtyard, followed by Girard, her constable Guy de Dampierre, her chaplain, and her maidservant. They were followed by a small wagon bearing the one coffer she had brought with her.

"Welcome, my lady," said the *portière*. "We were expecting you. The prioress is waiting for you in her quarters." She turned to the men and maidservants. "The hosteller will show you where to put the countess's coffer."

The prioress opened her door at the countess's first knock. "Welcome, my dear lady." She tried not to show the shock she felt at first sight of the countess's appearance. Marie was so thin that her clothes hung formlessly on her body. Her face was slack, and wrinkles had appeared where there had been none before. Her eyes were hollow, with dark circles beneath them. "We are so pleased to have you once again in our presence. There are two other noble ladies staying with us at the moment, so you will not lack for companionship."

"Thank you, Reverend Mother, but yours is the only companionship I require. I desire solitude far more than company."

"I was so very sorry to hear about the death of your son," Prioress Edna said in a quiet voice, reaching out for Marie's hand.

Marie blinked away the tears that seemed to fill her eyes whenever Henri's death was mentioned. "Thank you."

The prioress was truly sorry about all that had happened. She had been annoyed to overhear one of the priory's three priests casting judgments on the death of the king of Jerusalem, contending that his fall was a symbolic fall from grace—God's judgment on his illicit marriage to a woman who still had a living husband. These were, of course, words she would never repeat to the countess or anyone else for that matter. And she thought the priest unkind for speaking so heartlessly of a man who had been in the Holy Land fighting for the freedom of Jerusalem. Above all, she understood a mother's grief.

"Do come in and take a seat," Prioress Edna invited.

"Perhaps for just a short while," Marie replied, grateful for the chance to sit still, but wanting to be in her room before her maidservant began to put away her things.

Once the two women were comfortably seated before the warmth of the small fireplace, the prioress asked, "Have you finally decided to take the veil?"

"Not yet," Marie replied. "I am contemplating it, but I'm not sure I'm worthy."

"Of course you're worthy. But I realize that you're accustomed to a very different kind of life. Being a nun will mean giving up many things, worldly things that I know you love. It is a life of intense discipline—arising at prime, even earlier in the summer, and during the night for prayers at matins and lauds, not to mention the vow of silence and the austerity of the garments. It is not an easy life."

"I just want to be sure before I take any vows that I do so from strength, not from weakness, that I am moving toward God and not just away from the world," Marie answered softly. "But I have retired from court life for good. It has lost its savor, and I think I have done all I can for my children. My son Thibaut is well prepared to be count."

"You have accomplished much from what I hear. The rumor is that the priest of the lady chapel at St. Étienne has described you to others as having the heart of a man but the body of a woman. It's probably the highest compliment he could imagine," she said with a soft laugh.

"They have no idea how strong the heart of a woman must be to endure all she goes through. The pains of childbirth are only the beginning. I have learned that losing a child is far worse," Marie added.

"Not to mention all the struggles in between. I agree. Men have no appreciation of a woman's courage in the face of adversity or the humiliations one feels at being considered 'an incomplete man,' just because we don't have male organs," the prioress commented dryly. "It can be hard to bear. But we console ourselves by knowing that, like our Lord Jesus Christ, we nourish our children with our body and blood. We give them the tender love their fathers don't know how to give. We raise them to be strong in spirit and not just in body, as you have done, for the body may perish, but the spirit is eternal."

Marie smiled at the prioress's words. "This is why I need to spend time here, Reverend Mother. Your wisdom is reassuring, and you make me realize even more the worth of women to our Lord."

"You have certainly done much in your own life to show the staunchness and determination of a woman's heart, her commitment to duty, and the value she has to the world."

"You are kind," Marie said, touched by the prioress's words. "But I must go and settle in now. I'm not sure how long I will stay here. Who knows? Possibly for the rest of my life unless I am needed elsewhere."

"Then would you go?"

"I will always go if my children need me."

"Spoken like a loving mother," the prioress said softly. "But you are welcome here as long as you wish to stay."

Life at Fontaines was completely different from that at the courts in Troyes or Meaux. Meals were sparse, but they suited Marie, for only a few bites seemed to fill her these days. Fasting posed no problem. The hardest part at first was her stiffened knees from the constant kneeling at prayer. Then there was the silence. Except for the frequent singing of the nuns, who sounded like an angel choir, and the birds chirping in the garden, it was a world of silence, but it was conducive to her hours of contemplation. At first, she missed some of the comforts of her previous life. Yet all the privation seemed to purify her somehow, to make her body seem less important.

Gradually, her days took on a sense of peace, a new calm. She no longer let her conscious mind dwell on the broken body of her son, which sometimes still haunted her dreams. During her waking hours, she tried to focus instead on his spirit, on the coming reunion they would share in Heaven. Although speaking was not forbidden to her, she did not miss it. She found herself beginning to prefer the silence that allowed her to hear the inner voice of God.

Although most of her companions had long since returned to Troyes, her priest, for the time being at least, had joined the few monks and priests the priory housed. And her loyal maid, Jeanette, remained at her side, worrying daily about her mistress. She feared that Marie's increasing silence, her almost nonexistent laughter, her refusal of rich food, even on those rare occasions when it was offered, were signs of increasing depression. But she was wrong. Although the body and the outward manifestations of the countess might be growing weaker, her spirit was growing stronger.

Mid-February 1198

When Marie's son Thibaut came for a visit, Jeanette took him aside and expressed her worry about her mistress. "I fear for her health, my lord. She seems to take little pleasure in this life, as she once did. She seems almost eager to die."

"Thank you for telling me this, Jeanette. And thank you for taking such good care of her. I will ask the pope and all the prelates in my territory to pray for her. As I will do."

When he saw his mother, he was shocked at first. Her skin was almost transparent. He could see the bony contours of her face and wrinkled hands. Her body was covered by a loose garment, not a nun's habit, but a simple tunic of black wool without ornamentation. She was only fifty-three, though she looked seventy. But he also sensed a curious serenity about her he had not seen before, as though she had already left the world behind. *There is a new kind of strength in her*, he thought.

"Do you fare well, my dearest son?" she asked.

"Well enough, *Maman*. The king has agreed to knight me and to accept my homage in April in Paris. I hope you will come."

"If it's the Lord's will, I will be there," she said with a faint smile.

He dreaded the task for which he had come. He feared her reaction. Would it have any impact at all, he wondered now—or perhaps too much? Since that was the purpose of his visit, however, he gave himself no choice.

"*Maman*," he said gently, "I'm afraid I bring more bad news."

Marie's eyes opened wide. "Not one of your sisters, I hope?" She held her breath as she waited for his answer.

"No, *Maman*. This time it's Aunt Alix. She died recently in Blois. They said it began with a simple fever that worsened day by day."

Her face took on an expression of sadness, but she received the news calmly. She had no more tears to shed.

"I wish we had been closer," she said thoughtfully, almost in a whisper. Thibaut had the impression she was speaking more to herself than to him. "I wish she had gone with the rest of us to visit our mother in Poitiers, but she refused. She missed so much love in her bitterness. Although we saw each other occasionally, we were not close as sisters should be, but I'm sorry she's gone." It was the most she had spoken aloud for months. Then her face took on a look of contentment. "Our time here may be over, mine and Alix's, but we shall meet again."

Thibaut was relieved that she reacted so calmly. They talked on for a long time, as he told her about events in Troyes and any news he thought might interest her. She listened, nodding, and occasionally smiling and adding a brief comment. Finally, he got around to the other news he wanted to share with her. "I have sent an emissary to King Sancho to see when we could arrange for my marriage to his sister. The messenger should return in a few months. I will let you know when the wedding will be."

Marie nodded and smiled with contentment. "That's good," she said, recalling how her mother had helped to arrange this betrothal.

"Before I go, there's one more thing I want you to know," Thibaut said, taking his mother's hand. "I realize how well you have prepared me and taught me what I need to know. I have also watched you rule and learned from your example of justice and tolerance. I am very grateful."

She smiled once more and reached out to squeeze his hand. "You are a good son and a good man." It was comforting to know that her youngest child's future was settled, that the world of Champagne would go on without her—the world she had preserved for her sons throughout her long regency. It was solace to know it was intact and in good hands.

Less than a week after Thibaut's visit, Marie grew too weak to attend holy services. She could no longer kneel on the hard floors, nor could she stand for more than a few moments. Jeanette, fearing for her life, had her taken to the infirmary, where she could be more easily cared for. By the end of April, they both knew she was dying.

"Please send for Prioress Edna," Marie asked the nursing sister.

When the prioress arrived, she sat beside Marie's bed. "I hear that you are no longer eating, save for a few spoonfuls of soup each day," Edna said, a worried frown on her face.

"It's nothing to be sad about," Marie told her. "You and I both know that I am only weeks away from death. You should rejoice instead."

The prioress forced herself to smile. "Of course," she said, "you're right, for it is the destiny of us all—and our heavenly reward awaits."

"I want to take holy vows," Marie said. "I am ready, and I want to die as a nun."

"Is it not enough that you have been virtually living as one these recent months?" the prioress asked, surprised by her sudden request.

Marie sensed a hesitation. "My husband Henri's father asked to be buried as a Cistercian monk, and his wish was honored. Is my request any less worthy?"

It was true. When Count Thibaut was in his last days, he had been dressed in the white robes of a Cistercian monk and taken holy vows on his deathbed. No one questioned his sincerity or the appropriateness of the act. The countess Marie had been a great benefactor to the priory, even to the prioress herself. She was a good Christian woman, and she was indeed worthy.

"Of course it's not, my lady." Such deathbed vows were not uncommon among the nobility, even though they bypassed all the usual preparations for monastic life the Church required. Since it was the first time such a request had been made at Fontaines-les-Nonnes, at least in the time of Prioress Edna, she had no idea whether such vows were considered entirely valid by the Church, but Marie's would be certainly recognized and honored at Fontaines, for the prioress knew her goodness, her strength, and her conviction. Besides, she had been living almost as a nun already.

And so it was done. Marie asked that Queen Adèle be invited to witness her vows. In the meantime, Edna ordered the mistress of the wardrobe to bring the necessary garments. On the morning of the day the countess was to take her vows, the nursing sisters bathed her thoroughly in a symbolic purification and clothed her in a white tunic, setting aside the surplice, black girdle, veil, and cowl of the order of Fontevrault that would be added during the ceremony.

When Adèle arrived just before the hour of sext, she rushed to the infirmary and sat down beside Marie's bed. "I hear you have finally decided to abandon the world and take the veil," she whispered, reaching out to hold Marie's hand.

"I have and just in time. Thank you for coming. I am grateful for all our happy days together."

"As am I. You are closer to me than any of my sisters. We've shared so much, haven't we? Both joys and sorrows. I will always love you." Adèle leaned forward to kiss Marie.

When the time came for her to renounce the world and profess her solemn vows, the priest arrived to celebrate the Mass and the taking of the veil in the infirmary's chapel. Once the ceremony ended, Marie, now dressed as a nun of the order of Fontevrault, having taken the necessary vows of chastity, poverty, and obedience and received the priest's blessing, Prioress Edna leaned over her bedside and whispered, "Welcome to our order, Sister Maria."

The countess smiled. "I suppose I should have done it sooner, but I've never followed all the rules, have I?" She thought of her mother's words—that if one did only what the Church prescribed, life would be dull indeed. After all, man's rules were not necessarily God's rules.

"God knows what is in your heart," said the prioress.

Less than a week later, on Sunday morning, eight days into March, the bells were ringing for mass when Countess Marie took her last breath and closed her eyes to this world. The birds sang with joy at the coming spring.

Prioress Edna notified Count Thibaut at once of his mother's death. Thibaut sent messages to his two sisters as well as to the king and Queen Adèle, informing them that he intended to have his mother's burial at the cathedral in Meaux. Realizing after his last visit that her death was not far off, he had already ordered a splendid stone effigy for her tomb, depicting her in the garments of a countess rather than those of a nun, for he had not known of her intent to take the veil.

He sent for his uncle, Archbishop Guillaume, to participate with Bishop Ansellus of Meaux in the burial service. Marie's body was laid to rest between two pillars of the cathedral on the Gospel side of the sanctuary. Although her effigy was not yet ready, Thibaut had arranged and paid for a candle to burn perpetually before her tomb. It was lit during the service, and the bishop promised that each time a processional passed by her tomb, the censer would swing his incense in its direction, blessing it three times.

The cathedral nave overflowed with nobles and common people from Meaux and various other parts of Champagne who had come to say goodbye to the countess. There were many who wiped away tears during the solemn service. When it was over, the archbishop called Thibaut aside.

"I want you to know that Pope Innocent did not ignore your request for intercessory prayers for your mother." He pulled from his vestment a sheaf of parchment. "He wrote to me, as well as Bishop Ansellus and the archbishop of Sens to support and comfort her. I received this the day after her death." He handed the letter to Thibaut.

Thibaut read it over, touched by the pope's concern and his expression of "unfeigned compassion" and shared grief. The letter urged the bishops to protect Countess Marie and her possessions from ill-intended people. But as he read to the end, he was struck by the pope's contention that his mother stood in special need of the aid and counsel of the prelates "because of the weakness of the female sex in dealing with adversity." It almost made him laugh, thinking how infuriated his mother would have been by such words. He had never known a stronger woman, more capable of dealing with adversity or one who resented more the ways in which men, especially those of the Church, considered women inferior.

"It's just as well she never saw this letter," he said. "While I appreciate the pope's sympathy, my mother—albeit a woman—was never a weak person. Yes, my brother's death was a blow to her, but she was already ill. Yet even as she grew physically weaker, God gave her a new kind of spiritual strength."

Guillaume tucked the letter back into his cassock and said no more about it. He had heard from Prioress Edna that what Thibaut said was true.

Mariette caught up with her brother as they walked from the church back to the castle. "I'm sorry Scholastique was unable to be here, though I know she wanted to come." Thibaut nodded. "The candle was a nice tribute," she said. "I'm glad you thought of it."

"It seemed to me to be the most appropriate symbol for our mother. Do you remember the song of the troubadour Rigaud de Barbezieux, the poet who in her youth called her the 'wise and joyful countess' who 'illuminated' Champagne?"

"I do. I hadn't thought of that for a long time. No one sings his songs much anymore."

"That's why I had the Latin lament written for her funeral, referring to her as 'the light of Champagne' and 'the star from which so many lights have shown on us.' I'd rather she be remembered that way than as some weak woman who the pope wants us to believe died of depression at our brother's death."

"So would I." Mariette touched her brother's arm in appreciation. "Prioress Edna told me that her spirit was strong, that only her body was wasting away from the kind of physical sickness God sometimes sends to those he loves. I was also pleased that the poet referred to her as 'Marie, mother of grace.'"

Thibaut nodded. "I want her remembered for the beauty of her spirit, her learning, and all the determination she had to make sure the world knew that women too could be strong and independent. I hope my new wife will be like her."

"And when is the wedding?"

"One thing at a time, dear sister." Thibaut laughed. "Let me pay my homage to the king first—next month. As for the wedding, next summer maybe? I hope you and Baudouin will attend."

"We'll try," Mariette said.

Life would go on, they both knew, albeit diminished without their mother. It was their turn now to try to fill the void she left, to put into effect the lessons she had taught them, and to follow the example she set.

Thibaut took his sister's hand to walk the rest of the way to the castle through the cobbled streets of Meaux.

AUTHOR'S AFTERWORD

Voltaire has written, "There is no history, only fictions of various degrees of plausibility." If that were not the case, we could have no revisionist history. To be reputable, history must limit itself to what can be demonstrated through documentary evidence. However, documents can also be subject to interpretation, and written sources are frequently incomplete, ambiguous, or contradictory. Professional historians must often make choices and find plausible interpretations of events for which only partial and incomplete truth can ever be known.

The writer of historical fiction, on the other hand, seeks to retell events from the past in a way to make them come alive to the general reader rather than to be a resource to professional historians. Good writers of historical fiction include incidents or interpretations that are plausible and possible, but for which there may be no documentary evidence. In my view, however, no reputable writers of historical fiction would include an incident or event that can be *disproved* by the documents, unless, of course, at some point they acknowledge their sins and explain why, for aesthetic reasons, they may have chosen to make such changes. In my view, such deliberate alterations should be extremely rare.

Winston Churchill once described history, with a "flickering lamp," stumbling "along the trail of the past, trying to reconstruct its scenes, to revive its echoes, and kindle with pale gleams the passions of former days." Historical fiction does precisely the same thing, only trying to make the "pale gleams" more vivid and put the general reader into the heart of the narrative by the creation of plausible scenes of action and dialogue. It is not an easy process and requires considerable research, not only involving the same documents the professional historian must use, but also experiential research and a thorough grounding in the details of daily life in the past. It is a quest to make a place or time come alive in the mind of the reader. A historical novelist is not set on breaking new ground, but on interpreting what we know or may surmise as a coherent narrative that brings people and actions of long ago alive to the modern world.

Writing about medieval women is particularly challenging, for their lives are notoriously ill documented. Many of the things we think we know about Marie's famous mother, Eleanor of Aquitaine, are the accumulated conjectures of historians and even writers of historical fiction over a period of many centuries. Relatively speaking, she is rarely mentioned in the documents of the time compared to her husbands and sons, who were doing what was considered important things like making war, plotting against one another, and plundering their neighbors.

Nevertheless, having published both scholarly books and articles, particularly on events and works of twelfth-century France and Anglo-Norman England, and having done extensive archival research in France and England, as well as repositories in other countries, I offer the following historical notes to anyone who may be interested:

- The burning of Vitry in 1143 is recorded in a large number of chronicles, among them the *Historia Francorum*, *Historia regum Francorum*, the *Historia gloriosi Regis Ludovici VII*, and the *Chronica regum Francorum*, to name only a few. The date of the burning of Vitry is given as 1142 in some of the sources. It is the *Chronicon Turonense* that dates it specifically in January. According to the styles of various courts and sources, the year changed either at Christmas or Easter (as it did in Champagne), which explains why some chronicles date it as 1142 and others 1143.

- No chronicler recorded the year of Marie's birth. It is only thanks to the life of Bernard de Clairvaux (*Vita Sancti Bernardi*) that we have that information, which suggests the importance of the "miracle" to Bernard's biographer. Even in this account, neither the month, day, nor place of her birth is recorded. Historians have generally assumed with no particular proof that she was born in Paris. However, charter evidence places King Louis in Saintes in 1145, when he settled a dispute between Notre-Dame de Saintes and one Pierre de Niol. King Louis is still (or again?) in the general area in 1146 when he gives a charter of privilege to S. Viviani de Saintes at Poitiers. Present with him in Saintes is the husband of Eleanor's sister, Raoul de Vermandois. Both Queen Eleanor and her sister, Aelith, are mentioned in several of the charters drawn up in the region. We also know that Eleanor granted many privileges to the convent of Notre-Dame de Saintes, where her great aunt was abbess for forty years. Of the four charters to survive in Eleanor's name alone, three are related to Notre-Dame de Saintes. It would certainly have been in character for Queen Eleanor to insist on accompanying Louis to her own lands, away from the Paris court, to bear her hoped-for son under the watchful eye of her paternal aunt, Agnès de Barbezieux, abbess of the Benedictine convent of Notre-Dame de Saintes. The Abbaye-aux-Dames, as it was commonly called, was certainly an abbey fit for a queen, one that was very wealthy and much sought-after by women of the higher nobility. And Countess Marie bears the name of its patron saint.

• Concerning Marie's possible birth at Saintes, there is a curious reference in the printed text of a manuscript originating at the Couvent-des-Blancs-Manteaux in Paris, "Ex Anonymi Opusculo de Origine Regum Franciae," which refers to her as *Marie Santerrensem*. The reference is puzzling. I have been unable to find any connection between Marie and Santerre (in Picardy) or Sancerre, except indirectly through her brother-in-law Étienne. There is, however, the possibility of a scribal error or misreading in the printed text. It is possible that *Santonensem* may have been misread as *Santerrensem*. Such a misreading could suggest Saintes as her birthplace. Valid or not, it was this reference that first led me to consider Saintes as the place of Marie's birth. The information cited above seemed to add strength to that possibility.

• The name of Queen Eleanor's sister is given in various documents as both Petronilla and Aelith. Historians for the most part assume that the two names refer to the same woman. I have offered in this book a plausible, though undocumented, explanation for the change of her name.

• The portion of the *Codex Calixtinus*, which I mention in the text, is known as the *Liber Sancti Jacobi*. Book four, also known to scholars today as the *Pseudo-Turpin*, tells the story, as Eleanor reminds Louis in my novel, of the lances planted in the soil that bear leaves during the night. Book five of the *Codex* contains a pilgrim's guide to Santiago de Compostela. The first two books of the manuscript include sermons, letters, and miracles pertaining to St. James, while Book three describes the moving of his body from Jerusalem to Compostela. The manuscript also has an appendix that contains polyphonic works.

• The death I describe of Jaufre Rudel is of my own imagining. He did apparently die on the second crusade, though his death is mentioned in none of the chronicles or other documents thus far uncovered. His romantic *vida* suggests that he made it to the shores of Tripoli, where he died in the arms of Countess Hodierne. While it is tempting to embrace this melodramatic ending for the troubadour, it is far more likely that he died of wounds or disease during his travels. I have invented a way for him to reach the shores of Tripoli in his work alone, rather than in his person.

• The translation of portions of King Louis's letter praising young Henri and of Abbot Bernard's letter to Manuel Komnenos is used, with permission and only minor alterations, from Theodore Evergates's *Feudal Society in Medieval France*.

• Abbot Bernard's intervention in the betrothal of Henri and Thibaut to the daughters of the king is documented in the chronicle of Radulfus Niger, who reports that: "Louis King of France … took as his wife, Eleanor, daughter of Guillaume, count of Poitou, by whom he had his daughters, one of whom married Henri, count of Champagne, through the intervention of the holy Bernard, abbot of Clairvaux, and the other, Count Thibaut of Blois, seneschal of France."

• There are many events in Marie's life about which scholars still do not agree. Among these are the dates of Marie's marriage to Henri and of Scholastique's birth. The date of Marie's marriage to Count Henri was considered for many years (and still is by some historians, including her biographer, Theodore Evergates) to be 1164, a date championed by Henri d'Arbois de Jubainville in his nineteenth-century magisterial work on the county of Champagne. However, a well-respected historian, the late John Benton, who collected a large number of charters during his work on the court of Champagne, brought to light a document from 1159 that refers to Marie as countess of Champagne. Evergates argues that she could have been referred to as countess even though she was only betrothed to the count. I know of no other document that takes such liberties. Since many medieval betrothals ended in rupture—as did two of those of young Henri—it seems unlikely that the title would be used, especially five years before the wedding, or that she would actually witness the charter, as she does, with the title of "Marie, Trecensis comitissa." What muddies the waters is that the document refers to her both as *comitissa* (countess—a term used twice) and *sponsa*, which usually means "betrothed." Benton has suggested that it can also mean "bride" to indicate that the marriage is recent. Certainly it has that meaning in the well-known Latin term that refers to a nun as the *sponsa Christi* (the bride of Christ). I am following Benton's logic in placing the marriage, as do many other scholars, in 1159.

There are, I believe, other reasons for accepting the earlier date. The traditional marriage age of girls in medieval France was twelve to fourteen, or when they had become nubile. Since the betrothal took place when Marie was seven and was never disputed, it would seem illogical for the count to delay the marriage for twelve years, until she was nineteen and he was nearly forty. It seems far more plausible that the couple would be wed shortly after the completion of the count's new palace and the adjoining church of St.-Étienne, when the count was thirty-two and Marie was fourteen. It appears, however, that there was some sort of rupture in the marriage, for the chronicler Robert of Torigni indicates that in 1164 Count Henri "took back the daughter of King Louis whom he had earlier sent away." It is Benton who suggests it may have been caused by the failed meetings of the king and emperor at St. Jean-de-Losne.

• We do not know the exact birth dates of the daughters of Henri and Marie. However, because of the betrothal agreement arranged with Philip of Flanders, we can conclude with some accuracy that their daughter Marie (Mariette) was born in 1171. However, the date of Scholastique's birth is completely unknown. Some argue that she was born after Marie and before Thibaut. However, she was married (before her sister's marriage) to Guillaume de Macon somewhere between 1180 and 1183. I have thus placed her birthdate in 1169, which would have made her fourteen by 1183, the year before her husband became count. It is also the year suggested some decades ago by the late archivist and *bibliothécaire* in Troyes, Françoise Bibolet.

• The dates and order of composition I suggest for the romances of Chrétien de Troyes are not the traditionally accepted ones, though I believe they are far more plausible. I refer anyone who wishes to explore my reasoning beyond the scope of this book to my article entitled "Reconsidering the Order of Chrétien de Troyes's Romances," published in *Li Premerains vers: Essays in Honor of Keith Busby* (see below).

• The story of Anne Musnier has been preserved in several accounts with differing details. A thirteenth-century Latin *canticum triumphale*, cited by Félix Bourquelot, and dated variously from about 1200 to after 1290, is the earliest known version. In that report, the culprits were three angry knights (*Irati tres milites*), whom Anne encountered in a tavern. Later and somewhat different versions have been preserved in the seventeenth-century *Traité de la noblesse* of Gilles-André de la Roque and the eighteenth-century *Essais historiques sur Paris* of Germain-François Poullain de Saint-Foïx. Bourquelot cites the charter of privilege in which Count Henri had bestowed certain significant privileges upon Anne's husband, his wife, and their heirs as bestowing nobility upon them. The only known historical document contemporary to the event that corroborates a connection between Anne and Count Henri is an 1175 act by Count Henri issued in Provins. It grants, in exchange for a small annual sum to be paid in alms, that Anne's husband, Girard de Langres, as well as his wife and heirs, be exempt from all taxes and exactions, from military service and expeditions, and gives them the right to be brought to justice only before the count himself.

• Only one contemporary recorded a sexual relationship between Countess Marie and Philip of Flanders, and many scholars assume therefore that it never happened. However, the one place the allegation appears is in the chronicle of a thirteen-century abbot of Andres, who cites it as the reason their marriage negotiations were ended. The author of that chronicle was the successor of the earlier abbot of Andres who led the expedition to seek papal dispensation for the marriage and who may well have known the thirteenth-century chronicler. It is plausible to assume, therefore, that Philip did indeed provide that as an excuse to the abbot for calling off the negotiations. The tale seems to have spread no further.

• Some readers may be surprised that I have chosen to use the Old French version of *fine amor* (sometimes written as *fin'amor*) to describe what we often call today "courtly love," a term that was not invented until the nineteenth century by a scholar named Gaston Paris. However, since *fine amor* is used in both secular and sacred contexts at Marie's court, the translation "courtly" does not seem apt. *Fine* (f., fin, m.) has also been translated in conjunction with *amor* as "pure," "true," "noble," and "excellent." Rather than select among them, I have chosen to use the Old French term. Although the modern French word *amour* is masculine, that was not the case in Old French, except where it referred to Cupid, the God of love, as *Amor*.

• It seems odd today that the Church would frown on laypersons reading the Bible in any form, but in 1199 Pope Innocent III publicly proclaimed his disapproval of such biblical translation, for "[t]he depth of the divine Scriptures is such that not only the illiterate and uninitiated have difficulty understanding them, but also the educated and the gifted." That position hardened over time, and thirty years after Marie's death, the Council of Toulouse in 1229 passed the following resolution (canon 14): "We prohibit lay persons from possessing the Books of the Old and New Testaments, except for devotional purposes the Psalter, the Breviary, and the Book of Hours of the Blessed Virgin.

But we strictly forbid their having any translation of these books." Five years later, in 1234, the Council of Tarragona ruled that anyone who owned such translations "must turn them over to the local bishop ... so that they may be burned."

• Names are always perplexing in writing about medieval France, since so many people bore the same name. Spelling was not fixed by any means at the time, and we may find the name Alice, for example, given as Alix, Alais, Aelith. I have used all these spellings to differentiate among various women with the same name. For similar reasons and to avoid confusion, I have chosen to use the English spelling for Philip of Flanders, but the French spelling for Philippe-Auguste, as well as Henri for the count of Champagne, but Henry for the bishop of Reims. I can only trust the reader to be indulgent in such matters.

• There are various versions of the death of Henri de Champagne, all involving a fall from a window. I am inclined to accept the version in the *Chronicle of Ernoul*, which contains the most quotidian detail and reads more like an eyewitness account than any of the others. Since Ernoul was a squire of Henri's father-in-law before his death, it seems logical to assume that he may have then entered the household of Henri. It is this chronicle of Ernoul that reveals the financial difficulties that Henri faced in Acre. Sometimes, he noted, Henri "could find no one who wanted to give him credit. Then he would pawn some possession and send out for meat. Thus, it happened on many a day." He also noted his dependence on Countess Marie for funds. "When Count Henri de Champagne went overseas, he held onto and took from the county of Champagne. He'd left it in the charge, care, and keeping of his mother; and she sent him the income from the land as he needed it. And thus he paid the debts that he contracted at Acre, for she sent it to him to pay each year." Her borrowing from moneylenders to make these payments is well documented. It is also interesting to note that Ernoul ends his writing in the year of Henri's death. Ernoul has been tentatively identified as a squire of Balian d'Ibelin named Ernoul de Gibelet, whose family, both noble and wealthy, had intermarried with the Ibelins.

• One account from the following century of Marie's death, left by Thomas de Cantimpré, contends that she died, surrounded by the trappings of wealth, and that those who were supposed to be caring for her stripped her room and even her body. When her confessor, Adam de Perseigne, arrived, he found the door bolted and had to have it broken down, at which point, over her dead, nude body, he delivered a rather tactless sermon on vanity and condemned the love of worldly things. If, in fact, she died as a nun in a convent, as the necrology of Fontaines-les-Nonnes suggests, this story seems highly unlikely. I agree with Theodore Evergates that it is more logical to follow the obituary at Fontaines, which describes her as a "*reverendissima monacha*," a most reverent nun. It also suggests that she was much beloved there for her benefactions to the convent.

• The laments referred to at the funerals of Count Henri and Countess Marie are based on a series of *planctus*, set to music by Philip, the Chancellor of Notre-Dame de Paris, in the early thirteenth century.

• None of Marie's children survived beyond 1204, except Scholastique, who lived another fifteen years or so. Marie's daughter, the wife of Baudouin of Flanders whom I have called Mariette to distinguish between her and her mother, reached Acre in 1204, trying to rejoin her husband on the fourth crusade. Upon arrival, she received news that the crusaders had conquered Constantinople and that her husband had become its new emperor. Like her Aunt Marguerite, she contracted a fever shortly after her arrival and died without ever seeing him again, leaving behind two daughters, Jeanne and Marguerite, who would both become countesses of Flanders.

• Marie's successor, Blanche de Navarre, married Thibaut and bore him a daughter and a posthumous son. His death in 1201 left her a widow who followed in Marie's footsteps and never married again. She was befriended by Queen Adèle and successfully ruled Champagne as regent for two decades. Blanche faced various challenges, including a war of succession on behalf of her son against Érard de Brienne, who claimed that his wife, Philippa, the last daughter of Count Henri, was the rightful heir. Blanche prevailed, and her son, Thibaut IV, became not only count of Champagne, but also king of Navarre and a well-known *trouvère* whose songs are still remembered and studied today. Henri's daughter Alix became queen of Cyprus. Marie, the daughter of Isabella and Conrad, became queen of Jerusalem.

• Three of Marie's descendants would become kings of France—Louis X, Philip V, and Charles IV—the last of the Capetian kings, who ruled from 1314 to 1328. Under the reign of Louis X, Champagne was absorbed into the kingdom of France.

• Marie's candle burned for almost 400 years and was known as *le cierge de la comtesse*. The three swings of the censer were called *les coups de la comtesse.* On June 25, 1562, protestant hordes, led by Louis of Meaux, lord of La Rame, a man popularly known as Peter the Devil because of the role he played in a local performance of the *Mystère de la Passion*, swarmed over the town, wreaking havoc against everything Catholic. The cathedral was a primary target. They allegedly overturned altars, broke crosses, smashed statues, and trampled on holy relics. The tomb of Countess Marie met the fate of so many others that day. Her sleeping effigy was overturned and broken. Her candle was snuffed out and would never burn again.

ARTICLES BY THE AUTHOR ON MARIE DE CHAMPAGNE AND HER COURT

"Marie de Champagne and Eleanor of Aquitaine: A Relationship Reexamined." *Speculum 54* (October 1979): 698-711.

"Marie de Champagne's 'Cuer d'ome et cors de fame': Aspects of Misogyny and Feminism in the Twelfth Century," in *The Spirit of the Court,* ed. Glyn Burgess and Robert Taylor. Cambridge, England: D. S. Brewer, 1985, pp. 234-245.

"*Eructavit cor meum*: Sacred Love in a Secular Context at the Court of Marie de Champagne," in *Earthly Love and Spiritual Love, Love of the Saints*, ed. Susan Ridyard, *Sewanee Medieval Studies 8 (1999)*: 159-78.

"Chrétien's Patrons," in *A Companion to Chrétien de Troyes*, ed. Norris J. Lacy and Joan Tasker Grimbert. Cambridge, England: D. S. Brewer, 2005, pp. 15-25.

"Reconsidering the Order of Chrétien de Troyes's Romances," in *Li Premerains vers: Essays* in Honor of Keith Busby, ed. Catherine M. Jones and Logan E. Whalen. Amsterdam: Rodopi, 2011, pp. 245-260.

ACKNOWLEDGMENTS

My work on Marie de Champagne began some forty years ago, thanks to a fellowship from the National Endowment for the Humanities that allowed me to spend a full semester in Troyes, France, and the surrounding area doing research. As a consequence, I have written various scholarly articles involving Marie (listed above), as well as an unpublished biography that has, over time, evolved into the historical novel you have before you.

In the interest of historical accuracy, I have consulted colleagues and scholars who specialize in various aspects of medieval history and literature, and I am beholden to them for their helpful suggestions and answers to all my questions. They should, of course, in no way be held accountable for any flaws the book may contain.

One among them is Theodore Evergates, who has also studied the region and court of Champagne for many years. He has been most gracious in sharing information throughout the process and asking me to read and comment on his then-unpublished historical account of Marie's life, *Marie of France: Countess of Champagne 1145-1198*, while it was still was in progress. I am also very grateful to him for his reading and commenting on an early version of my manuscript. We do not agree on all matters or always come to the same conclusions based on the evidence (or lack thereof), but our exchange has been very cordial and fruitful.

Rupert Pickens, a well-known medievalist from the University of Kentucky, and a good friend for many years, has also read and commented on the manuscript, and is no doubt responsible for many of its merits. Similarly, Monica Wright, also a friend and one of my former students, now an expert in medieval clothing and fabrics in medieval literature, has saved me from various sartorial pitfalls.

I also had the good fortune in past years to meet and correspond with two now-deceased scholars who assiduously studied the court of Champagne, namely John Benton, who shared with me his collection of the charters of Henri and Marie de Champagne, and Françoise Bibolet, archivist and paleographer who directed the Bibliothèque de Troyes for twenty-eight years. I am grateful for their encouragement and assistance. I would also like to thank the many other friends, scholars, and writers who have made suggestions or whom I have consulted about various details along the way, Ron Akehurst, Suma Clark, Paula Gerson, Susanne Hebden, Norris Lacy, Donald Maddox, Joan McRae, Ron Messier, Patricia Price, Helena Schrader, and Valerie Wilhite.

Special thanks go to Margaret Ordoubadian, a friend and former colleague of many years, who has read my manuscript with her keen eyes and made many helpful suggestions, as well as to members of the Murfreesboro Writers group, whose comments have no doubt enlivened the text. As always, I am grateful to my editor, D. Michelle Adkerson, and to my book designer, Art Growden, for their contributions.

CPSIA information can be obtained
at www.ICGtesting.com
Printed in the USA
BVHW081531210120
569944BV00003B/292